WILD BELLS TO THE WILD SKY

Other Avon Books by
Laurie McBain

CHANCE THE WINDS OF FORTUNE
DARK BEFORE THE RISING SUN
DEVIL'S DESIRE
MOONSTRUCK MADNESS
TEARS OF GOLD

WILD BELLS TO THE WILD SKY

LAURIE McBAIN

 AVON
PUBLISHERS OF BARD, CAMELOT, DISCUS AND FLARE BOOKS

WILD BELLS TO THE WILD SKY is an original publication
of Avon Books. This work has never before appeared in
book form.

AVON BOOKS
A division of
The Hearst Corporation
1790 Broadway
New York, New York 10019

First Avon Printing, November, 1983

AVON TRADEMARK REG. U. S. PAT. OFF. AND IN
OTHER COUNTRIES, MARCA REGISTRADA, HECHO EN
U. S. A.

Printed in the U. S. A.

COM 10 9 8 7 6 5 4 3 2 1

For
Kathleen E. Woodiwiss
with
affection and continuing admiration

WILD BELLS TO THE WILD SKY

She shall be lov'd and fear'd. Her own shall bless her;
Her foes shake like a field of beaten corn,
And hang their heads with sorrow. Good grows with her;
In her days every man shall eat in safety
Under his own vine what he plants; and sing
The merry songs of peace to all his neighbours.

SHAKESPEARE

Prelude

"THE Queen is dead. God save the Queen, Elizabeth of England!" And with those fateful words, proclaimed on a November morning in 1558, Elizabeth Tudor, daughter of Henry VIII and Anne Boleyn, succeeded to the throne of England. The death of Elizabeth's half-sister, the childless Mary Tudor, a devout Catholic and daughter of King Harry by his divorced Spanish wife, Catherine of Aragon, brought the Protestant princess, who had been declared a bastard and banished from the court shortly after her birth, the crown of a country that had yet to become the great seafaring nation that was to build a world empire.

The realm that the young queen inherited was facing bankruptcy, rising inflation, civil and religious unrest, and a heightening of hostility from its powerful Catholic neighbors, France and Spain, who saw England as an uncivilized island of heretics. Ever since Henry VIII had renounced the supremacy of the pope and severed all bonds with the Church of Rome, England had become the revolutionary symbol of the great Reformation sweeping through Europe and, in the eyes of the papacy and its zealous defenders, threatening the very heart of Christendom.

King Philip II of Spain, fanatic champion of the Catholic

1

Counter-Reformation, ruled an empire that not only dominated the Continent but had conquered the New World. From her colonies in the Americas and Indies, Spain filled her royal coffers with gold and silver, precious stones, and the riches reaped from unrestricted trade with the Far East. By papal decree nearly a century earlier, Pope Alexander VI had established a demarcation line across the seas and lands of the newly explored western world, which forbade crossing by other nations, and allowed Spain and Portugal a monopoly on the wealth of the New World. And enforced by the unchallenged superiority of their well-manned and heavily armed fleets, the Spanish seemed destined for world dominion.

Across the English Channel, in France, Mary Stuart—daughter of Mary of Guise, a French princess, and of James V of Scotland, and the great-granddaughter of Henry VII—married the Dauphin of France. The marriage presented a grave threat to England and her queen. It united two ancient, Catholic enemies of an ever-growing Protestant England. And Mary Stuart, Queen of Scotland, and the future queen of France, also claimed the English crown. Under Catholic canon, which had never recognized Henry VIII's divorce from Catherine of Aragon, Elizabeth Tudor had been born out of wedlock and had no right to wear the crown.

Raised and educated in the French court, the devoutly Catholic Mary Stuart would find that her heretical English cousin would be a difficult rival to overthrow, and her native Scotland would be an even more difficult land to rule. The Reformation, which until then had been confined to England and the Continent, now took root in Scottish soil. The ancient faith found itself under attack by parish ministers, inspired by the soul-stirring speeches of the Protestant reformer John Knox, repudiating papal edict. And in the highlands and glens of Scotland, rebellious lairds and clan chieftains, aspiring for wealth and power through the dissolution of the monasteries and acquisition of church holdings, actively plotted the overthrow of their Catholic, foreign-bred queen.

In 1560, Mary Stuart had to meet that challenge, for in December she became a widow and, childless, lost her right to the French throne. In the summer of 1561 she returned to Scotland to rule an impoverished country of lawless subjects. Falling prey to the divisive politics of the time, as well as having ruled with her heart rather than her head, Mary Queen of Scots was dethroned by Protestant nobles only seven years after returning to her homeland. Her reign, which had been beset by murder and intrigue, was over, and fleeing for her life she sought exile in England.

Elizabeth was faced with a difficult decision. Despite her personal feelings for Mary Stuart, she was a staunch supporter of a hereditary sovereign's right to rule, and she would never willingly become a party to the shedding of royal blood. However, because England needed an ally on her unprotected northern border, she had secretly supported and aided the rebellion in Scotland. Mary Stuart had abdicated in favor of her infant son, James VI, who was protected by a Protestant regent. England need no longer fear a French-supported invasion from her northern neighbor. Elizabeth wished to preserve that alliance. She could not allow Mary Stuart the freedom to join forces with England's Catholic enemies on the Continent.

Queen Elizabeth would not sentence her cousin to death nor give her her freedom. And because Elizabeth Tudor never wed and had no heirs to inherit the crown, the Catholic Mary Stuart was heir-presumptive to the English throne. As long as she lived there would be those who would conspire to place that crown on her head prematurely and see the ancient faith restored to the heretics of that rebellious northern isle ruled by the Protestant usurper. The threat of assassination was an ever-present danger to Elizabeth and to the destiny of her kingdom.

During the following years of her reign, Elizabeth I sought to maintain peace with her neighbors while she restored order and stability to her realm and began to build a fighting force, especially a naval fleet, far superior to the might of her powerful foes. Elizabeth Tudor was a master in the fine art of diplomacy. Until she felt England could successfully defend her shores, she would not involve her people in a war. War was to be avoided at all costs. Elizabeth knew the end result would be far more devastating to her nation than a mere wrecking of the country's economy and a draining of the royal treasury. And tax her people to keep her armies fighting in a war on the Continent she would not do, for that would only promote further unrest and rebellion in the land, abetting the Catholic cause.

She would only engage in warfare to protect her people and defend her land from invasion. It was with reluctance that she allowed Englishmen to fight on the Continent, and it was with grave reservations that she even sent money and arms to her Protestant allies to aid in their struggle against the armies of Spain and France. Although she wished to keep the Netherlands in Protestant hands, she felt it would be only too easy for the papal-inspired armies of Philip II to cross the Channel and shed blood on English soil.

Elizabeth I remained stalwartly determined to keep her crown and her loyal Protestant subjects safe from the armies of Spain and the Roman Church's Holy Inquisition. She would not provoke Philip II's all-consuming ambition to make England a part of his empire or return her people to the orthodox faith. Despite increasingly strained relations, Elizabeth patiently continued to pursue a nonaggressive course and maintain an outwardly friendly diplomacy with Spain. But, privately, the queen and her council worried, knowing that it would be but a matter of time before the religious fanaticism of Philip II and his belief in a holy crusade of conquest in the New World would involve England in direct conflict with the Spanish crown.

Spain's aspirations for a world empire depended on her unchallenged supremacy in the New World. The religious and civil wars that had dominated western Europe throughout the century were bankrupting Spain, whose royal treasury financed the armies of mercenaries hired to suppress rebellion and restore the true faith.

Mountains of silver and temples of gold, masks studded and sparkling with emeralds and pearls were no longer legend when the *conquistadores* returned to Spain. Their ships' holds were filled with incredible riches plundered from a savage New World that existed beyond the western seas. This dazzling wealth raised Spain to its pinnacle of power. King Philip II came to depend on the great treasure fleets sailing home from the Spanish Main, a territory that stretched from Trinidad and the mouth of the Orinoco River at its southernmost point, to Cuba and the Straits of Florida at its northernmost, and encompassing Central America and Mexico to the west and the Bahamas to the east.

Spain's claim to all of the lands and seas of the New World would not go unchallenged for long. For years, French, Dutch, and English pirates, sailing along the coast of Europe, had been harassing the heavily laden Spanish galleons that had become lost from the well-protected fleet sailing home to Seville, but few sea rovers had dared to venture into the Spanish Main.

Now a few bold men, intent on winning a share of the plunder and wealth of the New World, sailed into these Spanish waters. Adventurers and privateers, backed by merchants hungry for access to the trade routes and natural resources so abundant in the New World, challenged the almightiness of Spain and Philip II's ordained right of sovereignty over the lands and seas of this once fabled terrestrial paradise.

Though Elizabeth was constrained by the precariousness of her position and vulnerability of her people to appear content with Spain's monopoly of the New World and its bounty, some of her more impatient and reckless seafarers now openly defied Spain's claim to a world empire. Seldom did these adventurers receive public support from their queen, in whose name they made their courageous voyages for gold and silver, honor and glory. But each captain and crew knew that they sailed with the silent prayers and good wishes, and some even with the private monetary backing, of Elizabeth Tudor. The white flag bearing the red cross of St. George flew proudly on the mainmasts of their trim ships. These enterprising, defiant Englishmen steered a course into the heart of the Spanish Main.

PART ONE

The Journey

We must take the current when it serves,
Or lose our ventures.

Chapter One

January, 1571—West Indies
  Fifteen leagues northeast of the Windward Passage

WHEN the *Arion* had set sail from Plymouth Sound the church bells had pealed. Many a Godspeed followed in her wake. It was the heart of winter and she was not more than thirty tons, with fewer than forty hands manning her. She made her way out into the Channel and turned her prow into the fierce, storm-driven seas of the Atlantic. Within a fortnight the Canaries were sighted, where fresh water and provisions were taken on board. Keeping a northeast wind off her quarter, she steered south by west with the trades filling her sails.

Her captain was an English gentleman by the name of Geoffrey Christian and one of Elizabeth Tudor's most illustrious privateers. Also on board the *Arion* was Geoffrey Christian's wife, the former Doña Magdalena Aurelia Rosalba de Cabrion y Montevares. The captain of the *Arion* had met Doña Magdalena seven years earlier when boarding and capturing the Spanish galleon on which she and her family had been passengers for the journey to Madrid from Hispaniola, where the Montevares family had a sugar plantation.

The Montevareses had been journeying to Spain to celebrate the birth of their first grandson. Their eldest daughter, Catalina, who now lived in Seville, had been married for five years. She had given birth to three beautiful daughters, but until young Francisco there had been no male heir. Don Rodrigo Montevares and his wife, Doña Amparo, knew that the lack of a son to inherit his father's name and titles was a grave disappointment to their son-in-law, Don Pedro Enrique de Villasandro. Don Pedro was a scion of an ancient, aristocratic family of Andalusia, and he exerted an influence at court that few rivaled and many envied. For him to have chosen a colonial for his wife, even one whose blood was pure Castilian, had been the greatest honor and had filled Don Rodrigo with pride and great expectations. Not only was Don Pedro master of many fine estates in Spain but by royal grant he held great estates in Hispaniola and Cuba. He captained his own ship and had traveled extensively throughout the Spanish Main. He was a gentleman and a soldier and held in the highest esteem by all who knew or served him. There had even been talk that he was to be the next governor of Hispaniola. It would be the culmination of all of Don Rodrigo's hopes and dreams if his daughter Catalina were wife of the future governor, and her family were to take up residence in Santo Domingo. And if he succeeded in his plan to marry off his only other daughter, Magdalena, to Don Pedro's recently widowed cousin in Córdoba he would no longer have to concern himself with trying to save the family's once thriving sugar plantation which now, due to his mismanagement, was failing. Although the bridegroom, Don Ignacio de Villasandro, was old enough to be Magdalena's father, he was a gentleman of impeccable respectability and considerable fortune. Magdalena, however, was less than pleased with her father's endeavors on her behalf and refused to believe that anything good would come of her father's intentions or of the voyage.

It was aboard Don Pedro's ship, *Maria Concepción*, that the Montevares family was sailing to Spain. Don Pedro had very graciously offered to escort them personally to Seville, where Catalina and her newborn son awaited them, then on to Córdoba, where Don Ignacio awaited Magdalena. Setting sail from Santo Domingo, the *Maria Concepción* had joined the treasure fleet sailing from Havana and had made her way through the treacherous waters of the Straits of Florida without incident. The Gulf Stream carried them northward to Bermuda, where they caught the westerlies and the *Maria Concepción*'s bow swung eastward toward Spain. It was near dawn of the third day after they'd survived a sudden squall, which had blown them off course and separated them from the protection of the rest of the fleet, that the red cross of St. George was seen flying atop the mainmast of a ship bearing down on them.

Don Pedro had been momentarily stunned by the daring of the English captain. What madness was this? The *Maria Concepción* was a five-hundred-ton galleon with sixty bronze cannon and over two hundred seamen and soldiers defending her. Calling his men to arms, Don Pedro, from his exalted position of command on the deck of the towering sterncastle, fully expected to disable the smaller ship within minutes of firing a deafening volley of broadsides. Grappling irons would have brought the English ship close enough to have been boarded and the English captain to his knees before the unconquerable might of Spain. It was, therefore, with a look of incredulity that Don Pedro watched the royal arms of Spain fluttering at the mainmast-head of the *Maria Concepción* blown into the sea along with the mizzenmast and rigging.

The Englishman's ship seemed to sail out of danger almost magically, then, through some sorcerer's trick, or so Don Pedro would later swear, maneuvered to windward of the slower-moving Spanish galleon. With her long-range cannon, broadside after punishing broadside wreaked death and destruction on the crowded decks of the *Maria Concepción*. Listing dangerously, her quarterdeck in shambles, her masts splintered, the *Maria Concepción* surrendered when the English ship ranged alongside, her crew armed with sword and musket and standing ready to board.

Don Pedro Enrique de Villasandro's humiliation had only just begun. Catching sight of the frightened passengers, Geoffrey Christian insisted they come aboard the *Arion*. Unrepentantly he warned them that the *Maria Concepción* might very well sink before the rest of the Spanish fleet could rescue her. He felt responsible for their safety, since it had been the *Arion*'s cannon fire that had left the Spanish ship foundering. With a mocking smile that had Don Pedro reaching for his sword only to be bitterly reminded of an empty scabbard, the English captain informed the Montevareses that they need have no further cause for fear once aboard his ship, which was still seaworthy, for he would personally guarantee a safe, uninterrupted voyage to England. Once there, he assured them that they would be able to continue their journey to Spain.

The *Maria Concepción* was in far less danger of sinking, however, after her hold was emptied of its treasure and loaded aboard the victor's ship. As the *Arion* gathered way, the furious Don Pedro swore vengeance against the swaggering English captain who had caused him such mortification.

Geoffrey Christian's thoughts had not lingered long with the vanquished captain of the *Maria Concepción*. The Spanish captain might have lost his ship in the battle, but the Englishman had lost his heart. Doña Magdalena was an ivory-skinned, bronze-eyed beauty with hair of darkest Venetian red. Although it was the fairness of her face and figure which first caught Geoffrey Christian's roving eye, it was the beautiful Spanish girl's undaunted spirit that finally captivated him. She had not experienced a fit of the vapors and been confined to her bed, as had Doña Amparo, nor had she remained in her cabin weeping or sulking. With exceptional grace, Doña Magdalena accepted the challenge of being aboard an English privateer's ship. Soon, even the most prejudiced crew member was enamored of the vivacious, laughter-loving young *señorita* who, despite the elegance of her appearance and her unfamiliarity with the English language, could mimic their captain to perfection as he roared his orders, much to the amusement of the crew.

The captain had shown unusual patience, even smiling at the jesting and good-natured pranks, for the game was his and, soon, so would be the lady. Pursuing the dark-eyed Castilian with all of the reckless determination that had so successfully marked his career as a privateer, Geoffrey Christian captured the beautiful Magdalena's heart by the time the *Arion* reached the shores of England.

With a wrathful indignation that left him purple in the face, Don Rodrigo refused Geoffrey Christian's request for Magdalena's hand in marriage. Thinking the unfortunate affair ended, he booked passage for himself, his wife, and his shameless daughter aboard a Spanish ship sailing for Spain. But Don Rodrigo's daughter had a mind of her own, and the heady memory of Geoffrey Christian's kisses and the disturbing thought of a portly Don Ignacio awaiting her in Córdoba helped Magdalena to make the most important decision of her young life. Despite the vehement objections of her father and tearful protestations of her mother, Doña Magdalena eloped with her handsome, fair-haired inamorato. In a quiet ceremony performed by a minister and witnessed by several of Geoffrey Christian's friends—without the blessing of her church and against the wishes of her family—Magdalena made her sacred vows to the man she loved.

The years passed in contentment for Magdalena. Never once had she regretted her decision to marry a man of a different faith and nationality from her own, even though it had resulted in a painful, inexorable rift with her family.

Although Geoffrey Christian was often away for long periods of time during his voyages, Magdalena's life at Highcross Court was full of happiness. The house of gray-brown Kentish stone had been in the Christian family for over two centuries and was surrounded by meadowland grazed by sheep and cattle, deep woods thick with pheasant and partridge, clearwater streams full of trout, orchards of sweet cherry and purple plum flowering in spring, and golden wheat and hops ripening in late summer. It was a haven found appropriately close to the banks of the River Eden, which meandered through the fertile countryside southeast of London.

The fulfillment of Magdalena's happiness had come with the birth of her first child. As Geoffrey Christian came to know his firstborn, he proudly declared to all that the babe had been born laughing. Never had there been such a happy, healthy little girl who brought such great joy to all who knew and loved her. Lily Francisca had inherited her mother's dark Venetian red hair and cheerful disposition and her father's pale green eyes and love of adventure. She could never be found where she was supposed to be. An open window having beckoned her outside to explore, an apple on a branch having been just out of reach of her small hand until she climbed higher, a duck having paddled to the far side of the pond, his quacking a challenge to follow—all of these temptations and many more had resulted in misadventures that left her nursemaid, Maire Lester, feeling far older than her years.

The quince apples had been harvested and made into jams and preserves, when Doña Magdalena, marking her seventh Michaelmas at Highcross Court, received a message from her father that her mother was dying. It was the first time her father had broken his silence since their bitter parting.

Don Rodrigo could no longer remain deaf to his wife's anguished pleadings to see her youngest daughter once again. Not even certain that Magdalena would respond to his entreaty, for he had greatly abused her character when she had defied him and he had banished her forever from his sight over seven years earlier, he sent her word of her mother's failing health. He asked, in as humble a manner as his pride would allow, if she would agree to come home.

Fortunately for Magdalena, Geoffrey Christian was at Highcross Court, having returned in early summer from a voyage to Egypt and Africa, and soon the *Arion* was being refitted and provisioned for a voyage to the Indies. It had been over two months since the *Arion* had set sail from England. Running swiftly before the winds, their first landfall on the far side of the Atlantic had been the green hills of San Salvador Island rising up before them and looking little different than they had when sighted by Columbus seventy-nine years earlier. They had slowly threaded their way through the Bahamas, finding a port of refuge on the lee side of a small island, just northeast of the Windward Passage, when storm clouds had darkened the noonday sky. By evening the squall had blown itself out without causing any damage to the *Arion*, riding safe at anchor. By dawn the sea would be calm and the skies clear, and the *Arion* would continue her journey. Above the rain-washed deck, the blackness of the night sky was already brilliant with stars.

"How many stars are there in the sky, Father?"

" 'Sdeath, but you're up early, child!" Geoffrey Christian exclaimed, thinking he alone walked the quarterdeck of his ship just before first light.

"At least a hundred, Father?"

"A hund—" Geoffrey Christian repeated absentmindedly as he measured the angle between the horizon and the North Star with a cross-staff. "By my faith, child, but 'twould take us till the crack of doom just to count all of these above our heads alone, and then we would still have all of those we can't even see," he said with a deep chuckle of appreciation, for it was an inquiring mind that pondered such thoughts. And in a child of six, and a female at that, it was truly amazing, he mused with fatherly pride.

Lily Christian continued to stare up into the early morning sky. Above her head, beyond the tall, swaying and creaking masts that stretched into the heavens, the sky was black with myriad shimmering lights. The east, whence they had come at noon of the day before and anchored in the cove to escape the storm, was faintly illumined by a sun that still hid just beyond the horizon. The sea and sky to the west were dark and silent and seemed to converge mysteriously before the bow of the *Arion*. Her captain now charted a course toward the channel that offered safe passage out of the dangerous waters of the sunken coral reefs and hidden sand bars surrounding the Bahama Islands.

"How can there be stars in the sky that we can't see? And how can we count them if we can't even see them? And what happens to the stars when the sun rises? Why do they disappear? Where do they go? Do they fall into the sea?" Lily demanded, her small brow knit with puzzlement as she stared up at her father, certain he would be able to answer her questions.

Geoffrey Christian's teeth gleamed whitely in his sun-darkened face as he grinned. "Ho! What devilment have ye got planned, my sweet Lily, with all of these questions to plague a man while he's about his measuring? Would ye have us run aground, then, on some heathen shore?" he exploded with a laugh that rumbled across the deck like thunder.

Lily's squeal of pleased fright filled the air as her father swung her up and tossed her high above his head. He caught her tumbling figure easily against his chest as she fell back into the safety of his arms.

"Well, fondling? Want to touch the stars?" he asked her with a gleam in his eye. "They're fading fast," he warned her as she giggled and hid her face against his shoulder.

"Yes, Father! Please! Let me touch them, please!" Lily said quickly, raising her face to gaze longingly at the few sparkling jewels that beckoned still from a sky streaked with the first glowing light of dawn.

"Wrap your arms around my neck and hold on tight, Lily Francisca. We're going to climb high into the heavens," Geoffrey Christian declared loudly, defiantly, before he placed a reassuring kiss against his daughter's flushed cheek. "Just for luck, sweeting," he added softly this time.

"You do not need luck, Father," Lilly corrected him. "You have always said that a man makes his own. And 'tis only a fool or a weakling who waits for good fortune to come to him or sits idly by while his fate is sealed," Lily solemnly repeated her father's philosophy of life.

"A mocking child, as I live!" Geoffrey Christian said with a hearty laugh that threatened to shake the very timbers of his ship. "Do you never forget anything? I see I shall have to take great care in future, lest I look the pickle-herring should you repeat my most ribald comment as if quoting scripture. Now, up we go!" he said, his laugh fading as he set his mind to the task.

Sir Basil Whitelaw, a gentleman of unusual equanimity, which was why he was one of his queen's most trusted advisers, had come up on deck and was carefully straightening the elegant lace edging the high ruff about his neck when he glanced upward past the tangle of rigging overhead. He was thinking that it most likely would be another uncommonly warm day as he took note of the incredible color of the sky. Never had he imagined such colors, even in his wildest dreams. To an Englishman, especially one whose memory of rain-heavy gray clouds hanging low over the barren hills of a winter landscape were to be cherished, these colors were not natural; a plum-colored sky slashed with the brightest scarlet, molten copper, and aquamarine, which when it faded under the full light of day would still be the brightest blue of his recollection, seemed incredibly barbarous. Even the waters of this sea they sailed were unusually clear and bright, and warm, compared with the somber, unfriendly seas surrounding England. *Ah, England,* he sighed, and not for the first time since leaving those mist-enshrouded shores.

It was during the most nostalgic part of Sir Basil's melancholy reflections of home that a high-pitched giggle intruded along with a small velvet shoe that struck Sir Basil upon the shoulder, causing him more amazement than pain.

"What the—" he cried out, momentarily thinking the ship under attack by cannon fire from a Spanish galleon or a French corsair. "The devil!" he exclaimed in growing concern, for he suddenly realized that there had been no accompanying roar and flash of gunpowder; there had, however, been a giggle, and that he now remembered only too clearly.

Picking up the offending object from the deck, Sir Basil examined it, then glanced up into the rigging again, this time searching out with a keen eye what he disbelievingly sought.

"Oh, ho! We've been spied!" Geoffrey Christian called out, his devil-may-care laugh having become only too familiar to Sir Basil during this voyage.

Although suspecting the worst, Sir Basil could scarcely believe his eyes. Far above him, in what seemed to be an endless crisscross of ropes, was the captain of the *Arion*, his nightdress-clad daughter clinging like a monkey to his shoulder as Geoffrey Christian sat astride a yardarm.

Sir Basil felt sick, which wasn't unusual since he was not a good sailor, but this time it wasn't because of the motion of the ship. Should Geoffrey Christian have lost his balance, Sir Basil did not even want to think of the tragic consequences of such a mishap. He prayed now that Lily Christian's mother still slept peacefully below.

"Ah, Sir Basil, 'tis a gloomy face you show to the world this fine day," Geoffrey Christian called to the finely dressed gentleman standing in silent disapproval on the deck below. "Cheer up, then! All is not lost, for soon you will once again feel solid ground beneath your feet, Sir Basil. Hispaniola lies not too many leagues distant."

Had England been the *Arion*'s next landfall, Sir Basil would have rejoiced of that sighting but the Spanish island of Hispaniola promised little pleasure for him. He feared that he was not the adventuring kind. Privately, he had to admit that he found it difficult to understand the desire to travel to faraway places, much less to venture into uncharted seas. In future, despite even the direst threats from his queen, he would leave the adventuring to the likes of Geoffrey Christian and to his own dear brother, Valentine, who actually seemed to enjoy the dangers of sea-roving.

"Ah! The sun comes, Sir Basil, and, unless I miss my guess, Mr. Saunders has prepared a most splendid feast for his captain and the stouthearted crew of this good ship," Geoffrey Christian declared with a wide grin. Then, spying a figure moving quickly along the port rail below, he called out in his sternest voice, "And God pity the fool who has yet to finish his ale and biscuit and get on deck."

"Aye, Cap'n, sir," Master Randall, the bos'n, answered without hesitation as he hurried below, determined to light a fire beneath the sluggards before his captain found need to repeat his command.

"Do I get stewed apples and buttered eggs, Father?" Lily asked hopefully.

"At the very least, my child. And, perhaps, poached chicken and sweet potato pie. We might even be able to find some sherry for Sir Basil," Geoffrey Christian added, thinking Sir Basil was looking a bit green.

Sir Basil inclined his head in acknowledgment of Geoffrey Christian's kind offer. He even managed a slight smile, for he was not completely humorless, and despite their disparate views on life, he had been a good friend of the *Arion*'s captain for many years. He had even stood witness to the marriage of Geoffrey Christian and Doña Magdalena. And what a surprise that had been to the captain's friends and family, although, now Basil thought about it, it shouldn't have surprised any of Geoffrey Christian's acquaintances, for he was a man who did as he damn well pleased.

Actually, it had been the taking of a bride at all that had been the surprising part of the affair, for they had all come to accept the fact that Geoffrey Christian would remain a bachelor until his dying day. Hartwell Barclay, Geoffrey's cousin, and next in line to inherit Highcross Court, had not taken the news of his cousin's marriage at all well. It had been rumored at the time that he had taken to his bed for a week and had yet to forgive his cousin for his treachery in marrying—and a Spanish Papist at that.

Despite such a stigma, Magdalena had managed to become a favorite at court and had a large circle of friends and admirers. The fact that Geoffrey Christian had always been a favorite of his queen, and had even managed to remain so after his marriage, had helped in Magdalena's complete acceptance at court. She had often accompanied Sir Basil and his wife, Elspeth, to London, staying with them in their house in Canon Row, when Geoffrey was at sea. Magdalena and her daughter had even stayed with them at Whiteswood for months at a time until his safe return.

At the thought of London and the court at Westminster and his queen, Sir Basil sighed again. Shaking his head in disbelief, he wondered with yet another sigh how it was he had ended up a passenger on board the *Arion* when she had set sail from Plymouth. After presenting his gifts to Her Majesty and enjoying the merrymaking and festivities so abundant in town, he had had every intention of spending Christmas through Twelfth Day in his own home, his feet stretched out before a roaring fire in the hearth of the great hall at Whiteswood, his wife and young son at his side.

However, it had been his incredible misfortune to have been in attendance to his queen the day that Geoffrey Christian had sought an audience with her. Sir Basil had always experienced a certain feeling of nervous trepidation when conversing with Her Grace, for Elizabeth was of a volatile nature, and one never knew exactly what mood she might be in.

Her regal appearance humbled the most arrogant courtier and silenced the most glib-tongued. With red-gold hair elegantly coiffed in curls and draped with pearls and diamonds, her dark eyes missing nothing, she swept into a room in a swirl of silk embroidered with gold and precious stones, her imperious commands ringing forth for all to hear and obey. She was quick-witted and short-tempered and spared none who displeased her, but with a smile of genuine warmth and affection she could just as quickly win the undying devotion of a recently admonished subject.

Geoffrey Christian's request for permission to travel to the Indies, along with his wife and daughter, had been given careful consideration by Her Grace and by Sir William Cecil, secretary of state and Her Grace's most trusted counselor. Francis Walsingham, one of Cecil's proficient young protégés, had been summoned to join the discussion. It was a disquieting circumstance for Sir Basil. Walsingham, now ambassador to France, had set up an intricate spy system on the Continent. He was personally involved in the apprehension and subsequent questioning of plotters against the Crown. Sir Basil hadn't even known Walsingham was in London, which, he supposed, gave indisputable evidence of the man's capabilities at espionage.

Up until the moment it had actually happened, Sir Basil continued to hope that Walsingham had been called in solely to advise Her Grace on Geoffrey Christian's voyage to the Indies.

Walsingham was an avid supporter of such daring enterprises, having contributed heavily to many of the voyages of exploration into the Spanish Main—Francis Drake, Gilbert, and Frobisher, as well as Geoffrey Christian, having benefited from Walsingham's sponsorship. Her Grace had previously invested in several of John Hawkins's slave-trading voyages to the Spanish West Indies from Sierra Leone and had enjoyed a 60 percent share of the profits.

Sir Basil wished to heaven that he'd had the foresight to excuse himself before he heard Walsingham's extraordinary proposal of sending someone along on Geoffrey Christian's next voyage. He must be one in whom Her Grace and Sir William had the greatest confidence, and one whom they could trust implicitly. He must be completely objective in his impressions and observations of the Spanish Main, and, of course, whatever information he might accidentally overhear concerning the treasure fleet, future expeditions in the lands north of the Indies, the location of gold and silver mines, and anything else which might be of interest to the Crown would be most appreciated.

"I believe that your wife's brother-in-law, Don Pedro Enrique de Villasandro, is quite often seen leaving the Alcazar in Madrid," Walsingham murmured thoughtfully, his eyes meeting Geoffrey Christian's for a meaningful moment, and if Geoffrey Christian was surprised by Walsingham's knowledge of his wife's family, then he didn't show it. "It might be worthwhile to learn what your Spanish brother-in-law is about. He may have spoken boastfully, perhaps indiscreetly, to your wife's father. We must never lose an opportunity to learn. The information may prove useful one day," Walsingham said. "Sir Basil, you are fluent in many languages, including Spanish, I believe. And you and the captain are also longtime friends. Yes, that will serve quite nicely. And Doña Magdalena is a favorite of—"

"—of mine, Master Spy, and I know where your mind leads you and I want to hear none of it. Enough of treachery and deceit! They plague my very footsteps in my own palace," Elizabeth raged. "I am giving Geoffrey Christian license to journey to the Indies because I do not wish to have anyone's death on my conscience. Whatever else may come of this voyage is incidental," she proclaimed with a reproachful look at Walsingham. "However, if Sir Basil is determined to travel with his good friend, which is most commendable, then he might as well carry my personal good wishes to Doña Magdalena's family. And I certainly shall not turn a deaf ear to Sir Basil's report when he returns," she assured a stunned Sir Basil.

When all eyes turned to him, Sir Basil felt himself growing pale, especially when Geoffrey Christian's laugh rang out when he fully understood his Queen's tactics.

" 'Sdeath! 'Tis about time you saw some of the world you've only been reading about until now, Sir Basil," Geoffrey Christian declared much to Her Grace's amusement, for Sir Basil Whitelaw was considered to be quite the scholarly gentleman, having taken a degree at Cambridge and studied law at Gray's Inn.

"Well, I—" Sir Basil began, a blush of painful embarrassment appearing on his pale cheeks as he sought the proper words of refusal. He was slow to realize that he had been expertly outmaneuvered by Walsingham and the queen, who knew exactly what she was about.

"We cannot always choose how we would wish to spend our time, Sir Basil. God knows I fear the truth of that, but too often the best purpose is served when we put our personal wants aside," Elizabeth said quietly, earnestly, as if talking to a child.

Sir Basil felt shamed and quickly spoke to reassure his queen of his loyalty, and unthinkingly so in his haste. "I would serve Your Grace through an eternity in Hell."

"By my faith! 'Tis where my enemies, especially His Most Catholic Majesty, would see me soon enough. Daughter of the Devil indeed!" she laughed, apparently finding more humor in Sir Basil's unfortunate remark than had either Cecil or Walsingham, both of whom remained unsmiling.

"Good sir. You need not go that far on my behalf, only as far as the Indies," she added, her black eyes twinkling with mirth, and this time even Walsingham had to smile slightly.

Geoffrey Christian, his laughter abating, couldn't help but feel sorry for poor Basil. He was such a sincere yet serious fellow that he never quite knew how to react to Her Grace's jesting.

"Rest assured you will have my most hearty thanks, Sir Basil, for the venture you are about to set out upon for the good of England," Elizabeth told him, holding out her hand for him to kiss.

* * *

For the good of England, that was what Sir Basil had to keep repeating to himself as they'd crossed the Atlantic. Now, as he stood on deck watching the sunrise, he idly wondered whatever would he do when they reached Hispaniola. He was not a spy. He could translate Greek and Latin better than he would be able to deciper any Spanish missives he might stumble across. And only too obviously *stumble* it would be, he feared.

"Such a beautiful morning following a storm should bring a smile to your face, Sir Basil."

"Indeed, madam, it is a glorious morning, and all the more beautiful for your presence," Sir Basil greeted Doña Magdalena, who had come up on deck and now stood beside him, with a courtly bow and phrase.

Doña Magdalena smiled archly. "Were not Geoffrey watching and listening from above, I would suspect you of a flirtation, Sir Basil," she said.

"Doña Magdalena, truly, I meant no such thing," Sir Basil said in order to quickly disabuse her of that idea.

"You think I am not beautiful enough to flirt with?" she asked, looking offended before she hid her expression behind a feather fan she expertly wielded.

"Madam, please, you misunderstand me," Sir Basil said in growing concern. "You are one of the most beautiful women I have ever seen." He did indeed speak the truth. Doña Magdalena, dressed in a gown of gold-patterned green brocade with a richly figured underskirt worked in gold threads, was breathtakingly lovely. A fiery emerald dangled from several long ropes of gleaming pearls. A girdle of precious stones and golden chains sparkled around her waist and emphasized her slimness in the tight-fitting, stiff bodice. A high lace ruff accentuated the long slenderness of her throat and framed the dark red curls crowned with a heart-shaped lace headdress.

"Sir Basil, I had no idea you felt that way about my wife. What will Lady Elspeth have to say when she learns of your indiscretion?" Geoffrey Christian called down from above.

"No, really, 'tis not true. I—" Sir Basil began, then, hearing their laughter, realized that both Magdalena and Geoffrey had been making sport of him.

"Dear Basil," Doña Magdalena said, a smile of genuine affection curving her lips as she stared up at him, for Sir Basil was a

tall man who often had to stoop when in conversation if he intended to catch what was said. "Will you never learn not to be
quite so serious a gentleman?"

"I fear not, madam," Sir Basil admitted, very seriously.
"Not at all? Hmm? Not even a little?" Doña Magdalena teased
him while watching him carefully, for no one could be so grave.

Sir Basil laughed softly, for he could not resist her charms.
"Perhaps just a little, but only when on board the *Arion*. I do
have a reputation to live up to in London."

"There, did I not tell you, Magdalena, that we would make a
changed man of Basil by the end of this voyage?" Geoffrey reminded her as he and Lily carefully began to make their way
down from the rigging.

"Now, if only I had the other Whitelaw brother on board
. . ." the captain of the *Arion* speculated, allowing the rest of his
sentiment to remain unspoken, which left Basil in little doubt of
what Geoffrey Christian's influence on his spirited, adventur-
ous brother would have been. He was thankful that he had not
had to witness the many years of gentlemanly training go completely unheeded while Geoffrey Christian taught Valentine the
finer points of being a successful privateer.

"So, I've been betrayed, have I, and he signed on with
Drake, eh, Basil? Preferred that Devonshire sea dog to me?
'Sdeath, but there's no loyalty among the thievin' rascals,"
Geoffrey Christian complained good-naturedly, for he had
supped with Drake on the eve of their departure.

"He was most disappointed that he could not sail with us,
Geoffrey," Basil called up to the captain. "But he could not
break his word to Drake."

"Nor would I have wished him to. Wouldn't want a man
who could break his word as easily as that on board the *Arion*.
Besides, 'twill serve us well having those hungry sea pups sailing these waters. The Spaniards will be too busy worrying about
what mischief the *Swan* and her hot-blooded young crew is
about to give us more than a passing thought."

Basil Whitelaw frowned. "You think they will find trouble?"

Geoffrey Christian grinned, and Basil would have sworn that
his friend was envious of the *Swan*'s chances of crossing bows
with a Spanish galleon or two.

"You needn't worry about Valentine," Geoffrey finally said,

relenting when he caught sight of his friend's worried expression. "Valentine is sailing with Drake, and he's learned his trade well. One day there'll be none finer, mark my words. Besides, Valentine reminds me of myself when I was that age. Bold as brass, he is, but then he has every reason to be; he's clever, that one. Inherited that from you. He'll be captain of his own ship soon enough," Geoffrey predicted.

That hardly set Basil Whitelaw's mind at ease.

"You worry too much about that one, Basil," Geoffrey advised.

But Doña Magdalena met Basil's look of concern with one of understanding. "There is little you can do, Sir Basil, once the sea gets into their blood. You must just continue to have faith. We have no say in what is meant to happen. Valentine could live peacefully in the city, perhaps become a wealthy merchant," Doña Magdalena said, then shrugged. "Then one day the plague comes, and he is dead. As long as he is happy, content. Is that not the best way to live a life?"

Basil could not fault her reasoning, for she was right, but still he could not stop worrying about Valentine. There were so many years between them, close to fifteen, that he had always felt more like a father to Valentine than an elder brother.

"Mama! Mama! Look at me! I've touched the stars, and now I'm going to touch the sun!" Lily called down excitedly to her mother as Magdalena calmly watched her husband and daughter make their way down out of the rigging.

Sir Basil stared in amazement at Magdalena's serene face. Not once had she caught her breath in fear or called out anxiously to Geoffrey. Feeling Basil's eyes on her, Magdalena smiled, and Basil would have sworn that she nearly reached out and patted his hand as if trying to comfort him for *his* fears.

"Her shoe?" she asked, noticing the small object Sir Basil still held in his hand.

"Yes, I thought it was a cannon ball when it landed on my shoulder."

Magdalena chuckled in appreciation. "There, you are already beginning to laugh at yourself. But not too much, we wouldn't wish Her Majesty to ask you to become the court jester when we return to London."

Sir Basil laughed, then seeing Geoffrey slip slightly as he

neared the deck, he asked with genuine curiosity, "Do you not worry?"

Doña Magdalena frowned, then she smiled when she caught his meaning as he continued to stare nervously at the pair coming down. "Geoffrey would not have taken her up there unless he knew she would be safe. He would never do anything to put any of us in harm. His own safety perhaps he is careless of, but never another's, and especially not his daughter's. If he had thought she would be afraid, then he would not have taken her aloft. But Lily is Geoffrey's daughter. I do not think she is afraid of anything. We debated bringing Lily along, but I could not bear to leave her alone in England, nor would she have allowed us to. I am certain she would have stowed away rather than have been left behind. Besides, I would like my mother and father to see my daughter. I am very proud of her and of my marriage. I want them to see that I am so very happy. That I have been blessed."

Sir Basil remained silent. "You must be looking forward to returning home, Doña Magdalena."

"Home?" Doña Magdalena shook her head. "I am looking forward to seeing my mother. I have missed her greatly, Sir Basil. I have also missed my father. He is a good man even if he is not a very forgiving one. I have also been lonely without my sister to confide in. We were a close family at one time. There was much love among us. But my home is now in England with my husband," Magdalena said firmly, and Sir Basil believed her. "Hispaniola holds treasured memories for me, *sí*, but not memories of longing or regret because I am no longer there. When I spent my first winter in England, I thought I would not live to see the spring; so cold and dark and strange it was. I could not understand half of what was said to me, but somehow, with Geoffrey's love and cheerful manner, I survived. Now, I actually find that I miss the cool rains and the mists. I think I would also miss the harsh tongue of the English. Geoffrey took great pains to teach me how to speak proper English, although he says he learned more of my language than I did of his." Magdalena laughed, then grew serious. "I miss Highcross. And you may believe me when I say this, Sir Basil. I look forward to returning home."

Basil Whitelaw, reluctant spy and homesick traveler, nodded his agreement, for he could not have put it more succinctly.

It is the stars,
The stars above us, govern our conditions.

SHAKESPEARE

Chapter Two

STRIKING her colors and topsails as a sign of courtesy and nonaggression to the Spanish authorities in Santo Domingo, the *Arion* sailed peacefully into the busy harbor at the mouth of the Rio Ozama. Half a dozen three- and four-masted galleons were riding at anchor when the English ship closed with the land and, having given the Spanish ships a wide berth, let go her anchor. Several of the galleons were riding light, while others were being refitted. Their cargoes of wine, olives, and cooking oil, clothing, household items, and necessities not to be found in the New World had been unloaded. Other galleons were surrounded by smaller boats, their crews busy hauling on blocks and tackle as they hoisted aboard the planters' valuable harvest of sugar. The casks joined the rest of the cargo carefully stored in the ships' holds, where bales of indigo, tobacco, cacao, and hardwoods; chests of silver and gold; pearls from the oyster beds off the coast of Venezuela; emeralds from mines high in the mountains of Columbia; and exotic birds and animals from the jungles of Guiana and Panama would further entice merchants and adventurers alike to seek their fortunes in the New World. The cargoes safely stored aboard, the galleons would sail for Havana, where they would join the treasure fleet assembled of heavily laden ships from Cartagena, Nombre de Dios, Veracruz, and other ports along the Main for the long journey home.

For a moment, Geoffrey Christian observed the ships with a

gleam in his eye, then he shrugged, for there would be other fleets sailing for Seville that he and his crew could raid. For now, he would bide his time and graciously welcome aboard the port officials who would soon be swarming over his ship. Fortunately, since there was an old score to be settled, Don Pedro Enrique de Villasandro had not become the next governor of Hispaniola, and Magdalena's second cousin was a high-ranking customs officer in Santo Domingo; he would see that they received no undue attention and were not unnecessarily detained in getting ashore.

Built on the west bank of the estuary, with a fortified wall for protection, Santo Domingo was a city of broad avenues lined with stately buildings and tall palms. The homes of the wealthy were two-storied, whitewashed stucco mansions built around center courtyards and gardens, the columned galleries, arched windows and iron entrance gates reflecting the Moorish influence of the Old World.

Warehouses and government offices crowded along the river front, and a plaza with a cathedral, a mission, and priests' quarters occupied a place of honor in the center of town. Near the river's mouth were the fort and the governor's residence, and La Calle de las Damas, a wide thoroughfare, led into the heart of the city, where plazas with shops and businesses and small chapels were located. Santo Domingo had once been the capital of the Spanish empire in the New World; the establishment of a hospital and university had helped it to remain more than a barely civilized colonial outpost after the capital had been moved to Cartagena.

Casa del Montevares, the home Magdalena had not seen since she had sailed for Spain over seven years earlier, was as grand as any wealthy hidalgo's home in Seville or Madrid. Thick walls and tiled floors repelled the heat, while high arched ceilings and long windows allowed the cooling breezes to circulate throughout the house. When storms raged, heavy shutters could be pulled tight against the winds and rains, but usually the windows remained unshuttered both day and night.

Although his shoulders were stooped slightly, as if from great weariness rather than age, Don Rodrigo was still a very proud man as he stood on the bottom step of the great staircase

in the entrance hall of Casa del Montevares when Magdalena
and her family arrived.

Geoffrey Christian, one of his hands clasped tightly by his
daughter as she stared about her in wonder, his other hand resting lightly on his sword hilt, eyed the stern-visaged Spaniard
and thought that some things never changed. Don Rodrigo still
looked the disapproving father who would never forgive his
daughter for having married against his wishes. Geoffrey hadn't
missed the arrogant lifting of Don Rodrigo's bearded chin when
he caught sight of the heathen Englishmen entering his home,
and in that instant Geoffrey had known that Don Rodrigo had
hoped his daughter would return home unaccompanied by her
family. Watching Magdalena's uncertainty as she greeted her father, Geoffrey wondered if perhaps they all had not made a mistake in coming. It was only too obvious by Don Rodrigo's curt
nod to his daughter, who had unconsciously held out her arms
to him when she had seen him, that the stiff-necked old gentleman wasn't about to forgive and forget.

However, Goeffrey hadn't missed Don Rodrigo's dark eyes
lingering on his daughter's face once or twice when he thought
himself unobserved, and Geoffrey would have sworn that Don
Rodrigo's thin-lipped mouth twitched just slightly when Lily
walked up to the Spaniard and brazenly demanded a kiss from
her *abuelo*, her words spoken in perfect Spanish perhaps as surprising to her grandfather as had been the request.

Don Rodrigo remained imperiously silent and apparently
unmoved as he stared down at his granddaughter for the first
time.

Magdalena held her breath, more concerned for her daughter
now than she had been when she and Basil had watched Lily
balancing on Geoffrey's lap when he had taken her high into the
ship's rigging.

"I do not think we have been properly introduced," Don
Rodrigo said sternly, for this small replica of Magdalena needed
to be taught some manners. She was an impudent little monkey
and apparently had never been taught to show proper respect
for her elders.

Lily frowned slightly, as if giving his words careful consideration, then she nodded. "Very well, sir. I am Lily Francisca
Christian. You are Don Rodrigo Francisco Esteban de Cabrion y

Montevares. Now I know you and you know me. Are you going to give me a kiss?"

Don Rodrigo seemed taken aback by her smooth recitation of his full name. As she continued to stand there with her hands planted firmly on her hips, staring up at him with incredibly bright green eyes, he bowed courteously. "Lily *Francisca*," he said, lingering with pleasure on the Spanish name, for it showed him that his daughter had not completely forgotten her heritage. He felt an impatient tug on the richly decorated silk of his slashed breeches and was reminded of his duty. Bending low, he met his granddaughter's steady gaze as she held her face up to his expectantly and unflinchingly. Lily was unaware that her grandfather was a strict disciplinarian and might have slapped her soft cheek for having been so disrespectfully forward. But Don Rodrigo, as he continued to meet that bold yet innocent stare, could not deny his own flesh and blood. *"Mi dulce batata pequeña,"* he murmured as he kissed the rose-petal smooth cheek held up so ingenuously.

Lily giggled. *"¡Batata!"* she squealed, repeating the word that Magdalena remembered as an endearment her father had been fond of calling her when she'd been Lily's age. "I'm not a sweet potato! I eat sweet potatoes," she said with another giggle.

"It would be wise to remember that *bad* little sweet potatoes often get cooked and eaten," Don Rodrigo advised her as Lily's mouth dropped open in amazement.

"But you said I was your sweet little sweet potato," Lily reminded him as she tucked her hand in his confidingly. "Papa says they are the true treasure from the New World, and he'd rather capture a ship with a hold full of sweet potatoes than one with a hold full of gold."

Don Rodrigo drew breath to speak then glanced over at Magdalena, a helpless look on his face. "Already she flirts outrageously. You taught her Spanish?" he asked. "You were allowed to do this?" he continued, his meaning obvious as his gaze moved to include the tall figure of Geoffrey Christian.

"Sí, mi padre."

"You may still believe that I stole your daughter from you, Don Rodrigo, but I never intended to steal her heritage from her. Although circumstances have brought about a certain heightening of hostilities between our countries, my daughter has been taught to have no shame of her Spanish blood and to be proud of *all* of her ancestors," Geoffrey stated, those pale green eyes of his, so like his daughter's, unshadowed by deception. Don Rodrigo could not doubt his English son-in-law's word, for did not his granddaughter speak her mother's native tongue?

"¿*Padre? Mi*—"

Magdalena did not have to finish her question, for her father knew what she had been reluctant to ask. "Your mother still lives. You have arrived in time to comfort her with your presence," he admitted, then turned his attention to the other Englishman darkening his door, a less than cordially raised eyebrow questioning the man's presence in Casa del Montevares. "I do not believe we have been introduced, *señor?*" he inquired in a tone that left little doubt that had he his wish they would continue to remain strangers.

Basil Whitelaw still stood hesitantly near the great door. He had been uncertain of Geoffrey Christian's welcome, much less his own when Don Rodrigo learned he came as special envoy from Elizabeth, but now he stepped forward and bowed deeply and deferentially to the Spaniard. With a fine flourish, he removed a stiff piece of parchment from the top of a packet he carried tucked beneath his arm. Basil Whitelaw handed the letter to Don Rodrigo. It was folded and affixed with melted wax, which bore the stamped impression of the royal seal of Elizabeth.

Don Rodrigo was startled, for who in England could possibly be writing to him? When he recognized the royal arms displayed so boldly on the letter that he, a loyal subject of Philip II, now held so gingerly in his hand, Sir Basil thought the Spaniard was going to drop it like a burning coal.

"*Madre de Dios*," Don Rodrigo muttered, turning pale as he fingered the high, stiff ruff about his neck. It suddenly felt much tighter than usual.

"With Her Majesty's sincerest compliments, Don Rodrigo," Basil Whitelaw said, urging the Spaniard to open the missive from the queen of England.

With a shaking hand, Don Rodrigo broke the seal and opened the folded sheet of foolscap. His expression was disbelieving as he stared down at the elaborate signature of Elizabeth.

"Her Majesty has instructed me to extend to you and your family her deepest sympathies and personal wishes for a quick recovery for Doña Amparo. Her Grace takes very seriously the welfare of her subjects, and she was most distressed to learn of Doña Magdalena's unhappiness concerning the ill health of her mother. Without hesitation, and indeed I speak from firsthand knowledge for I was present at the meeting between her Majesty and Geoffrey Christian, her Grace gladly granted him leave to travel to Hispaniola," Basil Whitelaw said with all of the smoothness of a born diplomat, which meant he only told Don Rodrigo what he needed to know and did not go on to mention the names of the other two gentlemen present at that meeting. "I am here, at her Grace's request, personally to lend support to Doña Magdalena and her family, and, on behalf of Queen Elizabeth, I hereby offer my services to you and your family should the occasion arise.

"Please understand, Don Rodrigo, that I do this not only because my queen has requested it, but because Doña Magdalena has become a dear friend of my family."

"Lady Elspeth, Sir Basil's wife, has become my dearest friend, *Padre*. They have welcomed me into their home and given me their friendship when I had no friends," Doña Magdalena said.

Sir Basil smiled. "It has always been our privilege. However, Doña Magdalena no longer is friendless. She has become one of Her Majesty's favorites at court. In fact, your daughter, Don Rodrigo, had the very great honor of being hostess to Queen Elizabeth and her court when they visited Highcross Court last year. Seldom have I seen or enjoyed such entertainment as was provided for Her Grace's pleasure. Several times I heard Her Majesty compliment Doña Magdalena on her gracious hospitality, declaring never had she eaten so well. She especially enjoyed the spicy sauces that Doña Magdalena seems to prepare with such excellence. You can be very proud of Doña Magdalena, Don Rodrigo," Sir Basil said, surprised by his own loquacity but thinking it was about time the imperious don heard a few truths about the honor his daughter had brought to his own family's name as well as to Geoffrey Christian's.

But Don Rodrigo surprised Sir Basil with his answer. "I would have expected nothing less from a daughter of mine. She is a Montevares, Sir Basil. She knows her duty. Now, I have been neglectful of my duties as host. You must be fatigued from your journey. Ana will show you to your rooms," Don Rodrigo said, indicating the maid who had quietly entered the hall and now stood awaiting her master's orders, her head bowed. "Magdalena, I will take you to see your mother now. Ana, take the gentlemen and Francisca to the rooms that have been prepared for their visit. I will have some refreshment sent up," he added. The maid, however, remained unmoving, and he had to repeat his order more sharply. "Ana!" he said again.

Finally, she curtsied and risked a quick glance at the two strangers. Her eyes were filled with fear, for she had never met Englishmen. She had heard that they were devils spawned of a heathen land, and here was her dear, sweet Magdalena married to one of the most notorious. Still, even Ana had to admit that Magdalena had never looked more beautiful. Bewitchment. That was what had happened. Her poor Magdalena had been bewitched and her soul was no longer her own, Ana thought, crossing herself before she moved any closer to Geoffrey Christian. He did seem harmless enough, though, as he lifted his daughter into his arms, tickling her beneath the chin in response to the secret she whispered in his ear.

"You have servants who will need quarters?" Don Rodrigo inquired.

Geoffrey Christian grinned. "We thought the smaller the party, the better. They are quite English and not fond of traveling far from home. My steward is acting as valet de chambre for both Sir Basil and myself. And I lend assistance to milady when the need arises. Lily, of course, is no longer in need of her nursemaid. Are you, heartling?"

"I'm a young lady now," Lily said proudly.

"I see. Maria, Magdalena's former maid, will assume those duties now," Don Rodrigo told them.

"A kiss for Mama?" Doña Magdalena inquired as she brushed a fold out of Lily's underskirt and straightened the lace on the sleeve of Geoffrey's doublet.

Lily gave her a tight hug and a kiss, then waved to her mother and grandfather as she was carried up the stairs by her father. Don Rodrigo shook his head as he continued to watch her, for now she was making comical faces at Sir Basil, who was following them upstairs. His gentlemanly dignity was being sorely compromised as he unsuccessfully tried to resist her childish pranks.

Sir Basil found himself in a dark-beamed, high-ceilinged room that fronted a long, arched gallery overlooking the tiled courtyard below. A comfortable-looking bed with a carved bedstead and lace spread was positioned against one wall, and a mahogany chest, a chair, and a small table with a candle and mirror completed the furnishings of the room. Walking over to the window opposite the door, he had a splendid view of the harbor, which afforded him the comforting sight of the furled masts of the *Arion* riding at anchor.

Awakening the next morning, Sir Basil was surprised that he had been able to sleep so soundly in strange surroundings. He was reluctant to admit, having always thought himself to be a man of moderation, that it had been because of the wine.

But seldom had he tasted such fine madeira or sherry. And Don Rodrigo had played the host to perfection. He had plied his guests with wine, never allowing a goblet to remain empty longer than it took his servant to refill it to the top. And with a negligible gesture of a ringed hand, he had kept course after delectable course coming, until Sir Basil thought he would have need of assistance in leaving the table.

The meal had not been quite the ordeal Sir Basil had been expecting. Don Rodrigo had even managed to be courteous to his son-in-law, although he had not pursued any more personal conversation with the man than the expected pleasantries exchanged amongst dinner guests. Strangely enough, the bulk of the conversation had fallen to Doña Magdalena and himself, while Geoffrey Christian and Don Rodrigo had sat in silence, neither one caring to contribute more than a murmured comment now and then. Doña Magdalena had spoken in great detail of her life in both England and Hispaniola. Don Rodrigo showed the most interest when she spoke of Highcross Court, and Geoffrey smiled more than once when she reminisced about her childhood in Santo Domingo.

Those remarks had elicited several comments from Don Rodrigo about the startling similarity between Magdalena and her young daughter. Lily had already been served her dinner and put to bed hours earlier, a situation Sir Basil had almost regretted when the dinner had begun with such uncomfortable formality.

Yes, Sir Basil thought now, it had been a very wise decision to bring the child, for Lily just might serve as a means of bringing Don Rodrigo and his daughter, and perhaps even her husband, closer together.

Sir Basil stood basking in the sunshine streaming in through the opened window. He had awakened earlier than the rest of the household, for all was silent except for the busy chatterings of brightly colored birds.

As he shielded his eyes against the glare off the water, Sir Basil realized that he felt quite refreshed. How nice it had been not to be awakened when thrown from his bunk or to find the floor slanting beneath his feet with each wave that pounded the ship. And as he thought of the blizzard-driven winds of January in England, he had to confess that it was rather pleasant not to have to hop about a chilled bedchamber in search of slippers and robe and then, huddling before a cursedly slow-to-start fire, try to melt the ice out of his stiff limbs.

Indeed, Sir Basil was quite surprised to discover that he was actually beginning to enjoy his journey to the Indies and his mission as special emissary of Queen Elizabeth. With a slight smile of satisfaction, Sir Basil thought of the tale of adventure, interspersed, of course, with appropriately imagined moments of suspense and danger, that he, courageous knight errant, would entertain his friends and family with when he returned home to England.

I'll note you in my book of memory.

SHAKESPEARE

Chapter Three

SIR BASIL was to find that the routine of the following days differed little from that first day of their arrival in Santo Domingo. Magdalena spent most of each day at her mother's bedside. Doña Amparo, who had suffered a stroke that had left her partly paralyzed, was confined to her bed and grew restless whenever Magdalena was out of her sight. What little nourishment she would take was by her daughter's hand. It was as if Doña Amparo knew she was dying and intended to spend what precious little time she had left in the world with the daughter and the granddaughter she had been denied seeing for so long.

Doña Amparo's own dark red hair was silvered with age and twisted into a thick braid that seemed far too heavy for the frail shoulder it lay across. Day after day she lay in bed, oblivious to the pain each breath cost her, and listened contentedly to Magdalena's soft voice telling her about every moment of her life since she had married her Englishman and made England her home.

Lily, her young hand caught and held tightly by the one blue-veined hand that still retained some of its former strength, would sit quietly on the edge of her grandmother's lace-covered bed and chatter tirelessly about her home and her friends and her father's adventures to faraway places. Doña Amparo's deep brown eyes, dulled into colorlessness by illness, grew bright and missed no expression crossing that small, animated face filled with all of the wonders life held for the young.

Often, when enjoying a moment or two of quiet reflection in the sunny courtyard, Sir Basil would hear the sounds of laughter coming from Doña Amparo's darkened room at the end of the opened gallery above, a child's infectious giggle carrying farthest. He was amazed by Lily Christian's unresentful acceptance of having to spend so much time in her grandmother's room, for it could not have been a very pleasant experience to witness one of Doña Amparo's frequent attacks. And yet never once had he heard Lily complain to be set free from so disheartening a responsibility as keeping a dying person company. With a wisdom and patience that even he himself would find hard to come by, especially at so young an age, Lily accepted the hour or so she had to herself in the courtyard, making the most of the time allowed her before returning to her grandmother's room. And Sir Basil often thought that never had he known a child who could manage to get into such mischief in so short a time.

The days numbered close to a week when Geoffrey Christian surprised everyone, except perhaps Magdalena, by announcing that he was heading back to sea. His men had been in port long enough now to have provoked censure from the authorities. The English crew's good-natured rowdiness and appreciative eye for a trim ankle had resulted in several heated arguments with outraged gentlemen demanding satisfaction on behalf of their insulted wives and mistresses. Before an incident resulted in the unfortunate death of one of Philip II's loyal subjects, the captain of the *Arion* declared he would have his lads back on board and too busy manning the capstan and making sail to be of any further annoyance to the affronted gentlemen of Santo Domingo.

The *Arion* would steer a course south, along the coast of Brazil—Portuguese territory—or, at least that is what Geoffrey Christian wanted the port officials to believe. Whether or not the *Arion* kept to that course would be known only to the captain and crew.

Don Rodrigo had not pretended to hide his relief at the sudden departure of Geoffrey Christian, especially since Magdalena and Lily would remain in Santo Domingo while the Englishman sailed the seas and most likely wreaked havoc throughout the Indies. There had been no lessening of hostility between the two men, and it had seemed to Sir Basil that Don Rodrigo had found it increasingly difficult to keep a civil tongue when around Geof-

frey Christian. It was not that Geoffrey intentionally antago-
nized his father-in-law, it was just that Geoffrey Christian was
so brazenly English with his fair hair and boisterous manner. Sir
Basil suspected that it had not relieved the tension any when
Doña Amparo, despite Don Rodrigo's objections, had requested
Geoffrey's presence on several occasions. Geoffrey's pleased expression when he had left Doña Amparo's room had left little
doubt in Sir Basil's mind that the captain of the *Arion* had made
use of his considerable charm and set at ease any fears Doña Amparo might have had about her daughter's happiness. Sir Basil,
however, knew that Geoffrey would not have had to say anything to convince Doña Amparo of his sincerity. His deep love
for his wife and daughter was only too evident in the gentle expression that entered his eyes whenever he gazed upon them.
Gone was the ruthless, rough-talking sea captain many an enemy had good reason to fear. And many a defeated foe would
have been comforted to know that the seemingly invincible captain of the *Arion* did have a weakness—Magdalena and Lily.
They made Geoffrey Christian as vulnerable and human as the
rest of them.

The morning the *Arion* sailed on the tide, Magdalena and Lily
stood on the quayside and waved until the last flash of sail disappeared beyond the horizon. Sir Basil had also remained in Santo
Domingo. He had reminded his friend that he was not a good
sailor and could be of more value on shore. He would use his
eyes and ears to learn all he could. Sir Basil had added this last
rejoinder mockingly, thinking he would idle away the days
playing chess with Don Rodrigo.

Sir Basil had not been wrong, at least not in the beginning.
He and Don Rodrigo had played a great deal of chess during the
next fortnight. They had also ridden out to Don Rodrigo's sugar
plantation near a small village south of Santo Domingo. Although he was no longer actively involved in the management of
the plantation, his recent partner having assumed those duties
and hired a new overseer, Don Rodrigo had personally given Sir
Basil a tour of the fields and the mill, where the cut cane was
ground and crushed, and the sweet juice boiled until a thick,
dark syrup formed before the sugar crystals were separated from
the molasses. Sir Basil, however, remembered little of the tour
after that or much of the return journey. Having developed a

thirst in the midday heat, he had mistakenly accepted a deep draft of rum from his host.

Don Rodrigo had even guided the Englishman on a tour of Santo Domingo. Sir Basil was so fine a gentleman, listening with such polite attention, that shopkeepers and dockworkers, seamen and wealthy citizens were eager to talk proudly and expansively about their city and their lives. Soon, Sir Basil's leather-bound journal was filled with entries. His neat script described every detail of life in Santo Domingo. The type of fortifications and number of troops at the fort were noted, as were the ships and warehouses, and the cargoes and goods loaded and stored in each. A detailed map of the city and the countryside south of Santo Domingo occupied two pages. Names and dates and interesting gossip concerning not only the people in Santo Domingo but persons in Spain and other parts of the Spanish Main were all reported, and Sir Basil never failed to be amazed at the startling amount of information people seemed to know without realizing that they knew something important. At least it became important when he added it to some other seemingly innocent remark.

Sir Basil had just completed his latest entry: the floor plans to the Alcazar—the viceroy of the Indies' mansion—and the governor's palace. With a sigh of dissatisfaction, he carefully placed the journal at the bottom of his trunk, beneath his finest silk hose. Although he had been successful in gathering his information, he felt only contempt for himself. At times he felt as if he were betraying a friend. He had come to enjoy his long conversations with Don Rodrigo. They had found that they had much in common, despite their different nationalities and faiths. He respected the Spaniard, and he despised himself for sneaking up to his room like some thief in the night and recording all that Don Rodrigo had confided to him.

Sir Basil found it hard to meet his own eyes in his reflection in the mirror as he cleaned the ink from his fingertips with a dampened cloth. Even the sad-faced Madonna staring down at him from the painting hanging above his bed seemed to be accusing him of some heinous crime. Rather than remain in his room any longer, which was his custom as well as that of the other occupants of the casa at this time of the day, he decided to seek a diversion from his guilty thoughts. Giving a last cursory glance at his appearance, he left the room, pausing for a moment to admire the brilliance of the exotic flowers in the courtyard. As he stood there staring down, he became aware of a child's voice raised in conversation. He searched the courtyard and was rewarded by a movement near a tall potted palm. Lily Christian was sitting cross-legged in front of a large wooden cage filled with brightly colored birds. The larger parrots and macaws with their scarlet, yellow, and azure plumage and strident cries caught and held the child's attention. Sir Basil smiled, wishing for a moment that he could join Lily in her childish amusements. It was then that he heard the commotion below, little realizing that his life was about to change drastically because of it.

Don Pedro Enrique de Villasandro, captain of the *Estrella D'Alba*, which had just docked, and former captain of the *Maria Concepción*, which was now on the bottom of the sea courtesy of Geoffrey Christian, looked around the entrance hall of Casa del Montevares with annoyance.

"*¿Qué es esto?*" he demanded in growing anger as he continued to stare at the empty entrance hall. "*¿Como está? ¿Como está?*" he called out but received no response. "*¡Madre de Dios!*" he muttered, not having missed the amused glances that passed between the two gentlemen standing just behind him.

"Pedro, *por favor!*" Catalina pleaded, not wishing for their arrival to be marred by an unpleasant meeting between her husband and her father, both of whom could be so unreasonable at times.

"You would think we were English raiders come to dine the way those servants ran and hid when they saw us," Don Pedro exclaimed, aware that his scornful words carried to the two gentlemen behind him, but unaware of how close to the mark his words really were.

"*No me siento bien, Madre,*" the little boy holding on to Catalina's hand whined. "*Me siento mareado.*"

"*¡Dios mio!* If you get sick on my gown again, Francisco . . ." his harassed mother complained, thinking that was all she needed with Pedro fuming, one daughter sulking while the other two traded pinches, her mother ill, her father disappeared, and, now, Magdalena coming down the stairs—

"Aaaah!" Catalina cried out, scaring poor Francisco into a fit of hiccups, her daughters into high-pitched squeals, and causing Don Pedro to spin around, his sword drawn and at the ready only to have its tip caught and pulled out of his grasp in the stiff folds of Catalina's gown as she hurried past him.

"¿*Qué?*" she said, spinning around just as Don Pedro made a futile reach to recapture his elusive sword. The laughter of the two gentlemen, not to mention the strangely muffled sounds coming from the deeply cowled priest standing just behind them, did not help to lessen Don Pedro's growing frustrations.

"¡*Sangre de Dios!*" he swore, then glanced apologetically at the priest. "Will you stand still, Catalina?" he pleaded as he pulled his dangling sword free of the silken folds just before his wife and his recently freed sword were encompassed in yet another entangling swirl of silk.

Don Pedro finally realized who was embracing his wife, and glancing over his shoulder at the laughing gentlemen, he spat, "You fools! That is my wife's sister. Geoffrey Christian's wife! Unless you want her to recognize you, and then, God forbid, have him come swaggering down the stairs next, then go into the courtyard before you are seen. Quickly!" he urged the two now serious-faced gentlemen, who quickly followed his bidding. The priest, whose dark robes whispered of his silent passing, was not far behind.

"Magdalena! *Mi hermana,*" Catalina cried, hugging her long-lost sister to her.

"Catalina! Oh, it has been so long!" Magdalena said tearfully.

Catalina, half-crying, half-laughing, held her younger sister at arm's length for a moment while she looked her up and down. "More beautiful than ever! Always, you were the pretty one," she said, but not jealously. "A good thing Pedro saw me first and that you were so much younger, or . . ." She let her words trail away as she hugged her sister close again. "Pedro!" she cried out, suddenly seeming to remember her husband standing at her side.

"It is Magdalena, Pedro! It is unbelievable, *sí?*" she demanded, far more delighted about the strange turn of events than her husband seemed to be.

"Indeed. I am surprised to see you in Don Rodrigo's home, Doña Magdalena, remembering as I do his bitterness at your betrayal," Don Pedro greeted his sister-in-law. "I find it difficult to believe that he has forgiven you. Or has that fine Englishman you wed left you for another woman, or, perhaps, even left you a widow?" he asked, hopeful of such a circumstance.

Magdalena raised her chin proudly. "*Mi padre* wrote to me and asked me to come home. He, Don Pedro, made the first gesture at reconciliation. *Mi madre* is very ill. I came to be at her side. I am also still very happily married to Geoffrey Christian, who is still very much alive," Magdalena said, taking great pleasure in saying the name she knew would cause her brother-in-law such irritation.

"A pity," Don Pedro murmured. "I did not see his ship anchored in the harbor. He did not accompany you to Santo Domingo?" he inquired. "Perhaps he has grown tired of going to sea and no longer captains a ship? Has he become one of those fat and lazy *inglés* surrounded by yapping hounds, and who cannot bear to leave his hearth and home? Lost his courage, eh? It has been known to happen," Don Pedro added sadly, hoping to bait Magdalena into telling him the exact whereabouts of the captain of the *Arion*.

"Should you wish to see how fat my husband has become, then please, you may see for yourself, for a pair of his breeches lies on my bed upstairs. I was darning a small rip when I heard your voices," Magdalena informed a rather startled Don Pedro, for even he had not expected that Geoffrey Christian was actually staying at Casa del Montevares. "Yes, *mi padre* has graciously accepted my husband as a guest in his home."

"Your husband sailed here with you? He is in Santo Domingo now?" Don Pedro demanded, his expression of concern causing Magdalena to smile.

"No, he has sailed, but we expect his return any day. Contrary to what you may believe, Don Pedro, the *Arion* sailed into Santo Domingo without a shot being fired. And nothing, thus far, has been looted. Unless, of course, you count the fluttering hearts lost to many a crew member aboard the *Arion*. It has happened before, if you remember the last time you met my husband," Magdalena reminded him, though she needn't have, for that was a memory that ate at Don Pedro every day of his life. The last time he had crossed bows with Geoffrey Christian had cost him his ship. That he would never forget.

"Magdalena, *por favor!*" Catalina requested nervously, for she herself would never have dared to speak to Pedro in so challenging a manner. Whatever had become of her sweet little sister? "You haven't met Francisco. Here, Francisco, come and kiss your *tía* Magdalena hello," she said, pulling her son between Magdalena and the glowering Pedro. "And I must know about *Madre*. She hasn't . . ."

"No."

"Ah, that is good then, for we could not sail until several unexpected passengers came aboard and delayed our departure from Seville. Had anything happened to *Madre* before I could arrive, and all because of *those* men," she confided, glancing around to give them a scathing look, but they had disappeared. "Where did they go?"

"Who?" Magdalena asked, glancing around curiously and setting Don Pedro's mind at ease, for it was apparent that she had not seen anyone but Catalina when she had come rushing down the stairs to greet them.

"Well, I could never forgive Pedro for insisting we wait for their arrival. For me, I have had enough of the sea. I intend to stay here with Francisco and the girls when Pedro sails with them for—"

"*Silencio*, Catalina," Don Pedro silenced his wife's prattle mid-sentence. "You do not know what you are saying," he warned her. "Magdalena is not interested in hearing about where next the *Estrella D'Alba* sails and what business my passengers are about. Merchants," he said, shrugging, as if he need say no more.

"We sail to France and *Padre* says that I will sail with them, and one day I will be a great sea captain like he is," Francisco told them proudly. "Only I don't think I want to be a captain. I get sick."

Don Pedro looked as if he were about to burst a blood vessel as he glared down at his son, but already Magdalena and Catalina were talking about everything under the sun, and his three excitable daughters were giggling and twirling around as they presented themselves to their aunt, each vying for her attention.

"¡Dios!" Don Rodrigo cried out as he came hurrying down the stairs and was engulfed by the new arrivals. In the confusion, Don Pedro took the opportunity of slipping away, one thought in his mind: getting his passengers safely back aboard ship before Magdalena recognized them as Englishmen.

But Don Pedro was to receive another shock. When he entered the courtyard, he found his passengers being confronted by a small, red-headed child of not more than five or six years of age. Were the surprises of this day never to end? The impertinent creature, he thought as he overheard her conversation and realized that his worst fears were confirmed—this could only be Geoffrey Christian's daughter.

"I've never seen anyone with one blue and one brown eye. Do you see different things out of each eye?" Lily asked the young gentleman standing so uncomfortably before her. "There's a man in our village, near Highcross, that is where I live in England, who has pink-colored eyes and white hair. He doesn't have very many friends, but Father says we should be kind to him. Did you know that they sometimes hang people or burn them at the stake for having one blue and one brown eye? They say they are witches," Lily told the gentleman, who found himself blinking uncontrollably. "Father says the officials are frightened fools. Are you a priest?" Lily demanded of the robed figure, turning her attention away from the other two gentlemen, much to their relief.

"We do not have many in England anymore. There used to be an abbey near Highcross, but it got burned to the ground and the priests fled to France. Hello!" Lily said as Don Pedro approached, his expression horrified. "I'm Lily Christian. Who are you? Are you sick?"

Don Pedro glanced at the two Englishmen, but the one who had caught Lily's attention was still staring in fascination at the child, and the other, his hat pulled low across his forehead, stood in the shadows. As Don Pedro drew closer, the priest beckoned him to his side and they began to talk in low tones, the Spanish words incomprehensible to the Englishmen.

Lily continued to stand nearby, staring at the strangers in growing curiosity.

"¡Váyase! ¡Váyase!" Don Pedro told her, those green eyes making him uneasy even if she couldn't understand what was being said. ¡Váyase!" he repeated again, never thinking twice about the fact that she immediately walked away, a hurt expression in those green eyes, for she had indeed understood his Spanish.

"Don Pedro." One of the nervous Englishmen now drew his attention, but spoke to the priest, who interpreted for him. "As you so timely brought to our attention, that woman was Geoffrey Christian's wife. She would remember my friend and, perhaps, me. What do we do now? What did she say? Do you not think it would be wise if we left before we have yet another encounter, and this time with Geoffrey Christian himself? Our cause may be lost, but at least we are still alive. And I have no desire to cross swords with Geoffrey Christian."

"You needn't worry about that. He is not in Santo Domingo. But you are mistaken. Our cause is not lost. Doña Magdalena did not notice you, but I do not intend to give her another chance to see you. Come, we will leave through the back passage."

"I don't suppose you would find us lodgings in town. I dread the thought of going back on board," the Englishman with the one blue and one brown eye said. "I've come to abhor the smell of the sea. I dare say I'll not eat fish again."

Don Pedro eyed the elegantly dressed Englishman with a look of distaste. Had the man not been on board the *Estrella D'Alba* at His Majesty's order, Don Pedro would have sent the man overboard long ago. "Come. You will at least be safe there. And getting you back to England without incident, *señor*, is far more important to me than your immediate comfort. I am surprised I need remind you of the importance of your task," Don Pedro told him.

"What of the child? She saw us."

"What of her? Did you speak to her?"

"No, but she spoke to us in English. She must have known we were not Spaniards."

"That was Geoffrey Christian's brat. Of course she would speak to you in English. Besides, you look English," Don Pedro added, for one of the Englishmen had silvery blond hair and very pale skin.

"She may say something about seeing us," the other Englishman said, speaking for the first time.

"And if she does?" Don Pedro said with a shrug of dismissal. "She saw two gentlemen and a priest. Guests of Don Rodrigo, nothing more. Does she know you are Englishmen? Do not concern yourself with her. She is but a child and can do no harm to you or to the ultimate success of our mission. Now, come before all is lost. We have delayed long enough.''

The Englishman who had held Lily's rapt attention glanced around uneasily. ''I wish I had your peace of mine, but as you may have noticed, I am a man not easily forgotten. I hope to God the brat doesn't speak of me.''

Don Pedro tried not to catch the man's eyes, for they were indeed unnatural. He resisted the impulse to cross himself as he walked past the man. ''I will hear of it if she should, and I will take the necessary steps to ensure your anonymity.''

As they disappeared through the narrow passageway leading toward the back entrance to Casa del Montevares, Sir Basil Whitelaw moved for the first time since the two gentlemen and the priest had rushed into the courtyard.

He shook his head in disbelief, for he had recognized one of the gentlemen. Unfortunately, the other man had kept his face averted, and the brim of his hat had hidden his features. He had also seemed of a more cautious nature than the other gentleman, preferring to stand in the shadows. But his style of dress marked him as an Englishman. The man who had entered last, a Spaniard, Sir Basil hadn't known, but there was no doubting the profession of the robed figure, the heavy cross dangling from his neck and glinting in the sun.

Sir Basil frowned, wondering why two Englishmen, a priest, and a Spaniard were meeting in Santo Domingo. Francis Walsingham would have been proud of him, for he was actually beginning to think like a spy.

For courage mounteth with occasion.

Chapter Four

THE fisherman, gold weighing heavily in his pocket, rowed as close to the *Estrella D'Alba* as he could without drawing the guards' attention. It was an overcast night, with no stars or moon to reveal the shallow-hulled craft's progress as it closed the distance between the shore and the looming bulk of the deep-drafted galleon riding at anchor in the bay. The fisherman smiled to himself. These fancy hidalgos were a greedy lot. But, he reminded himself, their greed had made him a wealthy man. He had often rowed one or two of them out to a galleon under cover of darkness so they could retrieve the contraband that had been so costly to smuggle in under the customs officials' long noses.

And this fine gentleman had been no different—except perhaps more nervous. Half hiding his face behind a scented lace handkerchief held to his high-bridged nose, his speech muffled yet elegantly spoken, he had certainly played the grandee until the first wave had lifted the boat's prow high into the sea spray. And without all of the finery, the simple fisherman imagined, he looked the same as any other man, and maybe not even as fine, for the gent was as rawboned and spindle-shanked as he'd ever seen.

Stripped down to his linen undergarments, Sir Basil slipped over the side of the boat and let the gentle swells carry him toward the galleon's curving hull. A block and tackle still hung from the stern where cargo had been loaded through an

46

afterport earlier in the day. A rope dangled from the pulley block, the frayed end conveniently close to the water and in reach of Sir Basil's outstretched hand. He pulled himself out of the water and began to shinny up the rope, his destination the carved balustrade, part of the gilded ornamentation gracing the stern, that guarded the small balcony outside the captain's cabin.

Climbing over the railing, he edged closer into the concealing blackness of the shadows beside the lattice windows, where a golden glow spread from the lantern-lit interior of the great cabin. His heart pounding more from anticipation than physical effort, Sir Basil risked a glance inside.

Three gentlemen and a priest were sitting around a table cluttered with silver plate and the remnants of what appeared to have been a sumptuous feast. Through a small, diamond-shaped pane of glass, he watched Don Pedro, whom he had been formally introduced to the night before at Casa del Montevares, raise a silver goblet in response to whatever toast had been made by one of his guests.

Sir Basil's gaze narrowed thoughtfully, for he had not been mistaken in his earlier recognition of a certain gentleman he had seen in the courtyard. Now, as the Englishman sat back down, Sir Basil saw for the first time the face of the other man. His identity was now fully revealed to Sir Basil's disbelieving gaze; it was a face he knew well. Not more than a year past, when he had dined with the court at Whitehall in celebration of the queen's accession to the throne, he and that very same gentleman, now dining on board a Spanish galleon, had toasted the good health of Elizabeth Tudor.

Turning his head, so his ear nearly touched the pane, Sir Basil listened intently.

" 'Twould be so easy to kill her. I have stood as close to her as I am now to you. Her palaces are not well guarded, and daily she takes the air, walking through St. James's Park and the streets of the City like some strutting courtesan. So very easy," the Englishman said, his pale blue eye glowing brighter, while the dark brown eye seemed to darken into blackness. "Should Elizabeth die, our true and rightful queen, Mary Stuart, would wear the crown that was stolen from her by that whore's daughter. A pity the king did not send her to the block when he sent the adultress.''

"You must learn patience, my son," the priest advised. ''The day will dawn when the true faith is restored to England. Until the glory of that day, you must spread our word to the devoted. You must make contact with others who still hold true to our beliefs and owe allegiance only to the pope. We must know of those we can trust to lend us aid when the time comes. By God's will we shall restore the faith. Until then, let the fires burn brighter and the blood stain the earth, and England will become an island of martyrs, and the heretics, spawned of Luther, will face eternal damnation," the Jesuit vowed, and the fanaticism in his voice sent a chill down Sir Basil's spine.

"By God's grace, Father, I will gladly sacrifice my life," the Englishman said, tears in his eyes. "I will tell the true believers of my audience with His Holiness, and of my meeting with His Most Catholic Majesty. Of His Majesty's promise to protect and defend our faith. And never to abandon our holy cause until England has been rid of the heretics and the harlot who wears the crown.''

"Your ardor, my son, will bring us victory, but, for now, you must remain cautious. There are others who wait for a moment to strike. Even as we sit here, there are those in England who plan for the freedom of Mary Stuart. I have seen her letters, smuggled out of England at great risk, and know that she has the unyielding support of His Majesty. Unless you bring suspicion upon that dear lady, and upon yourself, you must remain the queen's loyal subject. You must play the game well, my son. Bide your time and the glorious day will come by your hand if others fail, for you are in a position of trust that we must protect. But take heart, my son, for I have spoken with those who are prepared to invade England upon the assassination of Elizabeth. They stand resolute. That will be our ultimate glory. And you must be prepared to meet that day. Guard yourself against reckless actions and thoughtless speech, and you will know the rewards of your loyalty to Philip and the true faith. Remember that well.''

"I will, Father," he promised.

And I too will remember, Sir Basil vowed as he drew away from the stern window, the darkness engulfing him as he lowered himself into the warm waters gently lapping against the galleon's hull.

Doña Amparo died peacefully in her sleep. Her family and friends grieved deeply, for she had been a beloved wife and mother, and a true daughter of the Church. With death so close, Sir Basil's melancholy increased. Each day he nervously paced his room, his eyes anxiously searching the harbor for the familiar shape of the *Arion* sailing into port. But each morning he was disappointed. It was the feeling of helplessness that irked him the most. He had finally found the courage to act, to do what he had been sent here to do, and now he was powerless to do anything about his valuable information until Geoffrey Christian returned to Santo Domingo.

Of course, even had Geoffrey Christian returned several weeks ago, they still could have done nothing. To have left Santo Domingo so suddenly, when it had been obvious Doña Amparo had little time left, would only have caused suspicion in the already suspicious mind of Don Pedro.

However, Sir Basil speculated, if he felt frustrated in having to remain in Santo Domingo, so must Don Pedro and his passengers aboard the *Estrella D'Alba*. Don Pedro could no more have left Santo Domingo without causing comment than could Geoffrey Christian, were he here, Sir Basil thought in glum reflection of his predicament.

Although Don Pedro's presence at Casa del Montevares made Sir Basil nervous, he was thankful that the Spaniard remained. As long as the *Estrella D'Alba* rode at anchor in the bay, her passengers would be unable to implement their plot against Elizabeth. But Sir Basil was concerned, for now that Doña Amparo had died there would be no reason for Don Pedro to delay his departure from Santo Domingo. He would be surprised if Don Pedro did not announce plans for leaving Santo Domingo any day now. Catalina had already announced her intentions of remaining in Santo Domingo with her children while Don Pedro continued the rest of the journey without her.

Sir Basil was beginning to lose sleep worrying about what harm the two English traitors might cause before he could return to England and warn the queen. He was almost grateful to the priest for his words of caution to that young fanatic. The advantage, at least for now, was his, Sir Basil thought with a grim smile of satisfaction. Don Pedro did not know that his passengers had been seen and recognized, and when they returned to England, thinking themselves safe, they would be arrested. And that day would come soon, for if fortune were smiling on him, Sir Basil prayed, then Geoffrey Christian could not be far away, nor their return to England long off.

As it so happened, the *Arion* was one day's journey west of Santo Domingo when Sir Basil came down to dine that evening. Sir Basil was not looking forward to yet another meeting with Don Pedro, whose arrogance and rudeness were becoming exasperatingly difficult to accept without some response in kind. But as Don Rodrigo's guest, Sir Basil had been constrained to swallow many a cutting rejoinder about Don Pedro's own heritage. Should he, however, insult Geoffrey Christian's wife again, without Don Rodrigo coming to his daughter's defense, then he would not remain silent, Sir Basil promised himself as he took his seat at the long banqueting table.

Prepared to do battle, Sir Basil eyed the captain of the *Estrella D'Alba* as if taking sight along a cannon. But Sir Basil, even in his most satisfying imaginings, could not have foreseen the unexpected broadside that exploded in Don Pedro's lap as he sat sipping his wine.

"And how is Lily Francisca?" Catalina inquired with genuine concern. "I think she has taken the death of *Madre* very hard, sí. I have not seen the child in the courtyard since the funeral. Always she would sit there by the parrots and talk to them. I could hear her laughter, and I am afraid so could my daughters. They wondered why their cousin was not napping or working her embroidery. I do not think they understand her."

"Lily does not enjoy so—so docile an occupation, I am afraid. Although she does know how to tie a reef knot and mend a sail," Magdalena admitted with a sigh. "I am concerned, however, for she has not said anything about what has happened to her grandmother. Lily is such an inquisitive child. I am constantly at a loss to answer her many questions. And yet, not a word about *Madre*."

"Your daughter, Doña Magdalena, would do well to remember not to speak until spoken to. She is impertinent, but precisely what I would expect from a child sired of an English father," Don Pedro remarked. "Since the *inglés* do not teach their offspring to have proper respect for either the Church or the Crown, it is not surprising that they show little respect for their elders. Should the child have come under *my* guidance, I would know how to curb her insolence quickly enough," Don Pedro predicted.

"Don Pedro, you are a guest in my home, please remember that," Don Rodrigo said harshly, for it was one thing to speak ill of his English son-in-law, but to criticize his granddaughter, a child he found to be quite charming, was quite another matter all together. "If you remember, she is *my* granddaughter, and the Montevares blood that runs through her veins also runs through your children's. In future, when you insult Francisca, or Magdalena, you also insult a Montevares," the old gentleman said proudly, his defense surprising his daughter as much as it had Don Pedro.

"My apologies, Don Rodrigo," Don Pedro said smoothly, "but I had forgotten for a moment that Magdalena was, after all, Spanish. She has adopted so many English mannerisms."

" 'Tis strange, then, that Her Majesty should still think Doña Magdalena so Spanish in appearance," Sir Basil remarked. "Of course, Her Majesty was complimenting Doña Magdalena on her graciousness of manner, attributing it to her Spanish up-bringing. Quite naturally, she assumed that all Spaniards of good birth must be so refined. And, having enjoyed Don Rodrigo's hospitality, I have, until recently, seen no reason to disbe-lieve that assumption."

Catalina coughed and dabbed at her lips as she watched her husband's lips tightening ominously. Catching Magdalena's eye, she spoke quickly, "I thought I heard a scream and cries last night. Was it Lily Francisca? I know it was not one of my chil-dren, for I was up with Francisco half of the night. He does not like the dark, and he ate too much at dinner," she explained.

"If you would not baby him so, Catalina, he would act like a man and not a frightened mouse!" Don Pedro told her, despair-ing of ever weaning his only son from Catalina's excessive moth-ering. "He will never learn to stand on his own two feet if he is constantly clinging to your skirts, Catalina. I have decided that when I sail, Francisco will accompany me. He will learn—"

"It was Lily," Magdalena interrupted Don Pedro's threatened diatribe. "Ever since *Madre* died, she has been having nightmares about floating bodies and ships set aflame. She has even had the strangest dream about a witch with one blue eye and one brown eye who is—"

"¡*Madre de Dios!*" Don Pedro exclaimed as he choked on the sip of wine he had just swallowed. Coughing, he tried to catch his breath. Glancing around the table, his dark eyes didn't miss Sir Basil's relaxed and politely curious expression.

"Are you ill, Don Pedro?" he inquired solicitously.

"It is nothing, nothing. I will be fine," he said, but his complexion was still a pinkish hue.

"I am sorry to hear that Francisca is suffering so," Don Rodrigo commented. "If you would allow me, Magdalena, I will have a word with her."

"Please, *Padre*. I think it would help her. If Geoffrey were here, he would have her laughing at her fears. He always knows what to say. She is so terrified of this witch chasing her that I cannot even bring the subject up without her looking frightened to death. She keeps talking about those strangely colored eyes. How they stare at her with such hatred. She thinks the witch wants to kill her. She even said that this creature threw her into the water, and then stood on the edge of the pond and watched her drown. Which, of course, is nonsense, because Lily can swim. But she does not remember that when she is shaking with fear. I think she even believes that the witch is the cause of her grandmother's death. That is why she is frightened to speak of it. I truly believe she is petrified to mention it, lest the creature harm me, or Geoffrey, or even you, Sir Basil. She seemed concerned for your safety as well."

"How awful," Catalina murmured, clicking her tongue. "I myself should be scared senseless to be dreaming of such a horrid beast. And especially one with a blue eye and a brown eye," she said, crossing herself as a shiver shook her shoulders. Then her eyes grew round as she suddenly remembered where she herself had seen such a creature. "Why, do you know that sounds like"—she began to explain, then abruptly took a sip of wine, her eyes pleading with Don Pedro to forgive her for her slip of the tongue—"like a fable we once heard."

"I wish that were true, but I am afraid that Lily has actually seen a man with such eyes. He's English and—"

Don Pedro turned purple in the face as he choked on his wine again, only this time his eyes bulged and he made strangling sounds as he sucked air into his lungs and sought to halt Magdalena's confidences with an upraised hand.

Sir Basil left his place and hurried around the side of the table. Several lusty, well-aimed slaps on the back had Don Pedro no longer choking, and soon he was breathing easier. Sir Basil remained behind Don Pedro for a minute longer, giving himself time to think, then he returned to his seat, his face mirroring concern for the discomfited Don Pedro.

"Are you quite sure you are well?" he asked. At Don Pedro's nod, he glanced over at his host. "I am so sorry, Don Rodrigo," he apologized, gesturing at his overturned goblet, the spilt wine leaving a vivid, red stain across the linen tablecloth. "I must have knocked it over when I stood up," he said, although both he and Don Rodrigo knew it had happened moments before.

"Please, do not concern yourself with that," Don Rodrigo entreated him, for Sir Basil, despite his calm visage, seemed ill at ease.

"Thank you, Don Rodrigo. Hmm," Sir Basil continued on a thoughtful note. "You say one blue eye and one brown, and he's an Englishman. Sounds familiar, but I cannot quite place the gentleman. He is a gentleman?" Sir Basil asked mockingly, keeping the conversation light.

"Yes, indeed. I cannot remember his name, but he was a guest at Highcross when Her Majesty and the court came last year for a visit. That is where Lily must have seen him, and now that she is upset with the death of her grandmother, she remembers him. For a child, such a person might be disturbing. It is all very confusing for the child. Time means little. Today, yesterday, last year, it is all the same."

Sir Basil didn't dare glance over at Don Pedro, for he had heard the deep sigh of relief that the Spaniard had breathed when Magdalena had so convincingly explained away Lily's nightmare about the creature with one blue eye and one brown.

"Indeed, Doña Magdalena. Why, my son, Simon, who is not more than a year or two older than Lily, has had some bloodcurdling nightmares. Woke up the whole household one night when he claimed that an Awd Goggie was lurking in the corner of his bedchamber. I had to search the whole room before he would settle back down. And then I had to leave a candle, and his nurse, by his bedside before he'd sleep."

"What is an Awd Goggie?" Catalina asked in fascination.

"A demon, and not one to be trifled with, Doña Catalina. They say, or at least according to Simon's nursemaid who had told him the story, that the sprite protects orchards from thieves. And it would seem that Simon had raided the apple orchard that very afternoon, and 'twas a stomach ache and a guilty conscience that had him dreaming such nightmares," Sir Basil concluded with a chuckle, successfully dismissing such stories, and among them Lily's, as nonsense.

Later that evening, Sir Basil, safe in the confines of his room, slumped down on his bed in a cold sweat. And it was Sir Basil who suffered the nightmares that night about a man with one blue eye and one brown. When Sir Basil awoke the next morning, he could not shake the strange feeling of melancholy that hung heavily about him. It was, therefore, with a sense of foreboding that he glanced out his window to see the *Arion* anchored in the harbor.

" 'Od's heartling!" Geoffrey Christian exclaimed, and not for the first time since hearing of Sir Basil's daring exploits. "I should have stayed in Santo Domingo. There was more adventuring to be found at Casa del Montevares than off the coast of Nombre de Dios!" he said with another deep chuckle. He continued to eye his somber-faced friend, then glanced at the innocent-looking stern of the *Estrella D'Alba* anchored nearby, and the chuckle gradually turned into a rich laugh that had several busy crew members smiling as they went about their tasks.

"Ah, Basil, my old friend," he said, the laughter crinkling the corners of his eyes.

"I am glad that you find the situation so amusing. What, pray tell, would have kept you amused had I met my death that night?" Sir Basil inquired, slightly offended that his friend should find such humor in what had been an emotional experience for him.

"I do apologize, Basil," Geoffrey said with a grin that should have warned Sir Basil of what was to come. "But I find myself wondering about the scandal it would have caused had you been washed up on shore in your underclothes. Whatever would I

have said to Elspeth, or, 'Sdeath, to Her Majesty? For that re-
prieve alone, I am thankful you managed to get back to shore in
one piece.''

Sir Basil shook his head, for he would never fully appreciate
Geoffrey Christian's sense of humor, but he was learning. ''Indeed, better 'twas I than you, my friend. Think of the mortification it would have caused Don Rodrigo had it been his son-in-
law who had been found washed up on shore and clad only in
underclothes.''

Geoffrey Christian grinned. But as he glanced again at the *Estrella D'Alba,* his smile faded. ''So, it would seem that Don Pedro
plans to sail with the tide on the morrow? And Doña Catalina
and her children remain here in Santo Domingo,'' he mused. ''I
should be offended that the good captain sails immediately upon
my arrival in Santo Domingo. I do believe he has taken a
disliking to me.''

''I was afraid the two of you would come to blows when you
met accidentally in the entrance hall of Casa del Montevares. If it
had not been for the presence of the ladies and the children I
wonder if there would indeed have been bloodshed.''

Geoffrey Christian smiled crookedly, his handsome, bearded
face all innocence. ''I have no grudge against Don Pedro.''

''I wish he could say the same. He looked as if he could
scarcely contain himself from plunging his dagger into your
heart, my friend. I would not turn my back on that gentleman,''
Sir Basil warned. ''He disliked me so much that it was an effort
for the man to acknowledge my presence, and I was just an Englishman he hated as a matter of principle, but you—you he
hates with a personal vengeance.''

''Well, I do believe I gave him some small cause,'' Geoffrey
admitted modestly.

''Yes, I should say so. You blew his ship out from under him
and stole his cousin's bride, if I remember correctly,'' Basil reminded him.

''You do, and I believe it was one of my most inspired decisions. I've yet to capture a finer prize. I have never regretted taking Magdalena as my wife. She is a remarkable woman, Basil.
She is also the mother of my only daughter, and''—he hesitated
as if considering his next words with great pleasure—''perhaps
my son.''

"Magdalena is with child?"

"Yes, she told me yesterday that she has suspected as much for the past couple of months. Magdalena has desperately wanted to give me a son. I have told her that Lily is enough, that I am not disappointed in having no male heir, but she continues to think I long for a son. I suspect, however, that she wants to make certain that my dear cousin Hartwell does not inherit Highcross."

"I do not blame her," Sir Basil said, for he cared little for Geoffrey's pompous cousin. "Please accept my sincere congratulations, Geoffrey."

"Thank you. And I shall rejoice whether I have sired a son or another daughter. 'Twould be nice, however, to have another Christian sailing the seas and making life hell for any Frenchman, Spaniard, or Papist who crossed his bow. 'Sblood, but I'd like to get my hands on those two cuckolds sitting pretty in the captain's cabin," Geoffrey swore, his green eyes glinting as he gazed across the water toward the galleon taking on supplies.

"We will, Geoffrey," Sir Basil spoke softly as he stood at his friend's side.

"A fine piece of work, Basil," Geoffrey said, eyeing him with new respect. "No offense meant, but I didn't think you had it in you. At least not to pull off a feat like that."

"Neither did I," Basil admitted a trifle self-consciously, for he was not used to playing the hero. "I am relieved you have returned, for I am not accustomed to such a role. The responsibility weighs heavy on my mind, Geoffrey. I would see no harm befall our queen."

"None shall," Geoffrey promised.

"I aged a lifetime the night before last when Magdalena so innocently recited Lily's nightmare. Don Pedro was so surprised that I do not think he noticed how surprised I was. I do not think he is overly concerned that Lily actually saw the man in the courtyard and not at Highcross as Magdalena believes. And, I am certain that no one but the fisherman knows that I went aboard the *Estrella D'Alba*, and he has a purse full of gold and thinks I'm a Spaniard. I do not believe I have made any mistakes, Geoffrey. I would have known had Don Pedro suspected the truth. I most likely would not have lived to welcome you back to Santo Domingo had they known I was a spy. No, I think we will succeed, Geoffrey. We must."

Geoffrey Christian nodded, but he did not feel quite as confident about the situation as did Sir Basil, although he was hesitant to admit as much. He was not one to underestimate an enemy, and Don Pedro was indeed an enemy. Basil had not been wrong in his estimation of Don Pedro's desire to seek revenge against his old nemesis. Geoffrey had not missed the hatred that had flared in Don Pedro's eyes when they had met face to face for the first time since crossing bows nearly eight years ago. Sir Basil, he knew, would find it hard to understand, but Geoffrey Christian knew that the Spaniard would not leave Santo Domingo without a final reckoning with the man who had defeated him once before. Geoffrey Christian, because he would have felt the same need for vengeance had he lost his ship to his enemy, knew that the battle was not yet over, nor the victory theirs until they safely reached the shores of England.

"Lily seems a changed child since your return," Sir Basil commented, for he did not like the expression on his friend's face as the captain of the *Arion* continued to stare unblinkingly across the water at the *Estrella D'Alba* as she prepared to weigh anchor.

Geoffrey Christian seemed reluctant to withdraw his gaze from the Spanish galleon, but finally he turned to glance along the deck of his own ship. "My sweet Lily Francisca. A priceless jewel, isn't she? If you are fortunate, one day I might allow Simon the privilege of asking for her hand in marriage," Geoffrey said, and Basil believed he was quite serious. "He will never have a peaceful day once he loses his heart to my fairest flower, but then what is life without a challenge?"

"I would be honored to have Lily a member of my family, Geoffrey," Basil responded, although he had his doubts about whether or not Simon and Lily would make a match of it. He feared Simon was far too gentle and quiet a lad to handle so spirited a lass as Lily Christian. And Geoffrey Christian as a father-in-law might mean the premature death of the boy should he ever cause Lily an instant of unhappiness.

"Aye, I like the sound of Lily Whitelaw. We shall have to give this further thought, Basil," Geoffrey said, his gaze now centered on his daughter while she played on the deck with her new companion, a woolly monkey her father had traded a length of colorful silk for in Borburata, a Venezuelan coastal town.

"I think he likes you, Mistress Lily," Joshua Randall, the bos'n, declared with a wide grin. "What are you going to name him?"

"Is it a boy?" Lily asked curiously. "How can you tell, Master Randall?"

"Ah, well, uh . . ." Joshua Randall, who'd seen most everything there was to see, and had heard it all, now blushed brightly under Lily's frank gaze. "Reckon the critter's too young for it to really matter one way or t'other," he concluded lamely.

"I think you are probably right, though. He's got whiskers. Only men have whiskers, Master Randall."

"Ye be right, lass," he quickly agreed, for he'd hate to have it come to the captain's attention that he'd been telling Mistress Lily things a young lady shouldn't be knowing about.

"I'm going to call him Capabells. Do you know why?"

Master Randall rubbed his bearded chin in deep reflection. "No, can't say that I do, young mistress."

"Because he reminds me of the court jester. Father says we are going to make him a tiny velvet cap with bells on it so he can perform for Her Majesty when we return to London," Lily confided, then squealed when the little monkey with bright eyes climbed onto her shoulder and pulled her hair before scampering off, his excited chatter daring her to follow.

Joshua Randall had a moment's vision of what might happen should the monkey jump onto Her Majesty's slim shoulder and grab hold of one of the queen's red curls, for rumor had it she wore a wig. Then he noticed his captain's narrowed gaze lingering on him and quickly put that scene out of his mind and hustled below to complete his duties, which, he grumbled beneath his breath, would take him plenty of time to do. They had just gotten into port, and now they were setting sail again. At the rate they'd been taking on supplies, it seemed as if they really would be back at sea within the week.

It was two days later, in fact, that Doña Magdalena bid farewell to her father. Perhaps Don Rodrigo remembered now how much his daughter resembled his beloved wife, or perhaps he suddenly realized that he would miss his youngest daughter when she left Santo Domingo, maybe never to return.

The imperious façade he had maintained so steadfastly throughout the visit now crumbled, leaving Don Rodrigo looking like the heartsick man he was. Magdalena had made her farewells to her sister first, for Don Rodrigo had stood slightly apart, as stiff-necked and straight-backed as when she had first greeted him after so long and bitter a separation. With a sigh, she turned and faced him. She could delay no longer, for Geoffrey and Lily had already left with Basil and now they waited in the street beyond. Magdalena stood for a moment in indecision, then she rushed forward. Her arms were outstretched to him as they had been on her arrival. This time she found herself not repulsed as she had expected, but instead she was enfolded against his chest in a loving embrace.

"*Padre, mi padre,*" she cried softly, burying her tearstained face against the rich silk of Don Rodrigo's doublet.

"*Mi hija,*" he said huskily. "*Mi dulce batata pequeña.*"

"You forgive me?" she asked.

"All is forgiven, *mi hija,*" he said gruffly. His hand shaking, he caressed the softness of her dark red hair. "You are so like your mother. I shall miss you, as I miss her. Perhaps one day you will return and visit your father. I would like to see my granddaughter again. You can be proud of her. I am pleased she is of my blood. And I am proud of you."

"Thank you, *Padre.* If you knew how long I have ached to hear you say that. Maybe," she added hesitantly, looking beseechingly into his sad eyes, "one day you will come to England and visit me and my family in my home. You will always be welcome, *Padre.*"

"Well, we shall see," Don Rodrigo allowed, but he had not said no, which was more than Magdalena had even hoped for. "*¡Adios!*" he said simply. Then, pressing a lingering kiss against her forehead, Don Rodrigo turned away and disappeared into the courtyard.

As the *Arion* set sail from Santo Domingo, Magdalena stood aftmost and watched the coastline fade from sight, her thoughts her own. Sir Basil stood to starboard, watching the waves foaming against the ship's bow as she forged ahead. Lily, Capabells clinging to her shoulder, was watching the men climbing high into the rigging as they followed their captain's orders and made sail, their voices raised in a cheerful song that drifted on the wind. The *Arion* was homeward bound.

The sun's o'ercast with blood . . .

SHAKESPEARE

Chapter Five

SETTING every stitch of canvas she carried, the *Arion* sailed away from the convoy of heavily armed galleons that had been sighted at dawn off her quarter.

The sudden cry, "All hands to quarters!" still rang harshly in Sir Basil's ears. He had been enjoying a leisurely breakfast with the captain and his family when Geoffrey had been summoned on deck, and then it seemed to Sir Basil that all hell had broken loose as men swarmed across the deck and into the rigging, some climbing high into the shrouds. The men-of-war were out of Santiago de Cuba, the garrison that guarded the Windward Passage. Watching their progress as they increased sail and gave chase, Geoffrey Christian had smiled, for he knew the Spaniards could never bring their cannons within range of the *Arion*. She was too swift and her crew too experienced.

The rugged north coast of Jamaica had fallen astern as the prevailing winds filled the *Arion*'s sails and she held steady on her course. The Caymans had been sighted several leagues distant, and had the *Arion* not been under full press of canvas, with the enemy to windward, she might have found a safe channel through the sandbanks surrounding the islands and taken on fresh water there.

As each day passed the *Arion* steadily made her way closer to the Gulf of Mexico and the Straits of Florida, where the Gulf Stream would carry them through the dangerous channel of coral reefs, cays, and sandbars. Steering a northeasterly course as she beat into the Atlantic, she would catch the westerlies which would keep her sails billowing and her prow turned toward England.

But off Isla de Pinos, Geoffrey Christian began to suspect that the galleons giving chase had not come upon them by accident and were in fact part of a larger convoy, the vanguard of which could be now maneuvering athwart-hawse of the bows of the *Arion* as she steered toward Cabo San Antonio. Intending to round the cape and enter the narrow channel between Cuba and the outlying islets strung along the southern tip of Florida, the *Arion* might find herself cut off from escape.

Geoffrey Christian did not seem surprised to see the *Estrella D'Alba* assuming the position of flagship. It was all very clear to him now: Don Pedro Enrique de Villasandro was about to seek his revenge. The *Arion* had been flanked, with two of the galleons coming in to windward and taking the weather gage. She was outgunned and outmanned; she had nowhere to go. Thinking of Magdalena and Lily, the *Arion*'s captain was about to give the order to lower her colors and surrender. It was a cowardly act Geoffrey Christian was loath to do and would not have considered except for the presence on board of his wife and daughter. He'd rather fight to the death than give up his ship, but he would see no harm befall his family just so he could prove his bravery. But before he could give the order to heave-to, several puffs of smoke billowed from the *Estrella D'Alba* as she fired on the lone ship, the volley of screaming cannon balls and grapeshot cutting to pieces everything in its path as it rained down on the quarterdeck of the *Arion*. As Geoffrey Christian gave the order to sheer off, the captain of the *Estrella D'Alba* repeated his command to fire and the *Arion*'s deck shuddered beneath a raking broadside that splintered through the railing and planking and sent bloodied bodies of sailors flying across the deck. Another broadside damaged the rigging, cutting a halyard and slicing through canvas, but the *Arion*'s gunners managed to get off a volley of shot against one of the galleons that had fallen astern and was now within range of the *Arion*'s guns on her larboard side. Quickly they reloaded with powder and ball, ramming it down the cannon's muzzle; then, laying a trail of powder and taking new aim, they ran the gun forward and into position as the powder flared under a slow match, the gun recoiling when she fired with deadly accuracy.

With the *Arion*'s longer range cannon, Geoffrey Christian hoped to hold off the galleons while escaping into the channel. There was a strong, northerly current and already one of the galleons that had felt the fury from the *Arion*'s gunports was drifting precariously close to the reefs surrounding the pine-studded island lying southeast of the cape. Her rigging and sails hanging splintered and useless, her hull showing gaping wounds, she was certain to run aground. Another galleon that had felt the bite of the *Arion*'s guns was listing badly and taking on water.

Sir Basil choked on the acrid smoke and stench of death that permeated the ship as he made his way on deck in time to see the flash of fire from one of the galleons bearing down on them, then a roar filled his ears and he threw himself to the deck, expecting to find himself engulfed in flame as the cannon shot exploded around him. But the galleon had been out of-range, and her shot fell short of the *Arion*'s deck. In that instant, while the galleon's gunners reloaded, the *Arion* cut a path directly across her stern, bringing her guns to bear on the Spaniard's vulnerable backside. A deafening explosion followed in the *Arion*'s wake as she sailed past the galleon, now on fire, and made her escape through the hole in the net that Don Pedro thought he had so cunningly spread.

Making his way from the waist of the ship, where a tangle of rigging, spars, and splintered planking blocked his way, Sir Basil finally reached Geoffrey Christian's side. With a look of horror on his haggard face, Basil stared at his friend. A deep, jagged gash cut across the captain's skull, dripping blood down his temple and into his neatly trimmed beard. He was holding his left arm against his chest, and as Basil looked closer, he could see the red stain seeping from the wound.

"Geoffrey?"

"I look worse than I am, Basil. 'Sblood, but I'll have that Spaniard's heart before this battle is done!" he swore, his pale green eyes glowing with a fire that burned deep into Basil's soul. "Magdalena? Lilly?" he demanded, but his eyes never left the galleons that were closing ranks behind them and giving chase.

"They were fine, frightened, but unharmed when I came up," Basil reassured him.

"I didn't think we'd taken a hit in that quarter below decks. If Don Pedro lives, he will come to regret this day."

"The *Estrella D'Alba?*" Sir Basil for the first time realized what ship had attacked them and what Spaniard Geoffrey Christian was damning. "I cannot believe it! Surely he knows this is the *Arion* he has fired upon? And that a woman and child are on board?"

"Of course he knows," Geoffrey said, turning his attention to Master Randall and his mates, who were sent up into the rigging to repair the damage to the masts and sails. "I sank Don Pedro's ship. He will never rest easy until he evens that score. He will suffer no pangs of conscience because of the death of Magdalena and Lily, or you and the rest of the crew. He will merely think he has rid the world of a ship full of heretics."

Sir Basil felt ill. "How can Don Pedro explain to Philip, or the priest aboard his ship, his actions in risking his mission just to seek personal vengeance against you?"

"Perhaps he has told them of the incident where Lily spoke of seeing our nervous conspirator. When a man has something to hide, he is abnormally suspicious and quick to believe in threats to his safety, and he will sanction any act, however rash," Geoffrey Christian said, waving away a hovering crew member who was inspecting his captain's wounds with a professional eye. "Later. We've got sails to mend and rigging to secure. I haven't time now, James, for your coddling. We want to show Philip's swine what an Englishman can do when the odds are against him."

"Aye, Cap'n, we'll show them our stern all the way home, then we'll turn and spit in their eye."

Sir Basil had hoped they wouldn't come quite that close again, but he had to admit that he felt a similar bloodlust surging through his veins when he thought of Don Pedro's treachery.

"I think you should go below, Basil."

Basil started to protest, but he realized he would just be in the way if he remained on deck. He nodded his agreement. "You expect more trouble, don't you? I thought the battle was over. They won't catch up to us, will they?"

"I am not worried about what lies astern. I'm concerned about what waits for us ahead, in the channel."

"You think there might be more fighting?"

"Don Pedro probably alerted the fort in Havana. They control the channel. We must get through there as quickly as possible."

"There is something else worrying you."

Geoffrey Christian smiled. "Were I Don Pedro, I would have taken the precaution of stationing several galleons northwest of here in the Gulf, just beyond the entrance to the channel. When we round the cape, they will be in a position to intercept us, certainly to fire upon us. The *Arion*'s a sturdy little ship, but she can't hold up under much more unless we can make repairs. Our strength lies in being able to outmaneuver and outsail them, and our long-range cannon fire gives us the advantage. We shall need all of those if we hope to get safely through the channel. And then . . ." He paused, his gaze raking the damaged masts and torn sails rising above a deck that still bore proof of battle. "We are not out of this yet, Basil. Pray to God that Don Pedro was too arrogant to consider that the *Arion* might escape his net. That may just give us the time we need."

Later, Basil was to remember those words as the *Arion* made her way into the Straits of Florida. As he waited in the great cabin time seemed to have no meaning. All that existed for him was the past. He remembered things he had thought long forgotten. Moments of pleasure from his childhood at Whiteswood, of the years spent at Cambridge when he was a naïve young man who had spent all of his time studying and learning about the world from his books and tutors, of the excitement of London and life at court, and of the great change that happened to him when he'd met and fallen in love with Elspeth. She had been a vision of uncommon loveliness, and once he had spoken with her, and discovered that she had intellect as well as beauty, he could not imagine a life without her by his side. Basil felt the gentle touch of her hand on his, heard the wise word she would whisper in his ear, saw the loving expression in her soft blue eyes, breathed the sweet fragrance of spring flowers when he and Elspeth had walked through the gardens of Whiteswood, their son racing ahead. . . . Then the image faded as he heard the sound of explosions overhead and felt the sudden lurch of the ship to larboard. But the *Arion* continued on her way, her crew rallying again and again as they fought valiantly to keep her on course.

Sir Basil found himself almost smiling. He could have accepted his death with more grace had it been because of his actions for his queen and country—at least there would have been some reason behind it. But thinking that he would die only because of another man's desire for revenge left him shaking with frustrated anger. How ironic indeed, that Don Pedro would never know that he was a true hero; he would have to content himself with savoring his vengeance against one man, never realizing the service he had inadvertently performed for his king and his faith.

"Mother? They're hurting our ship. Why is Father allowing them to do this? Why doesn't he sink them? Father can do anything, I know he can. Father won't let us sink, Mother. I know he won't," Lily said firmly, her small, rounded chin stuck out with a determination that mirrored her father's. "Mother?"

At the sound of the childish voice, Sir Basil remembered the other two occupants of the cabin and opened his eyes to see Magdalena sitting across the table from him, Lily held against her breast as she prayed softly beneath her breath, the silver cross she usually kept out of sight now held to her lips.

"If anyone can get us out of this, Lily, then it is your father. I cannot think of another man I would more willingly trust my life to," Basil told Geoffrey Christian's daughter, and to his surprise, the green eyes that met his were without fear. He only wished he could say the same about his own, for he knew they must be wild with fright. "Nothing will happen to us. Nothing," he said again, trying to convince himself that was true.

Whether Geoffrey Christian would have been comforted or saddened to have heard those words he might not have known himself, for he knew he was in the most desperate fight of his life.

If any of them were to have the slightest chance of survival, then he would have to risk everything. "Hard to starboard, Master Evans!"

"Starboard, Cap'n?" the young helmsman repeated in confusion, for that course would take them right across the closest galleon's bows and within range of another devastating broadside. There was also a cay less than a league distant and lying directly across their path if they followed that sudden change of course. They'd run aground. The captain must be crazed, the young man thought in horror.

"Hard to, mister!" Geoffrey Christian yelled again. An old hand standing duty as lee helmsman took charge from the bemused helmsman and steered the ship as ordered. There wasn't time to question the captain's orders. "Stand on!" the captain called as the *Arion's* bowsprit swung into the wind.

As Geoffrey Christian had expected, the galleons trying to intercept the *Arion* off to starboard changed course, intending to catch the *Arion* as she headed into the deep channel between the cay and Great Bahama Bank, thinking the *Arion* might be trying to escape to the south to find a safe hiding place in one of the countless coves along the uninhabited Cuban coast. Several of the crew peered over the railing at the bright, razor-toothed coral just beneath the *Arion's* hull, their mouths gaping open as she rode over it and the sandy bottom so close below. A harsh scraping noise reverberated through the timbers of the ship as she touched the ground but she continued without any apparent serious damage. Unfortunately, the Spaniards aboard the galleon that had followed in the *Arion's* wake realized too late what she was about and ran aground. She was a deeper-drafted galleon, and her angle across the cay hadn't been as sharp, for the *Arion's* course had been just along the outer rim of coral before the captain had given the order to turn her back on her original course with the wind off her quarter. The deception had worked, and now the *Arion* headed back into the safe channel of deep water.

They were not safely out of danger yet, but at least the *Arion* had a little more room to maneuver, and Geoffrey Christian intended to make the most of it. The *Estrella D'Alba* had been far enough astern to watch the *Arion's* deception and avoid the cay, and now she gave chase, closing the distance with the smaller ship that, because of the damage she'd suffered in the battle, was not handling well and looked as if she were about to founder, as she fought her way north. With a heaviness in his heart, Geoffrey Christian knew that it was just a matter of time before the *Estrella D'Alba* overtook the *Arion*, if they continued north, riding the Gulf Stream into the Atlantic. His only hope was to keep a steady distance ahead until they reached the channel cutting through the Bahamas just north of the Great Bahama Bank. If he could steer a course into the islands, he might just be able to lose the *Estrella D'Alba,* if not, then . . . but he shook his head, wincing with the pain from his wound. He would not even think of the alternative. Not yet.

"Geoffrey?"

The voice he longed to hear, yet had dreaded hearing, now spoke his name. He turned to see Magdalena staring at him with tears in her eyes. Strands of dark red hair fell about her shoulders and several fine strands blew across her face as she stood staring at him, unable to move.

"Geoffrey. Oh, Geoffrey." Her eyes reflected the horror of seeing him covered in blood and the death she had witnessed throughout the day as she had tried to help the wounded. The blood of the dying stained her gown, drying now as she stood on the deck in the gentle warmth of the trades.

Geoffrey held out a hand to her. Magdalena rested her face against his chest, not seeing the look of pain that crossed his features.

"Why? Why? Geoffrey, must it end this way?" she spoke softly, sensing that all was lost.

"It won't, Magdalena. I won't let it end like this."

Magdalena looked up into his eyes. "I love you."

Geoffrey pressed her lips with his. "My only love. I do not think you realize how happy you have made me. My life would have been very empty these past years without you, my dearest little Spaniard."

Magdalena swallowed, unable to speak, but the love in her eyes spoke for her as she continued to stand in the curve of his arm.

Geoffrey's expression changed as he caught sight of the scattering of pine-studded cays and islets directly off to starboard. *Soon,* he thought.

"Magdalena, go below and gather up any belongings you can carry. Ask Sir Basil to do the same, my dear. Then wait until I send for you. Master Davis, give Doña Magdalena a hand. Then take care of that list of supplies and see that they are stored in the boat," Geoffrey ordered his steward, who was standing nearby and anxiously watching the sails that seemed to loom closer astern with each passing minute. "Have Masters Waterston, Randall, and Lawson on the quarterdeck immediately."

"Geoffrey? What is this? I do not understand," Magdalena said, an uneasiness beginning to show on her face.

"My dear, if we can't lose them in the islands, then we've got to turn and fight. It is our only hope. I don't want you and Lily on board if it comes to that."

"No, Geoffrey, I won't leave you. I won't!" Magdalena cried.

"I will not have you aboard, Magdalena. If I have to tie you up and put you in that boat myself, I will see you off this ship when we go into battle. Do you understand? I had no choice before. I do now, and I will not further endanger your lives. My dear, I would worry too much if I knew you were on board. Please understand. Besides, the men are a superstitious lot, and as charming as you are, they've not rested easy knowing a woman was on board. They will feel luck is on their side if you and Lily are not aboard," he told her frankly.

"Geoffrey, what purpose is there in my surviving should . . . ? No, I will not leave your side. Don't ask this of me, Geoffrey. Please!" Magdalena pleaded, her nails cutting into his palm as she held on to his hand.

Geoffrey raised her hands to his lips. "I do not ask it of you. You will go ashore in the boat. You will take our daughter out of danger. Nothing must happen to you, and to the child you carry, Magdalena. Sir Basil will accompany you. Have faith, heartling! Was there ever a ship that could best the *Arion?* They will regret crossing her bow, mark my words," Geoffrey Christian promised, sounding like the familiar, reckless captain of the *Arion*. " 'Sdeath, but I've not fired my last shot yet! Let them come, and we shall see who sails away with his colors still flying boldly for all to see. Ah, Master Waterston, and Masters Randall and Lawson, just the gentlemen I wished to see. We've got some business to attend to. My dear, please, do as I ask," Geoffrey told Magdalena, who continued to stand beside him, an obstinate look in her eye. With a last glance, which he ignored, she slowly turned away and followed the steward below.

"Master Lawson. When we get well into the islands, and if we can't shake the Spaniard, before our enemy gets within range, I want you to lower the boat and row my wife and daughter and Sir Basil Whitelaw ashore. Sir Basil is a very important gentleman with information vital to our country and the safety of the queen; we must protect him at all costs."

Master Lawson, who would gladly die for his captain, opened his mouth to protest having to leave the ship just before, the battle. But he realized the crew would feel easier having the woman off the ship. Nothing good had ever come of having a woman on board ship. Bad luck, it was, he thought. And the gentleman, Sir Basil, would only be in the way. "Aye, Cap'n, ye can count on me to see them safely ashore."

"Thank you, Master Lawson. Now, John, let us plan our strategy," Geoffrey Christian said to his first mate, but before he could continue he was racked by a fit of coughing which left a trickle of blood dribbling down his chin from the corner of his mouth.

"Cap'n, sir, ye'd best sit down and let me or Master Davis have a look at that. That wound in your side looks bad, Cap'n," Randall, the bos'n, said worriedly, realizing that the captain had not been wounded in the arm as he had led everyone to believe. "Cap'n, ye've got a mean-looking splinter stickin' in ye. We've got to get it out."

"He is right, Cap'n."

"Later," he said, but he sensed it was already too late, and he vowed he would die on deck, fighting, not below, not in the dark. "Master Randall. A word of warning, if you please. Say nothing of the seriousness of my wound to my wife. She'll never leave the ship if she learns of it," Geoffrey Christian told them.

"Aye, Cap'n," he said before hurrying off to prepare his men.

"You know I have faith in your abilities, Captain," Master Waterston said softly. "But, if the worst should happen, what about Doña Magdalena and your daughter? They will be stranded."

"My wife, Master Waterston, is Spanish. My daughter is half-Spanish. Sir Basil is an English gentleman who will seem of little importance to the Spanish authorities. If we should go down, then Lawson will row back out to one of the galleons. They will not fire upon a boat with a woman and child aboard, regardless of Don Pedro's intentions concerning my family. They will be rescued and returned to Santo Domingo, where my

wife's father will see to their needs and Sir Basil's ultimate return to England.''

"Ye've got it all planned, Cap'n," John Waterston said in admiration.

"Yes, I do.''

The sunrise held little beauty to Sir Basil as he came up on
deck with Magdalena and Lily, whose wide-eyed stare was
disbelieving as she saw the destruction. Capabells started chattering excitedly, for the smell of death and fear was strong.

"Geoffrey, I must protest," Sir Basil began, feeling like a
coward abandoning ship.

" 'Tis for the best, Basil. I cannot see you manning one of the
cannon, my friend. I will have more peace of mind, Basil, knowing you are with Magdalena and Lily. I would trust them to no
one else," he told his somber-faced friend.

Basil felt helpless. He didn't know what to say. A feeling of
desperation was spreading inside of him. "Geoffrey, I—''

"No words are necessary between friends," Geoffrey told
him, cutting him short as he watched the boat being prepared to
be lowered. "Please take this," he said as he handed Basil the official log of the *Arion.* "Just in case we go down, I don't want it to
get wet," he jested, as if making light of such a thing happening.
"I'll get it back from you later," he added with that familiar grin
of his as Basil tucked it under his arm with his own journal.

"All set, sweeting?" he asked as he bent down and hugged
Lily to him, the monkey wrapped around her neck scolding him.

"Do I have to, Father?" Lily said, her green eyes meeting his
for a long moment. "I want to stay on board with you. I don't
want to leave, Father.''

"Nor do I wish you to. But who will look after your mother
and Sir Basil? Now, now. No tears, Lily Francisca. You know I
am right. No questioning the captain's orders, mate," he told
her, his hand smoothing the dark red hair lovingly.

Lily hugged him tight, smacking a kiss against his cheek before he stood up and embraced Magdalena. Before she could say
anything, he kissed her. Taking her by the hand, he led her
through the tangle of debris to where the boat was being
readied.

They had rounded the headland of a small isle and Geoffrey
Christian had brought the *Arion*'s head into the wind, bringing

her almost to a standstill while the boat was lowered. Now, as he watched, Sir Basil climbed down the rope ladder and into the boat below. One of the crew carried Lily and Capabells down, while Geoffrey, his face paling with the effort, help Magdalena over the rail, his eyes holding hers for a long moment. Her footing secure, she slowly made her way down into the boat, where Sir Basil stood ready to catch her should she miss her step.

As the boat was shoved off, the oars dipping regularly as Master Lawson rowed toward shore, Geoffrey Christian gave his orders to ease the helm. Gradually the ship and boat drew farther apart as the *Arion*'s sails billowed, but Geoffrey Christian could still see the two people waving to him untiringly from the stern of the little boat as she drew near the shore; then she had disappeared behind a palmetto-studded headland.

Reaching the sandy beach, which curved along the leeward shore and out of sight of the *Arion*, Master Lawson quickly jumped out of the boat and into the warm waters lapping against the gentle slope of beach. Sir Basil hopped out on the other side and lent a hand in hauling the boat ashore.

With Magdalena and Lily standing high on the beach, just out of reach of the tide, Master Lawson and Sir Basil began unloading the boat of its tidy cargo of personal belongings and what supplies Geoffrey Christian had thought necessary for their brief stay on the island.

They had just about finished the unloading, when the sound of thunder echoed through the air. But when it was repeated again and again, they realized that it was cannon fire. Magdalena ran down to the edge of the beach, the tide breaking against her skirts as she stared hopelessly out to sea, wondering what was happening. The battle was some distance off. The *Arion* must have made some headway before she had turned to fight, Master Lawson guessed, his eyes straining as much as Magdalena's in searching the empty horizon.

The sounds of battle continued for nearly an hour before there was silence. Then there were several more volleys of shot fired, and that was when Master Lawson raced to the boat and pulling her from her beaching, floated her. Jumping in, he began to row out with a madman's strength.

"Lawson!" Sir Basil yelled after the young man. "Wait!" he

called, thinking the man deranged and about to abandon them. "Where are you going? Come back! Don't leave us here!"

"She's not firing back! She must've gone down! I got to rescue them. See if anyone is alive!" he cried, his face determined as he put his shoulders to the rowing. "I'll be back. I promised the captain I'd look after ye!"

Magdalena sank down in the surf, buried her face in her hands and began to weep. Lily was screaming after Lawson, and Sir Basil had to grab hold of her to keep her from racing into the surf after the rowboat and trying to swim out to where the loyal sailor was rowing through the narrow channel that cut through the reefs. As he disappeared around the headland, it was the last any of them ever saw of Master Lawson.

Sir Basil waded out to Magdalena and helped her to her feet. With her leaning against him, and with Lily held tightly in his other arm, her face still turned out to sea, Sir Basil staggered up the beach, Geoffrey Christian's family now his responsibility.

The hours passed in silence as they waited on shore. The sun sank in a fiery ball that reflected like blood against the water, then darkness fell.

Sir William Cecil shivered and pulled the fur rug closer about his knees as he studied the document spread out on the table before him, the candlelight sending a warming glow across them that did little to cheer him up. The rain blew against the windows and the cold drafts swirled into the room, apparently oblivious of his importance to the queen, he thought wryly as he shifted closer to the fire burning brightly in the hearth. It had been raining steadily in London for days now, and the storm would most likely would turn into a blizzard before they saw the sun again.

He rubbed his eyes tiredly, then glanced down again at the information Walsingham had compiled during the last couple of years against Ridolfi. Roberto di Ridolfi, an Italian banker and ardent Papist who had been in close contact with English Catholics unhappy with Elizabeth's reign. He had been interrogated by Walsingham about his frequent activities involving the Spanish embassy and the pope, as well as his connections with the French ambassador and influential Catholics in England, all known sympathizers of the Queen of Scots. He had been directly involved in the transfer of funds from secret sources on the Continent to aid the Catholic cause in England.

Unfortunately, they had not had enough incriminating evidence to hold him, and had to release him. But Walsingham had been keeping a close watch over him, and had discovered that Ridolfi had been very busy of late. More disturbing, however, had been the news that he, no longer confined to his residence, had left England for the Continent. Word had been received that Ridolfi had already met with the Duke of Alva, the Castilian grandee who commanded Philip's forces in the Netherlands and was next to meet with the pope, then Philip himself.

Cecil rested his bearded chin in the palm of his hand as he stared thoughtfully into the flames. What exactly were their plans? He didn't need to be a soothsayer to know what they were plotting—the death of Elizabeth. Now he needed to know who exactly was involved and how they planned it. They had lists of suspected traitors and malcontents, those seeking personal power and a return of the ancient faith, but he sometimes wondered if that was enough. All it would take was the one fanatic they had overlooked, that they had not detected in time. Then it would be too late, and all of the spying and counterspying would have been for naught. Elizabeth Tudor would be dead and England would face invasion.

PART TWO

Castaways

And pray, and sing, and tell old tales, and laugh
at gilded butterflies, and hear poor rogues talk
of court news; and we'll talk with them too, who
loses and who wins; who's in, who's out; and take
upon's the mystery of things . . .

SHAKESPEARE

Chapter Six

January, 1578—London
Whitehall Palace and the court of Elizabeth I

BLAZING torches cast flickering light against the rich-hued
tapestries and royal portraits which adorned the walls of the
Great Hall. As countless slender tapers burned low, strolling
musicians and singers, jesters, jugglers, and players vied jealously for the undivided attention of generous patrons and influential courtiers. Amusing themselves with gossip, games of
chance, and flirtations, serious matchmaking, business ventures, and politics, these privileged members of court whiled
away the hours awaiting their queen's pleasure.

The silver-gilt cups and tankards had been filled and refilled
many times over with red wines, Rhenish wines, sack, and ale.
The banqueting table had been emptied of the large platters of
venison roasts, oysters, river bass, stewed and pickled vegetables, salads, pasties, and tarts when the fanfaronade of trumpets
and drums announced the entrance of Elizabeth from her privy
chamber, where she had dined with a select few of her favorites
in attendance.

Resplendent in a French gown worked with Venetian gold

and a floral border encrusted with pearls, Elizabeth swept into the great hall. A starched, lacy ruff rose behind her head and framed her bright red hair and pale-complexioned face. A gold-wrought headdress studded with pearls crowned her head, while long ropes of pearls encrusted with gold and emeralds glistened against the tight bodice of her gown. The lace-edged sleeves were slashed to expose the richly figured brocade beneath, which was of the same golden material as the elegant underskirt revealed in front. A feather fan sprinkled with gold dust and attached to a golden handle entwined with exotic beasts fluttered in Elizabeth's hand, its various movements foretelling her volatile changes of mood.

Surrounded by her ladies-in-waiting and an assembly of court favorites, dignitaries, and officials, she moved easily amongst the crowd thronging the hall. Her loyal subjects knelt before her, hopeful of her notice and a kind word or jest spoken to them personally, and perhaps even a royal favor to be granted.

A lady-in-waiting, whose exceptional beauty in a stunning gown with a border worked cunningly with sparkling gems and pearls, and far richer seeming than the queen's own regal robes, received a glare of displeasure and a punishing pinch from Elizabeth, who would not suffer competition from one who served her, and who should remain no more than a shadow while in her presence. But a jester with a ready wit and comic antics soon had a smile curving his queen's lips as she laughed heartily at his fool's tricks.

By their queen's request, the court musicians, with lutes, viols, brass, and woodwinds, began a lively tune which heralded the dancing. Elizabeth, partnered by handsome courtiers who knew the steps well and showed a fine leg, enjoyed herself until she claimed the knaves would dance her to death and she retired to recline against silken cushions at the far side of the room. There, Elizabeth held court, summoning various people to her side and listening avidly until either boredom or anger overtook her patience for one who dallied too long before her or asked too many favors of her largesse.

From the crowded gallery overlooking the hall, the less fortunate watched in awe. And each dreamed of dressing in silk and jewels, with the finest lace scented with lavender, and on bended knee or with a deep curtsy would be presented to Elizabeth.

A young gallant who would soon draw the notice of his queen now stood in conversation with several other gentlemen near a deep window embrasure, where a certain amount of privacy could be found apart from the clamor.

He was dressed in a doublet of a deep burgundy color; the sleeves slashed and gold-embroidered showed the fine Holland linen of his shirt beneath. His trunk hose of a matching shade were only slightly puffed and slashed and were ornately embroidered in colored silks and golden threads. His netherstocks, gartered in velvet at the knee, were of silk and his shoes of cordovan leather. The starched whiteness of the plain ruff of cambric about his neck contrasted sharply with the darkness of his bronzed face. His hair was black and had a natural curl in its thickness, and an unruly strand curled against the single gold earring he wore in his left ear. As was the fashion, he wore a beard, but it was no bushy swallow's tail with curling moustache or long cathedral beard as was popular with academicians, nor did it serve to mask a weak chin. Dark as his hair and as neatly trimmed, the beard drew attention to the strength of his jawline.

Every so often, with a casualness that might have been deemed arrogance by one less sure of himself, he lifted a scented, gold pomander to his nose. It was indeed a noble profile, the nose patrician in cast. But when Valentine Whitelaw smiled, his mouth softened from its hard, chiseled lines and showed even teeth that gleamed in evidence of good health. His eyes, however, were the most startling feature about him, for they were heavy-lidded, the irises a bright turquoise shade that reflected like sunlight through clear water. They were fringed with long black lashes and set beneath beautifully arched brows.

He stood taller than his companions, and the severe cut of his doublet showed to perfection the wideness of his shoulders and the narrowness of waist and hips. Many an envious eye had been cast by less endowed gentlemen at the sleek muscularity of his thighs and calves, which needed no padding or tailor's tricks to enhance their masculine shape.

The gentleman standing just to his right was jostled as a group of people hurried past, too preoccupied with their conversation to realize they had rudely elbowed out of the way a rather short, elegantly dressed gentleman in their path.

"Clack-cackle, bibble-babble, gibble-gabble," the affronted

gentleman muttered as he watched the group barreling though the crowd. ''I swear this place has gotten as busy as Fleet Street during a royal procession, and with just as many riffraff milling about. Think I should see to my purse just in case it's been lifted. Since you've been away, Valentine, the court has tripled in size. Good Lord, I'm not acquainted with even half of this vermin,'' he decided as he eyed another noisy group approaching and took the precaution of taking a step backward. ''You know where to reach my family should I be trampled underfoot, never to draw breath again. They will have a moment's horror at the thought that I was in Smithfield Market, thinking I'd become a swineherd rather than a courtier, so you will have to explain the circumstances of my premature death, Valentine,'' he beseeched his friend. ''They will be overwrought at the thought.''

Valentine Whitelaw found himself smiling widely at George Hargraves's nonsensical talk. ''By your death, I understand completely.''

''No, by the scandal caused by the rumor that I was herding swine to market,'' he exclaimed with so serious an expression that anyone but a good friend would have been convinced of the shaken gentleman's concern.

''D'ye know, George, I think ye've missed your calling in life,'' Thomas Sandrick, another well-dressed gallant standing with them, drawled. ''The law isn't for you at all. 'Tis court jestering, and 'twould be one way of capturing Elizabeth's eye. Perhaps you might even manage to obtain a knighthood from your appreciative queen. Sir George Hargraves, first Earl of Doggerel, and his lady, the dancing bear!'' Thomas Sandrick intoned dramatically, much to the appreciation of the other gentlemen within hearing distance.

''Well, you, my late, unlamented friend, won't live long enough to congratulate me,'' George threatened.

''You mean you won't name one of the little cubs after me?'' Thomas demanded in outrage, a grieved look on his handsome face.

''Most likely I'll send one after you, teeth bared,'' George complained good-naturedly.

''I doubt seriously, however, that Walsingham acted the court jester to be rewarded his knighthood,'' Thomas Sandrick commented as he noticed the dour-faced Walsingham staring their way. "*Sir* Francis it is now," he reminded himself, for Elizabeth's current secretary of state, and onetime ambassador to France, had been knighted only the year before.

"Too serious by far for my tastes," George said. "That is why I shall be forced to turn down any royal appointments. Takes the humor right out of a man. Why, look at Lord Burghley, there. Did you ever see such a suffering expression?" he demanded as if resting his case, for all eyes followed his request and came to rest on William Cecil, still the queen's closest adviser, who was indeed looking a bit haggard.

"Gout," Thomas advised. "And he's becoming hard of hearing. Makes it devilishly hard to tell him any secrets," he said, winning a look of admiration from the quick-witted George.

" 'Tis a thought, becoming hard of hearing. Might not be half bad," George said, wincing as a loudmouthed individual walked past. "Lord, look at that!" he exclaimed with a loud guffaw of his own as he watched an elegantly dressed gentleman, overly anxious to be presented to his queen, trip over one of the silk pillows at her feet and fall sprawling to the carpeted floor in front of her, his face turning as bright a red as her hair as he quickly scrambled to his feet and tried to look dignified.

"Faith, but 'tis damned embarrassing the way some folks grovel," George declared before doubling over in laughter.

Valentine Whitelaw eyed his friend curiously. "I do believe, George, that life at court has had a peculiar effect on your personality. You used to be such a jovial fellow."

"Ah, Valentine," George said with a gasp, "I wish you wouldn't go to sea so damned much. I never seem to have as amusing a time when you're not here. And now that you've got your own ship and some land and a house in the West Country you never do come to London much anymore. 'Sdeath, but I nearly walked past you earlier, thinking you a stranger."

"I am sorry, George. I had no idea."

" 'Tis just that you are so difficult a fellow to get to laugh, that when you do, I know I've been especially amusing. You sharpen my wits," George said. "I suppose, though, 'tis a family trait. Basil wasn't the merriest of gentlemen."

Valentine Whitelaw was silent for a moment. "No, he wasn't, although because he did not laugh indiscreetly did not mean he was without a sense of humor."

"Of course, I was much younger then," George explained away his failure. "Hadn't quite developed my skills then. Depended more on physical pranks than on my sidesplitting witticisms. Have it finely honed now. Pity, though, Basil isn't here. 'Twould be the culmination of all of my long, hard years of study to get him to laugh uproariously," George wished aloud, then looked a bit chagrined when Thomas Sandrick jabbed him in the ribs and jerked his head meaningfully toward their friend.

"I wish he were standing here now," Valentine finally said, still finding it hard to believe that Basil had been lost at sea, along with Geoffrey Christian and his family, as well as all hands aboard the *Arion*.

"How long ago was that?" Sir Charles, an older gentleman, and a longtime friend of the Whitelaw brothers, asked now.

"This time seven years ago Basil set sail with Geoffrey Christian aboard his ship the *Arion*."

" 'Sblood, was it really that long ago?"

"Yes." The only surviving Whitelaw brother answered abruptly, for those years had haunted him.

"Can't be," the gentleman declared with a shake of his graying head. "Seems like yesterday I was dining with him and Lady Elspeth at Whiteswood. Still go there, but it isn't the same without good old Basil there to welcome me. Not that I blame Lady Elspeth for remarrying, she did have a son to raise, and she is still a damned fine-looking woman. Suppose you don't visit quite as often as you used to even though it is your family home. A fine place, that. I can certainly understand why Sir William has been in no hurry to build a place of his own. I've heard talk, however, that Sir William has had his eye on an estate closer to London."

"Elspeth may have remarried but Simon is still a Whitelaw and when he is of age he will inherit Whiteswood. My fondness for Elspeth has not diminished because she married Sir William. He has treated Simon like his own son. Since I am often away at sea, I am relieved to know that both Elspeth and Simon are well cared for."

"Generous of you, Valentine. Damned generous," Sir Charles declared. "No. Can't understand it, Valentine."

"What can't you understand, Sir Charles?"

"Well, why Basil ever sailed to the Indies in the first place.

We both know he wasn't one for doing much traveling. Not like you, he wasn't. He'd grumble about having to travel with Her Majesty during the summer months when she takes to the road and travels about the countryside. It suited him to travel between here and Whiteswood, but no further afield for him. That is why I cannot understand what he was doing aboard the *Arion*. Know he was a good friend of Christian's but still, I just cannot understand," Sir Charles said with a sigh. "Never told you why, did he?"

"No, he did not," Valentine answered.

"Surprised he didn't, or that you weren't on board. You used to sail with Christian, didn't you? Oh-ho, I remember now, you were with Drake, doin' a bit of adventurin', eh?" he chuckled. "You young sea dogs are a rovin' pack. France was the place for adventurin' when I was your age. Still is, if you ask me, that and Spain. Both need to feel the bite of a good English sword. But you hot-blooded young bucks have to go sailing off to godforsaken, faraway places where heathens and strange beasts are the only creatures roaming the lands. Waste of time and money," he muttered, his thoughts straying.

Valentine smiled slightly, for Sir Charles was a harmless gentleman. "I had not yet left England when Geoffrey Christian sailed, but I had already signed on with Drake. Otherwise, I would have been aboard the *Arion* the day she sank."

"Didn't know Christian that well, of course, but seems strange to me he'd attack the Spanish like he did, what with his own wife and child being aboard," Sir Charles commented in disapproval, for public opinion had turned against Geoffrey Christian's reckless act.

"He would not have," Valentine said.

"You sound certain of that."

"I am, Sir Charles. I knew Geoffrey Christian, and he would never have attacked a fleet of galleons, not with with Magdalena and his daughter aboard, and certainly not if he knew he could not win. Nor would he have jeopardized Basil's life, especially if—" he began, then shrugged and turned his gaze away from Sir Francis Walsingham and Lord Burghley. He had no proof that Basil had been working for them, but he did have his suspicions—even if they were just that.

"Wasn't it from a report by the Spanish ambassador that you

and Lady Elspeth were informed of the sinking of the *Arion?* The witnesses did say that the Spanish ships had to fire on the *Arion* in self-defense. You have to admit, Valentine, that Geoffrey Christian did not make his reputation as a privateer by turning tail. I imagine he made himself a few enemies, and the Spanish claim he'd been doing a bit of raiding along the Main before he was sunk. The man was fond of trouble, Valentine. He looked for it. Why get himself a Spanish wife, otherwise? No, I'm afraid he was a belligerent fellow, and this time he got in a fight he couldn't win.''

Valentine Whitelaw's lips were tight as he said, ''You have only the word of the Spanish ambassador, and your witnesses are the Spanish captains who would have rejoiced in sending Geoffrey Christian to the bottom. Even against the odds, Geoffrey Christian was unbeatable—if he'd even had half a chance, he would have survived,'' Valentine Whitelaw speculated.

Sir Charles looked pityingly at the younger man. ''You were not there, Valentine. I'm afraid that no one knows exactly what happened that day. The truth is buried with those unfortunates aboard the *Arion,* and she's on the bottom of the sea.''

''One day, I will find the truth. I owe Basil and Geoffrey Christian that much at least,'' he said softly.

Sir Charles coughed uncomfortably, clearing his throat. ''I'm sorry I missed out on Drake's latest venture. I hear, too late now of course since he's already sailed, that he needed investors. Sailing to Alexandria, is he? Would like to get in on some of that trade.''

Valentine Whitelaw smiled slightly. That was exactly what Drake, and his investors, among them Elizabeth, wanted people, especially the Spanish to believe—that Drake was bound for the Mediterranean, where he would trade English goods for spices. In truth, Francis Drake was up to his old tricks. He had devised a bold plan of attack against the Spanish, intending to sail round South America and into the mostly unexplored waters of the Pacific, where he planned to attack the port city of Panama and loot it of its gold and silver before the treasure could be sent by pack mule to Nombre di Dios on the Caribbean side of the isthmus. He also intended to try to establish a profitable trade with the islands of the Far East. Less than a month ago he had set sail in the *Pelican*, accompanied by four other ships and a company of over one hundred fifty men.

"If you ever need any private monies, Valentine, for your ventures, you just say the word and I'm committed for a handsome sum. Seems unnatural to me, seeing the other side of the world like Drake has," he said, a touch of envy in his voice. "Lord help us, but he'll be wantin' to sail to the stars next."

"Or at least around the world? 'Sdeath, but I can't even find my way safely around London, much less the world," George commented. "Still don't believe 'tis round," he added with a wink.

"Where was it you found that manservant of yours anyway?" Sir Charles suddenly demanded. "Don't mind telling you that he makes me more than a little nervous, Valentine. Made a wager with Roeburton that he's one of these eunuchs."

"God's light, I had no idea!" George said in amazement as he raised an inquiring eyebrow at the robust Henry Roeburton, who was standing not more than ten feet away.

"Not Henry, damn it!" Sir Charles said in exasperation, glaring at George's innocent expression. "The manservant! Valentine's valet de chambre, or—or—steward, or—or whatever he is!" Sir Charles said huffily.

"Oh, the Turk," George said, finally seeming to understand. "He's Turkish, and I for one am not about to ask him so personal a question," George advised them, thinking of the Turk's size and unsmiling countenance, and the curved blade of the scimitar that swung at his waist.

"Man doesn't say much, either. Did he have his tongue cut out? Hear 'tis the way these sultans keep their servants from giving away court secrets. He's not one of those dervishes, is he?" he asked with such a look of concern on his face, that George Hargraves nearly glanced over his shoulder expecting to see a bare-chested Turk come leaping and whirling into the center of Elizabeth's court with a bloodcurdling howl that would have the ladies fainting. "Can't see why you took him on as your servant," Sir Charles said, keeping an uneasy eye on George's grinning face and not daring to ask what he was thinking.

"I did not have much say in the matter," Valentine remarked, remembering how he had seen the lone, turbaned man fighting for his life against half a dozen armed men in a bazaar in Alexandria. . . .

Not liking to see anyone outnumbered in a fight, whatever the circumstances, he had come to the man's aid, and just in time, for the Turk had been wounded and was losing ground as fast as blood. Standing back to back, they had each faced with sword and dagger drawn a trio of angry Arabians, fanatically bent on beheading the Turk, and anyone unfortunate enough to be standing between them and their quarry. Valentine Whitelaw had found himself in a fight for his own life; with a fierce determination equal to the Arabs', but borne of wishing to see England again, he had vanquished two of the Turk's attackers. And with the timely intervention of several of his crew, who had seen their captain's predicament and charged in unmindful of the danger, they had quickly routed the others.

The fight over, the Turk had turned to face his unexpected ally. The dark, impenetrable eyes had met briefly the Englishman's clear-eyed gaze, then the seriously wounded Turk had fallen unconscious to the ground. Belatedly, Valentine Whitelaw had realized that he couldn't walk off and leave the man he had just saved lying helpless in the bazaar and at the mercy of his attackers, who were sure to return in greater numbers. Since no one stepped forward to claim the wounded man, Valentine had taken him back to his ship, where he'd seen that the stranger was nursed back to health.

Although the Turk had never spoken of his previous life, Valentine, assisted by a local merchant he had traded with, learned that the Turk had been a Janizary and had served the great Ali Pasha in the battle at Lepanto. The Turkish fleet had been destroyed by the Venetians and her Christian allies in their crusade against the Ottoman empire and the followers of Islam. Surviving the slaughter, the Turk had then joined Uluch Ali, an Algerian corsair, who had also been one of the fortunate few to survive the battle and who had returned to Constantinople a powerful man.

The merchant, a dealer in the finest Turkish carpets, had heard on one of his travels that the man Valentine knew only as the Turk was called Mustafa and had killed an influential pasha in the Sultan's court. The Turk had fallen in love with a slave girl who had been sold to a North African sheik by this same court official, despite the Turk's request for the girl and willingness to pay an exorbitant amount of gold for her. A northern European with the pale hair and eyes that would bring a high price on the market when she was sold as a concubine to a wealthy Muslim in Alexandria or Madagascar, she had been too valuable not to auction off to the highest bidder.

After taking his revenge against the pasha, the Turk had followed the girl to Egypt, and that was all the merchant could tell him about the man whose life Valentine had just saved. Although, the merchant had added after a quick glance around to make certain he was not overheard, since the Englishman had always dealt fairly with him, he could tell him this: Several sailors aboard a galley recently arrived from Constantinople had told a tale about a pale-haired girl jumping into the sea to drown rather than become a concubine to the sheik who had bought her. With a secretive look, the merchant had whispered the name of the feared sheik whose galley that had been and whose men had been the ones who had attacked the Turk in the bazaar. When the galley had docked, a madman had stormed aboard searching for the girl. During the ensuing scuffle, the sheik's favorite son and several guards who had been aboard at the time to protect the sheik's newly arrived concubines were killed. The attack on the Turk in the bazaar had been an act of retribution; that was why the Englishman should not have interfered. If he valued his life, the merchant had warned, he should leave Alexandria immediately.

A dagger thrown from an unknown assassin's hand the very next day had convinced Valentine of the expediency of following the merchant's advice, and he had wasted little time in leaving Alexandria. However, the Turk had sailed with them. Through the merchant's nervous translation, Valentine had understood the Turk to say that Valentine now owned his life, that he would serve him loyally and to the death. His life was his to command.

Valentine had no choice; the man had no place to go. He could not return to his home in Constantinople, nor could he stay in Alexandria or anywhere in North Africa. When Valentine had agreed to allow the Turk to stay on board ship, he had thought he might be able to find the man something useful to do, and then, when they reached a safe port, the man could go about his business or stay on board as a member of the crew. Never had Valentine imagined that the Turk would so seriously devote his life to serving him, or that the Turk would so quickly become indispensable to him.

To have called the Turk merely a manservant would have been incorrect as well as demeaning. He was a man of many trades. Although trained as a soldier, he easily learned the skills of a seaman. With a pride that none dared question, he now served his new master as steward, valet, and—many had learned to their regret—as Valentine Whitelaw's protector. Even Valentine had difficulty remembering the countless times during the past years when the Turk's sword had deflected a surely fatal blow meant for him.

"Eli— 'Sdeath, but *she's* coming this way," Thomas Sandrick said suddenly, an expression of awed appreciation spreading across his handsome face.

"Elizabeth?" George exclaimed, dropping onto his bended knee in anticipation of being presented to Her Majesty.

"No, Eliza Valchamps," Thomas Sandrick said reverently as his eyes feasted on the vision of loveliness approaching.

George Hargraves turned as bright as the fair one's gown. Pretending to straighten his hose, he quickly stood, not daring to catch anyone's eye. But he needn't have worried, for all eyes, including Valentine Whitelaw's, were held by the unparalleled beauty of the woman accompanying young Eliza Valchamps.

Cordelia Howard's black eyes flashed with amusement as she came to a halt before them and declared, "I do fear Elizabeth's wrath should she catch a gentleman down on bended knee before anyone but herself. Please remember that in future, George. I value my position at court too much to lose it over a smitten beau who forgets himself while in public. Sir Charles, Thomas," she greeted them courteously enough, but when she turned to Valentine Whitelaw her eyes were burning with an unnatural brightness.

"Cordelia," he murmured.

"I did not know you had returned from your latest voyage," she commented, a pout forming on her lovely mouth. "I never can remember where 'tis you go or why. By my faith, but it seems as if you've been away more during the last couple of years than you've been here. One of these days, Valentine, you will return to England to discover that few people of your acquaintance even remember you."

Valentine smiled. "I trust not everyone. One always hopes that the affections of friends . . . and acquaintances . . . will remain unchanged no matter how much time passes. Reunions can be so rewarding," he said. "Haven't you found that to be true?"

Cordelia remained silent for a moment, as if indeed remembering. "You know little Eliza Valchamps? She's a very distant cousin of mine, and Raymond Valchamps's youngest sister. Five more ahead of her, and it nearly bankrupted the family marrying them all off. Lord, what a feat," she said with a laugh that caused a painful-looking blush to spread across Eliza's paling cheeks. "That is why dear Eliza is in London. We must find her a husband, although, I fear 'twill be a bit difficult, since she has hardly more than pittance as dowry, and . . . well," Cordelia left the rest unspoken, for although Eliza had fine eyes and a delicate profile, next to Cordelia's raven-haired, dark-eyed beauty, she paled into a mousy insignificance.

Apparently, Eliza Valchamps, gray eyed and ash blond, was beautiful enough for Thomas Sandrick, for his eyes had never strayed from her. A discreet look from her lowered eyes was all the acknowledgment he'd received, but it was enough for a man in love.

Cordelia had not missed the masculine glint of approval in Thomas Sandrick's eye or the blush that had momentarily brightened Eliza's pale cheeks when she had greeted him. Her task might not be as difficult as she had imagined when first asked to introduce her nonentity of a cousin to a prospective husband in London, Cordelia thought. A speculative gleam in her eye, she watched the two young people. To wed little Eliza Valchamps to Thomas Sandrick would be quite an accomplishment, since the gentleman was wealthy and heir to a title and vast estates. And since they were both Catholic there would be no difficulty on that score. She would make certain the banns were announced before Eliza left London, Cordelia promised herself. And, she thought with a smile of anticipation curving her lips provocatively as she recognized one gentleman in particular amongst a lively group approaching, she would see that

Raymond Valchamps rewarded her handsomely for her efforts on behalf of his sister. As brother-in-law to Thomas Sandrick, dear Raymond, knowing him as well as she did, would soon have a far heavier purse to carry about. She would have to lighten it considerably for him.

"Dear, dear Raymond," Cordelia greeted him, the smile and look in her eye unsettling to the gentleman who had captured her notice. He knew his beautiful cousin too well to be flattered by her effusive attentions, Cordelia never did anything unless it suited her purpose.

"Cordelia, exquisite as always," Raymond Valchamps responded, ignoring his sister's presence as he acknowledged the other gentlemen at hand. "Whitelaw," he said, "I believe congratulations are in order."

"Oh?" Valentine Whitelaw raised a politely curious brow, for Raymond Valchamps had never been one of his close acquaintances.

"Yes, indeed. 'Tis all I've heard since doffing my cloak, how Valentine Whitelaw is stealing prizes right from under Drake's nose. Hear the man will have to chain his crew to the deck if he wants to keep them aboard, so many of them anxious to sign on with our latest hero. I understand 'twas a galleon loaded down with Philip's gold and silver that you boarded and took as your latest prize. Whatever will he say when he learns the treasure is in your pocket instead of his?" he exclaimed in amused speculation.

"Ask Valentine to finance Alva's mercenaries in the Netherlands," George bellowed, his next comment lost in the laughter which followed.

"More likely Elizabeth will grant our brave sea captain a title," Raymond Valchamps added, unable to hide his envy of the other man.

George Hargraves smiled slightly, for it was well known that the two men had been longtime rivals for the affections of the beautiful yet elusive Cordelia Howard, and from the seductive look in Cordelia's dark eyes when she gazed at Valentine Whitelaw it would seem he was the victor—at least for present, for Cordelia Howard was not known for her constancy.

"Sir Valentine Whitelaw. Has a nice ring to it," George commented. "Although, seeing how dangerous life at court can be, 'twould seem to me that Valentine would have a far better chance of being knighted if he'd stay in London and defend his friends' backs. Many more bloodthirsty mercenaries to deal with right here in Whitehall than in all the Spanish Main. Wouldn't you agree, Valchamps? I believe you have been involved in quite a few skirmishes of late," George remarked, for he suspected it had been Valchamps who had made certain that the queen had heard a particularly malicious piece of gossip concerning the reputation of a lady he was fond of.

For a moment Raymond Valchamps said nothing, allowing his gaze to rest on George Hargraves. And, as usually was the case, his adversary gradually grew ill at ease, losing his advantage to the other man. For it was difficult to hold Valchamps's gaze for long, and he knew it. With a slight smile curving his lips, and never reaching the one blue eye and one brown eye, he said, "Indeed? Can't say I remember, Hargraves. Most likely you've exaggerated the importance of whatever 'tis. In fact, I'd lay odds 'twas yet another one of your endless pranks. 'Sdeath, but one seldom knows whether or not to take the man seriously," he said to no one in particular as he glanced at George Hargraves's short figure with insulting speculation. "Ought to recommend the gentleman to Elizabeth as her next jester. 'Twould certainly keep us amused until the next village idiot comes along. I'll even supply the bells for your cap."

George Hargraves reached for his glove to wipe the sneering smile from Raymond Valchamps's face, but before he could challenge him to a duel, he felt a restraining hand against his arm. Despite his efforts, he could not shake Valentine Whitelaw's grip.

"Have caution, my friend. 'Twould not be worth the effort, George," Valentine advised. "Besides, Thomas would not thank you for causing him such an unnecessary hardship."

George Hargraves and his adversary, as well as Thomas Sandrick, seemed puzzled by the offhand remark. "Thomas?"

"What the devil does Sandrick have to do with anything?" Raymond Valchamps demanded arrogantly.

"Well, should George lose, and I do think it likely since you are a fairly capable swordsman and outreach George by several inches, I would then have to challenge you. Your subsequent death would, I suppose, result in your family mourning your passing. And that brings me to Thomas, who would not enjoy seeing the fair Eliza dressed in black. Nor indeed would Cordelia, a distant relation, or her many admirers thank you for causing her such an inconvenience.''

George slapped his thigh, his laughter mingling with his friends' as his anger was cooled by amusement. Unfortunately, however, it seemed that Raymond Valchamps found Valentine Whitelaw's conclusion anything but amusing. He met those mocking eyes, but they never wavered from his, much to Raymond Valchamps' discomfort for a change. He was reaching for his sword when he heard a commanding voice behind him.

''God's death, but I'll have no brawling in my palace!'' Elizabeth vowed. ''Have you *gentlemen*, and I use the word with some doubt, the need to prove yourselves on the field of battle, then there is the tilting yard beyond these walls. But take heed, my mettlesome ones, for if you continue with this dispute you may find your pretty heads rather than your proud shields hanging in the Shield Gallery. And beware! I would not thank either one of you for depriving me of the other's company,'' she warned.

'' 'Twould seem well-behaved and handsome courtiers are devilishly hard to come by nowadays,'' she remarked, her dark eyes flashing her disapproval and seeming to send a special message to the group of finely dressed gentlemen at her side. Amongst that elite gathering: Lord Burghley; Sir Francis Walsingham; Robert Dudley, Earl of Leicester, the queen's longtime favorite who seldom seemed out of favor with Her Majesty for long despite his indiscretions; Sir Christopher Hatton, darkly handsome and the finest dancer at court; Philip Sidney, a distinguished young gentleman poet who personified all that was honorable; Edward de Vere, ever quarrelsome and Cecil's son-in-law; and other notables and would-be notables jealously guarding their places at Elizabeth's side.

With a casual gesture, she bid her loyal subjects rise. Apparently satisfied that she had suitably impressed the two who would have dueled in her presence, she smiled. They were both such handsome rogues she found it difficult to remain angry. Indeed, she would rather flirt with them than have them banished from her sight because of such foolishness.

''Well, my roguish captain, 'twould seem we have just welcomed you back into our presence and already a storm is threat-

ening to blow you away from us," Elizabeth said with a twinkle
in her eye as she greeted Valentine Whitelaw.

"Your presence, madam, is like the sun shining through the
clouds," Valentine said softly before kissing the ringed hand
held out to him. On her finger sparkled a glowing emerald, his
gift to her at the New Year's celebrations, when he had been
given a private audience with her, and during which time he had
related his latest adventures.

" 'Tis lovely," she whispered, her eyes gazing down at his
dark head. *So young. So free,* she thought sadly.

"It pales before your magnificence, madam," Valentine
Whitelaw responded sincerely, and although Elizabeth was still
an attractive woman in the middle of her fifth decade, and entering the twentieth year of her reign, Valentine Whitelaw was
more impressed by the manner in which she had ruled England.
Her critics and friends alike might accuse her of many things; arrogance, wantonness, and pettiness, or kindness, loyalty, and
generosity, but none could say she lacked courage. And none
could claim that Elizabeth had ruled with anything but the best
interests of her subjects at heart.

"Ha! You will have to look to your laurels my fine ones," she
declared with a quick glance around her at her courtiers, "for
'twould seem my good captain is not only brave and adventure-
some, but courtly as well. We will have to keep you by our side
more often, Captain Rogue. Nay, that will not serve, for I do not
wish Philip to become too quiescent with one of my sea dogs
chained at my side," she said, and loud enough for the Spanish
emissary who hovered nearby to overhear.

"This may prove to be the year for hearty English ale rather
than sweet Spanish sherris sack," George Hargraves murmured
beneath his breath, and Elizabeth hearing him laughed loudly
despite the Spanish gentleman's flushed and angry countenance.

With a sly look, Elizabeth turned her attention to Raymond
Valchamps. Although his strangely colored eyes made some uneasy, Elizabeth was fond of him, for he was classically handsome, with finely etched lips and slightly flared nostrils, which
lent him an almost faunish look. Despite the delicate molding of
his face, there was no question that Raymond Valchamps was a
gentleman who enjoyed feminine company. Several of his well-

publicized affairs had resulted in his receiving the nickname of Satyr from his queen, who was fond of finding pet names for her favorites.

"Since 'twas my Satyr who was involved, I msut believe 'twas over a wench this argument?" she said with a look of displeasure cast in Cordelia Howard's direction, for she knew the dark-eyed she-wolf tempted both men.

"Indeed not, madam," Raymond Valchamps responded quite seriously. " 'Twas over George Hargraves."

"God's death!" came Elizabeth's favorite oath, which she had hardly uttered before her thin shoulders started to shake with laughter as she saw George Hargraves's astounded expression. "By my faith, but I'll knight all three of you for keeping me laughing—either that or have you drawn and quartered for your impudence."

" 'Tis not quite the manner in which I had imagined myself dying for my queen," Raymond Valchamps said, noting with satisfaction that she carried his New Year's gift as well as wearing Whitelaw's extravagant gift of an emerald ring. The whore did not deserve either, Raymond Valchamps thought with a smile as he pretended to gaze adoringly into Elizabeth's eyes.

Another year gone and a new one begun, and still she ruled England. But soon . . .

"I hear, my captain, that the ring you wear in your ear is Spanish gold. Is't true?" Elizabeth demanded, tapping Valentine's arm with her fan.

"Indeed, madam. The gold comes from a doubloon, one of many from the treasure of the first Spanish galleon the *Madrigal* took as her prize. A constant reminder, madam, of Philip's generosity to an enterprising Englishman," Valentine said.

"Your Grace! Really, I must protest so flagrant a boast of piracy!" the Spanish emissary expostulated angrily. "This man should be in chains for such an act, and yet here he is being presented at court as though having accomplished a heroic act. This is an insult to Philip and the honor of Spain. I demand satisfaction, madam, and certainly recompense for the man's thievery."

"Do not ask for too much, little man. Or you may receive more than you had bargained for. If Philip cannot keep the purse strings drawn, then do not expect me to," Elizabeth berated the flustered gentleman before turning her back on him.

"Now, which of my bold ones will partner me? My captain or my Satyr?" she asked with a flirtatious glance between the two men as she prolonged making the choice and ignored the hopeful faces of her temporarily forgotten courtiers.

"Satyr, let us dance," she declared grandly. "You, my Captain Rogue, I shall save the next dance for. 'Tis a slower one, so I may prolong the pleasure."

"The pleasure will be mine, madam," Valentine Whitelaw responded with a courtly bow.

"Then see that you keep your eye on the step so you do not disgrace me," she warned. "There would be those, deceitful and disloyal, who would try to distract you," she added with a gleam in her eye as she caught Cordelia Howard's impatient movement.

" 'Twould be like holding a farthing candle to the sun, madam," he said. Then, with a roguish smile that caused Elizabeth's heart to flutter, he added, "Besides, I have always had a penchant for red hair, madam."

"Ah, my captain, I shall not soon let you leave my side," she vowed as she moved into the center of the hall accompanied by Raymond Valchamps.

" 'Sblood, Valentine," George said with a laugh, "if you are not careful, she will never allow you to roam far from England. If I did not know you as well as I do, I would say you were a cunning knave. Half of the court would sell their souls to be as favored as you, and yet all you can think about is your next voyage. A pity I was born so short. 'Twill never be my good fortune to become one of her favorites when I can barely be seen in a crowd, and I certainly could not partner her without causing myself severe embarrassment. Ah, well. When do you plan to sail again, Valentine?"

"Not for some time," Valentine Whitelaw said, momentarily distracted, as Elizabeth had feared, by the dark eyes of Cordelia Howard as she moved closer to his side.

Foul deeds will rise,
Though all the earth o'erwhelm them, to men's eyes.

SHAKESPEARE

Chapter Seven

AT high tide, the waters of the Thames lapped over the river steps to Highwater Tavern. Built on pilings that stretched out beyond the river's edge, the half-timbered inn was popular with sea captains and sailors, most of whom enjoyed sharing an ale or two while a tale of adventure was related to appreciative mates. The sound of strange tongues could be heard as well when foreign travelers, newly arrived in port and anxious to find decent lodging after a long and perhaps perilous voyage, sought comfort before a cheerful hearth. Well-to-do merchants and well-dressed gentlemen of the city, some engaged in illicit business transactions with the proprietor and his patrons, were known to frequent the riverside tavern. The trapdoors concealed in the inn's floor allowed smuggled goods easy and free access into London. Many fine wines were enjoyed by the innkeeper's favored guests at considerable discount. And should there have been a few shekels left in a customer's purse, the affable innkeeper could also offer at thieves' prices, or so he innocently claimed, a pair of finely embroidered kid gloves that had eluded the customs officer, or the finest of imported silk ribbons and lace to trim a fair lady's gown.

Firelight danced against the aged darkness of oak beams in the low-ceilinged room when Valentine Whitelaw entered Highwater Tavern the evening following his attendance at court. He had just supped with Martin Frobisher at Devil's Tavern and had been delayed till late discussing Frobisher's next voyage. The Yorkshireman's enthusiasm had convinced even Valentine, as it previously had his investors, that this time he would find the Northwest Passage he had searched in vain for on his many voyages.

Cold rain blew in gusts about Valentine Whitelaw's cloaked figure as he swung shut the heavy door and made his way into the warmth of the inn. A frequent guest at the tavern, he was welcomed by the proprietor with opened arms when the gentleman captain had arrived a week earlier, no doubt just returned from a profitable voyage. He had even given his well-heeled guest one of his finest private rooms, for Captain Whitelaw never caused any trouble and paid his bill on time without haggling over each charge—fairly levied, the innkeeper was always quick to swear. And with their captain enjoying the tavern's best accommodations, the ship's crew could be counted on to spend a goodly sum of their well-earned pay in the taproom below.

It was a night few people wished to be out in and the taproom was packed with a multitude of shivering bodies. As Valentine moved through the crowded room he recognized many a familiar face. With nods of acknowledgment, he responded to the friendly hails. Several times he was halted in his progress through the crowd by an outstretched hand and hearty welcome for one safely home from the sea. Unable to refuse a toast to fellow captains and the success of future voyages, he found himself with tankard in hand time and time again, until the numbing chill in his bones soon fled before a spreading warmth that left him feeling well contented with his lot in life.

Few had noticed the silently moving man who had followed Valentine Whitelaw's cloaked form into the inn, but Valentine was ever aware of the Turk lurking in the shadows, never far from his side. And should someone, even one whose good judgment has become impaired because he had imbibed too freely, have taken notice of the strangely attired, turbaned man, he would have known instinctively not to voice his opinion of one so different from himself. The Turk's size alone should have been discouragement enough against a rash comment, but the intensity of the man's dark-eyed gaze would have convinced even the most drunken of sailors not to prolong the encounter.

Valentine Whitelaw was dressed in plainer doublet and hose than he had been the night before. He moved with as much ease amongst these men, some of whom were little better than ruffians a step ahead of the hangman's noose, as he had amongst the most foppish courtiers hovering around Elizabeth the night before.

"Let 'em try, the Papist dogs! I'd blow them out of the water fast enough. 'Sdeath, but I'd like to have Philip's head riding the bowsprit of my ship," a foolhardy captain boasted, and far more bravely in the taproom of a London tavern than he ever had while at sea.

"I've had enough of this poor-spirited business. Seems to me the queen and them fainthearted advisers of hers are more concerned about upsettin' the Spaniards than they are seein' that Englishmen have the right to sail where they will. What I'd like to know is who gave the Spanish the right to say nay to the course I set when aboard my ship. The Spanish must think we're a bunch of dunghill cocks and not to be feared the way we sneak about, afraid of our own shadows. Well, I am a freeborn Englishman and no one is goin' to tell John Danfield where or where not he can sail!"

"Aye! The devil take 'em all!"

"Here's to the Spanish! May they rot on the bottom!"

"Aye! To the Spanisssh," the well-oiled captain agreed before sinking beneath the table.

Valentine Whitelaw managed to slip away from the noisy crowd thirsting for Spanish blood and made his way up the narrow, rickety flight of stairs to his room overlooking the river.

Before Valentine could enter his room, the Turk had stepped in front of him and opened the door. His hand resting lightly on the hilt of the scimitar, he preceded Valentine into the room as stealthily as his size would allow. Valentine couldn't help but smile slightly, for every night they went through the same procedure, and the Turk had yet to confront any assassins hiding within. And Valentine doubted they ever would. But he would never convince the Turk of that, Valentine was thinking as he shook out his wet cloak and tossed his hat upon a chair. He was removing his sword when the Turk moved with a suddenness that caught Valentine by surprise, the scimitar rising in a deadly arc as he pulled apart the velvet curtains that had enclosed the four-poster bed set against the far wall.

The Turk's savage yell was echoed by the scream of terror from the woman who had been dozing peacefully amid the pile of soft pillows on the bed.

Cordelia Howard had never been so frightened in her life, nor was she likely ever to be so frightened again. Opening her drowsy eyes to see the maniacal face of a turbaned madman swinging a curved sword down upon her was enough to cause her to lose her wits or faint; she promptly did the latter.

"Damn, Mustafa," Valentine swore beneath his breath as he recognized the pale-faced woman lying unconscious in his bed, her dark, unbound hair streaming across her bare shoulders as she slumped against the pillows.

If Valentine hadn't been so concerned for Cordelia, he might have laughed aloud at the comical look that had replaced the fierce expression on the Turk's face when he had come face to face with his deadly assassin.

The Turk, who had learned English during the past few years but seldom chose to speak, now said with his usual pithiness, "Dead, Cap'n?"

Valentine sat down next to Cordelia and felt the pulse fluttering against the soft curve of her throat. "You are fortunate, Mustafa, for Cordelia will probably be satisfied just to see you hanged, and perhaps, since I may be able to convince her to be forgiving, not have you drawn and quartered."

The Turk did not seem to be overly concerned by the prospect and continued to stand staring down at the unclad woman, his expression now one of disapproval. The coverlet had slipped lower to expose more than even Cordelia might have wished of her womanly charms, and certainly more than was considered proper even for a harem dancer.

The sound of banging on the door drew Valentine's attention from Cordelia, who was beginning to moan as she returned to consciousness.

"Here! Open up in there! What the devil's goin' on?" the innkeeper yelled through the closed door. "Don't hold for any murderin' on these premises. Ye can take yer fightin' t'other side of the river," he warned, ready to evict the lot of them, even if this was Captain Whitelaw's room.

His ham-fist was raised to strike another blow and the heavy-set fellow behind him was prepared to ease a shoulder against the door when it suddenly opened and the innkeeper nearly fell against Valentine Whitelaw's chest.

"Yes?" he inquired politely. "What is amiss?"

"Huh?" the befuddled innkeeper mumbled. "Amiss? That's what I'm here to find out! Don't like to say what I nearly did in me breeches when I heard that howl," he confided, trying to glance past Valentine Whitelaw's broad form and see beyond. "Run a respectable place here, Cap'n. I'm sure, if ye killed someone just now, 'twas probably an accident. In fact, I'll swear to it," he allowed generously, thinking of how appreciative the captain was sure to be.

"Thank you. That is indeed kind of you, but 'twas merely the lady crying out at having seen a mouse."

"Oh, I see. Well, I s'pose—what lady?" he demanded, remembering that Valentine Whitelaw had entered the tavern by himself—except, of course, for that turbaned fellow.

The expression on Valentine Whitelaw's face never changed, but some instinct told the innkeeper not to pursue the matter of the lady's identity. "Well, as long as everything is all right. Could've sworn, though, there were two screams. But 'twas the one that came before the lady's that was the worst. Curdled me blood it did," he complained.

"That was Mustafa. He doesn't like mice either," Valentine said, closing the door on the astounded innkeeper.

Returning to Cordelia's side, Valentine took the dampened cloth the Turk had prepared for him and held it to Cordelia's forehead. As her lids began to flutter, he advised the Turk, who was still at his side, "I do not think that handsome turban of yours should be the first thing she sees when she opens her eyes."

"Valentine?" Cordelia murmured.

"None other," Valentine said softly, cradling her limp body in his arms.

She buried her face against his chest, sobbing so loudly that she did not hear when the door was quietly opened then closed.

"Oh, Valentine!" she wailed. "That madman was going to murder me! Where is he?" she demanded, risking a glance as she lifted her head from the security of his embrace and looked around the room. "I hope you beat him within an inch of his life," she said with a tearful sniff. "I don't think I shall ever be the same again. The heathen ought to be hanged as well."

Valentine smoothed back a long strand of soft black hair. "So bloodthirsty, my love," he murmured, pressing a kiss against her warm, perfumed skin.

"What did you do with him?" Cordelia asked, but with less interest in the man's punishment than she had displayed before Valentine's hands had started caressing her.

"I sent him from the room," Valentine told her, his lips leaving a trail of fire along the firm roundness of her breast as he drew her closer. "My love," he whispered against her fragrant skin. "I was not expecting you."

"I wished to surprise you."

"You certainly have succeeded," he said.

"I was expecting you last night," she said with a slightly imperious lifting of her chin. "Why did you not come?"

" 'Twas nearly dawn when I saw you leave, accompanied by Valchamps," Valentine reminded her, unable to mask the jealousy he felt when seeing the two of them together.

"His sister was in attendance, or did you not remember that I am sponsoring her at court?" Cordelia reminded him now. "Or were you enjoying the company of someone else?" she demanded angrily.

"The truth of the matter, my dear, is that I fell asleep," he admitted. "Am I to be forgiven?"

Cordelia raised a haughty shoulder, humiliated that he could actually have fallen asleep when he knew she would be waiting for him. She sent him a dark look from her eyes, thinking to leave him to sleep alone this eve as well, but when her eyes met his, she forgot her plans for revenge.

Valentine smiled, and Cordelia felt her blood quicken. He was so devilishly handsome, she thought as she threw back her head and allowed those turquoise eyes of his to roam freely over the silkiness of her pale-skinned flesh. And his ardent gaze alone was enough to excite her into a breathless anticipation.

But when his hands and mouth moved with accustomed familiarity over her body and elicited so wild a response from her that she felt intoxicated, she could hardly contain her impatience when he left her side to disrobe. And when he returned to her, she was so insatiable that Valentine gave a low laugh of surprise as her all-consuming passion made her forget any maidenly modesty she might have pretended or tantalizing seduction she had planned to prolong her pleasures as she sought immediate fulfillment from his lovemaking.

Slowly and sinuously, Cordelia moved her body against him, feeling the burning heat of his flesh against hers as he responded with increasing sensuality to her bold caresses, but still he remained apart from her. Fondling her and kissing her with leisurely thoroughness, his hands and lips left no part of her free of his touch. And when finally they came together as one, she knew again the sensations that sent shudders of delight through her body. She had come to crave that madness that raced like wildfire through her blood. It was as necessary to her as each breath she took. Feverish with desire, her nails raking Valentine's broad back, her pale, slender thighs locked about his hips, her long black hair tangled about them, Cordelia held him bound to her, refusing to allow their passion to die. Her mouth clung to his hungrily. Valentine stared down into the mesmerizing blackness of her eyes and saw his own face reflected in their fiery depths. He felt bewitched by the sorcery she practiced with her body and was lost to the ravening lust that now consumed both of them in its flame.

The noisy sounds of the river coming to life awoke them at dawn. For several moments they lay in companionable silence. A gray light was beginning to break to the east, but it seemed a halfhearted effort as the thunder rumbled overhead with the promise of more rain.

Valentine sighed contentedly and settled himself more comfortably against the pillows. He wanted to stretch, but he would regret losing the warm softness of Cordelia's flesh against his. Gently, he parted the veil of silk that concealed the beauty of her face from him. With loving tenderness, his lips moved along the delicate line of her jaw. The musky scent of the perfume she wore lingered against the heat of their entwined bodies and branded him her lover.

"Delia," he murmured against her flushed cheek, his mouth seeking a response from her slightly parted lips.

Pulling her long hair from beneath her, she deliberately pressed the curve of her backside against him as she curled

closer in his embrace, allowing his arm to drape across the tautness of her belly and his hand to rest intimately against her inner
thigh.

"When are you going to marry me?" Valentine asked softly.

"My love, you know Elizabeth will never give us her permission. She does not look kindly upon matrimony, especially
where her favorite subjects are concerned. She would have all
her ladies-in-waiting and any female at court live and die as
maids. Because she chooses to remain unwed, she would deny
us the pleasures of—"

"—of the flesh," Valentine said, his voice muffled as his lips
moved along her breast.

Cordelia laughed softly, shivering with delight under his caress.

Valentine's arms tightened about her. "I would marry you,
Delia, despite Elizabeth's wrath," Valentine persisted. "I will
convince her of my devotion to her, but I will not be denied you,
Delia."

"I am yours, Valentine," she reminded him, snuggling
against him with a seductive movement of her hips, her teeth
leaving a light impression in the flesh of his shoulder.

"I want you to bear my name and children," he breathed
against her warm body.

"One day, Valentine. One day," Cordelia promised him,
feeling him hard against her. "Until then, let us play her game,
but by our own rules. Elizabeth may continue to enjoy your undying devotion and admiration, but I shall have your love. And,
more importantly, I shall have you warming my bed. And yet,
we shall both continue to be welcomed at court, receiving her
favors," Cordelia planned. "A pity, Valentine, that you inherited that house in Cornwall. 'Tis so far away. I swear, 'tis in the
wilds, and the people little better than the savages of the New
World."

"You forget, my love, that I am half Cornish," Valentine reminded her. " 'Twas my mother's home. She was a Polgannis.
The last Polgannis. She knew that I have always been proud of
my Cornish heritage. She also knew that I had a great fondness
for her old home, and since Basil inherited Whiteswood, she left
the land and ancient seat of the Polgannis family to me."

"Well, I still think 'tis a pity. If only she hadn't been Cornish,

Valentine. You could have inherited an estate in Berkshire or Essex. Well, perhaps since you are so favored by Elizabeth, she will give you an estate much closer to London. 'Twill be much more convenient.''

"I happen to like my home in Cornwall. You will come to love it too, Delia," Valentine assured her. "I long to show it to you. I long to see you and our children within those halls.''

Valentine could not see the disgruntled expression on Cordelia's face as she stared at the glowing embers in the hearth. Living out her days in Cornwall was not what she had planned for the rest of her life. Nor did she have any intention of losing her feminine charms to motherhood so soon. Seeing herself abandoned in Cornwall in some drafty house, her plump figure surrounded by whining brats, while Valentine sailed away for months at a time and enjoyed himself at court was not to her liking at all.

Cordelia Howard knew what she wanted. Although Valentine Whitelaw was a charming rogue, indeed, she had quite decided he was her favorite lover, she had not yet decided whether or not she would marry him. Such an alliance would have to be to her advantage, and as she saw it now, marrying Valentine Whitelaw would not serve her purpose. He was an adventurer, certain to be away for long periods of time, perhaps never to return. His money was invested in his ship and his prized estate was in the wilds of the West Country. Although he was in favor with Elizabeth now, he might not always be so fortunate. And she suspected Valentine would not be overwrought by the prospect of being banished from court, as many a heartbroken courtier would have, for Valentine would contentedly sail away to spend the rest of his days in Cornwall, on that godforsaken estate of his. Of course, should she wed him, since he often would be at sea, she could take many a lover without his knowing. And, should he be lost, she would have his estate, which she could sell for a handsome profit. And in the meantime who could predict how wealthy and powerful he might become from these enterprising ventures of his?

Valentine Whitelaw was not her only prospect of marriage. There was Raymond Valchamps. He was handsome and witty, and he fully appreciated what life at court could bring to one with ambition. Although not as wealthy as she would have liked, he was one of Elizabeth's favorites, and she would most likely give him an estate one of these days. His expectations were quite good. He was certain to inherit within the year his family's estate, and he was heir-apparent to his grandmother's wealth—which was considerable.

Cordelia allowed a slight smile of remembrance to curve her lips. Raymond Valchamps had been her lover for years, long before she had even become aware of Valentine Whitelaw. He was indeed aptly named Satyr by his queen. He had never failed to arouse her fiercest passions, even when she was satiated from his lovemaking.

Then, there was Sir Rodger Penmorley. Odd that it should have been Valentine's brother, Basil, who should have introduced her to him, Cordelia speculated. He was a longtime friend of the family, having grown up on the estate next to the one Valentine had inherited in Cornwall. It would certainly be an interesting situation should she choose to marry Rodger instead of Valentine. Whatever would Valentine do, having her living so close, and as wife to his friend? The thought was intriguing, and not impossible. Although she would not enjoy having the family seat in Cornwall, Sir Rodger Penmorley was a very wealthy man. He owned large holdings throughout England, some of which were in the surrounding area. He even had a well-furnished house in the city, which was the fervent ambition of many an aspiring courtier. He was a member of Parliament and as a member of court had for years been seen at Elizabeth's side. He was deemed by all a worthy man; indeed, he was a man of noble character, a man of sterling reputation. But he was not a handsome, daring adventurer like Valentine, nor did he indulge in voluptuous pleasures like her libertine cousin; in fact, in Cordelia's opinion, Rodger Penmorley was dull. But he possessed greater wealth than either of them, and he was in love with her.

For now, Cordelia thought with a deep sigh of satisfaction as she lay with Valentine, she needn't concern herself with finding a husband. While she remained free, she had no one to answer to but herself. She could do as she saw fit, come and go as she pleased, and enjoy every moment to the fullest.

"Perhaps Elizabeth is quite wise in remaining unwed. She does as she damn well pleases, with no man to say nay to her. She has men serving her but not deciding her destiny, as would a husband. Such power, she wields. I swear I am envious of her," Cordelia admitted.

Valentine allowed his hands to move along the gentle curve of her hips and thighs. "I feel sorry for her at times. She is a lonely woman, Delia."

"Her loneliness is well compensated for when handsome rogues like you and Leicester vie for her affections and attentions by lavishing her with gold and jewels and fancies that would win any woman's heart. By my faith, but Elizabeth could not wear even half of the jewels she owns if she had a hundred years in which to do so. I have come to feel quite beggarly when in her glittering presence," Cordelia complained, remembering the countless strands of gleaming pearls that had dangled from Elizabeth's throat, several of which had been given to her by Valentine.

Valentine smiled. "You could never be called beggarly, my love."

"Had my father not left me well provided for, I would have been forced long ago to take a husband, even an impoverished one, just to keep a roof over my head. We cannot all be so fortunate as Elizabeth. I dare say she does not fully appreciate all of the jewels she has been given by her devoted courtiers. Were I in her position, I would certainly know how to thank so generous a gentleman," Cordelia said provocatively.

Valentine smiled. "Indeed, madam? I shall hold you to that boast," he said as he suddenly left her side.

With a curious glitter in her eyes, Cordelia watched him through half-closed lids as he prowled about the room. "Whatever are you doing? Come back to bed. I am becoming cold without you beside me," she cajoled, stretching luxuriously beneath the fur rug spread across the bed.

Valentine stood up from where he had been kneeling behind a large chest at the foot of the bed, a wide grin of satisfaction on his handsome face. Despite his obvious virility, he suddenly looked like a small boy with a prized secret he was about to share with someone very special.

Cordelia gave a squeal of delight as a handful of fiery gems scattered across the fur rug. Struggling from the covers, she scrambled across the bed, oblivious now to the cold against the bareness of her body. Frantically she moved her hands through the thickness of the fur rug as she sought the emeralds, sapphires, rubies, and pearls that were hidden from her sight.

They dazzled the eye. Cordelia's tongue licked the dryness from her lips as she held an emerald up to catch the light and stared through its translucent beauty in fascination.

"Where did you find them?" she demanded, her hands moving quickly now as she searched for any gems that had escaped her notice.

"I did not exactly find them, my dear," he said, watching her with pleasure as she knelt on the bed.

"Plunder! 'Tis from a Spanish galleon you sunk, is it not?" she said excitedly. The gleam in her eye brightened as she held a bloodred ruby against the whiteness of her skin. "I shall call this one my Spaniard's blood!" she exulted.

"I can see you have no qualms about accepting such a gift," Valentine remarked, slightly surprised by her lack of squeamishness. "I hate to disappoint you, my dear, but I took that from a French corsair."

"Hmm, 'tis a pity," she murmured, but her attention was centered on the sparkling gems she held in the palm of her hand. "I shall have these made into the most stunning pendant. 'Twill cause Elizabeth such envy when she spies it adorning my finest gown," Cordelia gloated. With a deep laugh of pure pleasure, she hugged the gems to her breasts and fell back against the pillows.

Staring up at Valentine, she eyed him lazily. "Come, let me thank you properly, as I promised I would, my dearest rogue," she invited him as she let the precious stones trickle through her fingers to fall in a fiery trail from breast to thigh.

A disturbance outside the door broke the spell she was weaving about them. Laughing softly, Cordelia did not seem annoyed by the interruption and quickly became absorbed in contemplation of her newfound riches. Valentine was less than pleased, however, especially when he recognized the voice calling so frantically to him.

"What the devil is George doing here at dawn?" he demanded as he found his dressing gown. Tying the velvet sash about his waist, Valentine had just reached the door when he heard low-voiced curses and scuffling noises coming from the far side of the door.

Opening it wide, Valentine stared in amazement at George Hargraves, who was standing rigidly against Mustafa's caftan-clad figure. George's head had been pulled back by a handful of his fine, sandy-colored hair which was grasped tightly in one of the Turk's hands. The curved blade of Mustafa's scimitar hovered within a hair's breadth of his throat.

"Not to enter captain's presence," Mustafa explained.

"Damn it, Valentine!" George choked, his ruddy-complexioned face becoming mottled with anger and desperation. "I can't take a breath for fear of having my throat slit."

"He is a friend, Mustafa. You may release him."

"Thank you," George said, straightening his manhandled doublet and cape. "Where the devil's my hat?" he demanded testily, and spying it beneath the Turk's turned-up, pointed-toed boot, he turned a disdainful shoulder to the man and proudly drew himself up to his full height, which still had him a good foot or two shorter than the Turk. "Friend indeed!" George croaked, having lost his voice more from fear than actual physical damage. Casting a baleful glance at the Turk before he stepped well away from him and that damned sword of his, he warmed to his grievance.

"Try to do a favor for a friend, and what happens? I nearly get beheaded by a Turk in a tavern in the heart of London! 'Sdeath, but 'tis becoming a dangerous town to be about in," George declared with a cantankerous glance at his too-quiet friend who could not completely hide his amusement at his unexpected visitor's predicament.

Glancing back into the room, he saw that the velvet hangings of the bed had been discreetly drawn to conceal Cordelia's presence within the bedchamber.

"I am sorry, George. Come in and sit down. I think there is some wine here that might settle your nerves," Valentine invited him, guiding the still pugnacious-looking George into the room.

"Need it more to settle my stomach," George said peevishly, but he was feeling a bit more mollified as he accepted the goblet of wine, even if the Turk was lurking near the opened doorway.

"Now what has you banging on my door this early?" Valentine asked, and seeing George's face still flushed, he wondered if it had been wise to offer him wine. "Not forgotten where you live, have you, George? Shall I have Mustafa escort you to your lodgings?''

"I am not fuddled," George insisted.

"What is amiss?"

"Valentine," George began, then hesitated despite the excitement glowing in his eyes. "I do not know quite how to tell you this? You will think me befooled, but—"

"But what, George?" Valentine spoke impatiently, thinking this yet another one of George's ill-timed and beef-witted pranks.

" 'Tis your brother! Basil lives!" George blurted out.

The web of our life is of a mingled yarn,
good and ill together.

SHAKESPEARE

Chapter Eight

IT was eventide of Twelfth Day Eve when Valentine Whitelaw approached Whiteswood. Crowning a hillside in the distance, twelve ceremonial fires burned in a circle around a larger one. Throughout the shire, in village, field, and vale, the ancient ceremony of blessing a bountiful earth was being followed by simple folk and nobles alike. A cup of well-aged ale was raised in toast. With shouts of *Wass hael* in the old Saxon tongue and cheerful songs echoing through the cold evening air, the revelers prepared for a night of feasting and merrymaking.

Through woods barren of leaf, Valentine Whitelaw, accompanied by the Turk, followed the familiar lane that wound deep into the valley. Every now and then pale stars winked overhead as the stormy weather moved south, leaving the skies clear. The ground was frozen and crackled beneath their horses' hooves. Directly in their path, the twin brick towers of the gatehouse rose before them. Blazing torches, set in heavy brackets on either side of the arched entranceway to Whiteswood, spread a welcoming glow into the darkness beyond the gates. The Whitelaw arms were cast in shadow as the riders passed beneath the arch and into the paved courtyard beyond. The noisy clatter of hooves striking against stone announced their arrival. As they dismounted, an elderly man, his shirtsleeves rolled up to his elbows, his jerkin unfastened, came scurrying out of the gatehouse.

"Who goes there?" he demanded, not recognizing the cloaked figure that now strode with such purpose toward the great doors of the manor. The sweating horses were already being led away by a dutiful stableboy; as if these uninvited guests intended to stay.

"Back to your warm fire, you old watchdog," Valentine told the gatekeeper.

"Master Valentine! 'Tis good to see ye!" the old man cried out as he recognized the intruder. "Heard ye had gone to sea again. Didn't know ye'd returned, and richer than ever, I'll wager. The master and mistress will be pleased to welcome ye back. And young Master Simon will keep ye up half the night listening to them wild tales of adventurin'. Lady Elspeth won't take kindly to that," he chuckled as he bent closer to see the young gentleman he'd watched over since the lad had been in swaddling bands.

"Still in one piece," Valentine told him.

The old man snorted. "Gotten too thin," he said, but was relieved nonetheless to see his former master's young brother looking so healthy. "Wish ye'd stay home, where ye belong, Master Valentine. This goin' to sea 'tisn't what a man was meant for. Otherwise, we'd all been born fish, eh? Worry about ye, I do. The sea be a cursed place to go. Brings misery, it does," he said, for Whiteswood wasn't the same without the Whitelaw brothers. *Sir William is a good man, but he isn't a Whitelaw,* the old retainer thought sadly as he eyed Valentine.

"No harm will come to me. You taught me too well how to get out of trouble, you old rogue," Valentine told him, smiling widely as the old man shook his head.

"Reckon I went to a lot of trouble for nothin', seein' how ye be goin' out of yer way lookin' fer it. But 'tis your good fortune to have the Whitelaw luck," Trent said, keeping a safe distance between himself and the tall gent with the strange-looking shoes, for their curling toes could not be concealed beneath the hooded cloak he wore. Had it not been for the exotic presence of Valentine Whitelaw's manservant, the old gatekeeper wouldn't have been so worried or believed a word of the heart-thumping stories he'd be sure to hear recited the next day by an overly excitable footman.

"Ye just make sure it don't run out on ye one of these days, especially when ye be with heathens and cutthroats and the likes of him. Can't trust 'em,'' he said, glaring at the Turk.

''Are Sir William and Lady Elspeth receiving this eve? It is urgent that I have a word in private with them.''

''They be gone nigh on an hour. Went to the festivities,'' Trent informed him. ''Be back soon, most likely. Maybe some folks comin' with them. Most of the village, I reckon, seein' how we got the most ale and cake hereabouts. Glad ye'll be here for the cuttin' of the Twelfth cake. Maybe 'twill keep yer luck good fer another year, eh? Now, ye just go on inside and warm yerself before the fire, Master Valentine,'' the old gatekeeper told him as the heavy doors were swung wide to reveal the well-lit interior of the great hall.

With mixed feelings, Valentine entered Whiteswood. There was a festive mood throughout the hall as the servants prepared for the celebration in which they would share equally with their master and his guests. A banqueting table held a large silver bowl filled with spiced cider. Pitchers of ale stood ready to be poured, while platters were being placed on the table by excited maids who bustled back and forth through the paneled screens that led to the kitchens. Dressed in their finest linen gowns, their hair woven with colorful ribbons, the young women cheerfully went about their duties, humming the songs they would soon be dancing to on the arms of attentive admirers.

Valentine's appearance in the hall was greeted with hails of recognition by a number of the older retainers, who still fondly recalled many an incident the younger Whitelaw brother had been involved in when growing up at Whiteswood. The steward, who had been a yeoman in the household when Basil had first become master, escorted Valentine through the hall and up the curving flight of stone steps that climbed to the first floor. There, in the privacy of the master's great chamber, Valentine awaited the return of Sir William and Lady Elspeth.

For more than an hour Valentine had stood contemplating the fire burning so brightly in the hearth of the quiet chamber. He glanced about the comfortable room where Sir William conducted the affairs of the estate and where the family dined in private. The plasterwork ceiling and ornate paneling were new, but the armorial glass in the darkened windows still bore the coat of arms of the Whitelaw family. Fine paintings had joined the tapestries hanging on the walls, and embroidered cushions on high-backed chairs set close to the hearth offered comfort to the master and his family. A backgammon board was positioned between two of the chairs and bore proof of recent play.

Valentine paced restlessly before the flames. How could he possibly tell Sir William that he might no longer be master of Whiteswood? That his marriage to Elspeth might be bigamous? That his beloved children might be bastards?

How could he relate the joyous news that Basil might still live, when such news could only destroy Sir William's life? And what of Elspeth? She had pledged herself to another man, thinking Basil dead. She had given birth to a son and a daughter by that man, a man she had thought to be her lawful husband. And what of Simon? He had come to accept Sir William as his father. There was a deep affection between the two.

How welcomed would Basil be at Whiteswood now? And it seemed almost certain that Basil would be returning, Valentine thought as he remembered how George Hargraves had burst in on him at Highwater Tavern with the startling news.

Calming the excitable George, Valentine had gradually gotten the story out of his friend. George had arrived with a group of friends at Devil's Tavern well after Valentine had left. George had been about to leave when he overheard someone demanding to see Valentine Whitelaw. His visitor, a rough-looking individual who had seen better days, had been told aboard the *Madrigal* that her captain was to be found with Frobisher at the Devil. George, being a curious fellow, and reluctant to send an enemy to his friend's door should the man have an old score to settle, demanded to be told of the man's business with Valentine Whitelaw.

The man had been reluctant at first to divulge his information, until several tankards of ale had warmed his blood and loosened his tongue. He finally told George that his name was Randall, and that his brother, whom he had thought dead for seven years, was back in London.

A strange occurrence indeed, George had thought, his interest piqued enough to buy the man another ale in order to hear the rest of the story and discover what relationship his friend Valentine had with the Randall brothers.

George Hargraves had not been prepared for the revelation

that Jemmy Randall's brother, Joshua, had been the bos'n aboard Geoffrey Christian's ship. When the *Arion* had gone down, Joshua Randall and several others had been pulled out of the water by the Spaniards. For years he'd been little better than a slave in the household of some grandee in Mexico City, but after he'd refused to convert to the old faith and tried to escape his captivity he had been made a galley slave aboard a galleon. For two years he had managed to survive, then, when he thought he'd die behind the oars, their ship had run afoul of several English privateers south of the Azores. The Spanish captain had surrendered, the victors freeing their English mates, and that was how his brother had managed to get back to England. He was a dying man, Jemmy said, but that didn't seem to concern Joshua; it was the passengers who had been set ashore and abandoned that had him worried the most.

Jemmy Randall had halted his story there, telling George that he expected Captain Whitelaw might be interested enough in hearing the rest of the story, and in seeing the map Joshua had drawn of the location of the island the castaways had been stranded on, to pay a fair price.

Valentine had gone to the lodgings where Joshua Randall lay dying. Although he wouldn't have recognized the emaciated man, he remembered the bos'n from his own days of sailing aboard aboard the *Arion* with Geoffrey Christian.

'' 'Tis young Master Whitelaw? Not dreamin', am I?'' the feverish man had whispered.

"I am here, Master Randall," Valentine had reassured him, grasping the man's shaking hand in his.

The warm strength of his hand had seemed to have a calming effect on Joshua Randall, even though tears streamed from his eyes as he told Valentine his story.

''. . . and the cap'n, he fought hard. Cursin' all the time, he was. I thought for a while there we was goin' to beat 'em. But the cap'n was hurt in the chest, bleedin' bad. He died before them bastards could gloat over the *Arion* goin' to the bottom. Laughed at them, he did. Broke me heart, when the cap'n fell to his knees. Then he was gone. 'Twas too late then, anyways,'' Joshua Randall said, a cough wracking his thin chest.

''Your brother says that Captain Christian sent his wife and daughter, and the other passenger aboard the *Arion*, Basil Whitelaw, ashore?'' Valentine questioned him gently.

"Aye, that he did,'' the bos'n agreed. "He sent young Lawson with them. Saw him row them ashore. Then we was fightin' them Spaniards. So many of them. And ye know, that Eddie Lawson, he comes rowin' back out to try to save us when the *Arion* went down. Good lad, he was. But d'ye know, them bastards blew him right out of the water. Poor little Eddie,'' he mumbled thickly. "I thought at first Doña Magdalena and sweet Mistress Lily were in the boat, that was the way the cap'n had it planned. Glad the cap'n didn't see that.''

"What did he have planned?''

"That when we went down, Lawson would row them out to one of the Spanish galleons. The lady was Spanish, and he said they would be returned safely to Santo Domingo. The cap'n was wrong. If Doña Magdalena and the little one, and Sir Basil, he was an important gentleman the cap'n said, had been aboard, they would have been killed. The Spaniards pulled some of us who tried to swim away out of the water. Wish the sharks had got me, I do. They got some of the lads.

'' 'Twas a trap, Master Whitelaw! They was waitin' fer us before we even got into the Gulf,'' he cried, his hands gripping Valentine's shirt, but his passion was soon spent and he dropped back against the pillows. "But we beat 'em through the Straits, then tried to get into the islands and lose them. But we couldn't make it.''

"You survived, Joshua. You beat them.''

"Aye, I did, didn't I?'' he sighed.

"You drew a map of the location of that island?''

"Aye, Master Whitelaw,'' he said, a secretive look entering his eyes. "Always worried about young Mistress Lily bein' left like that.''

"I'll find them, Joshua. I'll find Doña Magdalena and Lily. Sir Basil is my brother. I'll find them, and I'll bring them home,'' Valentine promised the dying man.

Joshua Randall had almost smiled, and there was a look of contentment on his face when he drifted into a restless sleep. The map was now in Valentine's possession. Jemmy Randall, plenty of money jiggling in his pocket, seemed almost relieved when told that a physician and his attendants would see to his brother's care and any arrangements after that would be handled as well.

Valentine was startled from his thoughts when a log fell in a shower of sparks in the fireplace. He felt the parchment, folded so carefully against his breast, and wondered what he would find when he reached the destination marked with a crude X on Joshua Randall's map.

Valentine was still pondering that thought, and dreading the meeting with Elspeth and Sir Willian, when the door opened.

"Uncle Valentine!" Simon Whitelaw cried out as he caught sight of the tall, bronzed man standing so quietly before the hearth. "I knew you'd come! I knew you would! I told them no one, especially a Spaniard, could sink you!"

"Simon! You've grown a foot since last we met!" Valentine exclaimed, holding the youngster at arm's length while he took his measure. "Can't keep you in the same doublet and hose longer than a month, I'll wager. The tailor will be cutting your hose as long as Sir William's by next Twelfth Day," he predicted, much to his nephew's delight as he offered his hand to him, then grasped Simon's thin shoulders in a hearty hug, for the lad was not too adult yet to mind a relative's fond embrace.

Valentine hoped he had been successful in masking the start he'd felt when first seeing Simon. The boy was tall for his age, and his bones seemed to stick out of his flesh at all angles. With eyes and hair black as midnight, and with a profile that was becoming more hawkish every day, at fourteen, Simon Whitelaw bore a startling resemblance to his father. There could be no mistaking whose son he was. Valentine glanced over Simon's dark head, realizing that his nephew must be a constant reminder to his mother and Sir William of the man who had fathered him.

"Valentine, my dear," Lady Elspeth greeted her former brother-in-law fondly. "I am so pleased to see you. I had feared the holidays would pass without your presence at Whiteswood. I had hoped since you were away that Quinta and Artemis would join us, but, alas, they would stay in Cornwall. Thinking you might arrive, they did not want you to find your home closed up. Trying to persuade a Whitelaw to a change of mind is like speaking to the winds. Ah, how thin you have become. We shall have to put some flesh on those bones of yours, Valentine."

"Elspeth." Valentine kissed her hand, then her soft cheek, with brotherly affection. "More beautiful than ever."

"And you more glib. No doubt you have been at court and paid your respect to Elizabeth. Court life can tarnish a shining armor, my dear," Elspeth responded with a low laugh. "I shall remind myself *not* to believe half of what you say."

"Too sharp-tongued by half," he laughed as he held out his hand to Sir William.

"Good to see you, Valentine," Sir William Davies now greeted him, gripping his hand firmly. "Despite Elspeth's concern you seem fit. A good voyage?"

"Aye, a good one," Valentine allowed.

"How many galleons did you sink?" Simon demanded eagerly, his boyish face full of admiration for his adventurer uncle. "I'll wear a ring of Spanish gold in my ear one of these days!" Simon vowed with youthful zeal.

"Simon, please, there will be plenty of time to hear of such things," Elspeth requested with gentle authority. "Stokes says you declined to sup and would only take ale," she said with a disapproving shake of her beautifully coiffed, fair head. "I am told that you were reluctant even to accept our hospitality overnight."

"What is this, Valentine?" Sir William demanded, his face becoming flushed. "Whiteswood will always be your home. Now, hear me out. I know you have your mother's home in Cornwall, but I have always hoped from the first day I became master of Whiteswood, that you, and your aunt and sister would still consider this your home. And that you would all feel free to come and go as you pleased."

"Thank you, Sir William," Valentine said, feeling more awkward than before. He glanced at Simon for a moment, then at Elspeth and Sir William. "We have need to talk. I cannot stay longer than this night. When we have spoken, you will understand the need for my unseemly haste."

"Simon. Although you ate enough for two when in the village, I know you grow impatient to sample the fare on the banqueting table below. Elspeth? Come, let us start the festivities, then we will return and speak with Valentine. I fear something weighs heavily on his mind," Sir William correctly interpreted the slight frown marring Valentine's brow.

"Yes, of course," Elspeth agreed. " 'Tis getting late for the children to be up, and yet we cannot deny them their pleasure of the feasting," she said smiling down at her daughter who was leaning tiredly against Elspeth's hip.

"Can this fair maid truly be Betsy?" Valentine demanded with grave consideration of her shyly hidden face. "The fair curls seem vaguely familiar. And were they not turned away from me, I would swear those eyes were as bright a blue as a summer sky. But what is this? Bows!" Valentine said, his hand gently cupping the little girl's small, rounded chin. "Now I am certain 'tis Betsy, my own cosset, for she was always fond of red satin bows," he cajoled as he noticed the profusion of bows sewn to the underskirt of her gown. And as he sighed, apparently heartbroken, he was rewarded by a quick peek from a pair of very bright blue eyes before giggling Betsy buried her face in her mother's gown.

"And you remember Wilfred?" Sir William said, beaming down proudly as his five-year-old son stepped forward like a well-bred gentleman greeting a guest in his home, although his courtly bow was slightly off balance.

"Of course I do. Wilfred has certainly grown into a fine young gentleman who does the Davies name proud," Valentine said with proper seriousness to Betsy's older brother, whose gap-toothed smile was widening as he giggled.

"You will accompany us, Valentine?" Elspeth asked softly.

"Please, we would be honored," Sir William added. "There are many in the hall who would be pleased to have two White-laws welcoming the new year with them," Sir William said without animosity, and little realizing how prophetic his statement might become as Valentine accompanied them to the great hall below.

The fire in the hearth of the great chamber had burned low when Valentine finished telling Elspeth and Sir William the strange tale that had begun so dramatically the day before.

Elspeth sat with her head downbent, her slender hands folded together in her lap. Her expression was hidden from them. Sir William sat stiffly in his chair, his eyes never straying from the softly glowing coals in the hearth.

"I will be riding for Highcross Court on the morrow. Geoffrey Christian's cousin must be told. Then I will return to London, where my ship, the *Madrigal*, is docked. I will sail to Cornwall and inform my aunt and sister of what has happened. Then," Valentine paused, "I will sail for the Indies."

Elspeth gave a slight nod but did not look up.

Sir William cleared his throat. "Of course." And for the first time since Valentine had begun his story Sir William glanced up, and Valentine saw that his eyes were red.

Valentine spread his hands, feeling a strange helplessness. "I would not have had you hear this from anyone else. The news that Basil may be alive will have spread throughout London."

Sir William stood up. He suddenly looked old and beaten, and his step, which had always seemed so self-assured, was slow and hesitant. Valentine hid the pity he felt for the slightly older man, whose pleasant-featured face only an hour earlier had been so full of happiness as he had stood with his family and friends around him and toasted a new year full of prosperity.

Sir William's hand trembled now as he placed it on Valentine's firmly muscled arm. "I know you must go, Valentine. You can do nothing else. Whatever happens, 'tis God's will," he said.

Without another word, Sir William Davies left the room.

"Elspeth?" Valentine spoke softly.

Elspeth raised her head, her expression still serene. But when Valentine looked into her eyes, the torment was revealed.

"Seven years, Valentine, I have thought him dead. I loved him as I have loved no other. It was difficult at first to accept his death, but finally I could. I came to accept that the happiness I had come to believe would always be mine was lost to me forever. I never thought I could love another man, not after Basil. I did not want to love again. I wanted those feelings to be as dead as Basil. But I found happiness again, and I have come to love William very deeply, Valentine. Do you understand what I am saying?"

"Yes."

"How can there be such great happiness and sadness? When I heard you say that Basil might yet live, my happiness knew no bounds. To think that he is alive. Dear God, how I prayed to hear that news. But now I know that if he lives my life with William and our children is over. Whatever are we to do, Valentine?'' she asked, but before Valentine could speak, she held up her hand pleadingly. Turning it palm up, she held her hand outstretched to him.

Valentine took her slender hand in his and drew her to her feet.

"Godspeed you on your journey, Valentine," she said quietly. For a long moment she stared into Valentine's face. Then she followed Sir William from the great chamber, where Basil Whitelaw had once sat as master of Whiteswood.

Highcross Court, home of the Christian family for generations, seemed deserted when Valentine Whitelaw rode into the courtyard. It was a far different house than the one he remembered. When Geoffrey Christian and Magdalena had resided within its walls, Highcross Court had been filled with light and laughter.

A surly-looking groom was crossing the yard from the stable block with unhurried strides. And from the straw sticking to his jerkin and hose, he had either been sleeping or rolling in the hay. Whichever activity he had been involved in, he seemed less than pleased by the interruption.

"Master know ye be callin'?" he asked doubtfully, eyeing the new arrivals up and down as he stood, arms crossed, blocking their path. "Where the divil ye be from?" he demanded insultingly, his eyes widened as he stared disbelievingly at the Turk.

"Tell your master that Valentine Whitelaw awaits his pleasure."

"Reckon ye be waitin' a goodly spell then, seein' how the master be sittin' for his portrait. Some fancy gent come down from London to do it. Reckon his nabs was thinkin' of giftin' the queen with his likeness at the New Year's celebrations, so fond of it and himself, he be. But then he weren't invited to court. Fit to be tied, he was," the groom chortled. " 'Tweren't done anyways. Couldn't give Her Majesty a paintin' of himself with only half a face and no hair, though, comes to think 'bout it, his nabs might look all the better fer it. Anyhows, he won't like bein' interrupted," he warned them. "Reckon he be mighty cross, seein' how he's most likely missed his meal. Strainin' at the bit, he is, thinking about that cold joint of mutton left over from last night's meal.''

"I'll risk incurring his disfavor," Valentine said, the look in his eye advising the groom to step aside.

"Door be open. Ye wants I should stable yer horses?" he asked with a speculative gleam in his eye as he took note of Valentine's fine clothes and the quality of his mount.

"We will not be staying."

With a shrug the groom moved out of Valentine Whitelaw's path, and well out of the way of the big, mean-looking fellow with the puffed-up hat on his head. Those dark eyes made him uneasy; never left him all the while he'd been talking to the well-dressed gentlemen. With a sly look over his shoulder as he hurried back to the stables, he wondered what business they could possibly have with the master.

Inside, the hall was cold and empty and unwelcoming. No fire burned in the great hearth, and Valentine doubted that even when darkness fell would tapers be lighted to brighten the room.

As Valentine glanced around the hall, trying to imagine where the master would be sitting to have his portrait painted, a young maid came hurrying out from behind the screens at the far end. Her arms were straining against the weight of the two buckets she carried. Soapy water sloshed out with each step she took and splashed down on her heavy clogs. The rags thrown across her thin shoulders were little better than the faded gown she wore.

Preoccupied with the task ahead of her, she didn't see the two men standing at the foot of the great staircase until she was nearly upon them.

Her squeal of fright echoed throughout the gloomy hall when she glanced up to meet the Turk's curious stare. Both Valentine and the Turk had to jump to avoid the wave of water that spread out around her as she dropped the two buckets. Her roughened hands covered her mouth and muffled the cry that followed when she realized that she had dumped the soapy contents of the two buckets across the hall and nearly on top of the finely shod feet of the tall gentleman standing before her.

"Please, sir, don't be tellin' the master what I've gone and done. He'll beat me, he will," she pleaded, pushing back a straying wisp of pale blond hair, then wiping the tears from her cheek with the back of her hand. "I didn't get any supper last night 'cause I spilled his wine. I was hopin' fer some tonight, but if he finds out . . . I'm sorry, sir."

Valentine smiled. "No harm was done. I would like to speak with your master. Where is he?"

His request to see Hartwell Barclay seemed to disquiet the child, for she was hardly more than twelve or thirteen, and with a gesture that had become a nervous habit, she pushed back the strand of hair that had fallen across her face again.

"Oh, sir, ye don't want to be doin' that. Please, sir, I—I can't be goin' up there and—"

"You needn't. I will find him," Valentine interrupted her, silently damning Hartwell Barclay for the parsimonious, bullying master he apparently was, for the child was scared to death, as well as overworked from the look of her. "Where is he?" he asked, his tone brooking no argument.

"I-in the gallery," she finally whispered, pointing overhead.

"Thank you. Now you'd better get someone to help you clean this up."

"There be just me in the scullery. The master got rid o' the others, said there be too many idle hands around this house. I'll have this cleaned up in no time at all," she said, her spirits rising as she realized that the master would not learn of her latest mistake. "Are ye sure ye oughta be doin' this, sir?" she dared to question as the handsome gentleman started up the stairs. She didn't want to see him get into any trouble, and the master had a nasty temper even at the best of times.

Valentine smiled again, but this time his smile didn't set the girl's mind at ease as it had when he had smiled down at her. She found herself almost pitying Hartwell Barclay should this gentleman not be the master's friend.

She was still watching the two men when they reached the top of the staircase. Her mouth had dropped open in amazement as she had taken notice for the first time of the man accompanying Valentine Whitelaw. His turbaned head along with the curling moustache and shoes held her spellbound. The master wouldn't be pleased at all when he caught sight of that one, she thought with a shiver as she sank down onto her knees and began to mop up the slippery mess covering the floor.

The two men at the far end of the gallery did not hear the approach of the unexpected visitors to Highcross Court. A pale light streamed in from the tall windows and lighted tapers filled the small area with a misleading warmth and brightness. Hartwell Barclay stood with hand on hip, staring with a majestic tilt of his head at the lands beyond the windows.

"Oh, Master Barclay, this portrait will be my finest achievement," the artist exclaimed as he peered around the corner of the canvas at his subject, then back again to the likeness he was adding flesh tones to.

"At the price I am paying you, it had better be a masterpiece," Hartwell Barclay said, his voice rather squeaky for so large a gentleman.

Valentine paused a few feet back, his presence still undetected by either man. He looked at the portrait, then looked at the man posing for it; there was little resemblance between the two.

The man in the portrait was a Greek god. He had a classical profile beneath curling locks; a muscular leg clad in silk was elegantly posed; and the richly ornamented codpiece, painted in generous proportions by the artist, revealed the gentleman's unquestionable masculinity.

Despite how he might wish to be portrayed in a painting, Hartwell Barclay had a forbidding countenance. His profile was anything but classical, his nose bulbous, his eyes close-set, his chin doubling. His colorless hair was thinning on top, but his thickening waistline could indeed have been painted in generous proportions. Anything else so portrayed was merely wishful thinking.

" 'Sdeath, but I'm getting a stiff neck. 'Tis well past luncheon. I'm growing faint from lack of nourishment. One would think you were painting a mural, so long it has taken. Enough for now, I say!" Hartwell Barclay complained as his stomach growled its protest.

" 'Tis fine with me," the artist agreed, eager to look at something more appetizing for a change. "I could use an ale or two."

Hartwell Barclay snorted. "You've been drinking my cellar dry for the past few months. My cupboards are bare. And since I've been taking precious time to pose, my servants think themselves on holiday; lords and ladies all, sitting around doing nothing all day long. You've already cost me plenty. I may deduct such amounts as I see fit when it comes time to figure the cost of this painting. Remember that when you sit down to sup and spear a second slice of beef," he warned as he turned to face the smaller man, stretching his aching muscles as he stepped closer to view the portrait.

"Hartwell Barclay, always the gracious host. You haven't changed," Valentine greeted the man.

"Wha—Who is that?" Hartwell demanded, startled as he peered into the shadows of the long hall.

"Valentine Whitelaw."

"Who the devil let you in? Told you last time I wasn't interested in any of those cursed voyages of yours. Pah! Seeking revenge against the Spanish for sinking my cousin's ship! Did me a favor. Geoffrey Christian would've gambled away the family fortunes to finance those damned ventures of his. Geoffrey Christian is dead! I am now master of Highcross Court."

"Maybe not," Valentine murmured softly.

"What? You can't come into my home and speak to me in that tone of voice. You may have been welcome here when Geoffrey Christian was master, but you are no longer welcome now Highcross is mine. Who's that with you?" Hartwell demanded, moving closer, then quickly stepping back behind his portrait when he caught sight of the Turk. "A foreigner! And a heathen at that! Out of my house, begone, the both of you!"

"I had not planned on staying."

"If you don't leave now, I'll have the footmen throw you out! Where the blazes are they anyway? Odell! *Odell!*" he yelled. "You're just like him. So bold and brave. Have the ladies begging, I'll bet. Strutting around court like some prince of the realm. Geoffrey was like that. He had Highcross. He had wealth. He was handsome and witty. Oh, how he used to laugh at me!" Hartwell Barclay said angrily, still seething with jealousy of his dead cousin. "Thought he'd die soon enough on one of those voyages of his and I would inherit Highcross. Prayed for that every day. Then he married that Spanish bitch just to cheat me out of my rightful place. Made a Papist mistress of Highcross. But I got the last laugh," Hartwell crowed. "They all went down together!"

"Maybe not." Valentine took great pleasure in repeating those two words.

Hartwell Barclay's face grew increasingly flushed. He could see enough of Valentine Whitelaw's expression to know an uneasy sensation growing within. The man wouldn't have come to Highcross unless . . .

"What do you want?" he asked suspiciously.

"I do not want anything."

"What did you mean by those words? Tell me! I demand to know!"

Valentine smiled. "I thought you might be relieved to know that Geoffrey Christian is indeed dead."

Hartwell Barclay looked at Valentine Whitelaw as if he were crazed. "You are certainly slow to hear the news. I've known that for seven years."

"Yes, but what you haven't known is that Geoffrey Christian sent his wife and daughter and my brother ashore before the *Arion* sank."

Hartwell Barclay looked as if he'd had the air knocked out of him. "Lies! Lies! All lies! How dare you come in here and say such things! Odell! *Odell!*" he hollered hysterically, glancing wildly down the gallery. With a scream of rage, he stormed from behind the safety of his portrait to confront his tormentor.

"That Spanish whore and her brat can't be alive! She can't be! Highcross is mine!" he blubbered, stomping his foot as if stamping out such a possibility.

Valentine glanced at the man, then turned away in distaste.

"You're going to rescue them, aren't you! Damn you! Odell! Odell!" Hartwell Barclay cried again. Momentarily forgetting his fears of Valentine Whitelaw, he charged after the man who had turned his back on him with such a look of contempt and was now walking away.

"They're probably dead! My God, it has been seven years! They're dead! Dead, I say! You won't find your brother alive. I tell you they are dead! Waste of time and money to go in search of them! If you don't go, I'll reward you handsomely. I'm rich. Far richer than you! I could invest in one of your voyages. You won't find anyone if you go!" he yelled at Valentine Whitelaw's broad back.

Valentine and the Turk had reached the staircase and were

halfway down its length. The Turk was a step or two behind, his hand resting in its usual place on the golden hilt of his curved sword. But when he saw the two footmen standing at the bottom about to ascend, a gleam came into his eye as he stepped ahead of Valentine.

Farley and Fairfax Odell, one short and dark, the other tall and fair, stared up at the two men descending the stairs. Neither had missed that gleam, and with a quick exchange of glances they started to back away from the stairs. With a well-honed instinct for self-preservation foremost in their thoughts, they had decided that their master, who was charging down the steps in hot pursuit, wasn't worth dying for.

"Stop them! Stop them!" Hartwell Barclay cried frantically, actually believing for a moment that his footmen might be able to seize Valentine Whitelaw and his servant and keep them from leaving Whiteswood and from ever leaving England in search of the castaways.

But Farley and Fairfax Odell were not so foolhardy. With some haste, despite their feet slipping on the wet flooring, they headed toward the back of the hall. As they passed by the scullery maid, who had paused in her scrubbing when she had heard the disturbance, they lifted her to her feet. Fairfax's big foot swung wide, knocking over one of the buckets. There was little Hartwell Barclay could do to him when finding someone to blame for the mess that covered the floor. With widening grins on their faces, they carried the maid with them into the safety of the kitchens.

Valentine Whitelaw turned at the door in time to see Hartwell Barclay sliding across the wet floorboards, his feet spinning into the air as he lost his footing and landed with a thud on his beefy rear end.

Smiling slightly, Valentine mounted.

But as he rode away from Highcross, he couldn't help but remember Hartwell Barclay's words. And as the miles lessened toward London, he kept hearing the words echoed by his horse's hooves pounding against the hard-packed earth.

Dead . . . dead . . . dead . . .

"I hope to God you are right and Christian's brat is dead," Raymond Valchamps swore as he paced nervously to and fro.

"Seven years is a long time," the man standing before the window, his back to the room, said softly.

"Damn! Who would have thought Christian would have set them ashore? If that brat told Whitelaw what she saw in Santo Domingo, then we've been living on borrowed time for the past seven years. God, I thought we were safe when his ship went down. Do you think Don Pedro knows?"

The other man was silent. "I am beginning to wonder if Don Pedro hasn't known all along," he finally said.

"Damn his soul!"

"Why should he tell us? As far as he was concerned, they were dead. Who would rescue them if no one knew they lived?"

"We could have gone ashore and made certain they were dead."

"We?" the other man questioned doubtfully.

"Ah, yes, I had forgotten that you never have had much stomach for violence. I think you were even sorry that Christian's ship went down. Well, be thankful that it did, for if Whitelaw had had any suspicions that we were on board a Spanish galleon, he would have seen us swinging from the gibbets quick enough. You waste your pity on him, as well as on the child. She was a danger to us. And if she still lives, she is still a threat to us. If only I had suspected she had escaped the ship I would have killed her with my own hands. We would be free—not hiding here in the dark, afraid of a knock on the door."

"And on which island were they set ashore? There were countless islets within rowing distance of Christian's ship. You would never have found them. I had hoped all of that was in the past. An unfortunate incident, one that we could forget."

"In the past? Forget that Elizabeth still lives? Have you forgotten our purpose? Have you forgotten the true faith? The persecutions? I have prayed for another St. Bartholomew's Day. Not enough heretic blood was shed," Raymond Valchamps said unhappily.

The other man sighed. "I do not believe bloodshed is the means by which we will succeed."

" 'Tis the only way! You still believe Elizabeth might wed a Catholic? Oh, she is the cunning one. She has been playing that game since she was first courted by Philip. He thought to add England to his empire by marrying her, yet she spurned him.

She is old now and still she dangles her crown before their noses. You think she will marry that boy Alençon and form an alliance with France against Spain? Always, we are told to wait. Why are they so afraid of shedding a little English blood?''

"A rebellion could cost us everything. The wrong people could come into power," the soft-spoken man tried to calm his friend. "Although I would see the true faith restored our land, I have little desire to see the Spanish invade England."

"That is the only way we will overthrow Elizabeth's rule. And once they have defeated the heretics, we shall be the ones to rule."

His friend looked at him pityingly.

"Just remember, while we sit here taking no action, Elizabeth still rules. Remember that!"

"Remember too, my hot-blooded one, that we are fortunate to still be alive," the man standing by the windows cautioned. "Others have been arrested. Others have gone to the gallows. Even one as powerful as Norfolk failed. When they intercepted Ridolfi's ciphers, we could have been implicated then, but it was by the will of Heaven that we have been kept apart from the actual plotting. I have lost count of the priests I have given shelter to during the past years. I cannot even remember their faces, but they have helped our cause more than a massacre would ever have. Perhaps it is our fate to lend assistance to those who would bear the arms for us. We will sustain them and their efforts."

"You speak so eloquently. You have not suffered any these past years. You have done well, my friend. You have wealth, power, position. You would not care to lose that, would you?" Raymond Valchamps retorted. "Well, you had better pray that Valentine Whitelaw doesn't find anyone still alive on that island in the Indies, or you and I might find ourselves exiled on the Continent, or, more likely, we will both lose our heads."

It was the end of January, and the *Madrigal* was riding at anchor in Plymouth Harbor. While her crew took on supplies, her captain crossed the Tamar, the river that bordered Devonshire and Cornwall before emptying into Plymouth Sound. The miles of tumbling whitewater cut steep ravines through the bleak moors and dense forests along the border and isolated Cornwall from the rest of the West Country.

Valentine Whitelaw traveled west. He was going home. He rode within sight of the wild Cornish coast. The roar of breakers rolling against the rocky shore far below and the strident cries of cormorants soaring high above his head filled his senses.

Every so often he would turn inland to cross one of the many rivers and creeks that fed into the sea, passing quietly through sleepy hamlets before turning back toward the coast.

He halted his journey in St. Austell only long enough to down an ale and sausages, leaving the apple pastry with scalded cream only half eaten, much to the dismay of the innkeeper's attractive daughter. She had hoped to engage the handsome traveler in conversation after he had dined, despite the unfriendly attitude of the strangely quiet man who sat at the table with him.

Valentine Whitelaw's blood quickened when he sighted the fishing village of Poldreggan. On the far side of the bay, across the creek that meandered through the fertile valley that climbed inland from the scattering of cottages above the sands, was Ravindzara.

Ravindzara, named from a Madagascan word Valentine had heard used by merchants trading in clove nutmeg, the first cargo the *Madrigal* had brought home to England and made a handsome profit on. The good leaf had allowed him to reopen his mother's home. For far too long it had stood empty.

His mother, the last to bear the Polgannis name, had inherited the house on the death of her father. It had never been known as anything but the Hall. Until the Penmorley family had built Penmorley Hall it had been the largest house between Fowey and Truro, and the Polygannises had been one of the most influential families in the country.

Valentine paused on the edge of the property. In the darkness of early evening, little could be seen of the scaffolding that climbed the south face of the great hall, where a columned frontispiece was being added. Soon the old north entrance would lead into the new kitchens and servants' quarters, which would open on the original courtyard. Sweet-scented herbs would be planted. In summer, the vegetables grown in the kitchen gardens beyond the courtyard walls would be harvested and flavored with rosemary and thyme; then, with wild game from the forests and a plentiful bounty from the sea, they would be served on silver plate in the great chamber. One day the great hall would be flanked by wings running east and west, boldly faced with tall, diamond-paned windows that would reflect the dazzling, shimmering light of the sea. A long gallery, reached by the stone staircase that rose in broad flights from the great hall below, would connect the two wings. Terraced gardens and lawns would surround the house, and . . .

Valentine Whitelaw sighed as he stared at the gray stone house in the distance; still modest in comparison to his visions of the future. The *Madrigal* would have to return from many a profitable voyage before work could even begin on the first part of his dream for Ravindzara.

Then he smiled, for it was enough that Ravindzara was his. He had a roof over his head, and his sister and aunt had a home to call their own.

Valentine ignored the medieval bronze door knocker centered in the great arched door and entered Ravindzara unannounced. The traceried windows, deeply recessed in the stone walls of the hall drew the eye to the richly carved oak beams of the timbered roof that climbed high above his head. A roaring fire was burning brightly in the wide, hooded hearth, spreading a welcoming warmth across the stone flooring. Several footmen had lowered the heavy chain that anchored one of the circular, bronze chandeliers to the center brace in the ceiling. They were lighting the thick candles spaced round the circle before they raised it back into position.

Valentine watched in wry amusement as a couple of maids set the long banqueting table with silver plate. At least that part of his vision for the future was true, and as he noticed the table being set for more than two places, his smile widened, for it would seem as if his aunt and sister had been prepared for his arrival at any time.

"Who left the door unlatched?" the footman nearest the entrance complained as he felt the cold draft swirling around his legs.

" 'Tis the master!" a sharp-sighted maid exclaimed, brushing down her apron with nervous hands as she watched him with a bold eye as he strode across the hall.

"Tom, Willie, Zeke," Valentine greeted the footmen, then smiled at the maids who curtsied as he passed. "Are my aunt and sister in the parlor?"

"Aye, sir, that they are," Zeke, the oldest of the trio, answered importantly.

"Told ye he'd remember," Tom whispered. "Never forgets. A real gentleman, he be."

"Well o' course he be a gentleman. Wouldn't be master o' this hall if he wasn't," Willie declared, impressed that the master had remembered his name.

"What I wants t'know is what be that fella's name?" Zeke said with a wink as he elbowed his friends, drawing their attention to the Turk, who was following Valentine Whitelaw up the broad flight of steps like a swiftly moving shadow.

"What I wants t'know is who's goin' to be askin'?" Tom demanded.

"What I wants t'know is *who* wants t'know that bad?" Willie guffawed, side-stepping his friend's swinging foot as they scuffled.

"Enough o' that," Zeke said authoritatively, halting their rowdiness before things got out of hand. "We got another candleholder to light before the master comes back down to sup. Good thing ol' Ettie made extra pasties or ye might not be gettin' any, Willie," Zeke declared, hiding his grin as he moved off.

"Me?"

"Looks like they be havin' to set an extra place at the table," Tom speculated, wondering if he too would come up short on a pasty tonight.

Zeke glanced back at the table. "Maybe," was all he said.

With growing anticipation, Valentine sought his aunt and sister. "Aunt Quinta! Artemis!" Valentine called out as he entered the parlor.

But as he entered the low-ceilinged, oak-paneled chamber, his favorite in the old hall, he halted in surprise.

"Valentine!" his aunt and his sister chorused when they saw him hesitating in the doorway. Quinta, a tall and thin, dark-haired women in her mid-fifties, rose quickly and hurried to his side to embrace him. Dressed in a flowing, brightly colored silk ropa lined and trimmed with sable, Quinta Whitelaw was an attractive, if somewhat eccentric, woman. The fashionable ropa had undergone a transformation under her nimble fingers; it was now an exotic caftan with full sleeves and braided fastenings. A jeweled cap stuck with an ostrich feather was set at a rakish angle on top of her head, where her smoothly braided hair offered no concession to the tightly curled hairstyles of the fashionable ladies of London.

"Aunt Quinta," Valentine said, kissing her cheek. "Hello, Artemis."

He held out his hand to his sister as she limped slowly across the room. He enfolded her in his arms. "You are well?" he inquired, looking deeply into the blue eyes that were a shade paler than his own. Her hair was as black as his and fought to escape the braid she had coiled like a dark crown across the top of her head.

"How could I possibly feel anything other than well knowing that Basil is alive," she answered him, her eyes glowing with happiness. "Oh, Valentine. We have heard the miraculous news."

Until that moment the gentleman who had been enjoying the warmth of the fire had remained seated, but now he stood, nodding slightly to his host.

"Last week, when I arrived from London, I came to pay my respects to your aunt and sister. I am afraid that I assumed you had already returned to the Hall and told your family the news about Basil. I came to wish you well on your journey. When I discovered you had yet to arrive, well, I could hardly leave without sharing the heartening news with them," Sir Rodger Penmorley explained.

"Rodger," Valentine coolly greeted his neighbor, then noticing for the first time the lovely woman who had remained seated in the chair next to him, bowed slightly. "Honoria."

"Valentine," she said with a slightly haughty yet polite nod, her almond-shaped eyes barely meeting his gaze before she had turned her perfect profile away. Sitting demurely before the fire, her hands quiet in her lap, Rodger Penmorley's sister was all that a well-bred, virtuous young woman should be.

"We were quite shameless in our insistence that poor Rodger tell us all that he had heard concerning Basil," Artemis confided, her pale cheeks flushed rosily. "Except for my unhappiness that you will be sailing again to rescue Basil, I am so happy. I do not think I shall be able to eat or sleep until you and Basil have returned."

" 'Twould seem as if our prayers have been answered,"

Quinta said, her penetrating glance meeting her nephew's gaze for a moment before she turned back to her guests. "It is time we sat down to dine."

"We really must not intrude upon Valentine's first night here," Rodger protested, for although they met with an appearance of cordiality, there had been a longtime rivalry between the two families, and especially between the two youngest sons. The most recent of which had been for the hand of Cordelia Howard.

"I insist you stay and dine with us," Valentine said. "If you will forgive me, I will be but a few minutes in changing," he started to excuse himself. "I am splattered with mud."

"Certainly. I know how hard a ride it is from London," Sir Rodger allowed.

"Actually, I rode only from Plymouth. The *Madrigal* is anchored there. She is taking on supplies in preparation for our journey."

"I am surprised. I would have thought you would have preferred Falmouth. 'Tis closer to the Hall," Sir Rodger questioned, still referring to Ravindzara by its former name.

"I had business with several people in Plymouth," Valentine said rather noncommittally.

"Ah, yes. I believe Sir Humphry Gilbert is a supporter of yours, is he not? Should you ever need—well . . . perhaps another time. I look forward to our conversation over dinner, for I am most interested in hearing about your voyage to rescue Basil," Sir Rodger said, and Valentine believed he spoke sincerely, for Basil and Sir Rodger had always gotten along quite well. They had been friends at court for a number of years. And although Rodger Penmorley had been slightly younger than Basil, their common background and preference for intellectual pursuits had drawn them together in conversation while other courtiers had danced around them.

"I will return shortly to escort my favorite ladies to the hall," Valentine said as he took his leave of them.

He hadn't gotten far along the corridor, just to the first row of windows when he heard quickly approaching steps from behind and turned to find his aunt hurrying to catch up to him.

"My dear, I do not wish to detain you, but I must know how Elspeth and Sir William fared when you broke the news to them.

I did not wish to speak in front of Sir Rodger and Honoria. You did tell them, did you not?'' Quinta asked.

"Yes. I would have faced a thousand cannon rather than have to tell them what I did," Valentine admitted.

"A difficult situation, my dear. Simon?"

"He does not know."

"No?"

"What if—" But Valentine could not continue with the thought.

"What if Basil did not survive? It would not be fair to the boy to get his hopes up if it all comes to naught," Quinta spoke aloud Valentine's worst fears. "I only wish Artemis could have been spared. She adored Basil. He was like a father to her. It will destroy her if—no! I will not even think that. Basil *must* be alive. He must, Valentine," Quinta declared. "To have this hope given to us after so many years. It would be too cruel otherwise. Now, I have detained you long enough. Your guests will be starved, and you must be. We will await you in the parlor. My dear, I know you will leave us very soon. Please remember, for your own sake, that whatever you find on that island was destined. Remember that, please," she warned, afraid that he might not accept the truth that he would discover there.

Valentine stood for a moment longer by the windows as he watched his aunt walk away. He stared out into the darkness, hearing the restless sound of the sea in the distance. Never before had it sounded so mournful to him.

Full fathom five thy father lies;
Of his bones are coral made:
Those are pearls that were his eyes:
Nothing of him that doth fade,
But doth suffer a sea-change
Into something rich and strange.

SHAKESPEARE

Chapter Nine

EASTWARD, as far as the eye could see, there was shimmering, turquoise water. Closer to shore, the colors changed in hue, from palest green in the shallows, to indigo where the deep-water channel cut through the purple and rust of the sunken coral reefs ringing the island. Bright splashes of sea foam curled around the rocky headlands where tall pines bent to the winds. But it was now a gentle breeze that whispered through the palms fringing the sun-warmed, white sands of the beach.

A wandering trail of footsteps patterned the smooth surface of the sands until the tide swept high, washing away any trace of human trespass.

"He's been here, Lily! Look! Here are his tracks!" Tristram cried out as he raced ahead, his thin brown legs sending the sand flying out behind his bare heels.

Dulcie, who had been hunting for shells, squealed with fear. Her shrill cry startled the woolly monkey that had been contentedly grooming himself on the edge of the tidal pool. His frightened squeal echoing Dulcie's, Capabells scampered along the sand and reached Lily's side before the little girl. Clinging to Lily's shoulder, his long tail wrapped around her neck and one of his small black hands entwined in the thick braid hanging

135

down her back, he scolded Dulcie as she grasped Lily's hand and pressed close.

"Choco won't hurt you," Lily said reassuringly, but her gaze searched the densely wooded inland areas. Her eyes, the same shade as the shallows, were narrowed against the glare off the water as she sought a swiftly moving shadow, one that was far darker than those cast by the trees or the thick undergrowth.

"He'll eat us alive! I don't like him, Lily. Why can't he stay away?'' Dulcie cried, tears threatening as she pressed closer to her sister.

"Sshhh, 'tis all right. I won't let him hurt you. He likes you."

"He only likes you, Lily. He woke me up last night. He was right outside the window, and he sounded mad. He was screaming for a long time. I thought he was going to come inside and get me. Did you hear Cappie? He was chattering and running around the room. He knocked over the dishes, then he hid under my blanket," Dulcie said, shivering despite the warmth on her shoulders from the noonday sun.

Lily smiled slightly. She had heard Choco prowling close last night too. The bloodcurdling cries had sent a shiver down her spine, but she hadn't been frightened like Dulcie. She liked to hear the wild sound of the jaguar's cry in the night.

Black as the night he roamed freely, his eyes glowing like topazes; Choco was seldom seen or heard during the day. It had been different when the jaguar had been a half-drowned cub rescued from the surf a couple of years ago. She had held him in her lap then, snuggling him close while hand-feeding him bits of fish and crab. He had mewed and purred like a kitten, but her mother had warned her that Choco was a wild cat, a *tigre enojado,* captured from the jungles of the mainland. Basil had said the cub was a rare jaguar. Most were spotted, but Choco had soft dark fur with black rosettes that showed just faintly. For months Choco had followed her around like a puppy, jumping playfully at her feet, tripping over his own clumsy paws as he'd raced along the sands.

As he had grown, his muscles had thickened and rippled beneath his sleek coat. Soon he had been leaping into the surf and jumping into the tidal pools to catch his own dinner. Seldom did Choco come away without a struggling fish hooked on a curving claw before his jaws clamped down on the tasty morsel, which he guarded with an outstretched paw and warning growl should anyone have strayed too close.

With the passing of the years, the jaguar had sought less and less the company of the human castaways on the island. Every so often Lily caught the flash of something black in the tangle of lush undergrowth, but just as quickly it had vanished. Once, when she had been exploring deeper into the pine forest on the far side of the island, she had been startled to find Choco crouched menacingly above her on an overhanging bough. His golden eyes had been little more than glowing slits, and never before had she realized how long and curved his fangs were. For an instant she had thought he was going to leap down on her. Then he had caught her familiar scent, and making that strange, hoarse cry, his long tail twitching as if irritated at having been cheated out of his prey, he had disappeared.

"Looks like he caught himself a turtle," Tristram said as he examined an area farther up the beach and out of the tide's reach.

"We're next! We're next! *Prraaaa! Prraaaa! Praack!* He's goin' to eat us alive!"

"Keep quiet, Cisco!" Lily said as the bright green parrot perched on her shoulder squawked in imitation of Dulcie.

"*Prraaack!* Keep quiet, Cisco! Lift a leg, Tristram!"

Tristram pushed out of his eyes the thick lock of dark red hair that had fallen across his forehead and glared at the parrot. "What are we having for supper tonight?" he demanded with a warning glint in his brown eyes.

"*Prraaack!*" Cisco cried before beginning to preen his feathers.

"If you don't help me catch something, then we won't be having any dinner tonight," Lily reminded her young brother.

Tristram Francisco Christian, almost seven years old, stood up proudly. "Have I ever not done my duty?" he demanded, his bronze eyes flashing with indignation.

Just turned fourteen, Lily stood a head taller than her hot-blooded young brother. "How is it, then, that I found you snoring away the hours yesterday when you should have been watching for any sails on the horizon?" Lily retorted, her cheeks flushing with anger, for Lily and Tristram had not only inherited their Spanish mother's dark red hair but her quick temper as well.

"I didn't fall asleep," Tristram denied, but not quite as stoutly as before. "I was shielding my eyes."

"I am just thankful that you did not open them to find a French corsair's sword at your throat or a galleon flying the royal arms of Spain. Basil always said 'twould be far worse to be rescued by an enemy than not rescued at all. What if he hadn't been vigilant the day those French pirates came ashore. They murdered their own captain. A mutiny, Tristram! Father always said mutineers were worse than having the plague aboard. If Basil hadn't seen them before they saw us, well . . ." Lily left unspoken the rest of her speculations as she glanced down and met Dulcie's wide dark eyes staring up at her. "As captain of this isle, I may have to take severe measures to guard against such behavior happening again."

Tristram stared at his sister in growing dismay. "What do you mean? I am still first mate!" he squeaked. "I am, aren't I?"

"I may have to return you to the duties of a lowly swabber," Lily answered, apparently unforgiving. "Father wouldn't have had you aboard longer than it would have taken to toss you overboard. He'd the best crew that sailed the seas. He would have been very disappointed in his only son."

"Lily!" Tristram cried, crestfallen. "He would have been proud of me. He would've! He would've! 'Tis the only time I've ever fallen asleep while on duty. I won't do it again. I promise! I want to be first mate, Lily."

"I'm the bos'n's mate," Dulcie chimed in importantly.

"Well, I suppose you can still be my first mate. But I'd better not ever catch you not pulling your weight again," she warned, trying to keep her voice stern.

Tristram stared down at his bare feet and said sulkily beneath his breath, "I don't know who made you captain anyway. You're a girl. Captains are supposed to be men with beards."

"I hardly think you would make a very good captain, since I am the only one who has ever sailed the seas with Father," Lily reminded him. "Besides, you don't have a beard either."

"One day I will. I wish I had sailed with him. He would have let me, wouldn't he, Lily? He would've been proud of me. I would never have let him down. Basil said I was a good lad. He said I was just like father. Basil said he would have been proud to call me his son. Father would have too, wouldn't he, Lily?'' Tristram demanded hopefully. ''Wouldn't he?''

''Aye, he would have, Tris,'' Lily agreed, unable to hurt him, for he really was a good lad even if he did occasionally fall asleep while on duty.

''Do you think anyone is every going to come and rescue us?'' Tristram asked as he stared out to sea.

''One day we will see the red cross of St. George. 'Tis the flag Englishmen fly. Then, and only then, we will be rescued. Basil said not to show ourselves to anybody else.''

''I thought the wild white horses were going to rescue us,'' five-year-old Dulcie demanded.

''That's just a fable. There's no truth to it,'' Tristram told her bluntly. ''I don't even believe there is a red cross of St. George. No one is ever going to come here. We're goin' to get old and die here, our bones sticking out of the sand.''

''Now see what you've done,'' Lily said, trying to quiet Dulcie, who had started to cry.

''Are we goin' to die, Lily?'' she wailed, her small shoulders shaking.

Dejectedly, Tristram looked down at his bare feet. Glancing up, he asked Dulcie, ''You want to help me find some rock crabs?''

Dulcie raised her tearstained face from Lily's waist. ''I can help you? Truly?'' she asked, her tears vanishing.

''Do you want to come, Lily?'' Tristram asked hesitantly, for he was never certain nowadays what mood his sister would be in.

''You and Dulcie go ahead. I'll follow,'' she said, playfully kicking a spray of water over Tristram's feet.

''You are not mad?'' he asked, splashing her. When she shook her head, he grinned. ''Come on, Dulcie! I'll race you!''

At a slower pace, Cisco and Capabells still clinging to her shoulders, Lily followed her brother and sister toward the rocky headland in the distance. Beyond that, where the waves broke against the hidden reefs, a Spanish galleon had gone aground and sunk.

Its rotting timbers were all that remained. Tristram said it looked like some dead sea monster, its bleached ribs broken against the rocks and picked clean by the sea. Lily had to admit that its desolate appearance, especially when there was a full moon and a howling wind through the trees, made her uneasy. Tristram, whose imagination ran wild sometimes, said the rocks where the galleon had sunk were haunted. He claimed he'd seen the ghosts of the drowned sailors and passengers walking out of the shallows, crying to be saved from the storm that had carried their ship to its watery grave.

Lily turned her gaze away from the ship's skeleton and climbed after Tristram and Dulcie. They were busy searching the rocky crevices on the lower slope of the headland. Finding a comfortable spot beneath a scrubby pine, Lily sat down. Capabells swung into the tree, chattering to himself as he climbed to the top. Sitting cross-legged, Lily leaned back against the gnarled bark of the pine and gazed out upon the empty horizon, wondering if Tristram was right and they never would be rescued from the island.

Lily glanced down at the jeweled locket that dangled from a golden chain about her neck. She held it tightly in her palm, then unclasping the tiny lock, she stared down at the miniature portraits of her mother and father. With a sigh, she closed it. Poor Tristram. He had never known their father. She had tried to tell him of their father's bravery. She had told him how he had fearlessly sailed the seas. She had told him how he had taken her high into the rigging to touch the stars.

But it had been Basil who had told them such wonderful stories about him. At first, he only spoke of his friend when they were alone, when her mother was resting. But after Tristram was born, and after her mother started to laugh again, she too spoke of the daring Englishman she had fallen in love with. Lily could still remember how frightened her mother was the night she gave birth to Tristram. Basil had been there to comfort her. He was always there to give a word of advice, to say something that had them smiling and looking forward to the morrow. Lily never felt afraid when Basil was there. They had become a family, she and Tristram, her mother and Basil. The days passed in contentment, and gradually Lily became aware of a change in the way her mother and Basil spoke to one another; the way one would always watch the other when the other wasn't aware.

Lily didn't mind that Basil loved her mother. And she

thought her mother must have loved him, too, for they were always exchanging glances, and she had seen them lying together in the darkness. Basil said that they were his family, and when Dulcie was born, he said that he could not know any greater happiness.

Lily wiped away a tear. Basil had tried so valiantly to take care of them. He never seemed to lose spirit. He took such pride in building the palm-thatched hut that had become their home. He taught them how to start a fire, although not successfully at first. He wove nets and taught them how to catch and prepare the fish, crabs, lobsters, conch, and turtles that were so plentiful. He made a bow and arrows and hunted the wild fowl and pigs that roamed the inland forest. He made a game out of searching for fruits and nuts and discovered the fresh-water springs that bubbled up from the ground and made their survival on the island possible.

In his journal, Basil kept a careful record of the passing days. He always knew exactly how long they had been on the island. He had even set up a sun dial to tell them the time of the day. Although stranded in the wilderness, they would continue to live as civilized human beings, he declared, causing them to giggle because he was standing barefoot before them as he said it. But to Basil, being civilized meant being well educated, even if one was dressed in little better than rags. He decided, therefore, that daily lessons in sums, spelling, and writing; in the languages of Latin, Greek, and French; and in an understanding of history, literature, and religion, as well as the sciences, would be necessary.

Soon the days were passing with a regularity that seldom altered unless the weather turned foul. Up at dawn, hunting and fishing for the day's food, lessons, then a few hours to do as one pleased, then sunset and conversation, mostly stories by Basil and her mother, as they sat around the fire. At least that was the way their lives had been until the storm struck with such devastation.

Lily's gaze returned to the wreck. She could remember how excited they had been when they had discovered it several days after the storm.

* * *

They had been walking along the shore, collecting driftwood for their fire and scavenging for other storm-tossed debris they could make use of, when they came across an unbelievable assortment of wreckage that had washed into the bay.

Several wooden chests were half-buried on the beach. Some had been smashed open with their water-logged contents spilled out on the sands. All that could be seen of a bronze cannon was its muzzle, aimed harmlessly at the sky. Tristram raced ahead, scooping up handfuls of golden doubloons that lay scattered across the sands. Whooping with glee, he tossed them high above his head. Dulcie tottered along behind him, squealing excitedly as she scooped up handfuls of sand.

Lily could still remember how delighted her mother was when she had spied the silver tableware and the gleam of finely wrought plates of gold. They would now dine like royalty, she laughed, her excitement growing when she pulled a silk doublet from one trunk, the damp garment soon to be followed by a satin gown and all the necessary finery of a well-to-do gentleman and his lady.

They still drank cool spring water out of the wine decanter and glass goblets she had unearthed, and Lily smiled as she recalled how startled they had all been when Basil had strutted across the beach in a cape of brightly colored feathers, a grotesque golden mask held before his face while the plumed headdress he wore danced in the breeze.

Tristram came racing back, a gold link chain snaking behind him as he'd carelessly cast down the gold doubloons, forgotten now that his attention was centered on the exotic garb Basil was dressed in.

Lily touched the curved, gold filigree earrings she still wore. They had come out of that same treasure chest. Basil said he had read about such strange things in an account of the voyages of the *conquistadores* and the great empire of the Indians they had conquered in the New World. Her mother said the cape was made of quetzal feathers. In a nobleman's home in Madrid, she had seen a cape similar to the one they had found. The man's father had sailed with Cortes and had returned to Spain a wealthy man.

The flower-shaped emerald ring that winked up at Lily had come from their find on the beach that day. Lily smoothed the sun-faded green satin of the shift she wore, the careful stitches her mother had sewn along its seams still holding firm. It was too short now, for she had grown a couple of inches during the past two years, but it was still her favorite garment.

While she was searching the sandy bottom of the clear water shallows for more doubloons she had heard mewing coming from an upended wooden cage. A spotted jaguar cub in the cage with Choco had died, as had other animals she later discovered washed up on shore. Cisco, however, had been more fortunate. The cage he and several other exotic birds had been confined in had been tossed high on the rocks, where it had been wedged safely out of reach of wind and sea.

Tristram was the first to see the broken mast and broad sheet of canvas floating in the water. His cry of delight, however, turned to one of pure horror when he saw the bloated figures of the drowned sailors caught in the tangle of rigging.

Basil ordered them all back on shore while he cut the bodies free of the rigging. He then gave the men a decent burial. It took them several more days to complete their search of the bay and finish their salvage of the wreck. They collected quite a treasure, although the practical items, among them tableware and clothes, and the timbers from the ship, were of more value to them than all of the gold and silver doubloons and reales, ingots and rare stones they discovered.

Soon, everything seemed to return to normal. Lily's mother began to make them new clothes, and as she had predicted their next meals had been eaten off plates of solid gold. Lily had occupied her time seeing to the demands of her *tigre* and the parrot whose broken wing kept him from flying away with the others. Basil said that since they had no place to spend their considerable wealth, and since the pirates might return one day, he thought it wise to find a safe hiding place for their fortune. Remembering the underwater cave that had another entrance among the rocks on the cliff, he proposed that they hide their bounty there. The uppermost part of the cave, nearest the land entrance, stayed dry even at high tide. Their treasure trove would remain safely hidden.

Almost two weeks had passed, Lily remembered. She wandered alone along the beach that day. She climbed the rocks to get a better view of the stretch of beach that curved out of sight

beyond the headland. Lily shuddered. She could still feel the
terror she had felt when she had seen the hand reaching out to
her. It grabbed hold of her ankle. Her piercing cry had brought
the others running.

Basil had pried the hurtful fingers loose from her ankle and
pulled her away from the man who clung to the rocks. Except for
the sound of his shallow, rasping breath, they might have
thought the man dead. He certainly had looked dead. He had
used the last of his strength in his effort to attract her attention.
He had dragged himself across the sands from the raft that had
floated ashore on the tide. They could see the trail he had left.
He had not been alone on the small raft. There were two people
lying facedown in the sand; they were both women.

Basil had carried the feverish man and his two delirious companions back to the hut, where her mother and Basil had tried to
make them comfortable. From the gentleman's almost incoher-
ent babblings, they had learned that they were survivors of another ship that had gone down in the storm. All had been part of
a convoy sailing to Spain. They had survived the sinking of their
ship, only to find themselves adrift at sea until the current had
carried them to the island.

Lily did not understand why Basil had sent her and Tristram
and Dulcie away. He had built a temporary shelter on the edge
of the beach where he and her mother cared for the sick people.
At first it had all seemed like a game. There hadn't been any lessons, and she and Tristram and Dulcie spent their days
swimming in the gentle waters of the cove. Several times during
the day either her mother or Basil would call to them and reassure them that all was well. Then one day Basil told her that the
man had died. Four days later, the elder of the two women died.
She was expecting to hear the news when Basil told her that the
other women died shortly after that. She had been disappointed
when Basil insisted that they would remain in their lean-to on
the beach. She thought that they would return to the hut now
that the strangers had died. But Basil wouldn't even let them
come near. He said the people had died of fever.

Basil had not wished for them to become infected, Lily remembered. She could still smell the smoke from the fire when
Basil had burned all of the clothes and mats that had been in the
shelter. She left fresh clothes and supplies for them at the edge

of the forest and, under Basil's orders, left before he approached to collect them. It had been a week later when her mother had not called to them as she had every day before.

Hearing someone approaching from the beach, Lily left the others and ran forward, only to be halted by Basil's upraised hand. Lily was shocked at how ill he looked. She looked past him, searching for her mother's familiar figure, but the beach beyond was empty. Lily knew the truth when she met Basil's glazed, red-rimmed eyes. His haggard face bore the trace of tears.

"The fever took her, Lily," he said very softly. "I buried her under the tree she liked to sit under. You must look after your brother and sister, Lily. I am placing them in your care now." He was shivering uncontrollably even though he was standing in the sunlight. "If I cannot come again. If you do not hear from me in the next few days, do not come into the shelter. Promise me you will obey me, Lily. Promise me, Lily," he had begged her. "Burn the hut. That is the only way you will be safe. Burn it, Lily. Leave my body inside. You know I love you, Lily. You are my daughter as much as Dulcie is. I promised your father I would take care of his family. I always tried, Lily. I do not believe he would have wanted Magdalena to have lived out the rest of her life alone. Let me rest in peace knowing that his son and daughter, at least, are safe."

When she had nodded her agreement, she saw a strange look enter his eyes. He glanced past her to where Tristram and Dulcie stood waiting, and he waved to them.

That was the last time they saw Basil. A week passed before Lily approached the shelter where Basil lay. It was dawn, and the light was faintly illuminating the inside of the lean-to. She stood just outside, staring into its shadowy confines. She could see Basil clearly. She stood there watching him until the sun started to go down. He never moved.

That night, the sky was lit with flames. The next day, when the ashes had cooled, Lily and Tristram carefully carried all that was left of the fire to the grave they had dug next to the one marked with a delicate wooden cross.

Whenever Lily walked along the sands and glanced toward the tall pine on the edge of the forest, she could see the two simple crosses. Her mother and Basil were together, and it gave her comfort, for she felt as if they were still with them, sharing their days.

"Hey, Lily! You want to come in for a swim?" Tristram called out to her.

Lily stared down at Tristram, who had just dived into the clear waters of the cove. She could see him swimming just beneath the surface. When his head popped up, he held up a large, conical shell triumphantly. There was a wide grin on his face as he said, "Dinner!"

Tossing the pink conch shell up on the beach, he dove again, coming to the surface nearer the rocks this time. "Are you coming in?" he asked as he stared up at Lily, who still remained sitting underneath the pine, Cisco perched on her shoulder.

"No, I don't think I will. I should get the fire going before sunset."

"You haven't come swimming all week, Lily," Tristram complained. "Don't you like to swim anymore?"

"*I* like to swim!" Dulcie cried out as she paddled like a turtle in the shallows.

"Maybe tomorrow," Lily said noncommittally.

"That's what you said yesterday," Tristram grumbled before he dived back under the warm waters of the cove, swimming away with carefree abandon.

Lily got to her feet and smoothed the wrinkles in her shift. With a sigh, she noticed the rounding of her breasts. It seemed to her critical eye that they got bigger every day. Enviously, Lily looked at Dulcie, swimming in naked innocence in the pool, and she found herself wishing to be so free again.

The sky was ablaze with crimson and gold and purple when they finished their meal. Leaving the washing up until later, they walked down to the shore. The gentle, melodic lapping of the tide lulled them into restfulness as they stretched out on the sands that were still warm from the sun and began their game of searching for the first star of night.

Tristram was lying with his arms folded behind this head as he stared up at the darkening sky. Dulcie had snuggled close against Lily's side, while Capabells climbed onto her lap.

"Tell me about the legend of the wild white horses, Lily," Dulcie asked.

"You know it already," Tristram said. "I see it! I see the first star! Over there!" he cried.

"You always see the first star. It isn't fair," Dulcie said petulantly.

"There! See, Dulcie!" Lily said urgently, pointing out a glistening crest of white foaming against the sunken coral reefs beyond the cove. "They're coming!"

"The wild white horses," Dulcie breathed in awe.

"See how they dance and prance and jump so high. They might even jump over Tristram's star."

Dulcie giggled.

"They're going to race faster than the winds. Past the mermaid's cave and the sea dragon's lair. Past the jagged reefs and sunken ships. They kick up their heels in a giant wave of sea foam and sail past seahorses and flying fish. With seaweed strung with golden doubloons for the reins and a starfish for a saddle, bearded Neptune, astride his great horse, Pegasus, rises from his castle beneath the sea. He'll capture the wild white horses and in his chariot of brightly colored coral he'll ride across the waves and catch us up in his silver net sprinkled with twinkling stars and carry us far across the seas, past the sun and the moon."

"To England?"

"Yes, all the way across the seas to England."

"To Whitehall? To return the queen's wild white horses?"

"That's right. They are the queen's wild white horses. That is why her palace is named Whitehall. The wild white horses were stolen from their golden stables at Whitehall by the evil witch."

"And we are going to return them to the queen and save her from the evil witch with one blue eye and one brown eye," Dulcie continued. "And we will van—van—what will we do to the witch, Lily?"

"We will vanquish the witch with the one blue eye and one brown eye, and we will save the queen from the traitors who are plotting to kill her."

"The wild white horses . . ." Dulcie murmured.

Lily glanced down at Dulcie. Her dark head heavy against her breast as she slept peacefully, a slight smile tilting the corners of her mouth upward.

"I wish it were true, Lily," Tristram said.

Lily stared far out to sea. It was empty, even of wild white horses.

*Be not afeard: the isle is full
of noises, sounds and sweet airs, that
give delight, and hurt not.*

SHAKESPEARE

Chapter Ten

O N a field of white the red cross of St. George flew proudly
on the mainmast-head of the *Madrigal*. Her captain, Valentine Whitelaw, had ordered her brought to well beyond the reefs where the waves were breaking in white crests across the shallows.

The *Madrigal* was a three-masted galleon of eighty tons and eighteen guns, with over fifty men manning her. She was sleek and swift, with a low forecastle and upper deck. She was unadorned except for the figurehead of a sea maid gracing her bow and the gilded carving and coat of arms of her captain decorating her stern. A striped stern ensign in the queen's colors of green and white, with the red cross of St. George in the canton, fluttered in the breeze.

Standing on the quarterdeck, the captain of the *Madrigal* cast a sharp eye overhead as his crew scrambled up the rigging and along the yardarms, where they quickly and efficiently took in the ship's sails and secured them. She was swinging slightly, due to the tide, but her anchors and cables were proved. She wouldn't break free and drift into the dangerous waters of the coral reefs and shoals surrounding the island.

In the distance, Valentine Whitelaw could see a crescent of golden sand curving along the shore. Beyond that was a dense forest. Leeward of the *Madrigal* a rocky headland studded with pine and palmetto stretched out its spiny back to the sea. Off to starboard another headland jutted into the bay, but it bent sharply at a right angle forming a natural breakwater. The force of the waves broken, a peaceful cove beckoned beyond. It was sheltered on its far side by low cliffs that curved out of sight.

Valentine Whitelaw glanced down at the map he had studied almost every day since the *Madrigal* had set sail from Plymouth. Joshua Randall hadn't been wrong; the island was just as the *Arion*'s bos'n had drawn it. Little changed, in fact, from seven years ago. If only he could have banished those years in between and been there when Geoffrey Christian and the *Arion* had fought alone and her passengers had been stranded. With the *Madrigal*'s guns lending support, they would have beaten the Spanish that day, Valentine vowed. He knew a deep frustration at having missed out on the fight his brother and friend had found themselves in. Gradually Valentine became aware of the map now crumpled in his hand. Carefully he smoothed the creases and refolded it.

Feeling he was being observed, Valentine glanced up to find the Turk's dark eyes watching him. "Now we find the truth, Mustafa," he said softly, his eyes returning to the island, where as of yet no sign of life had been sighted by the lookout.

The Turk nodded, his gaze following his captain's as the *Madrigal*'s boat was lowered into the water, the oarsmen taking up their positions as they prepared to row the search party ashore.

Lily dived deep into the warm waters of the cove. Her long hair floated out around her as she swam through the turquoise undersea realm, where great domed castles were built of bright orange coral, twisted trees sprouted yellow coral branches, and curious, iridescent fish darted through waving sea grasses like flashes of the rainbow.

She saw a slowly moving turtle and grabbed a ride through a sandy-bottomed channel between the coral reefs. Through the clear, aquamarine waters in the distance, she could see the entrance to the cave. She dropped off the turtle's back and dived toward the coral arch. Sunlight cascaded down through the roofless ceiling of the entrance chamber and lit the interior like brightly burning candles.

Lily came up for air. Above her head, white fluffs of cloud

drifted across the blue sky. She dived back down into the cave, following the narrow passageway deeper into the reef. It grew darker as she progressed, for the corridor was roofed in stone now and only an occasional shaft of sunlight found its way in.

Her paddling feet struck sand and she surfaced in a large cavern formed of rock. Finding her footing, Lily climbed out of the water and onto the sandy shelf at the edge of the pool. She walked up the gentle slope, feeling the ground harden beneath her bare feet as she climbed higher in the cave. Light filtered in through a rough-hewn window formed between two ill-fitting rocks of the low cliff that rose out of the sea. On the top, the land entrance was reached by following a meandering stone path along the shore. Little more than a shadow in the rocks behind a stunted pine, the entrance was barely discernible, even to the searching eye.

Lily knelt beside the chest that held their treasure. The lid protested on its rusty hinges as she opened it. She shook out the feathered cape that had been carefully folded over the golden mask and headdress. Beneath those, the glint of Spanish gold and silver met her eye as she stared into the depths of the trunk. Lily captured an emerald in the palm of her hand, its fire darkened until she held it up to the pale light streaming through the aperture.

She foraged deeper inside the chest, looking for one of the gold fishhooks that Tristram used for fishing. He had several in varying sizes and needed to replace one of the smaller ones he'd lost the day before. As her hand moved about, it struck the grainy hardness of Basil's leather-bound journal. Next to it was the log of the *Arion*. A few days before he had fallen ill, Basil has asked her to place his journal in the sea chest with the rest of their treasure. At his request, Lily had also placed her father's log beside Basil's journal. One day, when she had more time, she would get them out and read them, she promised herself. Even though Basil had never allowed anyone to read his journal while he was alive, preferring to read aloud to them from its contents, she did not think he would mind now. Besides, she was running out of stories to amuse Tristram and Dulcie, and she was sure to discover something exciting in the log about one of her father's many adventures, and Basil's journal was certain to be full of interesting observations.

Lily picked up the cape, and unable to resist the urge, she

placed it across her shoulders. Busy with her game of make-believe, she tied on the mask of gold. Although it had been beaten by the Indian artisans to a paper-thin fineness it was still heavy and her breath sounded labored and muffled through the nose piercings. As a sudden thought struck her, she grinningly placed the headdress on her head and prepared to leave the cave by its land entrance.

If Tristram had fallen asleep again, she thought with a glint in her pale green eyes, then he was in for the fright of his life.

Valentine Whitelaw felt his heartbeat quickening as he stepped ashore. It was a sensation not unlike that he'd experienced during his first battle at sea. He felt both exultation and fear. What would he find? he wondered, his gaze moving swiftly along the ragged edge of pine forest that bordered the beach.

As they'd neared the crescent of sandy shore, the boat slicing through the dark blue waters of the channel, he'd thought of Lawson rowing out of the bay to rescue his mates that fateful day so long ago. The shallow hull of the boat, far lighter once he'd unloaded his passengers, would have skimmed over the razor-edged reefs. Valentine could envision Basil and Magdalena, and the child, standing on shore watching. Waiting no doubt for Geoffrey Christian to return and rescue them. No one had come back for them—not until now.

Valentine hid his disappointment when no one responded to his hails. He smiled wryly as he remembered the satisfying scene he had imagined. Basil had come running along the shore, a look of incredulity on his face as he'd recognized his rescuer.

"Are you certain this is the same island that is on your map?" Thomas Sandrick asked as he jumped from the boat. Still unsteady from being at sea, he staggered, losing his balance and falling onto one knee. He glanced down in dismay at the sea splashing around his legs and ruining his fine silk hose. With a sigh, he struggled out of the surf and came to stand beside Valentine. "The place seems deserted. Seven years is a long time," he advised his friend.

"Randall was very observant. He knew how many leagues distant the *Arion* had sailed through the passage before reaching the island. He made careful notations of landmarks to use as a guide in finding the island. The shoreline he sketched of the island is identical to this one. There can be no mistake," Valentine responded, unwilling to admit to any doubts that he himself might be feeling.

He glanced over at Thomas Sandrick and wondered if he'd been wise in allowing him to accompany them. He had been surprised when his friend had approached him with the request to sail with them to the Indies in search of Basil. Thomas had jestingly explained that if he were to invest in future voyages of the *Madrigal*, as well as other ventures in the New World, it would serve him well to learn more about these strange lands beyond the shores of England. Unfortunately, however, adventuring did not seem to come naturally to Thomas Sandrick. Continuing to dress as befitted a fashionable London gentleman, he seemed woefully out of place aboard the *Madrigal*. And he was not a very good sailor. Valentine doubted that his friend would see much of the New World spending most of his time below deck confined to his bunk because of seasickness.

" 'Ere, Cap'n! Tracks!" the coxswain called out excitedly. Having beached the boat, the crew had started to explore while their captain had stood daydreaming.

"Some of them 'ead up into the trees! Look! There be more 'eaded that way, down the beach, and some more toward the 'eadland!"

"We'll go this way first. If they've built a shelter, it will be in a protected area away from shore and near a spring," Valentine decided, for there were several different sets of tracks leading away from the beach and into the trees.

Valentine eyed his friend, who was fanning himself in the heat. "Are you up to it, Thomas?"

Thomas Sandrick nodded, managing to smile; Valentine had to admire him, for as sick as he'd been, Thomas had never once complained or expected special treatment. He had set his mind on sailing to the New World and nothing was going to stop him. Valentine had never realized quite how resolute a man Thomas Sandrick was. Not having fared well even on the short voyage through the Channel to Plymouth, he could have jumped ship there and saved himself further misery, but Thomas had stayed aboard, determined to sail with the *Madrigal*.

"Reckon the cap'n's brother ain't all that big a gent," one of the crew remarked as his own footprint stamped out the tiny one beneath. "Even the biggest footprint ain't very big. Ain't wearin' no shoes, either," he added.

"Ye don't s'pose there still be them man-eaters hereabouts?" his portly mate asked, glancing around nervously and praying he wouldn't see a savage face glaring at him from the bushes.

"If there are any, reckon ye'd be lastin' them a month or two," chuckled a seaman with a bright red beard and crinkling blue eyes.

"That ain't very funny!" the nervous one said as they made their way up the beach.

" 'Tis too quiet," a thin, lantern-jawed crew member said as he blinked his eyes. He could've sworn he'd seen a shadow moving through the thick undergrowth.

To anyone watching the intruder's progress from the concealment of that shadowy undergrowth, the rescuers might very well have appeared frightening. They certainly would have seemed a rowdy, ungentlemanly group even to adult eyes, what with their unkempt appearance and ribald talk. But to a small child, especially one unaccustomed to strangers, they would have looked like bloodthirsty brigands stalking the sands.

And that was exactly how they appeared to Dulcie, who was hiding behind a palm. Her dark eyes were like saucers in her small face as she stared in open-mouthed terror at the group. If she could have moved her feet, she would have raced up the beach to find Lily and Tristram, but she could only stand behind the palm and watch as the men stomped along the path toward their hut and the only home she had ever known.

Valentine Whitelaw's long strides had put him in the lead as they left the beach and made their way along what seemed to be a path between the trees; constant use having beaten down the waist-high grasses that were swaying with the gentle breeze.

Valentine felt his excitement growing as he saw the hut in the distance. Although roughly finished, it was apparent that great care and pride had been taken in the building of it, for above the modest doorway a crude likeness of the Whitelaw family's coat of arms had been carved on a flat piece of wood.

Thomas Sandrick nearly stumbled as he saw the hut. Shaking his head in disbelief, he murmured, "So you were right. They are alive. How I envy you your faith, Valentine. Once you discovered the map, you never doubted that you would find your brother and the others.''

In response, Valentine quickened his pace and entered the hut. But even Valentine was unprepared for what awaited them inside the house that his brother had built with his own hands.

"God's light! They be eatin' off plates o' gold!'' the red-bearded seaman exclaimed as he stared in amazement at the elegantly laid table, the gold plates, silver tableware, and goblets of fine glass rich enough for a royal banquet. "Lord love us, all we be missin' is a throne made o' gold!'' he said, forgetting for a moment whose brother it was they were searching for.

"Lookee here! They even fish with hooks made out o' gold!'' another awed crew member said in disbelief as he spied the gleaming metal hooked to a neatly coiled length of string.

Liam O'Hara, an Irish gentleman-adventurer who'd signed aboard the *Madrigal* for a bit of excitement and profit, fingered the gold plate, his eyes narrowing as he took note of the engravings. "This is Spanish. So is the silver. And look at that rapier and dagger on the wall. From Toledo, or I'm a Dutchman and Protestant to boot. I'd know that workmanship anywhere. Wouldn't mind owning that myself,'' he said with a look of envy. Eyeing Valentine Whitelaw more closely, he asked, "You are certain that was your coat of arms over the doorway and not some Spanish grandee's? Faith, but I'd no idea you were Catholic,'' he suddenly exclaimed.

Thomas Sandrick glanced at his friend in surprise, but Valentine Whitelaw was frowning, until O'Hara pointed at the gold crucifix hanging from the wall.

"Geoffrey Christian's wife, Magdalena, was Catholic. She was also Spanish,'' Valentine responded. His explanation might have explained the crucifix, but it left unexplained the remaining Spanish items, for he seriously doubted that Magdalena would have brought such things off the *Arion*, even if she'd had the time.

"Maybe Captain Christian sent the valuables ashore with his wife. Didn't want them Spaniards to get their 'ands on 'em,'' the bos'n said, voicing his captain's speculations. "These things could've come off one of the cap'n's prizes.''

Valentine had to admit that the idea had merit, for he himself ate off gold plate won in battle from a Spanish captain's table, and he drank madeira and port from another Spanish captain's prized cargo of fine wines, and most of the rare gems he had given Cordelia came from that same captain's personal coffers. He could still remember the voyage and subsequent battle during which Geoffrey Christian had acquired the fiery emerald that Magdalena had worn with such pride.

But still Valentine was puzzled. He glanced around the room. There was a simple table and *five* stools. The table had been set for five; Basil, Magdalena, and the child—but for whom else? And yet, only three mats with neatly folded blankets were placed against the far wall. A sea chest had been positioned beneath a window. Opening the lid, Valentine stared down at the neat pile of clothes inside. They were an odd assortment of men's and women's, and of varying sizes and styles, although nothing very fashionable. Sitting on top of another, smaller chest across the room Valentine saw a doll. Woven from a rough, cottonlike material, it had eyes and nose formed of tiny shells and a dress made from a strip of elegant lace. Inside the chest, he found a woman's combs and personal items, including a rope of pearls and the emerald pendant he recalled so well.

The place had obviously been lived in—and by Basil and Magdalena, and a child—and yet there was a strange emptiness about it, Valentine thought as he picked up the ornately engraved, gold plate occupying the place of honor at the head of the rough-planked table.

'' 'Twould seem as if your brother has been enjoying all of the comforts of home,'' O'Hara commented with a smirk as he lifted up to the crew's curious eyes a frilly-edged, silk chemise. ''We should all be so fortunate to find ourselves stranded on a deserted isle with a beautiful, hot-blooded *doña*,'' he said, and glancing away to wink at a couple of other gentlemen seamen who'd signed aboard, the Irishman wasn't aware of the cold, unfriendly gleam that had come into his captain's eye. He was even more unsuspecting of the Turk's quick movement, at least until he glanced back to find a sword point hovering periously close to his throat.

Red-beard eyed the fancy gentleman contemptuously. He could have told his nabs not to say what he was thinking, at least not in the captain's presence if it was something rude about a lady, or the captain's brother, and especially if the Turk was by his side.

Valentine shook his head at Mustafa, who, rather reluctantly it seemed, sheathed his sword.

Liam O'Hara swallowed, although it was more like a gulp. " 'Twas a jest, nothing more. I didn't mean any harm by it," he explained without further delay and wondered how it was he'd ever thought Valentine Whitelaw so refined and sporting a gentleman when sharing a tankard of ale in London. In fact, Valentine Whitelaw had become a dour-faced, iron-handed stranger ever since they'd set sail, O'Hara decided peevishly, thinking this voyage had not been as amusing a venture as he had been led to believe. Indeed, Valentine Whitelaw had even seemed to forget that there were gentlemen on board and had treated them like the rest of his men, expecting them to eat and sleep with this rabble he called a crew. Even Sandrick had not been the amusing shipmate he'd hoped for when first learning of the man's presence on board. The man had been either sick or silent for most of the voyage. O'Hara wondered why he was even on board, since he was a wealthy man who had power and position at court. What could he possibly have to gain on this voyage? O'Hara grumbled to himself, thinking he'd be sitting pretty in London if he had even half of Thomas Sandrick's fortune.

"Cap'n! The ashes of a fire I found out back are still warm!" one of the crew called out as he came running to the door of the hut, his face flushed with excitement. "There's a spring just beyond the clearing. There's even a pot they use for cooking. 'Tis drying in the sun on a flat rock beside the pool."

The portly seaman exchanged a knowing look with his slightly pale and unusually quiet friend with the red beard.

"There's even a spit set up over the fire."

The portly seaman eyed his friend up and down, as if trying to figure out how long the spit would have to be to skewer his friend.

Valentine Whitelaw's eyes were bright with determination as he gave his orders, certain now he would at last discover his brother's whereabouts.

Scattering his men, sending half toward the headland with O'Hara and half into the woods to search, Valentine, Thomas

Sandrick, and the Turk headed in the opposite direction toward the cove.

They hadn't gotten very far when a shout from the group that had gone toward the headland drew Valentine's attention. Valentine halted, but the Turk kept walking, gesturing to the point of the other headland, just before it bent to parallel the shore. He had spied something and wanted to investigate. Valentine let him go while he and Sandrick waited to see what his men were yelling about as they hurried toward them, carrying something heavy under their arms.

" 'Tis a cannon, Cap'n!"

"We found it half-buried in the sand."

"Off a Spanish galleon!"

"Look out there, Cap'n. There she is!"

"Broken up on the rocks."

"Some of her cargo must have washed up on shore."

"Might even have been survivors!"

"No tellin' who we might be findin' on this island now."

"We could be attacked! Maybe that's what happened to yer brother, Cap'n?"

"Gives me the jitters, it does. Where the divil is everybody, Cap'n?"

Valentine Whitelaw stood staring around him in growing dismay. Where indeed was everyone? Might Basil, Magdalena, and the child have been attacked by the survivors of this wrecked galleon?

"Cap'n? Ye think we might have a closer look at that galleon? Reckon there might still be something salvable from it. Since we got a boat, we might find something interesting out there in the bay that didn't get washed ashore. There just ain't any way, unless he'd a boat, that yer brother could have gotten to it that far out," one of the crew suggested, thinking of the gold and silver he'd seen on that table in the hut. There was bound to be more treasure in the sunken galleon's hold.

But his captain was more interested in discovering what had happened to his brother to worry about the cargo of the wrecked galleon. "There will be time enough for that later. Take your men across the headland, Michaels. I want to know what lies beyond."

"Aye, Cap'n," the crewman said, exchanging disgruntled looks with several of his mates.

Valentine Whitelaw hadn't missed his men's disappointment. "Gentlemen. So there will be no further misunderstandings concerning this: Should there indeed have been survivors of that wreck you are so anxious to explore, then I would urge caution, for I would not want the Spanish to catch any of my men with their breeches off. Or were you gentlemen planning on swimming fully clothed? Were you intending on setting a guard, or were you all going to dive in and come up with your hands full of gold doubloons? And the gentlemen in the boat, what were you going to do should you have been fired upon? A fine pair of sitting ducks you would have made. Once we have discovered whether or not we face an enemy, and have dealt with that threat, then, and only then, will we have the pleasure of exploring the wreck. Do I make myself clear?"

"Aye, Cap'n," they chorused, some of them slightly shamefaced, although O'Hara's eyes remained turned out to sea and the wreck that held such promise of riches.

"Good. Now let us waste no more time," the *Madrigal*'s captain requested as he turned away, certain his orders would be followed this time as he started back along the beach. He glanced in the direction Mustafa had gone, but the Turk had long since disappeared.

Thomas Sandrick stared about him curiously. " 'Tis so quiet," he said. "Almost unnatural."

They had just reached the headland when the silence Thomas Sandrick had remarked upon was shattered by a horrible cry. Valentine looked up in time to see the strangest figure flying through the air in pursuit of Mustafa as the Turk came tumbling down the rocky side. He landed with a splashing thud in the middle of a tidal pool on the beach below.

Tristram Christian had fallen asleep while on duty, just as Lily had suspected. Sitting propped against his favorite pine, his bare, brown legs crossed at the ankles, he hadn't sighted the ship flying the red cross of St. George anchoring just off shore. Nor had he seen the boat load of men being rowed ashore, nor later the shadow that fell across the rocks and blocked out the sun.

He hadn't heard Capabells's agitated cries in the branches

above his head until too late. Opening his sleep-drowsy eyes, he had yawned lazily, wondering what the ruckus was. Stretching, Tristram had glanced up to see a horrifying sight.

The tallest, cruelest corsair he'd ever seen was standing over him. The man was even more terrifying a sight than the French pirates. Later, Tristram was to remember little about the man who had been about to attack him other than the fierce face and curved sword; both were certain to haunt his dreams for many nights to come.

Crying out, Tristram had jumped to his feet, or perhaps he had been pulled to his feet. Tristram was never to remember exactly, for the ferocious-eyed man had hooked his fingers around his arm in a murderous hold, or so the young boy believed as he started kicking and clawing at the madman who had caught him napping. But even more heart-stopping for the lad was wondering how he would explain all of this to Lily, if he lived; and then she would probably kill him for not having taken heed of her warning to keep watch at all times.

Tears of fear and desperation had been coursing down Tristram's face when he had been as startled as his attacker. Suddenly, like some fantastic winged serpent, Lily had flown at the man. Or perhaps it had been Cisco he had seen and he had just thought Lily was flying. The parrot had been in the tree, at least the last time Tristram remembered hearing him, but whenever Cisco spied Lily he would fly down to her.

That was exactly what had happened. Cisco had landed on Lily's shoulder as she walked beside the cove, and he had been perched there, curious about the feathers that had sprouted on his mistress's shoulder, when she had come stealthily up the other side of the headland. Intent on surprising her brother, she had seen instead a horrible man shaking Tristram by the scruff of the neck.

She hadn't stopped to think, she had just come running, forgetting for a moment the bizarre outfit she wore. Cisco had flown into the air, green wings flapping. At the same moment that Lily had landed before the Turk, Capabells had swung out of the tree, his little face twisted into a mask of ferociousness as he squealed at the interloper who had so disturbed the quiet.

The Turk had released the squirming boy to shield himself from what had become an attack from all quarters. Taking a step backward, he had stumbled, his balance thrown off even more by the hands that had pushed against his chest and sent him over the edge of the cliff. The last thing the Turk had seen as he'd disappeared over the edge had been two green eyes glowing like emeralds in a grotesque face that reflected like the sun.

"Come on, Tristram!" Lily cried, grabbing his arm and pulling him after her down the other side of the headland and out of sight of their attacker.

Capabells scampered along beside them and Cisco swooped low over the sands as they raced along the shore and into the safety of the trees.

Out of breath, their hearts beating wildly, they stood staring at each other. With shaking hands, Lily removed the headdress and mask. "Who the devil was that?" she demanded.

Tristram continued to stare at her, unable to find his tongue or catch his breath.

"How did he get so close that he could grab hold of you like that?" she asked, pulling off the cape and folding it across her arm. "You fell asleep again, didn't you. I've warned you, Tristram. Did you think it was just a game?" she said angrily, for she'd never been so scared in her life and she still didn't know what they were going to do now that the pirates knew they were here.

"Where's Dulcie?"

Tristram's eyes grew wider than they already were, his horrified expression answering Lily's question.

"She was down on the beach looking for shells. I remember seeing her down there just before I—"

"—fell asleep," Lily finished his sentence for him.

"Oh, Lily! I didn't mean to! Honest. I just closed my eyes for a second. What are we goin' to do? Do you think they got Dulcie? Oooh, I'm sorry, Lily. I'm sorry," Tristram cried.

Lily stood watching the beach, just in case their attacker or any of his scurvy friends should be in pursuit. "I don't think they would've gotten her. Unless she had fallen asleep," Lily speculated, not seeing Tristram wince at her choice of words, "she would have seen them coming ashore. Dulcie is probably hiding somewhere, waiting for us to come for her."

"What are we going to do, Lily?" Tristram asked with a sniff.

"He was a horrible man. He didn't look English. I would've known an Englishman, Lily," Tristram said.

"They must have just come ashore. Their ship is probably riding at anchor beyond the reefs. I don't think they would have come from the far side of the island. I bet they haven't found the hut yet. That must be where Dulcie is. She's waiting for us by the spring," Lily decided. "We've got to get to the hut first, Tristram. The table is set. Mother's things are in her chest. All of our belongings are there. They're a bunch of thieves and they'll steal everything," Lily predicted.

Taking the cape, Lily wrapped it around the headdress and mask, then hid them at the base of a nearby tree, covering them with several overlapping palm fronds.

"What were you doing with those?" Tristram asked, then frowned. "Why were you dressed in them?"

"No one will find them now. Come on, Tristram. We have to find Dulcie and clear out the hut."

"What if they're already searching for us?"

Lily smiled, her pale green eyes glinting, and in that instant she would have reminded many of Geoffrey Christian. "This is our island, Tristram. Just let them try to find us," Lily vowed before dragging him after her deeper into the forest.

Valentine Whitelaw eyed Mustafa curiously as the Turk drew his sword. The curved blade gleamed dangerously as he brandished it to the sky in what appeared to be a gesture of ceremonial significance.

All eyes were centered on the Turk, who had just survived a deadly confrontation with a strange creature. Someone said it had been a sea serpent, but the red-beard said he'd seen it fly and it'd had feathers. There was a lot of mumbling amongst the crew, and several had glanced for reassurance at the *Madrigal* riding at anchor just off shore, their beached boat within easy running distance of where they now stood.

"Mustafa," Valentine tried once again to draw the man's attention. "What exactly happened? Mustafa?"

Finally, the Turk turned to face him, but Valentine could not get the man to meet his eyes. Valentine began to suspect what was bothering the Turk. He felt he had lost face. He had been frightened by the strange apparition that had so suddenly con-

fronted him. Fear was something the Turk was not accustomed
to dealing with. It was a matter of personal pride. He had vowed
to serve the man who had saved his life, and now, because he
had shown fear, he felt he had betrayed that sacred vow.

"What did you see?" Valentine asked again.

"A young boy was asleep under the tree," he finally said in
his low-voiced, thickly accented English.

"A young boy?" Valentine demanded doubtfully. "Are you
certain it wasn't a girl?" he asked, thinking of Geoffrey Christian's daughter. "She would probably be small and thin."

The Turk shook his head. "It was a boy. Asleep. He woke
up. I grab him. He fights me. Then"—Mustafa paused, his
mouth tightening—"then, jinni come. Bad. Evil. Should leave island, Cap'n, before it is too late."

"Jenny? Who the devil's she?" one of the crew who'd been
listening intently now demanded.

"Mustafa, listen. That was no supernatural creature you
saw. That was no jinni," Valentine told him. "There was a human being beneath that feathered cape and mask. And he was
probably just as startled as you, perhaps even more so."

The Turk muttered something beneath his breath, his eyes
scanning the woods.

"Don't like the sound o' this at all," murmured one of the
crew.

"How old was this child, this boy, you caught, Mustafa?"

The Turk held out his hand about waist-high, maybe a little
higher.

"Not very old then. Too young to have been . . . :" Valentine
paused. "Did he speak?"

Mustafa frowned, tyring to remember. "He cried out."

"What did he say? What language?"

A sudden look of surprise spread across the Turk's swarthy
complexioned face and he grinned, startling the crew, since
they'd never seen the man smile.

" 'SDeath! It's pirates!" the Turk said, remembering now
the small boy's cry of alarm when he'd glanced up to see him
standing there. "*Lilyhelp. Lilyhelp*. He say again and again.
Lilyhelme. Lilyhelme."

"*Lilyhelp? Lilyhelme?*" Valentine puzzled. "At least we know the first thing he said was in English. Lily,'' Valentine said the name softly. ''That was Geoffrey Christian's daughter's name.''

'' 'E wanted this Lily t'elp 'e, eh?'' said one of the men understandingly, considering it was the Turk who'd caught the lad.

'' 'Lily help me,' '' Valentine said with a slight smile, but it quickly faded when he realized the boy had not called out to Basil for help.

''I thought there be just one child, Cap'n?'' one of the men asked, then began to turn a mottled color as he realized some of his mates were snickering while others were beginning to look uncomfortable as they caught their captain's eye and remembered O'Hara's snide remarks in the hut.

''Take several men and return to the hut,'' Valentine ordered, unwilling, at least for the moment, to speculate on what might have happened on the island during those seven years when Basil and Magdalena had found themselves stranded. ''They may try to return to it while we're here. If you do see them, I do not want them hurt. Try to catch them if you can, but do not harm them. They are just children. Remember that.''

He sent the rest back the way they had been headed when they'd discovered the cannon. With Mustafa and Thomas Sandrick and a handful of men accompanying him, Valentine started toward the headland and the peaceful cove beyond.

''Here, Cap'n! Ye be right. The footprints head out across the sands toward that tall pine on the edge of the forest. Reckon they scurried off like a couple of scared rabbits. They be little ones, too. Ye know, I don't think they be quite as small as the ones o'er yonder, Cap'n,'' one of the crew said curiously as he knelt down to examine the imprints dotting the sand. ''Well, I'll be,'' he said, rubbing his chin. ''Don't likely know what kind these be here? Ain't human, Cap'n,'' he declared as he looked more closely at the monkey's paw prints.

''Jinni,'' Mustafa murmured, causing the man walking beside him to cross himself nervously.

They had nearly reached the row of trees bordering the sands when Valentine suddenly halted. He gazed at the tall pine, his eyes narrowed against the glare off the water as he stared intently at something in the cool shade beneath the tree.

Slowly, Valentine approached the two graves marked with simple crosses. In silence he stood before them.

"Basil."

Valentine closed his eyes against the pain, all hope gone now. Basil had been dead for over two years. Next to his grave was Magdalena's. Valentine opened his eyes. He stared down at the crosses. The lettering of Magdalena's name had been carved with such precision and care, as had the date of her death. There was no doubt in Valentine's mind that Basil had made that cross and buried Magdalena less than two weeks before he himself had died. Valentine stared at the cross that marked his brother's grave. The lettering was ill-spaced and lopsided, as if carved by a child's unsteady hand, but the same "Our Beloved" that had been carved above Magdalena's name had been carved above Basil's.

Valentine knelt down on one knee beside his brother's grave. He reached out and touched the cross; then he stood. Without a word, he started to follow the tracks into the woods, his men hurrying to catch up to him. Only Thomas Sandrick remained a moment longer by the graves. His face was shadowed as he stood there deep in thought. Then he turned away to follow Valentine Whitelaw. He met the others halfway, for they hadn't gotten far before they'd lost all sight of the trail in the thick undergrowth and had to return to the beach.

During their search, they had traveled back toward the bay. They emerged from the woods on the far side of the headland, close to where they had beached the boat. Valentine started toward the path that led to the hut when suddenly a thin, black-haired child broke from the underbrush like a bird on the wing.

Valentine could hear the excited cries of his men just behind the child, whose small bare feet were carrying it directly toward them. When the child saw the men approaching from the opposite direction, cutting off its escape, it froze, and then bolted toward the surf.

Fast as the child was, Valentine's long strides quickly outdistanced it and with an arm outstretched, Valentine captured the child before it could reach the water.

Valentine felt as if he'd trapped a wild cat. The top of her head caught him on the point of his chin, slightly bloodying his lip as he bit into it. Cursing mildly beneath his breath, he felt her teeth sinking deep into his hand. He grimaced as her feet, kicking against his thighs, struck a vulnerable spot.

"I am not going to hurt you, child," he said softly, for he could feel her trembling against him even as she struggled. "I want to help you. I won't hurt you."

Suddenly she stilled, but Valentine could still feel her shaking uncontrollably in his arms. He lowered her to the sand, but kept a firm hold on her arm. A wise precaution, for as soon as her feet had touched the ground she had tried to race away.

Valentine turned her around to face him. Her eyes were dark brown and fringed with thick, sooty lashes. Her black hair was long and tangled and she had a smudge of dirt across one sun-browned cheek. Gold earrings dangled from her ears and a necklace strung with delicate pink shells hung around her neck. She was dressed in a plain, silk shift that was faded to a colorless shade by the sun and sea.

She jerked back her head when Valentine reached out to touch a dark curl. Her face was filled with fear as she stared at him. For an instant her eyes slid away from him as the rest of his men reached them. Keeping a wary eye on them, she watched as they formed a half-circle around their captain. Valentine could feel her tensing, ready to spring free if he gave her the chance.

"What is your name? Do you understand me?" he asked.

"Maybe she don't understand English, Cap'n. Could be she's off that Spanish galleon that sunk. She kinda looks Spanish, so dark she is."

"Looks more like some gypsy's brat to me," one of the men offered, eyeing the dark-eyed girl suspiciously.

Valentine captured Dulcie's chin, holding it turned up so he could see her face clearly. "A gypsy's brat?" Valentine spoke softly, shaking his head as his fingers caressed her cheek, then one of the silky eyebrows that arched so delicately above her wide eyes. Had anyone looked closely at Valentine Whitelaw's own arched brows, they might have remarked on the similarity, especially the odd way the left eyebrow rose slightly higher than the right one, which gave a slightly quizzical, sardonic cast to the expression on both faces. Valentine did not need to ask who her father was; he already suspected that this wild child was Basil's daughter.

"Won't you tell me your name?" Valentine asked her again,

smiling this time as he tried to get her to respond to him, but she continued to watch him distrustfully. He saw the tears welling up in her eyes before she began to cry, and he suddenly felt like the ogre he must appear to be in her young eyes. He glanced around at the men who had crowded close and did not blame her for being frightened.

"Ah, sweeting, I'm not going to hurt you," Valentine said, lifting her in his arms. "Did you see anyone else at the hut?" he demanded of the bos'n.

"No, Cap'n. Not a soul. We was making our way back there when we saw this one and she took to her heels. I left a couple o' men on guard, just in case t'others come sneakin' back."

"Good. I want you to take your men and go back to the hut and load up everything you can find. Strip it bare. And, gentlemen, I expect everything to be accounted for. Those are my brother's possessions, and they now belong to his family. Everything is to be stored aboard ship. We will camp out here tonight, and, if the children haven't shown themselves, we will salvage what we can from the wreck while we await their pleasure," Valentine told his men.

"Ye think we be havin' a long wait then, Cap'n?"

Valentine smiled. "These children know this island better than we do. Unless the others wish us to find them, I doubt we can," he said.

"Ah, Cap'n. We just heard about your brother," one of the men who'd been with the other group said, coughing uncomfortably before continuing, "and we be real sorry. Hear the lady is dead too. What ye think happened to them?" he asked, glancing down at the child. "Ye don't think this little one be Spanish then?"

Valentine tightened his arm around the child he held against his chest. She was quiet now, her head pressed against his shoulder, her face hidden. "Perhaps half-Spanish," he murmured.

"Why don't we just call to them, Cap'n? Tell them who we be."

"These children have no reason to trust us. Basil was a cautious man, he would have taught them to be on their guard, especially should any strangers come ashore. It is an impossibility. They disappear like rats. Lily Christian has grown up on this island, as have the other two, and I'm certain she's watching us at this very moment, trying to figure out how to rescue this one.''

"Lily is the captain. I'm the bos'n's mate,'' Dulcie suddenly spoke. There was such pride in her voice that the *Madrigal's* bos'n grinned back over his shoulder as he headed back to the hut with his men to do his captain's bidding, his step quickening as he watched Thomas Sandrick disappearing out of sight. He snorted. What did that one think? That only gentleman could count? He had ten fingers, didn't he? He could carry out the captain's orders without any assistance, he vowed, running to catch up to the gentleman hurrying ahead.

Valentine Whitelaw stared down at the dark head, a smile curving his lips as he heard the muffled voice.

"She is? Well, that is not surprising since she is a captain's daughter. Did you know that Geoffrey Christian, Lily's father, was my very good friend? I sailed aboard his ship the *Arion*. I even met Lily when she was about the same age as you. I knew your father, too. Do you know what my name is?''

There was silence.

"My name is Valentine Whitelaw. I am your father's brother. Did he never mention my name?'' Valentine asked. "Did he never talk about England?''

The child remained silent and Valentine sighed. She was so young. She would hardly remember Basil and Magdalena, much less anything they might have told her about themselves. If he was to have his questions answered, he would have to find Lily Christian.

Dulcie stared across Valentine Whitelaw's shoulder. She watched the waves breaking in splashes of white, and beyond that, she saw a ship. Her eyes widened as she stared at the white flag and red cross flying on the mainmast.

"The red cross of St. George!'' she squealed, struggling to free herself. "Lily always said that one day we would see it and then we would be rescued. Tristram said that it didn't exist, just like the wild white horses that would carry us home to England, but it does. It does! Let me go! Let me go! Got to tell Lily! We've been rescued!'' she cried, trying to squirm free of the arm that still held her tight.

"That's right. You have been rescued, but I can't let you go, not just yet," Valentine told her, tightening his grip. "Lily will find out soon enough. Lily *is* your sister, is she not?"

Dulcie nodded.

"And Tristram?"

"He's my brother."

"Do you have any other brothers and sisters?" Valentine asked, wondering how many children might be running wild on this island.

Dulcie shook her head. "Just Lily and Tristram. There's Cappie and Cisco, too. And Choco, but I don't like him," Dulcie confided, a frightened look entering her eyes.

"Who are they?"

"Jinni," Mustafa said.

"Maybe savages, Cap'n."

Dulcie giggled. "Cappie is a monkey! And Cisco is a parrot. He talks!"

Valentine laughed. "And Choco?"

Dulcie shivered. "He's a *tigre*. He scares me, but Lily likes him. Cisco and Choco came from that ship. Did you know it is a ghost ship? Tristram says 'tis haunted," Dulcie said, her childish confidences causing several of the crew who had been so anxious to explore the wreck to glance uneasily at the rotting hulk on the rocks.

Valentine smoothed back a dark curl from her cheek. "And what is your name? Will you tell me? I would like to be your friend."

" 'Tis Dulcie," she murmured shyly.

"Dulcie. That is a pretty name."

"And Rosalinda."

"Sweet Rosalinda," Valentine said softly.

"That's what Lily says my papa used to call me."

"What happened to him?"

"He went away. So did Mama."

"Where did they go?"

Dulcie pointed toward the cove.

"Do you know why they went away?" Valentine asked.

"Lily says it was the fever. We played all the time and there weren't any lessons, Lily says. Then we made the cross. Lily let me help. We go there everyday to say hello. And even though Mama and Papa aren't here anymore, we still set a place for them at the table. Lily says 'tis so we won't ever forget them. We don't go to the other graves very much. Tristram says we don't need to go at all, but Lily says Mama and Papa would want us to. Lily says Papa always wanted us to be civilized.''

"What graves are those, Dulcie?"

"The other graves. The crosses aren't as pretty.''

"Who are the people buried there?''

"Castaways, like us. Lily says their ship sank in a storm and they were the only survivors. Papa and Mama tried to save them when we found them on the beach, but they all died.''

"Why didn't you become sick, Dulcie?'' Valentine asked his young niece.

Dulcie shrugged. "We built a big fire, the biggest ever. We burned everything on the beach. Papa told us to. I'm hungry. Can I go now? Lily will be looking for me,'' she explained, struggling to free herself.

"I'm sorry, Dulcie, but you are going to have to stay with us for a while, at least until Lily comes. You don't know where she is, do you? Is there a secret place where she takes you and Tristram when she thinks there is danger?''

A secretive look entered Dulcie's dark brown eyes. "We have lots and lots of secrets,'' she said. "I'm not going to tell you any of them. I promised not to.''

"Your father would want you to. He trusted me like you trust Lily, Dulcie. Will you call to her for me? If she would come out of the forest I could talk to her and tell her that I knew her father. She can stay hidden while she talks to me. I will not hurt her. You want her to come, don't you, Dulcie? When Lily and Tristram are here, I'll take all three of you aboard my ship and then we will sail away to England. That is what your papa would want, Dulcie,'' Valentine said softly, persuasively.

"Cappie and Cisco, too?'' she asked worriedly.

Valentine raised an eyebrow, then nodded reassuringly. "Now, will you call to your sister? I really would like to talk to Lily,'' Valentine told her, and, unable to resist, he pressed a quick kiss against her smudged cheek.

Dulcie's eyes grew wide, then she giggled. "That tickled,'' she said, then she gasped, putting her small hand over her mouth.

"What is the matter?" Valentine demanded, concerned by the look of uncertainty that had suddenly entered her eyes.

"Lily isn't going to be very happy when she sees you," Dulcie declared. "She won't be able to be the captain anymore."

Valentine Whitelaw grinned. "And why is that?"

Dulcie touched his bearded face, then quickly withdrew her hand as if stung. " 'Cause you have a beard. Captains are supposed to have beards and ships. Lily isn't a real captain. You will have to take command now, and I don't think Lily will like that. Lily has always been the captain," she said.

Valentine laughed softly. "Well, I shall have to try very hard then to make her like me," Valentine told Dulcie as he walked up the beach, little realizing how difficult a task he had set for himself.

"Where is Dulcie?" Lily asked as she and Tristram huddled close together under a low palm, their faces peering out between the long, sweeping fronds.

"I don't see her anywhere?" Tristram said. "Look! There! Two of the pirates are inside the hut. I saw one of them peeking out, Lily! Do you think they heard us calling Dulcie?" Tristram asked, looking behind them worriedly. "If she was here, she would've heard us. I don't see her anywhere. She wasn't by the spring. She knows to meet there, Lily. Where could she be? You don't think they have her, do you, Lily?"

"I don't know," Lily said uncertainly. Basil had never told her what to do if one of them got caught by pirates. He had only taught them how *not* to get caught.

"Look, Lily, here come some more pirates," Tristram whispered hoarsely as a group of men approached along the path and disappeared into the hut. Several minutes passed while Lily and Tristram listened to muffled voices and laughter. "Look at them! They're stealing everything, Lily," Tristram squeaked in growing indignation as they watched several of the men leave carrying their chests.

"That's Mother's chest," Lily said angrily. "Those are my clothes. And those are Dulcie's shells he's got," Lily hissed as she watched the finely dressed gentleman walk quickly by.

"That's my fishhook and line," Tristram muttered.

The *Madrigal*'s bos'n was carrying out his captain's orders with no lack of haste for there were only a few hours of daylight remaining. It hadn't taken long to clear the hut: The sea chests had been repacked and carried out; the gold plate and silverware counted under his watchful eye before going the way of the chests; the clothes, personal belongings, and food, even the coat of arms over the door, had been gathered up with the bed mats and blankets and dispatched to the beach. Soon, nothing but the bare furnishings remained in the hut.

His job completed, the bos'n followed his men back to the boat. Once or twice, hearing a rustling in the trees behind, he glanced over this shoulder, but there was nothing to be seen. When he reached the beach, the crew had just about completed loading the boat.

"We goin' to be stayin' ashore or goin' back aboard?" one of his men wanted to know.

The bos'n glanced over to where the captain was standing, the little girl still held in his arms. "Reckon the cap'n'll be tellin' us when he wants us to be knowin'," he said. "Finish this up now and be quick about it."

"Ain't nobody answered him so far, even if they be in there watchin'," one of the crew remarked as he followed the bos'n's gaze to where their captain, now in conversation with Thomas Sandrick, stood near the edge of the forest. "Called to them, but no answer, unless ye be countin' all the birds squawkin'. Reckon we might talk the cap'n into lettin' us catch something fresh to eat? Saw some wild pigs runnin' through the bushes on the far side of the headland and there's all kinds of wild fowl we can catch. Sure would taste good," he said, voicing the rest of the crew's sentiments.

"Ye think the cap'n and me was born yesterday?" the bos'n demanded with a contemptuous snort. "On the cap'n's orders, I've already sent out a huntin' party. We'll be dinin' on roast pig and pigeon tonight or I'm not the *Madrigal*'s bos'n for long. And since ye've got time on yer hands, mate, ye might as well get busy, or ye just might find yerself eatin' pickled mushrooms and sour biscuit."

Valentine Whitelaw watched as his men rowed the boat back to the ship, where they would unload it of its cargo, and then return to shore with the necessary supplies for their stay on the island. At first light tomorrow they would begin to salvage what they could from the wreck.

That night a large bonfire illumined the sands of the bay. The crew of the *Madrigal* dined like kings on roast pig and pigeon pie flavored with onions and potatoes, and fresh fruit. Plenty of ale from the ship's stores washed it all down. A chorus of loud belches following the evening's meal was satisfaction enough for the cook. A sailor brought out a hornpipe and began a lively tune. Several of the men partnered each other and started to dance a jig around the fire, while others were content to sit and watch, their voices raised in song and laughter that drifted through the balmy, smoke-filled night air.

The *Madrigal*'s captain sat slightly apart. His mood varied from moment to moment as his thoughts lingered on what had happened on this island where Basil had lived out the last days of his life. Once before, he'd had to accept Basil's death, but it was harder this time. Valentine ran his fingers through his hair, shaking his head in disbelief at how cruel fate was. How many times during the last few years had the *Madrigal* sailed these very waters and how close he had been to rescuing Basil if only he had known, Valentine remembered. If Joshua Randall had returned home to England sooner, how different the future would have been. Valentine glanced down at the sleeping child curled up on a blanket next to him. He touched her smooth brow. She was so innocent. What would happen to her when they returned to England? And the others, what was to become of them? Was the boy also Basil's son? It seemed likely that he was. And Geoffrey's daughter, Lily, she had no family to return to in England. Valentine stared into the darkness, thinking of those back home who would be wondering what he had found on this island.

He felt the warm trades against his face as the winds rustled through the palms. He could smell the sea and hear the waves lapping gently against the shore. The stars were bright in the black sky above. Sweet water bubbled from a spring and fish and fowl were abundant. Realizing they would spend the rest of their lives on this island, Basil and Magdelena would have accepted their fate and eventually found happiness. As grief for what had been lost passed, would it have been so very hard to find happiness here?

Valentine pulled the blanket over Dulcie's small shoulders.

She had cried when no one had answered her calls. Later, she had sat quietly by the fire and eaten her meal, but her eyes had never strayed from the concealing darkness of the forest, where they both knew Lily and Tristram must be watching from the safety of their hiding place. Valentine stared in distaste at the length of rope he had tied around his wrist before securing the other end to Dulcie's waist. He couldn't let her loose; Dulcie was his only hope of catching the other children.

And he would not leave this island without them safely aboard the *Madrigal,* he vowed as his gaze raked the forest and he heard again the jaguar's cry. The first time it had sounded, it had brought an uneasy silence to the camp. The men who had been dancing and laughing had suddenly stilled. Almost breathlessly, they had waited to hear that inhuman scream come again. When it came, it was accompanied by the agonized death cries of the jungle cat's prey.

Valentine stared down at the peacefully sleeping child. He had not believed her story of a *tigre* prowling the jungle, thinking it no more than a tale of childish imagination. But Dulcie had not lied. And with good reason, she should be afraid of the jaguar. Valentine thought of the other two out there in the dark with the big cat and he cursed beneath his breath in frustration, knowing he could do nothing until dawn.

"I think he sees us, Lily," Tristram whispered, closing his eyes even though he and Lily were well hidden in the darkness and the denseness of the tall grasses they had crawled through until stopping just short of the beach.

"He can't see us," Lily reassured him, although she had to admit that the man who had called himself Valentine Whitelaw and claimed to be Basil's brother had seemed to be looking directly at them. "Don't move, Tristram," she added, feeling him shaking beside her. "This one just might be able to see in the dark."

"Do you really believe he's Basil's brother, Lily?"

Lily bit her trembling lip, uncertain what to do. If only Basil were here to advise her, she thought, quickly wiping away a tear as she glared at the shadowy figures on the beach.

"If he is, Lily, we should go to him like he says," Tristram decided, thinking the man knew an awful lot about them.

"He could have learned all of that from Dulcie. You know she can't keep a secret. He looks like a rogue who could charm the devil himself," Lily predicted, quoting one of Basil's favorite phrases.

"He's English, Lily," Tristram reminded her.

"Have you forgotten the way his men raided our hut? What do you think they'd do if they knew about our cave? I only hope Dulcie doesn't say anything about it to him. He must never know about our treasure. Basil warned us not to say anything. It is our secret, Tristram. They're no different from pirates. And don't forget, he kidnapped Dulcie. I bet he suspects there is more treasure, and he's holding Dulcie for ransom. All pirates are greedy. That is why I think our plan will work."

"I don't think he's hurt her. I even heard her giggling, Lily. Do you think she likes being with them?"

"Dulcie is too young to know what she likes. We have to decide that for her. I know what is best, Tristram," Lily said slowly, not certain herself what she was feeling. "That is why I think we are doing the right thing." She tried to work as quickly as she could without making too much noise, but it was hard to see what she doing in the dark. "I've been thinking, Tristram, that once we get Dulcie back we should hide until they leave. I really do not think it would be a very good idea to be rescued. Even if he is Basil's brother."

"What?" Tristram demanded, forgetting to speak softly.

"Sssshhh!" Lily warned him, giving him a pinch for good measure.

"Ouch! Why did you do that, Lily?"

"Sssshhh! Listen. Do you want to go to England?"

"Of course I do. Basil always said we would return there one day."

"Basil and Mother are here, Tristram. They will not be in England. It was different when they were alive. We would all go to England and live together at Whiteswood," Lily told him, oblivious to what Basil's wife, Elspeth, and their son might think about such an arrangement. "Everything has changed now, Tristram. You and Dulcie were born here. I can't even remember Highcross Court. What is there for us in England?" Lily demanded, frightened more than she had ever been of the unknown; and England was the unknown.

"I never thought of that, Lily," Tristram said, worrried now.

" 'Tis a cold country. You'd have to wear shoes all of the time. And hose."

Tristram's mouth dropped open in dismay at such a thing.

"They might even try to take Dulcie away from us, Tristram," she added. "*He's* already separated us."

"No! Dulcie? Why?"

"Because Dulcie is Basil's daughter. If he's really a Whitelaw, then he and Dulcie are of the same blood. We aren't, Tristram. What does he care for us? He'll try to take Dulcie away when we get to England. She'll have to live with the rest of the White-laws."

"Can't we live there too?"

"No. We will have to live at Highcross Court. 'Tis yours now, Tristram. You are master of Highcross. I think we've a cousin in England. But I don't think Mother and Father liked him very much. That doesn't matter, though, because I could take care of us if we had to return to England. Highcross is ours. We could live there. Live off the land like we do here. At least when there isn't snow on the ground," she added in an innocent-sounding voice.

"I don't want to go to England."

Lily smiled, patting Tristram on the shoulder. "I'm glad you feel that way, Tristram."

"And he can't make me go, either," Tristram said trucu-lently, then added hesitantly, "What are we going to do if he doesn't agree to our terms, Lily?"

Her work completed, Lily squatted down and stared at the beach, where the glow from the fire was flickering across the sands. "First, we'll go back to the cave. We'll stay there until just before dawn. Then we'll come back."

Tristram sniffed appreciatively of the aroma of smoked pork drifting through the night air. "That sure smells good. I'm hun-gry, Lily."

"We can get some fruit on our way to the cave."

Tristram sighed, wishing this Valentine Whitelaw had caught him instead of Dulcie; then *he'd* be sitting by the fire eat-ing roast pig.

"Are you certain we're doing the right thing, Lily? Don't you think Basil would wish us to say hello to his brother?" Tristram questioned as he began to crawl after Lily and away from the beach. "Maybe we could call to him from the trees. At least we could talk to him."

"Basil wanted us to be safe. But he always intended for us to be together. I don't think we would if we left the island, Tris."

They were about halfway to the first row of pines when a ferocious cry sounded nearby. Lily and Tristram paused, realizing that Choco was prowling closer than before. The strange noises from the beach had drawn his curiosity. He must be somewhere in the tall grasses. The scream sounded again, but even closer this time. Tristram froze, his heart pounding.

Choco was too close. Lily could feel his eyes watching them as they moved slowly through the high grass. Lily tried not to be frightened, but they were downwind of Choco, and the night air was full of strange odors, he might not recognize their scent. They had always stayed inside the hut at night, when Choco stalked his prey. She knew he wouldn't hurt them, but what if he attacked them before he realized who they were?

"Come on, Tristram," Lily whispered hoarsely, determined to reach the trees. "Hurry." She grabbed hold of his hand and forced Tristram to move faster with little regard now for stealth.

There was a blinding flash of light, before the deafening roar sounded around them. Lily threw herself to the ground, Tristram falling on top of her. Lily could smell a different kind of smoke in the air. It brought back vivid memories of another time when she had been at her father's side and smoke had burned her eyes. That had been the last time she had ever seen him.

"You damned fool!"

"I think I got him!"

"You don't even know what you fired at. You could have hit anything in the dark. Those children could have been out there," Valentine said, glancing down at the sleeping child he held in his arms.

"It was the cat, Whitelaw!" O'Hara exclaimed excitedly. "You heard him yourself. I saw something moving out there. 'Tis mine! I'm going to have it hanging for all to see in the hall of my house in Dublin. A jaguar! If I don't sell the skin for a fortune, I might even line my cloak with it," O'Hara boasted.

"If you shoot that pistol one more time, I'll have your hide displayed for all London to see," Valentine warned, cursing the darkness that kept him from seeing if O'Hara had managed to hit anything. If he hadn't, then he'd certainly frightened away anything that might have been hiding in the grasses.

"Stick 'is 'ead on London gate," one of the crew murmured, hoping the Irishman would be fool enough to fire again, for he'd like to see the captain knock the wind out of his bloated sails.

"You're jealous. All of you!" O'Hara charged, glancing around at the unfriendly faces. "You're mad because I reacted faster than any of you. I wonder if you'd be feelin' the same if the cat had taken a bite out of one of you hearties while you were in the grasses mindin' your own business? Well, just wait 'til mornin'. Then you'll be seein' that Liam O'Hara didn't miss the mark," he promised angrily before stomping back to the fire, not overly eager to explore the tall grasses where a wounded animal might be lying in wait until morning—when hopefully, if the creature still lived, he would certainly be dead.

" 'Ope 'e didn't just wing it. Then it'll be comin' back lookin' fer the Irishman's blood."

"Let's 'ope 'e did, then."

Valentine stood staring into the darkness.

"You aren't going to wait until morning, are you?" Thomas Sandrick asked as he watched his friend impatiently cut the rope that bound him to the child.

"No," Valentine replied curtly as he tied the frayed end of the rope around a startled Thomas Sandrick's wrist. "I am leaving her in your care," he told him as he carefully placed Dulcie in Thomas's arms.

"B-but I don't know what to do with her," Thomas exclaimed, holding the child as if a burning coal had been placed in his palm instead. "What if I drop her?"

"She'll probably start to cry, so unless you want her to wake up, I'd hold her a little more firmly," Valentine advised his nervous friend as he drew his sword before turning away to take one of the torches Mustafa had lit from the fire.

Holding the fiery torches before them, Valentine and Mustafa started toward the tall grasses, most of the crew close behind, torches of their own lighting up the night sky with a smoky, reddish glow.

Liam O'Hara, belatedly realizing that the captain wouldn't

wait until tomorrow to discover what lay beyond, was not about to share the glory. The kill was his. Jumping to his feet, he grabbed a burning log from the fire and ran after them. Pushing ahead of everyone, Liam O'Hara had the pleasure of being the first one to see the specter lunging out of the darkness.

His scream of terror effectively halted the others in their tracks. The assembled torches revealed to astonished eyes what had attacked Liam O'Hara, who was crouched on the ground, his head and face protectively covered by his arms as he waited for the wild creature to tear him apart.

The last thing Liam O'Hara expected to hear, however, was laughter. Uncontrollable laughter. Choking as he gasped for air, Liam O'Hara glanced up, disbelief replacing the horror that had robbed him of his senses.

The creature remained where he had first sighted it. It had not moved at all. It could not move. It wasn't real. It was nothing more than a scarecrow dressed in a feathered cape and head-dress, its face a mask of gold.

"Lookee 'ere! 'Tis the same critter that attacked the Turk! Reckon the Turk's got first claim on 'im. If'n 'e wants 'im, that is!" someone chortled.

"Reckon if Master O'Hara lines 'is cloak wi' these feathers 'e might be able to fly. What a figure 'e'll be in London."

"When 'e said 'e'd winged 'im, 'e weren't lyin'."

"Don't let 'im get away now, Master O'Hara."

" 'E's quick, I bet!"

Liam O'Hara's face was flaming, with anger and embarrassment. "It was the cat! I heard it! That is what I shot at, not th-this . . . th-this . . . thing!" he declared indignantly.

The Turk was walking around the area, holding his torch as close to the gently swaying grasses as he could without starting a brush fire. His own heart had pounded momentarily when seeing the creature so suddenly for a second time. The Turk breathed a sigh of relief.

"Cap'n! Blood!" Mustafa called out, a smile curving his lips, for the captain was right, and the creature was not supernatural.

Valentine hurried over to where the Turk was kneeling just beside the scarecrow. He held up his hand to the light, and there was blood staining two of his fingers where he had touched the ground.

"Damn!" Valentine said beneath his breath.

The Turk was dismayed. He had thought the captain would be pleased to know that the creature could be wounded, forgetting for the moment that the captin had never believed in the jinni.

Valentine stood up. He turned to face Liam O'Hara. "You had better pray that your shot just grazed the child, or you will wish that you'd never set sail aboard the *Madrigal*, because you will never see England again," he promised the startled man, the expression in his eyes leaving Liam O'Hara in little doubt of the deadly threat of the softly spoken words.

He tried to smile, but it was a sickly-looking grin. "How do you know that blood comes from one of the children? You all heard the cat. 'Twas the cat I wounded," he blustered.

"I suppose the cat stood up on his hind legs and made this scarecrow?" one of the other gentlemen adventurers in the group commented sarcastically. "I've always given you the benefit of the doubt, but—"

Liam O'Hara was reaching for his sword when the man broke off the rest of his words, his attention caught by something pinned to the scarecrow's cape.

"What the devil's this, Valentine?" he said as he pulled the torn piece of paper free of the golden fishhook that had been hooked through it and the cape. "I believe 'tis addressed to you," he said with a look of curious surprise on his bearded face as he handed the note over to this captain.

Valentine unfolded the piece of paper. He began to smile as he read the words that had been scrawled across the page with little attention to neatness.

"What's it say, Cap'n?"

"It would seem as if I have been given an ultimatum," Valentine responded, his eyes scanning the surrounding darkness. "I am to release the child at dawn and leave the island. I may keep this mask of gold and the items I stole from the hut. And if I do exactly as I've been told, then I might expect a few doubloons as reward. They have obviously decided that we are a greedy lot and would do anything for gold."

"Why, the nerve o' the—"

"To send us packin' like a bunch o'—"

"They can't do that!"

"Who do they think they be anyways?"

"Gentlemen, I do not see that we have any other choice but to follow our instructions. At dawn, we leave the island," Valentine Whitelaw said, leaving his men speechless by his easy capitulation to the children's demands.

"Lily? Wake up! We've got to go now or it'll be too late," Tristram said. Pale light was already beginning to filter in through the window of the cave. It was almost dawn and they had to get across the cove and to the other side of the headland to discover if Valentine Whitelaw had done as he'd been told and had released Dulcie and left the island.

"I'm so tired," Lily said, pulling herself into a sitting position, but she would have fallen over if Tristram hadn't grabbed her.

"Are you sure you are all right, Lily?" Tristram asked for the thousandth time. "You don't look very good."

"I am fine. It is just a scratch," she said, lightly touching the tender spot on her head where the ball had grazed her. She took away her hand, swallowing her fear as she stared down at the sticky red blood staining her fingers.

"Oh, Lily!" Tristram breathed. " 'Tis blood."

"*Prraaack!* Oh, Lily, 'tis blood," Cisco repeated, his giggling laughter filling the cave.

"I told you I am all right. It doesn't hurt nearly as bad as it did," Lily lied, for she had a horrible headache. "Now come on. We've got to rescue Dulcie," Lily told him as she struggled to her feet, ignoring Tristram's outstretched hand as she momentarily lost her balance. Capabells jumping into her arms gave her some comfort as she walked unsteadily toward the entrance to the cave.

Tristram grabbed the square of silk that they had wrapped the doubloons in, and which he would leave in place of Dulcie when they rescued her. "I wish we didn't have to give them any of our treasure," he said resentfully.

"A bargain is a bargain," Lily reminded him as they left the cave, Cisco flying down to perch on Lily's shoulder as Capabells leaped onto the sand to race ahead, his chattering disturbing the birds still asleep in the trees. "We aren't thieves. This way he won't have any reason to return. We will have kept our side of the bargain the way Basil always taught us gentlemen did.''

When Lily and Tristram reached the edge of the forest bordering the bay, all was quiet.

''Look!'' Tristram whispered, pointing to a spot near the headland, where a lone figure stood. '' 'Tis Dulcie. She's alone. I'll go get her,'' Tristram said, starting to step out from behind the palm. ''I don't understand why she's just standing there.''

''Wait!'' Lily cautioned. ''What is that around Dulcie's waist?''

''It looks like a rope. It's tied to something in the sand. It's a stake! They pounded it into the sand. I guess they knew she'd run off if they didn't,'' Tristram said.

''He's making certain he gets his blood money.''

''Look, Lily!'' Tristram cried, less softly now. ''There's the boat! It's full of men. There! Just beyond the reef. That's Valentine Whitelaw. The one sitting in the stern, and look at the one sitting just in front of him. I'd recognize that funny-looking hat anywhere. That's the man who attacked me, Lily.''

Lily blinked. She'd have to take Tristram's word for it. She couldn't focus her eyes. Everything was blurred and she felt sick to her stomach. Taking a deep breath, she stepped from behind the palm and started across the beach toward Dulcie.

''Lily! Lily!'' Duclie cried out as she saw her sister and Tristram approaching. ''They left me here, Lily. He told me to be good, that nothing would hurt me. Why did he go, Lily? He was nice.''

''As nice as a snapping turtle,'' Lily said, reaching Dulcie's side. ''What's wrong?'' she asked Tristram.

''I can't pull up the stake. It's in too deeply.''

Lily fumbled with the knots around Dulcie's waist, but they wouldn't give. ''Why are you crying, Dulcie? I'll have you free in just a minute.''

Dulcie wiped the back of her hand across her nose. ''You have blood on your face, Lily. Are you going to die?'' she asked tearfully, her voice rising shrilly as she stared at her sister's pale face. ''I don't want you to die! I don't want you to leave me like Mama and Papa!''

''Of course I'm not going to die. I bumped my head. That is all,'' Lily tried to reassure her. ''Why didn't I think to bring the knife. You're going to have to go back to the hut and get it," Lily told Tristram, but he continued to stand where he was, staring at her as if she were crazy.

"Well?"

"Lily, don't you remember? They took everything from the hut. We don't have a knife anymore. They've taken everything. What are we going to do now?"

"You won't have to do anything," a voice spoke from the rocks near the headland.

Lily spun around, nearly falling to her knees as her head kept spinning. "You!"

"Hello, Lily," Valentine Whitelaw said softly. "Are you ready to go home now?"

"B-but you cheated! You're supposed to have left the island. I kept my side of the bargain. *You cheated!*" she yelled at him. "Run, Tristram!" she cried, trying to dodge past the man who had appeared out of thin air like magic.

Her escape cut off toward the headland, Lily started to race up the beach, but Tristram's yell of surprise halted her from the direction and she turned instead toward the surf. As she waded into it, she saw Tristram's kicking feet lifted clear off the sand by the same horrible man who had attacked him a day earlier, only this time he had caught him and was holding on tight to his captive.

Lily dove into the clear waters, feeling the waves sweeping over her and carrying her high into the air. Surfacing, she took a deep gulp of air, but the sky and sea blended together and she found herself choking on salt water instead. She was underwater again. The sea was warm and soft and she was sleepy. But no, she couldn't sleep. Not yet. She had to escape . . . there was so much to do . . . Tristram . . . Dulcie . . . they needed her . . . they were her responsibility . . . Basil had trusted her . . . she couldn't sleep . . . not yet . . . not until they were safe. . . .

She was floating. She felt the gentle movement of the sea around her. She opened her eyes and stared deep into the turquoise depths. So beautiful, the sunlight through clear water. She closed her eyes. She could sleep now.

Yet mark'd I where the bolt of Cupid fell:
It fell upon a little western flower,
Before milk-white, now purple with love's wound,
And maidens call it, Love-in-idleness.

SHAKESPEARE

Chapter Eleven

LILY FRANCISCA CHRISTIAN stared down at her feet. How she longed to kick off the shoes that pinched her toes and roll down the stockings that felt so strange against her skin. Lifting her heavy skirts, she would run barefoot through the surf. She could feel the West Indian sun warm against her face, drying the sea spray as she splashed through the waves and licked the salt from her lips.

Lily sighed as she heard the rain splattering in wind-blown sheets against the diamond-shaped panes of glass in the window. She shivered, unaccustomed to the coolness, and snuggled deeper against the velvet cushions in the window seat. Wrapping her arms around her knees, she drew them against her chest and rested her chin on top.

An unladylike position, Honoria Penmorley would have declared with a haughty, dismissing glance. Indeed, Honoria Penmorley would never have been found sitting thusly. Honoria Penmorley was a lady. But Lily Christian and her brother and sister were half-wild children who'd been raised without any thought to civilized behavior. Basil would have chuckled at that, Lily thought as she remembered the hurtful words she had overheard Honoria Penmorley speak to Valentine Whitelaw in the great hall the day before. But Mistress Honoria Penmorley had known a moment's discomfort, Lily remembered with a sly grin, when she had entered the room and greeted the woman in perfect French, then continued to converse in Spanish, throwing in a phrase or two of flawless Latin and Greek just to put Honoria Penmorley on her mettle.

Lily hugged herself, thinking of Valentine Whitelaw's smile and how he had winked at her conspiratorially before returning his attention to his genteel and now flustered guest. Even Thomas Sandrick, who had accompanied them to Ravindzara, had hidden a slight grin behind his hand, politely pretending not to have noticed Honoria Penmorley's flushed face. Lily wrinkled her nose in distaste as she thought of the many times Sir Rodger and Honoria Penmorley had visited since the *Madrigal* had docked at Falmouth over a week earlier and her captain and passengers had arrived at Ravindzara. Thomas Sandrick and several of the other gentlemen aboard the *Madrigal* had ridden with their captain to his home. Liam O'Hara, however, had left the ship's company with the intention of sailing home to Ireland, a wealthier, if no wiser, man than before. The *Madrigal's* crew awaited their captain's return to Falmouth within the week, when they would continue their journey along the south coast of England, bound for London this time.

Lily's thin shoulders slumped dejectedly. If only they could have sailed forever aboard the *Madrigal*. With the wind filling her sails and the stars above, they could have sailed around the world, never making port until they returned to the island.

She had not always been so fond of the *Madrigal* or her captain. She had no memory of Valentine Whitelaw saving her from drowning that day on the island. He had dived into the surf after her and brought her safely to shore. Tristram, however, remembered everything that had happened. He had recounted the tale to her when she regained consciousness. Of course, by then, the *Madrigal* had already set sail and whether she wished to leave the island or not had been decided for her by Valentine Whitelaw.

Tristram had thought she was dead when Valentine Whitelaw carried her out of the surf. She had reminded him of one of those bodies they'd found floating in the bay, he had confided to her, touching her arm just to make certain her skin had lost that clammy feeling. He told her how he had struggled to free himself from the Turk, who really wasn't as bad as they'd originally thought. Tristram had shuddered when he told her about the blood trickling from her head, and how Dulcie and Capabells had started howling. When Valentine Whitelaw had placed her on the sands, Cisco had flown down to land on her shoulder. Tristram's eyes had grown wide when he'd told her how he thought the captain was going to wring Cisco's neck when the parrot had started giggling and talking about blood, and every time the captain had given an order, Cisco had mimicked him. He had been afraid the captain wasn't going to let Capabells—who'd attacked the Turk again when he'd gotten too close—and Cisco—who'd never stopped giggling—aboard the *Madrigal* when she'd sailed. Of course, Tristram said with a wide grin, Cappie had jumped into the boat before anyone had invited him, scolding the coxswain when he'd tried to take up his oars. And Cisco had landed on Valentine's shoulder when the captain had started to carry her to the boat, Tristram told Lily, awed still by the remembrance of what Valentine had vowed he was going to do to the parrot feather by feather.

Only Choco had remained behind on the island. She hadn't even had a chance to say good-bye to him, Lily thought sadly. Then she grinned mischievously when she thought of the *Madrigal*'s crew trying to catch their *tigre enojado*. Not that they had even tried, for the jungle cat was the one pet of theirs that Valentine Whitelaw had declared he was not going to take aboard his ship. And Lily knew he had been right. Although Lily's concern had been for Choco rather than the crew, who would have had to sail with a caged beast aboard. Choco's home was on the island, just as theirs had been. He would be happy nowhere else.

Tristram had really believed she was going to die, Lily remembered in amazement. His voice had wobbled when he spoke of how she hadn't opened her eyes for two whole days and nights, and then she'd been delirious for over a week. The captain had been scared, too, Tristram said, impressed by the attention Lily had received. The captain hadn't even left her side when his men had started to salvage what they could from the wreck. Tristram's voice had risen excitedly when he'd described the chests of gold and silver the crew of the *Madrigal* had brought up from the bottom. They had celebrated all night long, dancing and laughing and singing those funny songs of theirs.

They had even held a wrestling match, Tristram had begun to tell Lily when she had interrupted him to ask if he'd told this Valentine Whitelaw about *their* treasure chest in the cave. Tristram had looked at her in surprise. Of course he hadn't said anything, it was their secret, he reassured her. But Lily hadn't liked the guilty expression on his face and had questioned him further. Tristram had to admit to her that Valentine Whitelaw had asked a lot of questions about their life on the island. Since the captain was Basil's brother Tristram thought they could have trusted him with their secret.

Lily reminded Tristram of the promise they had made Basil always to keep the chest and its contents a secret. And had he so soon forgotten what had happened to their possessions in the hut? They'd been stolen by Valentine Whitelaw's crew. Tristram had quickly told her that the captain promised him that everything was still theirs and he was just keeping it safe until they returned to England.

Her feelings still smarting from having been tricked by Valentine Whitelaw, Lily had decided it wiser to keep the secret to themselves, besides, Valentine Whitelaw and his crew had found their own treasure. What good would it do to tell him about the cave now, she was to tell Tristram later, when they were almost to England and her opinion of Valentine Whitelaw had undergone a dramatic change. She did not wish to anger him by telling him that they had kept the cave a secret from him when they'd told him everything else about their life on the island. And if she admitted the truth to herself Lily did not want to fall out of favor. She feared she would if he knew their secret now there was nothing he could do about it—especially since she had lied to him.

Actually, it had been Tristram's fault, Lily reminded herself. He had let it slip that Basil had kept a journal and had written down everything that had happened on the island. That piece of information had certainly raised an eyebrow or two around the captain's table that night when Tristram had so innocently mentioned it. Lily could remember almost choking on her food. Basil's journal had been the most important part of their secret and Tristram had blurted out its existence to strangers.

Her sudden uneasiness had drawn Liam O'Hara's attention. He had always watched her aboard ship, guilt from having been the one who'd shot her making him very solicitous of her health. But Lily suspected he was more concerned about his own skin and what his captain would have done to him should she have died. Thomas Sandrick, who'd been sitting beside the captain, had eyed her curiously, offering her a sip of wine to bring the color back into her cheeks. She could remember ignoring him, a stony expression on her face, resentment at her predicament still souring her disposition. Later, she had come to like Thomas Sandrick. Since he was little more than a passenger aboard the *Madrigal* himself, his time was his own and he spent the long hours of their voyage reading or walking the deck. Although he was often lost in thought, he was always interested in her recollections. He spoke in the same quiet manner that Basil had. She suspected that his mild-mannered appearance hid a very sharp mind, for she had questioned him upon many subjects and he seldom did not have an answer. Liam O'Hara, on the other hand, seemed to have an opinion on every subject, yet one seldom learned anything from him.

Lily still grew nervous when she thought of that lie she had told Valentine Whitelaw that evening. She could remember the excitement on his face when he'd asked about this journal of Basil's. His deep disappointment when she had told him that it had been with Basil when they'd burned the lean-to had pleased her at the time, but now she wished she had spoken the truth. Valentine Whitelaw still thought the journal had perished in the fire. It was too late now to change what she had said. It was of little importance, Lily reassured herself, allowing the incident to fade from her mind.

Lily curled into a more comfortable position, propping the velvet pillows behind her shoulders. Succumbing to the temptation, she unlatched the window and opened it slightly. The cool rain against her face and the sound of the sea in the distance reminded her of being aboard the *Madrigal* and the voyage to England. Tristram and Dulcie had been frightened, even sick those first couple of weeks, but soon Tristram was climbing like a monkey into the rigging under Valentine Whitelaw's watchful eye. Lily had stared enviously as Tristram had climbed higher, a rope tied about his middle in case he missed his step, but he hadn't. He was Geoffrey Christian's son, the captain had called up to the proudly beaming Tristram. Even Capabells had been allowed to climb into the rigging; of course no one could have stopped him had they tried, for the monkey had seen Tristram disappearing into the tangle overhead and had scurried after him.

Once she had recovered enough from her injury to escape from the small cabin she'd been confined in, she had ventured up on deck. Being aboard ship and sailing the high seas had brought back a rush of memories of her father and sailing aboard the *Arion* that she had thought long forgotten. Her timbers creaking and her sails sounding like thunder as they billowed with the winds, the *Madrigal* had ridden the waves as easily as the playful dolphins racing alongside the trim little ship.

And as the days turned into weeks, Lily came to feel as if she had always belonged aboard the *Madrigal* and by the side of her captain. Lily closed her eyes, reliving the moment when she had opened her eyes for the first time aboard the *Madrigal* to find herself swimming in a sea of turquoise again, only this time she realized that she was staring into the eyes of Valentine Whitelaw. Even thinking about him caused her heart to flutter. He was the most wonderful man in the world. Lily felt the rush of heat to her cheeks. She loved him, as much as she had her father and Basil, and yet it was a different kind of love. It was not the comforting kind of love she'd felt for the other two men in her life; this was a love that confused her and left her feeling empty and sad. Her heart had never acted so strangely before. And whenever she was with Valentine Whitelaw, her stomach felt like it was dancing with butterflies and she knew a sudden shyness that was unnatural to her. Never before had she been tongue-tied. It embarrassed her even to meet his gaze, and yet she found herself trying to catch his eye again and again. She wanted to see that slow smile of his come just for her.

She could have stood for hours on the deck watching him. Dressed in a plain leather jerkin and breeches, his shirt sleeves rolled high above his elbows and startling white against his bronzed skin, his feet braced against the roll and pitch of the ship, his tall figure could always be sighted on the quarterdeck; his voice always heard above the wind in the sails and roar of the sea when he gave his orders. It was strange to Lily that he should suddenly remind her so much of Choco. Valentine Whitelaw prowled his ship with such restless energy, his gaze always searching the horizon for the white flash of a sail, that she thought of Choco stalking his prey. His hair was black and shiny, glinting in the sun like Choco's velvety coat. His muscles seemed to ripple with sinewy strength, just like Choco's when he was about to spring. Sleek and swift, he moved with a quiet suddenness that caught one off guard. That was the way Valentine Whitelaw had moved the day he'd spied trouble on the mainmast. There was an unleashed power about Valentine Whitelaw that seemed to come of instinct rather than thought. That was what had sent him into the rigging before any of his men, climbing high onto the mainmast to rescue the foretopman when the seaman had slipped. Catching and twisting his ankle in a loop of rope, the sailor had dangled upside-down over the deck, his cries for help alerting the others after the captain was already halfway up the mast.

But it was another incident when Lily felt the first stirrings in her heart, changing her from a girl into a woman with a woman's desires for a man. It had happened after the storm, when the seas had calmed. She had been dreaming, but the dream had turned into a nightmare with her screams filling the small cabin as she tried to escape the creature chasing her. She couldn't lift her feet and the glowing eyes had kept moving closer and closer, swirling around her until she was lost in darkness.

Lily had awakened from the nightmare to find a warming glow flooding the cabin and strong arms holding her close, keeping her safe from the horrifying apparition. Burying her face against Valentine Whitelaw's shoulder, she had cried. His hand had caressed her gently, comfortingly. He had lifted her face to his gaze, and Lily could still remember how clear and bright his eyes had been. Then he had smiled and all of the shadows had vanished. She had felt his lips against her forehead and heard him call her his sweetest heart. Her fears quieted, her tears dried, and her breath coming less raggedly, Lily had gradually become aware of the man holding her so close against his bare chest and her heart had started to pound erratically all over again. Confused by the rush of emotions she could not understand, Lily had jerked away from him, startling both of them by her violent rejection of this touch.

He had seemed disconcerted, even hurt, by her apparent revulsion. She had wanted to tell him that she hadn't meant it, that she wanted him to hold her again, but she could only lie there staring up at him with tearful eyes. Without touching her again, he had covered her with the blanket, then stepped away from the bed. He had stood before her for a moment, staring down at her. Lily had closed her eyes, mortified at the heat rising in her cheeks as she stared at his bare chest, her eyes drawn to the muscular narrowness of his hips, covered only by the thin leather of his breeches. He seemed to have forgotten that he'd only had time to pull on his breeches when he'd heard her cries, but Lily was painfully aware of his near nakedness. Suddenly the innocence of the days when she and Tristram had swum naked in the cove was gone. She dared not open her eyes, or he would surely know what she was remembering. She squeezed her eyes tighter, afraid to meet his penetrating gaze. The minutes seemed like hours, then, finally, she heard the door. He had left. The cabin had seemed so empty without his presence, and snuggling deep beneath the covers, she had whispered aloud the words he had spoken to her, holding them close to her heart.

Her love for Valentine Whitelaw had deepened beyond a mere physical attraction as the *Madrigal* sailed closer to home. And a part of Lily's love came of a knowledge of Valentine Whitelaw that other women would never understand, nor even be privileged to experience. Lily came to respect the captain of the *Madrigal* the same way her crew did. She saw a man of courage, whose spirit was defiant and daring, yet whose intrepidity was tempered by his own deep respect for the sea and the men who had pledged to serve him aboard the *Madrigal*. Serve her captain well and every man from gentleman-adventurer to lowliest swabber was treated fairly. Only those unfortunate few who shirked their duty or disobeyed their captain's orders learned how uncompromising a man Valentine Whitelaw could be, showing no mercy in exacting punishment for the offense.

And yet, the man who could give the order to have a seaman who'd stolen from his mates flogged was also the man who held Dulcie on his lap, teasing her and kissing her until she hugged him tight. He was a thoughtful man, patiently teaching Tristram about the sea, untiringly explaining to him about charting and measuring the stars, even allowing him to take a measurement with the cross-staff he used to chart the *Madrigal*'s course toward home.

Once, when she had still been recovering from her fever and had yet to leave the cabin, Lily had caught his eye on her and had blushed rosily, modestly pulling the short shift she wore down below her knees as she sat on the bunk. For the first time, Lily had been aware of herself as a maturing young woman who would have to dress accordingly. The next day she had found on her bunk one of her mother's gowns from the hut. It had been shortened and taken in by a tuck or two in the appropriate places. Embarrassed and indignant, she had not thanked him. But when she had gone on deck and felt herself the cynosure of all eyes, she had belatedly realized that Valentine Whitelaw had acted to protect her from further embarrassment at the hands of his crew. Although not a woman yet, she was old enough to attract the roving eye and ribald comment of sailors who'd been at sea for months.

Valentine Whitelaw spoke eloquently of many things. He had traveled the world and could spin a tale as well as Basil or her father ever had. Lily had sat watching him, spellbound, her green eyes glowing like emeralds. Gradually she had become less ill-at-ease when around him, her curiosity and returning amiability drawing her more and more into the conversation, until one day she found herself smiling into his eyes unselfconsciously. And when he had come to stand beside her on the deck and placed his arm across her shoulders to steady her as the *Madrigal*'s bowsprit swung to starboard, she had not drawn away. She had gazed up into his face, responding to the smile that came into his eyes as he drew her closer and they stood there in companionable silence.

Lily's spirits had soared and reality had fled. She'd become lost in a young girl's romantic dreams, and Valentine Whitelaw, unaware of his godlike stature in her eyes, became the object of her tender passion. After that, the voyage to England passed all too quickly. Then one morning, just as dawn broke through the heavy clouds hanging low against the eastern horizon, she had heard the cry "Land-ho!" and hurrying on deck had seen the misty shoreline looming to larboard. England. From the deck of the *Madrigal*, it looked cold and forbidding, not the land of rolling green hills covered in wildflowers that Basil had spoken of with such fondness.

But Lily was still lost in the enchantment of having fallen in love. She was as yet unaware that her future might not be what she had so innocently envisioned in her most treasured dreams. It had not been until they had reached Ravindzara and Lily had met Valentine's family, and the lovely Honoria Penmorley, that she had discovered a very real world existed beyond their isle in the sun and the magical seas the *Madrigal* sailed.

Honoria Penmorley was a part of that unfriendly world, and Lily's spirits sank as she remembered the reflection of a thin, brown-skinned girl that had met her eyes this morning in her looking glass. Why couldn't she be as beautiful as Honoria Penmorley? she wondered despondently? The woman's skin was pale and soft, and there wasn't a freckle to be seen on her nose. Lily stared down at her own small, brown hands, then thought of the sprinkling of freckles across her own nose. Honoria Penmorley had slender hands with long, tapered fingers that moved gracefully when she spoke. Lily pushed back a long strand of dark red hair that had somehow managed to free itself from the neat braid Quinta Whitelaw had tried to pin fashionably on top of Lily's head. Honoria Penmorley never had a curl out of place. And her hair was a pale, soft color.

Lily puffed out her cheeks, trying to fill in the curving lines of her heart-shaped face. Her chin was too pointed, not nicely rounded like Honoria Penmorley's. Everything about Honoria Penmorley was pale and delicate and softly rounded, Lily thought in growing despair, afraid that she would lose Valentine Whitelaw to the unfairly favored Honoria Penmorley.

Hearing approaching steps, Lily quickly closed the window. Pulling the velvet hanging across the part of the window embrasure where she sat, Lily moved deeper into the shadows, unwilling to reveal her presence, especially when she recognized the voice that drifted to her along the hall.

''I did not think I would need my cloak whilst taking a moment's exercise in the hall, but there is an uncommonly chilly draft. 'Tis worse than if we were walking outside in the rain,'' the voice complained between chattering teeth. Safely tucked away in the darkened window seat, Lily watched the two people approaching.

Honoria Penmorley was dressed in a gown of brown and gold brocade of a severe cut with just a touch of lace at the wrists and a small, discreet ruff about her slender throat. Her light brown hair was dressed in neatly wound braids, and covered by a white silk attifet, the heart-shaped headdress sitting attractively on her fashionably coiffed head.

" 'Twas most hospitable of Valentine to invite us to stay overnight. It would appear as if the rain will continue till morning," she continued conversationally. "I had not looked forward to the ride back to Penmorley Hall in darkness. I fear the lanes will be virtually impassable."

"Yes, it was very gracious of Whitelaw considering he has more house guests than normal and the work on the Hall is not yet completed. Indeed, I would foresee many more years of construction before the Hall is agreeably habitable. 'Twould seem, however, that Quinta and Artemis have coped well enough," Sir Rodger responded.

"Did you know that he plans on adding two more wings?"

"Yes, I had heard. Soon the Hall will rival Penmorley once again. I trust his purse equals his enthusiasm," Sir Rodger advised. Cautious behavior was always uppermost in Sir Rodger Penmorley's mind.

"Thus far, I think his efforts have been quite successful, although why he wishes to have the new windows overlook the sea is a mystery to me. He will have to keep the hangings drawn most of the day because of the glare," Honoria said. With a sideways glance at her brother from her light brown eyes she added, "Now that he plans on living here permanently, he has great ambition for the Hall and for reestablishing his family in Cornwall."

"And you, my dear?" Sir Rodger inquired, glancing down at his sister's face, though little of her expression could be seen in the shadowy hall.

"I?" she asked coldly.

"I do not mean to pry, Honoria, but I am your brother, and I cannot have helped but notice a certain *tendresse* in your eye when you speak with our host."

"I will not deny that I have speculated on the possibility of becoming mistress of Ravindzara."

"I would caution you, my dear, that Valentine Whitelaw's affections may already be engaged elsewhere," Sir Rodger warned his sister.

"Cordelia Howard?"

"You know?"

"I may lead a very sheltered life here, but I am not ignorant."

"I never—" Sir Rodger began, then said kindly, "I only mentioned the lady because I did not wish you to harbor false expectations."

"No, of course not, and I appreciate your brotherly concern. But you must understand that I have given the idea more than a passing thought. My decision comes not of a lovesick young girl's penchant for her heart's desire, but of a woman's careful consideration of her future. Valentine may discover it rather more difficult than he imagines to find a wife when she discovers his intentions of making her mistress of Ravindzara. Not many young women, accustomed to the amenities of London and the peaceful countryside of Hertfordshire or Kent, would look forward to the isolation of Cornwall. I, on the other hand, would choose to live nowhere else. Why do you think I have turned down most of the proposals I have received, despite how acceptable they might have seemed to you? I can afford to be particular, Rodger, and I intend to remain in Cornwall, near Penmorley Hall.

"Therefore, the ideal arrangement would be to marry Valentine Whitelaw. He would be most suitable. His mother was a Polgannis. The name is still very much respected in the country. He inherited the Hall and intends to restore it in a fashion much to my tastes. When the Hall is returned to its former glory, under my guidance of course, I could accept this as my future home. Although I would prefer he made his fortune in a more circumspect fashion, it would appear Valentine is most successful as a privateer. It would also seem as if great profit can be realized from these voyages. I believe he will be quite wealthy one day. He is in good favor with Elizabeth. In these perilous times, it would be to our advantage, Rodger, to at least have one of us wed to a Protestant. It would bring us more influence and perhaps guarantee our safety should there be more riots against the Church. And, should the winds change more favorably and a Catholic monarch once again rule, then our family is of the Faith. We stand to gain either way," Honoria told him in her soft, thoughtful voice, but every so often, the dulcet tones became harsh, grating as much as surprising the listener. "I get along well enough with Quinta and Artemia, and I know they would respect my wishes and position as the new mistress. Valentine will expect them to remain in residence, and I shall, of course, welcome them into my home. I would not have it said that I would turn out of my home an old woman and a cripple. They will have comfortable rooms in one of the wings. Their presence will be companionable while Valentine is away on his voyages, and they will be able to help with the children.''

"I would hardly call Artemis a cripple, and I have never yet met a woman as capable as Quinta Whitelaw,'' Sir Rodger commented.

"I did not mean to be cruel, but Artemis does have a limp. Unfortunate, since she is a very attractive young woman, but I dare say she will always be something of a burden to Valentine. You cannot deny that, my dear. A pity, for I would have liked to have seen her married before I assumed my position as mistress. However, I think we will deal together well enough.''

Sir Rodger eyed his sister as if seeing her for the first time. It was apparent that she had every detail planned. "And our host? How would you deal with him? Are you in love with Valentine Whitelaw?'' he asked curiously, a slight smile curving his lips as he noticed her sudden agitation. Apparently Honoria was not as coldhearted about the affair as she would have wished to appear.

"Undeniably, he is a gentleman of honor and breeding,'' was all Honoria allowed before quickening her step to reach the end of the corridor without further delay.

"I must congratulate you, my dear, for you have indeed given this a great deal of thought. I would, however, remind you that you have yet to receive Valentine Whitelaw's proposal of marriage. I do not believe the gentleman is even aware of your intentions. How do you intend to convince him of the suitability of your plan?''

"I shall leave part of that up to you,'' Honoria replied.

They had not quite reached the window where Lily still sat in silence, her presence undetected, when Sir Rodger halted to stare in surprise at his sister.

"I happen to have complete faith in your abilities to capture the hand of Cordelia Howard.''

"I see,'' Sir Rodger said slowly, a strange look on his face that momentarily puzzled Honoria. "I am flattered, my dear, by your confidence in me. And with the fair Cordelia no longer available you expect Valentine Whitelaw to turn to you.''

Honoria glanced down modestly at her carefully folded hands.

''You are a very beautiful woman, Honoria. Our host would have to be blind not to appreciate your sterling qualities as a future wife and mistress of his home,'' Sir Rodger spoke the appropriate words.

''Thank you, that is very kind of you.''

''You know it is true. Indeed, Valentine Whitelaw should think himself lucky that I would even consider him as a possible candidate for your hand,'' Sir Rodger said.

''Oh, Rodger, please, you will not be difficult when Valentine comes calling. Promise me, you will not interfere,'' Honoria pleaded, concerned now that she had revealed her innermost thoughts to Rodger. If he ruined all that she had worked for because of a misplaced pride and need to prove himself superior to Valentine Whitelaw, a Polgannis. . . .

Reading her mind, Sir Rodger patted her arm. ''I promise I will not thwart you on this, Honoria. In fact, I promise that your wedding will be the envy of all of England and your dowry will rival that of a queen's,'' he told her. ''I only wish I were as certain of my future.''

''What do you mean? Surely you do not doubt that you can win the affections of Cordelia Howard? I admit that I am not overly fond of her, but that is because she prefers the gaieties of London. I am a far more serious-minded woman. However, she would make you a good wife, Rodger,'' Honoria said a trifle urgently, lest Rodger not continue his pursuit of the beautiful Cordelia. ''She is considered a great beauty. She is popular at court. She has a respectable fortune. She has influence which could be useful to you. She would prove a valuable hostess when you entertained in London. She is witty, indeed, she is far more intelligent than she would have her gentlemen friends believe.''

''You need say no more, my dear,'' Sir Rodger said, raising his hand in supplication. ''You do not need to convince me of the charms of Cordelia Howard. I am well aware of them. And I will do my best to see that Valentine Whitelaw marries you and not her. I only hope he will realize how fortunate a man he is.''

''Thank you, my dear. I knew I could count on you,''

Honoria said, smiling for the first time as she tucked her slender hand around his elbow.

"I think you may have forgotten something," Sir Rodger said as they resumed their walking.

"Oh?" Honoria inquired doubtfully. "And what could that possibly be? I think I have been most thorough."

"The child."

Honoria laughed. It was one of the few unattractive qualities about her. "The child? Oh, Basil's daughter."

"Yes, I should think Valentine, and Quinta and Artemis, being the child's only living relatives, would wish to have her live here at the Hall," Sir Rodger predicted, bringing up a possibility Honoria had not had proper time to deal with.

"That is a situation I will not allow. I will suffer his aunt and sister's presence in my home, but not his brother's illegitimate children," Honoria declared.

"There would be only one," Sir Rodger corrected her.

"Do you really believe that the boy is not Basil's son? I seem to recall that Geoffrey Christian and his wife had only one child when they left England. The boy is not old enough to be anyone's son but Basil's, despite what the brat claims."

Sir Rodger frowned. "Why, if the boy is Basil's son, would Basil have led the child to believe that he is Geoffrey Christian's son? He recognized the girl as his daughter."

"My dear, 'tis obvious," Honoria said rather impatiently. "Basil, thinking they might one day be rescued, wanted to protect the lady's reputation. To have become lovers so soon after her husband's death, especially when Basil still had a wife in England, would not have been at all seemly. Indeed, I wonder if they may not have been lovers even before they left England. Why else was Basil Whitelaw aboard that ship? Not that I am surprised about what occurred on that island. Magdalena Christian was never decorous. I was always of the opinion that Geoffrey Christian made a *mésalliance* when he wed that foreigner. And now the boy stands to inherit Highcross Court, if, of course, his claim can be proven. Which I think is doubtful. There is no record of his birth. He was born on the island within a year of their being stranded. I should think most people will find it hard to believe that he is Geoffrey Christian's son. He does not even resemble him."

"Either way, 'twould seem as if Hartwell Barclay loses. If the boy's claim is denied, then the girl, as Geoffrey Christian's only child, inherits the estate. And," Sir Rodger added a bit maliciously, for his sister's smug assumptions had irked him, "Valentine and his wife inherit Basil's children."

Honoria Penmorley's lips tightened into a thin, unattractive line. "We shall see," she said unpleasantly, her steps more purposeful and nearly outdistancing her brother's as she hurried along the hall, her ladylike decorum temporarily forgotten in her haste.

Lily's lips were trembling with anger as she listened to the footsteps fading down the corridor.

"She just can't marry him," Lily whispered. How dare she say that about Tristram, Lily thought, her fist clenched. It wasn't true. Worriedly, Lily wondered if Valentine would try to keep Dulcie. Artemis was always holding Dulcie on her lap and fondling her and kissing her, as if she were her own little girl.

Lily pulled back the heavy curtain and crawled from the window seat. Standing up, she straightened her gown and tried to smooth the wrinkles from her underskirt. With a look of dismay, she noticed the streak of dirt marring the pale yellow silk. She must have dirtied it when she'd crawled beneath the bed to catch Cappie, who had been chased underneath by one of the maids.

As Lily looked closer, she became aware of a rip along the seam of the bodice, and that she'd caught the toe of her shoe in the hem. Lily could imagine the horrified expression on Honoria Penmorley's face when she caught sight of the elegant gown she had donated to Valentine's orphaned charge out of the goodness of her heart. But Lily had heard Honoria claiming later that she seldom wore the gown since she found the color less than agreeable.

Lily stared down at the yolk-colored material of her gown and for once had to agree with Honoria Penmorley. The color was ugly. It made her sun-darkened skin look sallow and dirty, and the dark red hair Basil had always claimed was so beautiful suddenly seemed a brassy color.

With a defiant shrug, Lily stomped along the corridor, knowing she could delay no longer in joining the rest of the guests in the great hall below. But when she reached the top of the stairs, she hesitated and stood looking down at the crowded room, a sudden awkwardness overcoming her. Surely all eyes would be watching her and noting the ripped seam, stained underskirt, uneven hem, and the strand of hair that hung so unattractively across her cheek. Lily swallowed the painful lump rising in her throat and knew that her cheeks were burning with embarrassment.

Lily saw Valentine Whitelaw standing in intimate conversation with Honoria Penmorley, who was nodding her head in polite agreement to all that he said. Lily's wide eyes clung to him. Never had she seen him looking so handsome. He was dressed in a black doublet and gold-embroidered black breeches, with a starched, white ruff about his tanned throat. The gold earring he wore gleamed softly against a black strand of hair that curled against his neck. As Lily continued to watch, she saw Honoria place her slender hand on his arm and he lowered his head to catch her softly spoken word, his deep laughter filling the room in appreciation of her witty remark.

If only she could have walked down the steps as proudly as a queen. Dressed in a gown of her own choosing, and the same color as her mother's emerald pendant, her hair woven with pearls, she would enter the great hall, and Valentine Whitelaw would be waiting for her, his eyes never leaving her until she reached his side, then he would take her into his arms and. . . .

"Are you all right, Lily?" Tristram said in his squeaky voice, standing where the captain of the *Madrigal* should have been standing.

"Of course I am. Why?" she demanded in disappointment, for Valentine Whitelaw still stood attentively beside Honoria Penmorley in the hall below.

"You look kind of sickly," Tristram said with brotherly candor. "I was just wondering if I could have your pudding tonight? Please, Lily, please. I love pudding, Lily. 'Tis my favorite thing in the whole world. If I'd known about pudding I would have built a boat of my own and rowed to England years ago. I would've loaded up a whole cargo, Lily, then sailed back to the island with it," he confided with a wide grin. "So can I, please? Please? Dulcie won't let me have hers. She started to cry when I asked, and Artemis promised her a second helping. You never eat all of yours. 'Tis just wasted. And, besides, I don't know when I'll get to eat pudding again. Did you know, Lily, we're leaving Ravindzara tomorrow and sailing for London. Valentine's aunt and sister are coming, too, and even Sir Rodger and his sister are sailing with us. I wonder if we'll ever get to come back here again? I heard Valentine say that we would be going to Highcross. I wonder if it is as nice as Ravindzara?''

Lily stared at her brother as if he were crazed. Pudding? Tristram frowned as he saw the look on Lily's face; then, much to his delight, Lily nodded, but before he could properly thank her, she had turned around and fled back down the corridor.

Had he really heard right and he could have her dinner tonight? Tristram watched her hurrying figure disappear and thought she had been wise to let him have her dinner, because from the look on her face he didn't think she could have kept it down.

A cheerful fire was burning in the hearth of the small chamber she shared with Dulcie when Lily entered, closing the door firmly behind her and shutting out the awful truth of Tristram's words.

"Prrraaaack! Prrraaaack! Cisco wants a kiss and something sweet to eat! Sweet to eat!"

Lily stared through her tears at the parrot sitting on his perch in the corner of the room, the sound of his voice comforting to her.

"Prrraaaack! Man the halyards. All hands! All hands! Avast heaving, me hearties! Prrraaaack! Land-ho! Ho! Ho! Ho! Prrraaaack!"

Lily struggled with the fastenings of her gown, pulling off the offending dress and tossing it with a vengeance across the room toward the fireplace. Cisco flapped his wings nervously as he watched the strangely colored yellow bird fly toward the fire.

Lily glanced around the oak-paneled room. The flickering firelight cast its warmth across the room and the big bed with its velvet hangings and fur coverlet that she loved to snuggle beneath. A linen chest sat at the foot of the bed and held most of her belongings—the rest remained aboard the *Madrigal*.

The room blurred as tears welled in her eyes. Lily ran to the big bed, her feet barely touching the shallow steps placed before it as she threw herself across the fur coverlet.

An outraged squeal caused her to sit up and roll over. Then a fuzzy face with bright eyes appeared from beneath the coverlet and Capabells, chattering angrily, scampered out.

"I'm sorry, Cappie," Lily said, her voice reassuring the excitable monkey that his demise wasn't at hand. He hopped onto her lap, his long tail curling around her arm as he rested against her, allowing her to comfort him for the fright he'd suffered.

"Are you glad to see me? You love Lily, don't you, Cappie?" Lily said, scratching the top of his head much to the little monkey's satisfaction.

Cappie had just dozed off when a firm knock sounded against the door, startling Lily, who'd been staring bemusedly into the flames.

The monkey quickly disappeared beneath the coverlet even though his mistress had made no move to answer the summons that was sounding less patiently now.

Lily continued to sit on the bed, staring in fascination as the door opened to reveal Valentine Whitelaw.

"Tristram tells me you are ill? That you are not going to join us for dinner tonight?" he asked as he shut the door behind him and came to the edge of the bed.

Lily nodded, unable to meet his eyes as she tried to hide her tearstained face from that hawkish stare of his.

"Are you certain that you do not wish to join us? I will be very disappointed if you do not. I had hoped to escort you into the hall."

Lily glanced up in surprise, a look of incredulous happiness crossing her face. "You did?" she whispered.

Valentine smiled. "Indeed I did. How could I possibly enjoy my dinner if I thought you were up here by yourself? Tristram told you that we leave Ravindzara tomorrow, did he not?" he asked, as if suddenly understanding the reason for her tears. "I would have this evening a celebration of our safe arrival in England, Lily," he said. Noticing the look of fear and uncertainty in her eyes, Valentine added softly, "Lily Christian. You needn't fear tomorrow, or indeed what the future may hold. I will never let any harm befall you. On my honor, Lily, I pledge to you now that I will always be there for you should you ever need me. You may be Geoffrey Christian's daughter, and for that alone I would befriend you, but I also happen to care about you very much. I will never let anyone hurt you. Will you always remember that?" he asked, and when she nodded, her eyes bright again with hope, he was relieved, not realizing that she took his words to mean something more. "Of course," he added with a twinkle in his eye, "you can hardly dine in your shift."

Crestfallen, Lily glanced over to where the yellow gown lay in a crumpled heap in front of the fireplace. "I cannot come."

Valentine frowned as he followed her gaze. Then without another word, he walked to the linen chest at the foot of the bed. "What about this gown? I rather liked this one better myself," he said as he shook out the creased skirt of the cream-colored, silk gown she had worn aboard the *Madrigal*. "Come, I'll give you a hand. You don't want young Tristram eating all of the pudding on the table, do you?" he said with a grin. "I want some myself."

Quickly wiping the tears from her cheeks with the back of her hand, Lily hurried to his side, afraid he might grow impatient and change his mind. Pulling the skirt and bodice over her head, Lily turned to face him, standing breathlessly before him as she felt his strong yet gentle hands fastening the gown together.

"Now, just a tuck here," he said, smoothing the stray curl back into place, "and you look as beautiful as any young lady of my acquaintance," he declared, satisfied with the results of his handiwork.

"M'lady," he said, holding out his arm to her.

Lily stared up into his face, her heart aching with her love for him as she placed her small hand on his arm and allowed him to escort her from the room. Proudly she walked beside him. With his promise warming her heart, she had no fear of what the morrow might hold. Valentine Whitelaw had promised he would always be there.

Past and to come seem best; things present worst.

SHAKESPEARE

Chapter Twelve

DOWNSTREAM of London Bridge, and in the shadow of the great tower that stood guardian over the city, the *Madrigal* rode at her moorings in the Pool of London, where the tall-masted, deep-hulled ships anchored against the tide.

Entering the estuary beneath the cannon of Tilbury Fort, the *Madrigal* had sailed up the River Thames along its meandering path through the marshlands and fens of Kent and East Anglia. Past fertile fields of ripening wheat and oats, green pastures of grazing sheep and cattle, dense woodlands, and peaceful hamlets of thatched-roofed, whitewashed cottages basking in the sun, the *Madrigal* had neared her journey's end.

Striking her topsails when sailing past the rambling brick and timber buildings of Greenwich, Elizabeth's river palace just below London, the captain of the *Madrigal* had honored his queen, whose gilded, royal barge was moored alongside the landing. Just upstream, the royal dockyards at Deptford had soon fallen astern, and cries and hails well-met had faded into the distance as the *Madrigal* held steady to her course.

As the *Madrigal* neared London, the open fields and commons had become enclosed by hedges and ditches, and farmsteads and cottages became more numerous as they spread outside the gates of the medieval wall surrounding the heart of the City. Church spires, turreted towers, and the steeply pitched roofs of three-storied, gabled houses rose in a jumble against the hazy skies over London. Smoke from thousands of chimneys mingled and thickened into blackness with the billowing smoke from the forges and furnaces in the workshops squeezed together along the narrow, cobbled lanes twisting through the City.

Open carts, drays, coaches, and pedestrians clogged the streets that wound past the shops and businesses of merchants and artisans. Every corner offered the loudest-voiced hustler a chance to hawk his wares, ever careful to avoid the open gutters of filth and the slop pails being emptied overhead. The great markets of the City—Billingsgate, Smithfield, Leadenhall, Cheapside, and Covent Garden—were crowded with tradesmen and shoppers haggling over the prices of all manner of goods from freshly caught salmon and oysters to bunches of sweet-scented rosemary and thyme.

The Thames, still the most popular and practical thoroughfare through London, was crowded with barges, boats, and wherries, all trafficking up and down the river and plying their trade. While the proud sailing ships continued to ride at anchor below London Bridge, with its two- and three-storied buildings tottering on either side of the narrow passage across the river, the watermen steered their boats through the arches underneath with well-practiced ease. Ferrying cargoes and passengers to the wharves, landings, and waterstairs that dotted the banks of the Thames from Traitor's Gate to Westminster, the coarse-talking oarsmen gave way to none but the royal swans that, in majestic splendor, sailed the river under the protection of the Crown.

Across London Bridge, on the south bank, was the borough of Southwark with its busy marketplace and yearly fair. Inns and taverns flourished. The dusty road wending into Southwark and becoming a footpath across the bridge was the only access into London from the south of England. Bridge Gate, crowned with spikes stuck with traitors' heads, allowed entrance to the City and stood as a warning to those who would challenge the Crown.

Westward along the north bank, the square tower of St. Paul's Church reached toward the heavens, leaving behind the City's steep, tortuous lanes abounding with alehouses, taverns, cookshops, and bawdy houses. Beyond Fleet Street, through Temple Bar, was the Strand, the thoroughfare that led to White-hall Palace and Westminster. On the heath rising to the north, past the open fields, pastures, and royal preserves, windmills with sails spinning in the wind were silhouetted against the sky.

Thomas Sandrick's London home, Tamesis House, sat in stately splendor on the south side of the Strand. Although a gate-house fronted the Strand, allowing access into the estate from the narrow road, most guests arriving at Tamesis House entered through the watergates on the river.

A broad flight of steps climbed from the river landing directly into the great hall. Tamesis House, a turreted and bay-windowed brick mansion of secluded, inner courtyards and spacious, richly furnished chambers, was surrounded by terraced gardens, orchards, and a wide expanse of green sloping down to the river's edge.

Three days earlier, the passengers aboard the recently arrived *Madrigal* had been set ashore at Tamesis House, where, at Thomas Sandrick's insistence, they were invited to stay during their visit to London. Thomas Sandrick's private barge met the ship and ferried his guests to the river mansion, where every comfort was to be afforded. Before the barge passed beneath the Bridge, however, it docked below the Tower to allow Sir Rodger Penmorley and his sister to disembark and continue to Sir Rodger's townhouse in Aldgate.

Lily stared out the window of the chamber she and Dulcie shared at Tamesis House. It overlooked the gardens and lawns sloping down to the glistening river beyond. Farther afield, she could see the church spires of London and hear the bells. They pealed in celebration of a birth or marriage, sounded a death knell for a loved one, or tolled in warning. She had awakened to the bells' ringing just after dawn, listened to the town crier throughout the day, then fallen asleep to the bells' sound at evening's end. Sleepless her first night in London, she had heard the faint sounds of the watchman announcing the striking of midnight, and she had drifted off to sleep hearing church bells and a ship's bell ringing in celebration as she dreamed of marrying Valentine Whitelaw.

Lily leaned outside the window, craning her neck toward the river, her eyes searching, but the landing was empty. She gazed back toward the Strand, her eyes following the brick path through the flower beds and hedges, but the gates remained closed against the traffic beyond.

Two days ago, Valentine Whitelaw had left London for Whiteswood, where he was to tell Sir William and Lady Elspeth that Basil would not be returning to England. Lily frowned, remembering Valentine's expression when he had spoken of sending word to Hartwell Barclay at Highcross Court. Valentine Whitelaw had no intention of informing their cousin in person of their arrival, and Lily wondered what manner of man this Hartwell Barclay was to inspire such a distasteful look on Valentine's face.

"Lily?"

Lily turned away from the window to see Dulcie standing in the doorway, her expression dejected.

"I don't like wearing these clothes, Lily," she complained, tripping over the long skirt as she took a tentative step into the room.

Lily had to agree that the clothes they now wore were far less comfortable than what they had worn on the island and even aboard the *Madrigal*. Indeed, she would hardly have recognized Dulcie. Dressed in a pale blue silk brocade gown with large puffed sleeves and a starched ruff about her neck, her black hair tightly braided beneath a lacy headdress, she looked like a fashionable but tiny woman with very mutinous dark eyes.

"Where is the cove? I can't go swimming anymore, Lily," Dulcie sniffed. "Lily, I can't keep my stocking up. It keeps rolling down around my ankle. I don't like these shoes, Lily. I can't wiggle my toes."

Lily smiled understandingly. "Come here and I'll see what I can do," she told her, sitting her down on the chest at the foot of the big bed they shared.

"I wish the captain would come back. I miss him," Dulcie said, watching curiously as Lily rolled the wrinkled stocking back into place beneath the garter she'd just adjusted.

"There," she said, smoothing Dulcie's underskirts back down.

"Are we going to live with him at Ravindzara, Lily?"

Lily pretended to straighten her own skirts. "I do not know," she answered, unwilling to speculate aloud about something she had been thinking of constantly since they'd arrived in England.

"Aunt Artemis says that I can stay with her if I want to. She said she wants me to stay with her forever. She said I was very precious to her and she wished I were her daughter," Dulcie confided to her startled sister, for Lily had heard nothing of such an arrangement.

"Aunt Artemis said that my father would want her to take care of his only daughter. She said I could have anything I wanted, Lily. And a pony, too," Dulcie said, her dark brown eyes glowing with excitement at the prospect.

"What about Tristram and me, Dulcie? Did she mention either one of us?" Lily asked in growing concern, for Valentine had yet to speak of their staying at Ravindzara rather than Highcross.

"No, just me."

"Where is Tristram?"

"Down by the river. He says he hears some of the strangest things from the boats going by," Dulcie told Lily.

"Tristram had better have clean feet and not come tracking into Thomas Sandrick's home with muddy shoes," Lily said worriedly, thinking of how she would be held responsible for his actions.

"*Bong! Bong! Bong!* Tristram had better have clean feet! *Praaack! Praaack!*" Cisco intoned as clearly as a church bell before his giggling laughter filled the room. "Muddy shoes! *Bong! Bong!* Past twelve o'clock, and rain! *Praaack!*"

"I do wish you would keep that bird quiet," Artemis Whitelaw requested as she entered the room. "And where is that monkey? If he gets into trouble again, well, I do not even wish to contemplate such a thing," Artemis said, glancing around to make certain the creature wasn't hiding in the corner. "I have been searching for you, Dulcie. Where did you go? I have been quite worried. You must not wander off again, dear."

"I wanted Lily to fix my stocking," Dulcie said, unconcerned, for she was accustomed to doing as she pleased and wandering wherever she wished on the island.

"There was no need to bother Lily. I would have assisted you. Why did you not come to me?"

"I wanted Lily to help me. Lily always knows what to do," Dulcie replied, unaware of the look of displeasure that crossed Artemis's face as Dulcie sang her sister's praises.

"In future, dear, please remember that I will see to your

needs," Artemis told Dulcie, her slender hands straightening Dulcie's headdress, then smoothing a crease in a pale blue sleeve before she bent low and pressed a kiss against Dulcie's rosy cheek. "So sweet," she murmured, her blue eyes gazing lovingly at her niece.

Temporarily forgotten, Lily watched Artemis Whitelaw fawning over Dulcie and wondered why Artemis did not like her. It was not that Artemis was not civil to her, Lily thought, but she never smiled as nicely either. Lily had tried to be pleasant. She had liked Valentine's sister and had wanted to talk to her about so many things she did not understand. Artemis, however, had never had time for either her or Tristram. She cared only for Dulcie, and Lily sensed that Artemis resented her and Tristram. She wondered if it was because Basil had not been their father, and they were not Whitelaws like Dulcie.

"Now, I want you looking your best, Dulcie, and I want you to act in a manner befitting a Whitelaw," Artemis said proudly.

"Why?"

"Because Valentine is down—"

"Valentine has come back!" Lily cried out, her green eyes glowing excitedly as she rushed to the door. Dulcie, not to be left behind, squirmed free of Artemis's arms and raced after Lily.

"Yes, but I would advise you, Mistress Christian, to present yourself in a more decorous manner. You are no longer running wild on that cursed island. You are a young woman of good family and yet you look and act little better than a street urchin. I fear you set a poor example for your brother and sister," Artemis berated the young girl who'd been halted in her steps by the harshly spoken words, and whose cheeks now flamed with embarrassment under the unexpected tongue lashing.

Artemis, seeing the distress evident on Lily's face, seemed to regret her outburst. Moving slowly across the room, she came to stand before Lily. Her words were still impatient, but more gently spoken as she said, "Here, let me wipe this smudge from your cheek."

Taking a slightly dampened and scented handkerchief from her sleeve, she carefully wiped the soft linen across Lily's flushed cheek, a slight smile curving her lips as she stared down into the young, earnest face tipped up to hers. "Please forgive me, I spoke unthinkingly. Now, you look quite lovely. Valentine is awaiting you in the hall. He requests your presence immediately.''

Lily hesitated. ''We will walk down with you,'' she offered, even though she longed to fly down the stairs to reach Valentine's side.

Artemis shook her head, bidding them leave. ''I have already greeted him. I will join you later,'' she explained, turning away and limping to the window as she heard them race down the corridor with little thought of so simple a pleasure.

Lily slowed her pace as she and Dulcie neared the entrance to the great hall of Tamesis House, for standing guard just outside the door was the Turk. Lily could feel his eyes watching her as she and Dulcie approached, and, unable to resist, she glanced upward to meet his gaze. He was always watching her, as if he still thought she was some kind of jinni. Valentine had once remarked that she was the only living being who seemed to make the Turk nervous.

Grinning widely, Duclie said hello to him as they passed, but Lily remained silent, defiantly returning his baleful stare and biting her tongue to keep from sticking it out at him. She did not think she liked the Turk, and she was beginning to suspect he didn't like her either.

''Hey! Wait up, Lily!'' Tristram called after them as he hurried to catch up to his sisters, Capabells scampering at his heels. ''Caught myself a salmon in the river, Lily!'' he announced, although unnecessarily, for he held proof of his claim before him; a huge fish. ''I showed it to the cook. She was surprised that I could catch anything. Wonder how she thinks we ate all of these years? She said we'd have it for dinner tonight,'' he told them proudly, pleased that he'd not lost his prowess as a provider since leaving the island. ''I wanted to show it to Valentine first, though. They told me he was back.''

As he passed by the still silent Turk, he pretended to pull a sword from his hip and flourish it in mock challenge before the man. ''Bet you could skewer a dozen of these with one sweep of that curved sword of yours, Mustafa,'' Tristram said admiringly. And Lily, watching curiously, would have sworn she saw a gleam of amusement enter the Turk's black eyes.

''I hope your shoes aren't muddied,'' Dulcie said, eyeing her brother up and down critically. ''You smell fishy, Tristram.''

"And you look fishy," Tristram retorted, blowing out his cheeks and opening and closing his mouth like a fish.

"I do not! Aunt Artemis says I'm as pretty as a princess!" Dulcie said, her shrill squeal of indignation having its usual effect on Cappie, who started squealing in response as he hopped into Lily's arms to avoid Tristram and Dulcie as they raced around Lily, Tristram trying to smack Dulcie with the salmon.

Still engaged in their boisterous antics when they entered the great hall, Lily was the first to see Valentine Whitelaw. She stopped just inside the door, suddenly unable to move her feet. Dulcie and Tristram, their voices rising louder as they began to lose their tempers after each had traded a pinch or two, bumped into Lily and were suddenly stilled as they followed her gaze.

Valentine Whitelaw was standing near the great hearth, but he was not alone. Around him was a group of people, and with the exception of Quinta Whitelaw and Thomas Sandrick, they were all strangers. And they were all staring in amazement at the three children who had entered the room in so rowdy a manner.

Lady Elspeth Davies stared in fascination at the three children standing just inside the doorway as if ready to bolt. Although Valentine had prepared her for an encounter with three rather precocious children, she had not been prepared for the high-spirited trio that stood before her now.

The tallest of the three she had met before. She recognized the dark red hair, so identical to Magdalena's, and pale green eyes, so wide and curious, that had been inherited from Geoffrey Christian. This young girl could be none other than their daughter, Lily. She was at that awkward age, not quite a woman, yet no longer a child. Dressed in an unattractive pink gown, her hair disheveled, she had yet to mature into the beautiful woman Elspeth knew Lily would one day become. But for now Lily Christian stood uncomfortably before them, unsure of herself as she fidgeted nervously. Elspeth thought sadly of the years that had changed the laughing child she remembered so well into this suspicious young girl.

The boy holding the fish before him like a shield she had never met before. He had also inherited Magdalena's unusual hair color, but the eyes . . . yes, they were like his Spanish mother's. Valentine had told them that the boy, called Tristram, was Geoffrey's son, and, although he bore no physical resemblance to Geoffrey Christian, she had no reason to doubt the claim.

Elspeth felt her heart miss a beat when, at last, she allowed herself to look at the youngest of the children. Dulcie Rosalinda. Elspeth knew she had tears in her eyes. This was Basil's daughter, this beautiful little girl with his black hair and eyes. Elspeth glanced toward her son, Basil's son, and could see the similarity between brother and sister.

Simon had been told the truth. His dark eyes had traveled quickly over the three. He had stared in curiosity at the girl who was about his own age and who was holding a chattering monkey in her arms. He had looked on in admiration as he'd taken the measure of the boy who'd caught the big salmon, but an unfathomable expression had entered his eyes when he'd stared at the little girl with hair and eyes of the same blackness as his own.

Sir William Davies stood off to the side, his son and daughter each holding one of his hands as they hid behind him and shyly peeked out at the three strange children. What he was feeling he kept to himself, for although saddened by the situation, he must have felt a certain amount of relief when told that Basil would not be returning to England.

"Are you satisfied, Valentine?" Quinta Whitelaw demanded with a laugh. "I told you the children would fare well enough while you were away. You have worried needlessly. As you can see, they have lost none of their exuberance. I, however, cannot claim to have been so fortunate, for I have lost my best hat to that monkey. I followed my hat's trail, piece by piece, throughout the house," Quinta said. "Come, my dears, and let me properly introduce you. I am afraid your entrance has confirmed the worst."

"I fear I shall be held accountable for all misfortune that befalls good folk in future. From hens not laying to sour milk, all mischief will be blamed on my small castaways if I set them loose in London," Valentine said, holding out his arms as Dulcie raced into them.

Lifting her high, he kissed her, laughing with pleasure as she hugged him tight, whispering in his ear that she loved him. Lily remained where she was, gazing on enviously.

"Captain, look what I caught!" Tristram said, holding out

his aromatic catch and waving it wildly, which caused Thomas
Sandrick to hold a scented handkerchief to his nose.

"A splendid catch, Tristram."

"I caught it for our dinner tonight," Tristram said, swinging
the salmon closer to Thomas Sandrick as he graciously offered it
to his green-hued host.

"That is very generous of you, Tristram. Why don't I have it
taken to the kitchens, where it can be prepared," Thomas Sandrick said with a sickly grin as he took a step back. But before he
could summon a footman, his attention was caught by a movement beyond the windows overlooking the river and he excused
himself.

"Lily," Valentine said, holding out his hand to draw her
near his side, "this is Lady Elspeth."

"Lady Elspeth," Lily replied, curtsying respectfully before
her.

Lady Elspeth smiled down at Lily. "I do not imagine that you
remember me at all, but I have very fond memories of you, and
of your mother and father. You and your mother often stayed at
Whiteswood when your father was away on one of his voyages.
Valentine has told me all about you and what your life was like
on the island. I think Basil must have loved you and Tristram,
and Dulcie, very much," Lady Elspeth told her, thinking of the
many stories Valentine had related to her about the children.

"We loved him very much, my lady."

"Yes, I know, my child," Elspeth said, the cross the children
had made for Basil, which Valentine had described for her in
such detail, still vivid in her mind. "Later, will you share with
me some of your memories of Basil, and your mother, and what
your days were like on the island?" Elspeth asked softly, exchanging a glance with Sir William, knowing he would understand her request.

Basil was dead. Although they both had believed that to be
true for the past seven years, the last few months, since learning
that Basil might still be alive, had been the most difficult of Elspeth's life. Whether he had been found alive or indeed had been
dead these many years, Basil had been there between them at
Whiteswood. Now that the truth was known, and she was secure in her love for William, Elspeth wanted to hear about Basil.
She believed she could accept the love he must have felt for Mag-

dalena. When Valentine had told her about Basil's life on the island, she had at first felt anger and a jealousy of Magdalena. She had even felt betrayed. But as she had listened to the story unfolding, she had come to understand how Magdalena and Basil would have sought comfort from each other, much the same way she had sought comfort from William. And she knew how that comfort would have gradually become love. Because she had loved Basil, she was not resentful that he might have found happiness on that island.

Lily nodded her acquiescence to Lady Elspeth's request, but the smile that had started to curve her lips faded when she saw Sir Rodger and Honoria Penmorley, accompanied by several people, entering the hall from the river steps.

Honoria, looking lovelier and haughtier than ever, and apparently well recovered from her seasickness, was being escorted by a gentleman who could not claim to be much taller than she, and whose grinning visage and casual utterances seemed to be causing her more irritation than amusement. For as soon as was politely possible, she removed herself from his proximity with a fastidious and elegant sweeping aside of her skirts and turned her attention to Thomas Sandrick, who had hurried to welcome his guests to Tamesis House and was now standing in conversation with Sir Rodger.

George Hargraves bowed deeply to Honoria Penmorley's retreating, stiff-backed figure, a look of mock despair on his face until he spied Valentine Whitelaw. With his usual irreverent expression back in place, he came sauntering over.

'' 'Sdeath, if it isn't Cap'n Rogue back from his travels,'' he declared. "And about time, too. Ever since Valchamps was knighted he has been lording it over everybody at court. Now that another of Elizabeth's fair-haired ones has returned, I look forward to seeing him cut down to my size,'' George stated as he gazed at his friend from head to toe, a suffering look entering his eye as he took Valentine's height. "Pity Elizabeth's hand didn't slip when she was knighting Valchamps,'' George speculated. "Have you heard about it?''

"I heard.''

"Thought you'd heard wrong, too, I'll wager,'' George said with a disbelieving shake of his head, still confounded by the affair. "A fool's luck, I say. If Valchamps hadn't happened to have been out riding with Her Majesty that day, and managed to out-maneuver me so he could be beside her, then *I* might be 'Sir' George Hargraves right now instead of just plain ol' George Hargraves who lost his seat and landed in the mud when Her Majesty's horse bolted. Valchamps went riding to the rescue and kept Elizabeth's horse from racing under the trees. Elizabeth could have been killed, Valentine," George said, still upset by the incident. "Missed my chance to play the hero," he grumbled, still humiliated by his unheroic participation in the affair.

"But Valchamps did not."

"Indeed he didn't. Even managed to hurt himself while trying to protect her. So grateful was Her Majesty, that she knighted him for risking his life for her," George said in exasperation. Becoming aware of the young girl Valentine still held in his arms, he added in a different tone of voice, "I've heard about your voyage, and I am sincerely sorry, Valentine."

"I am too, George," Valentine said as he set Dulcie down. "This is Basil's daughter, Dulcie."

"Hello, Dulcie. You certainly are the pretty one, and just about my size," George said, unable to resist poking fun at himself as he made one of his comical faces.

"Hello, George. This is Cappie, and he can make funny faces, too. Of course, he is a monkey," Dulcie responded to George's delighted amazement.

"Well, at least she did not say 'he is a monkey, too,' " George said with a loud guffaw.

"I don't believe you've met Lily Christian?"

"Lily, the fairest flower to find," George complimented Lily, for a brief moment no longer playing the court jester, but his seriousness only lasted an instant.

Suddenly George Hargraves was frowning, his nostrils flaring slightly as he glanced around. "Hmm, for a moment there I thought Raymond Valchamps must be nearby, but I perceive I was mistaken. 'Tis a freshly caught salmon the young man is holding so close beneath my sleeve," he said, eyeing a giggling Tristram with an amused gleam in his eye.

"Faith, Valentine," George said loud enough for his approaching host to overhear, "if I'd known Thomas expected us to provide our own fare, I'd have bagged a couple of pheasant on my way here. Or at least I would have stopped by Billingsgate and bought a barrel of oysters.''

Thomas Sandrick frowned. Then catching another whiff of Tristram's salmon, he beckoned to a footman, who promptly relieved Tristram of his catch. But Tristram hardly noticed. He was too busy watching George Hargraves, who was now frantically checking his doublet for stray oysters, much to the delight of the children now gathered around him.

"This has just arrived for you, Valentine," Thomas said, gesturing for the footman standing at his side to present the silver salver he carried, a sealed piece of parchment in the center.

Curious, Valentine accepted it. A smile of enlightenment curved his lips as he recognized the seal and opened the letter. " 'Twould seem as if I have received a royal summons. The queen has returned to Westminster and is now in residence at Whitehall. She requests my presence, as well as the children's, at court on the morrow. We are to have a private audience with her in the privy chamber," he remarked.

"Lily, we're going to meet the queen!" Tristram exclaimed in awe.

"Just like in the fable," Dulcie squealed, clapping her hands together excitedly. "Do you think the wild white horses will be there, too?"

"Wild white horses in court?" George repeated, momentarily dumbfounded by the prospect. "Now, that is something I would like to see," he murmured, his shoulders beginning to shake with mirth as he imagined the Great Hall crowded elbow to elbow with pompous courtiers thrown into a pudder as a herd of horses raced through.

"I believe Elizabeth's coach is pulled by six very beautiful horses," Valentine confirmed, ignoring George and whatever devilment he was about.

"Does she have a chariot made of bright red coral?" Dulcie demanded, her dark eyes round with wonder. "And does she have a starfish saddle and reins made of seaweed?"

George Hargraves's lips were twitching as he looked at Valentine Whitelaw, eagerly awaiting that gentleman's reply.

"Her Majesty rides in a chariot of gold, and her white horse's saddle and reins are woven with gold and jewels," Valentine replied, exaggerating slightly, but not disappointing his young audience. Especially Dulcie, who gave Tristram a smug, I-told-you-so look for ever having doubted the fable.

Then another, although far less pleasing, thought seemed to occur to her and she frowned. "The witch! The witch, Lily!" she whispered, remembering the rest of the fable. Glancing around fearfully, she squeezed between Lily and Valentine, hiding her face against Lily's gown. And only Lily and Tristram knew she was referring to the witch of their fable and not a real person.

George, however, misunderstanding her meaning, glanced around, his eyes widening as he recognized the woman entering the hall. "Good Lord! However did she guess?" he exclaimed, glancing back at the little girl. "What a rare child indeed!" he said in appreciation of the child's innocent remark—a remark he would have given dearly to have made, but could not because of gentlemanly restraint, and Valentine Whitelaw standing within earshot. But George's laughter was not so constrained as he watched Cordelia Howard make her grand entrance, his eyes narrowing slightly as he noticed the gentleman strutting like a peacock by her side.

Enraptured, Lily Christian stared at the breathtaking vision of the woman who had just entered the hall. Dressed in a gown of deepest rose with a gold-embroidered underskirt, Cordelia Howard was the most beautiful woman Lily had ever seen. Her beauty was all that a young and impressionable girl would wish to possess as her own; black curls, capped by a rose-colored, pearl-encrusted hat with a gold-dusted plume, framed her delicate, creamy-complexioned face; black amber eyes, fringed with thick lashes, sparkled with every emotion that crossed her flawless features; rose-tinted lips, curving provocatively with each smile or pout, were beautifully proportioned above a dimpled chin; and the close-fitting gown she wore accentuated the smallness of her waist and the gentle, feminine curves of breast and hip.

Cordelia Howard greeted her host, then allowed her gaze to encompass the assembled guests. A slight nod of acknowledgment was greeting enough for Quinta, Honoria, and Elspeth, but when Cordelia recognized their male companions, her dark eyes lingered invitingly before sliding away, leaving each man feeling that he'd been singled out as someone special.

It was only then, when Lily became aware of the burning in-

tensity of that gaze, that she realized the woman was now staring directly at Valentine Whitelaw. Looking up into his face, Lily
felt her heart miss a beat when she saw the expression on Valentine's face as he succeeded in holding the woman's eyes with
his. And as Lily watched, the slow smile she had come to treasure began to curve his lips, but this time the smile was not for
her.

Lily continued to stand beside Valentine as the woman and
her escort approached. She had not needed the introduction that
followed to know that this woman must be Cordelia Howard,
the woman Sir Rodger and Honoria Penmorley had mentioned
when at Ravindzara. Cordelia Howard was the woman Honoria
Penmorley feared. Lily, even in her innocence, could understand the reason behind Honoria's fear of her rival for the affections of Valentine Whitelaw. Although Honoria Penmorley was
as beautiful a woman as Cordelia Howard, when in the same
room with the other woman Honoria's perfect beauty remained
cold and lifeless. Cordelia Howard was a seductress. Her every
glance and gesture was captivating. She was a fascinating
woman who possessed a vivacity that drew people irresistibly to
her.

Even Lily was not immune to Cordelia Howard's allure as
she curtsied respectfully before her when introduced. But Cordelia Howard had given her little more than a cursory glance before turning her dark eyes on Valentine Whitelaw. Lily wished
she could have said the same about the man who had accompanied Cordelia Howard to Tamesis House.

Raymond Valchamps. Lily shivered, thinking of his strangely
colored eyes. It had been like awakening from a nightmare only
to discover that it was real. She had looked up into his face, a
face that had haunted her in dreams for years, and found herself
staring into the eyes that had terrified her for as long as she
could remember. As she stood there staring openmouthed at
Raymond Valchamps, all of the old terrors had returned. She remembered the day her grandmother had died. She heard the
sound of cannon fire and saw the blood staining the deck of her
father's ship. Then she saw the hooded priest and the heavy
silver cross that gleamed in the sun, and standing next to him
was the man with the strangely colored eyes. . . .

If it hadn't been for Dulcie, Lily thought she might have

screamed. At first, she had thought it was her own scream that had pierced the hall. Then, in the silence that had followed, she had heard muffled crying and felt Dulcie shaking against her.

"Good Lord!" Cordelia Howard exclaimed, beginning to laugh. "Those *beaux yeux* of yours, Raymond, have scared the child half to death. Apparently she has never seen anyone with one blue eye and one brown. My dear, do not be too dejected. Just wait until she is older, then she may find them quite attractive, certainly exciting," Cordelia said, for poor Raymond looked quite pale, stunned, in fact, by the child's frightened reaction when seeing him.

There was an embarrassed titter, quickly muffled from someone, then, after several softly spoken comments, the voices resumed their usual conversational intonations as everyone seemed to resume talking at once.

Artemis, who had finally joined the group in the hall, had rushed over when Dulcie had become hysterical, and, prying her loose from Lily's side, had taken her in her arms, trying to quiet her fears.

"I think there has been too much excitement for her. The children are not accustomed to so much noise and so many people around them," Artemis explained, dabbing at Dulcie's tears.

"Mistake, that. Can't mollycoddle the young," a gray-haired gentleman remarked. "Never did my own. Had my boy here in London as a page when hardly out of swaddling."

"I'm sure you were most wise, Sir Charles," Elspeth said kindly but dismissingly as she smiled at the old busybody. "I was just about to take Betsy and Wilfred upstairs for their nap. Why don't you bring Dulcie along," Elspeth suggested to Artemis as she came forward with her two children.

"Why don't I help you take her upstairs," Valentine offered, thinking the child looked ill. He glanced over at Lily and was surprised to see how pale she looked. "Lily? Are you well?" he asked in concern.

Almost without volition, Lily glanced toward Raymond Valchamps, her eyes widening slightly as she found him staring at her. Lily continued to meet his gaze, unable to look away. Embarrassed, she felt the heat rising in her cheeks.

"Lily?" Valentine questioned again.

Lily finally pulled her eyes away and as she looked into Valentine's warm, turquoise gaze, she felt her fears beginning to disappear. "I'll help Artemis get Dulcie settled," she offered, welcoming an excuse to leave the hall. She needed time to think. Why did Raymond Valchamps seem so familiar to her? Where had she seen him before?

"That will not be necessary, Lily," Artemis responded quickly as she lifted Dulcie in her arms. "I can take care of her. You might as well remain down here. You will only be in the way upstairs. If I am to calm Dulcie, I do not need that monkey racing around the room."

Lily continued to stand where she was, watching Artemis and Elspeth as they disappeared from the hall with the youngest children.

"Are you certain you wish to stay here, Lily?" Valentine asked in concern.

"Yes, I am fine, thank you," Lily said huskily, her arms tightening around Capabells.

"Well, I, for one, am befuddled," George Hargraves said with a perplexed look. "The child is raised in the wilds, and heaven only knows what kinds of beasts she has seen in the New World, and yet," he paused, casting a curious glance at Raymond Valchamps, "she is sent into terror at the sight of 'Sir' Raymond Valchamps. Hmm, now I think 'pon it, could be she had every reason to be frightened," he murmured as he brushed past the tight-lipped gentleman who was still staring at Lily Christian.

"Come along, Sir Charles, I'll lighten your purse in a game of chance. Dice? Cards?" George Hargraves suggested helpfully as he came abreast of the older gentleman and eyed him as if about to pick his pocket.

" 'Tis a fine afternoon," Sir Charles returned meaningfully. "The bowling green?"

"Let us see how accurate your aim is, young fellow. What say you to a shilling a—" Sir Charles was offering a worried-looking George Hargraves as he guided the younger man toward the door, his hand firmly beneath George's elbow and not about to let him loose.

Lily started to edge closer to Valentine, but Cordelia Howard moved between them. Grasping his arm, she led him toward his host, who was now engaged in conversation with the lovely young woman with pale blond hair who had entered the hall with Cordelia Howard and Raymond Valchamps.

Simon Whitelaw, who'd been avidly watching everything, especially Lily and her brother and sister, came hurrying over to her side now that she and Tristram stood alone. "Are you hungry?" he asked shyly.

Tristram's eyes brightened. "I am!"

Simon Whitelaw grinned. "That was a great salmon you caught. I caught a river bass almost as big once. Bet you've caught a lot of fish," he said, and even though the boy was younger than he was, Simon was willing to give him the respect he merited for having been raised on an island in the West Indies, and for having sailed with his uncle aboard the *Madrigal*.

Tristram puffed out his chest importantly, but that caused his stomach to start growling, and he eyed this Simon Whitelaw in speculation, curious if he was as good as his word. "Reckon I could tell you a few stories, but it might help if we had something to eat first," he bargained.

Simon Whitelaw nodded, his dark eyes glowing with excitement. He could hardly wait to hear about the island. "Come on. If I'm not mistaken, they'll be dishing up toffee pudding for the little ones to get them to go to sleep. We might be able to get ourselves some. Maybe even an apple tart or two," Simon Whitelaw enticed his young friend, willing to bribe the boy with anything in order to hear some of the more exciting stories of adventure about his father and the island. "I can even find something for the monkey. What do they eat anyway?" he asked as he eyed Lily and the fuzzy-faced creature peering over her shoulder with beady-looking eyes.

"Lily? Are you going to come with us?" Tristram asked, thinking she was awfully quiet.

Nervously, Lily glanced around, searching for Raymond Valchamps. Almost hypnotically, her eyes found his. He had joined the group in the center of the hall, but his eyes still watched her. Swallowing the fear that was beginning to spread through her, Lily looked away, desperate to escape him.

"Yes, I'll come with you," she said, her quick steps leading the way as the three left the hall.

"Lily?" Tristram said softly as they now hurried to follow Simon's long-legged gait down the corridor toward the kitchens.

"I know why Dulcie got so upset. It wasn't just because she hadn't ever seen anyone with one blue eye and one brown eye before. That lady was wrong. Don't you remember? It was the witch who scared her. The witch who's going to hurt the queen has one blue eye and one brown eye," Tristram reminded her.

Lily grasped Tristram's arm, surprising him by the coldness of her hand. "I know, Tristram. But listen, I don't think we should tell anybody about that," she warned him, not quite understanding the reason for caution herself, but she knew she was right not to say anything.

"Why?"

Lily frowned. " 'Tis a secret, that's why," she suddenly said. "Basil didn't want us to say anything about our cave, or the journal. Remember?"

"Yes, but the witch doesn't have anything to do with that, Lily," Tristram said in confusion.

"I don't know. But maybe it does, Tristram. That was a special story Basil told us. He said it was our secret. I remember now, Tristram, and we mustn't say anything about the witch. Besides, if *he* is the witch, then he could hurt us. He might steal Dulcie," Lily said, more loudly this time as she started even to scare herself with such thoughts.

"The witch could put a spell on her, Lily!" Tristram said, his voice rising shrilly.

"A witch?" Simon Whitelaw repeated curiously as he caught the one word. Glancing over his shoulder at the two who were whispering secrets, he said, "I know all about them. You want to be careful when around them. You don't want even to meet one, or make one mad. They can put the evil eye on you."

Lily and Tristram exchanged knowing glances.

"Do not let Sir Raymond Valchamps frighten you because he looks like a witch with those eyes. Some people might think that he really is a witch, but he is not. I can understand how little Dulcie, *my* sister, was scared," Simon told them, surprising both Lily and Tristram by his use of the word sister when talking of *their* sister, Dulcie. Seeing their shocked expressions, he said almost defensively. "Well, she is my sister. Basil was my father. He was Dulcie's father, too. Your mother was her mother. She is, therefore, *our* sister," he explained, suddenly reminding both

Lily and Tristram of Basil trying to explain some finer point to them and they started to giggle.

Simon frowned, halting in his tracks. He did not like being laughed at and was about to say as much when Lily said, "He's just like Basil, isn't he, Tristram?"

"Just like Basil," Tristram declared, a wide grin of pleasure on his face, for he was beginning to like Simon Whitelaw now that he reminded him of Basil.

"I am?" Simon said.

"Exactly," Lily told him honestly, knowing in that instant that he would become her friend.

"Well," he said awkwardly, feeling ten feet tall all of a sudden, "I am pleased to hear that. Now, what was I saying?"

"The witch. You were telling us about witches," Tristram urged him, despite Lily's warning glance, for although they might be related, it was still their secret.

"Oh? Oh, Sir Raymond Valchamps. Yes, even though he does have those odd eyes, gives me the shivers, he's not a witch. He's a knight. He even saved Elizabeth's life," Simon informed them, pleased to see that he had managed to impress the two, for they had looked at each other in amazement.

"There, you see, Lily. He's not the witch," Tristram whispered thankfully, for he had not looked forward to confronting the man, which he suspected Lily might think their honor would demand.

"Then he would never hurt the queen?" Lily asked, for although she was relieved to hear Simon's reassurances, her dreams had been with her for too long to be completely forgotten now.

"Hurt Elizabeth?" Simon asked incredulously. "Never. Sir Raymond Valchamps is one of her favorites," he said, increasing his pace as he appreciatively sniffed the aromatic smells drifting down the corridor.

But Lily's steps continued to drag behind. She could not forget the sound of Basil's voice when telling them the fable about the wild white horses and the witch with one blue eye and one brown, and how important it was for them to return to England and save the queen. But there was something more that was bothering Lily. She knew with a certainty that she had met Raymond Valchamps before. She had not recognized him merely from the fable or her dreams. Basil had never fully described the witch in the fable, except for the eyes. And the spectral figure in her dreams had always remained slightly blurred, except for the eyes. But she had known Raymond Valchamps. She had seen not only those eyes before, but his face and silvery hair. She could not remember where, but the meeting had left an impression in her mind that she would never forget.

Simon had not misled them, and with Tristram's stomach no longer protesting, they followed Simon into the gardens. Lily kept glancing back over her shoulder as they left the house, but there was no one there, watching. Still engrossed in her thoughts, Lily accompanied Simon and Tristram to the river's edge. But soon she tired of watching the boats sailing up and down the river, and, after her cheeks had flushed with embarrassment for the third time because of some ribald remark from an appreciative lad catching sight of her, she left Tristram and Simon to amuse themselves as best they could.

Lily had more important things on her mind than worrying about whether Tristram or Simon could skip his stone the farthest across the river. When she saw the tall, lean figure leaving the house and walking toward the gardens, she made up her mind.

She could not forget Raymond Valchamps. If it had been just a fable Basil had told to amuse them, or if her nightmares were unfounded, no more than childish fears, why did Raymond Valchamps watch her? Valentine would know, Lily had decided. She did not think that Basil would have objected to her sharing their secret with Valentine. She had to tell someone. And the only person besides Tristram and Dulcie she could trust was Valentine Whitelaw.

Lily's steps quickened as she hurried along the brick path through the gardens. The heady fragrance of lilies and roses filled the warm afternoon air as she ran past neatly clipped yew hedges and box-edged gardens resplendent with spring flowers. Water bubbling from a stone fountain muffled her steps as she approached the arbored entrance to one of the small gardens enclosed within brick walls.

It was there that Lily found Valentine Whitelaw.

He was sitting on a carved seat in the cool shade of the wall, and wrapped in his embrace was Cordelia Howard. As Lily watched, Valentine's lips touched Cordelia's. His hands caressed her as he pulled her closer against his body.

"I have missed you, my love," he murmured against her lips, unable to resist tasting them again as his mouth found hers in a long kiss.

"And I have missed you," Cordelia said breathlessly, her fingers sliding through his hair as she pulled his head down to hers again, not satisfied as she kissed him, her lips clinging to his, and she wished they had more privacy than the garden allowed.

Feeling his hand moving over her breast, she said, "I do not think you have missed me that much, or you would not persist in leaving England every few months on this adventuring of yours. I get lonely, and the winters are cold when you are away, Valentine. Never forget that I am a woman who needs constant companionship," she warned him, purposely allowing her mouth to part from his.

Valentine smiled. "I am with you now, and I will not be returning to sea for some time," he told her, his mouth stealing her breath away as he kissed her deeply.

"I suppose I should be thankful for at least these few moments of your time," Cordelia said impatiently, for she longed to have him in her bed again.

"What do you mean?"

"With that foolish child clinging to you all of the time, I scarcely could catch your eye all day. She is like a puppy yapping at your heels. Faith, but I expect to see her appear any moment. However did you manage to lose her?" Cordelia said, laughing.

"Lily?" Valentine asked in surprise.

"If that is the redheaded one's name, then yes, Lily."

Valentine laughed. "Don't tell me you are jealous of that child?"

"That child, my dear, is fast becoming a woman. Another few years and you will not even recognize her, except perhaps for that unfortunate red hair. And then, my roguish one, you had better keep on your guard, or you may find yourself married to the chit," Cordelia warned with an unpleasant glint in her eye.

"Don't be ridiculous, Delia."

"If I remember correctly, you said you had a penchant for red hair," she reminded him, pleased to see him frowning over her words. "I suppose, however, that only a queen could manage to receive compliments with hair that color," she added cattily.

"Lily is just a child. No different than Dulcie."

"I seriously doubt that she looks upon you as she would a brother or father," Cordelia said, thinking of the stable hand who had become her first lover when she had not been much older than this young girl.

Valentine stared at Cordelia as if she were mad. "Lily was the daughter of my very good friend. I could never think of her in the manner in which you seem to think. I feel responsible for Lily's welfare, that is all. I could never fall in love with her. I am very fond of Lily, but she is a child, and always will be in my eyes," he said again, this time with a mocking laugh. "Lily Christian means nothing to me beyond being the daughter of a friend of mine," Valentine said more harshly than perhaps he intended, but he was determined to end Cordelia's speculations concerning Lily Christian.

Hearing his laughter, which was joined by Cordelia Howard's, Lily turned away and ran. Tears blinding her, she did not see the figure that stepped out of the shadow of the hedge and grabbed hold of her as she ran.

Halted abruptly, Lily stared into Raymond Valchamps's narrowed gaze.

"You are certainly in a hurry. Why? Not spying on people, are you?" he asked, his fingers tightening punishingly around her upper arms. "You seem to make a habit of being where you have no business being."

Lily felt her breath coming raggedly. "Let me go!"

"Do I frighten you, little one?"

Lily continued to stare into his eyes, mesmerized by them.

"I won't hurt you. Why don't you come with me now? We can walk along the river. It is very peaceful down there where the current runs strongest," he said, smiling down into her wide eyes.

"N-no, I must go."

"No one is waiting for you, Lily Christian. No one cares where you go. Come with me. Come with me, Lily. My Lily. I've waited for you for so long," he said softly, and Lily felt her feet starting to move despite her resolution to stay rooted to the ground. Closing her eyes, unable to resist the soft sound of his voice, she moved through the garden.

Suddenly Lily could hear the busy sounds of bees buzzing in the flowers. She opened her eyes, startled to find herself standing alone—except for the Turk.

He was standing before her, blocking the path by which Raymond Valchamps would have led her down to the riverbank. Lily continued to stand where she was, her eyes held by those dark eyes that she had once thought so cruel and unfriendly, and she wondered how she could ever have been so mistaken.

The expression in the Turk's eyes was warm and understanding. He no longer seemed the fierce adversary she had been so mistrustful of, especially when he held out his hand, stepping aside to allow her to pass by in safety. Lily held his gaze as she walked by him. He nodded slightly, then Lily heard him following just behind until she had reached the hall. Turning around as she entered, she tried to force her lips to smile, but the Turk had already disappeared back into the gardens.

Raymond Valchamps paced back and forth before the balustrade of the terrace. So close. He could have ended right then any possible threat the girl might have been, except for that damned servant of Valentine Whitelaw's. He had been alone with the girl in the garden. It would have been so easy to have led her down to the river. She had been scared to death of him. He had felt her fear, and it had given him a strange sense of power. It had excited him, knowing that he could have killed her in that instant. He would have thrown her into the river, then stood there and watched her drown.

Raymond Valchamps smiled. Then his smile faded as he thought of that damned turbaned fellow's interference. He hadn't liked the look the heathen had given him. As if the man had known what he was about to do. But he couldn't have, Raymond Valchamps reassured himself. When he had become aware of the man standing there watching, he had quickly pretended to say something to the girl, as if he'd been guiding her back to the house. But next time, next time there would be no escape for her.

And there would be no escape for Elizabeth the next time either, he thought, his smile returning. Strange, that his attempt to murder Elizabeth should result in his being knighted for saving her. It had been his sword tip that had struck Elizabeth's horse. He had kept his horse racing wildly with hers, but when he had seen her personal guard almost about to catch up to them, he had turned his failure into triumph. Instead of being arrested for her attempted murder, he had been praised as a hero.

Raymond Valchamps's smile widened. Even if the girl did remember him, who would believe her word against his? He was a knight of the realm. He had saved Elizabeth's life. He was a hero. She was just a child, with a child's vivid imagination. No one would believe her. But, he would not rest easy until he was certain that she never spoke of having seen him in Santo Domingo.

Raymond Valchamps heard footsteps drawing close, and recognizing his friend, he carefully folded his hands. He would keep his own counsel concerning the girl. His noble friend would most likely disapprove of his actions, as he had of his attempt on Elizabeth's life. His friend was not one for shedding blood, he remembered, smiling in greeting as the man approached. His plans for Lily Christian would remain his secret.

The remainder of the day that had started out so promisingly with the return of Valentine Whitelaw to Tamesis House seemed to worsen as the hours passed. Lily never felt free of Raymond Valchamps's eyes. They continually followed her. She could feel them burning into her back when she turned away, trying not to meet that penetrating stare, but it was impossible. Again and again, she was drawn to them.

And to add to her suffering, Lily could not seek Valentine's comforting words or touch. Even had she wished, she would never have been able to get close to him. Cordelia Howard, or Honoria Penmorley, whenever she could manage it, was always there before her. Once or twice, she had caught Valentine's eyes, and he had smiled, but she had turned away, her heart breaking as she remembered his cruel words. She was just the daughter of his friend. He could never love her. He could never love Lily Christian. Then, after looking away, her eyes would encounter Raymond Valchamps's smiling face.

He had always been there, watching and listening. It had become unbearable toward the end, and Lily had nearly fainted when she had turned to find him standing beside her. The smile that flickered across his handsome face would have seemed friendly to anyone watching, but to Lily it was threatening and evil and she nearly fell into Simon's arms when he came to stand beside her, his cheerful face reminding her more than ever of her beloved Basil. And as she turned to face him, her eyes glowing with gratitude, Simon Whitelaw felt the first stirrings of love in his heart, and he contrived to stay by her side for the rest of the evening that had developed into something extraordinary for him.

Lily, however, was anxious for the evening to come to an end. And she had not lingered when the guests had at last begun to take their leave of their gracious host. With unseemly haste, or so it had seemed to a dejected Simon, she had hurried from the hall. Lily had hesitated at the top of the wide flight of stairs and glanced down, but what she had seen was enough to send her scurrying along the corridor to her chamber without another backward glance. Standing at the foot of the stairs and watching her had been Raymond Valchamps.

Safe at last in the seclusion of her bedchamber, Lily had wasted no time in changing into her nightgown and climbing into the big bed where Dulcie already lay sound asleep. Huddling beneath the coverlet, Lily began to shake, her teeth chattering. She closed her eyes to banish the darkness of the chamber that no longer seemed to offer her refuge. But that was even worse, for Raymond Valchamps's smiling face floated before her, then the mocking eyes of Cordelia Howard, and lastly, ringing in her ears, the laughter of Valentine Whitelaw.

Pulling the covers over her head, Lily sank down as low as she could against the feather mattress and prayed for morning to come, when her fears would fade with the darkness.

But the room was still dark when Lily awoke, her heart pounding. Next to her Dulcie had awakened and was sitting up, her cries filling the silent room.

Lily reached over and touched Dulcie, trying to comfort her.

"He's in here, Lily! The witch. He's coming after us. I saw him. He wants to kill us!" she cried, burying her tearstained face against Lily's shoulder.

"Prrraaack! Prrraaack! Witch! Witch!" Cisco cried out, his sobs echoing Dulcie's eerily.

"Hush!" Lily said into the darkness, rocking Dulcie back and forth.

"Hush! Hush! Past twelve of the clock and blacker'n hell," Cisco mimicked in a whispering voice before starting to giggle.

Lily heard footsteps beyond the closed door and hugged Dulcie closer, her soft, whispering voice soothing Dulcie's fears as she sniffed a couple of times, her tears beginning to dry.

"Lily?"

"Yes?"

"Promise me you won't ever, ever leave me. Promise?" Dulcie begged.

"Of course I promise. I'd never leave you, Dulcie."

"We're always going to be together, aren't we, Lily?" Dulcie asked, her small arms tightening around Lily's waist.

"Of course we are. No one will ever separate us. I promise," Lily told her, silently vowing that she would keep that promise.

"You won't let Artemis keep me away from you and Tristram and Cisco and Cappie?" she demanded.

"No, I won't."

"I like Artemis, Lily. But I like you better," Dulcie confided. "I wish we could go back to the island. I don't like England, Lily. Don't you wish we could go home?"

Home? Lily thought. "Yes, I wish we could go home. I wish we were on our island again. Just you, Tristram, and me, and Mother and Basil."

"And Cappie and Cisco?"

"Yes," Lily agreed dreamily.

"I guess Choco would be there too?"

"Most likely."

"Well, that is all right. As long as Choco doesn't come too close, I don't really hate him. The witch wouldn't be able to find us there, Lily. We would be safe," Dulcie murmured sleepily.

"Don't worry about the witch, Dulcie. I won't let him hurt you."

"Promise?" Dulcie said, yawning. "And you won't let him take me away from you and Tristram. We will always, always be together?"

"I promise you, Dulcie. We are a family. I promised Basil I would always look after you and Tristram. I promised, Dulcie. I told him I'd never let anyone hurt you, and I won't. Highcross is our home, Dulcie. It is where we belong, not Ravindzara," Lily said, her eyes closing as she leaned back against the pillows, Dulcie sleeping peacefully in her arms.

Artemis Whitelaw backed slowly out of the doorway, closing the door softly.

Turning away, she glanced up, gasping in surprise as she saw a shadow move beside her. "Oh, 'tis you."

Valentine Whitelaw took his sister's elbow and guided her along the corridor toward her chamber adjacent to the children's, for in the darkness it was difficult to find their way.

"You heard?" she asked softly.

"Yes, I did," he replied, and Artemis strained to see his expression.

"Oh, Valentine, I am so ashamed," she cried. "It has taken a frightened child's honesty to show me how selfish I have been."

"Artemis, don't. You are being too hard on yourself. What you have done has been out of the goodness of your heart. I have never known you to be anything but generous and kindhearted."

Artemis shook her head, denying all that he said. "No, I am dishonest. Deceitful. I have brought shame upon this family. I have only thought of myself since you returned with the family and told us of Basil's death. I saw little Dulcie as all that we had left of Basil. Oh, I know we've Simon, but he is nearly a man full grown. He has Elspeth. She is his mother. But Dulcie, she could have been ours, Valentine. She could have been mine," Artemis finally admitted. "I wanted her for my own. And yet even in that small wish am I mocked. Look at me. Useless. I could not even help her, so lame am I," Artemis said with self-loathing.

"Artemis, please, do not do this to yourself," Valentine pleaded, hating to hear his sister speak in such a heartless manner. "You have only wanted what would be best for the child. I, too, would wish to have Basil's daughter living with us. That is not wrong."

"It is wrong when it would destroy others, as I have finally realized that it would. But I did not think of them, only of my desires to have a child."

"My dear, please do not despair," Valentine said, placing his arm around her slender shoulders. "You only hurt yourself further by persisting in demeaning yourself—"

"You are not blind, Valentine. You do not wish to hurt me, but look at me. I am lame! What man would want to wed me? What man would wish to lie with me and have a cripple bear his children? Can I accompany my beloved to court and proudly dance with him? I cannot even walk by his side without calling attention to myself. Do you not think I have seen the pitying glances? I will not be pitied. I am a Whitelaw, and I will at least bear that name with some dignity and honor."

"Artemis, I—"

"No! There is nothing you can say, Valentine, that will change my lameness. I have accepted my fate. You are being far more cruel by continuing to pretend that I am not thus," she said, lifting the hem of her nightgown to reveal the foot that was twisted, the heel unable to touch the floor. "I will never be any different, Valentine. That is why I allowed myself, for just a little while, to believe that Dulcie could be mine. But now, I realize that it would not be right to separate her from Lily and Tristram. They are indeed her family. Not us. Lily is the one she turned to when she was frightened just now. Not me. I cannot replace Lily in her affections, much as I might have wished.

"I have been unfair to that child. I bitterly resented her closeness to Dulcie. I was jealous of a young girl who never wished me ill, who wanted only to be friends. Forgive me, Valentine. You trusted them to my care and I have betrayed you, and Basil."

Valentine kissed Artemis on the forehead, holding her close for a moment. "There is nothing to be forgiven. I still believe in your unselfishness, and in your goodness. None of us are saints, my dear."

Artemis signed. "I wish there were some way we could keep them with us. All of them," she said firmly, looking up at Valentine hopefully.

"I would have it that way as well, but we have no legal right to Lily or Tristram. Dulcie, yes, but it would mean separating her from her brother and sister. As we have both just heard, that would result in tragic consequences for the children. That is not what Basil and Magdalena would have wanted for their children. You heard what Lily said. She promised Basil she would always take care of the others. I wonder if Basil quite realized how serious a vow that was to Lily.

"And have you thought, Artemis, what Dulcie's life, or even Lily's and Tristram's, would be like at Ravindzara should we get guardianship of them? The house is barely habitable. There will be many more years of construction needed before it is a proper home. I even hesitate to allow you and Quinta to live there while the work is proceeding. And, remember, I shall have to be away for long periods of time during the next few years in order to earn the necessary monies to continue building on Ravindzara. I will not be here for the children. There is also another matter that concerns me," Valentine added in an unpleasant tone of voice.

"What?"

"By our sincere concern for the children, we might be depriving Tristram of his heritage."

"However could that be?" Artemis demanded, outraged by the suggestion.

"My dear, despite our belief in Basil, there are those, less knowledgeable and kind, who will continue to believe that Tristram is his son and not Geoffrey Christian's."

"That is wrong. He is not Basil's son. Basil would never have allowed the boy to believe otherwise."

"Nevertheless, it is true. The boy will have a difficult time in proving he is Geoffrey Christian's son, and in claiming Highcross Court."

"Hartwell Barclay inherited Highcross when Geoffrey Christian died."

"Yes, but only because Magdalena and Lily were thought to have died as well. And at that time Geoffrey did not know that he had sired a son. His will, however, left Highcross to his surviving heirs. He bequeathed his estate to his wife, Magdalena, and upon her death, to his daughter, if he had no son to inherit."

"So that leaves Lily Christian and Tristram now as the rightful heirs to Highcross."

"Certainly, Lily. But as to young Tristram. Where, except for the boy's claim, is the proof of his heritage?"

"It should not have to be proven," Artemis said angrily, for such accusations cast doubt upon Basil's good name. "At least Lily's claim cannot be disproven. Now that she has Highcross, she will of course need a guardian."

"Hartwell Barclay will, I am certain, be quick to assume that responsibility. As the children's only relative, he will, of course, have the right. And until Lily Christian is old enough to manage her own affairs, or marries, he will have control of Highcross.''

''From what you have told me of Geoffrey Christian's dislike of Hartwell Barclay, I cannot understand how he would have allowed such a situation to be develop. Surely he would have named another to be guardian of his daughter, should his wife have died before Lily could manage on her own?''

''He did.''

''Whom did he name as guardian?''

''Basil,'' Valentine said quietly. ''Geoffrey never foresaw the possibility of the tragedy that caused them all to be thought dead at the same time.''

''So, Hartwell Barclay will become the children's guardian. Is there nothing that we can do? He must understand, Valentine, that he must treat the children well. Dulcie is, after all, a White-law. We cannot allow the man to mistreat her, or any of the children. He may gain legal custody of them, but we are responsible for their welfare.''

Valentine smiled, but Artemis could not see his expression in the darkness. ''I will make it very clear to Hartwell Barclay that no harm must ever befall those children.''

''What if he won't take Dulcie?''

''Dulcie is Magdalena's daughter. She has a right to live at Highcross. Besides, Lily, for now, is the legitimate heir to Highcross, and I doubt very seriously that she would allow Hartwell to send Dulcie away. I imagine Hartwell Barclay will have more on his hands than he suspects,'' Valentine predicted. ''Believe me. I have come up against these children's ingenuity before, especially Lily Christian's. They are cunning little devils, and if Hartwell Barclay thinks he will have an easy time of it, then he is sorely mistaken,'' Valentine said with a chuckle, little realizing exactly how accurate a prediction that had been.

PART THREE

The Gathering Winds

This bud of love, by summer's ripening breath,
May prove a beauteous flower when next we meet.

SHAKESPEARE

Chapter Thirteen

January, 1581—Kent
East Highford Village, five miles south of Highcross Court

THE village of East Highford was nestled along the east bank of Little Highford River, which meandered through the Kentish countryside before joining the River Eden. To the west lay the Weald with its dense forests. To the east were the rolling hills and pasturelands of the North Downs. Farther south, toward the Channel, was Romney Marsh with its lonely villages isolated by dangerous marshlands and mists, and unfriendly smugglers suspicious of strangers.

East Highford was not an exceptional village. Grouped around the village green were a church dating back to Norman times, a tithe barn, a couple of conical-roofed oasthouses, and a bustling inn. The narrow, cobbled High Street that led to the market square was flanked by half-timbered cottages and shops. Beyond the village proper, across the stone bridge that spanned the sluggish waters of Little Highford, and past the outlying farms, was the great manor house, Highcross Court.

It was St. Agnes's Eve, and the skies overhead were dark with clouds that promised snow by evening. Earlier in the season rain had flooded the barren fields and even the waters of Little Highford ran swiftly. A cold north wind gusted against the figures hurrying along the village lane and sent them more

237

quickly about their tasks, anxious to reach the comfort of their homes and the warmth of a hearth. The uneven cobblestones were treacherous, and many a carelessly placed foot slipped. A cloudburst drenched those foolhardy enough to have lingered, sending them scurrying for cover as the icy rain fell in windblown sheets.

A bell jingled erratically over the door of a shop where a couple of buffeted figures now entered, accompanied by a shower of raindrops that splattered into a widening puddle just inside the door. It was a shop crowded with sundry items. One could find a bolt of taffeta sarcenet or coarse woolen; garden tools and seeds for spring planting; bottles of vinegar; ink and parchment; devotional primers; sweetmeats and salt; pewter spoons and trencher plates; sand for scouring pots; a sparkling-looking glass; assorted pieces of furniture; and, it was rumored, the proprietor was a moneylender should the need arise.

"Surprised I am to be seein' so many hearty souls about. 'Tis such a foul day," the proprietor commented cheerfully as he glanced past the customer he was serving to greet the latest arrivals. He shivered as the cold draft swirled around the small room and threatened to extinguish the only light; the flickering flame of a candle in a lantern suspended from the low-ceilinged crossbeams. On so dreary a day, little light penetrated the small, diamond-paned windows set beneath the deep overhang of the floor above.

Peering into the gloom, the proprietor, Benjamin Stubbles, said upon recognizing one of the women removing the hood of her cloak, "Oh, 'tis ye then, mistress? A long ride ye've had. And how are ye this rainy day?" he inquired with genuine interest, momentarily ignoring the buxom woman whose demands he'd been trying to satisfy for the best part of an hour while other customers waited impatiently.

"I am fine, thank you, Master Stubbles," the young woman responded with a smile that warmed his heart. "I came to collect those items I left with you earlier in the week," she explained.

"Why, bless me, mistress, I had indeed forgotten tomorrow was *the* day."

"They are not finished then?" she said, unable to mask the disappointment in her voice.

"Oh, they are indeed, mistress. Yes, indeed. They looks

mighty fine. Young Jane has worked her best on the one in particular, I might say most proudly, mistress," Benjamin Stubbles beamed, thinking of the fine embroidery his granddaughter had spent the evening stitching.

"I am so pleased, and so will—"

"*If* you could spare me a brief moment of your time, Master Stubbles. I was here first," the old harridan interrupted icily, her glance no warmer when encountering the young woman's, especially when she noticed her own son's eyes lingering on that delicate-featured face.

It was sinful indeed for anyone to be as beautiful as Lily Christian, the older woman thought, eyeing with disapproval the dark red curls that glowed in the candlelight like wine. Ann Fordham glanced down at her own daughter standing docilely beside her and gritted her teeth. Why couldn't her own dear daughter's skin be as smooth as alabaster, as was Lily Christian's? Not a pockmark to be seen on that heart-shaped face. And why did her own Mary Ann have such an appetite and, unfortunately, have to bear proof of it in so many of the wrong places? she wondered in despair, knowing that Lily Christian's cloak concealed a slender shape well-rounded in all of the proper places.

"Good afternoon, Mistress Fordham," the object of her disfavor greeted the woman politely, even though she had been well aware of the woman's critical gaze.

"Mistress Christian," Ann Fordham replied haughtily, glancing away uneasily from those green eyes that stared at her as if amused. *Daughter of Asmodeus, more likely*, the flustered woman thought as she remembered the previous Sunday's sermon upon the seven tempters of the soul. And catching her son's eyes straying again toward so great a temptation, she pulled his ear, even though he stood taller than she. "It would do you well, sirrah, to remember the sermon of Sunday last, warning against the vices the devil would tempt us with. You must beware of those who would paint themselves and lead a God-fearing man astray. You must cast out such thoughts or be lost," Ann Fordham warned her son, suddenly seeing Lily Christian as far more than her daughter's rival for an eligible male. It was no secret in the village that Ann Fordham's aspirations of marrying off her only daughter to Hartwell Barclay, master of Highcross Court, had been ruined when Lily Christian had returned to claim her rightful inheritance.

Otho Fordham turned a bright red, mortified that his mother might be reading his mind, or even be aware of such wickedness, for the sight of Lily Christian always resulted in sleepless nights full of lustful thoughts, which remained painfully unsatisfied.

Thinking her son well-reprimanded, Ann Fordham returned her attention to her task at hand. "I would like these items immediately. As I told you, Master Stubbles, the new parson is coming to dine this eve," she said loud enough for both her son and Lily Christian to hear, a self-satisfied smile curving her thin-lipped mouth.

"An honor," Benjamin Stubbles murmured.

"But surely not an unexpected one, Master Stubbles. After all, I am the widow of the former parson, and as such 'twas my right to welcome the good reverend to East Highford. Not that the same courtesy was extended to my dear husband and myself when first we arrived in East Highford. As I remember, the Reverend John Henderson could not even await our arrival, but was already aboard Geoffrey Christian's ill-fated ship and sailing to heathen ports, leaving his devoted parishioners without proper guidance," she declared with a condemnatory glance at Geoffrey Christian's offspring.

"Surely, madam, if we be truly faithful, we would remember the good reverend's teachings and remain true to our lessons for at least a Sunday or two without singing psalms in church," Benjamin Stubbles responded as he measured a length of lace.

"Really! I will remember your mocking comment, Master Stubbles, to the Reverend Buxby. I warrant he will remember it, too. They say the Reverend Samuel Buxby is a distant cousin to the Earl of Hadrington. A most auspicious relationship, I should think. Indeed, it has been said that the Reverend Buxby made quite an impression with the local authorities in the Hadrington witch trials. He was most instrumental in gathering the testimony needed to indict the witches for the bewitchment and death of the earl's wife. I understand that the Reverend Buxby was most unrelenting in his examination of the witches. Harlots that they were, they soon enough confessed to all charges, including the stillbirthing of several babies in the village. Devil's work, 'twas, and the judge quickly convicted them and rightly sentenced them to hang. A most grievous affair. Fortunately the earl has fully recovered from the dreadful experience, and I hear he has remarried. A lovely young woman, I am told. The only daughter of a most influential London merchant with court connections.''

"How fortunate for the earl," Master Stubbles replied.

"The Reverend Buxby found it most curious when I told him of the sheep that died so suddenly on the Carson's farm. He also thought it unusually strange about Mary Langley's stillborn son," she confided with a knowing look.

Benjamin Stubbles frowned. "Nothin' unusual in that. I don't s'pose ye told him that Mary Langley has never yet, in all the years she and Daniel have been wed, and that's been a score, given birth to a healthy babe. Too thin and nervous, she is, and always has been. S'pose next ye'll be blamin' the beer not brewin' properly on witchcraft," he muttered beneath his breath, winking at Lily Christian.

Ann Fordham sniffed, outraged by the man's attitude. "You would be wise to hold that irreverent tongue of yours, Master Stubbles, lest you find yourself under suspicion one of these fine days," she warned, her censorious glance including Lily Christian before it moved on to linger briefly on a man standing near the door. "Thieves, gypsies, harlots, and drunkards, Master Stubbles, have been tempted by Satan because they have turned a deaf ear to the pulpit. They are all destined to a heretic's fate. Mark my words upon that! Indeed, it might serve as a lesson well learnt if a cross were burnt into the left cheek of every heretic to serve as a constant reminder to those who would sin," she continued, eyeing Lily Christian's soft cheek as if she already saw it so branded.

"I will give yer kindly intended advice full consideration when next I sip my ale at the Oaks, Mistress Fordham. I am certain that we can all benefit from following yer fine example. Now, was there anything else?"

Apparently mollified, Ann Fordham pointed to a fine display of colorful ribbons. "We must have a length of red—no, no, the brighter one," she said, gesturing impatiently as Benjamin Stubbles reached for the satin ribbons. "And the yellow. Yes, that one. Perhaps a pale blue one, too. No," she said, changing her mind. "I want the peacock blue. 'Twill bring out the blue in Mary Ann's eyes. We want her looking her prettiest this eve," she said, pinching her daughter's cheek to bring out a rosier glow.

"Ah, now 'tis indeed a special eve fer fair young maids," Benjamin Stubbles said as he snipped the ribbons to the exact measurement requested, Ann Fordham's eagle eye watching closely lest he try to cheat her. "And will ye be pullin' the pins out and sayin' a paternoster, Mistress Mary Ann? Don't be forgettin' now, to stick the pins in your sleeve so ye dream of the lad ye hopes to marry," he warned a blushing Mary Ann, who cast a guilty glance toward the man who had moved in closer from the door and now stood nearer Lily Christian.

"How very opportune of ye to have invited the good reverend to dine with ye on St. Agnes's Eve. 'Twill not hurt young Mistress Mary Ann's divinin' any to have the good reverend on her mind tonight. I believe he is unwed?" Benjamin Stubbles continued conversationally as he added the ribbons to Ann Fordham's purchase.

"Of course! Why do you think I recommended him in the first pla—" Ann Fordham began hotly, then, seeing his grin, she said, "I believe that is so."

"And, ye, Rom? Ye haven't taken a maid to wife yet, have ye, lad?" he asked the handsome young man. "Shame on ye, lad, when three of the fairest in the village, nay, in all of Kent, are standin' within arm's reach of ye. If only I were a wee bit younger," he said with a twinkle in his eye as the young maid who'd followed Lily Christian into the shop, and now stood beside her mistress, grinned at him.

"I'm still fleet of foot, Ben Stubbles," he said softly, but his eyes never turned away from Lily Christian's face.

"Bah! Such arrogance! There's none who'd have ye, Romney Lee, and that's the truth," Jane Stubbles declared as she came down the narrow flight of stairs, a length of fur-lined velvet draped over her arm. "Ye be too pretty, lad, for there's no maid who'd wish to wed one prettier than she," Jane said with a wide grin spreading across her pert face. "But, if I hadn't already had the banns read with Hugh Moore, I might just see if I couldn't outdistance ye."

A devilish gleam came into the dark blue eyes of Romney

Lee. With his finely featured face and well-mannered ways, he gave the appearance of being a gentleman, if one didn't look too closely at the darned jerkin and hose, but everyone in the village knew he was part gypsy. Although he traveled the countryside from Rye in the south to York in the north and some said even to as far a distance as the moors of the West Country, he always returned to East Highford. Most said it was because his sister was married to the miller and Romney Lee knew he could always find a place to sleep under her roof. But others suspected it was because of the proximity of the marshlands he was named for. There were still some bands of gypsies, outlawed during Queen Mary's reign, that roamed the wild marshes. His mother and her family had lived there before they'd fled to the Continent, and speculation had it that half the smugglers and ruffians along the coast were Romney Lee's cousins.

Romney Lee was a man of many trades, although he had never been heard to admit to being anything other than a rover. Quick-witted, with a keen eye, and light-fingered some would swear, he journeyed with a vagabond band from fair to fair, never staying longer than a week in any one place.

"I wish you'd smiled at me sooner, Janey, for I would have managed to stumble one or twice," Romney Lee said with a glint in his eye that had Jane Stubbles wishing she had too.

Instead, she snorted derisively, for it would be doing no good now to be dreaming about the likes of Romney Lee. "Ye be the kind o' rogue to bring heartache to a lass, and a well-rounded belly and plenty o' promises, before ye disappear in the night."

Romney Lee laughed. "You've a shrewd, coldhearted granddaughter, Ben Stubbles."

"Aye, Romney Lee, that I do. Why d'ye think I trust her and no one else behind the counter when I've stepped across the lane to the Oaks?" he said with a grin as Jane came to stand beside him.

"Here 'tis, Mistress Lily," Jane said, spreading out the velvet cloak. "It turned out even prettier than I'd hoped. D'ye like it?"

Lily stepped up to the counter, although there was little space with Ann Fordham refusing to give way, and her son and daughter still standing dutifully beside her.

"Oh, Mama! 'Tis beautiful," Mary Ann Fordham sighed.

" 'Tis like a royal robe a princess would wear. I wish it were mine. I'll never have anything as pretty as this," she said with a disgruntled expression.

"It is lovely," Lily said as she examined the cloak. It was of crimson velvet and lined in sable. Delicate flowers and exotic beasts had been embroidered in colorful silk and gold threads along the collar and edges. "Dulcie will love this."

"Well, thank you kindly, Mistress Lily. The little one will certainly be snug once she bundles up in it," Jane said, pleased by Lily Christian's generous response. *Not like some who criticize every little stitch*, she thought, eyeing Mistress Fordham, who hadn't taken her envious eyes off the cloak. " 'Tis the finest velvet and softest fur I've ever worked with. Doña Magdalena had a real good eye fer quality. I had enough left over after I shortened the cloak to make an underskirt and bodice for Mistress Dulcie too," Jane said, shaking out the rest of the crimson velvet that had been too precious to waste. "I hope that was all right? I had her size from the last gown I cut down to fit her. I won't be chargin' ye extra fer it. 'Twas my pleasure."

"Thank you, that is very kind of you. This will be the nicest birthday ever for Dulcie," Lily said, her eyes bright with pleasure and excitement as she anticipated the hour when she could present Dulcie with her gifts. "I'm certain she'll be by to thank you herself for your generosity."

"Why, she's the sweetest, prettiest little girl, Mistress Lily. A bit on the quiet side, but she seems very bright. This crimson cloak will be so lovely with her dark hair."

"Hrrrumph!" Ann Fordham sniffed contemptuously, "Some people have no shame," she muttered under her breath. "Fancy finery cannot change the circumstances of a person's birth. Some people would be wise to remember that and not foster false hopes, for I warn you that the village has not forgotten."

Lily felt her cheeks warming with anger as she turned to face her sister's detractor.

Seeing the look that flashed into Lily Christian's eyes, Ann Fordham instinctively moved to a safe distance. "You are no longer living on that savage island, Mistress Christian. You and your brother and sister might have been raised like heathens, but you are now in England, where we have laws that decent, God-fearing people obey," she warned, for Lily Christian had always made her uneasy. There was a boldness and lack of humility about the girl that was unnatural. Of course, such wickedness was not surprising since her father had been a privateer and her mother a Papist. The Reverend Buxby had definitely been interested when she had told him about the wild animals the children had returned with and how Lily Christian had tamed those creatures of the devil. A talking parrot, indeed! Strange things had happened in the village since those children had returned to Highcross.

"There we are. Yer order be filled now, Mistress Fordham," Benjamin Stubbles said hurriedly, a broad smile stretched tightly across his face as he waited for her to make her own careful calculations. Never yet, for nearly fifteen years now, had she failed to question the total of her purchases.

"Now, Mistress Lily. See if ye be pleased with this while I go over these sums with Mistress Fordham," Ben Stubbles said, handing Lily a small leather bag.

Loosening the cord, Lily let the contents of the bag slide into her palm. The gold of the slender ring gleamed richly. Set with a single amethyst, it was of a medieval design and had belonged in her mother's family for generations.

Lily stared down at the ring that Benjamin Stubbles had cut down to fit Dulcie's small finger. It was one of the few possessions of their mother's that she could give to Dulcie. In a letter left with the solicitors, their mother had requested that her jewelry and clothes, and all personal possessions, be left to her only daughter. Hartwell Barclay, as guardian, had not allowed her to touch the more valuable pieces of jewelry, but this ring, inherited from their Spanish ancestors, he had not deemed worthy of safekeeping. All of her mother's clothes, including the crimson cloak, had been stored away in trunks and fortunately forgotten over the years by Hartwell Barclay.

Lily slipped the ring on her finger. It fit snugly; it would fit perfectly on Dulcie's.

" 'Tis a finely crafted ring," Romney Lee murmured close against Lily's ear. "An unusual design."

Lily glanced up in surprise.

"This, too, is for the little dark-haired one?" he asked curiously.

"Yes, my sister," Lily replied with a defiant stare into his eyes, daring him to speak further about Dulcie.

"I have often seen her with you," was all he said, his eyes wandering over her face and hair.

"Otho! Come!" Ann Fordham called to her son, who, even after his mother and sister had completed their business and stepped away, had remained behind, ogling Lily Christian.

"Better run along, Otho. There's a good lad," Romney Lee said dismissingly as he glanced at the awkward boy who'd been breathing down the back of his neck for the past few minutes.

"Ah . . . ah . . . M-Mistress L-Lily, I-I . . ."

"Otho! Come here at once!" the strident tones echoed across the room.

Lily Christian took pity on the young man and smiled at him. With his mouth dropping open in surprise, Otho Fordham gulped, then doffing his hat, he backed away. First he tripped over a sack of beans, then tumbled over a barrel of flour, before finding his mother's big toe with the heel of his shoe as he bolted out the door.

"You are too softhearted, Lily Francisca Christian," Romney Lee said with a rough laugh, jealous of the smile she had wasted on that beef-witted boy when she had not shared such a look with him.

At her startled look, Romney Lee smiled. "You do not remember, but 'twas I who sold the big white to your father. I was very young then, uncertain of myself and how to bargain. But your father, he did not try to cheat me. He paid me a fair price for the horse. 'Twas my first sale. You came running out of the house while he was sitting on the white's back and you demanded to ride too. You were very persistent. I can remember you stomping your foot, your hands placed on your hips as you stared up at him. He laughed, saying he could never deny his Lily Francisca anything, and asked me to lift you up to him," Romney Lee said, a strange look entering his deep blue eyes as he remembered that day. "You reached out your arms to me and smiled. Such big green eyes. You were very sweet, Lily Francisca."

Lily glanced away, made uncomfortable by his familiarity, for she had never spoken to him before. She had only seen Romney Lee from a distance, and her opinion of him had been formed from gossip she had overheard from the villagers and servants at Highcross Court.

"I was very saddened to hear about your father's ship going down. He was a fine man. I remember your mother. Until recently, I have always thought her one of the most beautiful women I have ever seen. I also remembered that little girl who let me hold her, smiling at me as if I were no different from anyone else. I was very unhappy to think she would not be coming home."

Curious, Lily glanced up at him, meeting his eyes for a brief instant before she glanced away again. "Why would I have looked at you any differently?"

Romney Lee shook his head. "That you do not know, even now, is the reason," he replied.

"Reckon ye'll be leavin' fairly soon what with spring comin' on in a couple of months?" Benjamin Stubbles said as he began to wrap up the cloak and gown. "Was there not some trouble at the St. Frideswide's Fair last year? Ye were there, weren't ye, Rom?"

"Now, Ben, you know there is always a bit of high-spirited rowdiness around a fair. 'Twouldn't be worth goin' otherwise. Sometimes a man can even profit handsomely during such confusion," Romney Lee replied with the kind of smile that would have had old Ben Stubbles betting a fortune that Romney Lee and his friends had been behind most of that confusion. And Ben Stubbles knew that the knife Romney Lee kept concealed up his sleeve would have flashed more than once doing its master's bidding.

"Perhaps ye won't be leavin' East Highford so soon this time, eh, Rom?" Jane asked with a sly glance between Romney and Lily Christian, pleased to see him looking a trifle disconcerted for once. "And Mistress Lily, ye'll be observin' the rites of St. Agnes's Eve? There must be a dozen young gentlemen who'll be hopin' ye'll be dreamin' of them this eve," she added with a wink at Romney Lee.

"Perhaps there is just one man that Lily Francisca Christian dreams of?" Romney inquired, his dark eyes searching her face for the truth of her feelings. His curiosity was to remain unsatisfied. Except for a slight flush staining her cheeks, whatever secrets Lily's heart held remained hers to keep.

"Of course, 'tis no secret whom Tillie is dreamin' of," Jane said, glancing at the young maid standing behind Lily. "Wasn't I seein' Farley Odell enterin' the Oaks not more than ten minutes past?" she said, eyeing with interest the surge of red that now came into Tillie's thin cheeks when one of the footmen from Highcross was mentioned. "Of course, there's been many who've tried to get one of them Odell brothers to wed them. I hope ye've been careful with the likes of that dark-haired one. He might be the least handsome of the two, but he's the wiliest and has often had a maid walkin' with him in the greenwood before the thought has even entered Fairfax's head."

"Remembering my last encounter with the big fair-haired one, I would say that having brains would just be a hindrance to his natural instincts," Romney said, recalling the ham-fist that had swung his way.

"They're both good lads, even if they are always a step ahead of trouble. Always were the mischievous ones, ever since their mother ran off with that tinker. Though she claimed they were both Tom Odell's sons, I'd swear Fairfax is the spittin' image of the Reverend John Henderson. Ye remember, Jane, he was a big, fair-haired man. When he was parson, 'twas the only time I can remember Leticia Odell goin' to church. Heartbroken, she was, when he signed on with Geoffrey Christian. Ah, well. Now, Mistress Lily, ye be pleased then with the ring?"

"Yes, you did a splendid job. I feel my mother would be very pleased that Dulcie will be wearing it. How much do I owe you, Master Stubbles?" Lily asked.

"Ah, that be fine. Thank you, mistress," he said, quickly counting the generous amount Lily had placed on the counter. Handing the package to Tillie, he said, "I thought I saw the lad, young Master Tristram, running by a few minutes ago. Hope he don't break his neck on them slick cobbles. I was hopin' he'd be comin' in to sample some of Jane's gingerbread."

"Made a fresh batch this mornin', I did. Figured the lad would be comin' in to town with ye," she explained. "Never knew a lad who liked sweets quite like young Master Tristram. Such a pretty boy, too," she added, and Lily was thankful Tristram hadn't been in the shop to hear such aspersions cast against his masculinity.

"Farley let him drive the cart into town. I told him not to

wander off. I suppose he tired of waiting, especially if Farley left him there to go to the Oaks.''

"I s'pose he's gettin' too old to enjoy gingerbread. Be losin' him to the Oaks soon enough, too, I reckon," Ben Stubbles said with a sigh.

"I think there may still be some time left, Master Stubbles, so I'll take a couple of pieces. I am certain he will complain of hunger before we reach Highcrosss," Lily said, placing enough coins on the counter for half a dozen pieces when she saw Tillie lick her lips, and, after all, Jane Stubbles did make the best gingerbread in the county and it was a long ride back to Highcross.

"Now, Mistress Lily," he said, pushing back the coins. "Jane made those pieces especially for the lad. No payin' fer them."

"'Just these extra ones, then,'' Lily said, pushing back most of the coins.

"She's a stubborn lass, Ben Stubbles," Romney murmured. "I don't s'pose your heart is big enough, Mistress Lily, to share something sweet with a poor gypsy lad?" Romney Lee's dark blue eyes were full of entreaty.

"Beware, Mistress Lily. This is when Romney Lee is his most dangerous. Loves t'have the maids feelin' sorry fer him. Charm the devil, and steal yer first kiss and more, he will, if ye don't watch out," Jane warned Lily, despite Romney's scowling face as he watched a suspicious look come into those green eyes.

Taking the package of gingerbread, Lily pushed a giggling Tillie toward the door. Lily bid the Stubbleses a good afternoon, while a grinning Romney Lee received a polite nod.

"And what can we be doin' fer ye, Rom?" Ben Stubbles asked.

But Romney Lee was already halfway to the door and called back over his shoulder, "I just came in to get out of the rain, Ben." Then he was gone.

The rain had stopped, but the wind continued to swirl along High Street as Lily hurried along the slippery cobblestones toward the stables where she had left the cart and her horse.

"I hope Farley has returned. I'd rather not linger in the village now that the rains have stopped. We might be able to reach Highcross before another downpour," Lily said worriedly, increasing her pace as she heard a distant rumble of thunder.

"Ye want me to call in at the Oaks, Mistress Lily?" Tillie offered as she scampered along beside, her arms full of packages and her mind full of dreams of Farley Odell. Unable to see where she placed her feet, she slipped and would have fallen except for a quick hand that reached out and steadied her.

The packages, however, did not fare so well and lay scattered acrosss the muddied lane. "You haven't hurt yourself, have you, Tillie?" Lily asked out of habit, for the young maid was always stumbling into something, bumping her shin, or stubbing her toe. In fact, Tillie was a menace to be around, Lily thought as she bent down to gather the packages up before they were ruined, but Romney Lee was faster and soon had them held firmly in his grasp.

"Oh, I'm fine, mistress, thanks to him," Tillie said breathlessly, risking a quick glance at the man who'd save her from taking a spill. She'd never been so close to him before. She could scarcely believe he was even more handsome than she'd thought. He was certainly tall, she realized as she stared up into these dark blue eyes. And he had the softest-looking chestnut curls. And when he grinned, as he was doing now, his teeth gleamed against the darkness of his skin and beard. He had the longest, thickest lashes, and he even wore a sparkling jewel in one ear. Tillie sighed as she tested her ankle for a sprain. Somehow she couldn't quite see Farley wearing a ruby in one ear.

"Good as new. Won't stop me scrubbin' the hall tomorrow," she said with a grin.

"Why don't you go warn Farley Odell that Mistress Lily is wanting to leave now?" Romney advised, his smile leaving Tillie breathless and wondering who Farley Odell was. "I'll see your mistress safely to the stables."

"Thank you, but that is not necessary," Lily began, but Tillie had already taken off down the lane, unmindful of her steps again as she hurried to the Oaks. "Please, I can take the packages now," Lily protested, holding out her hand.

Romney Lee smiled as he placed his hand beneath her arm and led her along High Street. But when he became aware of the curious stares following their progress, he dropped her arm and said, "I will leave you."

Lily glanced at him in surprise, wondering at such fickleness. Seeing her puzzlement, Romney laughed harshly. "I would walk by your side forever, Mistress Lily, but, alas, I am not considered a proper escort for a young woman of good reputation," he explained, boldly returning a woman's rude stare until, affronted, she looked away. "I would not wish to cause you any trouble."

Lily surprised him with her laughter. "As far as Mistress Fordham is concerned, I have little reputation to preserve. And I fear her tongue has already destroyed that. She has never cared for me or for my brother and sister. I wonder if she has ever liked any of my family. I truly do not understand her hatred of us. We have never wished her or anyone in this village ill, and yet many persist in being suspicious of us."

"It is because you are different from them, Lily Christian. They are frightened of things they do not understand. The superstitions of old fill their minds and they forget all that they have learned and know to be the truth. We gypsies get blamed for drought, famine, flood, and many a theft that we had nothing to do with," he said with a bitter smile as he doffed his hat to a woman walking by, the gesture more mocking than gentlemanly.

"Why do you allow them to treat you like that? You are only part gypsy. You speak in a refined manner and do not look like—" Lily began, then paused uncertainly. "I am sorry. I should have not said that."

"I do not look that much like a gypsy, and so I could pretend to be a gentleman? You have not offended me," he said. "But Mistress Fordham was right about one thing. You cannot change what you are, even if you wished to. I am proud, Lily Francisca. And so are you. Would you change the way you act just because of the disapproval of some narrow-minded, mean-thinking woman? Would you conceal that beautiful red hair of yours merely because someone else thought it unseemly? No, I do not think so," Romney Lee said, eyeing her thoughtfully. "Out of defiance you would braid bright ribbons in your hair just to make it all the more noticeable and all the prettier."

Lily met his gaze openly. He was so different from what she had thought he would be like. She had been mistaken about him, she realized, ashamed. She had been guilty of being just like the villagers who'd condemned her and her family so unfairly.

"My father might have been an Englishman, but I am still a gypsy. I cannot deny what I am. Neither could my mother, although she tried to be what my father wanted in a wife. He was a well-educated man, a gentleman some might have said. He was a schoolmaster. We lived in a small house in Rye. My mother tried very hard to become like the other women of the village, but they never accepted her. She was too different from them. She could not change what she was. Gradually she began to lose her spirit. She grew thin and sad. I remember her weeping all of the time. I think even my father knew she would die if she did not go back to her family and her old way of life. We stayed with my father. I never saw her again.

"I sometimes think my mother was the fortunate one. My sister and I were raised in a village, and yet we are gypsies. My father saw that we learned to read and write; but my mother spoke to us of many strange and wondrous things. We were also taught good manners so we might be accepted in polite society. My father had hopes that I would become a schoolmaster, but he forgot that others would not wish to have their children taught by a man whose mother was a gypsy. Besides, I would never have had the patience," he said with a mocking grin. "But I found that I possessed certain skills others did not, and I could put my mixed heritage to far more profitable pursuits. One day I am a gentleman . . . well, almost. And the very next day I am a gypsy, almost. I can move between villager and vagabond without causing too much suspicion for either. Strange that I should indeed have become a man of some importance and worth."

As if divining her thoughts and her changing opinion about him, he raised a cautioning finger. "I am still a rogue, Lily Francisca Christian. Never think otherwise," he told her, and although he smiled, Lily knew it was meant as a warning.

"How is the big white?" he asked suddenly. "I heard that he threw Hartwell Barclay many a time, until finally the new master of Highcross gave up trying to ride him. Rides a mule now, does he?"

The corners of Lily's lips twitched ever so slightly, but Romney caught the movement. "I always thought the white was a smart horse, if a bit high-spirited." Romney chuckled. "What did your father name him?"

"Merry Andrew," she said, laughing at his surprised look.

"My mother told me that my father always said that he thought the horse was laughing at him, and his efforts to ride him. He threw my father more than a few times too. But my father would never give up on him. He swore that no horse, especially one that was part buffoon, was going to get the best of him. They finally came to an agreement, although I am not certain Father would have called himself the victor. Merry would allow Father to ride him, but he had to be prepared to play Merry's game. Merry likes to bite. Mother said that my father was always rubbing his arm or shoulder where Merry had nipped him. Merry may have gotten a little older, but unless you are very careful, he'll take a piece of you, then bare his teeth and laugh. But he only bites once; then he seems satisfied."

Romney Lee stared at Lily in dismay. "I had no idea he was such a foul-dispositioned horse. I'm surprised your father didn't have me run out of the village for cheating him."

"I think my father would have thanked you rather than cursed you. He liked the challenge of trying to ride Merry. Every time he rode him it was an adventure."

"No wonder Hartwell Barclay never had a chance of succeeding. Why the devil hasn't he had the horse destroyed? I wouldn't think 'twas out of fondness that he hasn't," Romney said.

Almost sadly, Lily smiled. "My father was a very unusual man. He left a provision in his will for the protection of Merry. He's to have a home at Highcross until his dying day. Then he's to be given a decent burial under the old oak in the west meadow. The solicitor must have thought my father crazed."

Romney Lee's laughter drew the attention of several people standing in conversation nearby. "I would have given anything to have seen Hartwell Barclay's face when he heard that. But tell me, I have seen you riding the white. How is it that you have succeeded where others have failed?" he asked curiously.

Lily shook her head in denial. "I haven't succeeded. Merry has gotten fat and lazy and just tolerates me," she disclaimed modestly. "I've my share of scars. 'Tis Cappie and Cisco he likes."

Romney's frown of confusion wasn't unexpected and she continued. "The first time I approached him in the meadow, I had Cappie and Cisco with me. He was fascinated by them, and by me because I was with them. He has never thrown me. He will even let Cappie ride around on his back.''

''Ah, the monkey and parrot,'' Romney said with a smile of comprehension. He understood better now why the villagers were suspicious of Lily Christian.

They had almost reached the stables when they heard a commotion coming from within. Recognizing one of the voices raised in anger, Lily hurried inside, but she was stopped short by the scene that met her horrified gaze.

Tristram was surrounded by several boys, all from the village. Having ganged up on the lone boy, they were each taking a turn at shoving and hitting him, hoping to bait him into losing his temper. They weren't to be disappointed, for suddenly Tristram started swinging his fists with little regard for aim. But with so many boys crowding so closely around him, he connected more than once with a jaw or nose that had pressed a little too close. Tristram couldn't hold them off and was knocked to the ground, where he began to roll and trade punches with one of the larger boys. The others stood around yelling excitedly, except for one boy who was struggling ineffectively to free his ankle from attack. A big-pawed dog, hardly more than a puppy even though he stood nearly two feet high at the shoulder, had grabbed hold of the boy's ankle and was growling menacingly as he tugged on it, refusing to give up his prize.

Angered by their victim's luck, for the larger boy was now holding his stomach and rolling in pain, three of the boys jumped on Tristram. Two of them held him down while the other one began to hit him.

Lily's cries went unheard even as she rushed forward. It was then that she became aware of the two men fighting near the back of the stables. She recognized the thatch of blond hair atop the taller of the two. Fairfax. But what was he doing fighting the blacksmith? Fairfax wasn't even supposed to be in the village.

Before Lily could reach Tristram, however, Romney Lee had already scattered the group that had been standing around cheering. The icy contents of the bucket of water effectively having cooled their hot heads, they ran shivering from the stables. The boy who'd been fighting the pup managed to free himself and fled as fast as he could, his hose hanging in tatters. The pup, barking wildly, raced in pursuit. The two who'd been holding

Tristram down quickly retreated, disappearing out a back door. With his arms freed, Tristram's fist smashed into the larger boy's nose, sending him sprawling backward.

Finding himself fighting a losing battle now, the bully hastily scrambled to his feet. Romney Lee's hand, centered on the seat of the boy's breeches, guided him toward the stable door and sent him flying.

"Just wait 'til I tell my father that ye laid yer dirty hands on me, ye thievin' gypsy! He'll whip ye skinless," he threatened as he ran up the lane.

"I suspect I am safe for a while at least," Romney Lee predicted as he watched Fairfax Odell flatten the blacksmith with a bone-cracking punch that had the brawny fellow's knees buckling beneath him. "That"—Romney gestured in the direction in which the last boy had fled—"was the blacksmith's son. I don't think I'll lose any sleep over that bloodcurdling threat," he added, glancing back to see the blacksmith stretched out unconscious at Fairfax Odell's big feet.

Lily was kneeling beside Tristram. She stared at her brother in disbelief, hardly recognizing the bruised face that only minutes before had been described as being so pretty by Jane Stubbles. "Tristram," Lily whispered as she smoothed back the dark red curls from his swelling eye.

"The lad isn't hurt too bad, is he, Mistress Lily?" Fairfax asked in growing concern as he caught sight of Tristram's bloodied lip. Without a glance, he stepped over the blacksmith, who was starting to moan. "I come in here to find them beatin' up on the young master. And him," he said, spitting in disgust as he glanced backward at the blacksmith, "he was just standin' there watchin' with a big grin on his face. When I tried to break up the fight, he sneaks up behind me and hits me on the back with that poker. Made me awful mad. Should've twisted it around his bull neck. Figured, though, 'twas as good a time as any to settle an old score. He's been askin' fer it since we've been lads," Fairfax explained, sorry only that he had waited so long.

"Tristram?" Lily questioned worriedly as she helped him to his feet, steadying him as he leaned against her for a moment.

Tight-lipped despite the pain it must have caused, Tristram

pulled away from Lily's comforting embrace, his expression furious.

"They called me a bastard! A whore's son. She wasn't, Lily. She wasn't," Tristram cried, tears falling from his blackened eye. "I loved her, Lily. I wanted to hit them all for saying such things about her. Mother was a lady. She was. And Basil was a good man, a gentleman. Basil saved our lives. He loved us and Mother. Why do they have to say such horrible things? Why, Lily?" he said, choking on his tears. "I hate this place. I hate England! I wish we'd never left the island!"

Gazing into Lily's eyes, he asked in a quieter voice. "Why do I have to prove I'm Geoffrey Christian's son? Why? I am, Lily. I am!" he said again, his voice raised defiantly this time. "I am, aren't I, Lily? 'Tisn't a lie?"

Lily pulled Tristram into her arms and hugged him tight. "No, Tristram, it isn't a lie. You are Geoffrey Christian's son. Mother told you the truth. She would never have lied to you. Basil loved you as if you were his own son, but you are not his. You and I had the same father, never doubt that, Tristram. Never," Lily told him. She wished there were some way she could convince him of that, but staring down into his bruised face, she could still see the doubt in his eyes.

"Damn them," Lily said beneath her breath, wishing she had a couple of those boys within her reach right now. Her arm tightened around Tristram's slumped shoulders as she heard steps approaching from outside. Lily's green-eyed gaze narrowed dangerously as she recognized the swaggering figure that entered.

"Good Lord! What the devil has been goin' on here?" Farley Odell said as he entered and saw Tristram Christian's disheveled appearance. But when he spied his brother's broad grin, a look of comprehension dawned across his face. "I should've known ye'd be in the thick of things, Fairfax."

"I didn't start it, Farley. Honest I didn't," the younger but larger brother was quick to say. "But ye know he's been asking fer it fer years," he added, jerking his head in the direction of the blacksmith, who was still stretched out in the straw.

Farley Odell removed his hat, holding it nervously before him as he met Lily Christian's angry gaze, for although she was a slight young woman she had a lot of her father in her. "Mistress Lily, I'm really sorry about this," Farley Odell began contritely, his expression becoming woebegone when he looked more closely at the young master's face. "Did that damned bas—"

"No, he didn't hit Master Tristram. 'Twas that son of his and a bunch of his friends. They were pickin' on the boy when I come along and tried to stop them. Then he hit me, Farley. And from behind," Fairfax said, shamefaced that such a thing could have happened to him.

"Who? Him?" Farley demanded angrily, his baleful stare coming to rest accusingly on Romney Lee.

"No, not him, I think he came in with Mistress Lily," Fairfax quickly explained.

"He did?" Farley didn't like the sound of that. If the gypsy had been bothering Mistress Lily, then he'd have a thing or two to say to that bastard.

"And where have you been? Why weren't you here with Tristram?" Lily demanded.

"Well, I—"

"Oh, I found him over t'Oaks, just like they said. Drinkin' and laughin' as if he'd the whole afternoon to while away. Had the whole place in an uproar with one of his stories. Never met a better storyteller," Tillie supplied helpfully, that proud of Farley and always eager to please her mistress. But when she looked over at Farley and caught his jaundiced eye on her, she realized rather belatedly how that must have sounded to Lily Christian and her smile faded as tears filled her eyes. "Oh, Farley, I didn't mean it. I only meant to help," she cried.

"Now don't start blubberin' on me, Tillie," Farley complained, patting her hand comfortingly. "I know what ye meant by it. Ye be real proud of me and I'm appreciatin' that. If I'd have known this was goin' to be happenin', I wouldn't have left the lad alone, Mistress Lily. Ye got to believe me. I didn't leave him here. He come with me, Mistress Lily."

"You took Tristram into the Oaks?" Lily asked, growing angrier by the minute.

"Oh, no, Mistress Lily. Certainly not. The lad was goin' about an errand. A secret one, so he said," Farley explained, looking over at Tristram for confirmation. But the sight of the boy only made him feel guiltier, and more understanding of Lily Christian's anger, although he still didn't understand what Romney Lee had to do with it all.

" 'Tisn't his fault, Lily. Honest it isn't,'' Tristram said, his words sounding muffled through his quickly swelling lips. "I wanted to pick up my gift for Dulcie.''

"But the ring and cloak are from both of us, Tristram. You needn't have gone to any trouble.''

"I wanted to give her something special, Lily. Something just from me, that I got for her with my own money,'' he explained, glancing around dejectedly. "It's gone,'' he said.

"What did you get Dulcie? Maybe we can replace it if one of those boys stole it.''

"We can't. Besides, 'twouldn't be the same,'' he protested, kicking the straw beneath his feet in angry frustration.

"How did you pay for the gift?'' Lily asked, curious because she knew he had no money. Even she'd been saving for over a year most of the small allowance Hartwell Barclay doled out to her in order to pay for the alterations on the cloak and ring. The extras she treated Dulcie and Tristram to whenever they came into the village had come out of that allowance too.

Tristram remained silent and avoided meeting her eyes.

"How, Tristram?'' she persisted.

Lily heard Tristram draw a deep breath before he glanced up, but there was a defiant look in his eye when he admitted, "I broke into the coffer Hartwell keeps locked up in his bedchamber.''

"Tristram!''

Tristram looked around him. Tillie was staring at him open-mouthed, her eyes wide with disbelief. Farley and Fairfax Odell were grinning, and the stranger was watching him with a gleam in his eye, almost respectfully, Tristram thought.

"I took what was rightfully mine, Lily. I took one of the gold pieces from the island. He had no right to take that money away from us. Anyways, I only took enough to pay for my gift. I even brought back the change. I'm tired of having to beg from him. I get mad every time you have to ask him for something, Lily. I don't like the way he looks at you. We shouldn't have to beg him, Lily. 'Tis ours! Everything there belongs to us, not him. Highcross belongs to the Christian family. It was our father's. Now 'tis ours. I'm not sorry, Lily.''

Lily sighed. He was right, even if he was wrong to have stolen that money. But what worried her now was what would happen when Hartwell Barclay discovered the theft.

"You aren't mad at me, are you, Lily?" Tristram asked quietly, staring up into her face.

"No. I can't blame you for wanting to do something nice for Dulcie."

"What did ye get fer the little one, Master Tristram? Maybe if we look real careful like around the stables we'll find it. Might not have been stolen by one of them whelps," Farley suggested helpfully. "Come on, Tillie dear, give us a hand," he told the maid, who was wiping at her tears.

"Ooooh, we just got to find it, Farley," she sniffed, thinking there'd never been such a sweet lad as Master Tristram. Dropping down on her hands and knees she started searching the straw covering the stable floor, her fingers seeking out some small trinket, perhaps, or a fragrant bouquet of flowers tied with a pretty ribbon. So loving a lad, she was thinking as she crawled about determined to save the day. Suddenly Tillie let out a shrill squeal as she heard a growl and felt something sniffing around her backside. Ready to box Farley Odell's ears, she started to rise and turn around when something heavy landed against her, knocking her to the ground.

It wasn't Farley, she thought unhappily as she saw the flash of long, pointed teeth and gleaming yellow eyes and closed her eyes against the attack. She tried to cover her face against the foul hot breath panting against her face.

"He came back! He's back!" Tristram cried out as he ran to the barking dog, who was now slobbering excitedly as he licked Tillie's face with his wet tongue.

Spying Tristram, he raced to the boy, jumping up and down as he barked playfully. He rolled over, his big feet pawing the air as Tristram rubbed him on the stomach.

"Be careful, Tristram. This is the same dog that was attacking one of those boys," Lily warned as Fairfax grabbed a pitchfork and Farley a spade, even though Tillie was clinging to his arms.

"Good dog!" Tristram said, patting the dog's head. "He's my dog, Lily! Well, I bought him for Dulcie, that is," Tristram informed his surprised sister as he stared down proudly at his gift.

"She's always wanted a puppy, Lily," he added, just in case his sister needed convincing, which apparently she did.

"Puppy?" Lily said, eyeing the mastiff with a less than friendly eye, but that didn't stop him from trotting over and sitting down before her and staring up at her with large, soulful eyes.

"I knew he'd like you, Lily. Do you think Dulcie will like him?" Tristram asked hopefully.

"I'm sure she will. She's always wanted a pony," Lily said bemusedly, thinking of what Hartwell Barclay's reaction would be to this latest addition to their menagerie.

"We can keep him, can't we? It's my gift to Dulcie, Lily," he pleaded as he stared down at the big puppy with its sleek, dark, fawn-colored coat and dark brown ears and nose. "He's a beauty, isn't he? Just wait till he grows up."

"Where have you kept him all of this time?" Lily asked curiously.

"Looks like one of the litter from that bitch of Joe Riley's. She's a real fine-looking dog. Didn't realize he had any of the litter left."

"I got him to keep this pup for me until Dulcie's birthday," Tristram explained, patting the dog on its big head. "Had to pay extra for the food it has been eating all these months."

"Aye, Joe Riley drives a hard bargain, that he does," Farley agreed, vowing to find out later just what Joe Riley had charged the young master for the dog.

"Can I give him to Dulcie, Lily? Can I, please?" Tristram pleaded, staring up at her with his bruised face. Lily didn't have the heart to deny him.

"Well, since you have paid for him," she began, but Tristram did not allow her to finish as he hugged her, and the puppy, sensing he had been accepted, promptly started to bark excitedly and jump up and down as he raced around the two figures; then he was pawing at one of the packages that had fallen to the ground.

"Hey!" Fairfax cried out as he saw the dog's nose disappear inside the package, then reappear with a big chunk of gingerbread grasped in his jaws. Sensing this time that he had somehow erred, the puppy scampered across to where Lily stood, and with his tail wagging engagingly, he crawled as close to her skirts as he could.

"He's no fool," Romney Lee said as he began to gather up the rest of the packages, ignoring the Odell brothers, who were staring at him belligerently now.

The stable doors banged loudly as the wind blew against them. "You've a long ride home, Mistress Christian," Romney advised. "The boy will need seeing to. I've some salve of oil of roses and henbane you might wish to use if the bruises become too painful or infected." Romney eyed Lily Christian's brother with a professional eye. "And some white poppy if the boy has trouble resting. Please don't hesitate to ask me for anything." His eyes met hers as he continued to stare up at her.

"That—" Lily began to thank Romney, only to be interrupted by a red-faced Fairfax Odell.

"I think Farley and me have been in enough fights to be knowin' how to see to the young master's needs."

The look of battle in his eye, Fairfax stepped forward, seemingly to tower over the other man. "Farley and me might just be wonderin' what ye be doin' here with Mistress Lily," he said, glancing over at his brother for the usual nod of approval, but Farley was frowning.

Romney Lee had smiled, and Farley, having seen that smile before, called to his brother, "Get ol' Merry, Fairfax, I'll see to the cart. We oughta get back to Highcross. Don't want Master Barclay comin' into town after us now, do we?" he warned his brother.

That threat accomplished what the threat of rain had been slow to do, and soon Tristram, the puppy sitting happily on his lap, and Tillie, a place saved next to her on the seat for Farley, were sitting inside the cart. The packages had all beeen collected and safely stored on the floor of the cart.

Fairfax, holding Merry's reins, glared over at the gypsy as he stood watching as Farley gave Lily a lift up into the saddle. Standing there as if he'd every right to watch the young mistress, Fairfax grumbled to himself.

Muttering beneath his breath, Fairfax forgot to keep an eye on Merry, and before he was aware of it, the horse had nipped him on the shoulder. With a curse threatening to erupt, Fairfax rubbed the painful spot, daring Romney Lee to give vent to the laugh he could see widening the gypsy's grin.

Farley eyed his brother as if wondering if they could possibly be related. "That reminds me. What the devil are ye doin' in town anyways?" he demanded.

Fairfax frowned, as if wondering about that himself, then slapped his forehead. "Fergot all about it, I did! 'Twas Master Barclay who sent me to town in the first place. See, I did have a reason fer comin' into town, Farley. Come to tell ye, Mistress Lily, that the Whitelaw ladies and the gentleman be at Highcross."

Romney Lee was the only one who noticed the strange expression that crossed Lily Christian's face. As he stood outside the stable and watched the cart rumble along the lane toward Highcross Court, Lily Christian riding beside it on the big white's back, he was to remember that expression and wonder about the love he had seen in her eyes.

I am as constant as the northern star.

Chapter Fourteen

NEVER had the road between East Highford and Highcross Court seemed so endless. More than once Lily glanced impatiently at the oxen-drawn cart, its wheels churning so slowly through the thick mud. She wanted to touch her heel to Merry's flank and send him galloping up the lane. As it was, she feared they would never reach home. Fairfax was whistling contentedly and lazily tapping the oxen now and again to keep the cart trundling along at a steady pace.

Lily's impatience came more from anticipation than from a fear of the downpour that threatened to drench them at any moment. Although she had said nothing to anyone, secretly Lily had hoped that Valentine Whitelaw would arrive for Dulcie's birthday celebration.

Quinta Whitelaw and Artemis had been frequent visitors at Highcross, but it had been two years since last she had seen Valentine, and yet he had never been far from her thoughts. Her pride, wounded by the conversation she had overheard between Valentine and Cordelia Howard in the gardens of Tamesis House, had been slow to heal, but Lily could no more deny the love she felt for Valentine Whitelaw than stop her heart from beating. During the three years since their return to Highcross Court, her love for the man who had rescued them had not lessened. Carefully nurtured and guarded in her most secret dreams, her love had become her inner strength. It guided her and comforted her when her spirits were at their lowest. When the terrifying nightmares threatened, she would think of her love and would no longer be frightened of the dark. But it was a secret love, and it would always remain so—even to Valentine Whitelaw. The humiliation she had experienced when hearing his laughter and incredulous denial that he could ever fall in love with her still caused her to cringe in mortification.

Never, she had promised herself, would she allow him to know how she felt. Never would she give him the chance to laugh at her again. And never would he know how much she loved him and always would.

Romney Lee had been right. There was only one man Lily Christian would be dreaming of on St. Agnes's Eve, and that was Valentine Whitelaw.

"How are we going to get him inside without Dulcie seeing him, Lily?" Tristram asked, trying to avoid the drooling tongue licking his face. "I don't want to leave him out in the stables," Tristram continued worriedly as he met the pup's trusting gaze. "Hollings isn't a very nice man. I don't think Dulcie's dog would like him at all." He patted the pup on top of his big, bony head.

"Be no secret. Probably bark all night long anyways," Farley said, wishing he'd had time for another ale. He huddled closer to Tillie. The wind was cutting through his bones like an icy knife. *She must be frozen stiff, the skinny little goose,* he thought. "How are ye doin', dear?" he asked, taking her cold hands in his and rubbing them together to warm them.

"Ye're goin' to start a fire rubbin' them sticks together if ye're not careful, Farley," Fairfax muttered. His brother had not been the same since he'd started sweet-talking Tillie. Although, Fairfax thought scratching his square chin ruminatively, he had to admit that he liked Tillie a whole lot better than that bold wench at the Oaks whom Farley had been eyeing about this time last year.

"Reckon the ladies won't even be recognizin' ye, Master Tristram, what with yer face all puffed up and turnin' black and blue, and ye've grown another couple of inches since last they were here," Farley said, hoping the ladies wouldn't faint dead when they caught sight of the boy. Of course, if the elder Whitelaw lady—a more acid-tongued, steely-eyed woman he'd yet to meet—had ever fainted, then he was fair game.

"Is it really?" Tristram asked in awe, less concerned than excited about his appearance, for it had been the first fight he'd ever been in—and he'd just about won it.

"Aye, there'll be no doubtin' what ye be made of fer the next fortnight at least, Master Tristram," Fairfax grinned, proud of the lad. "Yer father, the cap'n, he would've been real proud of ye. I know that fer certain. I reckon t'others will be chewin' mighty carefully, if they got any teeth left in their fat heads that is," he said with a chuckle. "Ye should've seen him, Farley, swinging away at them louts. Smacked a number of them good, he did. Ain't many run out of there with the same-shaped noses they swaggered in with. No one's goin' to be sayin' anything against this young gentleman fer years to come," he declared, his large hand slapping Tristram heartily between the shoulders and nearly knocking the boy off the seat.

Suddenly Tristram didn't mind the ringing in his ears, or that he could barely see out of one eye and his bruised lip was throbbing while his skinned knuckles stung like the dickens.

Lily was less impressed by her brother's show of bravery than either one of the Odell brothers, who were known brawlers. Tristram was right, Lily thought as she remembered his angry words; they should never have left the island.

Shivering, she glanced ahead. She could see the great brick chimneys of Highcross rising above the trees.

Highcross Court. Life there had been anything but pleasurable. Lily could still remember entering the cold hall that once had been her home. It was like a stranger's house, she'd thought, her gaze traveling up the flight of stairs, hopeful of spying her mother standing there, arms outstretched to welcome her children home. Those first few days, when Lily had explored the house and recognized so many familiar places and possessions, she had found herself pausing to listen for the sounds of laughter that used to ring throughout the house. Hearing a step behind her, she would turn, expecting to see her father come striding through the door.

Gradually, however, those memories had faded as the days numbered into months and were filled with new experiences as Tristram, Dulcie, and Lily began to live out their lives at Highcross Court. Another impression Lily had not soon forgotten had been her first sight of Hartwell Barclay. Upon receiving word of their rescue, he had wasted little time in traveling to London. He had arrived at Tamesis House with half a dozen grim-faced solicitors marching behind him, well-prepared to present their client's case as sole, rightful guardian of Geoffrey Christian's children. And, to strengthen his position should any questions have been raised as to the suitability of his guardianship, he had brought along the one person who might be able to convince the authorities that Highcross Court was the proper home for the children: Maire Lester, Lily Christian's former nursemaid. The ensuing, tearful reunion would have convinced even the most hardhearted judge that the children would be happiest with the kind-faced, matronly woman who would love the children as if they were of her own blood.

But he had worried needlessly, for as Geoffrey Christian's cousin, his case had been strong. The only other relative who might have challenged his claim had been Magdalena Christian's father, but that old gentleman had died long before the children were rescued. Soon Hartwell Barclay had been smiling broadly, the embodiment of affability—or so it had appeared.

He had also come to some manner of agreement with Valentine Whitelaw concerning Dulcie, for there had never been any question of her not accompanying them to Highcross Court. During that first year, Lily had been grateful to Hartwell Barclay, innocently believing his oft-stated claim that it had been out of the goodness of his heart that he accepted without question Tristram's claim of being Geoffrey Christian's son and had allowed Basil Whitelaw's daughter to live at Highcross. But even the most accomplished actor would have found it difficult to carry on such a charade for long, and soon Hartwell Barclay's true nature had begun to surface. And when Lily had discovered the stack of letters and reference to what seemed a generous amount of money sent by Valentine Whitelaw for Dulcie's care, she had known the truth.

It would have seemed an unfortunate predicament the children found themselves in, for quite naturally Hartwell Barclay would have resented their claim on the inheritance he had come to think of as his own. A less God-fearing man in a similar situation might have speculated on the intriguing possibility that should the children not have lived to inherit, he would have stood to gain everything. Accidents had been known to happen.

And children seemed especially prone to such incidents. If a man were very careful in his planning . . .

Although Hartwell Barclay had managed to remain in control of Geoffrey Christian's estate through guardianship of his children, and perhaps might even have held aspirations of becoming master of Highcross again, he had not triumphed completely. It appeared the children had a guardian angel as well as a legal guardian, not to mention an avenging knight should the need have arisen.

Unbeknownst to either the children or Her Majesty, it was Queen Elizabeth who stood between them and what might have been an unfortunately premature death. The day Hartwell Barclay had arrived at Tamesis House had been the day Lily and her brother and sister were to be presented to the queen. Accompanying the children he so despised, Hartwell Barclay had finally succeeded in appearing at court. His grand entrance, however, had hardly been in quite the manner he had so often and fondly dreamt—although it had certainly been memorable.

Dressed in all of his finery, Hartwell Barclay, much to his dismay, found himself having to share the honor and a seat on the barge with a curious monkey who couldn't keep his paws to himself, and a wise-cracking parrot whose beak was cursedly sharp. It had been a shock to him even to discover the creatures at Tamesis House, much less to discover that they belonged to his wards and that they too, had been invited to court. The short journey by barge to Whitehall Palace had not lessened his anxiety any as he'd listened with increasing unease to the parrot's indiscreet chatter. And in his opinion the children were little better than the wild creatures they had brought home to England as pets. Savages, all. Poor Hartwell Barclay. He had even had visions of himself, as guardian of the trio who were certain to insult the queen, traveling back down the Thames, not to Tamesis House but to the Tower, where he would await his tragic fate.

Entering the palace, they'd become the cynosure of all eyes. So impressed was he by the grandeur and importance of the people he saw, Hartwell Barclay stared openmouthed, looking more the fool than the dignified gentleman he thought himself to be. Enviously, he had watched Valentine Whitelaw return the many greetings that had come his way from well-known courtiers, lords and ladies, and those influential in the affairs of state.

And it was Hartwell Barclay, not the children, who forgot his manners when introduced, and cleared his throat incessantly in order to mutter some inane remark when spoken to. To the delight of several women, young Tristram had bowed and kissed their hands with an expertise that would have several young courtiers practicing their art in front of looking glasses in the privacy of their chambers before the night was out. With her big dark eyes and angelic face, Dulcie was enchanting and had no need to worry about the impression she made. Her shy smile, and the esteem her father, Basil Whitelaw, had been held in, was enough to secure her a place at court.

Lily Christian, however, drew most of the interested stares. Her exotic appearance created quite a sensation when she entered the hall. Perched on her shoulder was a green-feathered parrot and clinging to her arm was a bright-eyed, fuzzy-faced monkey in a green velvet doublet and cap sewn with bells. Quinta Whitelaw had not only made the amusing outfit for the monkey, she had also cut down one of her own colorful ropas for Lily to wear. She had been determined to remedy the unfortunate choice in clothes the child had been forced to wear. She wanted Lily Christian to be able to walk proudly into court, unashamed of herself and lowering her eyes to none.

Although she would never have allowed the softening expression to enter her eyes, her heart had been touched by the young girl. She could well understand the child's awkwardness and unhappiness. Being tall and thin, a less than beautiful woman, who had always been unable to bridle her sharp-tongued retorts or hide her intelligence, she had suffered the ridicule of many. Realizing that she could not shorten her height, and would not dull her wit, she had decided to make herself all the more unusual. So unusual, in fact, that people would not expect the ordinary from Quinta Whitelaw. She was eccentric, not comical. She was interesting, not pitied. She walked proudly, without embarrassment.

Lily Christian was never going to be ordinary, Quinta had wisely decided, and it was about time the child accept that fact and give up trying to resemble Honoria Penmorley. Lily was certainly not going to be plain; that was not her problem despite how unattractive she might seem now. One day Lily Christian was going to be too beautiful for her own good, but until then, perhaps she could help the child get through a difficult time. Selecting one of her favorite gowns, a pale green silk ropa shot through with golden threads, she had shortened it and made a matching hat, trimming it with a turquoise plume. An underskirt and bodice worked in a richly patterned material lavishly embroidered in colorful silks completed the costume for a most extraordinary young girl.

Quinta Whitelaw could not have been prouder of Lily Christian had she been her own daughter, and with a keen glance around the room, she had not seen a pitying look or smirk on one face. Lily Christian, daughter of an English adventurer and his Spanish wife, shipwrecked on a wild island in the West Indies for seven years, was exactly the exotic creature people expected to see. And to Quinta's satisfaction, the child had walked unhesitantly into the Great Hall, her pale green eyes surveying the room and its people defiantly. She had received more than one admiring glance, as well as several disapproving ones, but then, that was to be expected. Quinta Whitelaw would have been disappointed otherwise.

The queen had been all that the children had expected from the stories Basil had told them. Dressed in black velvet and white satin studded with pearls and rubies and red satin bows, with a lacy ruff starched high about her face and a crown of gold set with precious gems glittering atop her red curls, Elizabeth was awe-inspiring.

The parrot had squawked excitedly and, frightened of the people crowded in the Great Hall, had flown from Lily's shoulder and across the room with a flapping of wings. Not content to scatter the milling crowd, he had disgraced himself over several important heads as he swooped toward the queen. Landing on the arm of her throne, he had started to giggle and declared in a loud, censorious voice, ''*Praaack!* Pirates! Lift a leg, mate! A scurvy bunch! *Praaack!* My, aren't we a beauty, my pretty one.''

An uncomfortable stillness had fallen over the room as Elizabeth had sat staring in disbelief at the parrot perched beside her. Eyeing her glittering gown curiously, he had tried to steal one of the gleaming pearls before ruffling his feathers in annoyance as he strutted on his royal perch.

The silence in the Great Hall had become unbearable by the time Elizabeth had started to laugh. Her courtiers, apparently as well-trained as the parrot, started to laugh with her, but more likely out of relief than amusement. The laughter grew louder when the monkey, dressed in his green velvet doublet and cap, scampered with a jingling of bells onto her lap, his long tail curling around her arm as he stared around him at the startled faces and began to scold them.

Elizabeth's sharp-eyed gaze had found the familiar face she'd been searching for and with a sly smile curving her lips she had beckoned Valentine Whitelaw and the three children standing so uncertainly by his side to approach her.

Overly anxious not to lose his golden opportunity of gaining Elizabeth's attention, Hartwell Barclay quickly stepped forward and bowed deeply. He felt the heat rising in his face as he heard the ripping noise and felt the cool draft caressing the flesh of his inner thigh along the ragged edge where the seam of his hose had torn. Swallowing, he slowly straightened, hoping no one else had heard the sound and praying that he would remain beneath Elizabeth's notice, for if he had to bow again . . .

To Hartwell Barclay it had seemed an eternity that Elizabeth had conversed with Valentine Whitelaw and the children, who seemed to be getting along splendidly with their queen, for her laughter rang out continually, especially when the parrot began to mimic it. For the first time in almost an hour, Hartwell Barclay breathed easier when Elizabeth rose to retire to her privy chamber. She had requested Valentine Whitelaw accompany her for a private conversation, and had been about to leave when she spied the chagrined-looking Hartwell Barclay starting to back away. His knees pinned together to maintain his modesty, he was taking mincing steps and for the first time in his life trying not to be the center of attention.

"Master Barclay, is it not?" she inquired softly, her dark eyes gleaming with what was either malice or humor.

"Your Majesty," he replied with a sickly looking grin and bowing only slightly this time.

"I trust you will take good care of my young subjects. Guard them with your life, good sir, for I wish to see them at court again. Naturally, as their guardian, you will escort them, and I will hold you responsible for their welfare."

"Your wish is my command, madam," he replied grandly.

Hartwell Barclay had sighed with relief when she had started to walk away, but then she had paused. Crooking her finger, she had called him to her side and whispered in his ear, "You would do well to get that tear repaired before you catch your death of cold, Master Barclay. And I would have a serious word with my tailor, were I you, lest he cut your hose too small next time as well. And with far worse consequences."

For at least a quarter of an hour Hartwell Barclay had remained standing where Elizabeth had left him, unable to take a step and feeling as if every person in the hall was eyeing the exposed flesh on the inside of his thigh. And as Hartwell Barclay stood there feeling little different from the monkey dressed up in that ridiculous green velvet cap and bells, he began to savor his resentment of that Spanish Papist's brats.

The insolent little beggars might have befooled everyone else, including the queen, but not him, not Hartwell Barclay. And he was, after all, their guardian. He was the one they would have to answer to in future, not these perfumed fools. And Valentine Whitelaw's warnings hadn't frightened him, he thought with so odious an expression that George Hargraves, who was standing next to his friend, wondered what the big gent had smelled.

With a smugly complacent look, much like a fat cat's with cream on his whiskers, Hartwell Barclay anticipated their return to Highcross Court, where he would see that the children lived to regret they had ever returned to England. At least for now, he had decided, the children were more useful to him alive.

Three years, Lily sighed, pulling her cloak closer against the cold as Merry entered the stable yard of Highcross Court. Poor little Dulcie. She could never seem to get warm enough. They had nearly lost her at Christmastide. She had caught a chill, which had developed into a chest fever. Lily still could not understand how the window in Dulcie's bed chamber had been left open, nor indeed how Dulcie had been allowed to wander the grounds on so stormy a day. Hartwell Barclay's explanation had been that he'd had no idea the foolish child would take him seriously when he'd told Dulcie that Tristram had been playing hide and seek out of doors, especially when he knew Tristram had gone into the village with her.

If only Maire had still been at Highcross. She would never have let such a thing happen. But there had been a lot of changes at Highcross since last summer, when Tristram had almost broken his neck in a fall from the steeply pitched roof of the west wing. Hartwell Barclay had blamed Maire Lester for the accident, declaring that she had been at fault for ever having related the story about Geoffrey Christian having accomplished the same climb. But Lily remembered it as having happened differently. For it had been Hartwell Barclay who had told the story in the first place, his words daring Tristram to prove himself Geoffrey Christian's son.

The near tragedy, or so Hartwell Barclay had claimed, had proven to him that Maire Lester's services would no longer be required. Dulcie was old enough now to no longer need a nursemaid. She would also now have her own bedchamber, no longer sharing a bed with her sister. And it was about time Tristram was sent away for proper schooling, where he would be well disciplined, Hartwell Barclay had proclaimed. So Maire Lester had been discharged and sent packing to her sister's somewhere in the West Midlands.

Although Lily was anxious to greet their guests, she suddenly felt that same sense of foreboding that she experienced every time she thought of entering Highcross. She was frightened, and yet, should she have spoken of her fears, what would she have claimed? Hartwell Barclay had never threatened them or abused them. There were many in the village who would claim he was a decent, God-fearing man who had unselfishly accepted the burden of raising his wards. They were still bound by the law to Hartwell Barclay. It would only worsen their situation should she speak against him. She had no proof that he was trying to injure them. She was not even certain herself that he intended them harm. It was just a feeling. There was nothing she could do, except keep a more careful watch over Tristram and Dulcie.

It was Fairfax who finally lifted her down from Merry's back. For Hollings, as was his custom, was in no hurry to lend a hand, and by the time the groom came sauntering across the yard with his usual surly expression, Lily had gathered her courage to enter the hall.

"Lily?" Tristram questioned hurriedly as he watched the groom approaching. "If I take him inside, Dulcie will see him. She's probably looking out the window right now." Tristram glanced toward the row of windows flanking the entrance to the hall. "But I'm not going to leave him out here with him."

"Here, hold him still." Lily pulled a blue ribbon from her hair and wrapped it around the pup's neck and tied it with a big bow. "If Dulcie sees him, then you can present her with her present right now," Lily declared with a smile, but it faded when she saw Tristram's painful attempt at a grin, his bruised face, now that it was swelling, looking worse than ever.

"Well, well. What have ye got here?" Hollings asked, eyeing the pup. "Looks like he'll make a good ratter, unless he stumbles into a nest of them and they get him first, that is," he said with a harsh laugh. "Little small right now, but we could make a tidy sum with this one in the bear gardens. Once he's full grown, he could worry one o' them beasts half to death before he gets clawed into two."

"You leave him alone! He isn't going to be doing any ratting or fighting. He's Dulcie's dog!" Tristram said angrily.

"Good Lord! What got its fangs into ye, *Master* Tristram?" Hollings demanded with a sly grin. "Ye been sneakin' around that ol' toothless hag's garden agin, *Master* Tristram? Pickin' a lily flower fer the young mistress here, eh?" he snickered.

"Reckon yer good friend over t'smithy didn't fare much better'n that no good son of his," Farley said with a widening grin. "Both be pickin' teeth and straw outa their clothes thanks to *Master* Tristram, and Fairfax here."

Hollings's thin cheeks turned ruddy with his anger, but with Fairfax standing so close he didn't dare try to wipe that stupid grin from Farley's face. "Reckon ye'll be comin' to see me tonight, Tillie, seein' how ye'll be needin' a man to keep ye warm, and from where I'm standin' ain't none around exceptin' meself," he said as he quickly stepped to the far side of the cart and started to lead the oxen toward the stables.

"Can ye be seein' to these, Tillie dear?" Farley asked, tight-lipped as he handed the packages to a speechless Tillie.

"Farley, I've never been in *his* bed!" she squeaked in denial as Farley stomped off toward the stables, leaving Fairfax to lead Merry.

"Not to worry, Tillie. Reckon Farley knows ye got at least that much sense," Fairfax said with a gleam in his bright blue eyes as he quickened his step to follow his brother into the stables.

Tillie watched until he'd disappeared inside. She waited a moment, but there was only silence. She heard a grunting noise coming from within, then Fairfax reappeared to close the doors, his smiling nod sending her hurrying to catch up with her mistress, who had just disappeared inside the great hall.

The wounds invisible
That love's keen arrows make.

SHAKESPEARE

Chapter Fifteen

FOR once the great hall seemed welcoming. Several wall sconces had been lit, a fire was burning in the great hearth, and the enticing aromas of a meal in preparation filled the room.

"I think we're in the wrong place," Tristram whispered, glancing around in surprise, for they hadn't even had a Yule log to burn at Christmas. "I wish it were like this all of the time," he added with an appreciative sniff, his stomach growling its agreement, for he'd never gotten his piece of gingerbread.

"It used to be like this when Mother and Father were alive. When you become master of Highcross we can have a fire in the hearth even in summertime if we wish," Lily told him, hoping to cheer him up, but her words seemed to have just the opposite effect on her brother.

"I'm never going to be master of Highcross, Lily. No one believes that I'm Geoffrey Christian's son."

"Well, then, I'll give Highcross to you. 'Tis rightfully yours, Tristram." Lily spoke aloud the thought that had been in her mind for some time now. "As our father's only son, you deserve to inherit Highcross. He would've wanted it that way."

Tristram looked at his sister incredulously, his lip trembling slightly. "You truly mean that, Lily? But even if I did become master of Highcross, the villagers would never accept me. They will always think of me as a bastard," he said dejectedly.

"Don't ever let me hear you say that again. It isn't true!" Lily told him angrily. "What do we care what they think? I don't, and they don't like me any better than you," Lily added contemptuously. Curious, she looked around the empty hall. "Our guests must be in the great chamber. It was probably colder in here than outside when they arrived. For once even Hartwell must have seen the need to light a fire down here. He does have his pride."

"I'm surprised the hall isn't full of smoke. We haven't used the hearth since last winter. You'd think the chimney would be full of birds' nests. I bet he grumbled about having to light this one," Tristram guessed with a widening grin that caused him to wince.

"We may be able to get the pup into your room before anyone sees him," Lily told him, thinking she would have time to reach her own bedchamber and change her damp and muddied gown before anyone, especially Valentine, saw her. She wanted to look her best.

"Come on," Lily said, pulling Tristram and the puppy after her toward the stairs. "If we hurry we can get down the corridor without anyone seeing us."

Lily, her arms full of the packages Tillie had handed over to her before rushing toward the kitchens, and Tristram, half bent over with his fingers hooked underneath the pup's ribbon collar, had nearly reached the stairs when a stout woman with a quarrelsome look in her eye came stomping through the screens leading to the kitchens and servants' wing.

"I see ye be back. I thought I saw Tillie scamperin' through, nothin' more on her mind than that ruttin' Farley Odell and trackin' up the floors. I hope ye haven't ruined this hall. The master has guests, and I—" The cook, who was warming to her subject, paused, dumbfounded as she stared at the pup. Forgetful of the dough sticking to her hands, she clapped her hand across her open mouth.

Sputtering, she demanded, "What's that flea-bitten cur doin' in here? Does the master know? Ever since ye three brats showed up here there's been nothin' but trouble. All I had to worry about before was fixin' the master's meals. Now he's more tightfisted than ever and there's hardly a crumb left over fer the rest of us. And I bet ye be the one behind this latest bit of mischief," she muttered, a wrathful gleam coming into her eye as she stared at Lily, hoping to make the girl cower, but Lily returned her stare defiantly.

"I brought the pup inside. 'Tis my gift to Dulcie," Tristram declared, stepping forward to take the blame.

"Oh, it is, is it?" she questioned, then becoming aware of his bruised face, she nearly choked. "Well, the fat's in the fire now. Wait till them Whitelaws see yer face! Whatever will they think? Not likely ye walked into a door. The poor master will have a lot of explainin' to do, especially once that sharp-tongued Whitelaw lady sets her eyes on ye. The lame one is always askin' questions about how he's treatin' the little dears. Are they in good health? Are they happy? Do they need anything? Nearly split a gut, she did, when she learned about ye fallin' off the roof, and Lord help us, but when she caught sight of that sickly little sister of yours, thought she was goin' to faint. Never heard such carryin' on over a child. If she cares that much, she oughta take the brat off the master's hands. Good thing the master's plannin' on sendin' ye away to school. About time someone taught ye some manners, and they'll beat it into yer thick skull until it cracks," she warned him, a satisfied smirk on her face when she saw his frightened expression. "And that would leave just ye, Mistress Lily, and I'm sure the master has plans fer ye, too!"

"Be quiet," Lily said softly. "You forget that *I* am mistress here, and Hartwell Barclay is merely my guardian. Soon he will not even be that, and I may find it necessary to hire a new cook."

"Well! Aren't we the bold one now that them nosy Whitelaws be here. Well, ye just wait. We'll see, missy, we'll see," the cook said, but Lily could see that it was mostly bravado, for she had given the woman something to think about.

"I'm not going! I'm not!" Tristram yelled heatedly, forgetting the pup wiggling impatiently at his heels as he raised his fist to the woman. "And I'll tell the queen that Hartwell Barclay set those boys on me in the village. We've been to London and the court. I've had an audience with the queen," he said proudly. "I might even tell the captain that 'twas Hartwell who did this to my face if he tries to send me away. And when Lily gives me Highcross, I'll send you to the devil!"

A loud, wheezing gasp came from the top of the stairs, where Hartwell Barclay and his guests now stood. They were staring down in stunned amazement at the confrontation between the angry, bloodied boy and the red-faced cook.

Lily and Tristram stared up at the horrified expressions. Hartwell Barclay, standing with arms akimbo, had turned purple in the face. Quinta Whitelaw and Artemis seemed unusually pale. Lily's heart had skipped a beat when she caught sight of the tall gentleman standing behind them, but she had quickly realized it wasn't Valentine. It had taken her a second to remember the man. It was Sir Rodger Penmorley. With a sinking of her heart, Lily looked for the ever-graceful Honoria, but that fair maid was not to be seen, and Lily was left to wonder why Sir Rodger Penmorley was at Highcross in the company of Quinta and Artemis.

He'd done it now, Tristram thought as he stared up at those disapproving faces, his hands falling limply to his sides. The pup, seizing his chance, began to race around the hall in widening circles, his frenetic barking echoing through the silence.

With a quick sniff, hungry bark, and spinning of paws on the hard floor, the pup shot behind the cook and through the screens. He had hardly disappeared into the kitchens for more than an instant when he reappeared, a tasty-looking leg of mutton clutched in his jaws.

"Why, ye thief! Stop him! That's meant fer the master's breakfast tomorrow!" the cook hollered as she raced after him, her waving hands sending clumps of dough flying through the air.

But the pup thought it all a game and continued to race around the room, halting only to drop the leg of mutton long enough to bark encouragement to the breathless woman before picking it up again and racing away, his tail wagging excitedly.

"Good Lord!" Quinta Whitelaw said as she stared in bemusement at the ruckus below.

"A puppy! A puppy! Is it yours, Tristram?" Dulcie cried out as she ran down the stairs, her dark brown eyes dancing with merriment. Since her illness, there was an almost ethereal quality about her. Dressed in a pale yellow gown, her black hair tied with a yellow ribbon and flowing free, she seemed like a well-dressed sprite as she flew down the stairs.

"Oh, Dulcie, please, be careful!" Artemis called after her young niece. *If she should miss her step* . . . "Rodger, please, do something," she pleaded, glancing at Sir Rodger Penmorley, who was standing beside her, his hand steadying her at the top of the steep staircase.

But Dulcie had safely reached the bottom step and now stood laughing in amazement at the puppy's antics. "What's his name, Tristram?" she asked, clapping her hands together in excitement as she hopped up and down.

"I don't know. I never thought to name him, besides he's yours, Dulcie," Tristram told her, almost sorry now the pup wasn't his.

"Mine?"

"I wanted to give him to you tomorrow on your birthday," Tristram explained with a shrug. "But I guess now is as good a time as any," he went on, thinking there wasn't too much Hartwell Barclay could do to him with the Whitelaws here.

"Mine, really?" Dulcie asked breathlessly, glancing toward the puppy just in time to hold out her arms to him as he catapulted into her, knocking her to the floor and standing above her licking her face as she giggled.

"Oh, don't, Dulcie! Don't let him get so close, dear. The dog might bite," Artemis called out as she hurried toward the top step, unmindful of her lameness for once.

"Be careful, Artemis," Sir Rodger cautioned, his arm now locked around her slender waist as he guided her down the stairs. " 'Tis just a playful pup, and unless I'm mistaken, 'twill grow into a very big, playful dog one of these days," he warned as he recognized the breed.

"A mastiff!" Hartwell Barclay stammered in disbelief. "Here at Highcross? Out of the question. Impossible! However will we feed it?"

Quinta Whitelaw eyed Hartwell Barclay's plump, silk-clad legs and smiled slightly. "How very perceptive of you, Hartwell, to realize that a dog would make an admirable companion and protector for a young girl, especially now that Dulcie has that cavernous room all to herself. What absolute . . . brilliance . . . you display at times," she declared before sweeping down the stairs with a splendid rustling of silken skirts.

"He's wonderful! My very own dog! Oh, thank you, Tristram! Thank you!" Dulcie cried, hugging the puppy around its thick neck. Struggling to her feet, she flung herself against Tristram while the pup raced around in circles chasing its tail.

Staring up into Tristram's face, she was about to give him a kiss when she became aware of his bruises and gave a frightened squeal of horror. Much to Tristram's dismay, Dulcie started to cry, drawing everyone's attention to his sorry-looking countenance.

"Good Lord!" Quinta said again. In the confusion she had momentarily forgotten her first sight of Tristram's face, but now the blackened eye, swollen lip, and bloodied doublet left her in little doubt of what must have happened in the village.

" 'Ere, I ain't laid a finger on the boy! Came swaggerin' in here lookin' like that, he did! Most likely got that fat lip 'cause of his smart mouth, but 'twasn't me who done it! No sirree!" the cook was quick to say as she made a sneaky grab for the leg of mutton despite the pup's warning growl. Wait until she got a handful of that Tillie's hair, the cook muttered beneath her breath as she made her way back to the kitchens, convinced Highcross wasn't a safe place for decent folk anymore. She'd make certain Tillie was kept busy cleaning up after that creature, she vowed.

"Horrible woman. Quite impertinent. You really should dismiss her, Hartwell," Quinta commented.

"Tristram, your face," Artemis said, her hand reaching out to comfort him, but Tristram was not in the mood for coddling and stepped out of reach of them all.

"Obviously the boy has been defending a point of honor. Regrettable, but often necessary," Sir Rodger spoke understandingly, his arm keeping Artemis from embarrassing the boy with her well-intentioned mothering.

"Yes, sir, I was, but I'd rather not say anything further about it. What's done is done," Tristram said in a husky voice, relieved that at least someone seemed to understand. But if he didn't get up to his room soon, he was afraid he was going to start to cry and disgrace himself before them all.

"Of course, very gentlemanly of you. We understand completely," Sir Rodger murmured thoughtfully as he caught the glistening of tears in the boy's eyes.

"Do we indeed?" Quinta remarked, raising her eyebrow at

the man, for Sir Rodger seemed to be assuming quite a lot nowadays.

"I intend to know what happened, Rodger," Artemis disagreed. "I shall lodge a complaint with the proper authorities about this. How dare anyone raise a hand against Tristram! He's a—"

"He's a bastard!" Tristram said, his threatened tears overflowing. "That is what the fight was about!" he cried, and dodging past them he raced up the stairs.

"Good Lord," Quinta said softly this time as she watched his forlorn figure disappear.

"And you, Hartwell Barclay," Artemis said, turning an indignant eye on that flustered gentleman, "I am surprised you would allow such a thing to happen."

"B-But I don't even know what happened! And I hardly see why I should be held accountable for the boy's ruffianism. A more churlish-natured lad I've yet the misfortune to encounter. If you knew what I have to put up with from him, why—" Hartwell Barclay began, eager to proclaim his innocence in this affair, besides, the lad probably deserved it.

"What did happen, Lily?" Quinta interjected calmly, for Hartwell Barclay's shrill voice was beginning to irritate her.

"A group of village boys cornered Tristram in the stables and started a fight with him. They called him names and insulted our mother. They ganged up on Tristram and were beating him. He was only trying to defend himself. I don't know what would have happened if we hadn't come along when we did and stopped it," Lily was explaining when the heavy doors to the great hall were swung open to admit a tall, cloaked figure.

Lily recognized that long-legged, impatient stride and felt her cheeks becoming hot with an uncontrollable blush as she stared at the quickly approaching figure.

"Thank goodness you have returned safely. I've been worried sick about you. Looks like a blizzard brewing out there. We might be stranded here for days."

"Simon?"

Simon Whitelaw grinned widely as he came to stand before Lily, his black eyes full of undisguised admiration. "Lily. And, I vow, more beautiful than ever," he greeted her. Pulling off his glove, he took her cold hand in his and bowed with gentlemanly courtesy. Lily felt his breath warm against her skin as his lips just barely grazed her hand. She was surprised to feel his hand tremble slightly.

"But where—" Lily began, looking behind him for another figure to come striding into the hall.

"Where have I been?" he asked, misunderstanding her query. "They told us you and Tristram had gone into the village. But that was hours ago. Hartwell Barclay sent that big fellow after you, but when he didn't return, I became worried lest you'd lost a wheel off the cart or become stuck in the mud. Devil of a lane," Simon explained good-naturedly. "Ought to do something about that Master Barclay," Simon suggested, and although he addressed Hartwell courteously enough, there was an underlying lack of respect in Simon's tone of voice.

Quinta Whitelaw had caught that tone and gave her nephew a disapproving glance. Hartwell Barclay might be a pompous fool, but it was not Simon's place to remark upon it.

"Look, Simon! Look what Tristram gave me for my birthday!" Dulcie cried, her small hand easily guiding the pup by his blue collar until he came to rest before Simon. "Sit!" she ordered and giggled when he did as he was told.

"Well, what have we here?" Simon exclaimed, squatting down beside her and showing proper admiration for the ungainly pup. "What is his name?"

"I don't know."

"He must have a name, Dulcie. I've never yet met a decent dog without a proper name," Simon said so seriously that Dulcie patted the pup reassuringly.

Dulcie frowned as she met the pup's expectant gaze. "Raphael. That is what his name is. Raphael. He'll always watch over me like one of the archangels," Dulcie sighed, pleased with her choice, and apparently Raphael was pleased too, because he yawned and stretched out at her feet. Resting his chin against his paws, he gazed up at her lovingly.

"Ruff for short, eh, Dulcie?" Simon said with a chuckle.

"You're silly, Simon," Dulcie admonished, a serious expression on her young face as she stared thoughtfully at her dog. "I do love this blue ribbon around Raphael's neck. Do you think we can keep it on him all of the time?" she asked. "It makes him look so pretty."

Simon shook his head regretfully. "By the time Raphael's full grown, we most likely will not be able to find a length of ribbon long enough to tie around his neck. As big as a bull this lad's going to be," Simon pronounced, eyeing the pup's big, clumsy paws and the track of mud leading from the entrance.

"I had better go see to Tristram," Lily excused herself, starting toward the steps, but before she had reached them she turned and glanced around expectantly. "Valentine?" she asked.

"He sailed just after Christmas. Probably somewhere off the coast of Africa by now, if you can believe what he says about the *Madrigal*'s destination," Simon said with a conspiratorial wink. "I wanted to sail with Valentine, but my mother has such an aversion against it that I can't even bring the subject up. Even Sir William hasn't had any success convincing her that I am quite capable of making my own decisions. Besides, there is none better to be sailing with than Valentine and the *Madrigal*'s crew. But try to convince my mother of that, and she becomes distraught. I've never seen her become so agitated. Whenever Uncle Valentine comes to call, she gets nervous. I sometimes think she suspects he is going to kidnap me and force me to serve aboard his ship," Simon said, and although he was smiling, there was a tinge of bitterness in his voice.

"Your mother has already lost one man she loved very dearly," Quinta reminded him. "You are all she has left of Basil. And I suspect that she is more concerned about Valentine's safety than annoyed that he chose to become a privateer. She has always been very fond of him. And should she ask my opinion, I will tell her that I agree with her decision completely. And it won't do you any good to glare at me, Simon," Quinta told him. " 'Twas enough to lose Basil and now to have to worry constantly about Valentine. Had I my wishes, you would be one Whitelaw never to set foot outside of England."

Simon sighed. What was the use in trying to convince them? "I know, Aunt Quinta, and I respect your feelings and Mother's, but I am eighteen," Simon responded. "I am a man," he added more quietly. "She, and others"—his eyes lingered on Lily's red hair for a long moment—"should realize that."

"How long will Valentine be away?" Lily asked curiously, trying to mask her disappointment.

"Months. He was gone almost a year last time."

"I haven't seen him in over two years," Lily said, her feet dragging slightly as she started up the stairs.

"You were ill with a fever last time he was at Highcross, weren't you, dear?" Artemis remembered. "Valentine was very sorry he couldn't say good-bye to you. He is very fond of you. I know he thinks of you as if you were our youngest sister," Artemis said helpfully, little realizing what a slap in the face her words were to Lily.

"You'll be interested to know, Lily, that Valentine has for the past few years—since he rescued you from the island—been plaguing a certain Spanish captain. He's been raiding the Main, then, with a hold full of treasure, sailing to Spain, where he raids along *their* coast, and then do you know what he calls out for all to hear, Lily?" Simon asked, his eyes glowing with admiration. "Valentine says to tell Don Pedro Enrique Villasandro that Valentine Whitelaw is waiting for him. *If* he has the courage, he'll know where to find him. Valentine's not one to boast, and the only reason I've heard about this is that people are beginning to question Don Pedro's valor, both here in England and in Spain."

Lily paused, turning around to stare at Simon, who was grinning in satisfaction.

"The cowardly Don Pedro, your uncle by marriage and the man who helped sink your father's ship and leave my father abandoned in the West Indies. One of these days, Lily, Valentine will send that Spanish bastard to the bottom," Simon said. "I intend to be aboard the *Madrigal* that day," Simon vowed.

"Simon, really!" Quinta shook her head at such bloodthirsty sentiments.

"You and I both, Simon," Lily said, and meeting his ardent gaze she held out her hand to him.

Simon grasped it eagerly.

"Promise me, Simon, you won't leave me behind if you do learn something about Don Pedro," she requested of him.

"I promise," Simon readily agreed, not even thinking how he could possibly fulfill that promise.

Quinta shivered, feeling as though someone had walked over her grave. If only she could convince them that their seeking of vengeance would not bring them happiness. It would not bring back Basil, or Lily's mother and father. Even Valentine seemed a stranger to her when he spoke of this Spanish captain. She could only pray that his revenge against the man would not destroy him.

"Why don't I go with you to help Tristram, Lily," Quinta offered. "Now that Maire Lester is no longer at Highcross you may need some help in tending to Tristram's injuries. I would also like to discuss her departure," Quinta said as she hooked her arm through Lily's. "Rather sudden, was it not? I had hoped to have several discussions with her concerning childbearing. She seemed a most intelligent woman."

"Lily?"

"Yes, Simon?"

Simon smiled, and for an instant Lily thought he looked uncomfortable. " 'Tis good to see you again," he said almost shyly.

"I am glad to see you, too, Simon," Lily murmured, recalling the very first time she had met him. He hadn't really changed much. Undeniably, he was a handsome young man. But he was still taller than average, and thinner than most. It seemed to be a physique common to the Whitelaw family, Lily thought as she remembered how Valentine had looked climbing the mast, his muscular chest bared to the waist. Simon also had the black hair that all of the Whitelaws seemed to possess. But he had inherited Basil's black eyes, the same as Dulcie. And staring at his hawkish profile, Lily realized that she would never be able to look at Simon without thinking of Basil. She wondered sometimes if Simon truly knew how like his father he was, not only in a physical resemblance, but in the gestures he made, and in the way his eyes crinkled at the corners when he laughed. They had used to tease Basil about that. Maybe that was part of the reason she liked Simon so much. He was almost like a brother to her, Lily thought, her smile softening as she stared down at his familiar face.

"I look forward to dinner, when we will have a chance to talk," Simon told her, his heart pounding so loudly in his ears that it nearly deafened him and he hoped he wasn't speaking too loudly.

"You should consider yourself quite honored, my dear,"

Quinta said softly, a gleam of enlightenment entering her dark eyes as she glanced between the two young people.

Quinta Whitelaw was not the only one to notice the tender exchange of glances between the two. Hartwell Barclay stood watching them with a growing unease. He sensed what Quinta had, that Simon Whitelaw was in love with Lily. Hartwell Barclay's fingers tightened into frustrated fists by his side. In the light of the wall sconces that red hair of hers glowed like captured firelight. Over the last two years, Lily Christian had grown into a beauty. Hartwell Barclay continued to stare unblinkingly. Chewing his thumbnail, he watched the way she smiled, the way she moved. Her cloak concealed the sway of her hips, but he had watched that seductive movement enough times to be able to imagine now how they moved. And those green eyes of hers, the way they glinted so mysteriously, so provocatively from beneath those thick lashes.

Hartwell Barclay wiped his forehead nervously. He would not allow it. Simon Whitelaw must not be allowed to marry Lily Christian. If he did, then the Whitelaws would gain control of Highcross. They had wanted to do that all along. He would never allow that to happen. He would never lose Highcross. Highcross was his—and Lily was his.

"Shall I accompany you? I might be of some assistance," he heard Artemis call to them.

"Where is Raphael?" Dulcie's high-pitched cry broke into his reverie.

"Raphael! You come back here!" Dulcie called to the pup, and to Hartwell's horror he saw the dog heading toward the corner of the hall.

"Oh, no! Raphael, don't!" Dulcie cried out.

"Assistance? What is wrong?" Simon demanded, pulling his gaze away from Hartwell Barclay, who was hotfooting it across the hall. "You are not ill, are you, Lily?" he asked.

"No, 'tis Tristram. He was in a fight," Lily explained, touched by Simon's concern. "He took quite a beating."

"I'd better come along," Simon decided, but when Quinta eyed him doubtfully, he spoke defensively. "Tristram will need a man to talk to."

"I have some salve of henbane in my trunk. I'll have that woman prepare him a posset," Artemis suggested. "The poor little lad is probably chilled to the bone after that long ride from the village.''

''That will do wonders for him. You might give her your recipe, Artemis. I really don't think she uses the proper blend of spices or enough eggs. The last one we had here wasn't near thick enough for my taste. Until she gets it cooked, you might have her fill a drinking horn with some burnt wine, 'twill help the lad sleep better. But I will find the salve, dear,'' Quinta called back to her. ''You needn't come back upstairs. I do not think Rodger would approve of you climbing up and down the stairs so much. You must remember your condition. You would coddle Tristram too much anyway. 'Twould embarrass the poor boy. You will have plenty of time to practice in the years to come,'' Quinta told her, smiling down at her niece.

Lily glanced back at the two people standing so closely together at the foot of the stairs. Sir Rodger was whispering something in her ear, much to her delight. Frowning, Lily glanced at Quinta, a questioning look in her eye.

''Oh, my dear! You don't know! Of course you are quite outraged. Scandalous behavior, is it not?'' Quinta laughed, patting Lily's arm apologetically. ''You were not here when we arrived. Artemis and Sir Rodger were wed this summer. She is now Lady Artemis Penmorley. Is it not wonderful? But what a surprise, I must admit. No one knew, not even I, that the two of them were so inclined. Hardly ever a glance exchanged. Such mysterious goings-on. Why, I half thought 'twould be Sir Rodger and Cordelia Howard, but the woman cannot seem to make up her mind. Now, however, I do believe that she and Valentine will wed before summer next. She came to stay at Ravindzara last spring and you couldn't separate the two for longer than a second. There must indeed be some truth to the belief that spring is a time for lovers. You do remember Thomas Sandrick? Well, he married Eliza Valchamps, Sir Raymond Valchamps's sister, that same spring. Quite a good match. We attended a magnificent banquet at Sir Raymond's estate just outside of London. Elizabeth gave him the house and land. He saved her life. I know he is not a favorite of Valentine's, but he was a very charming host. I do rather enjoy his wit. Even Elizabeth attended. There were fireworks, plays, routs, and even a masque ball. He has recently inherited a fortune from a relative, and he was very lavish in his entertainments. Even Elizabeth was impressed. Quite wonderful. Do you know it is quite extraordinary, but with all of the acquaintances Sir Raymond must have, he always finds the time to inquire about your welfare, dear. Most thoughtful, but I believe he did mention that he'd met you here at Highcross years ago and that you'd enchanted him.

"Well, enough of that gossip. Where was I, dear? Oh, yes, we were so amazed when Sir Rodger came to us and asked to wed Artemis. Actually, 'twas Valentine he spoke to. It was most unexpected. There has been a bit of awkwardness between our families over the years, I'll not deny that. And there is a difference in religion. However, all Valentine wanted to know was if Sir Rodger loved Artemis, and, more importantly, did she love him? There was, of course, no need to question the man's antecedents. I hardly think we could find a more gentlemanly courtier in all of England. And we all know how wealthy Sir Rodger is.

"Well, it really has been such a whirlwind. But I have never seen Artemis so happy, nor indeed, Sir Rodger," Quinta said, her words droning on in Lily's ears as Lily tried to smile; but her effort felt stiff and unnatural. "We really must have you attend Valentine's wedding if he does marry Cordelia when he returns from this voyage. Perhaps he will have less desire to leave England with a beautiful, bored wife staying behind. And with Cordelia, he will certainly have reason to worry," Quinta said, but her laughter came less easily this time.

Valentine and Cordelia Howard to wed by summer. Cordelia had been to Ravindzara. Lily bit her lip, her knuckles whitening around the packages she held to her breast like a shield against the pain caused by Quinta's casually uttered words.

"Are you all right, Lily? You're so pale," Simon asked worriedly.

"Why, my dear, you are shivering. Why don't you go to your bed chamber and get out of those damp clothes. Simon and I will see to Tristram," Quinta ordered, her tone of voice brooking no argument. "You need a rest after that ride. I can see that you are taking far too much upon yourself. I'll have that woman send you up a nice warming posset. There really is nothing quite like it for fighting off a chill," Quinta told her with a comforting smile.

Pressing her hand to Lily's forehead, she frowned. "You are a bit flushed, my dear. I really must have a talk with that guardian of yours. He really should have his head examined for allowing you to ride into the village on a day as foul as this one. He has a coach, he ought to use it for more than traveling into London once a year. Now, run along, and I'll make certain you've a fire in your room. Come, Simon," Quinta said as Simon continued to stand gazing after Lily. "I swear, sometimes this place is as cold as the grave," Quinta added uneasily as she glanced back at Lily's lone figure disappearing along the shadowy corridor.

We have heard the chimes at midnight.

SHAKESPEARE

Chapter Sixteen

THE storms of February blew into March with a vengeance
and proved false the old proverb:

> If Candlemas Day be fair and bright,
> Winter will have another flight;
> If on Candlemas Day it be shower and rain,
> Winter is gone and will not come again.

It had been a chilling ride to the parish church on Candlemas
Day to offer up candles in honor of the Virgin Mary. A fortnight
into February, lightning struck the steeple of the church and
burned it down to the square tower. And even the grumbling
cook at Highcross had been anxious to rise from her cold bed and
stir the banked fire in the great hearth of the kitchens for the
preparation of the traditional pancakes on Shrove Tuesday.

The narrow lane between Highcross and East Highford became impassable except on foot or horseback, and the waters of
Little Highford threatened to rise above its banks. It had been
with cold, stiff fingers on St. Valentine's Eve that Lily had written upon a billet Valentine Whitelaw's name and tucked it safely
away inside her bodice. And shivering with the other maidens of
the village, she had carried a garland of flowers, sweet herbs,
and ribbons before the casket of the shoemaker's unmarried sister, certain her fate, too, was to die an old maid. Throughout the
forty days of Lent, the Candlemas-eve winds continued to bring
the icy rains of winter.

Lengten-tide had been a long time coming, but finally it was spring, and already the days of April were becoming warmer and longer as they stretched toward summer. That afternoon had t en uncommonly warm, and Lily had unlatched the window in her bedchamber for the first time in months. The soft breeze caressed her while she poured the steaming water Tillie had brought up from the kitchens into the large, wooden tub. With care, she measured a couple of drops of rose oil into the water. The rising steam carried the heady scent on an aromatic cloud throughout the chamber.

Lily had begun to undress, proceeding as far as her under-skirt and chemise, when she paused for a moment and listened to the nightingale's song beyond the casement window. It came so sweetly, yet there was an underlying sadness to the notes that drifted to her from the woodlands. It was the first she had heard since winter's passing, but overnight the pale green leaves seemed to be unfolding on the bare branches, and the first cro-cuses were blossoming under the friendly warmth of the sun.

Lily breathed deeply, expelling her breath on a sigh of plea-sure. Although Hartwell Barclay had recently purchased fine carpets for the great chamber and his own private chamber, she still preferred the meadow-sweet fragrance of the fresh rushes strewn across the floor of her bedchamber. Dried lavender and roses scented the sachets tucked beneath the pillows and cover-let of the bed and sweetened the folds of clothing placed in the gilded chest at its foot. Sandalwood, clove, marjoram, and pen-nyroyal in a pierced potpourri jar on the mantelpiece lent a spicy redolence to the room. A vase on the windowsill held a spray of woodbine, a wild daffodil nodding on its slender stalk, and sev-eral delicate musk-roses plucked from the woods by Tristram. Inside an elaborately carved ivory box on the small bedside table was an assortment of prized vials of exotic perfumes of Araby—jasmine, orange blossom, hyacinth, violet, and patchouli—which had been a gift from Valentine Whitelaw on his return from one of his journeys to the Mediterranean.

''*Praaack!* Me arse is half frozen! Lift a leg, my pretty! *Praaack!*'' Cisco declared, strutting back and forth on his perch in the corner of the room. ''I'll have that bird roastin' on a spit if he don't shut up! *Praaack!*'' Cisco cried, his last statement mimicking the cook to perfection. "He nipped me! Ye bloodthirsty knave!"

Lily glanced over at him in surprise, a slight frown marring her brow. At times, it was fortunate that Cisco repeated whatever he heard. Lily would make certain she kept an eye on the cook in order to keep intact those green feathers Cisco preened with such inordinate pride.

"Oooh, Mistress Lily, I don't know how 'tis ye haven't shriveled up or caught yer death of cold by now," Tillie exclaimed as she entered the room, two more buckets of steaming water swinging from a yoke balanced across her shoulders. Setting them down by the tub, she quickly emptied the contents, careful for once not to spill any of the water. With a sigh, she straightened, her hand massaging the small of her back.

"Are ye certain, mistress, 'tisn't harmful bathing? I've heard some bloodcurdling stories, I have. Haven't done it very often, meself, and both times I nearly caught me death of cold. Nearly broke off all me teeth, I was chattering that much. Sneezed fer days afterwards and me skin started to flake off. Thought I was goin' to die," Tillie recalled with a shudder. "Reckon a spot of cold water against me face is all I'm needin'," she decided, but Lily could see her eyeing the warm, scented water almost wistfully.

"If you add a drop of oil to the water your skin won't dry out like that. Why don't you soak in the tub after I've finished? 'Tis so sweetly scented, 'twould be wasteful to pour it out. You must be all aches, Tillie. You've been on your hands and knees the whole day. I promise no harm will befall you. And think how pleased Farley will be," Lily added as a final inducement.

"Oh, Mistress Lily, why, whatever ye be talkin' of?" Tillie blushed and looked away nervously. "Now, mistress, ye do worry too much about the likes of me," she protested, shrugging off her lady's concern. She'd heard Mistress Lily's mother had been a fine gentlewoman too, always concerning herself about others. Tillie bit her lip, wondering if she should confide in Mistress Lily.

"And with good reason, for you were scrubbing the kitchens when I was distilling some flower waters, and later you were soaping down the hall," Lily reminded her as she stepped out of her underskirt. "Surely you have completed most of your duties for the day," Lily asked, thinking Tillie was looking more haggard than usual and vowing that she'd hire two more scullery maids when she became mistress of Highcross. She would also make Tillie her lady's maid.

"I've washed up the dinner plates and scoured the pots, but most likely the master will find something else fer me to do. Ah, but that do smell nice, mistress," Tillie sighed, scooping up a handful of water and patting it on her cheeks. "Hmm, smells like a whole garden of roses. Kinda deep, though, mistress. Ye could drown in less water; why the old Widow Hubbs slipped in a puddle t'other day and could've drowned right there on High Street if that cart hadn't run over her first. 'Tis the truth, mistress. Why, just before ye comes to Highcross, young Dan Barber drowned in a trencher plate at t'Oaks. But then, Farley Odell has always said that Dickie Sawyer serves watered-down gravy at t'Oaks. Too thin, 'tis. If it'd been thicker, bit of oatmeal in it maybe, why, Dan Barber would most likely be alive today."

Lily smiled. "I don't think I need worry." Pulling off her stockings and chemise, Lily climbed into the tub, sinking down until the water rose just above her bare shoulders.

"Ye can swim, can't ye, mistress? That be amazin'. Not many folk can," Tillie said as she hefted back up the wooden buckets. "I'm always wonderin' how them folk learn in the first place, 'cause if ye don't know how, then how are ye goin' to learn before ye drowns?" she puzzled. "Ain't goin' to do ye no good knowin' how if ye be on the bottom," Tillie said wisely, heading toward the door. "I'll be fetchin' some wood now, then start that fire, mistress," Tillie added with a backward glance over her shoulder.

Lily ducked as the buckets swung around. "A fire?" she questioned doubtfully, glancing over at the hearth that hadn't felt the heat of a fire in almost a year. Not since she'd been ill with a fever and Quinta Whitelaw had demanded the unhealthy damp be driven from the cold bedchamber. If she hadn't been so ill, Lily would have laughed aloud that day, for Quinta had certainly known how to light a fire under Hartwell Barclay, warning him he'd have many questions to answer if anything should happen to his ward because he was too cheap to allow a fire in her bedchamber.

"Oh, yes, mistress. The master, seein' me bringin' up yer

bath water, says 'tis still too chilly fer ye to be bathin' up here without no fire. Says he doesn't want ye to become chilled. Can't have that, no sir, he says with a big smile," Tillie told her, eyeing her mistress curiously.

Lily's gaze narrowed thoughtfully.

"Reckon he be tetched in the head?" Tillie asked, for the master had never before worried about Mistress Lily falling ill.

"I wonder," Lily murmured.

"I wonder he can still stand. Ain't seen him without that fancy silver wine cup of his all day. Started the day off with several tankards of ale, then had his claret at luncheon, and more at dinner, and now he's in the great chamber sippin' from a drinkin' horn full of hot spiced wine. Must have drunk up half a hogshead by now. Thinks he's ol' King Harry sittin' there lordin' it over the household," Tillie muttered as she hurried to the door, but before she reached it, it was opened just wide enough for a small face to peek inside.

"Oh, Mistress Dulcie! Ye're lettin' in a draft. Want to bring about the death of yer sister?" Tillie told the child.

"Come in, Dulcie," Lily called to her, smiling reassuringly when the door opened wider to allow Dulcie's thin figure to enter. Lily continued to watch the door and was not surprised when it was nudged wider and Raphael's big head poked inside. He had grown another foot and weighed twice as much since coming to Highcross, and Lily wondered idly if he would ever stop growing. He looked like a small pony trotting into the room. And sitting on his back, a small black hand hooked beneath the tattered blue ribbon, was Cappie, bedecked in his green velvet cap and jacket.

"If they ain't the pair," Tillie said with a grin, but giving the mastiff plenty of room as she slipped out the door.

Humming some unrecognizable song to herself, Dulcie came to stand beside the tub. Cappie hopped off Raphael's back and scampered along the curving rim, his chattering voice rising excitedly when Dulcie began to swirl the water, disturbing his reflection in its surface.

"What have you been doing?" Lily asked, flicking water on Dulcie's cheek in response to the splash that had drenched her face much to Dulcie's giggling delight.

"Nothing," Dulcie replied. "I'm glad 'tis warmer. I wish the lake didn't freeze every winter. Our pool on the island never froze over. We could swim all year long. Only time I get to swim now is when I take a bath, and that's not any fun," she said, her hand sending a wave of water toward Cappie's tiny feet. Scolding her, he leapt onto the bed where he took off his cap before curling up against the pillows.

"You left your embroidery in the hall," Lily told her sister. "I noticed you have almost completed it. It is very lovely, Dulcie," Lily complimented her. She had been surprised by the beauty of the needlework. Dulcie was becoming an accomplished needlewoman, just like their mother.

"I tried to work slowly, but I just couldn't wait to see it finished. I was very careful with my stitches, just like Jane showed me," Dulcie said.

"It's quite unusual. The flowers remind me of the ones on the island."

"I tried so hard to remember, Lily, but I couldn't remember exactly," Dulcie said, pleased by her sister's remark.

"I think they are all the prettier because of that. They look like mythical flowers. We will have to go into the village and buy some more silk thread now that the weather is warmer."

"Really! Do you think we can find some brighter colors this time, Lily? I'm always using up the red. I don't like the pale colors. My flowers and butterflies have to be bright as the sun," Dulcie explained very seriously. With a shy glance, she added, "I was thinking of giving an embroidered length of silk to the queen next New Year's Day if we are invited to court. Do you think she would like it?"

"I am certain she would be delighted," Lily told her, remembering some of the New Year's gifts she had watched Elizabeth receive with a queenly graciousness and an almost childlike delight last year. Jeweled pomanders, scented, lace-trimmed gloves, purses full of gold coin, and all manner of expensive gifts she'd received from her courtiers and others seeking royal favor, and with equal excitement Elizabeth had also accepted the more simple gifts from her loyal subjects: a nosegay from a scullery maid, a freshly caught trout from one of her bargemen, an orange studded with cloves from a gardener, and even a freshly baked quince pie from one of her bakers. And their generosity was returned in sundry gifts she handed out to her favorites. "If

Jane does not have the silks we need, then I'll have her order some special from London.''

"Oh, thank you, Lily!" Dulcie exclaimed, dancing around the room. "This is my favorite room at Highcross," Dulcie confided as she spun on her toes, her skirts floating around her until she came to a halt near the window. She reached out her hand and cupped one of the musk-roses, sniffing its fragrance. "Your room reminds me of the island, Lily. There are always flowers, and even in winter, when there aren't any fresh ones from the gardens, it still smells like spring. Even the bed hangings smell like roses," Dulcie said, throwing herself on the bed with a flying leap that had Cappie scrambling between the pillows and the bolster set against the headboard. Rolling onto her stomach, Dulcie playfully slid her hand beneath the pillow. A moment later, Cappie's dark face appeared, but unable to resist a bit of petting, he crawled out and sat next to her. His eyes closed with contentment as she scratched him under the chin. "I'm glad 'tis spring. Winter is too dark. I don't like it when there's not any sunshine.''

Tillie came staggering through the door with an armful of kindling and a couple of split logs, her steps somehow finding their way safely around the sleeping form of the dog stretched out in the middle of the room. Down on her hands and knees before the hearth, she grimaced when a spider came dangling down from the flue, his web undisturbed until now. But soon a crackling fire was spreading its warmth throughout the room and replacing the light that was fading fast beyond the windows.

"A fire?" Dulcie said, staring openmouthed at the dancing flames. "Are you sick, Lily?" she demanded, glancing over at her sister worriedly.

"No," Lily declared with a laugh. "Indeed, I shall wash my hair now that the room will be warmer," she suddenly decided, determined to make the most of this unexpected treat. Pulling the ribbons from her hair, she allowed the long red strands to reach into the soapy water. Closing her eyes, she sank beneath the surface, dampening the thick mass of hair so she could work the soap through it.

"Oh, mistress, ye be temptin' fate," Tillie sighed, for everyone knew migraines and madness came of getting your head wet, and no telling what might happen if a person got water in his ears, she thought, terrified. Saying a silent prayer to protect them both, Tillie helped Lily rinse her hair with the clear water from the earthenware jug on the bedside table, then held up the blanket she'd placed close to the warmth of the fire for Lily to wrap herself in when she climbed from the tub.

By the time Lily moved closer to the hearth, Raphael had changed his position and now lay toasting himself before the fire, his eyelids fluttering now and again as he no doubt dreamt of chasing rabbits across the fields. But he had to share his enviable position, for Dulcie had climbed down beside him and was now lying with her head propped up on his chest.

"Lily?" Dulcie questioned, wiggling her toes closer to the heat.

"Hmmmm?" Lily's voice was muffled as she shook out her hair and tried to wring the water out of its dripping length. Threading her fingers through the long strands, she spread them out to catch the warmth.

"May I brush your hair until it sparkles and crackles with fire?"

Lily smiled, remembering how she used to brush their mother's hair after they'd bathed in the pool behind their hut on the island. They'd sit on the edge of the pool, basking in the warm afternoon sun while they waited for their hair to dry. To pass the time, they would sing songs and talk nonsense until their laughter eventually drew Basil's curiosity. Those were the special times, Lily thought. "Yes, I would like that, Dulcie."

"Lily?"

"Yes."

"Do you think I could sleep in here tonight?"

Lily looked down at Dulcie's dark head resting so trustingly on Raphael's chest, her thin hands held out to the warmth of the fire, and Lily knew she couldn't deny her. Even though she had Raphael for company, Dulcie had never liked having a room of her own.

"May I go get on my nightdress now?" Dulcie asked. It was growing dark, and soon she'd have to light a candle to undress by.

"Run along," Lily told her. "Where is Tristram?" she called after her.

Dulcie and Raphael paused in their flight to the door. "Right after dinner, since it was still light, Tristram went out with Farley and Fairfax."

Lily raised an eyebrow. She didn't like the sound of that, for wherever Farley and Fairfax were to be found, trouble soon followed.

"Do you know where they went, Tillie?" Lily asked, not feeling any easier when she saw the guilty expression crossing Tillie's face.

"Me? Oh, Mistress Lily, now I wouldn't be knowin' about such things," Tillie was too quick to deny. "Oughta empty this tub."

"Why don't you leave it until morning? 'Tis getting dark," Lily advised, beginning to worry about Tristram's whereabouts, especially if he was in the company of Farley and Fairfax Odell.

"Oh, I really should, mistress," Tillie said. "Oughta help Mistress Dulcie into her nightdress," she suggested, edging toward the door.

"Tillie?" Lily said softly.

"Yes, mistress," she answered uneasily.

"Why don't you and I have a little talk while I finish drying my hair?" Lily murmured, eyeing Tillie's stiffening shoulders with interest.

"Yes, mistress."

"Now, where have Farley and Fairfax and my brother gone?"

Tillie swallowed nervously. "They truly be gone, then?" she questioned doubtfully.

"Where?" Lily repeated.

"Thought fer sure I heard them come back just minutes ago," Tillie said, cocking her head as if listening to approaching footsteps. "Shall I run down to see?" she offered eagerly, not liking the glint that had come into her mistress's eye. "Reckon they could even be out in the stables."

"I did not hear anything. And where exactly would they be returning from, Tillie?" Lily asked, slipping into the dressing robe Tillie had been busying herself with finding for the last few minutes.

"Well?" Lily asked as the silence continued.

"Reckon they just might've ambled into the village," Tillie finally admitted.

"Into Highford? What on earth for? Except for the Oaks, all of the shops are closed," Lily asked, amazed by Tillie's answer.

"Reckon they might not be goin' in to do any shoppin', mistress."

"Why did they go into Highford?"

Tillie started to chew her bottom lip.

Lily sighed. She knew Farley and Fairfax too well. "What mischief have those two planned now?"

Tillie took a deep breath, meeting Lily's gaze bravely. "Well, Farley says he ain't never met a man who don't have something to feel guilty about, even if 'tis just in his mind, and 'tis about time the good reverend was reminded that he's human, too. Reckon Farley has gotten tired of the Reverend Buxby always pointin' his long finger at him and Fairfax in church each Sabbath. Ye'd think they was the only two who spent any time in t'Oaks. Reckon, too, Farley don't like the way the reverend's been casting suspicion on yer good name, Mistress Lily," Tillie admitted, still feeling uncomfortable about the way the reverend had talked of sin and damnation, and all the while staring down at Lily Christian.

"And just exactly how are they going to achieve their purpose?" Lily asked almost reluctantly.

Tillie's lips twitched just slightly, and Lily could not have sworn if it had been out of fear or amusement. "Reckon the good reverend might see the ghost of St. George a-wanderin' and a-moanin' and a-callin' his name in the graveyard this evenin'. Real eerie, with a full moon risin' over them headstones. Farley swears there really is a ghost a-hauntin' that place," Tillie said with a shiver of foreboding.

But it was nothing compared to the dread Lily was experiencing. "And Tristram went with them," she said.

"Well, the young master overheard them talkin', mistress, and he said he had a right to be there too. Besides, Farley said 'twould be better if there were three of them, one to be the ghost and two to play the dragon. And ye know Master Tristram's been so awful upset of late, mistress, what with the reverend talkin' of . . . well . . . you know the way he carries on about . . . well . . . you know. . . ."

"Yes, about the children of sin being more easily led into the evils of this world than those of God-fearing parents," Lily said, and suddenly she wished Farley and Fairfax had invited her along, too, for she'd love to see the good reverend's face when the ghost started moaning his name.

"You said Tristram is to be the ghost?"

"Oh, yes. Ye see, Fairfax found this old boar's head, and they've fixed it up to look like a dragon's head. Fairfax is goin' to wave a torch before him, like the dragon's breathin' fire. Then Farley, who'll be underneath the blanket behind Fairfax, will be carryin' Master Tristram on his shoulders. Ooooh, mistress, ye know what they did? They got the breastplate and helmet from that suit of armor in the hall, and they put it on Master Tristram. They even got the shield and sword. 'Twill look just like St. George fightin' the dragon, what with Master Tristram swingin' that sword and the fire roarin' from the dragon's mouth," Tillie said excitedly.

"I just hope Tristram doesn't behead Fairfax by mistake," Lily commented, thinking that if anything went wrong, which it was certain to since Farley and Fairfax were involved, then they were all going to be in very serious trouble.

"And Farley's goin' to cry out the reverend's name, and maybe even name some of them fine folks of the village. Half the village is likely to be at the church this eve, seein' how they be preparin' the dragon fer the procession. Day after tomorrow will be the festival, though I s'pose if Farley gets caught we won't be goin' to the feastin', or walkin' in the procession," Tillie worried, then suddenly cried out and rushed over to the window.

"Whatever is wrong?"

"Can't ye hear it? Oh, no!" Tillie wailed, wrapping her arms around her middle as she rocked back and forth on her heels.

Lily listened, expecting to hear the sound of angry villagers coming up the lane and shouting for the blood of Farley and Fairfax Odell. But all she could hear was the nightingale's singing. " 'Tis just a bird complaining about the darkness."

"Just a bird? 'Tis a cuckoo!" Tillie cried with a sniff of despair. "And I heard it call at least six times! Oh, what am I goin' to do? I'll never marry now! Not fer six years. 'Twill be too late by then!" Tillie cried.

"Tillie, hush!" Lily said, trying to calm her, but Tillie kept crying, and her wails were growing louder by the second.

"Tillie, please. Hush! Do you want to disturb the whole household? I tell you that was a nightingale. Not a cuckoo," Lily entreated her, wondering what difference it made whether it was a nightingale or a cuckoo. "Now, come over here and let me dry your tears," Lily cajoled, her arm around Tillie's shaking shoulders as she led her toward the tub. Dipping her handkerchief in the rose-scented water, she dabbed it against Tillie's cheeks.

Tillie sniffed back the tears still threatening. "Are you certain 'twasn't a cuckoo?"

"Of course I am," Lily reassured her. "But why are you so alarmed, Tillie? And what is this about never marrying? After all, you are still a very young woman. There will be plenty of time for you to wed."

" 'Tis the legend. Maire Lester used to tell it to me. She heard it, and she never wed. I've heard his cry now, and six times. I won't marry fer six years, if at all. It'll come true, I just know it! I'm never goin' to get married," Tillie bawled.

"Of course you will, but even if you didn't, well, would that really be all that bad? You will always have a home here at Highcross. Besides, you're worrying for nothing. I thought you and Farley were certain to wed before the year was out," Lily said, trying to be helpful, but when she saw the expression on Tillie's face, she realized she'd said the wrong thing.

"He won't wed me now that I've heard the cuckoo. Maybe he don't love me anymore now that we've—or," she cried shrilly, her fears worsening, "maybe something will happen to him tonight. He might get shot! Or maybe he fell into the river while crossing the bridge. And now no one will wed me! Not now that Farley's gotten me with child! The master will kick me out of the house. Reckon he'll be findin' out soon enough, what with that cook stickin' her porker's snout in my business all the time. Askin' me questions about why I'm gettin' sick in the mornin'. Told her 'twas seein' her ugly face so early! I'll be run out t'village once they hears about it. Maybe they'll lock me up in the stocks. I'll be left on the village green fer all of them to jeer at and throw rotten eggs and cabbages at. Oh, what am I goin' to do, Mistress Lily? I got nowhere to go. I was born in the almshouse. I can't go back there. Oh, what am I to do, Mistress Lily?" she wailed, throwing her arms around a stunned Lily.

"What's wrong with Tillie? I could hear her crying all the way down the corridor," Dulcie said, waiting long enough for

Raphael to enter the room before she closed the door behind her.
"Do you want a bite of this tart, Tillie?" Dulcie offered, holding
out the mincemeat tart she'd been hiding behind her back, willing to share if it would make Tillie stop crying.

"*Praaack!* Ye knaves and tarts! Ho! Villains, me pretty! Villains! Damn them all and sink 'em! *Praaack!*"

With a watery hiccup and an almost comical expression on
her face, Tillie stared at the innocent-faced little girl and then at
the sharp-tongued parrot and started to cry all over again.

"Did I do something wrong, Lily?" Dulcie asked, looking
down at the soggy tart. "I snuck down to the kitchens and found
some in the cupboard. I knew they weren't all gone like the cook
said," Dulcie explained, going to sit before the fire, Raphael keeping close beside her lest she forget to share her prize with him.

"Will you tell me some tales, Lily?" Dulcie asked, taking a
bite out of the mincemeat tart, then handing a portion to Raphael, who promptly swallowed it. "I want to hear the tale of
the wild white horses and how they defeated the witch when
they reached England. I bet the queen would like to hear the
tale, too, Lily. How does it begin? 'On the isle of pines and
palms, where the waves . . .' "

The fire had burned down to glowing coals when Lily heard a
footstep outside her door. Yawning, she stretched from her
cramped position before the hearth, reluctant to leave its
warmth. She remained still, listening for the sound again, but
there was only silence.

Lily glanced over toward the bed, but all she could hear was
quiet breathing. She'd finally managed to calm Tillie down, and
unable to watch her return to the narrow mat she slept on in the
servants' wing, she had tucked Tillie into her bed beside a peacefully sleeping Dulcie, who'd dozed off during her own telling of
her favorite tale.

Unable to sleep until Tristram returned, Lily had curled up
close to the fire. During the long hours that had passed while she
waited, she thought of the conversation she'd had with Tillie,
and of the conversation she would have to have with Farley
Odell, the father of the child Tillie now carried. Tillie had said
that Farley wanted to wed her. Although she had said nothing to

Tillie, Lily had promised herself that she'd see that Farley Odell did exactly that.

Lighting a taper from one of the glowing coals in the hearth, Lily lit a candle and slipped out of her room. Making her way along the darkened corridor toward Tristram's room, she opened the door and stepped inside without knocking.

In the flickering candlelight, Lily could see Tristram sitting on the edge of his bed, his head bowed, his fingers clasped together tightly.

"Well? Aren't you at least going to say good night after I've stayed awake waiting for you to return?" Lily greeted him.

Startled, Tristram jerked his head up, looking as guilty as he should after a midnight raid on a graveyard. "Lily!"

"I am certainly relieved to see that you are in one piece. Can we say the same of Farley and Fairfax, your cohorts in this escapade?"

"You know?" Tristram asked with a sigh, but he sounded relieved.

"What happened in the village?" Lily asked him, moving to sit beside him on the bed.

"Oh, Lily," he said, his spirits momentarily lifting as he remembered, "I wish you'd been there. Farley rubbed this strange, glowing, green, slimy stuff on the blanket, then he put it over Fairfax's head before he got behind. Fairfax had this boar's head, only you would have thought 'twas a dragon's. Then I was wearing a suit of armor, just like St. George, and sitting up on Farley's shoulders. We went running through the graveyard, Fairfax waving the torch, and I was slashing through the air with the sword, and Farley was moaning and crying and making this awful dragon's roar. You should have seen those villagers come racing out of the church," he said, nearly doubling over with laughter.

"The Reverend Buxby tripped over that woman, Mistress Fordham, and she must have thought the dragon had her, because she cut loose with this horrible scream and grabbed hold of a shovel that had been left by one of the graves. Then she swung around with it and caught the reverend smack in the middle of his seat. Sent him flying over the nearest headstone."

Lily tried not to laugh, but her shoulders were beginning to shake as she envisioned the nightmarish scene.

"Of course, that's when everything started to go wrong. Fairfax tripped, and the blanket caught on a branch and got pulled off," Tristram admitted, glancing over at Lily.

"So you were recognized."

"I think so, Lily," Tristram said dejectedly. "I heard someone call out Farley's name, and Fairfax is the biggest man in the village. Don't suppose he'd be hard to miss."

"You had the helmet on. They wouldn't have recognized you, Tristram."

"I dropped the shield. It has our coat of arms on it," he said glumly. "I guess I'm in a lot of trouble. Hartwell will have every reason now to send me away to school."

Lily placed her arm around Tristram's shoulders comfortingly. "You do realize that it was wrong for you and Farley and Fairfax to do what you did," she told him, wondering how their father or Basil would have handled this situation.

"They deserved it, Lily," Tristram responded. "Even if I do get sent away, it was worth it to see them all racing around like scared rabbits."

"I'm not excusing the villagers, Tristram. They've been unjust in their actions too, but that doesn't mean we have the right to even the score," Lily tried to explain.

"I think Father would have laughed tonight, Lily," Tristram said softly. "He wouldn't have let those villagers say things about you and Dulcie like they do. And he would have defended our honor, just like I have, only maybe I did it a little differently than he might have. I haven't done any harm to anyone. I just made those people feel like the fools they are. I don't think Basil or Mother would have been ashamed of me, do you, Lily?"

Lily took a deep breath, wondering how to answer that. She was searching her mind for an appropriate parable to tell him when a frightening bellow filled the silence, followed by high-pitched squealing and wild barking and cries of "Rape!" and "Murder!" and "Lily, help me!"

Lily nearly dropped the candlestick when she jumped to her feet. Tristram had already reached the door and was racing down the corridor to her room. A couple of steps behind him, Lily stumbled against him when she entered. And unable to move as they stared at the scene, they continued to stand in the opened doorway.

Tillie was standing on the bed, clutching to her breast the nightdress Lily had lent her and which was now torn almost in two. Her howls, coming between gasping breaths, were almost deafening and rivaled Cisco's screeching as he flew around the room, until finally coming to roost on top of the bed, where Cappie was clinging to the tall headboard and chattering non-stop. Dulcie sat huddled against the pillows, her black eyes full of wonder as she stared at Hartwell Barclay's bare legs protruding from the tub. Next to it, Raphael, who had a death-bite on one of Hartwell's slippers, was growling and pawing at the offending object that had dropped from his enemy's foot.

"He attacked me!" Tillie cried, pointing an accusing finger at Hartwell Barclay. "Out of the dark like some demon, he came! Jumps on the bed and pins me down. He tried to . . . to . . . well, I'll not repeat such a thing before young, innocent ears. He slobbered all over me! I thought at first 'twas Raphael, until he started talkin'," Tillie told them, but all the while keeping a watchful eye on the tub.

"Oh, Mistress Lily! He said terrible things, he did. And he thought I was you! He's drunk, mistress. Said them Whitelaws wasn't goin' to get their greedy hands on his money. Nor was that Simon Whitelaw ever goin' to wed ye. Said that after tonight ye'd marry him, or ye'd be a ruined woman! Said he'd see ye dead and buried before he'd let ye marry anyone but himself."

"Lily?" Tristram said, eyeing the tub. "Do you think he's dead?"

"I didn't kill him! I'm no murderess! 'Twas the dog! He jumps up on the bed when Mistress Dulcie started screamin'. Thought he was goin' to tear the master apart, I did. The master started screamin' then and leaps out of the bed. Then there was a funny noise, kinda like a splash, then a gurgling sound, and then I didn't hear him again."

Slowly, Lily walked over to the tub and peered over the edge.

"Oh, mistress!" Tillie cried. "Remember the Widow Hubbs and Dan Barber. Ye don't think the master has drowned?"

Lily stared down at Hartwell Barclay's pale face bobbing in the tub.

"He's dead, Lily," Tristram said, startling Lily. "The constable is bound to come tomorrow morning, or maybe even tonight, because of what happened at the church. He and a group of them vil-

lagers will show up here at Highcross, Lily, and demand that we
all be brought to trial," Tristram warned her, clutching Lily's
arm and trying to drag her away from Hartwell Barclay's body.

"But he tried to attack Tillie. It was self-defense, Tristram,"
Lily said, as if explaining to the authorities. "He was crazed with
drink. He might have killed Tillie, or me, if I'd been in my bed,"
Lily suddenly realized.

"Do you think they are going to believe us?" Tristram asked.
"After tonight, they aren't looking for much of an excuse to send
me to Newgate Prison. Farley and Fairfax said that's what would
happen if we got caught. Oh, Lily, please, listen to me. They'll
think you murdered Hartwell. They'll think you murdered him because he was your guardian. They'll hang you, Lily," Tristram
pleaded with her, still pulling on her arm. "And they'll take me
and Farley and Fairfax away. What are we going to do, Lily?"

Lily stared at Hartwell's body. "We'll tell the truth, Tristram.
We have friends, we'll get help."

"There is no one to help us. Valentine Whitelaw is at sea. Artemis is married now, and she's back in Cornwall. She's going to
have a baby, Lily. She can't come to help us. Remember the letter from Quinta we got just last week? She's in the North Country. She's going across the border into Scotland. She won't even
know they've hanged you until 'tis too late, Lily!" Tristram
cried, shaking Lily's arm frantically.

"They mustn't hang Lily! They mustn't!" Dulcie cried, hopping down from the bed and flinging herself against Lily. "Are
they going to take Tristram away? Are they going to hang you,
Lily? Don't leave me, Lily! Don't ever leave me, Lily!"

"Who's going to believe us, Lily? Who's going to help us? No
one. No one, Lily."

"Oh, Mistress Lily! They'll think *I* killed the master. They
won't believe me when I tell them that he attacked me. When
they see that I'm with child, they'll think *he* was me lover!
They'll think I murdered him 'cause he wouldn't do right by
me," Tillie said wildly, her eyes darting around the room as if
seeking escape until they came to rest on Lily. "What are we
goin' to do, Mistress Lily?" she asked with a pitiful look. "What
are we goin' to do?"

I know a bank whereon the wild thyme blows,
Where oxlips and the nodding violet grows
Quite over-canopied with luscious woodbine,
With sweet musk-roses, and with eglantine:
There sleeps Titania some time of the night,
Lull'd in these flowers with dances and delight;
And there the snake throws her enamell'd skin,
Weed wide enough to wrap a fairy in.

SHAKESPEARE

Chapter Seventeen

"RARE phoenix birds from the deserts of Araby! Gold-spun silks and precious spices from the Kingdom of Kublai Khan! Marco Polo himself brought back this fine piece of jade from Kinsai! Oranges from Baghdad! Ivory tusks from Malabar! Musk, given to me by the black-eyed daughter of a Tartar chieftain! I, myself, have seen the wonders of the world! Come closer, fair maids and gentleman all, and listen to my tale of desert caravans and golden-domed palaces. And see for yourselves these priceless gifts!"

Overhead, the summer sky was as bright a blue as the lapis lazuli held in the outstretched palm of a dealer in rare gems. Colorful pennants and flags, strung along the length of stalls and tents lining the narrow thoroughfare, seemed to dance to the dissonant sounds from drummers, pipers, and strolling minstrels strumming lutes.

True Thomas lay o'er yon grassy bank,
And he beheld a lady gay,
A lady that was brisk and bold,
Come riding o'er the fernie brae.

307

> Her skirt was of the grass-green silk,
>   Her mantle of the velvet fine,
>   At ilka tett of her horse's mane
> Hung fifty silver bells and nine . . .
>
> She turned about her milk-white steed,
>   And took True Thomas up behind,
>   And aye when'er her bridle rang,
> The steed flew faster than the wind.

A fortnight earlier, on St. Bartholomew's Day, the Lord Mayor of London, dressed in his scarlet gown, had read the proclamation that opened the revels of the Bartholomew Fair. With bells ringing and trumpets blaring, acrobats, jugglers, and dancers romped at the head of the procession of mummers, giants, and knaves dressed as hobbyhorses. Prancing to and fro into the crowd, they cajoled, bantered, and goaded, and singled out a likely dupe or two to be made sport of. Singers, musicians, and pranksters followed to keep the onlookers full of merriment and moving toward the booths of the fair. Horse peddlers, tinkers, and gold sellers; actors, palm-readers, and conjurors; fortune-tellers, herbalists, and mountebanks; strollers, beggars, and pickpockets awaited.

Across the thronged midway, a tightrope walker balanced precariously on a tautly stretched rope, his dangerous antics eliciting gasps and cries for more daring feats.

Astride a white horse, a parrot perched on her shoulder, a beautiful maiden with dark red hair flowing free and dressed in a robe of green velvet caught the eye. Tiny silver bells braided into the horse's mane jingled melodically, while a funny-faced monkey dressed in his finest sat like a prince on the horse's rump. A young girl with black hair and eyes danced beside the horse and shook a gaily colored tambourine. Her slippered feet hardly seemed to touch the ground as she pirouetted around a large, playful dog with a ridiculously big ruff tied around his neck. A young juggler deceived and dazzled the eye with his tricks while he cavorted behind them and picked up the coins tossed from the appreciative crowd.

"A thirst! Have ye a thirst!" cried a wine vendor, holding out a leather flagon and a cup.

"Hot sausages!"

"Peppered meats, still sizzling!"

"Apples! Pears!"

"I've almonds and raisins!"

Inside a tent, close by the wrestling ring, cakes and ale could be had. Children playing games of hotcockle, leapfrog, blindman's-bluff, and logget paused only long enough to purchase a piece of gingerbread or cup of cider from the booths nearby. Beyond the stalls, where artisans were displaying their wares, where ribbons and lace, tobacco from the New World, Turkey carpets and antique vases were offered for sale, the grounds had been given over to jousting and dancing. In the distance, pens of geese, pigs, and sheep were grouped in a wide meadow. Under the nearest copse of oak, mares and their foals, frisky colts, and strong-chested draft horses were being auctioned.

In a space cleared behind one of the tents, servants and laborers sought to be hired on the spot. Cheers and horrible cries drifted through the air from the makeshift arena where bull and bear baiting drew its share of eager sideline participants. Opposite, a stage full of players tried to attract the attention of the passersby, their voices raised in bawdy verse, after droll wit had failed to interest an audience.

"Have ye an ache? Losin' yer hair? Trouble sleepin'?" a charlatan cried, holding up a small bottle of a strangely tinted liquid. "This magical potion, secret of the Pharaohs of Egypt until now and bottled on the banks of the Nile, will cure it all."

"Find out what yer future be! Fortune? Adventure? Marriage, my fair one?" an astrologer, dressed in Oriental robes, his long white beard snaking beneath the silk-covered table, enticed a young woman standing before the booth. "Let me read the stars and tell ye what tomorrow holds. So much knowledge, fer so small a coin pressed into my palm. Come, before the moon rises and the planets move."

"Dice? Cards? Primero! All Fours! Trump! Riddles? Any game of chance! Why, a hod carrier not more than half an hour past won a fortune! Told me how he now intends to *buy* not build a rich lord's mansion!"

Scattered around St. Margaret's Hill, the Southwark Fair had opened within hours of the final day of the Bartholomew Fair across the river near Smithfield. Michaelmas was less than a month away, and the many festivals and celebrations accompanying the harvest were already being eagerly anticipated.

A handsome man dressed in a jerkin of forest green, his shirtsleeves of the finest linen, stood before a booth decorated with green boughs and garlands of wild flowers. With a roguish smile and a gleam in his laughing blue eyes, he indicated the drawn curtains of the booth.

"A quarter past the hour! Don't be late! Don't miss it! Get a seat up close. That is when the next performance of 'The Wild White Horses' will be presented. Get here early, for 'tis the most popular show at the fair. A quarter past the hour! Don't forget!" Romney Lee warned, and after bowing to those who were already finding a good seat before the booth, he sauntered off, his smile widening with satisfaction.

"Rom! Rom, wait!" a young woman called to him. With no attempt at maidenly modesty, she lifted her skirts high as she ran to catch up to him. Her slim ankles, stockinged in scarlet silk, drew many an appreciative and outraged eye as she flew by, unmindful of all but the tall man making his way through the crowded midway.

Romney Lee casually glanced over his shoulder, not slowing his pace. He'd recognized the voice.

"Rom!"

With a sigh of impatience, Romney Lee halted. A boisterous group now blocked his way.

"Did ye not hear me?" the woman demanded breathlessly, her slender arm entwining around his possessively.

Romney Lee smiled down into her slanting eyes. "Hear? In this din? Now, am I a man to turn my back on a beautiful woman? And I've seldom seen ye lookin' prettier, Navarre," he said. He did not lie this time, for the gypsy girl, with her black hair and amber eyes, was one of the most beautiful women of his acquaintance.

" 'Tis a long time since last I heard ye say so," Navarre murmured, pressing closer, her lips parted enticingly. She was dressed in a gown of black velvet, cut away in front to expose the richness of her scarlet petticoats. The bodice, cut low and square, and trimmed with black lace and red satin rosettes, revealed the roundness of her breasts. About her small waist she had tied a rectangular piece of fringed, Indian cloth. Gold chains glistened against her dark skin and reflected the amber fire in her eyes when she stared up into Romney Lee's face.

"My voice has been just one of many," Romney replied mockingly, the heavy scent she wore filling his senses as she leaned against him and boldly allowed the bodice of her gown to gape wide to reveal a seductive expanse of warm, soft flesh.

"But 'tis the only voice I wish to hear, Rom," Navarre said softly, her gaze seeking to hold his glance, but Romney Lee had already looked away, as if searching the crowd for something or someone important.

Navarre's full lips tightened into an unattractive thinness. "Ye be lookin' fer *her*, aren't ye, Romney Lee?" she demanded jealously. "Ye'd do well to listen to me, Rom, and ferget her. She's no good fer ye. I've read it in her palm. She brings the evil eye on us. Ever since she and that little band of hers joined up with us we've all had a spell of bad luck. I say get rid of her and the others before 'tis too late."

Romney laughed, pulling his arm away from her grasp. "You expect me to take heed of your warning because of a simple palm-reading? You forget, I'm not one of these fools to be duped. You're just envious, Navarre. When Lily Francisca rides through the crowd, all eyes follow her—as well as most of the coins. You and the others ought to be grateful that we've an attraction like Lily Francisca. There is something captivating about her . . . but you shouldn't be greedy, my love, for with your dancing you've received more than your fair share during the past few years.

"Alas, times change, and I believe even the little one counted more in her tambourine than you did today," Romney commented, smiling unpleasantly. "You shall have to keep on your toes, for Dulcie Rosalinda's mother was Castilian, and the little one dances from the heart. I noticed you were strolling rather than dancing during most of the procession. You must be tiring easier than you once did, eh, Navarre? We may have to replace you with someone more spirited. I believe the Webbs need someone to serve ale in their booth. . . ."

"Ye swine!" she spat, raising her hand to strike, but Romney's fingers closed around her wrist and forced her arm behind her.

"Don't ever raise your hand against me, Navarre, or against those who belong to me," Romney warned her, his grip tightening painfully.

Navarre spat at his feet. "Ye think this Lily Francisca belongs to ye? I'm goin' to laugh in your face, Romney Lee, when she breaks your heart. And she will, my fine one. Ye think ye be good enough fer the likes of her? Pah! Ye be dreamin', lad. Ye just wait, Rom. Ye're nothin' to her. Try to take her, if ye can get past them watchdogs of hers that are always fallin' over themselves to keep everyone at a distance. I don't know which is worse, that flea-bitten, four-legged one, or them other two. There isn't much difference between 'em now I think about it," she said with a harsh laugh. "But if ye manage to get close enough to her to hold her in your arms, Rom, and knowin' ye like I do, ye will, then we'll see how much in love with ye she be," Navarre told him, her eyes narrowed to little more than slits. "Ye don't believe me, d'ye? Ye think she smiles just fer ye? She'd smile that way at a stinkin' beggar."

"Be quiet, Navarre."

"Oh, that cuts, does it, Rom, to know that she thinks of ye like she does them half-wits who'd do anything fer her? Oh, she likes ye, yes, Rom. But as a friend! Or, maybe like some servant, or one of them animals of hers. Not as a lover! Never that, Rom!" Navarre said, her narrowed amber eyes full of malice. She wanted to hurt Romney Lee the same way he'd hurt her when he'd brought Lily Francisca into their camp.

"Lily Francisca. Such a pretty name, don't ye think? Like a fair flower, and as easily bruised, I'd wager. Remember that, when ye climb into bed with her. She's still innocent of a man's touch, Rom. She's not woman enough fer the rough kind of man ye be. The fair maiden will remain exactly that till the right man comes along, and ye aren't him, Rom. I've seen the look in her eye when she thinks no one is watchin' her. She's dreamin' of some other man holdin' her and kissin' her and makin' love to her. Not ye, Rom. 'Tisn't your face she sees. She doesn't look at ye with that lovin' glance in them cat's eyes of hers. She's not fer a rogue like ye, Rom. What d'ye have to offer her? Not even a heart that will remain true, I'd wager. Ye like the taste of women too well, Romney Lee. Ye've never been faithful to me, have ye, now? And I know ye care fer me more than ye have any other woman. D'ye really think ye'd be true to *her*? 'Tisn't meant to be, Rom. If her father were alive d'ye think he'd let ye anywhere near his fair daughter? He was a fine gentleman, wasn't he? And her mother, the lady of the manor, she was. Like a princess, Lily Francisca is, ridin' that fine steed of hers. So cold. So haughty. So out of your reach, Romney Lee.

"Don't be fergettin' who and what ye are, Rom. Ye be mine. Remember that, too. We be two of a kind. Not of the true blood, either of us, that's why our blood mingles into one when we're together. We become like fire when we lie together, Romney Lee. It burns in both of us. Ye can't deny it. No one can make ye feel like I do. I am of your blood, Rom. Same as ye be of mine. Neither one of us can change what we are or what we've meant to each other. Listen to me, Rom," she pleaded, staring up into his flushed face, at the angry disbelief written there, at the pain in the dark blue eyes she loved so. "Oh, ye be a fool, Rom! Can't ye see she's bewitched ye with dreams that can't ever come true?"

Romney Lee pushed her away from him. Stumbling slightly, Navarre spun around, her hand resting lightly on the hilt of the knife tucked inside the scarf about her waist, but she was smiling when she said, "Go to her then! But ye'll come crawlin' back to me, Rom. And I'll be waitin', as I always am. I'm not too proud to admit that I love ye, and I always will. Ye think this comes of just bein' jealous?" Navarre asked with a contemptuous laugh. "She won't be able to hold ye. I'm not frightened of that *gorgio* with her pale skin and gentle ways. I'm not the only one who thinks *she* and them others are bad luck. There's been talk. There are others who—"

Romney reached out and grabbed her arm. "What lies have you been spreading, Navarre? If I find out you've been causing trouble for Lily Francisca, I'll—"

"Ye'll what? I haven't said nothin' that hasn't already been said by others. Ye be so blind, Rom, that ye can't see that she and them others have been takin' money out of the pockets of the rest of us. Well, maybe not yours, eh? Ye be pocketing half of what they get, so ye be doin' quite nicely. But there be some, and not just of my family, ones who've been travelin' with this band fer years, who aren't happy, Rom. She's not one of us, and she never will be. She's takin' bread out of the mouths of those of us who don't have no other way of livin'. Ye think that be fair? I got no other place to go, Rom. But her, ye think she'll starve, or she'll let that little black-eyed sister of hers go hungry if she can't make enough money with us? Will she watch that innocent-faced brother of hers turn to thievin'? No, she'll run back to her family. She's an heiress. Soon enough, Rom, she'll tire of playin' the fairs, and then she'll ride out of here without a backward glance, and right into the arms of some fancy gentleman who'll keep her in silks and well rounded with child. If ye think otherwise, then ye truly be livin' in a dream. Ye go ask the wise one, Rom, see what Old Maria has to say about your fair flower. Ye have to believe her words, Rom. We both know she sees the future. 'Tis no trick with her. Ask her, Romney Lee. If ye have the courage,'' Navarre dared him, and with a seductive swing of her hips, she sauntered away. She hadn't gotten far before several male members of the troupe joined her, laughing as she flirted with them, knowing Romney Lee stood watching her.

But Romney Lee had turned away and was walking toward a group of performers who were sitting in the cool shade of the trees beyond the clamor and congestion of the midway.

They were sharing a meal of coarse brown bread, cheese, and fruit. Countless apple cores were strewn about the big feet of the man stretched out full length in the shade, his snores rising and falling in time to the tentative tune the young boy was trying to play on a hornpipe.

''He ate my act, Rom,'' Tristram said with a wide grin as he nodded toward the apple cores at Fairfax's feet.

''You did well today, Tristram,'' Romney said, for the boy had been quick to master the rudiments of juggling and could now proceed to more complicated tricks. ''We'll have to start practicing with fire soon.''

''You mean it, Rom?'' Tristram exclaimed.

''Ye be that good, lad,'' Romney responded, but his gaze now lingered on the young woman sitting against the tree, her eyes closed while she rested peacefully on the grassy bank.

''Romney, no, 'tis too dangerous,'' Lily protested, opening her sleepy eyes.

''Lily! How am I ever going to become the greatest juggler in the land if I can't juggle blazing torches! I'm going to try and walk the tightrope next. Maybe I'll even try to juggle up there above the crowd. And I bet there'd be a crowd. Hey, Fairfax, listen to this idea . . ." Tristram said, throwing himself down beside the fair-haired giant who had yet to stir. "Fairfax? You aren't really asleep, are you?" he demanded, giving one of the broad shoulders a shake.

"He is certainly braver than I," Romney said. Dropping down beside Lily, he carefully pulled up a delicate pink bloom before his foot trampled on it. He breathed its sweet fragrance, then held it out to her. Slowly, his eyes took in her flushed cheeks and the rosy softness of her lips. Just like a child awakening from slumber, he thought, then frowned, for the image brought to mind Navarre's venomous observations.

"Is there anything wrong?" Lily questioned, reaching out to touch his hand rather than the flower.

Romney stared down at the slender hand covering his. Taking her hand in his, he lightly touched his lips to it. "No, nothing is wrong, Lily Francisca. In fact, this has been one of our better days thus far. I've never seen the booths so crowded. I came to remind you that you've a performance in less than half an hour."

"How's the audience?" Tristram asked, his question causing Romney to smile, for the lad was learning quickly.

"By now there won't be a place to stand within hearing distance of the booth. So, another ten minutes, no more," he warned, reluctantly getting to his feet. If only he could lie here in the shade beside this maid forever. *The rest of the world be damned,* Romney thought as his eye roved along the slender curve of thigh he could see beneath Lily's gown.

"Will you be there for the performance?" Lily asked.

"I've never missed one yet," he said, grimacing slightly with the unexpected pain when he accidentally punctured the tip of his finger on the prickly stem of the flower. Unthinkingly, he crushed the blossom in his fist as he stared at the drop of blood dripping from the wound. With a strange expression on his face, Romney stared at Lily's heart-shaped face, so flowerlike in its delicate perfection.

"Are you hurt? Here, let me see," Lily asked in concern, holding out her hand.

"It is nothing," Romney said brusquely, allowing the

bruised flower to fall to the ground. "Don't be late, Lily. I don't want to lose any of the crowd that is gathering."

"I won't, Rom. You've been such a good friend to us, I don't know what would have happened to us if it had not been for you."

"You will never forget your debt to me, will you, Lily Francisca?" he murmured.

"Never, Rom," Lily reassured him, puzzled by the strange look that had entered the friendly blue eyes, darkening them almost to black.

Romney Lee glanced away from the earnest expression on her beautiful face. Then, with a curious smile, he walked off.

Lily's gaze followed Romney Lee's figure as he made his way into the crowd. She frowned as she stared at the flower; its delicate petals now crushed and lifeless. Sometimes she didn't understand Romney Lee. He could be so gentle, so understanding, especially with Dulcie and Tristram, and yet, at other times, she had seen a violence in him that frightened her.

Although he had never been violent with any of them, Lily had watched too many times how easily he dealt with troublemakers at the fair. Sometimes, it seemed to her that he would join in the brawl too quickly. With a wide grin of pleasure on his face, he would swagger through the mob swinging the cudgel he handled with such skill. But it had been the expression in his eyes when he'd drawn his knife on another member of the troupe one evening that frightened her the most. The man had been drinking, and when Lily had wandered too close to where he'd been sitting, he'd dragged her into his arms. Romney Lee had been quicker than either Farley or Fairfax to come to her rescue. Lily had wanted to ignore the incident, but Romney Lee had not been willing to allow the insult to go unchallenged. For a long time, there had been bad blood between the two men, and as Romney Lee had turned away, the man had jumped him. When Lily had seen the knife blade glinting in Romney Lee's hand, then seen the look in his eye, she had known what the outcome would be and that Romney Lee would show no mercy.

Lily turned her gaze away from where Romney Lee had disappeared into the crowd and glanced toward the river and the tall-masted ships she could see riding at anchor downstream. Shielding her eyes against the glare, she searched the tall masts, looking for the ship she had once sailed aboard to England. Where was the *Madrigal*? Was she sailing the seas of the Spanish Main? Was her captain pacing the deck, searching for a distant sail on the horizon? Was he safe? Would he soon return to England and to Ravindzara? Where was Valentine Whitelaw? Lily wondered.

"Lily? Will we get to see the queen?" Dulcie asked, waking from her nap where she'd been curled up next to Raphael's sleeping form.

"Not this time, Dulcie."

"Why not? Doesn't she like us anymore? I've almost finished my gift for her."

"She may not be in London this time of year," Lily tried to explain without bluntly stating that Elizabeth might not wish to have criminals presented to her. A warrant for their arrest had most likely already been signed. If they tried to get to the queen to tell her what really happened that night, they'd be arrested on the spot and sent to the Tower before they could open their mouths, Lily thought.

"Where is she?"

"I'm not certain. She may be at her palace in Greenwich, or upriver at Richmond or Windsor. She has many palaces and royal manors she visits, Dulcie. She may even be traveling on one of her great progresses through the realm. She doesn't like to stay in London during the summer months."

"She came to Highcross once, didn't she?"

"Yes, but that was a long time ago," Lily answered, glancing away from the tall masts.

"Will we still be here when she returns to London?"

"I doubt it, Dulcie."

"Where are we going?"

"To the North Country."

"Is that where Maire lives?"

"Yes."

"Are we going to see her again?"

"I hope so. 'Tis why we joined the troupe, Dulcie, so we could travel north to where she now lives. Maire will know what we should do. She will help us."

"I'm glad we joined the fair, Lily. I like dancing all day long. I don't ever want to return to Highcross."

Lily shivered, remembering the night they'd fled High-cross—the night Hartwell Barclay had died. . . .

It was a nightmare she had yet to awaken from. She could still hear Tillie's wailing, accompanied by Raphael's howling, echoing around the chamber. Hartwell Barclay's big, bare feet were sticking out of the scented bath water, while Cisco, who'd swooped down to investigate so strange a sight, sat perched on the edge of the tub, his giggling laughter and unfortunate comments ringing in Lily's ears. Dulcie was huddled on the bed, her eyes wide with shock, but when Tristram started talking about hanging, Dulcie began to cry and hurried to her side to be comforted. Cappie started to chatter and, swinging down from atop the bed, had scampered over to the tub. He was examining Hartwell Barclay's big toe when a high-pitched scream brought a sudden stillness to the room.

Standing in the doorway, her mouth hanging open, was the cook.

"Ye've murdered him! The master be dead! He be murdered! Ye witch! Witch! Always knew ye'd bring misfortune to this house!" she cried, pointing a shaking finger at Lily.

"But I—" Lily began, taking a step toward the terrified woman.

"Don't come near me, murderess! Ye'll be hanged fer this! Don't come near me! Murder! Murder!" she cried, running down the corridor.

"Murder! Murder! *Praaack!* Witch! Witch!" Cisco hissed, ruffling his feathers.

" 'Sdeath! What's happened?" Farley Odell had demanded, standing in the opened doorway, a stunned expression on his face. "Fool woman nearly knocked me down," he complained indignantly.

"Oh, Farley! He tried to rape me! Only 'twas Mistress Lily he wanted. Oh, Farley, I'm goin' to have a baby!" Tillie cried, hopping down from the bed and flinging herself against Farley's chest.

Farley Odell, for once in his life, was speechless.

"Ah, now, Tillie dear, don't get yerself excited. Can't be knowin' something like that so soon," Farley tried to calm her, wondering how on earth they'd deal with Hartwell Barclay's bastard child, for if it was true, then he'd personally see that Hartwell Barclay sired no more brats in this world.

"Nooooo, 'tisn't *his*, 'tis yours, Farley Odell!" Tillie cried, burying her tearstained face against his chest.

"Mine?" Farley said, dumbfounded.

"I'm goin' to have yer baby, only they'll think 'tis his, and that *I* murdered him, instead of the mistress, Farley!" she cried. "They'll hang us both!"

"Murdered? He's dead, then?"

"Lord help us, Farley! What the devil's goin' on?" Fairfax demanded, his large form filling the doorway. "I thought ye just came up here to tell Tillie we were leavin'."

"Leavin'! Ye're runnin' out on me? Oh, Farley Odell, how can ye be doin' such a thing to me after ye said ye loved me? And me growing big with yer child?" she squealed, pushing Farley away from her.

"Now look what ye've done, Fairfax," Farley muttered, trying to quiet the moaning Tillie.

" 'Tweren't me who did the deed, Farley," Fairfax responded with a sly grin as he walked over to the tub. "Good Lord! 'Tis Master Barclay! What's he doin' in here, and in his nightgown?" he demanded, glancing around for some explanation, but Farley was busy trying to explain to Tillie that he wasn't running out on her.

"Ye mean ye came here to get me? To take me away with ye and Fairfax?" Tillie exclaimed, her tearful sobs quickly silenced.

"Of course, what kind of man d'ye think I be, Tillie Thaxton? Ye oughta be ashamed of yerself for even thinkin' such a thing of me," Farley said with a grievous glance at her.

"Be Tillie Odell, now, won't it, Farley?" she asked shyly.

"It'd better," Fairfax answered for his brother. "Don't want my nephew growin' up a bas—" he began, then turned a bright red as he remembered Dulcie, and Tristram, for despite what they'd said, no one had ever completely believed Tristram to be who he claimed to be.

"What are we going to do, Lily?" Tristram asked, unable to draw his eyes away from Hartwell Barclay's crumpled figure in the tub. "The cook thinks you murdered Hartwell. I told you no one would believe you. She'll tell the constable that. They've always hated us. They'll hang you, Lily. And after tonight, after what Farley and Fairfax and I did, they'll probably hang us, too," he whispered, his voice quivering.

"They can't hang Lily!" Dulcie screamed, her shrill cries causing Raphael to begin barking excitedly.

"Surely they will listen to my side of what happened," Lily said, looking at Farley and Fairfax, but their doubtful expressions told her otherwise. "I will tell them the truth. They must believe the truth," Lily repeated softly, but her heart was pounding as she remembered the way the cook had looked at her and called her a witch. Then Lily remembered Mistress Fordham's angry, suspicious words of just two days before when she'd accused her of bewitching her son and causing her daughter to trip and break her leg so she couldn't go a-Maying and wouldn't be crowned Queen of the May. And, Sunday last, the Reverend Buxby had ranted from the pulpit about harlots and those who would lead innocent men into sin. The village would be certain to believe Hartwell Barclay had been the innocent victim.

Lily swallowed the fear rising from the pit of her stomach. Who indeed would believe her? Tristram was right, no one would.

"Mistress Lily?" Farley had interrupted her desperate speculations. "Fairfax and me, well, we've got to leave Highcross. Nothin' else for us to do after tonight. And we've been thinkin' that ye oughta come with us. Won't do any good to remain here. Them villagers are likely to burn the place to the ground before they give ye a chance to make any explanations."

"Oh, Mistress Lily, please listen to him. Farley is speakin' the truth, and I'm that powerful scared fer ye safety, too," Fairfax added, and the fear in his eyes was what finally decided Lily to take their advice—at least that way they might live long enough to tell their side of the incident.

While Farley and Fairfax carried down to the stables the trunk Lily quickly packed with her clothes and possessions, she helped Dulcie and Tristram gather up their own belongings, taking only what she thought would be necessary for the next few weeks. She couldn't believe that they would be fugitives for much longer than that. It was while she was feverishly hunting under Dulcie's bed for the red slipper, that Lily realized where they must go. Maire Lester. She would know what to do. She was the only one who could help them. And they would have a safe place to stay until they were cleared of all suspicion in Hartwell Barclay's death.

Farley and Fairfax hitched the oxen to the cart and brought it around to the entrance. Tristram, Dulcie, and Tillie squeezed in, along with the trunks and bundles and an excited Cappie and Raphael. And from somewhere in the jumble, Cisco's giggles caused Lily more than one nervous glance over her shoulder as she rode Merry Andrew alongside the cart. Farley and Fairfax did not inform her until later that the reason they'd had so little trouble in the stables, was that the groom, Hollings, hadn't been there. The cook must have sent him to the village to warn the authorities. A horse had been missing, and Hollings had been sound asleep when they'd returned with Tristram after their escapade in the churchyard. The cook they had found barricaded in her room and crying murder. And just in case she found her courage, they'd blocked the door from the outside as well.

A pale sliver of moon was the only witness to their escape from Highcross as they rumbled down the lane. Entering East Highcross, Lily felt as if every window held a pair of peering eyes even though the village remained quiet. But Lily held her breath with every clop of Merry's hooves and creak of the cart along the village's narrow, cobbled street. The only lights came from the Oaks and the church at the far end of High Street, but before reaching the church they turned off the main street and followed the lane winding along the river.

Safely through the village, they traveled slowly along the deeply rutted road. They had no destination, just a desire to put distance between themselves and Highcross. The moon had risen higher by the time they reached the mill just north of the village and a figure suddenly stepped into the lane, blocking their path and startling the animals.

It was Romney Lee. He'd been walking back from the village, and an evening spent at the Oaks, when he'd heard the sound of the cart. He'd heard about the scare at the church and hadn't been surprised to find Farley and Fairfax on the road. But Romney Lee was startled to discover who was accompanying them.

Hoping to convince at least someone of their innocence, Lily told Romney what had happened at Highcross. His good humor quickly fled when he realized the danger. Convincing them that they could not get very far before dawn, when the villagers would surely be out looking for them, he insisted they hide the cart at the mill until evening, when they could travel under darkness.

That day seemed the longest Lily had ever spent. They remained hidden behind the mill, believing every sound threatening and every minute brought them closer to being arrested. Romney Lee left them to go into the village to learn what he could about the search for them. He'd even gone to Highcross, to discover what had happened after they'd fled. Returning just before dusk, Lily read in his expression the hopelessness of their predicament.

But Romney Lee did not despair, nor did he abandon them. He made a suggestion. Would they like to join the troupe of vagabonds and gypsies he traveled with? Farley and Fairfax were at first reluctant. They didn't trust Romney Lee, but as he spoke, they began to realize how helpless they were.

What better way to travel north, without causing suspicion, than with a group of players, dancers, jugglers, and peddlers going from fair to fair, Romney Lee asked? Where were they going? North? A long journey, indeed. Did they have money? No? Where were they going to stay during the nights? Where were they going to hide during the day when the authorities were searching for them? Farley and Fairfax exchanged glances, nodding slightly, for Romney Lee's reasoning held the answer to the problem that had been worrying them since they'd made their decision to flee Highcross.

Hearing about the angry mob of villagers that had arrived at Highcross, and how there had been talk at the Oaks of gallows and burnings at the stake for witches, Lily agreed.

It still amazed her, she thought now, gazing down at the crowded booths and tents of the fair, how easily they had adapted to traveling with Romney Lee's vagabond band. At first, their arrival had been greeted with suspicious, unfriendly glances, but when they'd started bringing in customers and paying their own way, they had been grudgingly accepted. But Lily knew that for some, suspicion had turned to resentment.

They asked nothing of anyone. They had their own cart, which they'd arranged with their trunks and possessions so she,

Dulcie, and Tillie would have a comfortable, safe place to sleep in at night. Since it was warm, Tristram, Farley, and Fairfax slept on the ground beside it. Lily hadn't thought what would happen when winter came and the weather grew cold, or when Tillie's time came and there would be a newborn babe to care for. But for now their oxen proved strong and sturdy and pulled their cart, now decorated in bright colors, along the dusty lanes. They had never fallen behind or caused the rest of the troupe to be delayed.

Until recently they'd done little more than take part in the procession and stroll through the fair to attract customers to various booths and games. But because of Romney Lee's inspiration after overhearing the tale Lily had been telling to Dulcie and Tillie one evening, they now had their own booth and puppet show, performed several times a day before an appreciative audience that seemed to grow larger after each performance.

"Oh, there ye be, Mistress Lily. I've been searchin' all over fer ye."

Lily glanced up to see Tillie approaching, her step slow and her breath labored, for she was well into her pregnancy now and had a difficult time in getting around. Lily eyed Tillie's ballooning shape worriedly. She'd never seen anyone get so big. Poor Tillie. Lily wondered sometimes how Tillie's thin legs managed to hold her upright when she tottered around, unable to see her own feet.

"Farley is gettin' mighty nervous. Says the show starts in just a few minutes, mistress. Ye don't want to be late, now. Oh, 'tis such a crowd, mistress! I've never seen so many people. Where do they all come from?" she said in awe. "Ye'd best be stirrin' them bones of yours, Fairfax. Ye've got another wrasslin' match within the hour. I hope ye can win this one, Fairfax. There's a goodly sum in the purse fer the winner," she told him with the candor her position as his sister-in-law allowed her.

Fairfax yawned and stretched and opened one eye. " 'Tis only one match, Tillie, that I've lost. And I wouldn't have lost that one if that cider squeezer's mother hadn't hit me from behind when I had him eatin' mud," Fairfax defended his only loss as he got to his feet. "Come along, I'll walk ye both back to the booth," he offered, and unable to glance away from Tillie's bulging belly, he shook his head and wondered about that brother of his.

Lily stood up and shook out her skirts and petticoats, then brushed the grass from Dulcie's while she straightened the ruff around Raphael's neck. With a shrill cry, Cisco flew out of the tree and perched on Lily's shoulder, receiving an almond from Lily's palm as he settled. Cappie put on his hat and hopped up on Raphael's back, ready for the ride through the crowd.

"Oooh, me back aches. Never ached this much when I was scrubbin' floors at Highcross," Tillie murmured, wondering that she'd ever found pleasure in Farley Odell's arms.

"I'll get you a stool to sit on behind the booth, Tillie," Tristram offered, coming up beside them and handing Merry's reins to Lily.

"Reckon ye'll be lookin' fer a bench soon, if her backside gets any broader," Fairfax guffawed, dodging as Tillie took a swing at his shin with the toe of her shoe and would have lost her balance and fallen if he hadn't steadied her.

"And surprised I am, Fairfax Odell, that ye haven't snow capping that thick-skulled head of yours, so high in the clouds ye be," Tillie retorted.

Lily smiled as she listened to Tillie and Fairfax's good-natured banter. Glancing around as they followed a weaving path into the fair, she had to admit that Romney had been right about the size of the crowd today. But she could see little beyond Merry's shoulder bumping against her on the right or Fairfax's tall figure overshadowing her on the other side, and so Lily didn't see the tall man who passed within a foot of her.

Many things, having full reference
To one consent, may work contrariously;
As many arrows, loosed several ways,
Fly to one mark; as many ways meet in one town;
As many fresh streams meet in one salt sea . . .
So may a thousand actions, once afoot,
End in one purpose, and be all well borne
Without defeat.

SHAKESPEARE

Chapter Eighteen

SIR RAYMOND VALCHAMPS had been a contented man during the past few years. Knighted for his valor by the grateful queen whose life he had risked his own to save, or so she believed, Sir Raymond had continued to enjoy Elizabeth's royal favor. Her largesse had included the gift of a great estate, where he lived as if he were a royal prince of the realm, a townhouse on the Strand, and thousands of fertile acres in the Midlands. Valuable licenses of export had been granted to him, the profits of so lucrative a trade giving him the advantage over less fortunate courtiers who found life at court a continual drain on their resources.

The family home in Buckinghamshire was finally his. He had inherited a fortune from his grandmother, as well as an estate and lands with a considerable yearly income collected in rents from the tenants. And his sister, Eliza, was now wed to the noble and wealthy Thomas Sandrick.

And soon the most beautiful woman in all of England, Cordelia Howard, was to become his wife. He had beaten Valentine Whitelaw to the prize. While the brave captain was sailing the

seas in search of Spanish gold, Cordelia accepted his proposal of
marriage. Quite a shock it would be to Valentine Whitelaw when
he returned to England to find his mistress wed to his most
hated rival.

"Not too warm, m'dear?" Sir Raymond inquired solicitously
of the woman walking by his side, his gaze taking in the lovely
line of her brow.

"Not at all, my love," Cordelia Howard replied as she neatly
sidestepped a steaming pile of manure centered in the path before her. "Oh, Raymond, really! You weren't watching where
you stepped. I do believe you've ruined your slipper," she berated him.

Sir Raymond Valchamps stared down at his fine, silk slippers. One of them was now coated with a noisome substance. A
look of dismay replaced the smug expression on his handsome
face. "Damn! I knew this would happen. Nothing good ever
comes of mixing with rabble like this, Cordelia. I don't know
why you insisted we come. By evening the place will be little better than one big brawl," he warned.

Cordelia stared down at his foul-smelling shoe in distaste.
"You needn't worry on that score. We will leave the fair early,
for we are to dine this evening with Sir William and Lady Elspeth Davies. You cannot have forgotten that? I intend to have
ample time to prepare, after all, 'twill be quite an occasion. I hear
the house Sir William has built is magnificent."

"No, I have not forgotten. I've heard scarce little else since
you received the invitation."

" 'Tis amazing the bargains one can find at a fair. I bought a
rare piece of gold cloth last month at the Bartholomew Fair. And
look at these silks I've just bought. And I've still some of the
scent I found here last year. I can see that I shall have to be quick
about finding more," she said, pressing a perfume-soaked
handkerchief to her nose. "Besides, I seem to recall you were
suddenly most eager to escort me."

"If I get out of here without having either my purse or my
throat cut I'll consider myself damned fortunate," Sir Raymond
complained, his contemptuous glance causing more than one
person walking by to give the fancy, sour-faced gentleman
plenty of elbow room. "And, if you recall, 'twas *I* who bought

the silks. And surprised I am that I've any coin left in my purse.''

"I do wish you would do something about that cursed shoe," Cordelia was quick to remind him as he stepped closer to her side and nearly lost his balance when he slipped.

Swinging a gold pomander as if warding off any other evils lurking before him, Sir Raymond glanced around. "As soon as I find somewhere to sit, I will have Prescott clean it," he said, much to his manservant's annoyance.

"Why, 'tis George Hargraves, isn't it?" Cordelia demanded as she caught sight of a short gentleman making his way through the crowd, a wide grin on his face as he spoke with several well-dressed gentlemen accompanying him. "I wonder what he's up to? I swear George can't be trusted not to have some trick up his sleeve. Damned irritating. Who is that with him?" Cordelia questioned, squinting as she tried to recognize the man just a step behind.

Sir Raymond followed her curious gaze. "Which one? Looks like Sir Charles Denning to me."

"Well, of course, I know that! I meant the other man."

"Thomas Sandrick?"

"No, no, not him. How strange. Eliza said nothing to me about attending the fair today. And I spoke with her yesterday noon."

"Perhaps she did not accompany Thomas. She does have many more duties now as his wife and the mother of his son," Sir Raymond reminded her.

"There! You see! I thought 'twas him," Cordelia said, a gleam in her dark eyes as she stared at the tall, bold-faced man who reminded her so much of Valentine Whitelaw.

"*Him?* I am surprised, my dear, that you would deign to glance his way," Sir Raymond commented with acerbity as he recognized the gentleman who'd recently arrived at court and was fast becoming one of Elizabeth's favorites. With growing unease, Sir Raymond had watched the obscure young rustic worming his way into the queen's inner circle. For now, he seemed to amuse her with his brashness, but one misstep and he would soon find himself banished from court.

"Walter Raleigh. That is his name, is it not?" Cordelia asked with growing interest, unaware of Sir Raymond's ire. "I vow, he is the fine-looking one."

"Sir Walter Raleigh I'm sure he wishes, but it won't become more than wishful thinking if I can help it," Sir Raymond promised, for there were others, like himself, who'd belatedly come to realize that the blunt-spoken Devonshireman might be a threat to their own positions at court.

"I have heard that he is quite a wit," Cordelia speculated, eyeing the gentleman's finely shaped leg.

Sir Raymond snorted derisively. "If you can understand him. I swear these West Country men speak with more of a burr than those heathens in Scotland," Sir Raymond commented.

"I've never had any trouble understanding Valentine, and he lives in the West Country," Cordelia said, a slow smile curving her lips. "In fact, 'twould seem that most West Country men are uncommonly tall and dark. 'Tis indeed a bold face both Valentine and this Walter Raleigh show to the world. 'Tis quite fascinating."

"To my knowledge, neither Whitelaw nor Raleigh are well-known wits. Of course, you would have more personal knowledge of Whitelaw, wouldn't you, m'dear? I've always been of the opinion that one doesn't need to listen very carefully to him. Indeed, doesn't say much at all, does our fearless sea captain? I dare say, when you and he were together, you didn't waste much time on useless conversation, now did you? But then, he hasn't been in England enough of late to put either one of us to the test. Pity, that. I s'pose, m'dear, your charms weren't enticing enough to keep him chained to your side," Sir Raymond remarked maliciously, for even he was not so conceited as not to have wondered what would have happened had it been Valentine Whitelaw who'd been knighted rather than himself. "However, in all modesty, my dear, I do believe you have made the best choice in accepting my proposal rather than Whitelaw's. He would have bored you to death within a month. You've become too jaded, my dear, to remain content for long with his unimaginative devotion to your beauty."

For perhaps the first time in her life, Cordelia Howard blushed. The truth of the matter was that Valentine Whitelaw had not asked her to marry him. At least he had not since she'd turned him down. And that had been over three years ago. They had continued their affair, with no lessening of passion between them, and she had mistakenly thought she would be able to change her mind any time she so wished. That he would remain devoted to her she had never doubted. At least she had thought that until last spring when she had visited his home in Cornwall. After that visit, which had been less than successful, there had been a definite change in their relationship. In her conceit, Cordelia had not realized that a man who took great pride in the home and land that for the first time he could truly call his own would not wish to hear it criticized even by the woman he loved—and certainly not by the woman he had hoped to bring to Ravindzara as its mistress. Valentine Whitelaw had heard nothing but criticism of his home, his servants, and his beloved Cornish coast. There had never been a kind word for anyone, and Valentine had gradually seen another woman revealed to him. And it was not the woman he had loved almost blindly. He saw a vindictive and greedy woman who thought of no one but herself.

And it was there, at Ravindzara, that Valentine Whitelaw had known that Cordelia Howard, beautiful though she might be, was not the woman to share his life. Had either admitted the truth, their relationship had not, during the last few years, fared as well as Valentine Whitelaw's voyages. And Cordelia Howard had been quick to place the blame for their estrangement on those long absences. Had he not been away from her side for so long, they would still have been in love with each other, or so she tried to convince herself. But Cordelia now had to face the unpleasant realization that Valentine Whitelaw might no longer wish that she become his wife. And even worse, that he had fallen out of love with her.

It had been a difficult time for the beautiful Cordelia Howard. Never before without her admirers and suitors, now she was suddenly faced with the reality that only Raymond Valchamps still sought her hand in marriage. It had been a bitter blow for a woman who, only three years earlier, had thought she could have any man of her choosing. Not only had she lost Valentine Whitelaw, but Sir Rodger Penmorley had surprised them all when he'd asked Valentine Whitelaw's crippled sister to wed him. That had stung Cordelia; to lose out to *that* woman, a woman she'd never even considered a rival. She had waited too long. Of course, she would have chosen Raymond anyway, she told herself. He was, after all, a knight and a favorite of Elizabeth's. They would live in London for most of the year, then, when not in residence on the Strand, they would travel to his numerous country houses. What more could she ask? She had what she wanted. But, sometimes, in the middle of the night, when she remembered a pair of warm turquoise eyes . . .

"This Walter Raleigh of yours cuts quite the figure. That silk doublet must have cost him a fortune. I've never seen such an exquisite color or such fine lace. I vow, I am envious," Cordelia spoke harshly, banishing the image of Valentine Whitelaw from her mind. "I imagine Elizabeth gave it to him. She is becoming rather fond of him, is she not, my dear?" Cordelia asked with an innocent-looking expression. "If it were not for those exceptional eyes of yours, my love, I dare say you might seem quite ordinary when standing next to Walter Raleigh. I fear you will have to make more of an effort to be noticed in future."

"Damned if I'll dress like a struttin' peacock. But let me give you a riddle, m'dear," Sir Raymond said, the tight smile on his face warning Cordelia of the insult before she heard it. "How can it be that a *lady* may not be a lady at all? Stumped you, have I?"

"I'm sure you will not keep me in suspense for long."

"Why, 'tis when a harlot marries a titled gentleman, of course!"

Cordelia smiled. "Have you thought, my dear, that you might jeopardize your treasured place by Elizabeth's side by marrying me? She prefers, nay, demands, complete devotion from her courtiers. How do you think she will take to having to share you with a wife? And that wife a woman she does not have much fondness for?" Cordelia demanded. "I believe Walter Raleigh remains unattached. My, my, intelligent as well as ambitious?"

Sir Raymond Valchamps shrugged.

"You are not concerned, are you? Are you so favored by Elizabeth that you do not fear anyone? I am impressed, my dear. I expect, however, that you are breathing easier because she will change her opinion about marriage soon enough when she weds the Duke of Alençon," Cordelia predicted, looking startled when Sir Raymond said something rude beneath his breath.

"She will never wed him. We have all been made fools of to have ever believed it likely," Sir Raymond said in disgust, thinking of the years that had been wasted while the whore had dangled her crown before that French pup. "Two years now she has been playing this game. At first, I did not believe she would marry him. 'Twas just another ploy to keep the French and Spanish from forming a closer alliance. But when he came to England and I saw how they amused one another, how she pampered him and kept him at her side, how very fond she became of him, why, I actually began to believe that she would wed him," he complained bitterly, thinking of all of the opportunities he had missed to rid England of Elizabeth because he'd hoped to achieve their goals through Elizabeth's marriage to Alençon. Little had the queen realized how safe she'd been during the last two years while he'd bided his time, believing her intentions were true.

"Well, she may yet do so," Cordelia said, wondering why Raymond should be so upset about it. Perhaps he'd been counting on his own marriage being more acceptable to Elizabeth if she were contemplating nuptials of her own.

" 'Tisn't important," Sir Raymond replied, a strange expression in his eyes. " 'Twill make it more difficult, that is all. But, not impossible, I think," he added, smiling as if at some private joke.

He would, however, miss the monies he'd been receiving from the French ambassador for the past several years. In exchange, he'd used his influence at court to further France's cause. He glanced down at the ruby glowing on his finger. A gift from a grateful Alençon, who needed all of the allies he could find in the English court. There were many, among them Sir Francis Walsingham, who were bitterly opposed to such an alliance. The Protestant preachers throughout England had been warning against Elizabeth's proposed marriage to a Catholic prince. Crowds had come close to rioting in the streets and Elizabeth's popularity had never been so low. There had even been an attempt on her life several years earlier when an unknown assassin had fired on the royal barge. A pity, thought Sir Raymond, that her assailant had missed and hit one of her attendants instead. Had Elizabeth died then, it would have ended forever Protestant rule in England.

Most likely there would have been civil war, but during the confusion, a group of loyal followers could have freed Mary Stuart from her imprisonment. Fourteen years now the Queen of Scots had been held prisoner in England, Sir Raymond fumed. But with Spanish troops landing in Ireland, Spain's army just across the Channel in the Netherlands, and Catholics rebelling in England and Scotland, they would soon have won the war and returned England and her people to the true faith.

Actually, he would be sorry if Elizabeth did not wed Alençon, for he preferred the French to the Spanish. Although he had in the past held closer ties with the Spanish, he had no special love for them. Until recently, he'd thought the French would be more useful to their cause, but now, it looked as if he might have to resume his relationship with the Spanish; indeed, he had an appointment with Bernardino de Mendoza, the Spanish ambassador, the very next day.

Whatever, it mattered naught to him, Sir Raymond thought, not unduly worried as long as the end result was the assassination of Elizabeth Tudor.

"We really should greet them," Cordelia was saying as she quickened her step toward where George Hargraves, Sir Charles Denning, Thomas Sandrick, and Walter Raleigh were standing in conversation.

"I'll be damned, Cordelia, if I am going to greet anyone, even George Hargraves, with *this* on my shoe," Sir Raymond declared. "I'll be over there, near that booth," he told her as he diesppeared into the crowd, determined not to give Hargraves anything to jest about on the morrow, and spying dung on his shoe, George Hargraves would not have been able to resist a ribald comment.

Damned crowded, Sir Raymond Valchamps thought as he squeezed into the crowd, wondering if he'd be able to find a seat. With an impatient gesture and coin pressed into his palm, he sent away his surprised manservant, allowing the man to think his master a most generous gentleman. Sir Raymond felt the stiffness of the ciphered letter tucked safely up his sleeve and smiled despite the press of unwashed bodies surrounding him, for that was the real reason behind his separating from Cordelia and not wishing to meet the others. Not a half hour past, the cipher had been passed to him. At the proper time, he would pass the secret document to a courier, who would then pass it to an agent who had access to Mary Stuart. Raymond Valchamps felt a shiver go through him as he thought of the pope's hand having touched the missive he now carried. At times, despite the comfort he found himself enjoying as a knight of the realm and court favorite, he wished to be more actively involved in the plotting against Elizabeth.

At the beginning of the year he'd been on the Continent, having received Elizabeth's permission to travel abroad under the excuse of making necessary business contacts concerning his exporting of cloth. Once on the Continent, he had quickly made for Paris, where he'd met with English Catholics in exile and with agents of Mary, Queen of Scots. It was there that he'd heard more of the plan, backed by the pope and Philip II, to invade England. And should the ultimate deed fall unto him and he be chosen to strike the blow against Elizabeth, then he would do it with a clear conscience, having been promised a papal dispensation.

Sir Raymond Valchamps sighed, glancing around curiously, wondering when he would be contacted. Who would the courier be this time? Except for the dark blue velvet hat with a red feather on the left side, the man would probably be a complete stranger to him. He would be nothing more than someone accidentally bumping against him and whispering the password, at which he would hand over the cipher and be about his way. He eyed those closest around him, his mind wandering while he waited. Idly, he listened to the performance that had just begun in the booth close by.

It was with a sense of disbelief that Sir Raymond Valchamps continued to stand there. It took some effort to turn his gaze toward the booth where the puppet show was in progress. Strange that he should feel so chilled on so warm a day in summer, he found himself thinking, oblivious now to the crowd pressing so close, like a noose about his neck.

On the small stage, where several puppets were engaged in various antics, a tale was unfolding. A team of wild white horses, drawing an incredible chariot formed of coral, came prancing out onto the stage. The stiff wooden legs stomped up and down almost rhythmically as unseen hands pulled their strings and guided them. A princely figure was addressed as

Prince Basil by a small puppet called Sweet Rose, who held the reins. On a voyage of great importance, they had discovered an evil jinni's plot to murder Elizabeth, Queen of the Misty Isle. They had been trying to return to England when they had fallen under the spell of the witch of the Northland, who had pretended to befriend them. But the witch had blown a storm into their path and wrecked them on a strange western isle where they were destined to spend the rest of their days.

But Lily, Queen of the Indian Isles, granted them each a wish. And in their chariot of coral, with a team of wild white horses, they would fly through the skies to the Misty Isle. Then the dark, cowled figure of a priest swept threateningly from out of the shadowy palms of a tropical isle painted on the backdrop, while a bizarre, feathered figure with a tall headdress and a gold-painted mask jumped in front of the horse-drawn chariot. There was a battle, and the prince and Sweet Rose were taken captive.

A puppet with flowing red hair floated across the stage on a sea horse. Uttering words of warning, Lily, Queen of the Indian Isles, confronted the menacing bird-figure from the New World. The jinni knew no fear and flung her off the cliff. A bearded puppet wearing a crown and brandishing a sword rose from out of the sea and rescued the fallen heroine from death, but both fled before the cannon fire from a troop of Spanish soldiers marching across the small stage.

The curtains closed, to great applause, then opened to reveal a painted backdrop of a mythical, undersea kingdom with strangely colored turreted towers and grotesquely shaped trees. The sea maiden and King Neptune floated down to a cave where a treasure chest lay half buried in the sand. Sitting on a golden throne, the king called his troops from the sea. Dolphins, turtles, starfish, and all manner of horrible, finned beasts appeared. Leading them was a young merman, the brave Count Tristram. Fearful for their safety, and that of Prince Basil and Sweet Rose, the sea maiden went in search of help and exited the stage.

Sir Raymond stared at the stage almost impatiently while he waited for the curtains to part on Act Three. The painted backdrop had become an ocean, with the distant shore of the isle rising from the mists in the background. Across this sea sailed a galleon with golden sails, the red cross of St. George flying above the masts. Courageously, the ship's captain sailed into the raging battle, sinking the Spaniards' ship, which disappeared from the stage accompanied by a roar of approval from the crowd.

The cowled priest was hiding behind a palm tree, but soon he was routed as a black jaguar leapt from behind the flowery underbrush and landed on the robed figure. The jinni attacked Prince Basil and Sweet Rose, but the prince, escaping his bonds, drew his sword and did battle with the jinni.

As Sir Raymond Valchamps stood mesmerized before the stage he saw the golden mask flung from the puppet in the feathered cape. A gasp of surprise came from the audience as a horrible face was revealed. The jinni was not a savage creature from the New World after all, but the evil Northland witch with one blue eye and one brown eye. Unblinkingly, Sir Raymond watched as Prince Basil beheaded the witch to the crowd's bloodthirsty delight.

The final scene opened at court, with Elizabeth, an elegant puppet with a bright red wig and velvet gown, knighting the captain of the ship and granting permission for the captain and the Queen of the Indian Isles to wed, while Prince Basil, Sweet Rose, and Count Tristram stood before her. And the head of the witch, with its one brown eye and one blue eye and colorless hair, was stuck on a mock Traitor's Gate.

"Saved the queen, they have. God bless her!"

"Aye, got the witch with the one blue eye and one brown eye," someone commented next to Sir Raymond Valchamps.

"Stuck the ugly head on Traitor's Gate! Let the crows have it!"

"Lord 'elp us, but d'ye think there really be traitors like that 'ere in England?"

Standing up on the ledge at the top of the booth, five figures cloaked in black, with expressionless, black-masked faces, took their bows.

Sir Raymond pushed his way through the crowd, not hearing a woman's cry of fear before she fainted when he shoved his way past her, his gaze catching and holding hers for a terrifying instant. Blindly, he walked right past the man in the dark blue velvet hat with the bright red feather who had been trying to move closer to his side for the past ten minutes.

Sir Raymond Valchamps was never certain how he managed

to make his way through the crowd and around to the back of the booth. Standing near a booth close by, as if interested in the display of brass gleaming along the counter, he watched as a tall man dressed in a green jerkin lifted a small, cloaked figure down from the ledge in back. Pulling off the concealing mask, a young girl's face met his eye. Another figure had climbed down unassisted. Removing the mask, a boy of about ten started laughing in response to the jesting remark made by another cloaked figure, which when the cloak and mask were removed revealed a short, dark-haired man.

But Sir Raymond continued to watch. He saw the man in the green jerkin reach up again, this time to give a hand to the last cloaked figure, safely guiding the puppeteer down the rickety steps to the ground.

Sir Raymond's breath quickened as the robe fell from the figure.

Lily Christian.

Sir Raymond leaned against the side of the booth, suddenly unable to support himself. Geoffrey Christian's brat seemed to haunt him as surely as if her father had returned from the grave to seek revenge for his murder.

Sir Raymond stared at the beautiful young woman, her dark red hair glinting in the sunshine. *Why? Why?* he asked himself. He dropped his eyes, almost guiltily, when she glanced around. How well he remembered those pale green eyes staring at him so curiously in the courtyard of her grandfather's villa in Santo Domingo. He had been lulled until today into forgetting the threat she was.

After that meeting with her at Tamesis House, when she and her brother and sister had returned to England, and when he had failed to end her life, he had made certain that everyone knew he'd met her before; but at Highcross Court, when Elizabeth and the court had visited. No one would have believed the child should she have spoken of meeting him elsewhere, and certainly not in Santo Domingo. But the child had never said anything; at least he'd never been questioned about such a meeting. The years had passed and he'd seen her at court and had even delighted in seeking her out and forcing her into casual conversation with him. He knew she was frightened of him, although he was the only one who knew why. Even she was ignorant of the truth. What a fool he'd been. She had tricked him, deceived him into believing that she was no longer a threat to him.

Sir Raymond swallowed, feeling the cold perspiration beading his upper lip. But now, if anyone of their acquaintance should witness this puppet show . . .

"The last performance of the day. It went well, Lily Francisca," Romney Lee congratulated her. "I think you should practice more with the horses, Odell. You nearly got the wires tangled up," he told Farley, who was handing his cloak to Tillie.

Farley Odell sniffed. "I'd like to see you do as well. Nor am I hearin' ye complainin' any about the share of the profits ye've pocketed for *our* day's work," he reminded him.

Romney Lee smiled. "Now, d'ye really think they'd be comin' just to see your pretty face if it weren't for my sweet-talkin' them up to the booth? I ought to be taking more than I am. Damned generous of me, actually. I've been thinking that you might do better in future to wrestle in the ring with that ox of a brother of yours. In between serious matches, that is. Perhaps we could get a bear cub for you to tangle with."

"Why, ye—"

"Farley, please!" Lily interrupted, stepping between them. The Odells and Romney Lee had never gotten along, and the situation had been growing worse of late. "Romney?" she questioned. She hadn't missed the instinctive movement of his hand toward his wrist.

"Only for you," he murmured, the look in his dark eyes when he gazed at Lily causing Farley Odell more unease than the knife the gypsy carried strapped to his forearm.

"Down, Ruff!" Tristram ordered, trying to keep the dog's nose out of the box where Tillie had carefully folded their cloaks and placed the masks.

"His name is Raphael, Tristram," Dulcie corrected him, patting the big dog.

"Ruff! Ruff! *Praaack! Bong! Bong!*" Cisco chimed from Lily's shoulder.

"I wonder how Fairfax did?" Farley said. "I think I'll head over that way and see," he decided.

"Lock up the booth, first," Romney told him, his hand sliding under Lily's elbow.

"I'll do it, Rom," Lily protested as Farley puffed out his chest. "Go on, Farley."

"Thank you, Mistress Lily," Farley said quickly, a smug grin spreading across his face when he saw the gypsy opening his mouth to object.

"Can I come with you, Farley?" Tristram asked.

"All right by me. Mistress Lily?"

Lily nodded her agreement. "But don't stay too long, or you'll miss dinner, and I don't want you anywhere near the bull bating. You had horrible nightmares last time you watched it."

" 'Tis just goin' to be meat pie again, Lily," Tristram complained.

"I haven't the time or the money to make anything else, Tristram. 'Tis good and hearty—"

"—and cold," Tristram said glumly.

"I did a bit of barterin' today and managed to find enough for a baked custard," Tillie offered shyly.

"Well, aren't ye the one?" Farley beamed proudly. "We definitely won't be late," he said, wondering if there was any left, for Tillie ate enough for a whole troop of soldiers nowadays.

"Keep an eye on him, will you, Farley?" Lily requested, although she feared she was wasting her breath.

"Right, mistress. Come on, Master Tristram."

"I've told you before, Lily Francisca, you are too kind-hearted," Romney Lee said, eyeing her thoughtfully. "You've gotten too thin. I've seen you giving your share of food to the woman," he said when Tillie had walked around to the front of the booth to place the box of cloaks on the stage. "You should let me deal with the Odells. They take advantage of your kindness. Everyone does," Romney added beneath his breath. "Including me."

"You? You've done more than enough for us. I am the one indebted to you, Rom," Lily reminded him. "If you hadn't helped us escape from Highcross that morning, well, I hate to think what might have happened. But the Odells are my responsibility. Farley and Fairfax have worked at Highcross since they were boys. They have always been loyal to my family. Have you forgotten that Tillie is going to have a baby? 'Tis her first one, Rom. She's scared. Except for Farley and Fairfax, I'm the only person she has. She needs the food more than I do," Lily said, climbing back up the steps.

"Where are you going?"

"I want to get this puppet of the witch. He's a bit worse for wear since we behead him so many times a day," she said, taking the puppet down from where it was hanging in the row with the others.

Romney Lee shook his head. "You always refer to the witch as a 'he.' Most are women."

Lily stared down at the wooden head with its pale thatch of hair and one blue eye and one brown eye, a strange expression on her face. "I don't know why I know the witch is a man, except perhaps because Basil always referred to the witch as a he. And I suppose he reminds me of someone I have never cared for," Lily said, looking away from that lifeless stare as she hurried down the steps.

"Careful!" Romney said, reaching out to steady her when she nearly lost her footing. "I can't have anything happen to my best performer."

"How can anything happen to me when you are forever keeping an eye on me?"

Romney laughed as he closed and locked the doors that opened in front and back of the booth. "I am merely protecting my property," he said with a wicked grin as he checked to make certain everything was secure. "There are too many rogues wandering around this fair for you to go about unguarded. One can't even leave the booth open anymore. The old spirit is gone. No more honor among us," he sighed. "But no one who knows me would dare to steal from me."

"I do have Raphael," Lily protested.

"Him?" Romney Lee asked incredulously as he eyed the big, clumsy dog with its comical ruff and the velvet-clad monkey sitting astride its back. "A most frightening appearance and about as ferocious as a lamb. All he does is cost money by eating our food."

"He's my watchdog! Raphael is brave!" Dulcie cried angrily, staring up at Romney in dislike.

"Ah, now I meant no harm, Sweet Rosalinda. With that silly face, he does bring in a fair amount during the procession,"

Romney allowed, reaching out to pull a strand of her long dark hair.

Dulcie jerked away from him and moved between Lily and Tillie, the latter giving the little girl plenty of room when her dog followed, pushing his head between them.

Romney Lee laughed. "I don't think she likes me, nor does her dog," he said. "I usually have a way with pretty little girls and wild beasts."

"Don't listen to him, Raphael. I think you're wonderful," she whispered in his droopy ear, patting him on his head affectionately.

Lily put her arm around Dulcie's thin shoulders. "She means no offence. She just doesn't understand your teasing."

"As long as her sister never takes a dislike to me, that is all I am concerned about," Romney warned. "Are you taking Merry out this evening? I do not like it. You shouldn't ride alone, Lily Francisca."

"Merry has to have exercise. I just take him for a run along the riverbank. Besides, no one can catch us. We race like the wind," she said, dismissing his fears with a smile as their figures became lost in the crowd and they were no longer visible to Sir Raymond Valchamps, who stood alone, watching them.

Lord Burghley stared down at the clutter of papers scattered across the table. Some things never changed, he thought a trifle sadly as he felt the warm breeze wafting in from the windows. Glancing toward the fading twilight, he knew a sudden longing to be strolling along a garden path, breathing the sweet scents of a summer's evening and hearing his grandchildren's laughter drifting to him from the terrace. He shifted his gouty foot, wincing slightly with the pain.

Even had he the leisure, there would be no long walks for him this eve, he realized, returning his attention to the parchment opened before him. It had been of particular interest to him. It was a report concerning Don Pedro Enrique Villasandro, captain of the *Estrella D'Abla*. It seemed that the good captain had been making inquiries as to the whereabouts of Valentine Whitelaw. Lord Burghley frowned. Their bold Englishman had been an unusually sharp thorn in the Spaniard's side ever since

he'd become captain of his own ship and since Valentine Whitelaw had learned of the Spaniard's part in his brother's death.

A slight smile crossed William Cecil's aging face as he remembered back to another time, when Basil Whitelaw and he
had engaged in many a diverting conversation. He and Sir Basil
had been of a similar mind concerning their philosophies of life.
How he missed those times of reasonable, rational thought.
Theirs had been calm voices heard even by the belligerent. But
now one had been silenced, and the constant threat of war
seemed to loom ever larger in the minds of those less patient
with diplomatic measures. Such a pity Sir Basil had been lost to
them for there were too few voices speaking out and cautioning
against rash acts.

Perhaps it was his own guilt or his suspicions aroused because of the assignment Sir Basil had been carrying out for the
government, but he had never felt completely satisfied with the
explanation of his friend's death. An old score to be settled between Geoffrey Christian and this Spaniard? No, 'twas too co-
incidental. Often, he and Sir Francis had speculated on the
possibility that Sir Basil had indeed discovered something in
Santo Domingo. He shook his head. Idle speculation, that was
all. They had no proof—and what good could it possibly do them
now to have in their hands what information Sir Basil had gathered ten years ago?

There was a knock on the door and he bid enter the man he'd
been expecting for close to an hour.

"Well?"

"He didn't make contact."

Lord Burghley raised an incredulous brow. "The cipher was
not passed?"

"No, m'lord. I never lost sight of the man. I followed him to
the fair. I watched him. Never once did I lose sight of that cursed
blue bonnet with the scarlet feather. One time, m'lord, I thought
he was about to make contact, but no one came close to him.
There was some kind of commotion by one of the booths, some
woman fainted, but I kept my eye on the courier, and he never
received as much as a nod from anyone. I'm sorry, m'lord," the
agent said.

Lord Burghley shook his head. "I do not understand. We
know there was a missive from the pope to Mary Stuart. Well,

perhaps tomorrow. You have someone watching the man now? Good," he said when the young man nodded.

"I followed him to the ambassador's residence. He stayed but a few minutes, then left. I then followed him to his lodgings on the wharf, where one of my men is stationed. If he leaves, we will know."

"Make certain the Spanish ambassador's residence remains under constant surveillance. I want to know of everyone who arrives there, whatever time of the day or night. Have you placed an agent on that priest we tracked from . . . let me see, yes, from the Tramorgans'?" he asked, checking the name of the Catholic family where the priest had stayed when first he'd arrived after entering England surreptitiously two days ago. Their agents had been awaiting his arrival in the small coastal village where he'd been set ashore.

"Yes. He's traveling north."

"Fine. Keep me informed on his movements. And don't lose him."

"No, m'lord," the man said, then was gone.

Due to Sir Francis Walsingham's diligence, or some might have said fanaticism, for he had a deep Puritan streak in him, they had agents sending them information from France, Spain, Germany, the Netherlands, and even Rome. Sir Francis's foresight in placing agents in the seminaries had paid off handsomely, for they now knew beforehand when to expect certain priests to arrive in England. From the time they set foot on English soil, they were watched and every move detailed in reports sent to the government.

Slowly the net was being drawn in, and soon they would have quite a catch. There would be many to share in a traitor's death at Tyburn, William Cecil thought without pleasure, carefully folding up the dispatches, ciphers, and incriminating lists of names before preparing to retire for the evening.

Valentine Whitelaw stood on the *Madrigal*'s quarterdeck, his gaze raking the skyline of the city. He saw church spires instead of ships' masts. He heard the ringing of bells rather than the roar of cannon. The haze hanging low over the city came from hearth fires, not the smoke of battle. It was good to be home, he thought. The *Madrigal*, riding at anchor, had returned safe from yet another profitable voyage.

Valentine glanced up at the creaking masts, the sails taken in and furled. And they would remain that way until he sailed for Ravindzara. He would not leave England again until Artemis had given birth. He had promised her, and himself, that he would be nearby. His nephew, or niece, a Penmorley, he thought with a disbelieving shake of his head. He had nothing against Sir Rodger, and as long as Artemis was happy, then he was happy.

"Joke?" Mustafa asked, having come silently to his captain's side.

Valentine laughed softly. "Not really. Just questioning the fates."

"Not good to do that, Captain. No one can understand why things happen the way they do," Mustafa said quietly. "One must accept what happens."

"I do not think that has always been your philosophy on life, Mustafa," Valentine challenged him.

"My mistake in the past, Captain. I was young and arrogant. I accept now what must happen," he said, turning his gaze to the distant shore.

Valentine smiled, juggling the oranges he had bought at the fair. "Well, I am pleased that the fates brought you and me together in that bazaar in Alexandria."

The Turk bowed his head, honored by his captain's words.

"Now, that is what I call a fateful sighting," Valentine murmured, his gaze narrowed as he stared at the shore. "Do you see what I do, Mustafa, or have I been misled by the mists? Is she mortal, or a Nereid sent to bewitch a weary sailor?"

The Turk followed his captain's gaze to the riverbank.

Sitting astride a white horse galloping along the shore was the most beautiful woman either man had ever seen. Dressed in green velvet, like the tall grasses growing along the river, her red hair flowing out behind her like a wild flame, she raced the wind with innocent abandon. She would disappear, then reappear almost magically out of the mists rising from the river. Only once did she seem to pause, and then she sat staring at the river, as if searching the clutter of masts for a certain ship.

"I wonder who she is," Valentine murmured, vowing he

would find out. "She is riding toward the fair. Strange, I didn't see her when we were there this afternoon. Tomorrow, after I've met with Elizabeth and paid my respects to certain people, I will return there and see if I can find her," he promised himself.

The silken hangings drawn back from the wide windows with their panes of heraldic glass moved imperceptibly with the soft breeze. The walls of the banqueting hall were covered with allegorical murals and tapestries, while the ceiling was crowned with elaborate plasterwork. A carved overmantel depicting Orpheus and the Muses graced the wall fireplace. A long table displayed a prodigious amount of silver plate laid with refreshment, while a small ensemble of six musicians played at the far end of the hall and filled the chamber with music.

"The gardens aren't planted quite the way we wish yet because the work on the banqueting house is not completed, but by next spring I think they will be quite lovely," Lady Elspeth said to one of her guests. "We've the orchards planted, and even a small vineyard. Oh, yes, an orangery, too. Oh? Why, yes, that is good advice."

"I really think you should consider the merits of the classical design rather than the Oriental. Let me have a look at the plans before you add the trim. Never let Charles handle these details. He gets too carried away," Lady Denning advised. "I've supervised all of the building on Denning House. Haven't had four husbands like Bess, Countess of Shrewsbury. We should all be so fortunate," she added as her husband approached.

" 'Tis a fine, stately home, Lady Elspeth," Sir Charles Denning stated as he joined his wife.

"Have you seen the solar room, Charles? 'Tis quite magnificent. The sun must be simply stunning coming through those oriel windows," Lady Denning remarked.

"Fine Turkey carpets, Lady Elspeth. Can't ever keep the dogs off them at home, though," Sir Charles said much to his wife's mortification. "Yes, indeed, 'tis a fine, stately home you and Sir William have built," he commented again as he took note of the inlaid paneling of the walls carved with the emblems and initials of the Davies family.

"Thank you, Sir Charles. Sir William and I are quite pleased with Riverhurst," Lady Elspeth responded, glancing around the room with pride, and even a sense of relief. Although she had loved Whiteswood, it was now a part of the past. It was where she had begun her married life with Basil as husband, but Riverhurst was where she would live out her days with William and their children. Simon was now master of Whiteswood.

". . . buttery, pantry, brewhouse, and bakehouse," an admiring woman was saying nearby. "A wine cellar, chandlery, and six ovens in the kitchens. Can you believe that? They've even a spicery. No, I haven't seen the chapel. I would rather see it during the day, I hear the stained glass is breathtaking. Is it true, Lady Elspeth, that you've an open gallery beneath the great gallery? Whatever for?"

"My physician tells me that there is nothing better than walking to keep one in good health and spirits. When 'tis rainy or perhaps too hot, I can take leisure in either the closed gallery or the open one below. Both overlook the courtyard," Lady Elspeth explained.

"I notice you've put in one of those wooden staircases. Nice touch those mythical beasts serving as posts. Been thinking about tearing out the old stone one at my hall," a gentleman commented, going on to explain in fuller detail the problems he'd come up against when adding another wing to his home.

"Have you seen the lodge? No? Splendid, absolutely splendid. Hope to be invited back to do a bit of hunting this fall. The gatehouse is bigger than my townhouse. Fine horses in the stables, I hear. Oh, you have, eh? 'Sblood! Didn't realize you were the one who outbid me on that little mare."

Lady Elspeth glanced around, making certain her guests were enjoying themselves. A number of young ladies were being partnered by the gentlemen in a lively galliard, followed by a coranto with its fast, running steps. Breathless from their endeavors, they joined with the more sedate guests who were moving closer to the banqueting table which had been cleared of dinner and now was being set with sweet wine and desserts.

"I hope everyone is enjoying himself?" Sir William inquired, exchanging a proud glance with his wife as he joined her at the end of the banqueting table.

"Indeed, Sir William," Sir Charles said with a mouth full of quince cake. "Must have this recipe, Lady Elspeth."

"Certainly, Sir Charles. I'll see that Lady Denning receives it before you depart."

" 'Tis going rather well, my dear," Sir William said softly, his hand entwining with hers under concealment of her skirts.

"Yes, it is. Why, thank you, I am so pleased you are enjoying yourself," she responded to a complimentary remark from one of her guests.

"Wish Simon were here," Sir William said with a frown.

"I know," Lady Elspeth said, patting his arm. "I had hoped he would arrive in time to attend our party, but he is now master of Whiteswood. He has the responsibility of his retainers. He must learn to concern himself with the running of his estate."

"Still just a boy, Elspeth."

"A boy who is fast becoming a man, William," she said.

"What do you mean?"

Elspeth Davies smiled. "He may not be living alone at Whiteswood for long. Do you remember when he accompanied Quinta and Sir Rodger and Artemis to Highcross Court last winter?"

Sir William eyed his wife curiously. "Yes, nothing odd in that. The little girl is, after all, his sister," Sir William spoke unthinkingly, then wished he hadn't when he saw a slight shadow cross Elspeth's serene face.

"He is fond of Dulcie, but, I suspect, he is just as fond of Lily Christian. He was strangely quiet after that visit—at least until he'd come down out of the clouds. After that, all we heard about was how beautiful Lily Christian was. He could not say enough about her."

Sir William seemed dumbfounded. "Well, I suppose if the lad is in love with a girl, then Lily Christian would make a fine daughter-in-law," he decided, then glanced at his wife. "I have no objections. You agree?"

"Whether I do or not will not concern my son if he is truly in love; however, I do happen to approve of the match. We shall have to invite Lily and her brother and sister here for a visit."

"Cordelia Howard is looking lovely this evening," Sir William commented rather abruptly.

"Yes, as always," Lady Elspeth agreed, but there was a glint in her eye as she stared at the beautiful woman dancing now with a handsome young man. In fact, Cordelia Howard had not left Walter Raleigh's side since she and Sir Raymond Valchamps had arrived. "I did not think they were going to attend. They nearly missed dinner."

"That late, were they? I didn't see them arrive," Sir William said, nodding to George Hargraves, who was partnering an uncommonly tall young woman around the room, his short legs hardly managing to keep pace with her long steps as they danced to the music. "I swear he does these things on purpose," Sir William grumbled as he caught the laughter of several of the guests as they watched the gentleman's comical antics.

"You needn't concern yourself that Minerva might be suffering an insult. She has an absolutely wicked sense of humor. That, and her height, scare most of the young gentlemen away. I am positive, however, that she is enjoying herself tremendously," Lady Elspeth advised him. "In fact, she is one of the few young women who has managed to interest George Hargraves."

"When is Valentine due back from his latest voyage?"

"Any day now. Why?"

"Watching Cordelia Howard dancing with Raleigh reminded me of when she and Valentine used to be lo— Well, I just wondered if he knew about Cordelia Howard and Sir Raymond. I had always thought that she and Valentine would wed. After all, she did visit his home last year," Sir William said almost disapprovingly.

"From what Artemis has told me, the visit was not what any of them had hoped," Lady Elspeth said.

"Speaking of Valentine's sister. Surprised to see Sir Rodger here. Didn't know he'd left Cornwall, especially now that Artemis is expecting."

"Well, I am pleased we saw him in town and convinced him to accompany us to Riverhurst and stay here while he awaits Quinta's return from Scotland. Apparently, she became concerned over Artemis and insisted on returning to Ravindzara before she had planned. I believe Sir Rodger is here to escort her to Cornwall, as well, I suspect, to find a good physician to accompany them back."

"Nothing wrong, is there?"

"No, but this will be Sir Rodger's first child, and he is anxious. I believe his sister, Honoria, is staying with Artemis. You remember how nervous you were when I gave birth to your first-born.''

''Was a damned sight more nervous over the second birth; knew too much then to rest easy,'' he said. ''Ah, Thomas, how is everything? Eliza, looking lovelier than ever. Can I get you anything?'' Sir William asked as Thomas Sandrick and his wife approached.

''Wonderful banquet, Sir William.''

''I am enchanted with Riverhurst, Lady Elspeth,'' Eliza Sandrick said shyly.

''Thank you. And how is young Henry Thomas?''

''A bit fretful of late, Lady Elspeth. He cries constantly. I fear 'tis the rash. I just don't know how to ease the pain of it.''

''I have had too many sleepless nights to remain a proud father for much longer,'' Thomas Sandrick said with a rueful glance.

''I will have my old nurse give you her special salve. 'Twill do wonders, I guarantee. If you will excuse me for just a moment, I will get you some now lest I lose the opportunity later,'' she offered.

''Thank you. I would also appreciate any advice your nurse can give me.''

Lady Elspeth laughed. ''I warn you now you will come to regret asking. Lanny likes nothing better than to share her views concerning child-rearing. I will not be long, William,'' she said, excusing herself.

''Mary Worthington is looking our way, Thomas,'' George Hargraves commented as he quickly stepped behind his taller friend.

''I have nothing to fear, or have you forgotten I am married?'' Thomas reminded his fearful friend.

''That has never concerned her before,'' George said, risking a glance at the woman heading their way. ''It merely means that I am a bit fairer game than you, my friend.''

Eliza eyed the two as if they were still in swaddling. ''She wishes a word with me,'' she said, deflating their egos. ''We never finished our conversation of earlier,'' she said with an understanding smile as she walked off to meet the woman.

''No offense, Thomas, but since you wed Eliza, she seems more and more like her brother. Never knew she had a tongue in her head, and certainly not a witty one, until now," George complained good-naturedly, wishing he'd paid closer attention to Eliza Valchamps when she'd been unwed.

"Raymond cannot stand competition from anyone, especially a sister he had come to look upon as little better than a mouse," Thomas spoke dryly.

"Become a bit of a tigress, eh?" George guffawed.

"At least where I and our son are concerned, yes," Thomas said quite seriously. "So guard your tongue when around her."

"I stand warned."

"I wonder where Sir Raymond is," Thomas Sandrick commented, for he hadn't missed Cordelia Howard's flirting with Walter Raleigh. Indeed, it had been scandalous.

"Most likely off sulking. He was looking daggers at the man earlier."

"I am indeed fearful for Raleigh," George Hargraves said, helping himself to a goblet of wine and a piece of spice cake. "But not because of Sir Raymond. Crossing swords with him would be a joy compared to falling prey to that she-wolf. Think we should warn our friend?"

"From what I've heard of Raleigh," Sir William advised, "he can take care of himself well enough."

"That isn't exactly the way I've heard it told," George said with a grin, lowering his voice as he confided. " 'Tis actually that . . ."

Not more than fifteen minutes had passed when Lady Elspeth reentered the hall and glanced around curiously. "We seem to have been abandoned, Eliza," she greeted the young woman who had come quickly to her side. "Where is everyone?" she asked, for she did not see her husband or the either of the gentlemen he'd been talking to when she'd left. "Here is the salve, and a few other items Lanny insisted I give to you."

"Oh, thank you. I am indeed grateful."

"Perhaps William took the gentlemen upstairs to the gallery. Let us go speak with Minerva, she seems to be having some difficulty with Lady Denning. Even Sir Charles has disappeared."

"My future sister-in-law seems quite entertained," Eliza said, surprising Lady Elspeth by the criticism. "I wonder if she is aware of what they say about Walter Raleigh?"

Lady Elspeth eyed the demure Eliza, not quite certain what

to expect. "What might that be?" she was intrigued enough to inquire.

"They say he loves a comely wench well," Eliza astounded Lady Elspeth by remarking.

Lady Elspeth found herself watching the two more closely, and she came to the conclusion that Walter Raleigh had met his match in the beautiful Cordelia. She only hoped that Sir Raymond, Cordelia's intended, did not watch as closely, but as she glanced around, she saw that he too was missing from the hall.

"Well, you certainly took your time. The moon has nearly set while I've been out here waiting for you," Sir Raymond Valchamps greeted his friend.

"I was delayed. I could not leave the hall sooner without causing comment," the man replied, his face hidden in the shadowy darkness of the uncompleted banqueting house in the gardens. "But why did you wish to meet? What is wrong? You've seemed nervous all evening."

"What is wrong?" Sir Raymond slowly repeated the question.

"Are you ill?"

"*We* are in serious trouble, my friend."

"What has happened?"

"You know I went to the fair today?"

"So?"

"I was to pass a ciphered letter from the pope to a courier who was to deliver it to Mary Stuart," he explained.

"I know. You weren't caught, were you?" his friend was concerned enough to raise his voice.

"Worried about me, or your own precious neck? Had I been apprehended, I wouldn't be here tonight. But if you are that concerned, then here 'tis. You deliver it. I've more important things to take care of," Sir Raymond said, tossing the letter at the man.

"Good Lord! You've still got it? What went wrong? Why do you still have it? And to bring it here, with all of these people about? You're mad!"

"Mad? No, I am desperate, my friend. You would do well to feel the same."

"What are you talking about?"

"I witnessed a stunning performance today. 'Twas at a puppet show."

The man in the shadows choked. "A puppet show? You had me meet you here to tell me about a puppet show?"

"Yes, I am sorry you missed the performance. I am personally going to see that it was the last one they ever perform. Would you like to hear about the wild white horses and the evil witch?"

"Really, Raymond. A child's play? I'm going back to the house."

"Oh, please, humor me for just a few minutes more. I want to tell you about this evil witch with one blue eye and one brown eye who plans to assassinate Elizabeth, Queen of the Misty Isle, and how Prince *Basil*, who was a castaway on a western isle, must come to her rescue. He has three helpers, Lily, Sweet Rose, and Tristram. I believe the Spanish for sweet is Dulcie, is it not? Do those names sound slightly familiar? They should. They are the names of the same three children who are now traveling as vagabonds and putting on a puppet show for the whole world to see and hear. What? Not laughing now, are we? Oh, don't worry, the queen's guards are not racing to arrest us. But it could happen, my long-suffering friend. If someone else should have seen that puppet show and made the connection between this evil witch and us, then all we have planned and waited for is ruined."

"Us?"

"Oh, I see. You think just because I am the one with the memorable face, that you are safe. Remember this. If I get arrested for treason, I will be tortured if I keep my silence. When I face the rack, when my limbs are twisted and I cannot stand the pain any longer, I will give them your name with the utmost pleasure. If I am to die a traitor's death, so shall you, my friend, so shall you," Sir Raymond warned the silent man.

"You speak of this puppet show as if it were no more. Is there no longer any danger from it?"

"I have dealt with it. But now I must deal with Lily Christian. As long as she lives, she is a threat to us. My God, Basil seems determined to avenge his death, doesn't he?" Sir Raymond laughed bitterly. " 'Tis obvious, isn't it? He couldn't tell what he knew to the queen, so instead he amused the brats with a tale of betrayal and revenge. Oh, I would laugh if I were not the man who will hang if anyone else understands the moral of Basil Whitelaw's fable. Damn him! May he rot in hell!''

''Why now? After all of this time. What is Lily Christian doing traveling with a group of vagabonds? I understood her to be at Highcross. Why has she left there? What are we going to do?''

''I am grateful that you have finally seen fit to concern yourself. But you really do not want to know. You are too soft-hearted, my friend. I will deal with this threat. Why she left Highcross Court does not concern us. All that matters is that she is here, within my reach, and I will not fail this time. Soon, Lily Christian will die. And no one can save her now.''

Dawn had yet to break as Simon Whitelaw sent his horse galloping along the road. In his eagerness to reach Highcross Court, he threw caution to the winds.

Lily and Dulcie and Tristram, of course, would be surprised to see him so soon after his last visit. He would tell them he had been in the vicinity and had suddenly realized how close to Highcross he'd been. How could he have possibly ridden by without stopping to say hello? As the miles passed, and he dreamed of Lily Christian, Simon Whitelaw rehearsed his excuse until it came easily to his tongue. This would be a visit he would not soon forget.

All is not well;
I doubt some foul play.

SHAKESPEARE

Chapter Nineteen

"WHAT a mess," Tristram said, raking his shoe through the rubble. "There's nothing left. What are we going to do now, Lily?" he asked, surveying the destruction of their booth. The fire that had raged the night before had burnt itself out by morning, leaving only smoldering ashes and a few charred pieces of wood.

"Did everything burn up?" Dulcie asked, her eyes filling with tears. "All of our puppets died, Lily," she cried, thinking of the wild white horses that she had embroidered the harnesses for. "Poor Prince Basil. He was my favorite," she murmured. "It's just like on the island, isn't it, Lily?" she asked, unnecessarily reminding Lily of the hut where Basil had lain and that she had set aflame.

Lily cleared her throat.

"Lily?"

"I don't know, Tristram," Lily said in a low voice, glancing away from his puzzled expression only to find suspicious, unpitying faces watching her. Lily lifted her chin proudly. But she was tired of having to decide what to do. With their puppet show destroyed, they had no way of earning their keep at the fair. They could still collect a few coins during the procession that opened the fair every day, but not enough. What they managed to make was shared with all of the performers. After being divided—and not always equally for there were those who'd

353

been with the fair longer than others and demanded a larger share—there would not be enough even to buy food. Because of the success of the puppet show they had been able only recently to set a small sum aside for their journey to Maire Lester's. Once there, Lily had fully expected to pay their own way. Had they not been so desperate, she would have hesitated in seeking out Maire Lester, for she knew their old nurse was living with her widowed sister on sufferance.

"I'd like to know how the fire started in the first place," Farley demanded, glancing around at those unfriendly faces surrounding them.

"Ye been careless, maybe," someone commented.

"Got what ye deserves."

"Or, maybe what *someone* thinks we should be gettin'?" Farley charged, meeting several of those glances accusingly. "Reckon there be some who've been jealous of us. Showed ye how to make some money for a change."

"Should've burnt ye out long ago."

"Yeah? Who said that?"

"I did! But I didn't burn down your booth."

"Trust you about as far as Fairfax could toss ye," Farley said hotly.

"My own booth be too close by. Otherwise, I would've carried the torch and set it meself. And I would've admitted it, that proud of the deed I would've been! Maybe I been losin' customers to yer puppet show, but I didn't burn ye out."

"I wish I had!" a low voice commented.

"Come out and face me! Ye coward!" Fairfax yelled, stepping forward to glare at the suddenly quiet group. "Thought as much," he said, spitting at their feet.

"Are ye sayin' we burned yer booth?" someone found the courage to demand, although he stayed well in the crowd and safely out of reach of Fairfax's fists.

"Maybe we are, and maybe we aren't," Farley said.

"Accusing each other isn't going to do any of us any good. We'll still have empty pockets by nightfall unless we get busy," Romney Lee advised. "It was probably a spark from the fireworks display that set it off. It has happened before," Romney Lee explained reasonably, trying to calm everyone's fears before things got out of hand. "All that has happened is that there will be no puppet show for a couple of weeks while we make new puppets."

"So what do we do in the meantime? Starve?" Farley demanded, thinking Romney Lee had explained away their misfortune rather too glibly. He hadn't, however, explained why their booth and no other had caught fire. And the fireworks hadn't even been close, unless, Farley thought, casting a grim eye at the assembled knaves, someone had purposely placed a flaming candle in their booth.

"Might be a good time fer some people to be goin' about their own way."

"Could leave the fair before something worse happens," someone suggested.

"Have ye forgotten what Old Maria's been predicting?" Navarre chimed in as she stepped to the front of the crowd, pleased with the growing discontent she was hearing amongst her friends.

" 'Tis right, she has!"

"Aye, been predictin' tragedy ever since Romney Lee brought them here."

"Told us to beware the flames, or murder would follow."

"Aye, we hold ye responsible, Rom."

"Old Maria has been predicting misfortune for the last three years," Romney scoffed. "She does every time her other predictions don't come true. 'Tis easy enough to predict bad omens, since there is always something going wrong. Keeps us afraid of our own shadows and quick to believe in her and cross her palm with silver."

"Ye be askin' fer trouble, Romney Lee."

"Surprised I am to be hearin' yer mockin' voice, Romney Lee, and ye with gypsy blood in ye. Why, yer mam would be turnin' over in her grave to hear such talk."

" 'Tis the girl, she's the one who has deceived ye. Not old Maria. Ask the old one what she saw, Romney Lee," Navarre baited him.

"It doesn't matter what she thinks she saw," Romney told Navarre, the glint in his dark blue eyes causing Navarre to take a step closer to her uncle's side. "I say they stay."

"And who said ye speak fer the rest o' us, Romney Lee?" Silver Jones demanded. "I, and a council of elders, have always made the decisions for this band. Seems to me Navarre is right, and ye've been misled by the girl. We all know she comes o' some highborn family. Ye think to better yerself by weddin' her, Rom? Think ye'd do better with the likes o' her rather than my Navarre? Ye be a fool, lad! That one is bad luck. Ye can see it in her eyes," he said with a superstitious crossing of himself as Lily glanced over at him.

"You say throw them out? We've never made as much money in our processions until Lily Francisca rode Merry through the crowd. And their puppet show, that you all complain so heartily about, draws more of a crowd into the fair, and to our booths nearby, than we've ever seen before. And yet, because of some old hag's crazed talk and the gossip of a woman jealous of one more beautiful than she, you would take money out of your own pockets? You can't be that foolish, Silver Jones. You say you and the council speak for the rest of us? Then go, talk it over. And when you've cooler heads and can hear the jingling of money in your pockets, then tell me again to send them away. Are you going to let Navarre's jealous whisperings in your ear speak for the rest of us?" he challenged them.

"Aye, right he is, Silver."

"She was run out of her village fer being a witch! She's cast a spell over him. Don't listen to him. Uncle Sil, don't. He's crazed fer her. Don't listen, I tell ye," Navarre cried out angrily.

"Aye, we all know Navarre is angry 'cause Rom seeks his comfort elsewhere now," someone snickered, then yelped when Navarre's hand cuffed him a stinging blow on the side of his head.

"Enough!" Silver Jones bellowed. "The fair opens in less than an hour. We've got the procession and our booths to set up. Get about yer business, ye thieves and sluggards! And I'd better be countin' all that I think I should afterwards," he warned, eyeing one family of performers with special interest. "I've heard talk some ain't sharin' like they should. Go on, now! Get about yer business. The council will be meetin' this evenin'. Ye'll have yer chance to speak before us, Rom. Then and only then, and by vote, do we decide what happens to Lily Francisca and the others," Silver Jones pronounced. "And don't ye be glarin' at me," he warned, slapping Navarre across the face as she muttered something.

Wiping the blood from her lip with the back of her hand, Navarre sauntered over to where Lily was standing. "Ye'd do well to stay close to yer friends. No tellin' what accidents can happen at night if ye're up and about and wanderin' where ye shouldn't be," she warned, then laughed harshly as she eyed the mastiff. "Reckon we could get a pretty collar like this fer Rom's neck? This one's got him actin' as tame as some fine *lady's* pampered lap dog," she said. "Don't think he'd be man enough fer me now," she added as a parting shot, her smile turning seductive as she sidled up to a young man who had not been shy in his pursuit of her favors. "Now there's no doubt that *he's* a man," she said with a deep, throaty laugh as she moved her hip against him. "No doubt at all."

Romney Lee flushed angrily as he heard the laughter of those who were still standing nearby, but Silver Jones sent them, and his niece, about their tasks as he roared his orders and raised a threatening fist at them. Shaking his leonine head of silver hair, he stomped off, but not before Romney Lee had seen the grin on his grizzled face and heard the low chuckle.

"I'm sorry, Rom," Lily spoke beside him, her hand resting comfortingly on the bunched muscles of his arm. "We should do like they say and leave. We really do not belong here. Now that we no longer have the puppet show, we can't continue to travel with you. I would sell the oxen and give you half for the trouble we've caused you, except that we need them to reach Maire Lester's. After we're there, I'll sell them, then send you half. You have done enough for us, and what have you gotten in return? All we have ever brought you is misfortune. Old Maria is right. We are bad luck, and not just for you. No one fares well when they become involved with us—with me," Lily added.

"Don't say that, Lily Francisca. I don't want to hear any talk about you leaving the fair. This is where you belong. You have been happy here, haven't you?"

"Yes, but it cannot continue. We've just been playing make-believe this summer, Rom. I've tried to pretend that all is well, but I can never forget that we left Hartwell Barclay dead at Highcross. The authorities are still searching for us, Rom. Perhaps it is time that I faced them, told them the truth," Lily said, not looking forward to having to defend herself before the good people of East Highford.

"No!"

"Rom, you must understand—"

"I do understand, Lily Francisca. I understand far better than you. You would never have a chance with those villagers. They think you caused Hartwell Barclay's death. I know, I spoke with them in the village. Don't you remember? I went out to Highcross. I heard the cook talking to the authorities. I spoke with the stable hand. They had already found you guilty and had you hanging from the gallow's tree. Please, listen to me, Francisca. You must never try to return to Highcross."

"For once I agree with him," Farley said. "Them villagers can hardly wait to try you for Hartwell Barclay's murder. Even your powerful relatives couldn't save you, Mistress Lily. Besides, ye'd never get the chance to get word to them. Like the gypsy says, ye'd be swingin' from the gallows, or burnt at the stake as a witch, before they could rescue ye. Listen to him, Mistress Lily."

For the first time Romney Lee eyed Farley Odell with respect and even gratitude. "There! Farley Odell was born in that village. He knows them even better than I, Francisca. Would it be that bad to stay with the fair a little longer, at least until winter comes? We will manage well enough until we've made new puppets. Fairfax can continue to wrestle. I'll match him up with more opponents," Romney Lee said quickly, glancing over to the big man who nodded his agreement.

"I can juggle," Tristram piped in eagerly.

"That ye can, lad," Romney agreed.

"I s'pose I could bake some cinnamon cakes," Tillie offered. "I'm afraid I won't be very good at sellin' them. Can't get through the fair very easily," she explained, glancing down at her rounded belly self-consciously.

"By the time ye got down to the midway, reckon there wouldn't be many left either, Tillie," Fairfax said with a chuckle.

"Raphael and I can sell them," Dulcie cried excitedly, causing the mastiff to bark and sending Cappie into a somersault on his back. "I can dance with my tambourine like I do in the procession."

Romney Lee grinned in satisfaction. "Yes, that would catch the customers' interest. But we must have a way of displaying our goods. We can harness the dog to a small cart filled with the cakes, and perhaps flowers and ribbons, whatever we can find. We will put the monkey and the parrot in the cart, too. They will amuse the customers and keep them entertained while they decide what to buy. But, while Sweet Rose is dancing, we must have someone watching the cart. Lily?"

"Have I any choice?" she asked with a laugh, her spirits a bit higher.

"No, I will never let you have a choice," he said.

"How about me?" Farley demanded aggressively, for the gypsy wasted no time in getting things done, and usually just the way he wanted. He was the smooth-tongued one all right, Farley grumbled to himself, not liking to be maneuvered into doing something he wasn't certain he wished to do—whatever it was.

For once Romney Lee didn't respond with his usual sarcasm. "I've been thinking that you might stroll through the crowd calling various booths to the people's attention. I would see that each booth contributed something for your efforts on their behalf. You could tell some of those amusin' stories of yours while you make your way along the midway, leavin' the end of the story, of course, 'til ye've reached the booths," Rom suggested helpfully.

Farley grinned. "I can see that I've never underestimated ye, gypsy," he said, bowing to the other man. "If I was wearin' a hat, I'd take it off to ye, Romney Lee."

"What is that?" Romney asked, noticing for the first time the object Lily was holding in her hands.

"The witch," Lily said, holding up the only puppet that had survived the fire. The one blue eye and one brown eye painted on the ugly face glared up at her malevolently, and even though it was just a harmless puppet, Lily shivered. "Strange, but of all our puppets, this is the one I liked the least."

"Well, at least that is one we won't have to worry about," Romney Lee said, gesturing for them to follow him. As they walked away, he glanced back at the charred remains of the booth. He frowned slightly, for he too had his suspicions about the fire.

Simon Whitelaw rode up the narrow lane to Highcross Court. He couldn't quite stop his grin from widening boyishly as he anticipated walking into the great hall. It wasn't afternoon yet, so he'd be in time for lunch, he thought as his stomach rumbled hungrily.

There were several horses, as well as a cart harnessed to a tired, old mare, in the courtyard. He didn't recognize any as belonging to the Highcross stables. Wondering who was visiting, Simon Whitelaw dismounted, glancing around for the groom, but no one came to assist him. The visitors had not come any great distance, for the horses were sweating only slightly and hadn't lathered up at all.

Curious, Simon Whitelaw hurried up the steps and knocked soundly on the great doors of Highcross. Schooling his expression into one of polite inquiry, he stared at the door that had yet to open and allow him access into the great hall. He tried again. But still no answer. Frowning, he was about to turn away when one of the doors swung wide and he found himself staring into the face of a stranger.

"Yes?" the stern-visaged footman inquired haughtily, his expression seeming to indicate that he doubted that the dusty-booted young gentleman standing on the doorstep had any business at Highcross.

"I am Simon Whitelaw."

The man continued to stare at Simon expressionlessly. "Indeed?"

"Yes! I've come to visit my sister, Dulcie, and Lily and Tristram Christian. Please inform your mistress of my presence," he told the man without any further attempt at gentlemanly behavior, for he'd not missed the strange look that had crossed the man's face when he'd mentioned Lily Christian's name. "Well?"

The footman opened the door wider to allow Simon to enter. "If you will wait here, sir?" he said, gesturing vaguely toward the oak settle against the wall.

Simon opened his mouth to protest, but the man had disappeared too quickly up the stairs. Simon tossed his hat onto the bench, but he'd be damned if he'd sit there like a good little boy. He stared about him, thinking the hall awfully quiet. He hadn't even heard Raphael's barking when he'd ridden into the courtyard. The dog had never stopped barking the last time he'd been here.

Simon walked over to the stairs. He'd thought he had heard approaching footsteps, but all was quiet at the top of the stairs. With an impatient sigh, he sat down on one of the steps, his long legs stretched out to the floor. Hearing steps again, he popped up, frightening the young maid rounding the bottom of the stairs.

"Oh, I'm sorry, sir," the maid apologized, abruptly stopping her singing. "Scared me half to death, ye did. Didn't know there was anyone in here," she said nervously.

"Who are you?" Simon demanded. He'd never seen the girl before. "What happened to Tillie?"

"Oh, sir! Why, she be gone, nigh on four, no five months now, same as t'others."

"What others? Who has gone?" he asked, making the girl more nervous than ever by the question.

"Why, ah, why the young mistress and t'others. The little ones and the Odells. Tillie, too. She went with them when they run away. I weren't here then, not when the accident happened, but I've heard tell 'twas horrible. Why, the cook, she still has nightmares—oh, no! Wait, sir! Ye can't be goin' up there!"

With his long strides, Simon Whitelaw wasted no time in reaching the top of the stairs. He quickly made his way along the corridor toward the great chamber, where he assumed the master of Highcross would be entertaining his visitors. Whether Hartwell Barclay was receiving or not, Simon Whitelaw was determined to have some explanations.

The door to the great chamber was slightly ajar when Simon approached it, and pausing just outside, he stood for a moment and listened to the conversation coming from within, an incredulous expression beginning to form on his face.

"I still think prudence dictates that charges should be brought against this Lily Christian. I have had some dealings in the past with witch trials, and I tell you now that the evidence points very strongly toward her being in league with the devil. A few hours under my questioning and I would have her confession to having practiced witchcraft while under this roof. Naturally, I would expect your cooperation in this matter, Master Martindale. As constable, you would, of course, figure greatly in the proceedings. Your name would become quite well known throughout the shire, indeed, throughout all of England. And,

Doctor Wolton, as the family physician, your testimony will be most influential in indicting the witch.''

Simon Whitelaw stepped closer and inched the door a shade wider. The footman was standing just inside, waiting for the opportunity to speak. He was partly blocking Simon's line of sight, but glancing around him Simon saw a rather plump, pompous-looking individual, dressed in somber clothing. He was gesturing wildly with his arms as he addressed two women, who were seated before him as if sitting in the front pew of a church. Two gentlemen, nodding their continual agreement, stood near the window.

"I can indeed testify to the strange incantations Lily Christian spoke while feverish just a year ago,'' the doctor promised.

"And, of course, I have investigated many strange occurrences since Lily Christian and her brother and sister arrived at Highcross,'' the constable was quick to confirm.

"Oh, Reverend Buxby, 'tis absolutely sinful what she has done,'' the whey-faced young woman sighed, staring in fascination at the parson. "I am indeed fearful of such bewitchments as you have described. I am certain 'twas she who caused me to fall and break my leg. And, of course, poor Hartwell . . .''

"Now, now, Mary Ann, calm yourself lest you faint from a lack of breath,'' Mistress Fordham cautioned her daughter, afraid she was going to start hiccuping any second.

"Oh, indeed, Mistress Mary Ann, I am positive she has bewitched this village. I will present such evidence against her that she will burn in the fires of hell!''

"Oh,'' Mary Ann whispered, catching her breath.

"Does she not have familiars? What of that horse she speaks with and that none but she could ride? What of those wild creatures from the New World where savages worship the devil and all manner of false idols? The unspeakable acts they perpetrate in the dark caverns of the underworld. Lewd dances and human sacrifice!''

"Ooohh.''

"Mary! Mary! Calm yourself, now,'' Mistress Fordham warned her daughter, slapping her on each cheek to bring back the color.

"And how can you explain the ease of her escape?'' the Reverend Buxby demanded, his face turning mottled with frustrated rage at having lost his intended victim. "Upon that dreadful night, she jumped upon the back of her familiar and raced into the sky, with lightning and thunder marking her path through the gates of hell. To some far distant place she was spirited. Not a sign of them could we find. Not a word heard concerning them. Not a sighting by any mortal being! Vanished into thin air. We have evidence, right here in this house, of her devilish lusts. To mislead us, she sent her instruments of Satan to mock us in our own house of worship. Upon sacred ground they came! Were we all not there to serve witness to their desecration of our holy place?

"Does she not float on water? Is there not proof of her sorcerer's ways in the heathen charms from the New World she wears with such wickedness? Have we all not heard the incantations she chants to her prince of darkness?" the reverend demanded, then, with hands folded complacently before him, he gazed at the doctor. "You have examined this Lily Christian. Perchance you remember seeing the devil's mark upon her person? It would indeed be irrefutable proof of her guilt."

"Well . . ." the doctor paused, a thoughtful look in his eye. "I might be able to recall such a mark. Naturally, I would have to examine her again."

"Indeed, doctor. Witches are clever at hiding so damning a mark where the devil has touched them. But Lily Christian will not be able to deny her sins after I've applied the proper sort of persuasion. Not many can stand for long having their heads tightly bound or their bodies stuck with pins, unless, of course they are guilty; then they feel no pain. Before I am finished, I would see her and that brother and sister of hers burn!"

"How dare you!" Simon Whitelaw cried out, storming into the room and startling the occupants so by his sudden appearance that Mary Ann Fordham screamed and began to weep hysterically, actually believing it was the devil himself. And even the Reverend Buxby had a moment's horror, thinking he had gone too far in his exhortations this time.

"Really, sir!" the affronted footman began, picking himself up from the floor where the rude young gentleman's shoulder had sent him sprawling. "I must protest!"

Simon Whitelaw ignored the fellow and faced the other occupants of the room, who still remained speechless. His expression

was one of outrage as he stared at them. But his gaze centered on
one man as he said, "You, sir, have much to answer for! I would
have an explanation from you, Hartwell Barclay!"

Hartwell Barclay, sitting in a plush velvet armchair close to
the hearth, his leg stretched out before him and supported on a
small, upholstered footstool, opened his mouth to speak, but
couldn't seem to find anything to say.

Simon Whitelaw turned his wrathful indignation on the Reverend Buxby and the two gentlemen. And when he spoke, his
cold, imperious voice sounded like a distant echo of Basil Whitelaw's when presenting a case to those he intended to deliver a
scathing rebuttal to. "Before you begin this witch hunt of yours,
I would caution you to remember exactly whom you are dealing
with. The innocent child you would burn at the stake happens to
be my sister, and the daughter of Sir Basil Whitelaw, once the
trusted adviser to Elizabeth Tudor and longtime friend of William Cecil, Lord Burghley. My stepfather, Sir William Davies, is
a highly placed member of court. My aunt, who happens to be
exceedingly fond of Dulcie, is Lady Artemis Penmorley, wife of
one of the wealthiest, most influential gentlemen in England.
My uncle, Valentine Whitelaw, is one of Elizabeth's favorites
and not without influence of his own. A privateer, whose
exploits you may well have heard about, he has never had trouble dealing with the enemies of his queen," Simon Whitelaw
boasted, conjuring up the image of a bloodthirsty pirate in the
minds of the Fordham ladies.

"The *witch* you speak of has been received at court by Elizabeth. There is even talk that she is considering making Lily
Christian one of her ladies-in-waiting. Her Majesty would be
most displeased to hear such false, slanderous rumors as you are
spreading. And Sir Christopher Hatton, Thomas Sandrick—who
was aboard the *Madrigal* when Lily Christian was rescued and is
devoted to her—and Philip Sidney are all ardent admirers and
would be eloquent, convincing voices raised in her defense. I am
certain you know the Sidney name, since Philip Sidney's home,
Penshurst, is here in this shire. He is a most respected member
of court. I believe he intends to visit Highcross in the near future
to see how the young woman who so charmed him is faring,"
Simon added for good measure.

"So before you pursue beyond this room this witch hunt of

yours, remember the powerful friends of Lily Christian you will have to challenge as well," Simon Whitelaw said, his voice quavering with his rage and fear, but he need not have worried, for his case had been most effectively presented.

Hartwell Barclay finally found his voice. Spreading his hands in supplication, his expression one of confounded innocence, he said, "Please, please, you misunderstand. As I have been trying to explain to the good reverend and the constable, who have my best interests at heart, there was no attempted murder. Good gracious no. The cook, an excitable woman, simply misunderstood when she entered Lily's chamber and found me unconscious in that tub."

When Hartwell Barclay saw Simon Whitelaw's expression, he quickly continued. "Oh, yes, indeed, I can see that you are wondering what I was doing in the dear girl's bedchamber, well, 'tis a long story," he said with a sickly grin.

"Ah, but I have plenty of time, Master Barclay," Simon said softly, causing Hartwell Barclay to reassess his opinion of this young man.

"Yes, well, the girl is prone to nightmares, and I merely had come to see if all was well. Let me remind you, young man, that I am her guardian. Upon entering the chamber, which, unfortunately, was being occupied at the time by young Dulcie and that—that—dog, as well as those other creatures, and the maid, although what she was doing in Lily's bed I still do not understand," he said with a ruminative rub of his chin, "I found myself involved in quite a ruckus. The silly creature thought I was trying to attack her. Bless me, what a fright she gave me when she started shrieking. Sounded like a banshee. Then that dog attacks me. Ought to be shot. Well, fleeing for my life, I stumbled into the tub, breaking my ankle when I twisted it and knocking myself unconscious. I still do not know where Lily was during all of the commotion, but I understand she was in the room when the cook came running in, and the woman assumed some foul play.

"Naturally, when I regained consciousness, I told the authorities, who had been summoned by Hollings, the groom, that there had been a tragic misunderstanding. Why, we had everything cleared up the very next day," he laughed dismissingly. "However, Lily, the dear child, thinking herself responsible for my death, had fled Highcross with the Odells and that slow-witted Tillie. If she hadn't started screaming, none of this would have happened. But these good people, and only out of their deep concern for my welfare, were hesitant to believe my story. They have had some suspicions in the past concerning Lily. A most eccentric young woman, you must admit. Thought I was merely trying to protect my wards and so they have continued to pursue the investigation of what happened that night. They continued to search the countryside. They questioned everyone. But no one had seen my frightened wards. But, as I was about to say before you entered so suddenly, I really must insist that the matter be dropped in its entirety," he concluded magnanimously. "Don't you agree, Reverend Buxby? Doctor Wolton? Constable Martindale? I wish to hear nothing further concerning this matter. I am certain you will agree with me?"

"Of course! An unfortunate mistake."

"Naturally! No other actions will be necessary. No charges have been filed. There are no warrants for their arrest. Best forgotten."

The Reverend Buxby was the only one who remained ominously still, but Simon suspected it was merely because he'd had all of the hot air knocked out of him.

"The dear girl. Such a tragic accident. If only she had come to me. Why, like a mother I am to her," Mistress Fordham sighed, handing her daughter another handkerchief. "Oh, do be quiet, Mary Ann!" she hushed her weeping daughter.

"B-but, Mama! You said if Lily Christian were out of the way, then I'd get to become mistress of—"

"What nonsense, child!" Mistress Fordham sputtered, shaking the girl until she stared dazedly at her mother's flushed face. "You are becoming fretful again. I don't know what I am to do with you. Such a disappointment to me, both you and your brother."

Simon Whitelaw continued to stare at Hartwell Barclay, who was wiping the perspiration from his face with an oversized handkerchief. "When did this 'unfortunate affair' occur?"

"Why, uh, not too long ago," Hartwell Barclay answered, glancing around at the others, but they were all busy; the doctor picking lint off his sleeve, the constable straightening his hose with unusual care, while the reverend seemed lost in his next week's sermon.

"Not long ago?" Simon questioned politely. "I would think five months was rather a long time for your wards to be missing. Indeed, I am surprised, Master Barclay, that you have not found the opportunity of informing my family of this situation."

Hartwell Barclay cleared his throat. "I have been desperately ill. Not quite myself since the accident. I had hoped they would return before I had to send such disquieting news to your family," Hartwell Barclay explained. "I fear even to speculate upon what might have happened to the dear children traveling unescorted and unprotected across the countryside."

"You had better have the good reverend pray for you then, sir, as well as for himself and these other good folk, for if anything has happened to my sister, or Lily and Tristram, then you will wish you had died that night," Simon Whitelaw warned the astounded group, and turning on his heel, he walked from the great chamber.

Simon Whitelaw could not get out of Highcross fast enough. He was still shaking with anger when he vaulted down the steps into the courtyard. His horse was still standing where he'd left it, unattended, but as he mounted, a surly-looking groom crossed the yard.

"When I recognized ye enterin' the hall, didn't figure ye'd be stayin' long enough fer me to bother about yer mount," he greeted the young gentleman.

Simon stared down at the man, none too impressed by what he saw. "How perceptive of you."

"Well, don't know about that, whatever it be, but I ain't no fool, that much I can tell ye, and, maybe more, if'n the price was right, of course. A man has to take care o' himself 'cause no one else is."

"Quite."

"Yeah, well, reckon how I pretty much watch the comin's and goin's of anybody visitin' Highcross, I'd be the man with some o' the answers if'n I was asked the right questions," he said with a smug grin as he eyed the finely tooled leather of Simon's saddle. "Reckon a fancy young gentleman like yerself might find that kind o' information of interest. Reckon he might even be real grateful, if'n ye knows what I mean?"

"Hollings, isn't it?"

"Well, now, ye be real smart too. Always thought that about ye, Master Whitelaw. Always figured ye to be the smart one. Not like others I might mention," he said with a broad wink toward the house.

"What exactly can you tell me about the night, and the following morning, that Hartwell Barclay was thought to have been murdered?" Simon inquired as he took a small leather bag from his pocket and casually weighed it in his palm.

Hollings smiled. Wetting the dryness from his cracked lips, he said, after a conspiratorial glance around, "Reckon fer one ye ain't quite as bright as I was thinkin' if'n ye believe the master's tale o' havin' heard that pretty young Mistress Lily havin' a nightmare and wantin' to comfort her."

"You doubt the sincerity of such a statement?"

Hollings stared up at Simon Whitelaw as if staring at some strange creature. "Ye sure we both be Englishmen? Ain't never heard no one speak such words."

"He's lying?"

"Huh? Oh, sure. The master's been tryin' to get into that little lady's bed ever since she come home. Especially of late, since she's got so pretty. Ye oughta see the way he eyes her. Wouldn't mind that fer myself," he wheezed, laughing unpleasantly, but when he saw the expression on the young gentleman's face and realized the bag of money had been moved out of his reach, he hunched his shoulders and glared up at Simon Whitelaw. "Can't hang a man fer his thoughts. But the master, now, I bet if ye was to find the mistress, she might tell ye a thing or two different about that night."

"And where might I find Lily Christian?" Simon asked, lowering the bag closer to the man's reach.

"Reckon she and them others had to have somewhere to hide, seein' how she thought they were being hunted down fer murderin' the master. And since ye didn't know about what happened until today, figure 'twas exactly what I been thinkin' all along, and the master never sent word to ye. At least, I never was sent to tell any o' ye folks about what happened here. So . . ."

"Yes, go on!"

"So . . . I reckon she went to find ol' Maire Lester. The old woman was the only one who ever cared about them three."

"Of course! The nurse. Lily was upset when she was dismissed. She would go to her for help. She knew that Uncle Valentine was out of the country, and Artemis is in Cornwall, and heavy with child by now, and Quinta is in Scotland. But why didn't she come to me?" he said, thinking aloud. "Of course! I'd told her when last I was here that I intended to study law, but thought I might travel to the Continent first. She didn't realize I'd changed my plans. Damn!"

"Uh, Master Whitelaw, haven't ye forgotten something?" Hollings reminded the young man, who still held the bag of money clutched in his fist.

"Where does this Maire Lester live?" Simon demanded, still holding the money out of the groom's reach.

"Well, I don't know that," Hollings whined, growing impatient, but as the tightfisted young gentleman continued to hold onto his purse, Hollings sighed, scratching his head of dirty, matted hair. "Well, s'pose I do recall her havin' some widowed sister livin' up north."

"Where up north?" Simon prodded.

"Could be Warwickshire."

"The village?"

"Ah, Master Whitelaw, now ye be askin' too much o' me. I can't be knowin' such things."

"If you think a moment longer, I am certain you will remember, and what name you do give me had better be correct," Simon warned. While he'd been speaking, he had opened the purse and had allowed some of the coins to trickle into his palm.

"Said something about havin' a niece upriver in Coventry. 'Twould take at least a day or two to reach her from the farm. 'Twas just outside o' the village—now what was the name o' that place? A real funny-sounding name, 'twas. Two names? No, three! Like 'twas on something. The river. 'Twas on the river. That's it! Let me see."

"The Severn? Perchance, the Avon?"

"Aye, now there ye be. That's the one. Ye be the smarter by far o' the two o' us. The village be similar to East Highford. On the river, ye know. A market town," he said with a wide, toothless grin of pleasure as he anticipated his reward.

"Stratford-upon-Avon?"

"Oh, sir, ye have impressed me, that ye have."

"My family visited the Comptons at their home, Compton Wynyates, 'tis just south of Stratford. And we traveled with the queen to Kenilworth Castle, the Earl of Leicester's home. 'Tisn't far from Stratford."

"Did ye really now, sir? Well, if that ain't amazin'," Hollings said, wiggling the fingers of his outstretched hand.

"Here, you deserve it all, and thank you," Simon Whitelaw said, dropping the plump bag of coins into the man's palm. "I had better find them at Maire Lester's," he added as warning to the man.

The groom shrugged. "Can't help what happened to 'em after they left Highcross. But I do know they reached the mill, 'cause Romney Lee, the miller's wife's brother, he come here to Highcross to find out what was goin' on, and when I told him what had happened, that the master had an accident, but was goin' to be all right, more's the pity, he says that he saw Mistress Christian and her brother and sister and them damned Odells headin' up the road way past the mill. Reckon they was headin' toward London. Sent out the villagers after them, but never found them on the road," he puzzled. He must have misunderstood the gypsy, he thought. Glancing up, he watched as the young gentleman galloped out of the courtyard. Long ride ahead of him, he thought unconcernedly as he poured the coins out of the purse, his smile widening.

Simon Whitelaw was looking grim as he rode toward London. Hartwell Barclay hadn't heard the end of this yet, he vowed, wishing Valentine Whitelaw had returned to England. He would know how to deal with these people who had driven Lily, Tristram, and Dulcie from Highcross. He would know what to do. He would know how to find Lily.

Chapter Twenty

"CINNAMON cakes! Cinnamon cakes! Freshly baked cinnamon cakes!" the little girl called out, shaking a blue and red tambourine over her head while she twirled in front of a small, gaily decorated cart being pulled by a mastiff.

Dressed in crimson velvet, with a richly embroidered kirtle sweeping the ground, and a brightly colored scarf of fringed, Indian silk crisscrossed over her bodice, she seemed an exotic creature with her golden earrings, necklace of pale pink shells, and an amethyst stone gleaming mysteriously from the gold ring on her finger.

"Posies! Posies! Sweet-scented posies!" she cried, curtsying prettily while holding out a bunch of colorful wildflowers tied with a length of silk ribbon.

"Dance, Sweet Rose, dance!" a handsome young man strumming a lute called to her, his nimble fingers plucking a lively tune while the little girl danced faster and faster.

On the toes of her dainty velvet slippers, with petticoats flying, she raced away. She returned quickly with a cinnamon cake for him, then danced away again to entice the crowd with an armful of posies. The troubadour, spying the fair maiden who was standing beside the cart and who had bestowed a smile upon him as well as a cinnamon cake, began another ballad:

My lord's daughter went through the wood her lane,
And there she met the cap'n, a servant to the king.

He said unto his livery man, "Were't na agin the law,
I would tak her to my own bed, and lay her at the wa."

"I'm walking here my lane," says she, "among
my father's trees;
And ye may let me walk my lane, kind sir, now gin ye please.
The supper bell it will be rung, and I'll be miss'd awa;
Sae I'll na lie in your bed, at neither stock nor wa."

He said, "My pretty lady, I pray lend me your hand,
And ye'll hae drums and trumpets always at your command;
And fifty men to guard you wi, that weel their swords can draw;
Sae we'll both lie in one bed, and ye'll lie at the wa . . ."

"O keep awa frae me, kind sir, I pray don't me perplex,
For I'll na lie in your bed till ye answer questions six . . ."

"O what is greener than the grass, what's higher than the trees?
O what is worse than women's wish, what's deeper
than the seas?
What bird craws first, what tree buds first, what first
does on them fa?
Before I lie in your bed, at either stock or wa."

"Death is greener than the grass, heaven higher than the trees;
The devil's worse than women's wish, hell's deeper
than the seas;
The cock craws first, the cedar buds first, dew first
on them does fa;
Sae we'll both lie in one bed, and ye shall lie at the wa."

Little did this lady think, that morning when she raise,
That this was for to be the last o' her maiden days.
But there's na into the king's realm to be found a merrier twa,
And she must lie in his bed, but she'll not lie next the wa.

With a fine flourish, the troubadour ended his song. Sweeping his velvet hat from his head, he bowed deeply, then rose,
and with hat in hand strolled through the crowd, smiling now

and again when he was favored with a coin from a blushing maid or a bold and comely wench.

" 'Tis a harsh winter comin' on! I can feel it in me achin' bones! Come! Feel the softness of this fur! The richest, blackest sable! Siberian wolf! Touch this soft, Persian fleece! A king's ransom I should be sellin' it for!"

"Silk! Every color of the rainbow! God bless her, but the queen herself took my last bolt of crimson! Not even unloaded from the ship's hold yet, that fine was it!"

"Have ye seen this ebony chess set! Carved under the watchful eye of the Russian czar himself!" another vendor called a bit louder.

"Clove and nutmeg from the Indies!"

"Venetian glass!"

"Sandalwood and aloes!"

"Cherry ripe! Spanish lemons! Fine lemons from Seville!"

The aroma of cooking meats, of pigeons slowly turning on spits while they roasted over open fires, of great cuts of beef and mutton, and wild boar, filled the air. The juices were caught in pans and blended with claret and spices, and thickened with eggs and butter, to be served in trenchers with a thick slice of bread. Aromatic steam rose from the big kettles of stewed crabs and oysters, while plates were heaped high with a tasty mixture of quartered potatoes and apples, sweetened with sugar, cinnamon, ginger, and oranges, and served piping hot. Minced pies, puddings, and tarts, still warm from the ovens, were set out for close inspection on rough-hewn counters, while tall pitchers, kegs, and larger barrels stood ready to be emptied of ale, cider, beer, and wine. The row of drinking cups and tankards never remained constant as they exchanged hands over and over again to be filled with the best, well-aged March ale or the cheaper and far weaker penny ale.

"We've sold all of the cinnamon cakes, except for this one, Lily," Dulcie said, eyeing the last cake hungrily.

"We can't have that. 'Tisn't good for business. You had better do something about it quick, Dulcie," Lily advised.

Dulcie grinned, and quicker than a magician's sleight of hand, she made the cake disappear, the only evidence of its existence a sprinkling of crumbs around her mouth.

Leaning against the cart, Dulcie scratched Cappie under his whiskered chin.

"Tired?" Lily asked when Dulcie yawned widely.

"A little. 'Tis so warm. I danced all day, didn't I, Lily?" she asked, hugging Lily around the waist and staring up into her sister's face for her approval.

"You were never still. I shall have to put a bell on you to keep track of you, fairy-child," Lily said, smoothing a soft black curl from Dulcie's cheek as she pressed a kiss against her forehead.

"Hey!" Tristram called out, approaching them from somewhere out of the crowd. "Gee, you sold *all* of the cakes? Not even a crumb left," he said with a disappointed glance at the empty tray in the cart. "*Except,* for those on Dulcie's chin. How ya doin', Ruff?" he said, patting the big dog whose tail had started wagging when he'd recognized Tristram's figure.

"Tristram!"

"*Prrrraaack!* Ruff! Ruff! *Prrraaack!* Buss us a nice one, sweeting! Buss us a nice one, Tristram sweeting!" Cisco repeated, eyeing the frowning lad with a cool yellow eye. "Ruff! Ruff!"

"Tristram!"

"Oh, all right. *Raphael,* your highness. Looks like we sold everything but these posies. Can't eat them, though. I wonder how roasted parrot would taste?"

"You haven't eaten all day?"

"Been too busy juggling, Lily. Haven't had a hand free. Although, Old Maria gave me a bun when I was near her booth earlier. Sure did eye me strangely," he added. "Said to come by later and she'd read your palm for free, Lily."

"My palm?" Lily questioned, surprised by the offer, for Old Maria never did anything for free unless it served her purpose.

"Raphael's thirsty, Lily."

"Why don't you take Dulcie and the cart back to the camp and get Tillie to feed you? She has probably baked a whole new batch of cakes. She had a wedge of cheese and some tarts in her basket when I saw her earlier, and she said Fairfax was going to put some cider in the brook. I'm certain 'tis well-chilled by now. And don't forget to feed Cappie and Cisco, Tristram."

"And Ruff?" Dulcie added unthinkingly, much to Tristram's delight for he laughed and turned a cartwheeling handspring in front of her squealing figure.

"Yes, and Ruff. I'll see if I can sell the rest of these," Lily said, gathering up the remaining bunches of flowers. If she hurried, she might be able to sell enough to buy several of the roasted squabs that had been tantalizing her for most of the day. It would be a nice surprise for the others, she thought, remembering Tristram's comment about cold meat pie.

Tristram heaped the unsold posies into the woven basket Lily had hooked over her arm, then turned Raphael and the cart around. "See you later, Lily," he called as he began to lead them through the crowd.

Lily stood watching until they'd safely reached the edge of the fair and disappeared underneath the trees. Positioning the basket more comfortably over her arm, Lily pushed her way into the heart of the midway. She needn't have worried about selling the remaining posies, for even before she started to call out, "Sweet posies! Sweet posies for your sweetheart!" she was surrounded by eager young men anxious to catch her eye, even if they did have to buy a posy for a nonexistent sweetheart.

Lily spun around angrily when she felt someone caressing her waist as if he'd every right to. Ready to slap away the hand and deal a stinging rebuke to the impudent fellow, Lily's indignation mounted when a soft kiss was pressed against her cheek before she could do either. But she smiled in relief when she saw Rom's grinning face.

"I thought I should let these young gallants know before they commit a serious mistake, that they may feast their eyes upon you, but nothing more if they value their lives," Romney warned, loud enough for a stubborn lad, determined to insinuate himself closer to Lily, to overhear and hopefully take heed.

Rom took pity on the callow youth, for he could well understand the lad's heartsick expression. Lily, dressed in a plain gown of violet silk brocade embroidered with gold and silver silks, was a temptation to yearn after. A delicate square of crisp linen was folded demurely against her throat, while a gauzy white veil trimmed with gold lace floated gracefully from her shoulders and almost touched the ground. The slashed, puffed sleeves of her bodice revealed the fineness of the linen chemise beneath. She had draped her kirtle high in front to expose her beribboned white petticoats, the scent of lavender drifting from them with every rustling step she took. Braided with fragrant,

delicate flowers, her hair hung down her back in a maidenly innocence that contrasted strangely with the barbaric-looking gold
earrings that gleamed through the dark red strands.

Rom stared down into her face. Even though the day had
been hot, and her cheek was warm and flushed, her brow damp
with a light coating of perspiration, the heat rising from her body
was sweetly scented. She always smelled as if she'd just rubbed
perfumed oils into her skin, Rom thought, feeling a manly stirring and wishing they were lying in the shade of a greenwood
far away from the noise and prying eyes.

"Rom?" Lily asked when he remained silent, staring down
at her with a troubled expression in his dark blue eyes.

But Rom didn't hear her. He watched her lips moving and
was reminded of the glistening pearls that were so treasured by
Jack o' Selsey, a dealer trading in precious stones. Once Rom
had come upon Lily unawares and had watched while she'd
rubbed her teeth with a small piece of soft cloth dampened in a
soapy-looking solution. Her breath was always fresh, never
soured with ale or the strong herbs and spices from the victuals
of the night before. He'd continued to watch when she'd started
to brush her long hair, until the strands had crackled with fire.

"Rom?"

"I'm sorry, just dreamin'," he said with an embarrassed
grin.

"You're tired. You are doing far too much, Rom. You cannot
continue trying to handle our problems while managing your
own affairs. We ask too much of you, Rom," Lily said, noticing
for the first time the lines of worry etched around the corners of
his mouth. Unaware of the interpretation he might put on her
gesture, Lily reached up to smooth the lines away, her eyes
warm with friendship as she tucked her hand under his arm and
walked with him in companionable silence.

Romney Lee was startled and uncomfortable, which surprised him even more. For so long he had waited, longed for
such a closeness between them. But now, knowing that he had
lied to her, he felt guilt not exultation. It was a strange, sobering
sensation for Romney Lee, for he had come to think of himself as
a man without conscience.

He glanced away, unable to meet her clear-eyed gaze. He
had cheated her, and now when she offered him her friendship

and perhaps more, he felt like the thief he was. He did not deserve her gentle ministrations and concern, he berated himself, damning himself for a liar. When he remembered the gratitude in her eyes that morning he had stopped them on the lane from Highcross, he felt as if he had betrayed the trust she'd placed in him.

So clever, he had been. He had only been thinking of himself. He hadn't worried about what fears she might be feeling, believing herself responsible for another's death. But now, all he could think of was what she would think when she learned of his cruel trick, of his deceit, how she would stare at him in contempt before turning away from him forever.

Romney Lee frowned. It had been too easy, like taking something from a child. At daybreak, leaving Lily and the others safely hidden behind the mill, he had ridden into the village to learn all he could about what had happened at Highcross the night before. Thinking Hartwell Barclay dead, he hadn't been surprised to find the groom drinking ale at the Oaks. There was little for that idler to do with his master gone. The groom was thoroughly enjoying being the center of attraction while he recounted his tale.

Listening to the groom's droning voice, it had been quite a shock to hear that Hartwell Barclay wasn't dead, but alive and well, if a bit groggy from the accident that had nearly cost him his life. The man could have drowned, hitting his head like that in the tub, the groom had declared with a smirk. When Hollings had returned to Highcross with the physician and constable, they had discovered Hartwell Barclay bellowing and struggling to remove himself from the tub of cold water. The groom couldn't quite hide the disappointment he must have felt when discovering that his master still lived. Hartwell Barclay had kept mumbling that it had been an accident. No harm had been done, he had kept reassuring everyone, almost guiltily so, some might have thought had they known what really had occurred. After that, Hartwell Barclay had fallen unconscious, or into a stupor from the prodigious amount of liquor he had consumed, for he'd still reeked of it despite his unexpected bath. But because Lily Christian and the others had not been properly questioned, and since the Odell brothers still had to answer for their rowdy behavior of the night before, the authorities had continued the search.

Rom remembered how he'd had to hide his grin of satisfaction when he had returned to the mill and told them the lie that they were being sought by the authorities for the murder of Hartwell Barclay and they must leave the shire. So hesitant, he had sounded, when suggesting they should join his band of peddlers and vagabonds. Lily and the others had been beholden to him, just as he had planned. Indeed, what had happened that morning could not have been planned any more ingeniously had he himself set the events into motion, and Lily, so trusting and innocent, had fallen right into his hands. He had seen his chance and he had seized it, uncaring of the consequences.

Later, he had tried to convince himself that he'd acted out of genuine concern for Lily and her family. He understood only too well what had really happened that night. Partly because of what Lily and the maid, Tillie, had told him, but mostly because he knew the kind of man Hartwell Barclay was. As he thought of that, he suddenly saw another face, the face of Geoffrey Christian, and Rom closed his eyes against the accusing glint in those green eyes so like Lily's. *I am not like Hartwell Barclay*, he told himself. "I am not like that. I'm not," he spoke softly, defiantly, and opening his eyes, he blinked, startled by the brightness of the afternoon sunlight.

Almost guiltily he glanced down at Lily Christian, but she was unaware of his softly spoken words. She was staring straight ahead, oblivious to all around her while she gazed at a man standing in the midway, a curious expression of both longing and aloofness on her face that puzzled Romney. But it was the unguarded look of desire that momentarily flashed in Lily's pale green eyes when her gaze was caught and held by the man's bold stare that alarmed him the most.

Romney Lee eyed the gentleman with growing suspicion and dislike. That the man was indeed a gentleman there was no doubt in the gypsy's mind. Although he was dressed rather casually, as if he'd been out riding, there was no question of the fineness of his attire, for the cut of his doublet and hose could not be faulted, nor the quality of the buff leather trimmed with a discreet touch of gold braid.

He still wore his riding boots, the soft leather coated with dust up to the middle of his thighs. His lacy ruff was fashionably starched and he held his gold pomander with an elegant air, but this man was no pampered courtier. The man's lean, handsome face was bronzed from the sun, and his shoulders and thighs were sinewy with muscle. A single gold earring gleamed against his neatly trimmed hair and beard, which were as black as a raven's wing.

The man's gaze was steady, unwavering, as he stared at Lily Christian, and Romney Lee knew a sudden fear of this nameless man.

Lily knew the name.

She felt her heart pounding so wildly in her breast she had trouble breathing. She tried to catch her breath, her lips parted slightly as she stared at Valentine Whitelaw. She hadn't been able to believe her eyes when she'd glanced up to see him standing so boldly before her. He was just the way she remembered him. The sensations that had spread through her had been both pleasurable and frightening. She had hoped she would feel different when seeing him again, that she had outgrown her young girl's blind adoration for him, but the attraction was stronger than ever, especially when his narrowed gaze had captured hers and she'd found herself unable to glance away.

Never before had he stared at *her* with that ardent look in his eye. She had seen that warm, interested gleam in his eye when he'd gazed at other women, at Cordelia and Honoria, but never when he'd gazed at her; never at Lily Christian. But today, Valentine Whitelaw had caressed her with his eyes. He had watched her as if he'd actually found her beautiful, Lily thought in disbelief, forgetting for a moment that she had become a woman during the years since last they had met. But all she could think of was that he'd been standing there alone, as if searching the crowd for someone, and then his eyes had met hers, and for a stunning moment Lily had felt her world reeling around her. She remembered another time and place when she had gazed up into eyes the same turquoise shade as the warm waters surrounding their island in the Indies.

It never occurred to Lily that he might not have recognized her.

"Valentine," Lily said his name soundlessly, her lips curving in a smile so gentle and loving that a man walking past forgot to

watch where he was going and bumped into a woman carrying a
yoke across her shoulders and balancing a couple of pales brim-
ming with ale. As she staggered, swinging around, one of the
pales caught the man in the middle of his back. The blow sent
him flying into another man, who was busy minding his own
business while he selected the proper coin for the gooseberry
tarts he'd just bought for his wife and himself. His wife
screamed when the ale splashed over her skirts. But the startled
gentleman only had time to stare in bemusement before his feet
were knocked out from under him and his purse sent flying into
the crowd.

"Hey! Come back here! Thief! Thief! He stole my purse!" the
man cried out angrily, struggling to his feet only to fall over the
gentleman who'd had the wind knocked out of him by the pale.
"Stop, thief! Stop him!" he yelled as he watched a thin boy
dressed in little better than rags race off through the crowd with
several of his brawny servants in close pursuit.

Romney Lee cursed beneath his breath, for he'd recognized
the boy as one of theirs. The boy's widowed mother worked as a
serving wench or laundress whenever she could find the work,
which wasn't often. Romney had to get to the lad first, for if
caught, the lad would be hanged. If he got away, they could all
face being fined or having their booths closed down. The man
the boy had stolen the purse from was a high-ranking guild
member in the city, who would use his influence to make things
difficult for the rest of them if his money wasn't returned.

Romney glanced quickly at Lily, unwilling to leave her, but
she had disappeared. He looked around in surprise, but she was
nowhere to be seen. As he hurried through the crowd, he risked
a glance at the tall gentleman who'd been staring so intently at
Lily, but he was now in conversation with another woman, and
a very beautiful woman at that, Rom thought with an admiring
glint in his eye.

She was certainly a beauty. Her hair was black and elegantly
coiffed in small curls high on her head and topped with a jeweled cap. Her silk gown was a blushing peach shade and of the
latest French fashion, although perhaps a trifle indiscreet. For
the bodice was cut lower than modesty allowed, a stiffened
corselet pushing her bare breasts precariously close to the lace-
trimmed edge. Around her throat, she wore a ruffled collarette

rather than the more discreet partlet, and it served to draw the eye to the swell of soft flesh below. Her waist was encircled by a jeweled girdle and seemed all the tinier for the farthingale worn beneath her gown, which allowed the heavy folds of silk to fall in undisturbed elegance. While she conversed, she fanned herself with a large feather fan dyed the same exotic color as her gown, even though she stood in the cool shade of a canopy being supported by two liveried footmen standing on either side of her.

Curious, Rom watched as the man lifted the woman's hand to his lips, and the seductive glance she gave him told Romney Lee far more than if he'd been close enough to catch the exchange of pleasantries. The two were lovers, and the man had most likely already forgotten Lily Christian's existence as the dark-haired woman smiled up at him, leaning provocatively close to whisper something loving in his ear.

Romney Lee breathed a sigh of relief. The man had only been admiring Lily's exceptional beauty. He could not blame him, he had to confess, quickening his step along the midway when he caught sight of one of the thick-skulled fellows who'd gone after the boy.

"So, you have safely returned from sea once again?" Cordelia Howard greeted Valentine Whitelaw, eyeing him as if memorizing every feature of his handsome face. "You were not gone as long this time."

"We journeyed only as far as Africa. I intend to be in Cornwall when Artemis gives birth," Valentine responded politely, but his eyes were searching the crowd impatiently as he looked for the girl who had so entranced him. But she had disappeared.

"A profitable voyage?" Cordelia inquired a bit shortly, trying to recapture his attention.

"Not as profitable as some, but enough," Valentine replied, smiling down at her and causing Cordelia Howard to realize, and not for the first time, that the greatest mistake of her life had been in not marrying Valentine Whitelaw when she'd had the chance.

Cordelia laughed harshly. "You and your damned voyages. I vow, I hate that ship of yours. If you had stayed in England more we would still be together."

Valentine smiled slightly. "I never got the impression that

you missed me all that much, Cordelia. You always reminded me that there were others to amuse you while I was away."

Cordelia flushed, not caring to be reminded of her past indiscretions. "I might have allowed others to amuse me, but I never forgot you, Valentine. I always missed you and longed for your return. I even missed you this time," she said, her dark eyes holding his, and for a brief instant, Cordelia thought she saw a flash of the old passion come into them.

"Not all that much, I think. I understand congratulations are in order?"

"From your tone, I gather that you do not approve?" she asked poutingly, hoping he was jealous, but he disappointed her by his response.

"I will not pretend that I have ever cared much for Valchamps, Cordelia. But if you are happy, then . . ." he said, shrugging as if it was of little concern to him.

Cordelia Howard affected a coquettish look which covered well the real regret she felt deep down inside. "You could have made me very happy," she said softly.

"I think we both realized the mistake we were making. We mistook our feelings for one another to be love. We would not have made each other happy, Cordelia."

"I wish we could have tried again," she surprised both of them by admitting. " 'Tisn't too late, yet," she reminded him, then sensing his withdrawal, she winked a trifle wickedly. If he declined, she would at least still have her pride for he would never know if she had spoken in truth or jest. "I will not be Lady Valchamps until next month."

"I do not think Valchamps would approve," Valentine commented without either accepting or declining her invitation.

"One never knows with Raymond," Cordelia said strangely. "Of course, were it anyone but you . . ."

"I do not think I will risk provoking the gentleman."

"Although he thinks himself almost a god, I do not believe Raymond is omniscient. He does not know everything that goes on. Besides, there is no reason why we cannot remain friends," she added softly, and had anyone overheard her, they would have believed in the innocence of her remark, but Valentine was staring into her eyes and knew differently.

"We can't go back, Delia," was all he said, but it was enough to convince Cordelia Howard that she had truly lost Valentine Whitelaw.

"A pity you were not at the Davieses' last evening," Cordelia said quickly, guessing he was about to take his leave of her and walk away. " 'Twas a wonderful banquet. Riverhurst is quite an estate. You haven't seen it yet, have you? Yes? Well, I vow poor Raymond was green with envy. He was unusually subdued the whole evening. Not at all himself. We arrived late, then I thought Raymond was going to demand we leave early. I dare say we will be rebuilding one of these days ourselves. Raymond can't stand to be beaten in anything, by anybody. I always let him think he has won, whatever the game," she said, glancing around curiously. "Where is that manservant of yours? I'm always uneasy when he's lurking about."

"He is selecting provisions for our journey, and for tonight's dinner," Valentine said, growing impatient to be about his way so he could find the girl.

"Journey? 'Sdeath! You just returned. I thought you said you wished to be here for the great arrival of Sir Rodger's heir? Faith, but I still become choked with laughter thinking of you and Sir Rodger being brothers-in-law. The family dinners must be uproarious with the two of you glaring at each other across the table."

" 'Tis for the journey to Cornwall. I shall sail there rather than travel across country," Valentine explained, ignoring her jibe.

"When do you sail? I thought I understood Sir Rodger to say that he would be attending several of the countless birthday celebrations for Elizabeth. Of course, so determined is our queen, one can always wait another couple of years for her to celebrate her half century of life. 'Twill be quite magnificent. The sky will no doubt be ablaze with fireworks. Who would ever have guessed *she'd* manage to survive so long?" Cordelia said with a note of grudging respect in her voice. She only hoped she would be so fortunate.

"We will not leave London until Quinta has returned from Scotland. 'Twill be at least a fortnight before we sail."

"You intend to stay in London, then?"

"Part of the time. I was at Riverhurst earlier in the day to pay my respects to Lady Elspeth and Sir William. I wish to visit my nephew, Simon, at Whiteswood, then call in at Highcross Court to see the children,'' Valentine said with a smile of anticipation, for he had a sea chest full of presents for them. It had been too long since he'd spent any time with them, he thought, deciding he would have a talk with Hartwell Barclay. It would be pleasant to have the children aboard the *Madrigal* when she sailed for Cornwall. A tender look came into Valentine's eye when he thought of them aboard his ship once again.

"Those children! I swear one would think you'd sired them yourself the way you worry about them, Valentine. I really shall have to find a wife for you, my dear, so you can fill your house with noisy sons and daughters,'' Cordelia said with a glint in her eye that had Valentine watching her warily.

"I think I can manage on my own, Cordelia.''

"Yes, I'm sure you can, but . . . of course! There is the lovely Honoria Penmorley. Such a *dear* young woman. Rather pale, though. However, she would make you the ideal wife. And now that your sister has taken over her duties as mistress of Penmorley Hall, she must be occupying all of her time with her embroidery. I dare say, there most likely isn't a bare chair in the whole hall. I do believe she would be eternally content to remain in Cornwall. Don't you think so?''

"Yes, now that you mention it, I believe she would. Indeed, she would make a most admirable wife. She is a very capable woman. She has managed Sir Rodger's home for these many years. She is intelligent. She converses well on most subjects. And she appears in very good health. Yes, she has splendid qualifications,'' Valentine said, his lips twitching slightly as he noticed the tightness around Cordelia's mouth.

"What you have described, my dear, is a housekeeper. Of course, unless you find a lusty one, and pay her extra, you would not stay very warm on a cold winter's night, now would you?'' Cordelia asked slyly, lightly tapping her fingers against his lean cheek. "And come to speculate 'pon it, I doubt even with Honoria in your bed you would fare any better. The woman's cold as a stone. And I must admit, my dear, you are a man who demands quite a lot of a woman when she is in your bed. Do you really think Honoria would be able to handle such unbridled passions?''

Valentine inclined his head slightly. "I am beginning to wonder if Raymond Valchamps quite realizes what a prize he has won for himself. Now, if you will excuse me, Cordelia? I must leave, I've several more people I must see before this evening.''

"Oh, dear me, I believe I have struck a sensitive nerve, haven't I?'' Cordelia murmured, her cheeks flushed with irritation. ''I believe you have already been considering taking Honoria to wife, and here am I speaking so ill of the woman. I am sorry, Valentine. I do hope I haven't cast any doubts in your mind. I am certain, m'dear, that Honoria would make you a very . . . ah, yes, a very *respectable* wife,'' Cordelia concluded, her smile understanding as she dealt her final insult.

"Good afternoon, Cordelia,'' Valentine said, and bowing slightly, he walked away.

Lily Christian was standing unnoticed beside the tent just beyond where Valentine Whitelaw had stood in conversation with Cordelia Howard. Her lips trembling slightly, Lily remembered Quinta Whitelaw's conversation of the previous winter, when she had spoken of Cordelia's visit to Ravindzara and how most likely by summer Cordelia and Valentine would be engaged, certainly wed by fall.

As Lily stood watching the two, hearing that cruel, mocking laughter of Cordelia Howard's, she remembered another time, when she had overheard the two in the gardens of Tamesis House, when Valentine Whitelaw had laughed so scornfully over the prospect of ever finding Lily Christian attractive. He could never fall in love with her, Lily remembered him declaring, reliving again the mortification she had felt that afternoon. It had been an afternoon much like this one, she thought as she saw Sir Raymond Valchamps sauntering along the midway, Thomas Sandrick and another gentleman accompanying. Lily stepped inside the cool darkness of the tent and out of sight before anyone could see her, for Raymond Valchamps was the last person she wanted to cross paths with.

Lily began to step back outside when something grabbed hold of her hand. Crying out in alarm, Lily spun around and stared blindly into the shadows of the tent.

"Ah, Lily Francisca, have ye come to Old Maria to have yer fortune told?'' the old woman cackled, her wizened hand fondling Lily's young flesh.

"So pretty. So sweet. So dangerous," she crooned, laughing huskily. "Come, do not be afraid, little one. Let Old Maria tell ye what yer future holds. Come . . . come . . . I won't hurt ye," she said, pulling Lily deeper into the tent, where the air was heavy with burning incense and potions.

"Cordelia, my love," Sir Raymond greeted his fiancée, pressing a kiss into her palm. Still holding on to her hand, he inquired, "I trust you were not bored while Thomas and I watched that wrestling match?"

"Not at all," Cordelia responded, not caring for Raymond's tone of voice. "My dear, you are hurting my hand."

"Oh, I am sorry, my love," Sir Raymond apologized nicely. "That wasn't by any chance the good captain I saw standing here talking to you not more than five minutes past?"

"Valentine? Here? At the fair? I had a note from him this morning inviting me to join him at the Devil for a light supper," Thomas Sandrick said, glancing around. "If you will excuse me, I'll try to catch up with him now. We could go on over. Devilish thirst," he said with a laugh. "I'd like to hear about his journey. Cordelia. Raymond. I'll see both of you this evening," Thomas Sandrick excused himself.

"Cordelia?"

"Not jealous, my dear?" She laughed, prolonging his uncertainty.

"Constantly," he confessed, his eyes searching the crowd. "And what did you and the good captain discuss?" he asked conversationally.

"Now, that would be telling, wouldn't it? 'Tis far more exciting for you to wonder," she said with a teasing smile that quickly faded when Raymond's fingers tightened painfully around her wrist. "If you were not about to break my wrist, I vow I would be flattered, m'dear. Let loose, Raymond," Cordelia said, no longer finding the conversation amusing.

"Don't ever try to hide anything from me, Delia. You will regret it. I give you fair warning. Now, what were you and the good captain discussing? I will know."

Cordelia moistened her dry lips. "We did not speak for long, he was in a hurry to leave the fair. Obviously to meet Thomas," she said a trifle indignantly. Had it been another woman, she would have understood. "We were merely discussing his journey and return to England. He will not be here longer than a fortnight, if that will set your mind at ease."

"Oh? And where is he journeying next?"

"To Cornwall. His sister is with child. He wishes to be there. Raymond, please, let me go," Cordelia pleaded, for her fingers were becoming numb.

"I see. What is he going to do before he leaves London? As if I didn't know," he said, smiling into her startled eyes.

"No, Raymond, truly. We have not planned to meet. I am to wed you, my dear. I chose you for my husband, not Valentine Whitelaw," she reassured him. "Valentine is going to visit Whiteswood, then travel to Highcross to see those damned children he rescued from that isle. He will have little more time than that. If we meet, 'twill merely be during a banquet. Raymond? You do believe me, don't you?" Cordelia asked, frightened of a man for the first time in her life.

"What? Oh, yes, of course," he replied, releasing her swollen wrist. "Yes, those children have always been a problem, haven't they?"

Cordelia stared at him in confusion, for what did Raymond care about those children? "Yes, I s'pose. Damned nuisance."

"Yes, quite. But not for much longer I should think. Did Whitelaw say why he was going to Highcross? He hadn't heard that anything was amiss, had he?" Raymond asked, a note of concern in his voice that surprised Cordelia.

"No, he has heard nothing about them. He just wants to visit. Feels responsible for their welfare, I s'pose. Why?"

"Oh, nothing, my dear. I thought if there was some trouble that he might be delayed there. Merely a selfish wish that he might be away from London longer than expected," Sir Raymond said, his mouth curving in that unpleasant smile of his. Apparently Valentine Whitelaw did not know that the children had left Highcross and were right here under his nose. He had nearly fainted when he'd seen the good captain standing in conversation with Cordelia. He had feared all was lost, that Valentine Whitelaw had known the children were here. But he hadn't. He was always just a step ahead of the good captain, Raymond Valchamps thought with a silent chuckle. He had thought he'd taken care of any immediate danger when he'd

burned to the ground their damned puppet show. At least that
was no longer a threat to him. And now, Valentine Whitelaw
was leaving the fair, without realizing how close to the truth he
had come.

Too late, however, would he discover his mistake. By then,
Lily Christian would be dead.

'' . . . the shadow of death lingers close by. Ye must leave
this fair, Lily Francisca. I've seen the omens of death walkin' in
my dreams. Ye be in danger, lass. Beware the witch. It stalks the
night searchin' fer yer blood, my fair one.''

Lily forced herself to sit still, for although she did not believe
a word of Old Maria's outrageous predictions, the woman still
made her nervous with her mutterings and strange moanings, as
if she were gasping out her last breath.

'' 'Tis a dark cloud surrounding us,'' she whispered, then
cried out, shivering as if deep in a trance. ''But the danger will
pass. Lily Francisca, ye hold the key. Ye must fly from here. Ye
must return to the beginning. The end will be the beginning. The
answer lies buried across the seas! Run from here! Run from
here! Before 'tis too late fer all of us!'' she hissed. ''Ye be bad
luck. The evil eye is upon ye! He brings death where he wan-
ders! The colors. They are wrong! They do not match! Bad!''

''I must go, please,'' Lily said frantically, trying to free her
hand from the woman's tight grasp.

''Yes! Go! Ye must go! Faster than the winds! Upon a singing
ship, across the waters. Yes! The waters, child. Fear them, but
do not fear them. They will try to take ye, but they will have to
release ye. If ye survive the waters the first time, then they will
protect ye the second time. Do not fail. The book, my child. Find
the book and all revelations will unfold as they were meant to
from the beginning. Do not deny what must be, Lily Francisca.
What was thought to be lost, is not. What must be, *will!* Ye cannot change what must happen. Yer fate lies with another! Yer
destiny lies along another path from ours, from Romney Lee's.
Ye're not fer Romney Lee, but another. Ye be of the sea, like
him. The colors! The clearness of a gentle, warm sea, drifting
into the shallows. The colors are now one. Ye must go with him.
He will protect ye from the evil. Go, child! Go! 'Twill end in trag-

edy if ye don't. Go! Tonight! Tonight! Do not stay here tonight! Death walks this camp tonight!''

Lily smiled slightly with understanding, for Old Maria was, after all, Navarre's grandmother. Naturally, she would wish to see her granddaughter's rival leave the camp, and Romney Lee, Lily thought, eyeing the old woman curiously.

"Maria? Old Maria?'' she questioned softly, but the woman sat slumped on the bench, her eyes closed. She hardly seemed to be breathing, Lily thought in alarm. "Maria? Are you ill? Shall I get help?''

"Go, child, go,'' the old woman whispered shakily, and Lily almost believed that she was not faking this time. Reaching into her basket, where only a couple of posies remained, Lily found a coin and left it on the table.

Pulling her hand free from Old Maria's clawlike hand, Lily broke the contact between them, but the sense of foreboding remained with her even when she stepped out into the sunlight. Old Maria certainly knew what she was doing, Lily thought with a grim look in her eye when she saw Navarre lingering near the tent with its mystical markings and signs of the stars and moon.

Lily shuddered despite her resolve not to take seriously Old Maria's mutterings. Frightening predictions and nonsensical riddles, Lily thought as she hurried away, feeling groggy from the incense that had filled the tent. But even as she cleared her aching head, she found herself wondering how Old Maria had known about her dreams of drowning.

Preoccupied with her thoughts, Lily did not see the tall shadow that fell across her path, nor the man who stepped directly in front of her until she'd nearly fallen into his arms.

Glancing up in surprise, Lily found herself staring into Valentine Whitelaw's turquoise eyes.

Chapter Twenty-One

VALENTINE WHITELAW stared into Lily Christian's face. He had not been mistaken. She was the most exquisite creature he had ever beheld. Never before had he gazed upon such incomparable beauty, and he vowed to have this maid who had tantalized him from afar. Standing on the deck of his ship, she had enticed him from the mist-enshrouded shore, drawing him irresistibly into the dangerous waters of the shallows.

Now she stood before him as innocent as if heaven born. And yet she had captivated him as surely as if she'd cast a spell over him, he thought bemusedly. Indeed, everything about her was bewitching. Never had he seen such soft, unblemished skin, dew-kissed like the petals of a flower. Her eyes were of the clearest, palest green, greener than a new leaf unfolding on the bough. Her hair, a darker, richer shade than the finest sherry, flowed across her shoulders and around her hips like a silken veil. It glistened in the sunlight, like wine reflecting fire.

And yet she seemed unaware of her fairness of face and the effect she had on a man. There was no false coyness in her expression or seductive lowering of her lashes, and he was all the more intrigued because of that look of tender passion so innocently revealed in her eyes. What manner of maid was this to stroll so gracefully through a crowd of thieves and ruffians, to single him out and smile at him as if they were long-lost lovers, yet remain so pure and virtuous of mind and body, as if she had never lain in a man's bed or shared his passion.

She was indeed a temptress, and a far more dangerous one than her legendary sisters in the sea. They would lead an unsuspecting mariner onto the rocks with their dulcet singing. This sweet maid would steal his heart if he gave her even half a chance. Could she really be as soulless as the water? Standing so close to her, Valentine Whitelaw breathed deeply of the delicate fragrance scenting her skin and knew he would welcome that risk. He would tempt the fates to have her in his bed for just one night, even if she disappeared into the sea afterwards, leaving him aching for her return.

"I could not allow you to pass by without at least discovering your name," Valentine said, his turquoise eyes raking her heart-shaped face and the seductive curve of breast. How he longed to hold this maid in his arms, to feel her flesh burning against his. He needed to know again the softness of a woman. He had been at sea too long to know gentlemanly patience now, he realized, remembering again the frustration of the hot, humid nights spent alone in his bunk while his ship had gently ridden the waves as if locked in a lover's embrace.

Lily remained silent. Startled. *What was her name?* That had been the last question she had been expecting to hear from Valentine Whitelaw. Was he not surprised to see her in London? Surely he would demand to know what she was doing selling flowers at a fair? Shouldn't he want to know why she had left Highcross? Did he not wonder where the others were? Was he so uncaring that he had little curiosity about them after so long an absence?

"You do have a name? I shall hold you captive until I know it, my fair one," he told her, and although he spoke lightly, there was a glint in his eye that warned Lily he was serious.

"My name?" Lily repeated. She met his gaze uncertainly, wondering if this was some kind of jest. She seemed to be a never ending source of amusement to him and his friends, Lily thought dejectedly, wondering if Cordelia was standing behind the nearest booth laughing.

"Yes," he said softly, curious why she suddenly seemed to shrink away from him. "Is that too much to ask?" he persisted, determined not to lose his prize now.

Lily swallowed nervously. She touched her tongue lightly to her lips to ease the dryness. She was unaware of the provocativeness of her action, but Valentine Whitelaw's gaze was drawn to the delicate shaping of her mouth and he knew a sudden determination to taste of it.

"You do not know it already?" she spoke huskily.

Valentine smiled. So, she wanted to play a game, did she? She acted as if surprised by his pursuit. She had been the one who had smiled so invitingly at him. Well, he would play, but by his rules. "I will when you tell me. I am not the fortune teller," he reminded her, and seeing her puzzled expression, he gestured to the tent she had stepped out of.

"But I am no—"

"—ly Francisca! A posy fer this lad's sweetheart! Here, catch!" someone called to Lily from the crowd, but the first part of her name was lost in the noise, and only the last part drifted to the tall man who still stood blocking her path.

Valentine easily caught the coin that spun through the air, and with a satisfied gleam in his eye, he reached into the basket and tossed one of the small bouquets to the fellow who had so obliged him with the maid's name.

"Francisca," he said with a smile as he dropped the shiny coin into the basket. He was about to look up, when his eye caught sight of something. With a strange sense of his own destiny, he fingered the small, pink-hued shells that lay scattered on the bottom.

"Be careful, please," Lily cautioned, her hand staying his when she saw him pick up several of the delicate shells she had placed in the basket for safekeeping. They had come loose from Dulcie's necklace earlier in the day and she hadn't had time to restring them. The necklace of shells was Dulcie's favorite one of her few possessions from the island, and Lily would not have any harm befall it.

"Shells," Valentine murmured in disbelief, his eyes narrowing almost suspiciously as he found himself beginning to believe his own flights of fancy about mermaids. "Why should I be surprised? And green eyes too," he said with a slow smile, his hand releasing the shells to capture her hand instead. "Later, I will know for certain," he added, his gaze lowering to her skirts. "Few people place any value on shells. But they seem precious to you," he commented with a look of amusement in his eye. "You have captivated me. Who are you really, Francisca? Have you been sent by my enemies to torment me? To destroy me, perchance? If that be so, then they have indeed succeeded, for I would gladly die while in your arms," Valentine Whitelaw said, and whether now in jest or truth only he knew for certain. "Francisca? 'Tis Spanish? Let me guess? You've a Spanish father and an English mother. I do not believe you are gypsy. From the look of you, I would say your father had been a gentleman, who, perhaps, fell in love with a fair English rose, but had a wife and family back in Madrid?"

"Perhaps," Lily whispered, almost tearfully. He really did not know.

"Tears? I swear, I am undone by a woman's tears. Now I am certain you have indeed been sent by one of my enemies. Well, I have no friends in Spain. And there would be many who would pay well to have you bewitch me, then stab me through my black heart when I am least suspecting an assassin's attack," he said mockingly. "But they know I could not resist the challenge of taking a Spanish maid to bed," he said, eyeing her speculatively. "But you have not been sent here to hurt me, have you, Francisca *mía*? You are here to give me pleasure."

"*Can* you be hurt?"

"Yes, if my enemy knows where to strike," Valentine admitted, smiling down into her face, a beautiful stranger's face, or so he believed.

Lily Francisca Christian stared at the man she had loved for so many years. He had not even recognized her. She meant nothing to him. She never had. He would never be able to believe that the woman who had caught his eye was the little girl he had rescued from that island in the Indies. The same girl whose heart he had broken that day in the gardens of Tamesis House. She was the awkward, leggy girl whom he had claimed he could never love. She was that very same girl, with the same green eyes and red hair, who had cried herself to sleep because of his laughter. And he was the very same man who could never gaze upon Lily Christian with desire.

"A fortune? You wish to have your fortune told true?" Lily surprised herself by saying.

"My fortune? You think you can read my future, little one?

Or, perhaps, 'tis your own you will be reading," Valentine¯
Whitelaw replied, his fingers entwining with hers as he tightened his hold on her hand. "Come, then. Into the shade of these
trees, where we may be alone. Tell me my fortune, if you dare,"
he challenged her.

But Lily Christian, daughter of Magdalena and Geoffrey Christian, was not to be intimidated by her enemy, and in that very second, meeting his mocking gaze, she came to think of him as
one—at least she did for the briefest of moments while her pride
sorely smarted because he had not recognized her. Very well, Lily
thought, she would teach him a lesson he would not soon forget,
nor would he ever again forget Lily Christian, she vowed.

"Come, Cap'n. I will tell your fortune," she said softly, with
just the slightest of accents, remembering the manner in which
her mother had spoken. "You were correct, for *I* am the teller of
fortunes, while you, good sir, are the hunter of fortunes. You
have become wealthy in your search for treasure," she surprised
him by announcing.

"Aye, I am master of a ship. Did you hear me addressed as
captain?"

"Your fortune, Çap'n?" Lily reminded him. Setting the basket down on the ground, she steeled herself to grasp the hand
that still held hers. Turning it palm upwards, she pretended to
study the lines revealed to her. It was such a strong, capable
hand, Lily thought, lightly tracing her fingertips across the
toughened palm, where hard work had worn rough callouses.

"Do you not wish to be paid first?" Valentine asked abruptly,
for even her lightest touch had the power to excite him.

"I will leave that to you, Cap'n. If you are pleased with my
reading, then reward me as you will," Lily replied without looking up into his face.

"Indeed I shall," he murmured softly, startling Lily when his
hand cupped her chin and tilted her face up to his. "I promise
you will not be disappointed," he said, a hunger growing deep
inside of him to bury his face in those soft, silken curls cascading
across her slender shoulders.

Lily glanced away quickly, freeing her chin from his disturbing
touch as she peered closer into his palm. "You've just returned
from afar, Cap'n. You have crossed the seas many times. You have
a ship that sings," Lily said, unconsciously mimicking Old Maria

with her riddles. "You never stay long in one place. You sail away, always searching for something. But there is a place that longs for you. A house where the sun sets. A beautiful house by the sea. It stands empty, waiting for your return," Lily said, beginning to enjoy the charade, for his sudden silence bore proof of his shocked dismay at her intimate knowledge of him.

Then in a low voice she added, "But the sea you love has treated you most cruelly. You have lost one you loved dearly. A wise, kind man whose words you took heed of. You have become famous sailing the seas, a man much feared by his enemies, but the sea will exact a price from you, Cap'n. Always remember that. You had to pay homage once before, my brave captain, when your ship nearly went down in a devil-brewed storm off a far distant shore," she spoke dramatically, waving her hand as if conjuring the vision to mind. "You cursed the sea that day, and from that day forward, you were left carrying the mark of the sea upon your back." Lily could not resist taunting him with the tale he himself had told her when she'd sailed aboard the *Madrigal*. She had seen the strange crescent-shaped scar that had been cut into his flesh like a brand when a tackle had swung loose and caught him across the shoulder, nearly sending him overboard. "It claimed the lives of several of your crewmen, and very nearly your own, did it not, Cap'n?"

Valentine Whitelaw stared at Lily Christian disbelievingly. How could she possibly know such things unless she really could see into the past, or, if indeed she'd been sent by one of his enemies, or even a jesting friend? It would explain why she was so very well informed.

Valentine Whitelaw smiled. "You have knowledge of many things for one so young. Were I not so certain that we'd not met before, I would claim you have the advantage of this conversation. But you have only spoken of what has already happened. What of the future? Can you not see where our paths cross, and where they will lead us?" he asked.

For the first time Lily smiled, her green eyes glowing mysteriously, and Valentine Whitelaw felt a painful tightening in his loins. To be so close to her and yet not know the feel of her in his arms was proving a difficult battle of self-restraint.

"Ah, but our paths have crossed."

"Now you mock me. Had our paths crossed, little one, I

would certainly have remembered. I am not likely ever to forget your face, although . . .'' he paused, frowning slightly when he heard her soft laughter.

"Although? You sound less certain. Could you possibly be mistaken? Beware, lest your arrogance lead you astray and you miss the right path to follow,'' she warned him, and for a moment Valentine had the distinct impression that they had indeed met before, but he was damned if he remembered where. "Francisca?'' he murmured, shaking his head. "A lovely name, but . . .''

"Oh, but our paths have crossed, just now,'' Lily said quickly, unwilling to forfeit the game so soon. To see him so disturbed, so in doubt, was a balm to her wounded pride. Soon enough he would learn the truth. And she would enjoy seeing his stunned expression when he discovered her true identity.

Valentine Whitelaw raised her hand to his lips, and feeling her tremble when his lips touched her flesh, he said, "I would have them become one, Francisca.''

For a moment, Lily stared up at him uncomprehendingly, then her cheeks grew hot with a rosy tint as she understood only too well his meaning. His gaze was traveling slowly and intimately over her body now, leaving her in little doubt of what his wishes were concerning her.

Lily pulled her hand free of his and picked up her basket, holding it between them. "I must go,'' she said, panicking, for this conversation was not progressing quite the way she had planned. He had caught her off guard. She needed time to think.

"Afraid?''

"No!'' she responded, but she glanced around nervously, noting that they stood alone, unseen, in the shade of the trees. Where had everyone gone? she wondered. The midway was unusually empty for this time of day.

"Has your heart already been given to another?''

Lily opened her mouth to deny that, but when she stared into his turquoise eyes, she knew she couldn't. She would always love Valentine Whitelaw, despite how he unwittingly hurt her.

"The man who kissed your cheek and fondled you. He is your lover?'' Valentine accused, startling himself by the sudden jealousy that kiss had caused him. Never before had the mere sight of a comely maid caused him to act like some lovesick swain tripping over his own feet.

"Rom? My lover? No! Of course not. Rom is my friend. He has always been there to help us," Lily said, outraged by such an accusation. "I have come to love him, but as I would a brother."

Valentine Whitelaw smiled. "I see. I wonder then, who is this gentleman who is so fortunate to possess your love? I vow, he is the fool to allow you to wander beyond his grasp. If you were mine, Francisca, I would never let you leave my side."

"If I were yours?" Lily said the words softly, disbelievingly.

"Yes, mine, Francisca," Valentine spoke urgently, his hand lightly clasping her shoulder. She was so frail, he thought, feeling the bones beneath his hand. It could so easily be crushed by the wrong hand, but never his hand. He would never hurt her. Despite the company she kept, she seemed so untouched, so innocent, and yet he knew differently. No woman who was innocent of love could have gazed at him the way she had earlier. He had not mistaken the seductive invitation in her eyes. "Do you not believe me? Come aboard my ship. She rides at anchor in the river, just beyond this bank, where first I saw you."

Lily's eyes widened in surprise. "You saw me?"

"Since first gazing across the waters at you, I have been able to think of little else but you," he admitted, his hand sliding from her shoulder and into the tangle of dark red hair. His voice was low and persuasive as he said, "I had never seen such beauty as yours. You enchanted me, little sea maid. Astride a white horse, you raced along the bank, disappearing into the mists, then riding out into the sunlight, your hair catching the fire from the sun. You were so spirited. So free. Can you blame me for wanting to capture you for my own? You were what I had longed for while I was at sea," he said, and while he spoke his fingers moved along the delicate line of her jaw to trace the soft contour of her lips.

"Please, don't," Lily said weakly, her heart fluttering wildly. If he only knew . . .

But Valentine persisted, his words soft and seductive. He would have his way with this maid. He could sense her confusion, and he knew how to tempt her into his embrace. He felt certain her curiosity, like a cat's, would be her undoing. She would not be able to resist. "Have you never sailed the sea,

Francisca? Come aboard my ship and we will ride the tide downriver, then sail into the sea. It seems to stretch away forever. Let me show you its magic, free you, for just a short while. You have longed for that, haven't you? I can see it in your eyes. It excites you, doesn't it?

"You will feel as if you are flying above the waves. We will sail with the winds. Far more swiftly than you did on that white horse of yours. Come, Francisca. Come with me," he urged her. "The *Madrigal's* hold is still laden with treasure. She is sweet-scented with the richness of spices. It fills the senses. Come aboard the *Madrigal* and I will wrap you in silk so fine you will think it had been woven by fairy hands. I would honor your beauty, Francisca, with jewels so precious, so full of fire, that you would believe them to be alive. Let me prove to you how enchanted I am. Come, tonight. Come aboard my ship. Feel the movement of her beneath you, and you will never want to leave. And, if you so desire, then on the morrow we will sail."

"No, please, don't say more. You mustn't. You do not understand," Lily pleaded, frightened by his words, by the ardent demand in his eyes. Would he be saying such things to her if he knew . . . ?

"You're shivering. But not from fear. You desire me as much as I do you. I can see it in your eyes," he said roughly, and taking the basket from her hands, he tossed it aside. "I saw the expression in your eyes when first we met. You did not bother to hide your passion then. You stared at me as if you recognized me. As if we had already been lovers. You cannot deny it, Francisca. I felt your gaze upon me even before I saw you standing there. I felt your eyes caressing me, wanting to know me. Do you think I would chase after every maid I chanced to see and admire? Something astonishing happened when I saw you. Call me planet-struck or perhaps spellbound, but I felt the same strange sense of recognition that I saw cross your face. I knew you. I felt as if I'd known you all of my life. There is something so tantalizingly familiar about you, about those green eyes of yours, and yet I know I have never gazed into eyes that burn through me like yours do. No, don't look away," he told her, his hand holding her face turned to his. "You seem so innocent, and yet you have seduced me as surely as if we had already lain together as lovers."

"No!" Lily cried, trying to free her hands from his.

"What game are you playing? You entice me, then deny me. Can you be that cruel and unfeeling? Or is it that you are afraid I will not pay you enough? Perhaps you fear I will be disappointed? Well, here, take it now," he said harshly, throwing his purse into the basket. "Now you owe me. One night, Francisca. Let us see if you are worth it."

Before she could move, he had pulled her against his chest, his arm tightening around her waist and hip while he held her against him, molding her body to his. She had started to protest, but his mouth closed over hers, the hardening pressure parting her lips beneath the demand of his kiss.

Lily stood unmoving in his embrace. Never before had a man kissed her mouth in passion. She drew a sharp breath in surprise when she felt his tongue touching hers, moving against its softness as if the taste was pleasing to him. His beard scratched her face when his mouth lifted from hers to leave a trail of fire across her cheek and throat before returning and stealing away her breath, for she was finding it increasingly difficult to breathe. And every breath she took was filled with him, with the taste and smell of Valentine Whitelaw.

A quivering sensation shot through her body when she felt his hand slide down to caress her buttocks and pull her against him. Even through her petticoats she could feel the hardness of him pressing against her. It frightened and excited her at the same time, confusing her with both guilt and pleasure that she should enjoy a man's intimate touching of her body. She was not so innocent that she did not understand what he was seeking. Never before had she completely perceived the reason why, but now, feeling an emptiness that left her aching for something more fulfilling, Lily Christian, tasting of passion for the first time, experienced a newfound awareness of her woman's body.

Valentine lifted his mouth from hers and stared down into her flushed face. Her breath was coming quickly between her parted lips, her lashes fluttering slightly. He tightened his arms around her, holding her even closer against him until he could feel the fragrant heat of her body warming him. She was so beautiful, he thought, lowering his mouth to taste of hers again.

Lily felt his mouth moving hungrily against hers, his teeth nibbling her lips, then his breath became hers. Never had she known such pleasure, and she wanted it to continue, she suddenly realized, her arms moving for the first time in response, to clasp his strong shoulders, to entwine behind his neck. Her fingers moved through the softness of his black hair, tightening in its thickness so he would not draw away from her again.

Valentine felt a surge of excitement when he felt her shy response to his kisses become more passionate. Her tongue moved slowly against his, tasting of him now, and he kissed her all the deeper, wanting a more intimate coupling with her as his arms held her closer against him, his hands caressing the curve of her buttocks with slow, deliberate strokes. With one hand he kept her close while his other hand moved to fondle her breast. Through the soft silk of her bodice he could feel the tautness of her flesh, the delicate nipple hardening beneath his thumb as he rubbed it. He pressed her back against the tree trunk, his mouth bruising hers with his increasing passion. Kiss after breathless kiss followed, her mouth opening wider to his, to let him explore her more deeply, her lips clinging to his time and time again.

His breath coming raggedly, Valentine lifted his mouth from hers and stared down into her green eyes glowing with passion. "Now? Come with me now. Come aboard the *Madrigal*. Francisca, don't deny me," he said, his hands caressing the delicate contours of her face. His fingers touched the slightly dampened curls that clung to her flushed cheek and brow. "Forgive me for my anger. But I was desperate to have you in my arms. To touch you."

Her scent clung to him. The sweet smell from her woman's body, warm with the pungency of healthy perspiration and spicy perfume, had aroused him so that had they indeed been aboard his ship, nothing on this earth could have stopped him from taking her.

"I—I must tell you. Please, this is wrong. I did not mean for this to happen. You don't know. I—"

"No, it is not wrong. It can never be wrong when two people feel as we do. Francisca, listen to me," Valentine began quickly, unwilling to allow her to leave him, to deny both of them the pleasure he knew they could share as lovers.

"Captain, there you are," someone spoke from beyond the trees. "You have to hurry. You have meeting with friend. Remember?" Mustafa reminded his captain, his dark eyes glancing away in embarrassment when he realized his captain was with a woman.

Slowly Valentine drew his gaze away from Lily's face. He stared at Mustafa as if he were the crazed man and not himself. "A meeting? Damn! That engagement. The Devil, I remember now," Valentine swore, glancing back at Lily, who was leaning against him, her head turned away as if embarrassed by what had happened while held in his arms.

Turning his face to her, he met her gaze and it shocked him, for there were tears in her eyes. He pressed a soft kiss against her forehead. "I must go. I will come back, Francisca. I promise you this is not over yet. I will come for you. Have your things packed, for I will not leave this camp without you," he warned.

"No, please. You mustn't come into the camp. They are suspicious of strangers. It would not be wise," Lily told him, thinking to set up a meeting tomorrow. She would know what to do by then. "Tomorrow."

"No. This evening. Agree to meet me or I will come for you and drag you out of that camp," Valentine told her, not to be denied. "Meet me on the bank, where I saw you riding yesterday. I will come in the evening, before it grows dark. My ship is anchored near there. I'll row ashore and no one will see us. I will not let you out of my life now. I do not understand what you've done to me, but I promise you I will know you as no lover of yours has before. This evening, Francisca. I will return for you in the evening," Valentine promised, reluctantly freeing her from his embrace as he stepped away from her and out into the bright sunshine.

He started to walk away from her, then turned around with a boyish-looking smile on his handsome face. "You never asked what my name was," he said, seeking her figure where she stood in the shade of the tree, leaning against the trunk for support. "Or, perhaps, you already know it? 'Tis Valentine White-law. Tonight, Francisca. Don't forget," he said, turning away.

The Turk continued to stand where he was, just beyond the trees, his gaze narrowed thoughtfully as he stared beneath them at the shadowy figure standing there so quietly. He could see the woman's face, the eyes staring at him so strangely, but the shadows masked their color and the true shade of her hair. Where had he seen her before? he wondered. With a shrug and a shake of his turbaned head, he followed his captain from the fair.

"I know your name, Valentine Whitelaw," Lily said shakily, a scalding tear falling from her eye as she watched his tall figure stride away. "I'll never forget you or what you have done to me."

What kind of man was he that he could stand here and make love to her when he had a fiancée waiting for him? His casually spoken words struck her once again. His engagement. He had forgotten his engagement? How would Cordelia feel about being dismissed so easily? Lily speculated bitterly. The devil, he had said. He was certainly that, Lily decided, feeling his sweat drying on her body. She would never feel the same. Her mouth tasted of him. Her body smelled of him. He had touched her intimately, as no man had ever dared to do before.

But more than that, he had made her feel a stranger to herself, and for that she would never forgive him. He had cheated her. He had made her feel emotions she'd never experienced before. He had stolen from her something precious—her love. She had given her love to a man who could never love her. A man who didn't even know who she was.

With shaking hands, Lily tried to brush back her hair, but the long strands were tangled, and some of the flowers she'd woven into them had fallen to the ground, where they had been crushed beneath his feet. Lily felt her lips, wincing when she touched their bruised tenderness. In her dreams, she had never thought love would be like this. For so long she had dreamed of Valentine Whitelaw, of his kisses, and yet the reality of it had been far different from her innocent imaginings. She sighed, trying to straighten her bodice. She felt hot and uncomfortable and longed to wash herself clean of his touch, but when she smoothed the silk covering her breasts, the flesh tender now from his touch, she knew a deep longing to be held in his arms again.

Picking up her basket, Lily walked from under the trees, her steps carrying her unseeingly through the fair and the mass of people crowding close around her. She stared without a flicker of recognition into the oddly colored eyes of a well-dressed gentleman walking by, never seeing the smile that crossed his handsome face as she passed. She stumbled slightly when she neared their cart, and glancing down, she noticed the small leather purse of money Valentine Whitelaw had paid her with. A glint of anger flared in her eyes as she thought of the insult. Had she been worth the price? she wondered, remembering how his mouth had devoured hers. Tonight, he had said. He would come for her this evening. He had told her to be there. He would not let her forget him. It was not over yet, he had promised. Indeed it was not.

Lily smiled in anticipation of that meeting. She would be there, all right. But Valentine Whitelaw was in for a surprise, especially when she threw his money in his face for humiliating her. Lily's smile faded when she thought about how angry he would be when he discovered that she was Lily *Francisca* Christian. He would be disbelieving, then full of rage, then mortified to remember how he had held her and kissed her and admitted his desire for her. Oh, yes, Lily vowed with a glint in her eye, she would be there tonight. It was an assignation she would not miss if her life depended on it.

For the moment, Lily put the anticipated meeting from her mind, for ahead, she could see Tristram and Dulcie, sitting in the shade, with plates balanced precariously on their laps while they ate. Raphael sat beside his young mistress, towering over her and her plate, watchfully. Every few minutes, his big paw landed on her lap, reminding Dulcie that he too was hungry. But when he saw Lily approaching, he stood up, eyeing her suspiciously until he recognized her, then his tail started its dangerous wagging, nearly sending Tristram's plate flying from his lap.

"Oh, Mistress Lily," Tillie said, trying to rise from her seat in the back of the cart, where she sat beside Farley, Fairfax having stretched out beneath the shade of a large oak nearby. "I'll get ye some supper. Ye look tried to death."

"Stay seated, Tillie," Lily said, and Raphael barked and sat back down, returning his attention to Dulcie's supper.

"Why, ye've sold almost all of the posies," she exclaimed. "Oh, but Mistress Lily, ye do look flustered something awful. Did someone hit ye in the mouth? Looks kinda swollen. I'll get some salve fer it," she said, starting to rise again.

"I'll get it, Tillie dear," Farley offered kindly, unable to watch her trying to rise yet again. It was making him nervous.

" 'Tis all right, please don't bother. It just stings a little," Lily said, placing the basket in the back of the cart, the purse of gold coins tucked beneath her waistband.

"Did you get in the fight, Lily?" Tristram demanded, nearly choking on a mouthful of food as he eyed his sister's disheveled appearance. "Sure looks as if you did."

"What fight?"

"You don't know, Lily?" Tristram asked, staring at her incredulously. "Where have you been for the last hour?"

"I've been busy. But what is this about a fight?" she said, glancing around. "Where is Rom?"

"He's in town, with the constable and them officials, trying to make peace. There was a big fight t'other end of the fair, nearly ended up in the town, over that boy who stole the gentleman's purse. Seems the lad got beaten up pretty bad by one of the man's servants. Pretty ugly scene. Everyone got involved in it, even some of the townspeople. Surly bunch of louts. Lot of broken bones with all of the fists flying."

"Rom wasn't hurt, was he?" Lily demanded.

"No, that one knows how to take care of himself, though I reckon some of those he fought with can't say the same. I wouldn't save any food fer him, 'cause I reckon when he finishes there, he'll go to the council meeting. The elders called it early to discuss the fight and to decide if we are to be sent packin'," Farley said worriedly. "Been thinkin', Mistress Lily, what with that, and with winter comin' on in a few months and Tillie about ready to have the wee one, that we oughta find somewhere else to stay. Been all right, travelin' like we have, sleepin' 'neath the stars, but what happens when it starts to snow? Ain't goin' to be very good fer any o' us, especially the young 'uns, mistress."

Lily nodded. "I know, Farley. I too have been thinking that it is time we left the fair. I do not think even Rom can convince the others to let us stay, despite how he feels about us staying with him.

"Damned jealous, they be," Fairfax muttered. "Haven't lost a match yet, I haven't," he chuckled. "Still think one o' them burned us out o' the puppet show. Reckon they ain't as smart as they think. Heard a number of them grumblin' about losin' business 'cause the show wasn't bringin' in customers. Can't please some folk."

"I hope Rom won't anger them. They are his friends, and I don't want him to get thrown out with us. He has already done

too much for us. We have another choice, but this is all Rom
has.''

''Reckon he'd like something more,'' Farley murmured.

''Where we goin' to go, Lily?'' Tristram asked in surprise.
''We can't go back to Highcross can we?''

''Are we still goin' to Maire Lester's?''

''No, I do not think that will be necessary now.''

''What do you mean, Lily? Did she die? She's kinda old, isn't
she?''

Lily drew a deep breath. ''I saw Valentine Whitelaw today.
He is back in England.''

''Uncle Valentine! He's here, Lily!'' Dulcie squealed excitedly.

''Valentine! Really, Lily?'' Tristram said, grinning widely.
''Where is he? Why didn't he come back with you? Didn't you
talk to him?''

Lily glanced away guiltily. ''No, I did not speak with him. I
needed time to think about how we would explain what had
happened at Highcross and why we are with the fair. I have sent
a note to him to meet with me this evening, and we will talk,''
she lied, then added truthfully, ''He will learn the truth then.''

''Tonight? Is he coming here?'' Tristram demanded,
belatedly realizing that Valentine Whitelaw might indeed think
it strange they were here in London. And he'd probably blame
him for all that happened, Tristram thought, wishing he'd never
gone into the churchyard that night.

''I thought it best to meet him away from the camp. It would
only cause suspicion to have him come here.''

''I always thought the captain was a good man, Mistress Lily.
Glad to hear he's returned. Reckon he'll set things right with
them villagers in East Highford,'' Farley declared, feeling better
about things already.

''Can I come, too, Lily?'' Tristram asked.

''Me, too!'' Dulcie cried.

''No, I am not meeting him until evening, and it might be late
before we finish our conversation. We have much to discuss,
and I would rather speak with him alone. 'Twill be hard to explain,'' Lily said, some of her anticipated pleasure disappearing
when she thought more about her proposed meeting with Valentine Whitelaw. ''I want to change,'' she said suddenly.

" 'Twas so hot today, I'm going to have to wash this gown before I wear it again," she added a trifle lamely, anxious to get out of her soiled gown.

Although he was hesitant to offer, Farley finally managed to find the nerve. "Maybe me and Fairfax oughta come with ye, Mistress Lily. Reckon I could explain about Fairfax and Tillie and me bein' with ye. Wouldn't want the cap'n to think we done something wrong. Reckon 'twill kinda look that way in his eyes," he said worriedly. And exchanging glances with Fairfax, who had opened a curious eye when he'd heard Farley's extraordinary offer, both remembered their first encounter with Valentine Whitelaw and his servant on the stairs at Highcross. No, Farley was certainly right, they didn't want the cap'n thinking ill of them.

"No, thank you anyway, Farley, but I do not think it will be a pleasant conversation. It might be wiser to allow Valentine Whitelaw to regain his composure before I even mention the part about you and Fairfax and Tristram hiding in the churchyard and frightening the reverend and the villagers half to death," Lily advised.

"Good idea," Fairfax quickly agreed, remembering the curved sword that foreign fellow wore at his hip.

"Might not even have to mention it at all," Farley went so far as to speculate. "Reckon if some people could keep their mouths shut about it . . ." he added.

"I wouldn't say anything, Farley!" Tristram declared stoutly; after all, it was his neck too.

Farley shook his head. "I wasn't thinkin' o' ye, Master Tristram," he said, eyeing his brother's lazy form instead.

"Ah, Farley, now ye know I wouldn't be sayin' anything. Why, remember the time when ye and that maid—now what was her name? Well, don't matter," Fairfax began, hiding his grin when he saw Farley glance quickly at Tillie, who was staring at him in amazement.

"Here, Lily, you haven't eaten anything all day, I bet," Dulcie said, handing Lily a plate with a small wedge of cheese and a cold tart sitting proudly in the middle. "It's the last one," Dulcie told her, thinking it might enhance it some in her sister's eyes, but instead, Lily began to cry softly. She had forgotten all about the roasted squabs for their supper.

"Oh, Lily, what's wrong?" Dulcie cried, tears hovering close in her luminous eyes. "I told Tristram not to eat that other tart. I knew you'd be hungry."

"I'm sorry, Lily. I thought you wouldn't mind. You always give me the extra one, anyway," Tristram said, feeling horribly guilty about having eaten that last tart. "I did give half of it to Ruff," he added.

Lily shook her head, pulling them both close to her and giving them each a hug. "I'm not crying about that. I'm just a little tired. Here, I'm not even hungry. You split this tart, and I'll just have the cheese. I ate something earlier," she lied, handing each of them a piece of the tart.

Tristram eyed her suspiciously. "Are you certain, Lily?"

"Yes, I'm certain. Now do as I say!" she said, quickly wiping away her tears. "I do not want to hear another word about it," she warned, not seeing Tillie shake her head and exchanging an I-told-you-so glance with Farley, for they had both said Mistress Lily was getting far too thin.

"I want to wash away the dust before it gets dark," Lily told them, making her way to the small tent they'd put up between the cart and one of the low branches of the oak. "I intend to look my best when I meet with Valentine Whitelaw tonight. We are not beggars asking for handouts."

"Ye want me to give ye a hand, Mistress Lily?" Tillie asked, starting to rise, Farley's hand giving her a lift up. "We can bring some pails of water from the stream."

"Thank you, but I'll just wash in the stream. I won't be long," Lily said.

Gathering up her green velvet gown, a cloth for washing and drying herself, and her favorite scents, Lily made her way toward the stream that flowed just beyond the camp and closest to where they'd set up their tent. A thick copse of trees grew close to the bank and provided ample privacy. There was no one around to disturb her as Lily placed her clothes on a flat rock. With punishing strokes, Lily brushed her hair free of tangles. Braiding it over her shoulder, she secured it high atop her head. Slipping off her gown and petticoats and clad only in her smock, Lily waded into the cold water. She took her prized bar of soap and used just enough to cleanse the dust and perspiration from her legs and arms. She scrubbed her face clean, rinsing away the touch of Valentine Whitelaw.

As she stood in the middle of the stream, listening to its soft murmuring around her, she breathed deeply of the cooling air, still heavy with the pungent scent of the woods. Lily continued to stand with the water flowing around her calves. It had a soothing effect and she found herself wishing she could lie down and float with the waters as they flowed into the Thames.

The shadows were lengthening as the light began to fade and the shapes of the trees became dark silhouettes against the mauve sky. Suddenly Lily was alerted by the sound of a twig cracking loudly beneath someone's foot and a flock of startled birds took to the sky in fright.

"Who is there?" she demanded, angry that someone might be spying on her. "Please, who is it?"

But there was only silence.

Even though she could see and hear the comforting noises from the camp through the trees, Lily hurried from the stream and wasted no time drying off and smoothing the scented lotions into her skin. She fumbled with the fastenings on the green velvet ropa, her smock and petticoats sticking to her damp skin as she struggled into her stockings and slippers.

Lily kept glancing over her shoulders as she walked back through the trees. The copse seemed far thicker than it had when she'd entered less than an hour earlier. With a sigh of relief, she left the dark underbrush and walked out into the clearing, where golden sunlight slanted down on her and where she heard the sound of cheerful voices and smelled the aroma of cooking meats, for some were just beginning to prepare their evening meals.

Passing by the back of the cart, Lily tossed the discarded silk gown over the edge of the tub. Leaving her toiletries in the cart, she neared the fire Fairfax was adding wood to. Farley sat close with Tillie napping beside him, and Tristram and Dulcie had moved in from the other side, for by darkness it would be far cooler, and even now the shadows held the chill of autumn fast approaching.

"Why don't you get ready for bed?" Lily asked, sitting down next to Dulcie, who was beginning to nod off, her head propped against Raphael's soft coat.

"Will you tell me a story first?" she requested, yawning widely.

"What would you like to hear?" Lily asked, smiling, for she knew before Dulcie answered what it would be.

"The tale of the wild white horses," she murmured sleepily, turning to lie in Lily's arms. "Tell me about the island too, Lily. I want to hear about Neptune and the cove."

"When we were on the island, she always wanted to hear about England and the queen. Now we're here, she only wants to hear about the island," Tristram complained as he helped Cappie out of his coat and hat, carefully folding them up and ready for the next day's performance.

"*Prrraaack!* Wild white horses!"

"That reminds me, Tristram. Did you remember to feed Merry?"

"Whole bag of oats, and a nip on my shoulder for my trouble," Tristram replied, stretching out his feet to the fire. "I think he's getting meaner, Lily."

Lily smiled. "He's just getting old."

"He's getting older and meaner, then," Tristram said. "Hey, look! I think I've seen the first star of the evening!" he crowed with delight, pointing up into the darkening sky, now streaked with mauve.

"Oh, Tristram! It isn't fair. You always find it first," Dulcie said, disappointed as she searched the heavens for a star. "I don't see any."

"Don't worry, soon there will be too many to count," Lily said. "After I tell you the tale of the white horses, I'll tell you a new one about the dancing stars," Lily promised, beginning the story. Soon, it would be time to meet Valentine Whitelaw.

Devil's Tavern was crowded to the beams with patrons. There was hardly more than enough elbow room to lift a tankard by, so packed were the oak tables. A fire burned brightly in the great hearth, helping to warm the damp chill creeping in on the mists rising from the river. Overlooking the Thames and the gallows at Wapping, where there was a convenient public landing place, the tavern was a hive of activity. It was within easy distance of the Pool of London, and the first place a knowledgeable seafarer might stop to meet with friends and quench a thirst.

Every so often, the bellowing voice of a bargeman answering the call for "Oars!" could be heard responding with a ribald cry. More often than not, a brief silence would fall over the taproom while they waited for the usual ear-burning oath full of unusually descriptive vulgarities that the watermen prided themselves on mastering.

Valentine Whitelaw had met Thomas Sandrick as agreed upon and had found a table against the wall, where they'd been served a light supper of beef and ale. But soon their party had grown in size, when his gentlemen friends, including George Hargraves and Walter Raleigh, and fellow captains had discovered his return to London.

The noise was deafening around him, and Valentine could only catch a word or two of any of several conversations going on at once.

"Ye've been away. Did ye not hear? 'Tis *Sir* Francis Drake now!"

"Aye, he's the devil himself, that one!"

"Her Majesty went aboard his ship in Deptford and knighted him right there on the deck. Ye should have been there. Says, just as bold as brass, she did, that them Spaniards were demandin' Drake's head, so she takes this gilded sword and with a devilish look, hands it to the French ambassador. Has the gent knight Drake instead of beheadin' him."

"Half a million pounds that treasure was worth. Made a tidy sum, I hear."

"I know! I served with him. He's the sly one!"

"Since he's been raidin' the Main, I hear them Spaniards have nicknamed him *El Dragón*. Got 'em scared senseless, never knowin' when he's goin' to strike and burn their cities and loot 'em of gold!"

"Hear tell there be a few of them pointed Spanish beards with hairs out of place since ye been sailin' them waters, Whitelaw. Learned a few tricks from Drake, eh?"

But Valentine Whitelaw didn't hear, he was too busy remembering a soft body pressed against his and the sweet fragrance of perfume that still clung to his clothes and skin. Impatiently, he glanced at the fading light. Soon, it would be dark. Already, he was late, but Walter Raleigh had been full of questions about the

New World, more interested in the continent that lay north of the Indies than the Main.

"Thomas, I'm afraid I've got to leave. I have another appointment I will not miss."

"A woman, no doubt!" someone commented wryly.

"Won't be seein' Valentine for some time then."

"That beautiful, is she?"

"No, he's just back from a long voyage. No women aboard! I'm never all that particular, myself. First pair of hips I see will do fer me," the grizzled-looking man said, eyeing a buxom serving wench with a lusty look when she passed by. Reaching out a long arm, he pulled her onto his lap; his hands slid roughly along her hip and thigh, and bussing her a juicy one on the mouth, he grinned down into her laughing face, her halfhearted protest going unheeded.

Valentine Whitelaw couldn't hide the look of distaste that crossed his tanned face. For the first time, Matt Evans's crudeness was offensive to him; even though the remarks might have been made in good-natured jesting, it bothered Valentine to have Francisca referred to in the same breath as the drab sprawled indecorously across Evans's lap.

Francisca was not just any woman to ease his lusts by. Despite what he might have said about just one night aboard the *Madrigal*, he knew he would want her in his bed for many nights to come. He had already thought about setting her up as his mistress. He would see that she had everything she needed. A fine house in the city. A coach. Clothes and jewels and servants to wait on her every whim. He would pamper her and keep her in silks and velvets, her dark red hair gleaming with pearls and her soft, pale skin scented with the headiest, most exotic perfumes he would buy for her in Arabia.

Perhaps he would even take her to Plymouth with him, since he would be spending more time in the West Country. It would be but a few hours' ride to see her whenever he wished. One day, he might even take her to visit Ravindzara. Thinking of Francisca, of having her in his bed, of her mouth trembling and soft from his kisses, of her pale, slender thighs entwined around his hips, of taking her until she was breathless with desire, the image of any other woman but a redheaded, green-eyed enchantress faded from his mind. So did the idea that had been forming in his mind of late that he needed a wife, and that he might make his intentions known to Honoria Penmorley.

Realizing he still sat lost in his daydreaming while the sunset faded across the river, where a woman was waiting for him, Valentine began to excuse himself, rising from the table with a determined glint in his eye to bid a quick farewell to his friends.

Valentine hadn't gotten as far as the next table, the Turk moving closely behind him, when he was halted by a man he knew only slightly. The man drew him aside, slipping him a note.

"Lord Burghley wishes to see you."

"Now?" Valentine questioned in disbelief.

"Yes, sir, now. If you please. His lordship has been busy with appointments all day, and only now has he found the time to see you. If you please?" the man repeated, but more insistently this time, and Valentine realized the man was not likely to take no for an answer. Nor indeed did one refuse to see William Cecil when he requested your presence.

Valentine hid his frustration well as he followed the man from the tavern. For a brief moment, Valentine Whitelaw stood outside, staring with a narrowed gaze at the distant bank. The first star of the evening had risen low in the darkening skies.

"Mustafa."

"Yes, Cap'n?"

"I do not know how long I shall be," he said, glancing over at the silent courier.

"I am afraid I cannot say, sir," was all he allowed as he headed toward the steps, where a barge awaited.

"I want you to go across the river and meet Francisca. I don't want her to think I am not coming. Damn!" Valentine cursed when he saw the night watchman, carrying his halberd and horn-lantern, wander past as he roared the hour and warned the residents to light their lanterns and hang them outside their homes to light the way for others. " 'Tis later than I thought."

"Francisca?" Mustafa said the name curiously. "The girl from the fair?"

"Yes, I've arranged to meet her. I want you to go instead. She saw you with me this afternoon. Explain to her why I cannot come. Take her aboard the *Madrigal*, and don't take no for an answer if she resists you. I don't think she will, though," Valentine added with the assurance, or perhaps the arrogance, of a handsome man who had seldom been denied the woman he was after.

"Bring her aboard, Cap'n?" Mustafa questioned, for the captain had never had a woman aboard the *Madrigal* before, except, of course, the women of his family.

"Captain Whitelaw? We must not keep Lord Burghley waiting," the messenger reminded him.

"Just do it, Mustafa. I will expect to see her in my cabin when I come aboard," he warned, and with one final glance across the river, the bank now lost in darkness, Valentine Whitelaw made his way down the slippery steps to the barge that waited to carry him back upriver, but not to meet the person he'd been hoping to.

"As you wish, Cap'n," Mustafa said, bowing his turbaned head deferentially, but he was more curious than ever about this woman who had so captivated his captain.

Lily patted Merry's flank comfortingly, although she suspected she derived more comfort from the contact than he did. It had grown dark so quickly. She could scarcely see the river anymore, except where the flickering glow from the stern lanterns of ships and passing barges reflected in the blackness of the waters swirling past. But a mist was rising, and soon she wouldn't even be able to see those few beacons.

Lily glanced around uneasily. There were so many strange sounds. The river kept up a constant gurgling as the waters lapped against the hulls of the ships anchored midstream, before rushing against the bank. Every so often she would hear voices calling through the night, but most of the words remained unintelligible to her innocent ears.

In the fading twilight, she had found Valentine Whitelaw's ship, the *Madrigal*. She'd recognized the carved figurehead of the sea maid riding her bow. Under different circumstances, Lily found herself thinking, she would have liked to go aboard his ship again. She was the most beautiful ship on the Thames. But now, never . . .

Lily sighed, jumping nervously when Merry snorted, his warm breath tickling the back of her neck. "All right, boy, I know you don't like standing out here in the mists any more than I do," she spoke to him gently, rubbing his soft nose.

He wasn't coming. Valentine Whitelaw was not going to

meet her. What a fool she had been to believe his lies. He had gotten all he had wanted under the trees. After all, he had Cordelia to hold in his arms whenever he chose. They were probably aboard his ship right now, standing on the deck watching her forlorn figure on the shore, laughing at her gullibility. Or perhaps he'd seen another comely maid and enticed her into his bed, Lily decided, her anger growing with each shivering breath she took.

She didn't know if she was more relieved or angry that he had not kept their assignation. Even though she had not been looking forward to the confrontation, despite her desire to see his shocked expression when she revealed her true identity, she did not like being made a fool of. And that was exactly what she was to remain here waiting for him any longer.

"Come along, Merry. Let's go," Lily whispered, and leading the big white horse over to a fallen tree stump, she climbed on his back and, with a light touch of her heels to his flank, she sent him back toward the camp.

Sir Raymond Valchamps lifted his scented pomander to his nose and eyed with increasing contempt the rabble of unwashed bodies crowded so close together in the small taproom of the inn situated on a narrow lane just beyond Traitor's Gate. It was absolutely breathtaking, he thought.

And they were an angry mob, too. It wouldn't take much to incite them to further violence after the beating many of them had taken that afternoon when they'd tangled with a group of ruffians from the fair.

Sir Raymond smiled. Things had gone rather nicely for him today.

"Damn those peddlers! Cheated me out of a fair price, that one did!"

"Sold me a lame horse last week. Tried to take it back, but they said the nag wasn't lame when I bought it. Accused me of lyin'!" a rough-looking man said angrily, taking a long swallow from his tankard of ale.

"Heard tell they be sellin' ale that's only a few days old, yet chargin' even more than this place does! Hate to tell any o' ye'se been drinkin' it what I thinks it be made of."

"How about that, John? Them cheatin' ye out o' yer customers with stuff like that," another one yelled at the innkeeper.

"Aye, cheatin' the public, I says. Oughta run the lot of them out of London."

"Lost plenty bettin' on ye in the ring. Why'd ye let that big fair-haired fellow beat ye?"

"Cheated, he did! Bit me on the shoulder!" the man defended his loss with a guilty glance away from his friend's speculative gaze.

"Not only did he beat ye, and steal my earnings, he was sweet-talkin' and fondlin' yer daughter!"

"Lizzie? He had them big ham-fists of his on me daughter? When? I'll—"

"What d'ye mean ye can't be payin' fer the ale ye sat here drinkin'?" the innkeeper demanded of the fancy gentleman who'd been sitting by himself in the corner.

"Exactly what I said, my good man," Sir Raymond declared, glancing around at the indignant faces glaring at him. "My purse has been stolen," he said, standing up so quickly he upended the small oak table, sending the plates the serving maid had set down when collecting his empty tankard scattering onto the dirty floor. " 'Twas the whore. The one traveling with the gypsies. Has red hair. She did it. At the fair, just a little while ago. She wanted me to buy some of the posies she was selling."

"Aye, remember her, I do," someone said.

"Smiled at me so sweetly, why, I couldn't keep her hands off my person, so bold was she."

"Wish she'd been as bold with me, eh?" someone guffawed, thinking he'd have dealt easily enough with the wench. The fancy gent probably needed his servants' help.

"Enticed me behind one of the tents for a bit of pleasure. Well? I'm a man, aren't I?" Sir Raymond demanded as several of the men nodded understandingly. "She was fair enough to catch my eye," Sir Raymond said, unfortunately drawing the attention of several to his eyes. "Then, before I could do more than put an arm around her, I was hit from behind. When I awoke, my purse was gone, as well as my rings!" he declared, his gold pomander safely tucked away inside his hat now. "My God! 'Tis an ourtage. So weak was I, that I could only get as far as this inn. I hope you will forgive me, good sir, for drinking your ale without being able to pay for it.''

''Oh, sir, never think that. 'Tis on the house. Why, after what ye've been through! They oughta be hanged! The nerve of them to do such a thing to a gentleman! Why, I never heard of such boldness!''

''Yes, quite,'' Sir Raymond murmured faintly, fanning himself. He glanced up in feigned surprise when two men who'd been standing in the crowded taproom, awaiting his signal, suddenly picked up a couple of torches, and lighting them, held them high over their heads much to the innkeeper's horror as he watched the flames licking against the rafters of his inn.

''Let's burn 'em out! Come on! Are ye with us?''

''Aye!''

''Burn the thieves and whores out of our town!''

''We'll take care of them gypsies!''

''I'm with you!'' Sir Raymond cried out, making his way through the crowded taproom.

Sir Raymond's elegant figure became lost in the crowd that surged through the streets of Southwark, growing larger as they passed by other inns and taverns. They neared the grounds where the vagabond band was peacefully settled around their fires while most ate their only hot meal of the day, and others were already asleep for the night beneath their carts or inside colorful tents.

The fires from the torches held to the booths and tents passed along the way spread quickly, surprising and even sobering some of the mob by the searing heat from the flames rising high over the fairgrounds.

Screams and cries filled the air. The smoke billowed in black clouds, choking and blinding the people as they staggered about. Animals and people began to rush madly through the mob, oblivious of the cudgels and fists being swung by many as gypsies and vagabonds met the vicious attack by the townspeople with an erupting anger of their own.

Reaching the campsites, Sir Raymond held back, watching the crowd. Women and children were running wildly along the outskirts of the fighting, many huddling together in little groups, while others quickly gathered up their belongings and, locating their scattered animals, wasted no time in hitching them up to their carts and wagons.

Staying close to the trees, and safely out of reach of the bloodthirsty combatants, Sir Raymond made his way toward the group, searching out the figure of Lily Christian. With a sense of disbelief at his good fortune, he saw her standing alone, near a cart where a couple of oxen stood tethered to a tree by a tent.

Slowly, he moved up behind her, the loud noises masking his stealthy approach out of the trees. Pulling the knife from his doublet, Sir Raymond raised it high above his head, his arm arced to strike the death blow.

Through a haze he saw a man approaching from the crowd, yelling something to the girl, a warning, but Sir Raymond's arm was already swinging down, the knife blade glinting in the fire-light as it inched closer, slicing past her dark red head to drive deep into her back, the soft flesh of her slender shoulder ripping apart as Sir Raymond stabbed deep into her body, the blood spurting from the wound splattering his chest and face.

The force of the blow spun her around to face him and Sir Raymond screamed with fear when her hair came loose in his hands.

Sir Raymond's mouth opened in horror as he stared down at the flimsy piece of dark red lace that floated to the ground at his feet. He looked up in time to see the girl's face as she fell against him. It had been a mask of death, the dark, sightless eyes staring at him in surprise.

The girl he had just murdered had not been Lily Christian. But Sir Raymond had no time to speculate upon his mistake as he himself was attacked by a knife-wielding fiend. The man's body hurled against his and sent them both flying into the dirt.

Sir Raymond cried out, feeling some of the searing pain that the girl must have felt when he'd driven his knife into her. For a moment, Sir Raymond thought he was going to die. The blade of the knife had felt so startlingly cold against his flesh; then it had become a burning sensation deep inside of him. Holding his own weapon against his chest as he tried to defend himself, Sir Raymond and his attacker rolled over. Then suddenly Sir Raymond found himself released from the death hold the other man had held him in.

Fearing another blinding pain striking him full force, Sir

Raymond remained unmoving, but when the other man didn't move, he cautiously rolled away. Staggering to his feet, blood dripping from the wound in his shoulder, Sir Raymond stared down at the man who had attacked him.

Sir Raymond stared bemusedly at his knife embedded in the man's chest. Had he truly struck the blow himself, he could not have had a surer aim. Gradually, Sir Raymond became aware that the fight had gone out of the mob, and many of them were running away, nursing wounds, as they sought the safety of their homes.

Taking a handkerchief from his doublet, Sir Raymond tried to stanch the flow of blood from his wound. Odd, now that his fear of having been attacked was over, his wound seemed strangely insignificant. What bothered him the most was that Lily Christian still lived.

Moving into the shadows of the trees, Sir Raymond stared down at the two people he'd killed. He couldn't understand how he'd mistaken that woman for Lily Christian. She was wearing the same dress he'd seen Lily Christian wearing earlier in the day. Of course she had been wearing that damned veil over her head. A pity it'd been the same dark red as Lily Christian's hair.

Suddenly, Sir Raymond caught his breath as he watched Lily Christian riding into the camp astride a white horse. Quickly, she dismounted and was racing directly toward where he stood in the quiet of the trees, when someone called out to her and she turned, then ran in the opposite direction, out of his reach.

A young boy and girl flung themselves into her outstretched arms. Hugging them tight, she hurried to the side of a woman who was trying to kneel near a man who had been felled by a blow to the head. Another, shorter man, assisted her, then knelt beside her as he examined the large man lying unconscious on the ground.

As Sir Raymond continued to watch, Lily Christian glanced up, looking his way. Unable to control himself, he stepped deeper into the shadowy concealment of the trees just behind the cart.

Sir Raymond knew she couldn't see him, but he could see her. She might have escaped death this time but not the next time, he vowed. He would not fail again.

O mistress mine! where are you roaming?

Chapter Twenty-Two

I T was just before dawn. Valentine Whitelaw stood on the deck of the *Madrigal* and stared broodingly across the river, toward the distant bank cloaked in mist and barely visible through the lightening gloom.

She was gone.

While he had been waiting to meet with Lord Burghley, she had fled. And after what the Turk had told him had happened at the vagabond camp, he knew he might never have seen her again. She could have been the one lying dead, stabbed through the heart, Valentine thought, damning the circumstances that had kept him from meeting her, from being by her side when danger had struck so close.

He had waited nearly five hours before William Cecil had been able to see him. When he'd entered Cecil's chambers, that tired gentleman had been hurriedly leaving. Ordered to attend the queen at once, his lordship had given him an apologetic glance and promise that he would not be long as he'd limped along the corridor, and from the flustered look of a member of the queen's guard who'd been sent to escort the Lord Treasurer, Her Majesty was most likely in one of her towering rages and needed to be quieted by the comforting, calming voice of her old friend.

Valentine had sat waiting patiently. Then he'd paced the long, darkened corridor with impatient strides as the hours had slowly passed and he'd thought too often of the woman waiting for *him*. But believing the Turk had brought Francisca aboard the *Madrigal*, and that she was comfortably settled in his cabin, he had not grown overly concerned, just frustrated not to have been with her.

Recalling now his dismay when he'd come aboard after midnight to find his cabin empty, then his shock when he'd heard the reason why, he realized that he had yet another score to settle with Don Pedro Enrique Villasandro, captain of the *Estrella D'Alba*. The Spaniard had plagued him long enough, Valentine mused, vowing to settle that score once and for all.

The Spanish captain had been the reason for Lord Burghley's summons, and Valentine now held Don Pedro indirectly responsible for having put Francisca's life in danger and for what had *not* happened last night aboard the *Madrigal*. Lord Burghley, ever one to advise caution, was concerned about the growing animosity between the two captains and had advised a more conciliatory attitude. Lord Burghley did not wish to see a personal grudge develop into a far more serious incident between the two unfriendly nations. An official complaint from the Spanish ambassador had been lodged against Valentine Whitelaw, listing in fine detail his piratical acts against Spain and her loyal subjects. And Drake, through his latest exploits of plunder throughout Spain's empire in the New World, was causing irreparable harm to the already fragile negotiations.

They did not need yet another Englishman giving Philip more cause to arm Spain against England. Valentine Whitelaw knew that Cecil and the queen were having a battle of their own to maintain England's peace while trying to restrain the warmongering voices of many members of her council, among them Walsingham's, Hatton's, and Leicester's, who were far less pacificatory toward Spain.

Cecil had gone on to inform him that when Don Pedro had been in England the month before, he had inquired about the whereabouts of his enemy, and through sources he would not care to divulge, they had learned that spies were watching Valentine Whitelaw's movements and had been asking quite a few questions along the docks about the future voyages of the *Madrigal*.

Valentine Whitelaw smiled, for Don Pedro Enrique Villasandro would not have to wonder for long. Cecil had also told him that the captain of the *Estrella D'Alba* had sailed for Spain over a fortnight ago, carrying high-placed members of the ambassador's household and other important dignitaries. Indeed, it seemed of late that all of the *Estrella D'Alba*'s voyages had been on the king's business. Her passengers were more often than not traveling on diplomatic missions rather than private business. It would be most embarrassing if an Englishman were to sink a ship in which the Spanish ambassador or any member of his family were sailing, Cecil had said with a judicious shake of his head. Of course, if the *Madrigal* was attacked first, her captain would have every right to defend himself, Cecil had added, not totally lacking in understanding of the situation.

Valentine Whitelaw had been in complete agreement. And, of course, he did have his own spies too, and he would soon know where Don Pedro next planned to sail, and whether his passengers were important enough to allow the *Estrella D'Alba* to go unchallenged. If not, then perhaps they would meet sooner than he had anticipated, Valentine speculated, thinking of his next voyage.

But that would have to wait. At first light, he would try to find Francisca. He *had* to find her. If only he had been there last night when that mob of townspeople had attacked the camp. Mustafa had told him of the stalls and tents set aflame, of the frightened women and children, some huddling in groups, others running blindly into the thick of the fray, and of the animals, driven into a frenzy by the fire, causing panic when stampeding through the camp.

The Turk had been deeply upset by his failure to please his captain. He'd explained that he had rowed over to the riverbank as his captain had ordered, but had found the girl gone. He'd already decided to go in search of her when he'd seen the flames and heard the cries for help. He'd hurried to the camp, arriving in time to see a group of people standing around a man and a woman who'd been wounded during the attack.

He had moved up closer to see if he could be of any assistance. He hadn't been able to see the woman's face, because of the people gathered so close, but her gown, of violet silk, had been stained with blood. Edging even closer, to peer over the shoulders of several people kneeling beside the fallen pair, he had seen the girl the captain had wanted him to bring aboard the

Madrigal, and it had been the same girl, the Turk had reassured his stunned captain. There had been no mistaking the dark red hair and green eyes the captain had described to him.

For a horrible instant, Valentine Whitelaw had believed the dead girl was Francisca, for he remembered only too vividly that gown of violet silk, and he'd felt as if the knife that had mortally wounded her had struck him instead. His mind had filled with the image of her lying on the ground, the blood seeping from her lifeless body.

But the Turk had gone on to say that this Francisca had been kneeling beside a man, who had apparently been wounded trying to defend the woman who had been so brutally attacked. The dead woman had looked like one of the gypsies, her hair black, her skin dark. A silver-haired man, now holding the woman in his arms, had given orders to move the man into one of the carts. The man was not dead yet, although, from the look of the wound, the Turk suspected he soon would be. The silver-haired man had ordered everyone to pack up their belongings. They were leaving the fair and London before dawn and before their attackers returned.

The girl who'd been sitting with the wounded man's head cradled in her lap, had glanced up, her face stained with tears and darkened by the smoke from the fires still burning out of control. The man lying in her arms had moaned in pain, calling her name. It had been Francisca. His hand had grasped hers with surprising strength, for the girl had given a start of surprise and quickly bent over him, listening to his whispered words. She'd looked up at the silver-haired man pleadingly, and the Turk had heard her ask if she and her family were to be allowed to travel with them.

The silver-haired man had shaken his head, saying something abusive to this Francisca, which had caused the wounded man to raise his bloodied shoulders, gasping for breath as he begged the older man to let the girl accompany them. The silver-haired man had hesitated, then nodded his agreement to the man's request.

The Turk had looked discomfited while he'd continued his tale, but Valentine Whitelaw had been insistent. The Turk had tried to speak with the girl when she had gotten to her feet, but she'd stayed beside the man, comforting him. He hadn't been able to get close because of the group surrounding them. He had walked out of sight, not wishing to attract any more attention and had waited. He'd watched the carts rolling out, toward the south. Then he had returned to the ship to await his captain's arrival.

Concluding his story, the Turk had frowned. It had bothered him at the time, this persistent feeling that he knew the girl, but he kept silent, thinking the captain would think him mad. But he did tell the captain something else he'd seen, which had bothered him even more.

Standing in the trees, he had become aware of another man, a gentleman, standing nearby, and also watching the group of vagabonds and gypsies leaving the burning camp. Sensing the man's desire not to be seen, the Turk had lingered, now watching the man instead. To his surprise, after the last cart had rumbled down the lane, the man had stepped from the trees, his face revealed by the flickering light of the flames that continued to burn, sending a reddish glow into the night sky.

The man had glanced around, searching for someone, then, when two rough-looking men had approached him, both carrying cudgels and torches that were still burning brightly, he had handed each of them a purse of money. The Turk had known it was money, because one of the men, less trusting than the other, had tossed down his torch and opened the purse. Pouring the gleaming contents into his palm and weighing the amount, he had nodded to the gentleman, and with a wide grin on his face, he and his friend had hurried away.

The Turk had recognized the fancy-dressed gentleman paying off the two men. It had been an acquaintance of the captain's: Sir Raymond Valchamps.

Sir Raymond Valchamps? Valentine Whitelaw couldn't get the name out of his mind as he continued to wonder why Valchamps had been at the gypsy camp, and why he had been paying off two men who had obviously been part of the mob that had set fire to the gypsies' encampment.

Valentine Whitelaw continued to stand on deck, lost in his thoughts. Quinta was not due in London for almost a fortnight. For now, Sir Rodger was content to remain in London, busy with business affairs. And by tomorrow, the *Madrigal*'s cargo would have been unloaded. He would have time to search for

Francisca. He had to find her, he thought again, unwilling to let her disappear out of his life after that chance sighting of her riding along the riverbank. He knew he would never be able to forget her, to stop wondering about her. The first pale streakings of dawn were lighting the eastern skies when Valentine, preparing to go ashore and begin his search, heard a hail from off the port side.

Much as he enjoyed his nephew's company, Valentine Whitelaw was less than pleased to see Simon waving to him wildly from a boat being rowed close to the *Madrigal* amidships.

"Valentine! Uncle Valentine! You're back!" Simon Whitelaw cried excitedly, and spying his uncle standing on the deck, he nearly fell overboard when he stood up in the small boat, forgetful of where he was as he tried to attract his uncle's attention.

Simon Whitelaw scrambled aboard, his young face mirroring his disturbing adventures of the last day. His doublet was dusty and wrinkled, and there was a rip in one of the sleeves. His hose hadn't fared any better, nor had his shoes, which were caked in dirt. He had a bruise on one thin cheek, and his eyes were bloodshot and heavy-lidded from lack of sleep.

"Good Lord, Simon! What has happened? Nothing wrong at Riverhurst, is there? I was just there yesterday morning to call on Lady Elspeth and Sir William," Valentine exclaimed, worried now that he'd seen his nephew's disheveled appearance.

"No. I was just there. That is how I knew you'd returned to England in time to help. I stopped there to tell them what had happened, and Mother and Sir William told me that you were back. Oh, Uncle Valentine, thank God you have returned," Simon said, his voice hoarse.

"Is there some trouble at Whiteswood? You are not having difficulties with the tenants or servants, are you?" Valentine demanded, but thought it unlikely, since they had known Simon all of his life. "What happened to your cheek? Not in a fight, were you?" Valentine asked doubtfully, for that did not sound like his nephew.

"No," Simon said, looking ashamed. "I fell from my horse. I wasn't watching where I was going. I think I fell asleep. But I'm all right. A few bruises. Kept me from falling asleep again. And everything is fine at Whiteswood. Uncle Valentine, she's gone!" Simon declared, his dark eyes full of anguish.

For a moment, Valentine Whitelaw thought he heard an echo ringing in his ears. Then, eyeing his nephew suspiciously, he wondered what game he was playing?

"Uncle Valentine? Don't you understand? She is gone. So are the others. Lily has disappeared!"

"Lily?"

"Yes, Lily Christian! Dulcie and Tristram, too! And Cappie and Cisco and Raphael and Merry! They've all disappeared. It was that Hartwell Barclay, Valentine. He's the one!" Simon said angrily. "If he hadn't gone into her room and fallen into that tub of water, Lord knows what might have happened, because I believe the groom when he says Hartwell Barclay has been trying to seduce Lily. They weren't safe there! And now, they've run away. The Odells and Tillie too!"

Valentine Whitelaw stared at his nephew in growing concern; never before had he seen Simon in such a state, and he wondered if the lad had been sowing a few wild oats and lifting too many tankards of ale. "Now, Simon, why don't you come into my cabin and lie down. You look tired, lad. We will discuss this after you've had a chance to rest."

"I am tired, Valentine. It seems as if I've been riding since night before last, but I can't rest until we've found them. They're gone, Valentine. They had to leave Highcross because of that Hartwell Barclay. Oh, he denies it all, but I know the truth. I never have liked him much. And now they're trying to say Lily is a witch! I think they wanted to burn her at the stake! Well, they've got me to answer to, as well as my family, and I told them as much. I'll see that reverend in hell first," Simon said, his voice rising heatedly again. "Of course, now that you're here, Valentine, I know you will wish to deal with these upstarts personally. But I shall accompany you. I want to see their smug faces when you toss the lot of them out on their rear ends! Especially the constable and that sour-dispositioned woman and her whey-faced daughter, sitting there like a couple of fat hens ruling the roost already."

Valentine Whitelaw sighed, his glance straying to the distant bank as he said, "Why don't you come below and tell me exactly what has happened."

"I knew I could count on you, Uncle Valentine. All the way back from Highcross, I kept wishing you were back in England. I knew you would know what to do. I think they've gone to find Maire Lester,'' he confided eagerly.

''Who is Maire Lester?''

''The old nursemaid. I know that is where they've gone. She's the only one they could trust. You were out of the country. Artemis is married now and going to have a baby. Quinta's up north somewhere. They must have been terrified, thinking they killed Hartwell Barclay and that the village wanted to burn Lily and arrest the Odells and Tristram for raiding the churchyard. I stopped off in the village to get an ale before riding back to London, and you should have heard the talk,'' Simon exclaimed. ''If we leave right away, Uncle Valentine, we can reach Stratford without any delay,'' Simon said.

''Stratford?''

''Yes, that is where this Maire Lester lives.''

Valentine Whitelaw eyed his nephew, an angry glint in his eye. ''If this is some kind of jest, Simon, by God, I'll—'' he warned.

''Jest?'' Simon croaked, his voice squeaky with indignation. ''Uncle Valentine, I'm telling you the truth. You can go to Highcross and talk to Hartwell Barclay in person, but my sister, and Lily and Tristram, are gone! We've got to find them. They're out there somewhere,'' Simon said, waving his arm so that all directions were encompassed. ''Anything could have happened to them, Valentine. They've been wandering the countryside for months now. Just think of the riffraff that travels the roads. Vagabonds. Deserters. Thieves. Gypsies!''

Valentine nodded slowly. Yes, gypsies, he thought. ''Stratford lies north of here. In Warwickshire, is it not?''

''Yes,'' Simon agreed quickly. ''Not too far from Coventry, or Kenilworth and Charlecote,'' he added, mentioning two of the greater estates Valentine might have visited.

''And you believe Lily, Dulcie, and Tristram have gone there?'' Valentine asked slowly, his gaze lingering a moment longer toward the south, then he glanced away, knowing that he had made his decision. There was no other decision he could have made; Dulcie and the other children were his responsibility. Suddenly, he found himself remembering the vow he had made to Lily Christian years ago. He would always be there for her, he had promised. His vow to protect her and Dulcie and

Tristram came before his selfish desire to find a woman he had wanted only for his bed.

With a bitter smile, Valentine Whitelaw realized that fate was against him this time and some things were not meant to be. "Very well, Simon. Let us hope you are right, and Lily Christian and the others have gone to this Maire Lester's."

"Francisca? My Lily Francisca," Romney Lee murmured feverishly. "Where are you, Francisca? Don't leave me, Francisca. Please, don't ever leave me. It is so dark. I wish there was sunshine. I'm so cold," he said, shivering, then pushing away the blankets and complaining of the heat.

It was afternoon, and although the shadows were lengthening the sun was still shining brightly. In a wide meadow, Silver Jones had halted their flight from London so the animals could rest, and the wounds of those who had been hurt in the fight could be properly treated.

Lily pressed a cooling compress against Romney's burning forehead. "I won't leave you, Rom. I'm here, right beside you," she reassured him, her hand gentle against his lips as she moistened them with a few drops of water.

"My love, my beautiful Lily Francisca," he said, his dark blue eyes staring up at her as if memorizing every beloved feature.

Lily hid her start of surprise well and smiled down into his flushed face.

"I love you, Lily Francisca. I think I always have. You have always been like the fine piece of silver I coveted but had no table to set it on, or the bolt of silk that was too fine for my roughened hand, and that embroidered armchair I wanted but only had a cart to set it in. Always, I have wished for that just beyond my reach. When I saw that man attacking you I felt as if I had lost the most precious thing in my life. I hurried over, but not quick enough. You had fallen. So much blood. Your blood stained my hands. Your blood. So red," he said, beginning to shake violently.

"It is all right, Rom. Please, don't think of it. I am not dead. No one has hurt me," Lily said, trying to quiet him. "I am here, feel me."

Rom grasped her hands in his. "No. You are not dead, are

you? I can smell the fragrance you wear. Your body is warm, not cold with death. Your heart is beating so strongly. I can feel it," he said, lightly placing his hand over her breast.

Lily remained still, allowing him to touch her.

"I am so confused. I thought you had died, and it was all my fault. I had lied to you, and because of my deceit, I had killed you. But then I saw Navarre's face. It was Navarre, wasn't it? She was killed in your place. I couldn't understand. It was like a nightmare. But she was wearing your gown. Francisca?" Rom muttered, both his hands clasping hers. "She was dressed in your lovely violet gown. Francisca? Where are you?" he whispered.

"I am here," Lily said softly.

Navarre. She was dead, and it almost seemed as if she had died by mistake, although Old Maria had seemed to accept what had happened with her usual lack of surprise—as if she had already seen it. Lily drew a shaky breath, remembering the feeling of horror she'd felt seeing Navarre lying there, her sightless eyes staring up at her accusingly. She had been dressed in the gown that she, Lily, had worn that very afternoon. The pale violet silk had been stained with Navarre's blood. Lily swallowed the painful lump in her throat. For an instant, she had felt as if she'd been staring at herself and a chilling premonition had spread through her that had left her shaking with fear.

She realized now that it had been Navarre who'd been watching her by the stream, following her through the copse that afternoon. She must have seen her toss the gown over the tub and, seeing her chance, had stolen it. Navarre had always envied her the gowns she wore.

She had probably found the purse of money too, Lily thought. Valentine Whitelaw's money. She had forgotten it after her wash, and when she'd gone back to get it, remembering she'd left it tied to the waistband of her gown, she'd found that both the purse of money and the gown had disappeared.

"Lily Francisca? Will you forgive me?" Rom pleaded.

"For what, Rom? You are my friend. I will always be grateful to you," Lily told him, smoothing back the chestnut curls clinging damply to his brow.

"Your friend? No, I do not deserve to be. But I have loved

you as I have no other. Do not hate me for stealing this summer from you, Lily Francisca. Do not hate me.''

"I could never hate you, Rom," Lily told him, pressing a kiss against his forehead.

Romney Lee smiled. "Never? I wonder?"

"Do you want to know a secret? I would not have missed this summer, Rom. I've loved traveling with you from fair to fair."

Romney Lee sighed. "We will be happy together, Lily Francisca. We will always travel across England, from fair to fair we will ride. Our puppet show will make us wealthy. We will buy a beautiful wagon. Carved and painted as bright as the sun. It will be our home. We will love there and raise our children. You will lie with me, won't you, Lily Francisca?" he asked, a boyishly innocent expression on his face as he stared up at her.

"Yes, Rom, I will lie with you."

"And be my lover? My only lover, Lily Francisca?"

"Yes, my love."

"My beautiful flower. You do love me, don't you?"

"Yes, Rom, I do love you," Lily told him, and truthfully so, although not in the sense he might wish.

"How I have loved you. Will you kiss me, Lily Francisca?" he asked, his dark blue eyes glazed with pain. "One kiss."

Tears filling her eyes, Lily lowered her mouth to his and let his lips touch hers in a gentle kiss that held the promise of a love that could never be.

Romney Lee stared up into Lily Christian's face, her pale green eyes like a clear pool of water above him, and he felt himself floating away, drifting out of his pain-racked body into a peaceful sleep.

Two hours later, Romney Lee died in Lily Christian's arms. Silver Jones had come up to the cart when he'd seen her climbing from it, his hand steadying her when she'd stumbled.

"We will take him with us to the marshes. 'Tis where both he and Navarre were born, and where they will both be laid to rest," Silver Jones spoke huskily, his bull-shoulders slumped with grief for his niece and the young man he'd always thought of as a son. "I will let Romney Lee's sister know of his death, but he will be buried by us. He was one of us and my Navarre loved him. She had a great deal of money on her when she died. I do not know where she got it, but I will use whatever I need of it to give both of them a decent burial. Navarre would have wanted it that way," he said, almost daring Lily to claim the money as hers, for both she and Silver Jones knew that the gown Navarre had been wearing had been hers.

"You and the others must leave."

Lily nodded. She knew they couldn't return to Kent.

"We only allowed you to stay because of Rom. He convinced us last night to let you stay. Maybe, too, because you did good," he added grudgingly. "You'd better leave soon. It would be best, now that . . ." But he let the rest of his words trail off. "There are some who will blame you for Rom's death. And for Navarre's. Go, now, while you still have some daylight left," Silver Jones advised before he walked away without a backward glance.

Lily walked slowly to their cart. Tristram and Dulcie sat quietly on the edge, their feet dangling while they waited for her return. Tillie and Farley were arguing in loud whispers, and Fairfax sat propped against the side, his head bandaged from the blow he'd received during the scuffle when he'd tried to protect the others from being attacked.

"We are leaving," Lily told them abruptly.

"Rom died, didn't he?" Tristram demanded, his eyes red-rimmed.

"Yes."

"Which way we headed?" Farley asked.

"North. We have no place to go but to Maire Lester's."

"Can't we get Valentine to help us, Lily?" Tristram asked. "Didn't you tell him what happened? Didn't he believe you?"

"He never showed up. He's probably already sailed for Cornwall," Lily said shortly, glad she did not have to face Valentine Whitelaw. There wasn't anything he could do for them. They did not need his help, or his pity, she thought proudly.

"Figured they'd send us packin'," Fairfax grumbled. He had one hell of a headache and he wouldn't be sorry in the least to see the last of this bunch of thieves.

"I'm getting cold, Lily. Can we have a fire tonight?" Dulcie asked, rubbing Raphael's thick coat. "I'm hungry. We haven't eaten all day."

"Yes, we'll have a fire, but let's find somewhere else. Hitch up the oxen, Farley, and we can get a goodly distance before dark. We will rest then," Lily told them, keeping her eyes turned away from the cart where Romney Lee lay. But as she turned away to saddle Merry, Lily's gaze encountered the wizened face of Old Maria. She was standing watching them, a strange, sad smile on her face. She raised her clawlike hand and pointed north, shaking her finger at them. Bent over double by her great age, she shuffled off to resume her vigil by her granddaughter's body.

"Never did like that old witch," Farley mumbled, quickening his work even as his fingers fumbled. "Ye think she just put a curse on us?"

The oxen hitched to the cart, Farley guided them along the road, tapping them every now and then to keep them moving. They followed the road north, and soon the gypsy wagons had been left far behind. They were delayed only briefly when waiting in line to be ferried across the Thames by barge, but soon they were trundling along the narrow, rutted lane.

None of them glanced behind to mark the miles left behind, and so no one saw the shadowy figure on horseback that rode under cover of the trees, or remained just beyond the last bend in the road, always keeping pace, never allowing his quarry out of sight.

*There was a star danced, and under
that was I born.*

SHAKESPEARE

Chapter Twenty-Three

THREE riders rode into Warwickshire. It was a countryside of rolling green meadows grazed by thickly fleeced sheep, densely wooded hills of cedar, oak, and elm, orchards heavy with ripening fruit, and golden fields under harvest, the piles of grain sheaves stacked to cure and dry during the last days of summer. The riders passed through peaceful villages of straw-thatched cottages, sending their horses splashing through the murmuring streams that fed into the gentle waters of the Avon.

The long street of Stratford, a small market town beside the river, was busy with pedestrians and wagons trafficking in goods gathered from other counties before being sent downriver to be traded in the larger towns. Herds of cattle, wagons groaning under the weight of barrels of ale brewed locally, bales of cloth and wool piled high in two-wheeled carts crowded the thoroughfare flanked by half-timbered houses and shops.

Valentine Whitelaw, followed by a curious Simon, who was stretching his neck back and forth in hopes of catching sight of a familiar figure, and the Turk, just behind, rode their horses slowly along Church Street. The droning sound of children's voices reciting memorized sums drifted to the street below from the opened windows of the grammar school directly above the guildhall, where Valentine Whitelaw had intended to stop and inquire of Maire Lester's whereabouts. He hailed a lad hurrying past, apparently late for his lessons, for the boy's expression was harried. Simon glanced at him pityingly, for he would feel the sting of a flogging for his tardiness.

Alas, the lad had never heard of Maire Lester and continued on to class with an apologetic shrug and a wide-eyed stare at the Turk's turban, something he'd have a hard time getting his friends to believe he'd seen.

However, a woman crossing the lane with a basket packed full of long loaves of freshly baked bread was familiar with the name, having met Maire Lester just a week ago last when she'd come into town to do the marketing. Her sister, though, wasn't there, she confided, eyeing the strangers curiously. Moll Crenshaw, Maire Lester's sister, had gone north, to Coventry, where her daughter who was about to have another child lived. Five children already, she'd had, and her husband just an apprentice cobbler. She wouldn't be at all surprised to hear that they were coming back with Moll to live on the farm; after all, Moll was widowed, with no sons, and needed help with the chores. But the woman's conversation came abruptly to an end when she was asked about any strangers staying at the farm with Maire Lester.

Valentine Whitelaw managed to extricate himself from the woman's confidences without satisfying her curiosity and rode on through the town, crossing Clopton Bridge to ride south toward the small farmstead where Maire Lester was living.

"She didn't know anything about them, did she?" Simon asked, frowning.

"Just because she did not have any knowledge of them does not mean that they might not be there, Simon," Valentine told him, but he too thought it doubtful that a woman as well informed of other people's affairs as that one appeared to be would not have heard about the children.

"I suppose Maire could be hiding them? They might fear the authorities will come here looking for them," Simon speculated, lightly touching his heels to his mount to keep pace with the other two riders.

They rode on as directed, passing the gnarled old oak that stood alone on a hillside, then past three farms, before crossing a stream, where an old waterwheel was turning slowly. They traveled another couple of miles, past undulating fields of wild flowers, across an arched stone bridge spanning a swiftly running brook, until at last they saw the farmstead.

"I think it's going to rain, Uncle Valentine," Simon muttered, unnecessarily drawing his uncle's attention to the worsening weather. He'd been watching the clouds darkening to the east for the last half an hour, and he could have sworn he'd heard a distant rumbling of thunder.

"You're probably right, Simon," Valentine agreed, thinking it would somehow be appropriate that they should get soaked in a cloudburst.

They left the narrow lane and followed what was little more than a path cut between hedgerows to the rambling outbuildings. A cow byre and hayloft were to the left, across from a humble-looking stable with a lean-to for pigs and poultry, while a dovecoat and large barn rose behind. They entered a courtyard surrounded by a low, stone wall and dismounted before a long farmhouse that looked deserted.

Simon, however, soon discovered that it wasn't. Impatient to learn if Lily and the others were there, with youthful exuberance he stepped ahead of Valentine and hurried to the door of the farmhouse, prepared to bang unceasingly until someone answered. To his surprise, a squealing pig came racing through the door, scooting between his legs as it shot into the yard beyond. Simon fell backward and rolled over and was crouched in an undignified position trying to rise when a woman swinging a broom barreled through the door after the pig, the broom coming into contact with his seat when she mistook him for the culprit who'd made a shambles of the kitchen.

"Oh! Good Lord! Who and what ye be then?" the woman, tall and raw-boned, but with a ready smile, demanded indignantly. Then, peering closer at the lad she'd just struck so insultingly, she exclaimed, "Why, Master Simon, whatever are ye doin' down on all fours?"

Simon snorted, sounding a bit like that pig, and drew himself up to his full height with as much dignity as he could muster under the circumstances. "I—we—have come in search of Lily Christian, Tristram, and Dulcie. Are they here?"

The woman stared at him dumbfounded. "Here? Now whatever would they be doin' here?" she asked, eyeing the other two gentlemen more closely. "Why, it be the captain?"

"Yes. Maire Lester, is it not?"

"Oh, aye, ye be rememberin' me, then?" she said, pleased for a brief instant, then she frowned. "Mistress Lily and young Master Tristram and the little one, here?" she repeated incredulously.

"They've run away from Highcross!" Simon blurted out, unable to contain himself or his disappointment as he slammed his fist against the doorjamb.

"Run away, have they?" she murmured thoughtfully, a glint coming into her eyes. "I'll bet that Hartwell Barclay has something to do with this," she said, meeting Valentine Whitelaw's curious gaze. "Always was after the young mistress, couldn't fool me, he couldn't with his blustering ways. Why ye think he got rid of me? Owed it to the good captain and that lovely wife of his, the Doña Magdalena, to protect their children, especially the young mistress. Always pawin' her, his nabs was. Reckon there be a lot of other things he was thinkin' about and plannin'. Never did understand how Master Tristram fell from the roof, or even why he was up there in the first place. And later, when the young mistress wrote to me to tell what was goin' on, never did I understand how that window got left open in Dulcie's chamber. Nearly caught her death of cold, she did. Poor little dear. How I do miss them. Reckon ol' Hartwell Barclay thought if there wasn't any heirs left, he could inherit Highcross. Oh, aye, don't be lookin' so surprised, wouldn't put murder past him at all. And when that failed, well, bet he was tryin' to get into the young mistress's bed, he was. 'Fraid, what with her bein' so fair and an heiress, that he'd be losin' his position at Highcross soon enough. Aye, I seen how jittery he got when young Master Simon here came a-callin'. Sweet on Mistress Lily, he is," Maire Lester said, her eagle eye having missed nothing all these years.

"I told you so, Uncle Valentine!" Simon exclaimed, although his cheeks were flushed with embarrassment by the nurse's bluntness concerning his intentions toward Lily Christian.

"Ye thought they might be comin' here, to their old nurse, eh?" Maire Lester speculated aloud. "Could be ye be right about that. Maybe they'll be showin' up soon."

"I doubt it," Simon said with a dejected glance around. "They've been missing since before summer."

"Lord! That long, is it? And how is it that ye just be lookin' fer them now?'' she demanded angrily, her hands on her hips as she stared at them, and both Simon and Valentine were momentarily reminded of their old nurses and having to face them after some misconduct.

"I have been neglectful of them," Valentine said shortly. He had been concerned before to learn that the children were traveling about the countryside unescorted except for the Odells, but now, to realize that they'd been in danger even at Highcross, he was heartsick and guilt-ridden at his own duplicity in having allowed such a situation to develop. He had been away on his voyages too often, and when in England he'd spent too much time at Ravindzara. He had seldom given the children more than a passing thought or visit through the years. He had left them to the mercy of Hartwell Barclay.

The Turk, watching his captain, saw the recognizable gleam that entered Valentine Whitelaw's eyes and he smiled in anticipation of the reckoning he knew would soon follow. Unconsciously, his hand began to caress the ornate hilt of the scimitar while he contemplated Hartwell Barclay's demise.

"The poor little dears. All by themselves. Alone and hungry, maybe even hurt, why, the kinds of folk that travel the roads nowadays, well, a decent, God-fearin' person has to beware," Maire Lester said, clucking her tongue. "Don't care to be here by myself, I don't. Had a troupe of actors stumble by the other day. The way they carry on, why, faith, but I didn't know when they was jestin' or not. Goin' to London, they were. End up beggin' in the streets most likely. Think they'd find decent work. And to think, my poor little ones out there by themselves."

"Oh, they're not alone. Farley and Fairfax are with them," Simon volunteered. "And that maid."

Maire Lester's eyes looked like black currants about to pop from her head. Opening her lips to speak, she found her breath had escaped her and she just stood there staring, her mouth hanging open.

"Well!" she finally managed to breathe. "Well, I never heard such a thing! The Odells! Lord, but I'm glad ye didn't tell me that right away or I would have fainted dead on ye. Farley and Fairfax and this maid—Tillie, I'll wager 'twas—there's never been a more misbegotten pair than the two of them beef-heads. And that Tillie, if she's got a brain in her head she don't know it.

I should have known them Odells were involved in this. If the children didn't have enough trouble before, then they sure as do now.''

Simon Whitelaw looked at his uncle. He wondered if it had been a good idea after all to come to Stratford in search of Maire Lester, conveniently forgetting that it had been his suggestion in the first place, for the woman was depressing him with all of this talk about the unsuitability of the Odells.

''Well, if the children are not here, and you have not seen them since you left Highcross, then all we can do is return to Highcross and speak a little more bluntly with Hartwell Barclay. He may know more than he is telling us,'' Valentine said. ''That is one conversation I am looking forward to.''

''I'll be comin' with ye, then,'' Maire Lester decided. ''Never did like it here. Can handle children better than I can animals, especially that porker. Meanest, sneakiest pig I've ever met,'' she said, glancing past them to where the old sow was rooting in the garden.

''I think it would be best if you stayed here, at least until we discover where the children are,'' Valentine advised. ''Simon may be right and they might be trying to travel here. We will search the roads and villages between here and Highcross. They may have met with an accident.''

''Very well, sir, but it don't set my mind any easier wonderin' about what has happened to them and where they be right now. I only hope they do show up here, and I'll have a thing or two to say to them Odells.''

''If they should, tell them that we are searching for them and that they have nothing to worry about. Hartwell Barclay is not dead. And he will no longer have any say in their welfare,'' Valentine told her as he walked to his horse and prepared to mount. ''I will deal with Hartwell Barclay. They need never fear him again.''

''More's the pity he's still alive,'' Maire Lester said, not in the least bit concerned about the health of Hartwell Barclay.

''You will tell them what I've said if they arrive?'' Valentine reminded her.

''Oh, aye, that I will. And ye will let me know if ye be findin' them?'' she reminded him, her gaze narrowed speculatively on his lean figure as he sat his horse so easily, as if he was a man who was always in control and seldom knew defeat, and she hoped Hartwell Barclay got everything he deserved and then some.

"When we find the children and return them to their rightful place at Highcross, then you will be sent for, Maire Lester. And thank you for the information about Hartwell Barclay," Valentine said, nodding to her.

"My pleasure. Looks like 'tis goin' to open up and rain on ye. Don't know that ye'll make the village before it does. I'd offer ye lodging here, but there's only the one bed, and, well," she added a bid defensively, "I'm not a very good cook. Never had to worry about fixin' more than a bit of gruel fer the babies. Never had to cook my own meals at Highcross, always ate with the rest of the servants in the kitchen. Plenty of food already set on the table. I've just got some bread and cheese and a little broth I'm goin' to heat up when I start the fire after dark. Moll counts every stick of wood," she added apologetically.

"Thank you, but I think we can make it back to Stratford before it begins to rain," Valentine reassured her, much to Simon's relief.

"Already gettin' cool in the evenings. Winter's comin' on. Hate to think of them without shelter," Maire Lester fretted, wringing her hands as if Hartwell Barclay's neck was stretched out between them. "Ye'll be stayin' overnight in Stratford, then be headed toward Coventry in the mornin'? Follow the road that way?" she asked.

"No. I do not think they would have come by the North road. It is too far out of their way, especially if they didn't go through London. And no one they might have gotten in contact with in London has seen them. We traveled west along the main road out of London. We came north through Cirencester. Although we expected to find the children here, we asked of them in every village along the road and we heard nothing. No one had seen them passing through. We know they took the cart and a team of oxen, so they would have to follow the roads, and no one has seen them," Valentine said, tapping his gloves against his thigh impatiently. "We thought to travel into Oxfordshire and Buckinghamshire this time, perhaps they took the road through Oxford. 'Tis well traveled."

"Aye, they might. Even if they came up through London,

then came as far north as St. Albans, they might have gone west there; the road meets with the one comin' out of Oxford. Ye might hear about them there. They might have gone north at the crossroads, come up past Buckingham and Towcester. Since ye already traveled the main road, there's a short cut ye can take that'll take ye right to the road somewhere between Burford and Minster Lovell. If they been through there at all, then someone will have seen them," she told them, going on to tell them how to find the shortcut. "Lord, but ye've got a lot of country to cover," she predicted, none too hopefully.

"It may take time, but we will find them," Valentine White-law promised.

Maire Lester continued to stand outside the quiet farmhouse after she'd watched the three riders disappear down the road and even after the first light rain started to fall. With a feeling of helplessness, she turned and entered the house, wondering where Lily Christian and her young brother and sister were.

"Are we there yet, Lily? How much longer?" Dulcie de-manded with a shiver, eyeing the deepening shadows of the wold that seemed to be closing in around them while they rum-bled along the lane wending through the thickly wooded slopes.

"How many nights have we camped out without seein' a livin' soul?" Farley asked of no one in particular as he walked beside the oxen, guiding the plodding pair along the lane.

"Seems like we been traveling through this valley fer years," Fairfax commented from his position at the side of the cart, his heavy shoulders, eased against the side every so often, helping the big wheels through the worst of the ruts. "And I'm not cer-tain I want to see anyone."

"Why's that, Fairfax?" Tristram asked, tossing a couple of sweet berries, plucked from a thicket they'd passed, into his mouth in quick succession as he walked behind with Raphael trotting at his heels.

" 'Cause we be strangers hereabouts. And 'cause, most likely, they'd be poachers," Farley answered. "And we don't want to get mixed up with the likes of them or any royal keepers out lookin' fer them. So no venison pie tonight," he advised.

Tristram glanced around worriedly, swallowing nervously when he saw a herd of fallow deer grazing under the trees nearby. "You don't think there are any poachers hiding around here, do you, Farley? I feel like there are eyes watching us from the underbrush."

Farley shrugged. "Could be they been busy stringin' their nets up between the trees, then they'll have their dogs run the deer into them. Makes a decent enough livin', I s'pose, if ye stay a step ahead of the keeper," he warned with a chuckle.

"Heard tell, Farley, that some poachers even have false bottoms to their carts. Don't reckon young Master Tristram and ol' Ruff have been doin' a bit of poachin' and we're sittin' on a load of venison?"

Tristram sighed. "I wish I had," he said, thinking of a thick roast of venison sizzling on a spit.

"Are there still wolves in these woods, Lily?" Dulcie asked, pulling her feet up into the cart just in case.

"I thought I heard one howling at the moon last night," Tristram said, mimicking a wolf despite the warning look Lily gave him.

"*Prraaack!* Wolves! *Aaaaaooooooooh!*" Cisco repeated the howl, causing Dulcie to squeal loudly in fear, while Cappie, echoing her cries, ducked beneath Tillie's arm and tried to hide behind her ample form where she sat half-leaning against the side of the cart, her swollen feet dangling over the back.

"Ye know, now ye mention it, Master Tristram," Fairfax said, rubbing the blond beard covering his square chin, "I thought I heard someone, or something, prowling about our camp last night."

"Probably a wild boar. Ye don't look so good, Tillie dear," Farley said, noticing the greenish tinge to her face.

"She kind of looks the color of green peas," Dulcie commented helpfully.

"She's seasick," Tristram said, stepping away from the cart.

"Seasick in a cart?" Fairfax roared with laughter.

"'Tis the same motion as aboard ship," Tristram said knowledgeably. "Back and forth. Back and forth. Up and down. Up and down. Swishing your innards back and forth, up and down, back and forth."

Lily, sitting astride Merry, eyed her brother with growing irritation. "I think you have explained well enough," she told him rather shortly, causing Tristram to eye her more closely lest she be coming down with the same ailment Tillie was suffering from. He sighed, mumbling an apology, but continued to watch his sister. She'd been so quiet since they'd left London and since Romney Lee had died. At night, when she thought everyone was asleep, he had heard her weeping and in the morning she sounded like she was coming down with the sniffles.

"If ye hadn't taken the wrong road back there in Cirencester, bet we'd be in Stratford already," Farley complained.

"If ye hadn't fallen asleep, then I would've had somebody to ask, now wouldn't I? Not that ye wouldn've known any better than me which road was which," Fairfax charged, not willing to shoulder the blame.

"Well, anybody who's got any sense can tell which way the sun is risin', can't they? Ye was headed east, Fairfax, not north!" Farley maintained. "That last village we was in was Burford. Now, if we was goin' through Burford, which we shouldn't have been if ye'd been on the right road, then we would've been goin' west, not east. We should have been in Northleach, headin' toward Stratford."

"Well, I can't be expected to know everything, Farley," Fairfax answered stoutly, thinking some people were beginning to expect too much from a fellow. "I never been outside of East Highford till a few months ago."

"No harm was done," Lily said placatingly. "We just lost a couple of hours. We're headed in the right direction again. If this shortcut takes us across-country like that farmer said, then we'll end up having saved hours and we should join the main road north of that other village."

"I sure hope that fella knew what he was sayin'; smelled pretty strongly of ale, if ye asks me. Don't think he knew what we was talkin' about half the time; probably went and tried to milk that bull he had out to pasture," Farley muttered, wishing he'd a spot of ale to quench his thirst rather than the fresh water he'd had to make do with for the last few days.

"Don't know if it be such a good idea to be way off the main road like this, Mistress Lily," Fairfax said worriedly, glancing over his shoulder. "What if we was to get stuck, or lose a wheel, or what if this path don't go anywheres near this road? No one would ever know what happened to us. 'Tis awfully lonely out here," he said, noting the rolling hills that rose around them, and where it seemed only wild hare and hart roamed.

"Well, one of us could always walk to the nearest village. That farmer said there was one called Chipping something not too far north of here," Farley suggested, but the look of worry on Fairfax's face bothered him. "What ye really be worried about?"

Fairfax hunched his shoulders, glancing uneasily at Lily Christian riding Merry a few strides ahead now. "I didn't take too kindly to the way them ruffians we passed on the road was eyein' Mistress Lily. She's too pretty, Farley, to be ridin' around on that big white horse, no gentleman with her for protection from the likes of them. Ain't a man this side of London who hasn't thought about her after she's caught his eye. And she's damned hard to miss. I've been real worried, that I have, Farley. They might not think she's a gentlewoman, seein' how she's with us. And nobody is likely to mistake us fer gentlemen."

"Aye, ye be right there," Farley agreed, eyeing his brother up and down. "Well, I reckon we can handle any trouble that comes along," Farley added, beginning to feel some of his brother's uneasiness. "Ye say ye thought ye heard something in the bushes last night?"

"Aye, prowlin' around 'twas. Ye know, I been feelin' fer the last few days like someone's been watchin' us. Just like Master Tristram has."

"Someone watchin' us?" Farley said with an incredulous glance around. "Who? No one knows we're here, nor even who we be. And them fellas, ye didn't see them until yesterday. Just yer nerves, Fairfax. Ye know how ye get when ye ain't eaten proper."

"Aye, s'pose ye be right. And, like ye says, Farley, the two of us can take care of anyone who thinks they got business with us when they don't," Fairfax said, a mulish look on his face that gave fair warning.

"It kind of looks like 'tis goin' to rain," Tillie said, eyeing the clouds with a frowning glance. "I hope we can find some shelter fer the night. 'Tis gettin' late. Maybe we should stop soon," she suggested, the green tinge to her face deepening when the wheels rolled over a large hump in the road.

"Just a little farther, Tillie dear," Farley told her. "Be on the lookout fer a nice-sized tree, Master Tristram. We'll pull right up under it, give us some protection fer tonight. Get our fire goin' and maybe trap a hare or a nice, fat trout, and if it starts to rain, then we'll sleep underneath the cart. Look fer a tree well back from the lane, that way we'll have plenty of privacy, Master Tristram. That's a good lad," he said, and only Fairfax knew that his brother intended for them to remain unseen by anyone passing along the lane.

Valentine Whitelaw glanced around. Nothing. Ahead, stretched the road. Behind them, stretched the road. And yet no shortcut.

They had left the inn in Stratford early, just after breakfast. They had wasted little time in reaching the road and turning south. They'd traveled along the narrow, muddied track, searching for the shortcut Maire Lester had told them about. But, if they had followed her directions correctly, they should have seen the old windmill a couple of miles ago. They had missed it.

"I think we've missed the shortcut, Uncle Valentine," Simon said. "I've looked and looked, but I haven't been able to see any windmill. I guess we'll have to follow the road all the way to Cirencester. We'll be hours and hours now."

"We have no other choice, unless we go back to Stratford and ask directions again," Valentine said, feeling time slipping away from them while they sat there in the middle of the road.

"Why don't you ask him? He looks like a local," Simon suggested as they watched a young man of less than twenty approaching along the road. He did not see them at first, so lost in his thoughts did he seem, but upon spying them blocking his path, he quickened his step.

"A good day to you, gentlemen. A fine morning, 'tis, after a storm," the young man greeted them, a bright curiosity in his eyes as he stared at them, his gaze lingering longest on the Turk.

"And a good day to you. We were told there was a shortcut through to the road to Oxford. We are strangers to this shire and unfamiliar with the countryside. Maire Lester, who told us of this path, directed us to an old windmill. Have you knowledge of this path?"

"Maire Lester? The name is familiar. Ah, Moll Crenshaw's

sister. Yes, I remember now. I visited the farm not less than a week ago when a troupe of actors was passing through Stratford. I fear she found them most tedious. But I must confess to having been entertained by their conversation and talk of London. Although, 'twas Maire Lester who entertained us the most with her stories of the family she once worked for. Now, the shortcut you speak of, sir, is not more than a mile or so back the way you have come. 'Tis understandable you missed it, for 'tis beyond a grassy bank, where the honeysuckle grows thick and sweet and where I have spent many an enjoyable hour lying beneath a stout oak; however, 'tis easy to miss if you are not familiar with the lane.''

"But where is the windmill Maire Lester told us about?'' Simon questioned. ''I don't see how I could have missed it?''

'' 'Tis enringed by ivy. One might believe 'tis a lofty cedar stretching to the sky. One night, a lone rider passing along this lane claimed to have seen the moon riding astride the sails. 'Tis the only time I've heard of it spinning since a noble roe was wounded through the heart and died beneath the windmill's shadow. They say it stopped singing with the winds out of sadness. 'Twould certainly have been an enchanted night,'' he said with a smile. ''I am going that way, so I will point it out to you,'' the young man offered, beginning to walk down the lane.

"Thank you. That is most kind of you . . .'' Valentine Whitelaw paused, unable to thank the obliging man by name.

"Will. William Shakespeare. I live in Stratford. My father owns a shop there. He is a glove maker.''

"Master Shakespeare. I am Valentine Whitelaw, and this is my nephew, Simon Whitelaw, and this is Mustafa, my friend and most trusted companion,'' Valentine made the introductions. ''We are in your debt, sir, for we would have lost valuable time if we had missed this shortcut.''

"Oh? Indeed, sir, then I am most heartily glad to have been of some service to you. I trust your business will be concluded to your satisfaction,'' he replied politely.

"You haven't by any chance seen three young people, strangers to these parts, traveling in a cart pulled by oxen? They would be in the company of two men, one large, the other short, and a woman? And, they might even have had a monkey and a parrot, as well as a mastiff traveling with them?'' Valentine questioned.

"No, I am afraid I have not seen them, and I would surely have remembered such unusual traveling companions—although, I am reminded of something. . . . Ah, they are the very same ones Maire Lester spoke of, yes? You are searching for them?''

"Yes, they've run away from their guardian, who mistreated them, and we have to find them,'' Simon said.

"How unfortunate. They seem to have led a life full of misadventure,'' Will Shakespeare said. "I do wish you well. Whitelaw?'' he murmured. "The name sounds familiar. Have I heard it before, sir?'' he questioned, gazing at the Turk more closely, his eyes narrowed with interest as if he longed to know the reason why a Turkish gentleman was traveling with an Englishman in the heart of England.

"My uncle is a famous privateer. He has sailed with Drake, and now he is captain of his own ship, the *Madrigal*,'' Simon told the young man proudly when Valentine remained silent.

"Of course. I am honored, sir. I have heard of your exploits. I have listened with great interest to news of such travels. Would it be too much to ask, sir, if you might share with me a few descriptions of the New World while we walk along the road? I would like to learn more of those strange lands and your travels,'' he requested, and for the next half hour his questions came without end while he listened attentively, his eyes aglow with dreams as yet unfulfilled.

"Perhaps one day you will travel to the New World and be able to see it for yourself,'' Valentine said with a smile for the young man's wide-eyed interest.

"Oh, I doubt that, sir, for I am to wed in two months' time. I shall not wander far from Stratford. I doubt I shall even travel as far as London,'' Will Shakespeare announced. "There 'tis, the windmill. If you look carefully, you might be able to make out the sails,'' he said, pointing to a bulky shape through the trees, and Valentine Whitelaw was not surprised that they'd missed it the first time. "It has been a pleasure, sir. Godspeed you on your next voyage. Master Simon, Mustafa,'' he nodded to them.

Valentine Whitelaw bid him a friendly farewell before he sent his horse up the grassy bank, toward the windmill.

"So long," Simon called when William Shakespeare glanced back and waved, and while Simon watched, the young man disappeared along the road.

"Dulcie, aren't you hungry?" Lily asked in concern, placing her hand against Dulcie's forehead.

Dulcie sneezed a couple of times in response, then grinned up at her sister through a tangle of black hair. "I'm starved," she said, fidgeting beneath Lily's hand while her sister tried to brush some order into her curls.

"I thought we were going to eat rabbit last night," she demanded.

"Farley couldn't catch one," Lily said, trying to hide her own disappointment at the stale loaf of bread and narrow wedge of cheese they'd had to divide up for dinner. They'd eaten the last of the meat pie they'd bought in Burford for dinner the night before, and the last of the fruit and nuts had disappeared at lunch.

"What about that fat trout?"

"Farley couldn't see in the dark, dear," Lily explained. It had taken Farley and Fairfax so long in their unsuccessful try to catch a rabbit, that it had grown dark before they'd had a chance to try their luck in the shallow stream that ran through the trees nearby.

"Things will be different today, I promise," Lily said, kissing Dulcie's wide brow. The sun was shining and Farley and Tristram had gone ahead to make certain the narrow track they were following was passable. Lily raised her face to the warmth of the sun. The rain, falling in cold sheets the night before, hadn't helped their dispositions, especially when it had put out their fire and the smoke had drifted eerily through the trees and hung in a haze over their camp while they'd huddled on the cold ground beneath the cart.

"Cappie's not hungry. He's been stuffing himself on berries and nuts all morning," Dulcie said enviously while she watched the monkey select another berry from the small pile he'd collected during his early morning foray in the woods. His velvet cap was covered with stickers from the brambles he'd explored, and he'd lost one of the tinkling bells from its pointed tip, which seemed to concern him, for he kept pulling his hat off and examining it closely.

Fairfax had reloaded the cart and wandered off to explore. Tillie was sitting in the space enlarged for her in the back of the cart in case she wanted to lie down and nap during the day. She was mending a pair of Farley's hose, while Cisco walked his perch on the rail, mimicking the chirping of birds and other animals he'd heard during the night. Hearing a startled neigh, Lily looked over in surprise to where Merry had been grazing peacefully in a small meadow, a long length of rope keeping him from straying too far. He was standing still, staring off into the trees. He neighed again, then when there was only silence, he began to feed.

Raphael, who'd been lying at Dulcie's feet, stood up, his ears perked as he listened to something in the trees. Lily was startled to hear him growl and see his fur rising along his spine with warning.

Lily handed Dulcie the brush and walked away from the cart to stare at the shadowy copse just the far side of the meadow.

"Fairfax? Is that you? Hello! Is there anyone there?" she called, shielding her eyes to stare more deeply into the trees. "Fairfax?" Lily called again, but there was no answer.

"What is it, Lily?" Dulcie demanded, coming to stand between Lily and Raphael, who'd followed just a step behind Lily like the good watchdog he was.

"I don't know. Probably a doe and more startled than we," Lily said, shrugging off the strange sensation she'd had of being watched.

"Oh, look! There! 'Tis Tristram and Farley, and Fairfax is with them!" Dulcie cried, racing to meet them as they approached from near the copse of trees Lily had been staring into just moments ago.

"Guess what, Lily?" Tristram said, hurrying ahead.

"You saw the road?" Lily guessed, her spirits lifting.

"Well, not exactly, but we did see a farm," he explained. "And we saw some people. There was a woman out feedin' the chickens, with a couple of little children hanging on to her skirts. I saw her husband coming out of the barn with some cows."

" 'Tis through them trees, other side the dale. I was figurin' that I might amble on over there with some of those fancy ribbons and sweet-scented sachets ye made and never got a chance to sell, Mistress Lily. Thought I'd trade them fer some food. Few eggs, bread, cheese, maybe even a nice roast chicken. Reckon the lady down there might want some pretties she can't get without a long trip into the nearest village. And from the look of them kids of hers, I'd reckon she don't get into the village very often. And, of course, I'd be sellin' the ribbons mighty cheap," Farley explained. "Even thought I'd dig into that trunk and get a couple of knives we don't use. Reckon they'd come in handy on the farm. Always use them fer something."

"Can I go too?" Tristram cried.

"Well, I don't know, Master Tristram. Ye'll have to ask Mistress Lily."

"You may go, but I expect you to give Farley a hand," Lily warned.

"Oh, I will, Lily. I will!" Tristram beamed.

"I've been thinkin', Mistress Lily, that the young master might be able to entertain the little ones, keep 'em busy, while I'm about my business. Ye still got them little boxes ye been jugglin'?"

"I can juggle?" Tristram asked, racing away to find the colored boxes before waiting for an answer.

"I was also wonderin', mistress, if ye've still got that one puppet. Ye know, the only one that survived the fire?" Farley asked curiously.

"The witch?"

"Aye, that be the one. Remember his ugly face, I do."

"Yes, I kept it in my trunk. I thought we'd be making more for another puppet show," Lily said, her expression becoming sad as she remembered Romney Lee. The show had really been his. He had been the inspiration behind so many things, she thought, missing him.

"I thought it might amuse the children and the older folks. Get them in the proper mood fer a little tradin'," Farley said, his smile widening as if he could already boast a successful trade.

"I'll find it. Don't you want to go, Fairfax?" Lily asked, for Fairfax had been unusually quiet.

"I thought I'd stay behind, Mistress Lily. Thought while Farley was away doin' the barterin' I might just catch us one of them fat trout I saw in the stream. Make a tasty breakfast, it would," Fairfax said, smacking his lips. "Have it all baked, ready to eat when they get back with the rest of our meal."

"Aye, and 'twould be best if there was someone here with ye," Farley added.

"Maybe I oughta stay, too," Tristram offered, but Lily knew he was eager to go with Farley, because he was already tossing the boxes into the air.

"We won't be gone long. We'll just be through them trees, other side of the brook. In fact, I think I saw where this track heads away into the trees this side of that farm. Bet the road ain't far after that. That farmer has to have a way to get to market. Reckon we're gettin' toward the end of our journey, Mistress Lily," Farley said, pleased with the fine way the day had begun thus far.

Climbing into the cart, Lily opened the big trunk that had been carried down from her bedchamber that night when Hartwell Barclay had met his death and they had fled Highcross. When she opened the lid, the aromatic fragrance of lavender and roses, and the spicy scent of potpourri drifted to her. It held most of her worldly goods—at least, her most prized possessions. It had traveled far with her since that night, she thought, staring down at the neatly packed clothes, boxes, and bundles that Tristram and Dulcie had added to it for safekeeping. Her thoughts went to Romney Lee again, for he had always come close when she'd opened it, staring down at the contents, his hands gently touching the items, occasionally holding one of the vials of perfume to his nose, or carefully handling a scented handkerchief or stocking, a devilish glint in his eye, as if daring her to scold him.

Lily's pleased expression faded when she saw the puppet. It was a horrible creature, she decided, suddenly finding the wooden face disturbing with its sightless blue and brown painted eyes staring up at her.

"I see ye found the wicked creature," Farley said with a grin. "I'll take real good care of him. He might just bring us good fortune, or at least a berry tart fer lunch," he declared, his rough hands taking hold of the dangling puppet and tucking it beneath his arm with the ribbons and sachets he'd unearthed from the cart.

"I hope ye be good enough fer a couple of them tarts, Farley. I'm awful hungry. I don't know what I'm goin' to do if I don't

get something to eat soon,'' Tillie said. ''Feel like a troop of soldiers be stompin' around inside of me.''

''Aye, we'll get ye them tarts. Better get hoppin', Fairfax,
'cause Master Tristram and me'll get back before ye can say Ol'
King Harry, who next will he marry! Come on, lad, we're off!''
Farley said, beckoning to Tristram, who was still practicing his
art.

Lily watched until they disappeared into the trees, Tristram
waving wildly before doing a handspring, and Lily found herself
smiling. Turning away, she saw that Tillie had returned to her
mending, another pair of hose, much longer ones these, waiting
in a rumpled pile next to her.

''Goin' to take more thread than I've got to mend Fairfax's
hose,'' she said with a halfhearted laugh, her stomach growling
so loudly that Dulcie and Raphael stopped their frolicking to
stand and listen. Lily tried to keep from laughing when Raphael
crept up closer, then with a whine turned tail and shot behind
the cart.

Fairfax couldn't contain his laughter. ''Couldn't figure it out
fer a second, how there could be thunder with blue sky above.
Reckon Farley oughta get a cartload of them tarts,'' he chuckled,
carefully winding a length of string around his big fist, his chest
shaking with suppressed laughter.

''Why don't you look for some sweet berries, Dulcie? We can
eat them while we wait,'' Lily suggested, much to Tillie's relief.

''Reckon I'll catch that trout now,'' Fairfax said, wandering
off toward the stream that ran beside the meadow.

''Here's a basket you can put the berries in.''

''You want to help me, Lily?'' Dulcie invited, taking the basket over her arm.

''I saw a deep pool yesterday before it grew dark. I thought
I'd wash by it since we've the time,'' Lily said, collecting her toiletries from the trunk.

''Give us a buss, sweeting,'' Cisco said, coming close to have
his head scratched, his eyes searching the trunk for a tasty
morsel his mistress always managed to find for him. Ruffling his
feathers with pleasure, he strutted off with a nut held in his
beak.

''Oh, Lily, do I have to wash, too?'' Dulcie cried. She didn't mind swimming, but washing with soap and water was different.

Lily eyed her little sister's grubby face. "It might not be a bad idea. But you can find those berries first," she decided, thinking of the stains that would be around Dulcie's mouth and on her hands by the time she returned.

"Can I go swimming?" she asked eagerly, Raphael barking his agreement as he sensed her excitement.

"The water is far too cold," Lily told her, wishing that they both could go for a swim. "Come on, I'll walk with you part of the way," she said, Cappie jumping onto Raphael's back so he wouldn't be left behind. "I'll be over there, in that small copse where the stream is dammed," she said, leaving Dulcie to race through the meadow with Raphael. Cappie was holding on tight, perched precariously on his back, while Raphael barked loudly at her heels.

The woods were quiet except for the chirpings of birds high in the trees, and even the stream seemed hushed as it fed into the pool. The forest floor beneath Lily's feet was soft, cushioned by a thick layer of fallen leaves. The sunlight filtered in through the maze of interwoven boughs overhead.

Lily paused, startled, when a doe and her fawns bolted from beside the pool where they'd been drinking. Lily found a bank that sloped gently toward the clear, deep water and dropped her soap, folded inside a soft cloth with her brush and comb, and her lotions into the tall grasses.

Standing beside the pool, Lily was reminded of the pool on the island, where she had often bathed, and where she and Dulcie had so often sat beside their mother on the bank. *So long ago*, Lily thought, unfastening her skirt and bodice and slipping out of them. She untied her petticoats, carefully folding them and placing them on top, then kicked off her slippers and quickly pulled off her stockings, anxious to bathe the grime of several days of journeying on dusty roads from her skin.

Clad only in her thin linen shift, Lily sat down on the edge of the bank and lowered her bare legs into the cold water, shivering slightly with the shock of the icy contact. After a moment, she splashed the water higher, until the edges of her shift were soaked and clung to her body.

Reaching for her soap, she rubbed it into the cloth and

soaped her legs and arms, the scent of lavender clinging to her flesh even after she'd rinsed the soap with clear water. Taking the sweet-scented lotion, she smoothed the oily substance into her skin, her hands rubbing along her thighs and calves, then her upper arms and shoulders. She took her brush and began to draw it through the long strands of hair while she brushed it across her shoulder.

Her head was downbent, toward the water while she brushed, and Lily found herself staring into the water, mesmerized by the gentle, widening circles that seemed to spread out from the center.

Suddenly Lily gasped. Behind her rose a cloaked figure. Slowly, unable to move, she watched as the arm holding the heavy stick lowered toward her. She screamed, then felt a blinding pain in her temple before the blackness of the pool engulfed her and the face of Sir Raymond Valchamps faded before her to be replaced by the grinning face of the puppet.

The puppet jumped up and down, his comical antics eliciting squeals of delight from the two children old enough to enjoy a puppet show, but the youngest, a baby still held close to his mother's breast, cried at the sight of the frightening creature.

Farley Odell scowled at the child, thinking this was going to be harder than he'd anticipated, for the farmer stood watching them, unimpressed so far by their performance.

At Farley's signal, Tristram began juggling the colorful boxes with an agility that soon had the farmer nodding his approval and the children begging to be taught such a feat.

While Tristram kept the children, even the bawling brat, spellbound, Farley drew out the brightly colored silk ribbons, allowing them to wave enticingly before the woman's face. He yawned slightly, as if bored, hiding his grin when he saw the woman's eyes gradually slide over to where the ribbons dangled from his outstretched arm.

"Henry, look at them. If they ain't the prettiest silks I've ever seen," she breathed.

Henry glanced over. "Got yerself a ribbon fer the Michaelmas fair. Reckon that be enough."

The woman's expression fell, but she couldn't draw her eyes away from the silken display of ribbons. Farley Odell eyed this

Henry fellow with growing dislike, thinking the woman deserved a ribbon, or . . .

Slowly, Farley withdrew several of the scented sachets from his pocket. Each one of the linen squares had been beautifully embroidered and edged with delicate lace and tiny ribbons. Without meaning to do so, he gestured toward the man, allowing a liberal whiff of the heady blend of scents to pass beneath his nose.

"Oh, I've never seen anything so beautiful," the woman sighed. "Oh, they smell good," she said when Farley obliged and held one close to her nose, making certain Henry got another good sniff of it.

"Aye, made by a beautiful young maiden they were. Think of these fancy sachets, soft as a woman's flesh, and smelling just as sweet, scenting your dowry chest and the linens of your bed. Ah, makes a man wish he were layin' there right now, hearin' the winds and rains outside, but knowin' he's warm and snug with his wife tucked in beside him and nothin' to do 'til mornin'," Farley said, a look of longing on his face.

"Henry?"

Henry eyed the short man with the dark hair a bit suspiciously; then remembering that sweet smell and the long winter coming, he nodded. "What ye want fer a couple o' them things? Don't got any money to spend on this, but maybe we got a few extra eggs and some cheese."

"I just baked a whole oven full of tarts!"

Farley Odell made a fine show of hesitating, as if deep in thought, but when he glanced Tristram's way, he winked broadly.

Tristram winked back, nearly missing one of the boxes, but he quickly got his rhythm again and began to throw the boxes even higher, much to the squealing delight of the two children. Feeling quiet pleased with himself, Tristram Christian was rather surprised, therefore, when one of the boxes suddenly disappeared and never came down.

Spinning around, Tristram felt his jaw drop as he stared at the tall figure standing just behind him, the missing box held in his hand.

"Cap'n! You came! I knew you would. I knew you wouldn't forget about us. Lily said you didn't care anymore about us, but I knew she was wrong! I knew it!'' Tristram cried, and, forgetting his audience, he threw himself into Valentine Whitelaw's outstretched arms with boyish abandon.

"Of course I haven't forgotten about you, lad," Valentine spoke, strangely touched by the boy's almost tearful reception. "Where are Lily and Dulcie? Are they all right?" he asked, still disbelieving of the sight that had met their eyes when they'd ridden up to the farm to ask directions and had seen Tristram standing there juggling as if he hadn't a care in the world.

Farley Odell was less enthusiastic than Tristram to find Captain Whitelaw and his stern-faced manservant staring at him as if waiting for an explanation.

"Lily and Dulcie are back at the camp. Fairfax is there keeping an eye on things. He's going to go fishing for trout for our breakfast—well, lunch now. Lily will probably cook it, 'cause Tillie can't get around very easily anymore," Tristram said, gazing up into Valentine Whitelaw's face for a long moment before glancing over at the other two men. "Mustafa! Simon! You came looking for us too."

Simon took a deep breath, he still couldn't believe that they'd found them. "We've been searching all over England for you, Tristram," he said, impatient now to find Lily and Dulcie.

"Everything is going to be all right. I just know it. Wait till Lily sees you riding back with us, Cap'n. Is she going to be surprised! She'll have to take back every nasty thing she said about you," Tristram laughed.

"Why don't we go give her that surprise," Valentine said, his pride smarting still from Tristram's remark that Lily thought he didn't care about them anymore. "You can ride with me," he said, and mounting, he reached down and pulled Tristram up behind him.

Glancing over to where Farley Odell still stood in silence, he said, "I think we must have a very long talk, Farley Odell."

"I want them sachets," Henry said, glancing between the two men, one of whom was obviously a gentleman, but he was determined to get his hands on those sachets. "Reckon I might even give ye a hen fer a couple, and the eggs she's laid."

Farley Odell swallowed, and gathering his courage, he said, "Aye, Cap'n, that we do. Reckon ye'll be wantin' some explanations. Oughta take care of this business first. Reckon ye and the others might even be a bit hungry after yer ride. Why don't I follow ye in just a wee minute or two. The lad can fill ye in on most of what's happened. Know ye want to find Mistress Lily and little Dulcie. I'll be right with ye, Cap'n," he added a trifle lamely.

"I'll leave Mustafa here with you. You can ride behind him back to camp," Valentine said much to Farley Odell's consternation as he thought of being so close to that wicked-looking sword of the Turk's.

"Oh, I can walk back. Ain't far. Just beyond them trees, other side of the meadow," Farley said quickly.

"Not at all. We wouldn't want you to become lost. Can you guide us to the camp, Tristram?" Valentine asked, turning away dismissingly from a flustered Farley Odell who was thinking of poor Fairfax looking up to see Valentine Whitelaw riding into camp.

Fairfax Odell thought he was hearing bells at first, so shrill and repetitious were the sounds. Gradually, however, he realized that it was screaming he was hearing, and that it was coming from their camp.

Dropping the fishing line, he bolted through the trees, his big figure crashing through the undergrowth like a mad bull's as he broke through the trees and raced across the meadow toward the screaming. He reached the cart, but it was empty. The horse was still grazing in the meadow, but Tillie had disappeared, along with Dulcie, whom he'd seen not more than fifteen minutes earlier picking berries near where he'd been fishing. Mistress Lily was missing too, he realized.

He stood listening for a moment, for the screaming had stopped, then he started to run along the edge of the meadow when he heard Tillie's cries for help. He saw the small copse ahead, then Tillie's figure came staggering out, waving her arms to attract his attention.

"Oh, Fairfax, hurry! Hurry! 'Tis the mistress, I think she's dead!"

Fairfax had never run so fast in his life. Nor had he ever been so frightened in his life when he came to an abrupt halt beside the pool. Lying facedown in the water, her red hair floating out around her pale body was Lily Christian.

"Oh, no! Oh, Lord! What am I goin' to do?" he cried, his blue eyes wide with disbelief.

"Save her, Fairfax! Ye got to do something!" Tillie cried, shaking his arm.

"I can't swim, Tillie!" he yelled.

Before he could do anything, Dulcie had jumped into the pool, her small figure bobbing up and down for a moment, then she had disappeared. Tillie screamed, thinking the little girl had drowned, but then the dark head reappeared near Lily and she was pushing her sister over so that she was no longer facedown in the water.

As they watched, horrified, both heads disappeared beneath the surface. Fairfax glanced around, and reaching out, he broke a large branch. Before Tillie could stop him, he'd started to wade into the pond, but it was deep and his feet slipped, his shoulders and head disappearing beneath the water. He came up gasping for breath, his arms flailing wildly. Tillie grasped the end of the branch that had drifted toward shore and called to him to grab the other end, then she pulled him close enough to the bank for him to struggle out.

Raphael was racing back and forth along the bank, his frenzied barking masking the sound of quickly approaching footsteps from behind; then there was a splash of water as a figure dived into the pool, followed quickly by another, smaller one.

Fairfax, still coughing up water, watched in amazement as young Master Tristram grabbed hold of his little sister and pulled her to shore, swimming as easily as a fish even though his arm was hooked around Dulcie's shoulders. Fairfax struggled to his feet to lend a hand, but stumbled weakly to his knees. But he wasn't needed, for Simon Whitelaw was suddenly there, and standing waist deep in the water, he pulled Tristram and Dulcie up on the bank. Fairfax sighed with relief when he heard the little girl's soft cries as Simon Whitelaw comforted her.

Turning his gaze back to the pond, he watched as Valentine Whitelaw swam toward the bank with Lily Christian, her long red hair floating around her like a veil. Finding his footing, he stood up and waded from the pool, the unconscious girl held in his arms.

Gently, Valentine Whitelaw laid her down on the grassy bank, his gaze taking in the pale, slender thighs and hips, and the softly rounded breasts that were rising and falling so wildly as she tried to draw breath into her body. He turned her over onto her stomach, moving his hands against her back as he forced the water from her lungs. He couldn't help but become aware of her shift which was soaked and clung to every curve of her body, leaving nothing to the imagination. He was startled, for his memory of Lily Christian had been of a young girl, hardly the woman he had been holding in his arms, or the woman now revealed to his gaze.

Breathing more steadily and deeply now, Valentine White-law turned her over and cradled her limp body in his arms. Slowly, he smoothed the long dark strands of hair from her face. Drawing in his breath in disbelief, he stared down into the face that had haunted his dreams.

The thickly fringed eyelids flickered open for just an instant. There was no mistaking the pale green of her eyes that gazed into his. "Francisca," Valentine breathed the name in disbelief.

"Lily! She can't be dead! Valentine, you can't let Lily die, not now that we've found her," Simon pleaded.

Chapter Twenty-Four

VALENTINE WHITELAW stood with his back turned to the room. Standing before the small, mullioned windows of the inn, he stared out through the diamond-shaped panes at the narrow, cobbled street below. It sloped steeply down to the bridge crossing the river. While he stood watching the sunset reflected on the water, the pealing of bells sounded from the old Saxon church across the marketplace. The church's spire had guided them all the way down the valley through the hills where the Windrush and Evenlode rivers flowed into the Thames.

To the east, where darkness had already cloaked the thickly forested slopes, was Wychwood, a royal hunting preserve where the kings of England, from William the Conqueror to Henry VIII, had hunted. Far away to the west, beyond the plains and vales of Gloucestershire, rose the Black Mountains of Wales.

The market square had been crowded with the stalls of wool merchants, farmers selling poultry and produce, and the locals hawking their wares, when the travel-weary strangers had ridden into the village and sought rooms at the inn.

Valentine Whitelaw turned away from the window and stared at the woman asleep in the bed. A fire was burning in the hearth, its warmth spreading throughout the small chamber and vanquishing the chill of an early autumn evening.

Lily Christian. Lily *Francisca* Christian, he corrected himself. Quietly, Valentine moved closer to the bed and gazed down at her. The dark red hair fell across the pillows like rich crimson

458

silk, framing the pale, heart-shaped face that was so familiar to him.

Too late, he had remembered the laughing, cherubic face of a child with curious pale green eyes so like her father's. Regretfully now, he remembered the awkward young girl with wide green eyes that had reflected her hopelessness when faced with her return to England. Orphaned, and with a young brother and sister to care for, she had tried valiantly to hide her fears.

But a slight smile curved Valentine Whitelaw's lips when he thought of the beautiful woman dressed in green velvet and riding a white horse along the riverbank, and then, later, the bewitchment of those green eyes that had, for just an instant, glowed with love when she had stared at him. That expression, revealed so frankly, was what puzzled him the most.

And now, he remembered only too vividly the deathly paleness of her face when he'd rescued her and bundled her up in blankets and carefully placed her in the cart, her bandaged head resting against the maid Tillie. Her green eyes, bright with pain, had fluttered open only for an instant, but Valentine had known that she'd seen him standing there watching her. He had heard her whisper his name, and he had taken her cold hands in his and promised her he would not leave her side. He would be there for her. The words had brought back another promise he'd made to her long ago, one that he had broken. He had not been there when she'd needed him the most and when she'd faced danger alone.

After the journey into this village, he would never again forget her face. His eyes had seldom left it while they'd ridden through the valley, the narrow path seemingly endless as it wended toward the river. Dulcie had sat curled up beside Lily, the big mastiff wedged in on the other side, and helping to keep Lily from being jostled on the bumpy track they followed, the monkey chattering worriedly from somewhere in the cart. Tristram rode behind Simon, oddly silent for one who was usually so full of insatiable curiosity, but the parrot had made up for his silence with a loquacity of its own. The two Odell brothers walked just ahead of the oxen, their feet seeming to drag, while the Turk had led Lily's horse and brought up the rear of their small procession, ever watchful of their surroundings in case of another attack from their unseen enemy.

Valentine stared down at Lily while she slept. Her expression was serene, innocent. She seemed so vulnerable lying there.

"You damned fool," he murmured beneath his breath, cursing himself for having been so blind. But could he really blame himself for the mistake he had made? He had not been expecting to encounter Lily Christian selling flowers at a fair in London. Lily Christian, the young girl he'd been so fond of, Geoffrey Christian's daughter, whom he'd thought was safely at Highcross. Rather belatedly, he'd realized that he'd not seen her for almost three years. A girl had become a young woman during those years. Indeed, he thought with a bitter smile as he watched the softly rounded contours of her breasts rising and falling beneath the covers, there was little doubt that Lily Christian had become a very beautiful young woman.

Unable to resist the temptation, he found himself reaching out to touch a long strand of her hair. She had made a fool of him. Why? he wondered. What had he done to her to cause her to play this charade? How she must have laughed, he suddenly thought, fanning his anger anew, for the mere thought and feel of her weakened him, and it was not a sensation he enjoyed, especially when he knew he'd been duped. But he would have the truth from her before he left this room.

He was still reeling from the startling revelation of her true identity. Thinking he had rescued Lily Christian from drowning, he had been stunned to discover instead Francisca, the woman he'd so desperately wanted to find. But rather than pursue her, he had chosen to follow another path in search of Lily Christian. Feeling the silken strand curling around his hand with a life of its own, he suddenly felt overwhelmed by the consequences of that act. If he had made the wrong decision he would have lost both of them without realizing that they were one and the same.

Damn her, he thought, for doing this to him.

Staring down at her, he was uncomfortable remembering the plans he'd had for her, for Geoffrey Christian's cherished daughter. He had wanted her to become his mistress—in his thoughts she already had. And marriage had been the furthest thing from his mind when thinking of Francisca. When he had found her at the fair and pulled her into the trees, he had taken what he wanted. He had kissed and caressed her as he would a woman he desired to bed, not an innocent, gentle-bred maid who should have been gently wooed and courted and given a chaste kiss upon the hand. Not Lily Christian, no; he had fondled her boldly, tasting of her lips like a man starved. He would have killed a man for touching Lily the way he had, and yet he had been the one guilty of the misconduct. He had betrayed Geoffrey Christian's friendship—he'd tried to seduce his daughter, Valentine thought with a groan of self-disgust.

He still could not believe that this seductive woman who'd had him lusting after her was Lily Christian, the same little girl he'd pitied when she'd stood before him at Ravindzara looking so forlorn in that unattractive gown. Valentine ran his fingers through his hair, leaving the black curls in disorder as he continued to stare down at her with the same sense of disbelief and pleasure he'd felt when he'd rolled her over after rescuing her from drowning to find himself gazing at the woman who had captivated him. No wonder he had felt he'd known her from somewhere before. In a sense, he had known those pale green eyes for most of his life; first when meeting Geoffrey Christian's clear-eyed stare, and, now, his daughter's.

How he had dreamt of this moment. To be standing here beside the bed she lay sleeping in. He eyed the pale softness of her bare shoulders revealed above the blanket and knew that she would have been his by now if . . . but everything had changed. They would never be lovers now.

Lily moaned softly, turning fretfully in her sleep. Valentine sat down on the edge of the bed and felt her forehead, but it was cool. There was no fever. Sitting so closely beside her, he found his gaze wandering over her lingeringly, capturing in his memory every feature until he felt he knew her better than she knew herself. He noted the thickness of her dark lashes and the curving line of her silken eyebrows. Her nose was straight and delicately molded, while her slightly parted lips were soft and full. A rosy blush stained the alabaster smoothness of her cheeks. Suddenly Valentine realized that she had opened her eyes and had been aware of his perusal.

His turquoise eyes, which had been so warm only moments before, grew cold and distant. "How do you feel?" he inquired solicitously, as if asking the question of a stranger.

Lily glanced away. "I am fine," she replied huskily.

"Eventually, yes, but right now I seriously doubt that," he

said, her refusal to admit to the way she must really feel irritating him. "Are you warm enough?"

"Yes. Tillie told me that you pulled me from the pool. I would have drowned if you hadn't been there. Thank you," she said simply, still not meeting his eyes.

"You do not need to thank me. Actually it was Dulcie who kept you afloat long enough for me to rescue you. She's a very brave little girl. And at least that bull-necked fellow, Fairfax, tried to rescue you. But I am more interested in hearing the answers to my questions," he said, startling Lily when he suddenly leaned forward. Some of her dismay must have shown on her face, because he momentarily hesitated, a mocking gleam entering his eyes. "You needn't fear my intentions now, Lily *Francisca*. If you can, try to sit up," he said brusquely when he saw the look of relief cross her face.

Lily tried to raise herself into a sitting position, but couldn't. Muttering something in exasperation, he reached out, pulling her forward to rest against his shoulder. Uncontrollably, Lily stiffened. The pungent smell of leather and horses, mingling with the scent of him, drifted to her from his body, and it was strangely exciting, not offensive. Her senses were filled with his warmth as she rested her head against him. His hands were gentle when they touched the large lump on the back of her head, probing it carefully.

"You're very lucky, *Lily* Francisca Christian," he murmured, easing her back against the pillows, but he remained seated close, staring at her.

Lily began to twist the end of the blanket nervously, refusing to meet his gaze, but that only made matters worse, for his muscular thigh clad in leather cannons and boot, stretched along the length of her thigh and hip, and even though she was covered by the blanket, she could feel the heat of his body and was reminded of the even closer, more intimate contact between them she had experienced when held in his arms. Her blush deepened and she glanced up quickly, only to find her eyes held by that turquoise gaze and she knew he must be able to read her every thought. It had been far easier to anticipate this encounter between them when she'd had the element of surprise on her side, having carefully planned to humiliate him by revealing her identity.

"Why, Lily? Why didn't you tell me who you were? Why, when you, and Tristram and Dulcie, were in trouble, didn't you come to me for help?"

"You were not even in the country."

"I realize that, but you saw me at the fair. You could have spoken to me then."

"If you will remember, you gave me very little opportunity to tell you who I was. And then you rushed away and I did not have the chance," Lily explained, but not completely satisfying him, because he began to frown.

"You could have told me you were in trouble when we met that first time at the fair. You saw me, Lily. I saw the expression on your face. Then you vanished into thin air," he reminded her.

"You were with Cordelia. I did not wish to interrupt you, and what I had to speak with you about was very private. I did not intend to speak before a stranger," she said, not admitting how all of the old hurts had returned when she'd seen them standing together. She could just imagine Cordelia Howard's malicious laughter and scorn when she discovered that they had left Highcross and had been living like gypsies for the past few months. Lily would not admit that it had been her love for him that had caused her to hide from him more than anything else. She would not humiliate herself further.

"When I said your name, at least the name I thought you were called, you did not correct me. Why not then? Why let me continue to believe you were someone else?"

"Because I"—Lily hesitated, realizing she couldn't reveal the truth to him or she would reveal her love as well—"I was startled that you did not recognize me. You thought me a stranger. How could I come to you with my problems? How did I know that you would care? I wasn't certain what to do when I realized that you knew nothing of what had happened at Highcross, that we were criminals. There were other people I had to think of, and, in truth, it wasn't any of your affair," she amazed him by remarking, lifting her chin defiantly. "I am no kin to you. We have managed well enough on our own," Lily said. "We cannot always presume upon your charitable nature."

"Well enough? You were nearly killed because of your lack of judgment. And as for my charitable nature," he began, his anger growing as he became aware of her resentment and could not understand the reason behind it. What had he ever done to her?

"I *was* going to tell you everything that night, when we were supposed to meet on the bank. But you never showed up."

"I was summoned to the palace to meet with Lord Burghley. I sent Mustafa to bring you aboard the *Madrigal*, but you'd already left," he said, wondering how she had managed so quickly to put him on the defensive. He was the one with the grievance, the one who'd been made a fool of.

"I returned to the camp to find it in flames and Rom wounded. Rom needed me. I had to go with him, and Fairfax had been hit on the head and needed attention. We had no other place to go but with the gypsies. How could I come to you when I did not know where you were? Besides, Rom was my friend, and I was not going to betray that friendship. And the more I thought about that afternoon, the angrier I became. Even though you thought I was little better than a serving wench, how dare you try to make love to me, especially when you had a fiancée awaiting you? What kind of man are you? Have you no sense of loyalty to anyone?" Lily accused him.

Valentine was almost speechless. "How dare you say such a thing to me?" he finally said, grasping her chin in his hand and forcing her to meet his gaze when she would have avoided it.

Lily was startled by the underlying anger in his voice.

"And what do you mean by 'fiancée'? I have no fiancée," he said, although he couldn't deny that his intentions toward her that afternoon had been less than honorable.

"Cordelia. She is your fiancée. Quinta said that Cordelia had visited Ravindzara and that you would be wed by summer's end. Then, when you left me, I heard you damning your engagement, yet trotting off to escort Cordelia while making plans to meet me later."

"Cordelia is not my fiancée. She is to wed another. I met her by accident at the fair. When you saw her with me was the only time I spoke with her. And I had a supper engagement with Thomas Sandrick, not Cordelia Howard."

Lily's green eyes momentarily brightened. He was not engaged to marry Cordelia?

"You speak very highly of this gypsy, Romney Lee. I understand from Tristram that he was the one who advised you to leave Highcross. He very conveniently managed to keep an eye on you by convincing you to join his band of vagabonds and thieves. He had you feeling indebted to him for his many kindnesses. He was the wily one, wasn't he? I saw him fondling you and kissing you at the fair. He could not keep his hands from you. And after that loving display, you allowed me to caress you and you responded to my kisses. What of *your* loyalty, Lily Christian?'' Valentine demanded, stung by her contempt.

Lily's hand struck his cheek, leaving a vivid mark against the tanned skin, but before she could even lower her hand, it had been caught by his and was held immovable between them while they stared angrily into each other's eyes. In her anger, Lily had forgotten the blanket covering her bare shoulders, which had now slipped lower to reveal the soft curves of her breasts, but Lily was unaware of the fact.

''He wasn't my lover, but we could have become lovers,'' she said, surprised by the sudden look of cruelty that crossed Valentine Whitelaw's hardened face. ''He was my friend. He was always there for us when we needed him. He cared. He was loyal. He did so much, risked so much for us.''

''For you, Lily, not for the others. He wanted you,'' Valentine told her, ''and what he did was for himself.''

''Yes, then, for me. Perhaps he loved me. Was that so wrong? He helped us escape those villagers who would gladly have seen me burned and the others driven from Highcross. He saved us, and, ultimately, he gave his life for me. He thought he was saving me when he fought off that attacker,'' Lily said tearfully. ''Perhaps, in time, I would have come to love him, and—''

''No, you would not, Lily. He lied,'' Valentine said, not feeling sorry for the man Lily Francisca was trying to convince herself she might have loved. He was not the man she could have loved, who would have become her lover, he thought, surprising himself by the intensity of that feeling.

''Lied?''

''Yes, except to escape the unwanted attentions of your guardian, there was no reason to leave Highcross,'' Valentine told her.

''But Hartwell Barclay is dead. Surely Tristram and the others have told you what happened? That was the reason we fled Highcross," Lily told him, unconsciously placing her hand over his while he still held her wrist in his grasp.

"But you see, my dear, Hartwell Barclay is not dead. He was slightly inconvenienced by that unfortunate episode, but it hardly proved fatal. And Romney Lee knew that because he went into the village and spoke with the groom. He knew when he told you to leave with him that there was no reason for you to have fled, or for your fears or your guilt. He lied to you, Lily."

"No, no, I do not believe you. You are lying. You are just saying these things about him because he helped us, and because he might not have been a fine gentleman like you. How do you know?" Lily demanded.

"Did you not wonder how it was that we happened upon you when we did? When I met you at the fair, I did not know what had occurred at Highcross, but I was planning to visit within the week, before I'd sailed for Ravindzara. Before I could do anything, even find you, Simon arrived. He had been to Highcross and discovered what had happened. He spoke with Hartwell Barclay, who had been laid up with a broken ankle, but that was all. Simon spoke with the groom, who told him that you might have gone to find your old nursemaid, Maire Lester, who lived in Stratford. The morning after that mob attacked the camp, Simon and I set out for Stratford. Little did I realize that we were riding ahead of you and that you traveled through every village we asked in *after* we had already inquired of you. When we found you had never arrived at Maire Lester's, we were returning, and, luckily, learned of the shortcut."

"No," Lily murmured, but not convincingly this time as she remembered Romney Lee's last words. She understood now his plea for forgiveness. He had asked her not to hate him for stealing this summer from her. Rom, she thought sadly. He had given his life trying to save her. He paid the ultimate price for having loved her. She could not hate him. Never would she hate him, Lily promised herself, trying to hold back the tears that threatened, but one tear escaped to fall onto Valentine Whitelaw's hand.

"You cry for him? A man who deceived you?" Valentine demanded harshly, unaware that his anger came of a jealousy of this man who had betrayed her, who would have stolen her love, and for whom she now shed tears. "The man used you. He knew you were an heiress, that Highcross was yours. He also knew there was no reason for you not to return there. Of course, by then he would have wed you and he would have been master of Highcross. You are a very beautiful woman, and he wanted you, and he wanted your fortune, and he would have stopped at nothing to get you," Valentine predicted, his jealousy of this man increasing, even though the man was no longer a threat, as he thought of the months Romney Lee had had Lily to himself.

"And were you any different?" Lily demanded, raising her shoulders proudly. "When you thought I was little better than a gypsy, you wanted to take me for a night's pleasure."

"Not just a night's pleasure, Lily Francisca," Valentine found himself admitting in a soft voice that held a wealth of meaning, and following his gaze, Lily saw her breasts fully revealed to him, the delicate-hued crests beginning to harden under that gaze. Quickly, she tried to pull the blanket back up, but only half-succeeded, for he still held her wrist.

"I was never in danger from Rom," Lily defended him. "Indeed, it would seem I was in more danger while in your company than I ever was while with Rom," Lily said, daring him to deny the charge.

But Valentine would not be baited. "Because of that gypsy, you were in that compromising situation in the first place. I cannot be blamed for admiring a beautiful woman and accepting the seductive invitation in her eyes when she stared at me across the crowd. Little had I expected to find Geoffrey Christian's daughter traveling with a band of gypsies. And because of that gypsy's deception, you, and Tristram and Dulcie, have been in constant danger of some mishap. I am only surprised it did not happen sooner. You very nearly lost your life when that ruffian attacked you by the pool. And he will not go unpunished, I promise you that. I will see that he is tracked down and brought to justice."

"Ruffian? I know who attacked me," Lily startled him by announcing.

"You know?" Valentine demanded. "Was it one of the gypsies from the camp? Or perhaps someone who accosted you at the fair?" he asked, realizing too late that the latter description fit himself.

"No, 'twas Sir Raymond Valchamps who attacked me," Lily

said, for until that moment she had told no one of the image she had seen reflected in the pool.

"Raymond Valchamps?" Valentine repeated the name incredulously.

"You don't believe me? I know what I saw. And I saw his face reflected in that pool as clearly as I see yours before me now."

Valentine Whitelaw stared at Lily as if the blow to her head had been more severe than he'd at first thought. "Sir Raymond Valchamps? Are you absolutely certain? I admit that I have little liking for the man, but I do find it difficult to believe that he should wish you any harm. He hardly knows you," he said, but he was suddenly remembering the Turk telling him about having seen Sir Raymond Valchamps at the fair the night the mob had attacked the gypsy camp. Mustafa had said that Valchamps had been paying off two rough-looking men who had been carrying torches and cudgels and who had apparently been involved in the mayhem.

Valentine's gaze narrowed thoughtfully as he stared at Lily, a strange expression on his face. A girl, one of the gypsies, had been murdered that night, and she had been wearing a gown remarkably similar to the one Lily had been wearing that afternoon at the fair. And Cordelia Howard had been at the fair that afternoon with Sir Raymond.

"Who was the girl murdered at the camp?" he asked.

Lily was startled by his question. "Navarre. She was the niece of the leader of the gypsy band we traveled with. Why?"

"She was wearing your violet gown, wasn't she?"

"Yes, how did you know? I remember how shocked I was to see it, for a moment, well . . ."

"For a moment you felt it could have been you lying there dead."

"Yes, I did. In fact, if I hadn't gone to meet you on the riverbank, I would have been in the camp during the attack, and I might very well have been the one struck down and not Navarre. Romney thought it was me, although I knew he would have helped Navarre too, but he fought the attacker thinking the man had stabbed me."

"But why? I wonder. What reason could Raymond Valchamps have to wish you dead? What threat are you to him?'' Valentine spoke his thoughts aloud. ''You are certain that it was Raymond Valchamps? There is no mistake? You have no doubts at all?'' he questioned, watching Lily's expression closely.

Lily shook her head emphatically. ''I saw his reflection in the pool before I was struck. His is a face one does not easily forget. He has one blue eye and one brown eye, and that pale hair, and . . .'' Lily hesitated, shuddering.

Valentine realized the blanket had slipped again from her bare shoulders and the soft curve of her breast was once again revealed to his gaze. Sighing, he pulled the blanket up higher, his hand lingering longer than necessary against her flesh. ''And what?'' he said gently, smiling slightly when he saw the wild blush come into her cheeks as her hand slid between and moved his away.

''You will think me mad. But he was smiling.''

''Had you told me anything but that, I might have remained unconvinced, but that sounds like Valchamps,'' Valentine said, the smile fading from his face as he thought of what Lily had told him. ''Why?'' he repeated more to himself this time, unaware that his hand was now caressing her palm while he sat there lost in thought.

''Maybe he saw the puppet show?'' Lily said half-seriously, smiling when she saw Valentine's puzzled expression.

''We had a puppet show at the fair. The day you came was the first day we didn't put on a show. Our booth was burned to the ground the night before,'' Lily explained, glancing down at his strong hand, the long fingers now tracing a random design in her palm before moving to entwine with her slender fingers.

She didn't see the look of interest that entered his eyes when she mentioned the fire that had burned only their booth. ''Why should he have been upset at having seen this puppet show? Surely it was harmless.''

''We were very popular with the crowds,'' Lily admitted. ''Sir Raymond, however, probably didn't like it because one of the puppets, a witch, resembled him. When we made them I thought of Sir Raymond. I have never liked him.''

''Nor have I, and I suspect I have injured his pride more often than you have with that puppet, but he has hardly tried to murder me," Valentine said. "Do you still have this puppet, or was it destroyed in the fire?"

"No, it was the only one that didn't perish. It's in the cart, in my trunk. No, Farley took it to entertain at that farm. He must still have it."

"Odd, isn't it, that your booth should burn down? I would like to see this puppet. What was your puppet show about?" he asked out of idle curiosity.

"It was a fable about wild white horses. I used to tell it to Dulcie to get her to go to sleep when we were on the island. Actually, 'twas Basil who—" Lily was beginning to say that it had been Basil who'd told the fable to them when there was a knock on the door before it slowly opened to reveal Dulcie and Tristram peeking in; seeing her awake, they both raced in, followed by Raphael and Cappie.

"Oh, Lily! You're alive!" Dulcie cried, climbing onto the bed and scrambling into Lily's arms. "I was afraid when you slept so long that you might have died. Uncle Valentine wouldn't let me come in to see you. He said I had to trust him."

Simon Whitelaw, who had followed Dulcie and Tristram into the room, now stood self-consciously near the door, a slightly puzzled frown on his face as he noticed his uncle sitting so close to Lily on the edge of the bed, and he could have sworn that Valentine had been holding one of Lily's hands.

"I told Dulcie you would be all right," Tristram said, neglecting to say that he had left most of his supper untouched.

"Tillie said you have a bump on your head as big as an apple," Dulcie said, eyeing her sister curiously.

"Not that big, Dulcie. More like a walnut, isn't it, Lily?" Tristram corrected his sister.

Lily managed a smile, even though Dulcie's jump onto the bed had left her head pounding sickeningly. "Thanks to you saving me from drowning, sweeting, I'm at least here to feel it, whatever size it is," Lily said, kissing Dulcie on her forehead. "That was very brave of you."

Dulcie snuggled closer. "I could swim, Lily, and Fairfax couldn't," she explained without taking any special credit for her act of heroism. "He looked so funny running along the bank. Kind of like a big chicken. I was afraid he was going to bump Tillie into the pool, and no one could have pulled her out.''

''We will have to find some special way to reward you and Tristram,'' Valentine said, tickling her under the chin while she giggled.

''I wish I'd been there earlier,'' Tristram said from his perch on the foot of the bed. ''I would have caught your attacker, Lily,'' he told her, thinking he hadn't done anything special in jumping in the pool to help Dulcie out, for he'd done that most of his life, especially when they'd been on the island.

''I understand we have you to thank, Simon, for coming in search of us in the first place,'' Lily said, noticing the tall, thin figure standing near the door.

Simon Whitelaw smiled, stepping forward eagerly when she held out her hand to him. He sat down on the opposite side of the bed from his uncle and took her hand, pressing a gentlemanly kiss against it much to Valentine Whitelaw's astonishment.

''I think I aged a lifetime when we rode up and heard the screaming, then saw you and Dulcie disappearing in that black water,'' he said with a rueful look. ''I hadn't thought I could be more frightened than when I visited Highcross and discovered you'd run away. I very nearly became the one to kill Hartwell Barclay that day,'' Simon admitted, and glancing over at Valentine, he was startled to see his uncle's expression, and, rather belatedly, he realized he was still holding Lily's hand with both of his.

He flushed uncomfortably and stood up. ''I know you must be tired, Lily. I'm so pleased to see you and know that you are going to be all right. I don't think I've slept in days worrying about you—and Dulcie and Tristram, of course,'' he finished lamely.

''You probably won't get any sleep tonight either,'' Tristram said. ''We've got Cisco in our room.''

Simon looked bewildered until he realized Tristram was referring to the parrot, and he laughed, for he wouldn't mind losing sleep to that parrot since he knew it meant Lily was sleeping peacefully in the next room. His gaze drifted to where she sat in the bed, her long hair cascading over her bare shoulders, and as Dulcie moved into a better position in Lily's arms, Simon's mouth opened and he gulped as he caught sight of the curve of a creamy breast.

"Where were the Odells when you left them?" Valentine asked Simon rather sharply, not having missed his nephew's admiring gaze.

"Down in the taproom. I've never seen anyone drink as many tankards of ale as that one."

"Fairfax?" Tristram said. "He holds the record in all of the shire," Tristram said proudly.

"No, the other one, the short one. Farley. Don't know where he's putting it," Simon puzzled, his eyes still lingering on Lily. Although she had pulled the blanket higher, he had never seen a more breathtaking sight than this woman with her hair flowing free over bare shoulders.

"Do you think Farley would remember where he put that puppet?" Valentine asked, rising from the bed and coming to stand by his nephew's side, effectively blocking Simon's view of Lily.

"I'm not certain he even remembers his name," Simon said, trying to glance around his uncle. He'd never before realized quite how wide Valentine's shoulders were, and irritatingly so, he thought.

"Why don't we go down and see if he does before the inn runs out of ale?" Valentine suggested. "I'm curious about that puppet."

Simon eyed his uncle as if he'd lost his mind. "Puppet? What puppet?"

"The one from our puppet show. The evil witch!" Dulcie squealed, sending Cappie beneath the pillows.

"Well, if he doesn't, I bet Tillie will know," Simon suggested. "All of the trunks and things from the cart are in the Odells' room."

"Where is Tillie? Lying down?" Valentine asked, for he'd never seen a woman so alarmingly pregnant.

"No, she hasn't left the table since we arrived, except to help Lily into bed. I've never seen a woman eat so much," Simon remarked, remembering the innkeeper's expression when the woman had asked for another meat pie after the two she'd put away practically by herself.

"Now that I know you are feeling better, Lily, I think I might go and get myself a couple of tarts before Tillie finishes that meat pie," Tristram said worriedly, feeling hungry now.

"Can I bring you something, Lily?" Simon inquired solicitously.

"Thank you, but Tillie is going to bring me something later."

Tristram glanced back, his expression conveying doubt that there would be anything left in the kitchens. "I'll save you a tart, Lily," he offered generously.

"I hope when we return to London—and after everything has been settled at Highcross—that you and Dulcie and Tristram will come to visit me at Whiteswood, Lily," Simon said shyly. "Mother and Sir William have Riverhurst now, so . . . well, I'd like to show you around the house and the lands. I know you'd love it."

"Can we really, Lily? When?" Tristram demanded, winning looks of appreciation and irritation from the respective younger and elder Whitelaws.

"We'll look forward to that, Simon," Lily responded.

"Shall we go, Simon?" Valentine requested, his hand closing around his nephew's bony elbow to speed him to the door.

"Good night, Lily," Simon managed to call over his shoulder, catching one last glance before being hustled from the room.

"I'll have the innkeeper prepare you something light," Valentine said before he followed Simon's lanky figure from the room.

"I won't forget the tart, Lily," Tristram promised, hurrying out as Valentine remained holding the door, a less than patient look on his face.

"Lily? Will you tell me a story?"

"What do you want to hear?" Lily asked.

"I want to hear about the dancing stars. Then, I want to hear about the wild white horses," she requested, settling herself more comfortably, while Raphael took the opportunity to jump up on the foot of the bed, his soulful glance begging not to be sent from the comfort of the soft mattress and blankets; after all, he'd loyally followed his mistress far from home.

"Very well," Lily said, resting her chin on top of Dulcie's head. "Once there was a twinkling star that loved to dance and there was this little girl who was born under it, and she loved to dance, too . . ."

Valentine Whitelaw wasn't gone more than fifteen minutes. He had managed to leave the others downstairs, slipping away unnoticed while Simon had been trying to engage a bleary-eyed Farley Odell in conversation, and had returned with a light repast for Lily. He now stood just inside the door and listened to her soft voice telling the mythical tale. Lily hadn't heard him enter and was continuing uninterrupted with the story of the wild white horses led by Prince Basil and Sweet Rose. Valentine Whitelaw's heart missed a beat when Lily described the witch's treachery in abandoning Prince Basil on the island in the Indies and of the plot to assassinate the queen.

Dulcie was sound asleep, her dark head resting against Lily's shoulder, when Lily finished the tale. Lily had just rested her head against the pillows when she became aware of Valentine's presence near the door. She glanced over, her eyes widening in surprise.

"You startled me. I did not hear you enter."

"I didn't want to disturb you."

"I see you found the puppet," Lily commented, spying the ugly creature's face tucked beneath his arm.

"Yes, I found him," Valentine said, his arm tightening around the puppet's neck. "I wanted to hear the end of your tale. Where did you learn that story, Lily?" he asked in a conversational tone.

"It was one that Basil told us while on the island."

Valentine Whitelaw placed the tray and the puppet down on the bedside table and stood staring down at Lily, his turquoise eyes glowing with excitement. "You don't realize the truth yet, do you? My God, I wish I could have seen Valchamps's face when he heard the tale. He must have been stunned watching your not-so-innocent little puppet show revealing all of his secrets for the whole world to hear. I'll wager 'twas he who burned down your booth so no one else would learn the truth."

"Learn what? It is just a fable Basil told to amuse us. I've heard it since I was seven."

"That is why you never understood. You always thought it just a fable, a story Basil made up, but don't you see, Lily? Were it anyone else but Basil who had told you this tale, I would think it mere fantasy. But Basil never did anything, Lily, without a reason. He knew exactly what he was doing when he told you that tale. He was giving you some very important information, but he was also protecting you, or so he thought, by the manner in which he told you. The story parallels what happened to all of you on that island and explains why you were on that island, Lily. By having the jinni unmasked as the witch, and by having that witch resemble Sir Raymond Valchamps, Basil was sending the warning that Sir Raymond is a traitor. He is plotting to assassinate the queen. I've always suspected that Basil was aboard your father's ship because he'd been sent by Lord Burghley and Walsingham. I am certain he must have been gathering information for them about Santo Domingo and whatever else he could learn on this journey. Somehow Basil discovered Sir Raymond's involvement in a plot to assassinate Elizabeth. I wonder now if Sir Raymond was not in reality trying to murder Her Majesty the day he claimed he was trying to save her life," Valentine speculated, still disbelieving the enormity of the plot he'd just uncovered. "Basil knew the truth, Lily. He suspected he would never live to reveal it to Lord Burghley and warn the queen of the danger she was in. So he told you an innocent fable, hoping that one day you might be rescued and the tale would be heard.

"Sir Raymond himself has convinced me that it is more than a fable. Why else, unless this story of yours is the truth, would Sir Raymond concern himself with it? He has now tried to kill you twice."

"Twice? The only time I've been attacked by him was at the pool," Lily said, beginning to remember more about Basil's tale than even Valentine suspected.

"He killed the wrong girl at the fair, Lily. This gypsy girl who was murdered by a strange man in the mob that attacked the camp. I think it was supposed to be you. But you were away, waiting for me," Valentine reminded her.

"My gown! Navarre had stolen it and was wearing it."

"Yes, and Mustafa saw Sir Raymond at the camp that night paying off two men. Damn!" Valentine said. "If only we had proof. Even though I know it must be true, no one else will believe a fable."

"I saw Sir Raymond when he attacked me," she reminded him. "I can swear to that."

"Your word against his. I fear, my dear, that his word would carry more credence than yours. Basil is the only one who could prove Sir Raymond's guilt," Valentine said, "and he is dead. I wish we had that journal."

"The journal?" Lily asked, glancing up quickly, a strange look crossing her face.

• "Yes, don't you remember that journal you spoke of when we returned from the island? You told me that Basil had written everything down in it, and that it had been burned in the hut. Basil would have written his suspicions down in that journal, Lily. He was always recording his thoughts and impressions of people and places. I am certain that it must be filled with everything he did and saw in Santo Domingo. He most likely would have reported the information to Walsingham on his return to England. Basil was very thorough and an untiring diarist. There is a whole room full of his journals at Whiteswood. If only it had not been destroyed. That, I am positive, would be our proof. Unless we have something more than your childhood fable and an attempt on your life, we have nothing to arrest Sir Raymond on. I will, of course, inform Cecil, but all I can do is warn him on the weight of my suspicions, which isn't much, I'm afraid."

"The journal," Lily repeated, a look of horrified amazement on her face. "I had forgotten it over the years. Basil always said it was important. He would never allow any of us to look inside it. He always read to us from it," Lily remembered.

Valentine couldn't hide his disappointment. "So you never saw inside it, then? You never read what was written there? You have no idea?"

Lily shook her head, staring down at her hands nervously, her face paling.

"Don't worry, Lily. I won't let Sir Raymond anywhere near you. We may not have the proof to arrest him, but now that I know the truth, he will have no reason to harm you. In fact, I will see that he is constantly watched. A man's reputation has been ruined by suspicion alone, and after I finish with Sir Raymond, he will find it healthier to leave England," Valentine vowed. "You need not fear him again. I only wish I had that proof, for who can say who else might be involved that we have no suspicions of now? I would prefer not to alert Sir Raymond. I would like to catch him and his coconspirators before they have a chance to flee.''

Lily glanced up, then away, unable to meet his gaze when she admitted in a low voice, "There still might be the proof you want. The journal did not burn in the hut. It is still on the island," she said, her head downbent.

Valentine Whitelaw stared at Lily as if he hadn't heard. When he said nothing, Lily glanced up, and taking a deep breath, she repeated her words more loudly this time.

"I said the journal is still there. I lied when I told you it had burned up. Basil made me promise to tell no one about the journal. He said what was inside it was for the queen's eyes alone. He said it was special. He always kept it hidden, with our treasure," Lily confessed.

"Basil's journal is still on the island?"

"Yes, buried with our treasure."

"What treasure is that?" Valentine asked, wondering what other secrets the island held that Lily had never shared with him.

"The rest of the treasure from that sunken galleon. We found quite a lot washed up on shore. It took us days to gather it all. Basil said we should hide it to keep it safe from the pirates that occasionally came ashore. He said it was rightfully ours and that we might need it someday. When you came that day I never had a chance to tell you about it. We had already sailed when I regained consciousnees, and by then it was too late. Since the journal was safely hidden, and we were returning to Highcross, I didn't think it was important anymore," Lily said, flushing now as she remembered her naïveté and the contempt Valentine Whitelaw must feel for her when she found the courage to confess another guilt she'd been hiding for so long. "I did not trust you when you first came to the island and tricked me aboard the *Madrigal*. When you first asked about the journal, I lied, partly because of the promise I'd made to Basil to keep it a secret, but mostly because I was still angry at you for having tricked me. You'd lied to me. I understand now why you did, but then I did not. Then, later, when I came to—to—" Lily paused, then continued, an embarrassed blush spreading across her cheeks, "to like you, I was afraid you would hate me if I told you I had lied. I did not want to know your displeasure, to lose your friendship," she said, looking up into his face, expecting to see his disgust.

But Valentine Whitelaw didn't react the way she'd suspected, instead he sat down beside her on the bed. Taking her face between his hands, he stared deeply into her pale green eyes, shadowed now by her guilt that she had somehow betrayed him. "I do not blame you, Lily. You mustn't hold yourself responsible for something you did not understand. You have been an innocent victim. You have suffered enough already because of Valchamps's treachery. You were but a child. Now . . ." he said, and before he could resist the temptation, he lowered his mouth to hers, touching her slightly parted lips in a gentle kiss, his hand straying to rest on the bareness of her shoulder, his fingers curving around it before sliding into the thickness of her unbound hair. Before he lifted his mouth from hers, his kiss deepened for a brief instant when he felt her response, the way her lips clung to his when he would have parted from her.

Her breath was warm against his face when his lips left hers. He stared down at her closed eyes, the lashes fluttering against the softness of her skin, and he kissed each of her lids, startling them into opening so he could stare into her eyes. "Nothing is settled between us. We still have much to discuss, Lily Francisca Christian," he warned before abruptly releasing her, his eyes holding the promise of that reckoning as they roved over her.

Standing up, he laughed, his sun-bronzed face full of triumph. "By God, I'm going to get that journal. The *Madrigal* is already prepared to sail. If you are up to it, we will return to London immediately. I'll have to confer with Burghley before we sail, then make port at Falmouth to send Sir Rodger and Quinta ashore. I trust she has returned to London by now. You and Tristram and Dulcie will stay at Ravindzara while I'm in the Indies. You will be safe there. You might even stay at Penmorley Hall, for Quinta will wish to stay with Artemis. That might be better. Sir Rodger will not mind, and he will be able to keep a closer eye on you. Of course, now I know the truth, I really do not think Sir Raymond need concern us. I shouldn't be gone longer than a couple of months," Valentine Whitelaw said confidently, his hands moving to bring the puppet within his grasp while he planned his next move against Sir Raymond Valchamps, and forgetting that he had yet to learn the exact location of the journal from Lily Christian, who was lying quietly in the bed making plans of her own. He was not going to leave her at Penmorley Hall with Honoria Penmorley to keep her company while he returned to the island—the island she had longed to return to for so many years. If anyone had the right to return to that island, then she did.

Glancing up at his tall figure standing before the window, Lily vowed that she would be aboard the *Madrigal* when Valentine Whitelaw set sail for the Indies.

"Well, you have certainly taken your time in returning to London. Have a good journey?" the man sitting quietly in an armchair in the corner of the great chamber inquired of Sir Raymond Valchamps.

"What the devil are you doing here at this hour of the morning?" Sir Raymond greeted his visitor with an obvious lack of pleasure. "I hope you've a good reason for getting me out of bed so early," he demanded, clad in a dressing gown, his silvery hair uncombed.

"I hear you've been seeing some of the countryside."

Sir Raymond glanced up curiously from the goblet of wine he'd just poured, and, taking a sip, nodded. "Yes, you might say that," he said with a smile as he took his seat opposite, hiding a yawn behind a casually raised hand.

The man watching him longed to strike that smug expression from Raymond Valchamps's face. "Warwickshire, perhaps?"

Sir Raymond Valchamps's smile widened. "Yes, I believe so. I had intended to mention my travels to you this evening. I do have considerable holdings, given to me by Elizabeth, which border Warwickshire and Oxfordshire. And have you forgotten my own family home is in Buckinghamshire? Not far away. I have been in the area for the last couple of days. Have an interest, do you, in what I've been up to?"

"Oh, I know precisely what you've been doing."

"Indeed? News does travel fast nowadays. When is the funeral? I suppose I shall have to attend. Rather enjoyable one, I should think," he said, laughing softly.

"What funeral?"

Sir Raymond's eyes blinked slightly. "I thought you knew.

What is all of this conversation about, otherwise? The girl's, of course. I have dealt with her," Sir Raymond informed him, taking a long, satisfying swallow of wine. "Damned thirsty. Lot of dust on the roads."

"Have you indeed?" his friend inquired icily.

"Ah, of course, that conscience of yours. You really must do something about it. You are becoming a bore, so please, spare me your usual remorse. I am fatigued from my journey . . . and Cordelia was waiting for me upon my return. She will make a splendid wife. Have some wine. We will toast our success. It had to be done," he reminded his serious-faced friend.

But the man surprised Sir Raymond by laughing harshly. "*If* done properly. All you have managed to do is draw attention to yourself. You and your damned obsession with Lily Christian have put us in more danger than we have ever been in—if indeed we haven't always. Fools, Raymond. We've been fools these many years. The executioner's ax has been hovering over our heads all along, my friend."

"What on earth are you talking about now?" Sir Raymond asked rather offhandedly, though he was beginning to become concerned. "You've no guts, that's your worst enemy," he said with a contemptuous look at the richly dressed man. "Wouldn't want to ruin our fine silk hose, now would we? What did you mean when you said *if* done properly?" he added, seemingly more interested in examining the fine leather of his slipper than hearing the explanation. "The girl is dead. I stood there and watched her drown. But just to make certain, I hit her over the head first," he added, his fingers tapping nervously against the arm of his chair.

"Oh? You actually watched her drown?"

"She went under. There was blood on her head. Good as dead. I heard someone coming. A dog started barking nearby, and I hardly wished to be seen standing on the edge of the pool with that stick in my hand while I watched the girl drown," he retorted with a defensive glance at his friend. "At least I had the courage to act."

"She did not drown."

Sir Raymond Valchamps remained unmoving. "Not dead? Surely you jest, dear friend?"

"No."

"Damn!" Sir Raymond said beneath his breath, his hands clenched around the arms of the chair.

"You were not very careful, were you? Nor were you the last time. You have made two very serious mistakes, Raymond, and you have endangered us all."

"Endangered you? I doubt that. I'm the one who struck her down. Well, 'tisn't of concern. She did not see me."

"Oh, but she did. She saw your reflection in the pool. Like a mirror held before her eyes, with your face revealed to her."

Sir Raymond wiped the wine from his lips with the back of his hand. "No one will believe her. 'Sdeath, but she's been living with gypsies. Little better than a whore. That gypsy who attacked me was probably her lover. You should have seen the way she brazenly bared herself in the woods. If I'd had more time . . . well," Sir Raymond speculated aloud, remembering the seductive beauty of her body. "My word against hers. I'm the queen's favorite," he chuckled.

"Valentine Whitelaw believes her, Raymond."

"Oh?" Sir Raymond responded easily, but he couldn't hide his momentary start of surprise.

"Yes. You were very sloppy when you tried to murder her at the fair. My God, Raymond, you started a riot, and then you stabbed the wrong girl. You were seen paying off those two henchmen of yours."

Sir Raymond's smug expression disappeared. "Who saw me?"

"Valentine Whitelaw's servant. He thought it strange you should be involved in the burning of the gypsy camp and told his captain as much."

"Damn! I didn't see him. There were so many people about, and I was more concerned with the girl."

"As usual, you were too busy enjoying yourself to worry about the consequences."

"But who will accept the word of a *Turk*?" Sir Raymond asked with a laugh. "People will merely believe that Valentine Whitelaw is trying to implicate me in this affair out of spite because I stole his mistress from him. I will make certain people hear of his insults and harassment of me. They will believe he is trying to get even. Nothing more. One day I will have my revenge against him. And no one will blame me."

"The man you should be seeking revenge against is this Hartwell Barclay."

Sir Raymond snorted derisively. "Hartwell Barclay? Good Lord, why on earth should I worry about that butt?"

"Because if he hadn't tried to rape Lily Christian, she would not have run away from Highcross. She would have remained safely out of your path. There would never have been a puppet show or two botched attempts on her life which have resulted in Valentine Whitelaw becoming suspicious."

"Damned Whitelaws, always interfering, sticking their noses where they shouldn't."

"Due to that interference, Lily Christian still lives. Valentine Whitelaw pulled her from the pool before she drowned."

"How the devil did he track them down so quickly? Took me days of following them, spending cold, wet nights huddling beneath my cloak. Did stay in an inn a couple of nights, knew I'd catch up with them the next day."

"Simon Whitelaw visited Highcross and discovered Lily and the others had fled. He knew they might try to reach their old nursemaid in Warwickshire. That is why Valentine Whitelaw was a step ahead of you this time, my friend."

"One of these days, he and I will have that reckoning," Sir Raymond Valchamps vowed. "He has cheated me of the prize too often."

"If you live that long. I fear this is one predicament that you will not be able to bluff your way out of, Raymond," the man advised him. "You were seen by Lily Christian before you attempted to murder her. You were seen at the gypsy camp when a girl, wearing Lily Christian's gown, was murdered, and for the last several days you have been mysteriously absent from London. Supposedly visiting your estates near where the attack against Lily Christian took place."

"Circumstantial evidence. No one can prove anything against me," Sir Raymond responded, almost convincing himself that he had nothing to fear. "No one can prove anything," he repeated softly, vowing to be more careful in future.

"Of course, there is the puppet. Ugly thing," the man said.

Sir Raymond shifted in his seat. "The puppet?"

"Yes, the one of the witch, with the one blue eye and one brown eye. Took me quite by surprise, I must say. Odd, it wasn't destroyed in the fire you set. It is now in Valentine Whitelaw's possession. You have mocked the fates far too often, Raymond."

"Well, even I can find a bit of humor in that. By God, that is rich!" Sir Raymond said, laughing uncontrollably. "The jest is on me!"

The man smiled.

"Of course, what the devil does a child's puppet prove? Everyone knows the girl has met me. I'm not easily forgotten. A cruel, childish prank, that's what it is. The girl made the puppet to frighten her sister and brother. It means nothing. If that is Valentine Whitelaw's evidence, then I shan't even bother to show up at the trial. A waste of time. There is no proof. He'll be a laughingstock."

"And the fable you told me about? The story of the evil witch who so fits your description and is plotting to assassinate the queen?"

"You have said it yourself: a fable. Am I to be executed because of a puppet show? 'Sdeath, but things have not gotten that bad for Catholics yet that I would be tried for treason on that proof alone. Lord, but I would indeed become a martyr for the cause."

" 'Twas a story obviously told to the children by Sir Basil Whitelaw, one of the queen's advisers, who happened to be in Hispaniola, and most likely at her bidding," Sir Raymond's inquisitor pointed out. "It is obvious that his friendship with Geoffrey Christian served as a cover for his spying activities. Do you not wonder that Walsingham and Lord Burghley might begin to have doubts? How very inconvenient for them that he should die before returning to England to report, and how very unfortunate if one begins to suspect that he knew something."

"Again, I say there is no proof. You are worried needlessly. Perhaps I will no longer be the queen's favorite because of these *unfounded* rumors casting suspicion on my good name, and I may even have to flee to France for a while rather than spend my days in the Tower, but that will not be for long."

"You and I will meet our deaths, Raymond, because we will be tried and convicted on very damning proof. Basil Whitelaw's journal."

Sir Raymond Valchamps paled slightly. "Journal?"

"Yes, the one he was taking notes in while visiting Santo Domingo. 'Tis obvious he saw us, or he would never have told the children that fable. He knew. He knew everything. Somehow he learned even more of our plans, or being the intelligent man he was, he guessed what we were about. He was far smarter than we, my friend. Whatever the case, he wrote down everything he saw while visiting Santo Domingo. Lord knows what else is in that damning journal of his. Basil Whitelaw was a very conscientious man, and he took his duties very seriously. I am certain, had I access to that journal, that I would discover both of our names inscribed neatly there."

"I seem to recall you mentioning, after Valentine Whitelaw had rescued the brats, that there was a journal, but that it had been destroyed with Basil Whitelaw when he died."

"Yes, I did."

"So?"

"So the girl lied."

Sir Raymond Valchamps got slowly to his feet. "She lied? Lily Christian lied?"

"Yes. The journal Basil Whitelaw kept of his travels and of his life on that island he was so cruelly abandoned on was not destroyed. Lily Christian solemnly promised Basil Whitelaw that she would hide his journal and keep its existence a secret. My God, the man was on his deathbed and all he could worry about was that journal. Makes one wonder what information could be so very important that Basil Whitelaw would be so concerned about its safety. Lily Christian kept her vow to him and hid the journal, and she never spoke of it to anyone. And now it is just waiting to be found and brought back to England. After so many years of believing ourselves safe, Raymond, the truth is about to be revealed. Basil Whitelaw has indeed had his revenge against us. As Geoffrey Christian has as well. He at least died quickly and with honor, while you and I have been hiding all of these years. Can you hear his laughter, Raymond?"

"You seem very well informed. How do you know all of this?"

"I've just come from Riverhurst, where yesterday evening I and several other privileged individuals—all trusted friends of Valentine Whitelaw—were privy to some rather startling information concerning you. All highly confidential, of course. Naturally, Valentine Whitelaw is at Whitehall this very minute informing Burghley of those suspicions you have been so contemptuous of. We were all properly shocked. No word will leak out concerning this, however, since Valentine Whitelaw wishes to catch the conspirators before they can escape the net he is spreading."

Sir Raymond Valchamps sat brooding, thinking of all of them sitting there at Riverhurst listening to Valentine Whitelaw's damning words. He could see them all. Valentine Whitelaw, with his host and hostess, Sir William and Lady Elspeth, and their guests—Thomas Sandrick, George Hargraves, Sir Rodger Penmorley, Sir Charles Denning, and others, perhaps even Walter Raleigh, for he'd become very good friends with certain people of late.

Sir Raymond sat back down. "Whitelaw will be sailing, won't he? He's going back to that island to find the journal. What are we going to do? There is no hope of keeping our identities secret now," he said, glancing toward the window as if he could already hear the sound of the queen's guard banging at his door. "We will have to flee. Damn, they are probably already watching my house. You took a chance coming here. Walsingham has spies all over London."

"Valentine Whitelaw sails with the tide on the morrow. But you needn't worry, at least not yet," the man said.

"Not worry? A fine reassurance coming from you. I'm surprised you spared the time to come and warn me. Or that you found the courage. I am a marked man, but you, you are still safe. At least," Sir Raymond added with a cruel twist to his mouth, "until I'm under torture. Then your name will come screaming from my lips."

"I said I have taken care of the matter."

"You?" Sir Raymond asked incredulously. "Well, I am reassured. What did you do, pray for us?"

"No," the man said quietly, "I sent word to Don Pedro Villasandro."

"My God! You what?"

"This very morning, I wrote a letter to the Spanish ambassador, explaining the seriousness of the situation, without mentioning names, of course, and asked that he would forward my letter to Don Pedro," he explained.

Sir Raymond stared at the man as if he were mad. "Don Pedro can sail into hell as far as I'm concerned, and I suspect he feels the same sentiments about us. Why on earth contact him? He's not even in England that I know. What good will it do to inform him? I'd do better trying to flee England aboard a fishing boat stinking of salmon. Of course, by the time Don Pedro arrives, he might be able to collect the various parts of my body after I've been drawn and quartered. Might be difficult getting my head down from Traitor's Gate, but I'm sure he'll manage. At least I might get a hero's burial on the Continent, having died for my beliefs. However, if that is your idea of escaping Elizabeth's wrath, then no thank you."

"Have you forgotten that it was while aboard Don Pedro's ship that we sank Geoffrey Christian's ship? Don Pedro knows where the island is, Raymond. I've sent word to him that he must get there in time to stop Valentine Whitelaw. Oh, I do not believe that he would sail just because we are in danger, but I do know that he hates Valentine Whitelaw as much as he hated Geoffrey Christian. They are two of a kind, and our Spanish captain would not hesitate to get rid of this enemy of his the same way he did the last one. He will sail to that island, and he will sink the *Madrigal*. Don Pedro is very capable at setting traps for his enemies. He will sail. He will not be able to resist the challenge I have given him, nor the opportunity of surprising his enemy. Don Pedro is a man who likes to have the odds in his favor before he acts."

"What if he fails?" Sir Raymond asked.

"We must have faith that he will not fail."

"That may satisfy you, but it hardly sets my mind at rest."

"We can do nothing else. I am an Englishman. I could never live on the Continent in exile. My life is in England. I have never known as much happiness as I know now. And if I were to flee today out of fear that Don Pedro might fail, how could I possibly explain my absence? Whether Whitelaw returns or not, my life would be ruined. I can do nothing but await my fate. It is out of my hands now. I've had to act to protect us all. I do regret what may happen because of my actions, but I had no other choice."

"On the Continent you would at least be alive. But I can see that you are determined to become that martyr. I, on the other hand, shall be preparing for my escape should Valentine White-law return to England with that journal.''

''Oh, I am no martyr, Raymond. I have no wish to die. So let us both pray that Don Pedro does not fail. For he is the only one now who can save us. He is the only one who knows where the island is. A special messenger has already been sent to Madrid with my letter, and within the week, Don Pedro Villasandro will be sailing for the Indies.''

Sir Raymond Valchamps smiled. ''And in the meantime I am going to settle the score with Lily Christian. Because of her, the life I've come to enjoy is finished. She owes me. I will see her dead before I leave England,'' Sir Raymond promised.

''I do not think you need worry about Lily Christian. For now, at least, she has escaped us. She is sailing with Valentine Whitelaw.''

Sir Raymond stared at his friend in disbelief, then his shrill laughter filled the room.

Come unto these yellow sands,
  And then take hands:
Curtsied when you have, and kiss'd—
  The wild waves whist—
Foot it featly here and there.

SHAKESPEARE

Chapter Twenty-Five

FROM the deck of the *Madrigal*, the island seemed quiet, basking peacefully in the late afternoon sun. Fluffy white clouds drifted over the low hills of pine and palmetto that seemed little changed since last Lily had viewed them. The gleaming crescent of sand ringing the bay was untouched except for the foaming surf spreading across its smooth surface.

The lone pine still stood sentry at the tip of the rocky headland, and Lily wondered how many times she'd sat beneath its sheltering boughs and stared out to sea, hoping to spy the white flag bearing the red cross of St. George. Lily glanced upward, past the tall, swaying masts to see the flag fluttering in the gentle breeze that caressed the isle that had been her home, and where she had known such happiness and sadness.

"O where have you been, my long, long love,
  This long seven years and more?"
"O I'm come to seek my former vows
  Ye granted me before."

Lily listened to the melodic voice that drifted from above. Shielding her eyes against the glare off the water, she continued to gaze upward, searching the masts for the balladeer. Through a maze of ropes she spied a sailor clinging to a ratline, the toes of his bare feet holding him firm on the rope rung while he worked at some task high in the topgallant shrouds.

> "I might have had a king's daughter,
> Far, far beyond the sea;
> I might have had a king's daughter,
> Had it not been for love o' thee."

When the call of Land-ho! had been sounded by the lookout high atop the foremast, the deck, rigging, and yardarms had suddenly been swarming with hands as the ship had closed the land and they'd prepared to lower and furl the sails, paying out the cable to drop anchor just beyond the reefs.

> "I have seven ships upon the sea,
> The eighth brought me to land,
> With four-and-twenty bold mariners,
> And music on every hand."

"Hand over hand, lads!"
"Heave well and heartily!"
"Avast ye, there!"

> She set her foot upon the ship,
> No mariners could she behold;
> But the sails were o' the taffetie,
> And the masts o' the beaten gold.

> They had not sailed a league, a league,
> A league but barely three,
> Until she spied his cloven foot,
> And she wept right bitterly.

Lily's eyes searched the uneven line of the forest fringing the shore. A tall tree rose above all others. At its base, in the cool shade, were the graves of her mother and Basil Whitelaw.

> "O what hills are yon, yon pleasant hills,
> That the sun shines sweetly on?"

"O yon are the hills of heaven," he said,
"Where you will never win."

"O what a mountain is yon," she said,
"All so dreary with frost and snow?"
"O yon is the mountain of hell," he cried,
"Where you and I will go."

He struck the topmast with his hand,
The foremast with his knee,
And he broke that gallant ship in twain,
And sank her in the sea.

Lily looked away from the island to where Valentine Whitelaw stood on the upper deck, his gaze raking the isle and the
bay. He turned to starboard, his eyes narrowing thoughtfully as
he stared out to sea for a long moment. He seemed to sense her
eyes upon him, for he suddenly glanced down to where she
stood against the rail. His turquoise eyes were a dazzling reflection of the sea and sky, ablaze with the brilliancy of the sun,
then, as if a shadow had crossed before it, he had turned away.

"Lower handsomely, lads!" Valentine Whitelaw called out,
following the progress of several seamen who were struggling to
lower a sail. "Away aloft, Master Turner. Bear a hand there,
that's a good lad!" he said as the young man responded quickly
to his captain's command and climbed the mast without question.

"I always wondered what this island looked like," Simon
Whitelaw said, coming to stand beside Lily by the rail. "I've
dreamt of it since hearing your stories, but I could never quite
envision it. Now that I see it, I realize that I never came even
close in my imagination."

"I sometimes think it truly is a magical isle. It cast a spell over
us when we first set foot ashore. It protected us from danger. It
kept us well-supplied with food and water, and it gave us happiness. And then, like most enchantments, it showed its cruel
side. It took from us, perhaps because we broke the spell by ·
letting strangers come ashore. Or maybe because we stole from
the sea its bounty of flesh and gold," Lily said, remembering the

bodies they'd pulled from the surf and the doubloons they'd hidden beyond its reach.

Hearing the seriousness in her voice, Simon Whitelaw stared down at her, a curious expression on his thin face, which was bronzed from weeks at sea. "I think you really believe that."

Lily glanced over to where the Turk stood watching the shore, a frowning expression on his dark face. "I do not think I am the only one who feels so strangely about this isle."

"From my own memories of my father, and from what I have gathered from others, I cannot quite believe that my father would have felt that way," Simon declared, unwilling to believe in such fantastic lore. Next she would be asking him to believe in mermaids and winged horses. "He was a very practical man," he reminded Lily.

Lily smiled, remembering Basil strutting along the sands, proud as a peacock in the feathered cape and headdress. And when she thought of the love that Basil and her mother had found together she knew that Basil had known of the enchantment.

"I am curious, Lily," Simon said, trying to recapture her attention. "Would you really not have told Valentine where the cave was if he hadn't agreed to take you on this journey?"

Lily eyed Simon speculatively for a moment. "What do you think?"

Simon grinned. "I think you put on a false bold front and dared Valentine to take the risk that you might be serious."

"False?"

"Yes. I know you too well, Lily. Valentine, however, must have had some doubts. You might be willful and stubborn, but you would never put your own desires before another's needs. You are far too conscientious to risk Elizabeth's life to satisfy a childish whim. You would have told him, wouldn't you?"

Lily glanced around, gesturing for him to bend low so she could whisper in his ear. "Yes, but that is our secret," she made him promise, placing her finger against his lips to seal them.

Simon caught her hand in his and shook an admonishing finger at her. "You dare what I would never have the courage to do. I could never have faced Valentine with that challenge, risking his anger and disapproval. He does not like to be defied. My knees would have buckled beneath me."

"He is well used to giving orders, even to those he has no authority over," Lily remarked. "I fear he has captained this ship far too long. 'Tis about time someone sent a couple of shots across his swaggering bow."

Simon laughed. "Lily, you are a far better adventurer than I."

" 'Tis the challenge I like. And had he left me behind, Simon, I would have found the way to have gotten aboard before the *Madrigal* sailed," she added with a glint in her eye that had Simon believing her claim.

"How?"

"I would have masqueraded as the *Madrigal*'s new cabin boy and gone aboard in Falmouth. Valentine might have thought to leave me at Ravindzara, or," she said with a grimace, "at Penmorley Hall under Honoria's hawkish eye. I would have raced the wind back to Falmouth and boarded before Valentine returned. I would already have been aboard, safely hidden behind a barrel of pickled herrings in the hold. Then, when well out of port, I would have surprised my captain with my true identity. I'm rather good at that," she said with a low laugh that had Simon laughing in response, although he did not understand the full meaning of her statement, for he'd never learned of the chance meeting between Valentine and "Francisca."

"Damn, I wish I'd half the nerve, Lily. Valentine swears you are much like your father, and I suspect he is correct. I, on the other hand, am overly cautious by nature, like my father."

"But you are too harsh on yourself, Simon. You confronted Hartwell Barclay and my accusers with great courage, then you came in search of us. And you are aboard the *Madrigal*, are you not? When at Riverhurst, I heard you speak most eloquently for the right to accompany us."

"Well, how could they deny me when you were going? And you are, after all, just a female," Simon said with an apologetic look, making light of his own attributes, as well as of his persuasive speech.

But Lily remembered it, and, earlier, the angry confrontation she'd had with Valentine Whitelaw while still at the inn. . . .

When questioned, she had remained silent about the location of the cave where the treasure chest and the journal had been safely hidden all of these years. She refused to be intimidated and met Valentine Whitelaw's incredulous stare with a bold one of her own. And had the *Madrigal* received a broadside across her beam Valentine Whitelaw could not have been more surprised by the challenge.

She told him that it was her right to return to the island and retrieve Basil's journal. Once before, when he had deceived her into coming out of hiding on the island, he had deprived her of the chance to bid farewell to her mother and Basil. He might not understand her feelings concerning that, but now was her opportunity to return to the island and she was not going to be cheated this time. After all, she and her family had been the victims of Sir Raymond's treachery. And there was a treasure to claim. With a chest full of golden doubloons, they would never have to fear Hartwell Barclay again, despite what Valentine had promised he'd do to the man for his abuse of them. Nor would they have to be beholden to Valentine Whitelaw either. If Valentine wanted to know the location of the cave, he would have to take her along. Besides, she added, even if she did tell him he most likely would not be able to find it for he was unfamiliar with the island.

Valentine Whitelaw remained silent, then he smiled that slow smile of his. "Very well," he said. "Where is the journal?"

He capitulated too easily, Lily thought.

"I will go with you when you sail?" she asked.

"Yes, now where is the journal," he repeated.

"Once we arrive at the island, then, and only then, will I tell you," she replied suspiciously, adding that if he would give her his word of honor that he would take her with him then she would tell him now.

She was surprised when Valentine remained silent, tossing the puppet that so resembled Sir Raymond Valchamps high into the air, its arms and legs flying out in all directions before he caught it in his grasp. A moment later he surprised her when he excused himself, leaving the tray of food on her lap with orders she was to eat it all. He returned less than a quarter of an hour later and gave his word of honor that she would be aboard the *Madrigal* when she sailed. Trusting him, she told him where the cave was located, having to pause several times in confusion when he questioned her in detail about the path and any identifiable markers they would be able to follow. But once on the island, she would be able to find it again, she reassured him. Belatedly, because of his questioning, she began to doubt his promise, but he didn't go back on his word, and when the *Madrigal* set sail for the Indies she had been aboard.

It had seemed to Lily, since she hadn't had to face a disapproving parental eye, that Simon had had an even more difficult time in convincing Lady Elspeth and Sir William to allow him to accompany Valentine on his voyage.

"My father lies buried there, where his only son has never been able to mourn for him, except in his heart. I have the right, Mother, to stand beside his grave. I will never know any peace unless I do. I want to pay my respects to a man who is only a vague memory to me now, to a man I knew for too short a while, but who is still my father. I would prefer to go with your and Sir William's blessing, but I will go, Mother. I am my own master now, and no one has the right to forbid my actions. I will stand on that island one day," Simon told them. "I have already spoken to Valentine, and he has given me permission to sail aboard the *Madrigal*. But he has also said that if you ask him not to allow me to sail with him, then he will abide by your wishes. Mother, please, give me your blessing," Simon implored her, and Lily, watching Lady Elspeth's expression, knew that she wished above all else that he would not venture from England and from her side, but wisely knew that Simon must make this journey.

Lady Elspeth and Sir William gave Simon their blessing and even came into London to bid him Godspeed when the *Madrigal* sailed with the tide. Valentine Whitelaw's trusted friends, Thomas Sandrick and George Hargraves, as well as Sir Charles Denning, all of whom accompanied them back to London, had been invited to join the voyage. Thomas Sandrick had declined. His wife was Sir Raymond's sister, and although he'd never been very close to his brother-in-law, he could not participate in gathering evidence against him; besides, he'd added on a lighter note, he had already proven himself less than a capable sailor. George Hargraves had looked astounded and claimed that he needed no further proof of his unseaworthiness; he got sick crossing the Thames. And Sir Charles Denning, sputtering while he hemmed and hawed, said he was far too old to go gallivanting around the world—nonsensical idea, surprised Valentine had even suggested such a thing, he'd declared huffily.

Sir Rodger Penmorley and Quinta Whitelaw, however, had been on board when the *Madrigal* weighed anchor and they began their journey down the Thames. Quinta had arrived two days after they'd returned to London. Upon hearing the news, Lily knew, had Artemis not been expecting her first child, Quinta would have been with them now, standing on deck viewing the island.

Fairfax and Farley and Tillie Odell, one tall, one short, one rotund, stood on the dock waving until the *Madrigal* had disappeared downriver. Soon they would travel to Whiteswood, where Simon Whitelaw had invited them to stay until Hartwell Barclay had been dealt with. Tristram and Dulcie, and the menagerie of animals, had been aboard for the brief voyage to Falmouth, where the *Madrigal* had docked and taken on fresh water and supplies while her captain and passengers had traveled by land to Ravindzara.

During the three years since she'd visited Valentine Whitelaw's home, Ravindzara had undergone a startling transformation. They approached Ravindzara from the sea. Riding across a wild heath, they entered the parkland along a lane planted with carefully nurtured saplings that were already beginning to plant their roots deep and stretch to the sky with strong limbs. The terraced gardens surrounding the house were interlaced with brick paths, bordered with sweet-scented plants and flowers rich in color, that led to rose arbors and fountains secluded behind clipped yew hedges.

Across the gray stone front of the great house were tall, diamond-paned windows flanking the columned frontispiece and overlooking the sea. On each end of the south front were curved oriel windows displaying a large expanse of glass on three sides that must have served more than one floor and allowed light to enter the great hall from dawn until dusk. Work was almost completed on the west wing. And next year, the master of Ravindzara proudly told them, work would begin on the east wing.

The lane had curved in front of the entrance and before they'd even dismounted attentive grooms had appeared from the stables to see to their horses. Entering the great hall, Lily felt as if she'd come home. Except for the sunshine streaming through the great wall of gleaming windows, and the additional furnishings, the hall was little changed. Colorful Turkish carpets in bright blues and reds covered the floor, while tapestries and paintings added color and warmth beneath the high-arched ceiling. The oak banqueting table, where a tall vase held fragrant dark red roses, was being set with silver plate, and already maids were lighting a fire in the great hearth.

But Lily's pleasure quickly fled when she saw Honoria Penmorley standing at the foot of the great stone staircase, waiting to greet them as though she were already mistress of Valentine Whitelaw's home. Dressed with her usual discreet good taste in a gown of tawny satin, she came forward, her slender, elegant hand politely extended in welcome, a complacent smile curving her lovely lips while a delicate flush pinkened that flawless porcelain skin.

With a martyred air, she sighed and glanced sadly around the great hall, claiming that she'd had to visit Ravindzara continually since Quinta's absence, for servants and laborers could never be trusted to do their jobs without proper supervision. And from some of the sour looks being sent her way from the servants in the hall, Lily suspected Honoria had carried out her self-professed duty with a vengeance. Lily doubted that Ravindzara possessed any secrets that Honoria Penmorley hadn't ferreted out by now, for she moved through the great hall like one well accustomed to her surroundings. Even Quinta Whitelaw raised an arched brow when Honoria presumed to reprimand a nervous maid who'd accidentally spilled a few drops of ale from a tray of refreshments she was serving to the thirsty riders.

Lily could smile now in remembrance of the momentary look of discomfiture that had crossed Honoria's face when she'd seen the visitors accompanying Valentine Whitelaw. Those almond-shaped eyes stared at her for a long moment before recognition entered them, leaving them coolly assessing. Lily felt only briefly ill at ease, then she nodded, meeting and holding the other woman's gaze with a proud one of her own. Throughout the following minutes, Lily felt Honoria Penmorley's eyes lingering on her and she even caught a slightly puzzled expression on Honoria's face when she turned her gaze to her host.

Lily was not sorry to see Honoria take her leave soon after that, returning to Penmorley Hall to greet her brother. Valentine's offer to escort her had been graciously accepted, her apologetic glance around leaving the impression that he'd chosen to escort her at the expense of his duties as host, when in reality he had stated his intention of visiting Artemis. Sir Rodger and Artemis and Honoria returned the following day to bid them a safe journey, for Valentine told them he would be leaving almost immediately for Falmouth.

Lily recalled her last sight of Tristram and Dulcie, Raphael racing around their small figures and barking excitedly, Cappie astride and clinging to his collar. Although Tristram had been sulky at first when denied his request to accompany them, he stood with Dulcie in front of the house and waved wildly until she could no longer see them. Quinta and Artemis were standing close to them, with Sir Rodger just behind, his hand resting possessively on Artemis's shoulder. It was odd, though, that it was Honoria she remembered the most, standing there watching their progress along the lane, a secretive smile on her face as she'd turned away to gaze at Ravindzara long before the riders had disappeared from view.

Boarding the *Madrigal* in Falmouth, they'd set sail without further delay. The journey had passed uneventfully, perhaps too uneventfully Lily was to believe later, but while the sails had billowed and the *Madrigal*'s prow had swung toward the Indies, she'd felt she had been destined to return to the island.

Unable to resist, Lily's gaze now drifted to the captain of the *Madrigal*. In the balmy, tropical air, he had removed his doublet and jerkin, and his shirt of snowy white linen, the gathered neckline opened to reveal a wide expanse of bare chest, and the long, full sleeves rolled up above his elbows to expose his muscular forearms, made his sun-bronzed skin seem all the darker. His leather cannons fit snugly, the tubelike breeches molding his hips and thighs and revealing the sinewy strength of muscles that rippled with his every movement.

His black hair had grown much longer since beginning the voyage and remained untrimmed. He kept pushing the thick curls, tousled by the winds, away from his lean face. The gold earring he wore glinted in reminder that some, especially the

Spanish, thought him little better than a pirate. And Lily knew
they had reason to fear him, for when he grinned at something
his first mate had said, there was a devilish light in his turquoise
eyes.

Lily's lips trembled slightly when she thought of the
coldness—or perhaps it had been more of an indifference—he'd
shown her during the voyage. He'd been like a stranger and she
knew he was still angry because she had blackmailed him into
taking her with him on this voyage. Never had he sought her
out, and very seldom had he even been alone with her or engaged her in conversation, and Lily sometimes wondered if it
had all been a dream: being held in his arms, feeling his lips
pressed to hers in a passionate kiss that had left her breathless
and stolen some of the maidenly innocence from her.

He had never spoken of that day at the fair. To him, Lily
thought, it might never have happened. And as soon as he'd
discovered that Francisca was Lily, he had lost interest. And yet,
for her . . .

"You're in love with him, aren't you?" Simon stated, but it
wasn't really a question, because the truth was revealed in her
eyes when she looked at the *Madrigal*'s captain.

Lily looked startled, and for a moment thought to deny it, but
then she shrugged. "I have always loved him, Simon. He
doesn't know that, nor does he return my love. And he will
never know how deeply I love him and always shall," Lily admitted, not realizing how expressively she'd spoken until Simon
took her hand in his and raised it to his lips before tucking it beneath his arm companionably.

"I fear I have even lost his friendship, Simon. How he de-
spises me," she said huskily, turning away from Valentine
Whitelaw, for it did little good to dream, especially when
Honoria Penmorley waited at Ravindzara for the *Madrigal*'s captain to return home.

"I would not despair, Lily, for I have begun to believe of late
that things have a way of working out for the best, even if at the
time we think all is lost and we cannot conceive of ever finding
happiness again," Simon said, his smile bittersweet, and
strangely adult.

Young Simon Whitelaw knew the truth, even if Lily and Valentine did not suspect it. He'd watched them the whole voyage,

and being a fairly objective observer, he had witnessed, at first idly, then in dismay, the meaningful glances that had passed between them, both openly and surreptitiously. He suspected what Lily did not, that Valentine had been fighting his feelings for her. Simon knew he was not mistaken, for he'd seen the gentle expression that had entered Valentine's eyes whenever he gazed upon Lily, and the caressing gaze had not been fatherly. Simon had watched the way those turquoise eyes had narrowed, following Lily's every gesture, the way her hips moved and the way her bodice tightened across her firm young breasts when she raised her arms to push back a stray curl. Never before had Simon seen such a look of tender passion in Valentine's eyes. But Simon also knew that Valentine was blind to the fact that Lily was deeply in love with him.

And yet something that he had no knowledge of had happened to cause an estrangement between them, to make them defensive and suspicious of each other. They seemed to make a special effort not to catch each other's eye, but every so often they had, and then Simon had been embarrassed by the exchange, certain that neither of them had been aware of the unbidden desire that had entered their eyes. He had felt as if he'd committed the unpardonable sin of spying on two lovers embracing. He glanced down at Lily's beautiful face and sighed. The hopes he'd cherished were gone, but then, they had only been dreams and would remain his secret. And unless he wished to lose Lily forever, as well as his uncle's friendship, he would have to be satisfied to remain her friend.

"Do you believe me, Lily? I do not claim to be omniscient, but I do believe that fortune is smiling on you. How could it not, when you are so lovely?" he couldn't resist remarking.

Lily surprised him by reaching up and pressing a soft kiss against his cheek, her eyes tender with love for him, as if he were a brother to her.

To Valentine Whitelaw, watching from the upper deck, they looked like young lovers, and he knew a sudden, all-consuming jealousy of Simon, his own nephew. Watching him fondle and kiss her was maddening. If he had thought Lily Christian beautiful when first seeing her riding along the banks of the Thames and then later when he'd held her in his arms in the greenwood, he knew now that he'd seen only a glimpse of her true beauty.

He had come to know all over again the girl who had matured into a desirable and fascinating woman of incomparable beauty. Watching her and listening to her, learning of her views and feelings concerning all manners of subjects, he had found himself falling deeply, irresistibly in love with her. It was Lily, his Lily of the island he found himself aching to hold and caress—and that desire came of an attraction that went far deeper than the physical lust he'd felt for the beautiful woman in green velvet whom he'd come to know as Francisca. Lily Christian possessed a humility and kindness that few other renowned beauties of his acquaintance even had knowledge of. She was a woman of thoughtful intelligence. She was spirited and headstrong. She was a young woman who could hold her own with anyone, and although she'd even challenged him, he admired her for her courage. There was no artifice with Lily, and yet she was a born enchantress with her pale green eyes that glowed with so many emotions. He'd watched the way the corners of her mouth turned up slightly when she was thinking of something amusing, and the way she would stretch like a child, her arms held out, unaware that it drew a man's gaze to her soft, womanly curves. And when she would sit on deck, brushing her long dark red hair, she never realized the effect it had on a man, driving him to the point where he would sell his soul to bury his face in its fragrant thickness. With an innocent wantonness, she had seduced him. When he lay in his bunk feeling the gentle movement of the ship beneath him, knowing she was lying close by, he was left with a painful ache in his loins that would not be satisfied until he had possessed her.

She stood on deck now, her dark red hair glinting in the sunlight like fire. The winds swirled around her figure, lifting long strands of her hair to float about her as if they were alive, molding her gown against the slender length of her thighs and gentle curve of buttock. After leaving the coldness of the North Atlantic, Lily had replaced the heavy green velvet gown she'd been wearing with a lighter gown of creamy silk. Since entering the islands, she had shed the voluminous petticoats beneath her gown and freed her breath from the stiffened corset.

Only Lily, whose untamed spirit seemed to guide her every action, would have thrown caution and propriety to the winds and done as she pleased in order to be more comfortable. Everything about Lily Christian fascinated him. But she was not for him, he warned himself. He was too old and cynical for one as young and innocent as she. And were he to take Lily Christian for his wife—*if* she would have him, he added with an uncertainty he was not accustomed to experiencing—then how could he ever bear to leave her to sail away for months at a time after he had once lain with her. And yet the sea was a part of his life. If it were not for the *Madrigal*'s voyages there would be no Ravindzara to return to. He would not be able to keep Lily in the manner in which he would wish. To love Lily would only serve to bring him heartache, for he knew he would never be content to be away from her for long. She inspired an uncontrollable jealousy, passion, and love that he'd never felt so deeply before and which would always keep him aching for her touch.

Valentine shook his head, thinking he must be feverish to be dwelling upon such things, like a lovesick boy who had yet to know the pleasures of a woman's body. But never before had he known a woman such as Lily Christian. He had thought he'd been in love with Cordelia, but the desires she had kindled paled in comparison to the fires that burned inside of him now. He wanted Lily and he knew he could win her if he tried. She was so innocent of passion that he could easily seduce her. She had trembled in his arms before, and her lips had clung to his. She had wanted him. She would be his, if he so desired, but what of her needs? he found himself thinking. Would he be able to make her happy, away as he was for most of the year? She would suffer loneliness and perhaps wish for another to warm her through the long, cold months of winter. And he had little doubt that there would be many who would hope, perhaps even conspire, to replace him in her affections.

Despite her claim that she and her family were none of his affair, she was a part of his life. He felt responsible for her; after all, he had been the one to rescue her from the island. He felt a certain proprietary interest in her that no other man could claim. He might even remind her of the debt she owed him for having rescued her. And she was Geoffrey Christian's daughter; that gave him the right, as Geoffrey's friend, to concern himself with her well-being. He would have wished Valentine to keep an eye on his daughter. And whether she liked it or not, he was in her life to stay, Valentine decided with a stubborn glint in his turquoise eyes as he watched Simon place an arm across Lily's slender shoulders.

If he had to lose Lily to another man, then at least Simon was a Whitelaw, and he could exert a certain influence in their lives. He would see to it that no harm ever befell Lily. If she chose his nephew, he would make certain Simon never brought Lily any unhappiness. Valentine ran a shaky hand through his hair when he envisioned any man other than himself lying with Lily.

Valentine Whitelaw forced himself to look away from Lily, to keep his mind on the task before him—there would be time enough later to worry about Lily Christian's future when they returned to England.

"Every inch of it, lads! I don't want to see any slack in that line," he called to a group of seamen hauling on a rope. "Haul taut, there!" he reminded, the unusual harshness and impatience in their captain's voice giving cause for several of the reprimanded hands to exchange curious glances.

The *Madrigal*'s captain signaled to the coxswain to prepare to lower the boat.

"Prepare to lower away!" the cry sounded.

"If you can manage to tear yourselves away from each other's loving caresses long enough to board, we might be able to beach the boat before nightfall," Valentine spoke brusquely to a startled Lily and Simon who'd been laughing at a shared jest and had not heard his quiet approach from behind, where he now stood staring, arms folded across his wide chest.

He did not miss the guilty flush that stained her cheeks, and he misunderstood the reason for it, thinking his nephew had wasted little time in whispering loving words into her ear.

"I'm sorry, Valentine," Simon began, although with a puzzled expression, for it wasn't yet noon. "We were just laughing at that porp—"

Simon's explanation was cut short, rudely interrupted when the captain spoke sarcastically, unable to contain the jealousy that had surged through him when hearing their soft laughter. "And in future, have the decency not to fondle each other in the presence of my crew. When we return to England I will see that the banns are posted and then you can find a secluded arbor to make love in, or you may boldly do so in St. James's for the whole world to see. But while aboard my ship you will maintain yourselves in a discreet manner," he warned them.

Eyeing Lily Christian up and down with his narrowed gaze, he said, "And you, Mistress Christian, would do well to remember to wear a petticoat. It would do much to help the morale aboard this ship."

Simon Whitelaw stared at his uncle, flabbergasted by the undeserved attack.

"Aye, aye, Cap'n, sir," Lily said with a defiant glance, but Simon could see her lips trembling under the harsh criticism. Without another word, Lily swung her skirts around and marched across the deck to disappear below.

"You know, Uncle Valentine, I used to think you could do no wrong, that you had the answer to everything," Simon said. "Indeed, you may know more about the sea and captaining a ship than most men, but you sure as hell don't know much about women," Simon declared, his dark eyes full of resentment, but before Valentine could try to explain or even apologize, the young man had walked over to the rail, prepared to board the boat that had just been lowered into the water.

Valentine Whitelaw began to feel like the fool he'd just played so well, and it did not help his disposition to catch the Turk's concerned gaze on him, as if worried his captain was losing his senses. Nor did it add to his temper a few minutes later to watch as Lily Christian sauntered across the deck to follow Simon into the boat below, the fine ruffles of her petticoat displayed for all eyes to admire.

"Up oars! Stand by to shove off!" the coxswain called, waiting for his captain to climb aboard.

Valentine Whitelaw glanced down below, where Lily and Simon and the boat's crew had taken their seats in the small boat. He nodded to his first mate, who came hurrying over.

"Master Blackstone, you have your orders and you will carry them out. Keep a vigilant watch."

"Aye, aye, sir," the first mate, a pleasant-faced man in his late twenties, responded.

"I leave you in charge then, Master Blackstone," Valentine Whitelaw said before following the Turk into the boat below.

"Bear off, now!"

The bowmen aboard fended off the boat, pushing it away

from the *Madrigal*'s side with long, wooden shafts with brass hooks on the ends.

"Let fall!" the coxswain called when they were safely away, the oars dropping into the water.

"Give way together, lads!" the coxswain called, the oarsmen starting to row, their oars stroking evenly through the water.

As the boat neared shore, Simon Whitelaw had a difficult time keeping his seat, and even once Valentine had reached out and, with a hand placed firmly on his shoulder, reseated him before he fell overboard.

Lily could understand Simon's excitement, for as the oarsmen sent the boat flying through the narrow channel that cut between the sharp-toothed reefs, she felt a shiver spreading through her as she recognized the curve of sandy shore and the rocky headland shielding the peaceful cove where they'd once frolicked, the rest of the world forgotten—until the sickness had come and, later, the *Madrigal* had appeared on the horizon.

Lily watched Valentine for a moment, wondering what he was thinking. Perhaps he was remembering the last time the *Madrigal* had dropped anchor just beyond the reefs and he'd come ashore hoping to find Basil. Lily's gaze moved away to encounter the Turk's dark, unfathomable eyes watching her and she had the strange sensation that he still did not trust her.

"Pull! Pull! Pull, mates, pull!" The blades dipped in and out of the water, propelling the boat closer to shore.

" 'Tis beautiful," Simon breathed, his wide-eyed gaze drinking in the lush beauty of the palms and the sea of tall grasses that moved restlessly in the warm trades. Staring at the sun-bleached beach that rose beyond the curl of waves foaming against the shore, he could suddenly envision his father walking along that lonely stretch of sand, perhaps staring north, toward England, and thinking of the family he would never again see.

"Way enough, toss and boat oars!" the coxswain yelled above the sound of the surf breaking against the shore as one of the crew jumped from the boat, a line of rope held securely in his hand, while two others jumped into the surf and lent a hand in pulling the boat up on shore.

Lily glanced around bemusedly. Her surroundings seemed so familiar, and yet, it was different. Lost in her thoughts, she was surprised when strong arms suddenly closed around her and lifted her out of the boat. Wading through the surf, Valentine carried Lily up onto the beach. She had flung her arms around his neck when he'd swung her off her feet, and now she was so close to his face that she could see the golden lights fanning out from around each pupil before becoming diffused in the turquoise irises.

"I wouldn't want you to get that petticoat of yours wet," he murmured, loud enough for her ears only before setting her down beyond the surf.

Lily straightened her bodice and skirts, then started along the beach toward the headland where, on the far side, lay the cove. She glanced back once, to see him giving orders, then, leaving one man on duty with the boat, he and the rest of his crew began to follow.

Simon hurried to catch up. "Hey, Lily, wait!"

"Insufferable man," Lily muttered, not risking another glance back, for a shadow with long strides was closing the distance behind.

"Lily. Will we go to the graves first?" Simon inquired, his gaze darting while he tried to absorb everything as they quickly passed. Once, he stopped dead in his tracks, thinking he saw a shadow moving swiftly through the trees. Shaking his head, he rubbed his eyes and hurried on. "I can't believe it, Lily. I am actually here, on the island. I've dreamt of this for so long," he said again, and indeed, he looked like a child newly arisen from a dream. His head was cocked at a slight angle as he listened to the strange cries of exotic birds drifting from the forest.

Lily smiled, taking his hand in hers. "See that tree?" she said, pointing to the one that stood above all others. "They lie beneath, Simon," she told him.

Simon nodded, his eyes never leaving the tall pine as they made their way along the curving beach, a trail of footprints left behind. Midway along the beach, Lily's steps slowed until she finally halted to stare worriedly at the thick underbrush of the forest.

Valentine came to stand beside her, watching her carefully, while his crew, some of whom had visited this isle before, eyed the concealing undergrowth with growing unease.

Lily stared around in dismay. "Everything has changed. I hardly recognize anything. I think there used to be a tall palm there. And that is where the path should be that we followed to our hut and the pool. It looks as if there has never been a path there, or that we had ever been here at all," she said, searching the shadowy darkness of the jungle for the opening, but the thick canopy of leaves let in little light from above and the grasses growing up waist-high were woven together like a living wall. "I feel like a stranger here," Lily said, shivering slightly. This had been her home, but now the enchantment was gone.

"It is as I feared. You've been away from the island for over three years. Not only has the vegetation altered all that you remembered, but the storms that have struck during the years have altered much. Even the shape of the bay has been subtly changed."

"The cave will still be there," Lily said, her step determined as she began to walk toward the headland, "and I can see the pine," she added, staring ahead to where the pine rose above the rest of the forest.

"You said the cave was part of a cliff? Was it this headland?" Valentine questioned.

"No, it was beyond the cove, amongst the cliffs that curve out of sight toward the far side of the isle," Lily told him, reaching out to take Simon's hand held out to her as she struggled up the bank and through the underbrush directly in their path.

"I remember crossing this headland. I believe this is where the Turk met you for the first time?" Valentine said, unable to forget the sight of the Turk tumbling down from the rocks, a feathered figure flying after him.

The Turk said something unintelligible, for it was in his own tongue, but Valentine was in little doubt as to the sentiment it expressed and he grinned in appreciation.

"Tristram used to stand guard beneath that pine on the headland. The ship—I didn't see the shipwreck," Lily suddenly realized, glancing back out into the bay.

"The storms have probably carried it back out to sea in a thousand pieces by now," Valentine said, holding a thorny branch safely clear while she and Simon passed. "She always reclaims her own."

Reaching the cove, which had been more sheltered from the sea and the winds than the bay, Lily could see that at least here little had changed. The beach stretched before them, untouched except for the sea lapping gently against the sands.

Simon, finding the tall pine, quickened his steps until he was almost running across the beach toward it.

"Simon! Wait!" Valentine called too late, afraid that the storms blowing in from the sea and the passage of time would have wreaked destruction beneath the pine. He did not want Simon to see Basil's grave desecrated.

He reached out in time to catch Lily's arm as she would have hurried after Simon.

"Please, let me go," she said, staring up into his harsh face in puzzlement while trying to free her arm from his grasp.

"Lily, you haven't been here to care for the graves. I don't want you to see something that may not be pleasant," Valentine explained, the old gentleness softening his eyes.

Lily remained standing where she was for a moment, then nodded. "Thank you," she said simply, then gestured toward the tree. "But I will eventually have to face whatever has happened."

Valentine smiled. "I should have remembered," he said, and when Lily frowned, he added, "that you are Geoffrey Christian's daughter. He would have been proud of you, Lily."

Lily looked up at Valentine Whitelaw in surprise, her green eyes glowing with pleasure at the unexpected comment.

"Thank you, Valentine," she repeated, but this time his name came like a caress from her lips.

Gently, he placed his hand beneath her elbow and began to walk with her toward the tall pine where they could see Simon's lone figure standing so still.

Lily gave a cry of relief when she saw the two pristine crosses. Miraculously, they had survived. Slender green grasses, waving in the warm sea breeze, and luxuriant plants, heavy with exotic blooms that scented the air with a heady sweetness, had grown up around the graves, almost hiding the crosses if one were not looking for them.

Simon stood with his head bowed, his face hidden from any prying eyes and Lily knew he was silently weeping. She moved closer, placing her arm around his waist comfortingly. He moved his arm to embrace her, holding her close against his side while both of them stood staring down at the two graves bearing the names of a beloved parent.

Valentine sighed. It seemed right, to see them standing there together. Turning away, he signaled for the others to follow him on down the beach, leaving Lily and Simon to grieve in privacy.

"Figured settin' foot here once would about do it fer me," one of the crew who'd sailed with Valentine Whitelaw for years, since before the first voyage to this isle, said, glancing around nervously.

"Aye, once was enough fer me, too," a red-bearded sailor agreed.

"Reckon the Turk ain't all that pleased either," another commented, nodding to where the Turk stood, his hand resting easily on the hilt of his scimitar, the silver scabbard with its ornate engraving gleaming dangerously.

"Aye, reckon that jinni might be lingerin' nearby," one snickered à little too loudly, for he drew the Turk's eye.

"Well, maybe he's got reason to be watchful," another one advised.

"What ye mean?"

"Didn't ye see them tracks up close by them trees?"

"No, where?"

"Over there aways. Don't know what kind o' creature'd be makin' them," the one who spied them speculated while his mates grinned, albeit sickly, wondering if he were pulling their legs.

Their captain had been eyeing the cliffs in the distance. He glanced along their uneven face but couldn't see anything that fit Lily's description of the cave's opening. He felt the heat against the back of his neck and glanced upward. The sun was almost directly overhead now. He wanted to find that cave and retrieve the journal before the sun went down or before the weather worsened. He could see the clouds brewing to the south, growing darker and rising higher into the clear skies as they grew turbulent with wind and rain.

He hadn't heard Lily's approach until she was suddenly there beside him, staring at the cliff face. He glanced back, but Simon was still beneath the pine, kneeling now beside his father's grave.

"Do you think you can remember where the path is that

leads to the cave?'' he asked, startling both Lily and himself by the harshness of his voice.

Lily bit her lip, moving her gaze along the cliffs. Shielding her eyes from the sun, and from revealing her panic, she stared at the confusing mass of dirt and rock.

"Much has changed," she murmured, embarrassed. She'd been so arrogant, so certain she would be able to lead him to the cave. It had all been for naught she was beginning to think, staring blindly at the cliffs.

"Take your time, Lily," Valentine told her, hearing the doubt creeping into her voice.

"I don't know where it is," she finally said.

"Listen. We will make a path through there and walk along the headland toward the cliffs. Something of the path may remain, and I think you will find that you will begin to remember all kinds of details about the cave that you'd thought forgotten. It will come back to you. If you were not here, we wouldn't even have the slightest idea of where to look, despite your and Tristram's directions," he told her, his voice confident and calming her fears.

"I've disappointed you. I've let everyone down. I've been so foolish, thinking I could return here and just walk right into that cave and get the journal for you," she berated herself.

"No, Lily, you haven't disappointed me. I never expected it would be easy, my dear," he said as he pushed through the thick foliage blocking their path.

Lily frowned, but continued to follow him. "What do you mean that you never expected it to be easy? And what directions did Tristram give you?" she demanded, growing suspicious, especially when she remembered what he'd just said about not knowing where to look at all if she hadn't been along, as if he'd known the directions she'd given him at the inn would prove worthless.

"You always intended to take me along, didn't you?" she demanded, humiliated now to think of the deceit he'd practiced by allowing her to think she'd outwitted him.

Valentine glanced back to see her face, no less stormy than the darkening skies to the south. "My dear, I was just playing the game you dared me to play, but by my own rules. I don't like to lose," he said unrepentantly.

"A game? That is all it has been to you? A game? Just another challenge?" Lily repeated, momentarily forgetting that she herself had fallen victim to that challenge.

"I had not planned on taking you at first," he admitted, ignoring her charge. "I had thought to get the location of the cave from Tristram, and he was most obliging, but his directions did little to set my mind at ease. He would have had us on the banks of the Orinoco. Then, when you told me your directions, which were only a little clearer, I realized that I would have to take you with me. I could not risk sailing here and then not finding that journal."

"But I only told you *after* you'd given me your word of honor that I would be aboard the *Madrigal* when she sailed," Lily accused him. "You would have broken your word to me."

Valentine laughed, which fanned her anger even more. "I would not have broken my word, my dear. If you remember, I gave you my word that you would be aboard the *Madrigal* when she sailed. I did not say, however, for what duration or where you would be leaving the ship. Originally, I had planned for it to be at Falmouth. I intended to leave you at Ravindzara, with Tristram and Dulcie, where I thought you would be safe."

"You cheated! You knew what I meant," Lily told him, her cheeks flushed with the heat of anger.

"I also began to think that you would be safer aboard the *Madrigal* than anywhere else, even safer than at Ravindzara," he continued, undisturbed by her anger. "I did not think Sir Raymond would try to harm you again, but I could not in good conscience take that risk. He is a very vindictive man, and you have brought about his downfall. That, my dear, is something he will not forgive you for, even though you have done it most innocently. And"—Valentine paused, not liking the thought that had decided him ultimately to bring Lily along—"we only know of Sir Raymond's identity as one of the traitors. The names of the others, if there are any, might be quite a revelation. Sir Raymond, and many other Catholics, move in high circles; they are members of court and very influential. What if someone I have trusted is involved in this plot? I could not take the chance of leaving you behind in England and allowing you to fall into our enemy's hands. Right now, you are our only witness to Sir

Raymond's attempt at murder. If the journal does not prove his guilt, then your testimony will be needed to convict him.''

Lily fought the tears that threatened to fall. She was important only as a witness against Sir Raymond Valchamps. Valentine Whitelaw did not care beyond that. "A game. That is all it ever is for you," she said bitterly, stumbling slightly over a vine and shaking off the hand that had kept her from falling.

"A game? Perhaps, my dear," Valentine Whitelaw agreed, a strange expression on his hardened face, "but one of life and death. Never forget that, will you, Lily?" he requested.

Lily glanced away from him, unable to meet his gaze. It was while she stood there, staring along the cliff face, searching for something, that she saw the grotesque tree, its limbs bent out of shape and driven into tortuous angles by the winds that battled across the headland. She remembered now that the path curved around that tree, although she'd never remembered that until now, to wend along the headland until it came precariously close to a ravine that dropped straight down into the sea below. At one time, it must have been a cave much like the one that hid their treasure, only the roof had caved in long ago and the sea had surged into it, cutting a jagged fissure into the headland.

At that juncture, there were two paths; one led down toward the cove, while the other wove higher along the cliff, leading to the summit.

"We turn here and follow this path," Lily said, indicating a stony path that seemed to lead nowhere.

"Are you certain?" Simon demanded, having caught up to the party that had almost disappeared out of the cove. "There's another path that climbs over the headland there," he said, drawing everyone's attention to a dangerous-looking path of little more than rough-hewn stone steps too far apart to be easily followed. It led over the top of the headland before disappearing into the forest.

"No, that one only leads down to the beach on the far side, then around the curve of the shore. We very seldom used it. On the far side it is slippery from the waves that splash across it," Lily said. "I know now where the cave is. Watch your step, the path closely follows the cliff edge," she warned.

"Lead the way," Valentine Whitelaw said, no longer in doubt of finding the cave.

Sensing his confidence, Lily started along the narrow footpath along the cliff. Without hesitation, she turned toward the summit of the cliff, several of the crew wondering if they would come out into thin air when they reached it, then fall into the sea below, for the sound of the waves was too close for many of them to take more than one carefully placed step at a time.

Almost reaching the summit, Lily suddenly vanished, and those same crew members froze in their steps, believing the end was near unless they could retrace their steps back to the shore below.

But Valentine, who was just behind her, stepped between the rocks, the path narrowing even more until they were standing directly before the cliff, where only a stunted-looking pine grew and the edge sheered off alarmingly close. They had nowhere to go.

Lily couldn't help but smile at his disappointed expression, for he believed she had been mistaken after all.

Even though he'd been standing before her, gazing at her, he still could scarcely believe his eyes when Lily stepped behind the pine and disappeared into the solid face of the cliff.

"My God! Where'd she go?" Simon exclaimed, having come up in time to see Valentine standing there alone.

But Valentine Whitelaw was not worried. Grinning at Simon, he stepped behind the tree and disappeared.

Valentine felt the coolness engulfing him. He continued to stand just inside the entrance, his eyes unaccustomed to the dark, especially after the blinding brightness outside. Slowly, his eyes adjusted to the shadowy confines of the cave, and a shaft of light shining down from an opening higher up lit the cave as if by candlelight.

He blinked slightly and stared across the cave to find Lily watching him. Beside her was a wooden chest. He could hear the sound of the sea as it surged into the cavern with the ebb and flow of the tide. And even in the filtered light, he could see the glint of water at the bottom of the sloping floor of the cave.

"You remembered, Lily."

He could see the smile that flickered over her face.

"How the devil did Basil get this chest in here?" he demanded, for it would have been no easy task for two men, much less one, to cart the heavy chest along that path.

Lily laughed softly, the sound echoing strangely through the cave.

"He took it apart and carrièd it into the cave in sections. Then he put it back together again. It took us weeks to haul the treasure inside," Lily told him, opening up the lid of the chest to reveal its startling contents.

"Ah, Basil," Valentine murmured, hearing Simon and the others entering the cave behind him as he stared down at the treasure.

"What an incredible place!" Simon breathed, awed by the curving rock formation arching above his head and in his haste nearly slipping on the dampness that coated the rock floor.

"Lookee 'ere! 'Tis a fortune!" cried one of the crew, his mouth dropping open as he came to stand by the chest, the glint of gold and silver unmistakable even in the shadowy light of the cave.

"And I thought we'd made a fine haul when we dove for the rest of the treasure out there in the bay. Must o' been the king o' Spain's biggest treasure ship that went down!"

"Emeralds and pearls. Lord, this one be as big as an egg!"

"Ooohwee! Lookee 'ere, 'tis a chain o' gold links. Must be a king's ransom in these two links alone," the sailor said, weighing the length of chain across his palm. "How we goin' to get all o' this outa here?" he suddenly demanded, crestfallen at the thought that they might have to leave it here for old Neptune to guard, because there was no way he was going to carry this chest down that path. "What d'ye think, Cap'n?" he asked.

But Valentine Whitelaw wasn't listening. He had found the journal.

Francisco Esteban Villasandro waited nervously, wondering how he would find the courage to carry out his father's orders. Although Don Pedro had placed his son in command of the landing party, he had sent along one of the ship's officers to advise the young man who had yet to prove himself a man by his father's inflexible standards.

But, Francisco thought, at least he was on shore and had been able to keep his dinner down for one night. And sleeping beneath the stars, with a fire burning brightly against the darkness and the frightening, savage cries sounding from the forest, he had found a certain measure of peace and the fortitude to tell his father that he did not wish to captain one of his father's galleons. He wished to become a priest and devote his life to the Church. He was not a soldier. And no matter how much his father wished otherwise, he was not and never could be a man of the sword.

Upon their return to Madrid, he would tell his father that he wished to join a seminary and study for the priesthood. He had spent many anguished hours in deliberation, and, after telling his pleased mother and their priest of his decision, he had been about to confide such a wish to his father, who had been unusually even-tempered since receiving a missive from a dust-stained courier. Then, before he could even broach the subject, his father had received another important message and hurried off to answer a royal summons. Two days later, and hardly a week after his father had returned from a voyage to England, the *Estrella D'Alba*, with a small fleet of ships accompanying her, had set sail for the Indies.

His father has requested his presence on board or, rather, had assumed that his only son would accompany him on this greatest of journeys to rid Spain and the seas of one of her most hated enemies. Francisco knew no more of the voyage than that his father intended to entrap an English privateer who had challenged his father on many occasions. The man had raided the Main and even been so bold as to attack the treasure fleet just off the coast of Spain. The devout in the coastal villages went in fear of spying the red cross of St. George flying on the mast of a ship sailing out of thin air. He had heard some of the men aboard the *Estrella D'Alba* refer to the man as *El Tigre*, because the man seemed to lie in wait for their captains, striking before they knew what had happened. He did not know, nor did he care to ask, what his given name was. If the man was to be feared as much as the other heretical Englishman, Drake, then it was indeed an honor to be aboard his father's ship and share in the glory of this Englishman's death.

Francisco clasped the heavy silver cross he wore tucked beneath his doublet, the cool feel of the silver comforting him. If accepted for the priesthood, he would carry God's word into a heathen England, and whether the heretics burned at the stake or drowned at sea, it was all part of God's will.

Shielding his eyes, he gazed out to sea, where he could just make out the mainmast of the *Estrella D'Alba* riding at anchor beyond the waves that rolled across the reefs and broke in foaming white crests that sent sea spray shooting high into the air. He couldn't spy the other galleons, for they'd anchored some distance apart, prepared to raise sail as soon as the word was given.

Francisco glanced around at the camp. The crew, which had rowed the small pinnace ashore the day before, were scattered along the beach beneath several palms. Some were resting peacefully in the shade, while others were jesting and playing games of chance in the sand with shells and driftwood they'd scavenged. The soldiers who'd come ashore with them stayed apart, their harquebuses and halberds close at hand. They seemed so calm, so unconcerned about their task ahead, Francisco thought almost resentfully, for he was weak in the knees and felt a quivering in his stomach that threatened to erupt at any moment.

No, he thought, he would not disgrace himself before these men, his father's men. He would, for this one time only, prove himself his father's son, he vowed. He opened his eyes to find Diego Calderon's dark eyes watching him, and forcing himself to draw in a deep breath and calm his fluttering heart, he stood tall, meeting the older man's gaze with dignity.

Diego Calderon nodded deferentially to his captain's son. He'd had his doubts when Don Pedro had given command to his son, thinking the boy a weakling, but the young man seemed willing to carry out his father's orders. Indeed, he had sounded quite authoritative when sending the scout to the other side of the island at dawn. His report to Don Pedro concerning his son's abilities to command would not disappoint his captain.

Diego Calderon scratched his head, leaving several graying strands standing on end. The scout should have returned by now with the news that *El Tigre*'s ship was anchored on the other side of the island, or that it had yet to arrive. Either way, they had to send word to Don Pedro so he could plan his next strategy. If all went as previously discussed aboard the *Estrella D'Alba*, then the landing party would, upon hearing the news that the Englishman's ship was anchored beyond the reefs on the windward side of the island, split into two units. They would then cross the island and cut off any escape for the English over land, for, by then, Don Pedro with his fleet of heavily armed galleons would have rounded the island and cut off *El Tigre*'s escape to sea.

But where was the scout? He'd had ample time to reach the other shore and discover if the enemy was within range. He should have been back by now.

Young Francisco Villasandro must have thought so as well. "*¿Cuanto tiempo lleva?*" he demanded, his warm brown eyes searching the forest for a sign of the scout. "*¿Cuanto dista de aquí a—*" he had started to ask the older gentleman, whose experienced eye could have estimated how far the scout had to travel to reach the far side of the isle, when he was interrupted by an excited hail from the trees he'd just searched.

"*¡El Tigre! ¡El Tigre!* He is here! I have seen him! His ship is anchored just off shore," the scout called out, nearly tripping over his own feet in his excitement to report his news.

Lily walked along the sands, skirting the tide as it spread higher on the beach as the afternoon waned. She stopped and looked back toward the distant headland. No one had even noticed that she'd wandered off. The crew was busy loading the boat. Several hours earlier, after the discovery of the cave and the treasure, Valentine had sent half of the crew back to the boat they'd beached in the bay. They'd rowed it back out beyond the reefs, then sent it skimming through the waters around the headland and into the cove, where they'd left it anchored in the shallows so it would be easier to shove off with the added weight of the treasure.

Lily paused by the tall pine for a few minutes before sitting down cross-legged in the sand, just beyond the graves, but still in the shade. She sat there for a while in companionable silence, watching the sunlight glistening like molten gold across the water, the light changing constantly as the sun sank lower on the horizon. She'd forgotten how warm it could get on the island, she thought, pulling her bodice free where it was sticking to her skin. On impulse, she kicked off her slippers, leaving them half-buried in the sand. She lifted her skirts and pulled off her garters, rolling down her stockings and tossing them into the air to float down. She stretched out her legs, wiggling her toes through the hot sand.

The memories came flooding back of another time when she, Tristram, and Dulcie had raced along these very same sands, past this tall pine, bare then of the graves that marked it now, for Basil and her mother would have been laughing and calling to them from the headland. Basil would have started the fire, and their mother would have cooked their evening supper, the aromatic odors drifting on the smoke-scented early evening air. Then, as the fire burned low, until there was little left but glowing coals, Basil would have told them a story, his deep voice lulling them to sleep on the sand that still held the warmth from the day, the sea lapping gently against the shore like a lullaby.

Lily stood up, brushing the sand from her skirts. She gathered up the front of her skirt and petticoat and tucked the ends into her waistband, leaving her legs bared to mid-thigh, the skirts draped high and clear of the surf as she waded into the shallows. She spied a shell and reached into the clear waters to capture it. She held the shell to her ear and listened; she could hear someone calling to her. Glancing toward the headland, she saw Simon approaching with several of the crew, who were carrying barrels over their shoulders.

"Lily!"

Lily waved and tossed the pink-tinted shell to him. Simon caught it, examining it carefully, a grin of pleasure on his face. " 'Tis beautiful. I've never seen one quite so big as this," he said in awe.

"The meat from it is delicious. But this one is empty. Would you like it?"

"You mean it? Don't you want it? It might be quite valuable back in England."

Lily smiled, deciding not to tell him that she'd seen hundreds just like it while living on the island.

"Betsy will love it. I'd better find something for Wilfred, too, or he'll set up a howl," Simon declared.

"I'll help you find some more. I know just where to look. Where are you headed?" she asked, eyeing the sailors who'd kept walking down the beach.

Belatedly, Simon became aware that he'd neglected his duty and raised an arm to hail them, but they'd already disappeared over the headland. "We're going to get fresh water. Valentine told me to ask you if you could lead us to the pool? Do you think you remember where it is?''

"The pool? I think I can find it," she said, slightly stung by the innocent reminder of her previous confusion. "I'd like to see if our hut is still there," she said, but she was curious about something else as she fell into step with Simon, who was hurrying now to catch up to the sailors, but she decided against telling him that the pool was also the main watering hole for many of the animals of the isle. And there was one particular animal she wished to find.

She glanced back, toward the boat being loaded, her gaze searching for Valentine's tall figure. She was surprised to see one of the sailors walking along behind them, but not hurrying to catch up.

"He isn't there," Simon told her, guessing her thoughts.

"Oh?" Lily said, pretending a lack of interest.

"He climbed back up the headland. He's posted a guard there, and that fellow following us is stationed at that pine Tristram used to guard," Simon explained.

Lily eyed the sailor again. "Valentine is very cautious."

"That is why he's alive today," Simon said. "I wish he'd let me see inside that journal. 'Twas my father's, after all," Simon said wistfully.

"He has been very strange since reading it," Lily commented, for Valentine had not allowed her to see inside either. "He is just like Basil, for he would never let any of us read what he'd written there," she said, thinking of how Valentine had tucked the journal under his arm after retrieving it from the chest. Once back on the beach, and after giving his orders to his crew, he'd separated himself from everyone, and sitting on the beach, he'd read the neatly penned words filling the pages, his expression becoming grave as he'd turned the pages. For an hour afterwards, while he'd awaited the return of his crew, he'd remained withdrawn, his expression thoughtful as he'd gazed out to sea.

Unable to contain her curiosity, Lily had asked if Raymond Valchamps's name had been mentioned and if he'd been involved in a plot to assassinate the queen. Valentine Whitelaw had gazed up at her, a dangerous glint in his eye, then he'd nodded, but he had said nothing.

Glancing down at her bare feet and slender length of leg, Simon blushed. "Don't you need your shoes, Lily?" he advised tactfully, not wishing to say that she was drawing attention to herself.

They'd climbed the headland and were descending to the sandy beach of the bay on the other side, where the three sailors were standing nearby, waiting for directions. But their eyes widened when they saw the display of leg revealed to their appreciative gazes.

To their disappointment, however, the skirts had fallen discreetly back into place by the time Lily had reached the beach below. She seemed unaware of their crestfallen faces as she walked past, her attention focused on the forest beyond. When Lily saw the group of palms, where two grew so closely together that they seemed one, she knew she'd found the old path to the hut and the pool just behind.

"The path lies here," she said, and the sailors quickly set about cutting a path through the heavy vegetation.

Lily was amazed by its thickness. Like the sea, the island had reclaimed that which had temporarily been stolen from it. The familiar cries of parrots and wild birds filled the air as the interlopers disturbed the peace of the forest.

If the sailors doubted Lily's decision to enter the forest through what had seemed an impenetrable tangle, they soon forgot those fears when the hut, sitting in a clearing, was sighted directly ahead.

"Coooeee, Mistress Christian, ye be a born navigator," one of the sailors exclaimed in admiration.

"Aye, a captain's daughter, she is," another one said, relief coloring his voice.

But to Lily, the scene was anything but a relief.

The hut that had given them shelter for so many years was little more than a hovel overgrown with vines. The frail walls had long since been blown in. The thatched roof had collapsed on top. To seal the destruction, a tall palm had fallen across the hut, crushing anything that had remained standing beneath its weight.

"Well," Simon said shakily, unable to find the words to describe the scene.

Lily nodded in understanding. "The first year we were on

the island, a storm hit. I remember the winds were deafening and the rain fell in torrents. We were scared to death. We had to leave our hut and seek shelter behind the pool. There is a bank that rises higher on one side. When the storm was over, we came out of hiding and there was nothing left of our hut. It had blown away. For days afterward we couldn't even go near the bay because the waves were so high," Lily said, amazing Simon by their closeness to death on that particular occasion. "Later, of course, we found enough driftwood for a month."

The sailors had already made their way around the rubble that had once been the hut and found their way to the pool. It hadn't changed. The waters bubbling up from deep in the earth were clear and cool. The area surrounding the pool was overgrown with grasses and thick vegetation, especially the high bank that overlooked the pool on the far side.

Lily knelt down on the low bank where they'd once sat basking in the sun, and cupping her hands in the crystalline waters, she drank deeply. Quenching her thirst, she sat on the edge of the pool, gazing up at the clear skies overhead, the echoes of voices filling her mind.

Simon stood watching her, wishing he could share her thoughts of another time, but he couldn't.

"Lily, we're ready to return to the beach with these casks. They've been refilled," he said, hating to disturb her reverie, for this pool obviously held special memories for her.

"You go on, Simon," she said, staring into the waters. "I won't be long," she added, glancing up with a smile.

"All right," Simon said. After all, if anyone was going to get lost, it wasn't likely to be Lily. "I'll come back after I've reported to Valentine," Simon said, already beginning to sound like one of the crew. "If you don't mind?" he said, not wishing to intrude.

"I would like that. I find myself remembering a lot of stories about Basil. Maybe you'd like to hear them?"

"That would be wonderful," Simon said with a wide grin of pleasure, some of the sadness he'd felt when standing beside his father's grave beginning to fade as he thought of hearing about their life here on the isle. "Well, I'd better shove off or they'll have reached the beach before me," Simon said, glancing around to find that the sailors were already disappearing hrough the trees. In truth, he had no desire to walk alone on his island.

Lily continued to sit by the pool. The warm, humid air was heavy with the spicy scent of pine and the almost overpowering fragrance of flowers, the brightly colored blossoms opened fully to capture the sun. Lily breathed deeply, stretching her arms high above her head and filling her lungs with the heady, perfumed air.

A sudden thought entered her mind, and, unable to resist the temptation, especially since Simon would be some time in returning, she stood up and began to unfasten her bodice, removing the stiff silk that felt so confining and uncomfortable against her flesh. Her fingers worked quickly with the fastenings of her skirt, and a moment later she was stepping out of it. Her slippers and stockings had long ago been discarded. With quick efficiency, she braided her hair into two long braids and wove the ends together on top of her head.

She was standing on the edge of the pool in her petticoat and chemise, when she heard a rustling nearby and glanced around quickly. She peered into the shadowy vegetation, but nothing moved in those cool depths. Even though she could not feel anything, she felt as if eyes watched her.

"Choco?" she called softly, making the low sounds and the whistle that had used to bring him running to her when she beckoned.

She stood unmoving, listening. In the distance, but moving closer, she heard the snapping of twigs and the rustling of branches.

"Choco?" she called again, more confidently, the whistle piercing, for the noises were coming in the opposite direction from where Simon and the sailors had disappeared.

"Choco!" Lily called more loudly this time. She had hoped she'd catch sight of the jaguar. She'd never forgotten him through the years and had always wondered what had happened to him, if he still lived. She had even wondered if he might have missed them after they'd left the island. He used to crawl close to the pool and watch them from the undergrowth. She'd always known when he was near, sensing his presence even when he remained silent. And quite often they'd heard his cries late at night outside the hut, as if he'd remembered a time when he'd slept inside curled up beside her, his purrs rumbling through the small hut and keeping her awake.

Lily smiled, thinking of Hartwell Barclay's dismay at the parrot and monkey when he'd first seen them. He would have been apoplectic if she'd brought her little *tigre enojado* back to England. She doubted Hartwell would have been doing any midnight wanderings with Choco prowling the halls of Highcross.

Lily frowned, disappointed, for there was only silence now. With a sigh, she turned away from the forest and sat down on the edge of the pool, dangling her legs into the warm water. Slowly, she allowed the rest of her body to slip into the water, hardly disturbing it as she paddled back and forth, the light petticoat floating around her.

Drifting dreamily through the water, Lily didn't see the dark shape that crept closer, making no sound through the shadow undergrowth. A palm frond whispered with movement, but could have been the breeze stirring it. A gaily colored parrot with red and yellow and blue feathers, sat on a branch overlooking the pool, his curious eyes watching the scene below. With a strident cry of warning, he ruffled his feathers and flapped his wings and flew to a safer perch deeper in the leafy branches overhead.

It felt so peaceful to be swimming in the warm waters, feeling the softness embracing her, and banishing the horror she'd felt the last time she'd sat beside a pool, only to find the face of Raymond Valchamps reflected before her. The engulfing blackness and coldness she'd felt then was gradually being washed away by the brightness and warmth surrounding her now.

Lily eyed the sky overhead as she heard a distant rumbling of thunder and remembered the darkening clouds she'd seen earlier far out at sea. She was surprised to hear thunder so soon. It usually took several hours for a storm to reach shore.

Regretfully, Lily began to swim toward the bank, knowing she could delay no longer when she heard another clap of thunder, even closer now. Perhaps Valentine would allow them to camp overnight on the island. She might be able to return in the morning and bathe properly next time, she promised herself as her feet struck the sandy bottom of the pool and she waded toward the bank.

The water was lapping around her thighs when Lily suddenly froze.

Some instinct kept her from moving, kept her standing perfectly still in the water. Her eyes gazed into the big cat's glowing amber eyes staring at her so intently from the shadows that had lengthened and darkened menacingly while she'd been swimming so peacefully in the pool.

Choco, she thought, her heart pounding. He wasn't her little *tigre enojado* any longer. During the three years they'd been away from the island, he had matured into a full-sized jaguar. Although he looked heavier and his muscles were even more pronounced than before, the dark fur with its black rosettes thick and shiny, he was still sleek and sinewy with unleashed power.

Lily continued to stand in the shallows of the pool, mesmerized by the golden eyes that had narrowed into slits. She felt she could have reached out and stroked the broad, velvety nose. Long whiskers drooped to touch his wide paws, the claws just barely visible. He was sitting in a semi-crouch, his muscular forelegs short and sturdy, ready to bear his weight when he sprang forward to capture his prey. As Lily watched, he bared his fangs, the long, curved teeth gleaming like ivory against the blackness of his fur.

His tail was twitching faster now, moving back and forth almost in irritation, as if he were undecided yet whether to attack or allow her to live. Lily knew that he was indecisive, because she'd seen Choco streak out of cover and catch a bird without hesitation, the poor creature never knowing that its death was imminent.

But Lily continued to face death, aware that it was just a foot away, waiting patiently for her to make the wrong move.

Anyone else might have dived deeper into the pool, but Lily knew better; Choco could swim.

Choco hissed and made his hoarse cry when the thunder sounded again.

The breeze carried her scent to him, she could see him sniffing the air and she was thankful now that she hadn't been bathing, the soap and perfumed oils masking her scent. And she hoped he remembered it.

That she was still alive, unharmed, seemed to prove that he

had remembered her, perhaps only something fleeting, but it was enough to have kept him from attacking her immediately.

So intent were the two, with the thunder so loud, that neither Lily or Choco were aware of the Spanish soldiers who'd been slowly and silently approaching the pool where they saw only a beautiful, partly clad girl standing in the water, afraid to move.

Beyond wishing to capture this woman for their pleasure, they had to take her captive to keep her from warning the English of their attack, for she had surely seen them passing by and, if not so frightened, would scream out for help.

Another deafening roar filled the silence and the violence that erupted after that happened so quickly that Lily was never to remember exactly the sequence of events.

When she'd finally become aware of the soldiers it had been too late to do anything, even to cry out a warning, although whether she would have been warning the jaguar or the soldiers Lily was never to know. It mattered not, because Choco sensed the enemy closing in around him at the same time Lily saw them.

The soldiers, however, did not know what it was that leapt out of the tall grasses, except that it must be from hell. A horrible, bloodcurdling cry sent a shiver up each man's spine, the bared fangs and claws that flashed past having every one of them praying for salvation.

Diego Calderon, who'd remained near the trees along with Francisco Villasandro while his men apprehended the woman, yelled for his men to find their courage. Couldn't they see that it was just a *tigre?* he had cried out, trying to stop his men from fleeing like frightened sheep.

The confusion, however, had given Lily the necessary time to climb out of the pool, and while the soldiers were halted on the far side of the pool, she ran toward the hut and headed for the beach to warn Valentine.

Lily hadn't even gotten past the jumble of thatch buried beneath the tree entwined with thick vines when something grabbed hold of her and nearly swung her off her feet.

Lily Francisca Christian stared up into the face Francisco Esteban Villasandro, never knowing that this was her cousin. All she saw was the face of a stranger. He was a handsome young man with brown eyes that were almost bronzed, reminding her strangely of Tristram's. His hair was black and he was dressed like a gentleman, not in a uniform like the others, nor did he wear the peaked metal helmet or carry a pike with its deadly spearhead.

Francisco stared down into the woman's frightened eyes, and although they were the palest green he'd ever seen and her beauty was breathtaking, he was struck by the color of her hair. The dark red shade was identical to his youngest sister's. Little Magdalena, named for his mother's beloved sister who'd been lost at sea, possessed the same extraordinary hair.

Francisco Villasandro blinked, for this woman had a look about her that was so tantalizingly familiar. So pure in line, he found himself thinking, almost the face of a madonna.

Lily struggled to free herself from this young man's grip, even though she wasn't frightened of him, not the way she had been of the soldiers when she'd suddenly seen them.

Loud sounds drifted to them from the other side of the hut. They heard the sound of gunpowder exploding, then Lily and Francisco turned to see the black jaguar sailing through the air as he leapt down from the tree that had fallen across the hut.

Francisco stared in horror at the hellish creature. But his courage did not abandon him as he might once have feared. Before Lily knew what he'd done, he'd pushed her aside and stepped in front of her at the same time, shielding her body from the slashing claws and terrible fangs of the jaguar as it landed against his chest.

The big cat had been driven into a frenzy of rage and fear by the soldiers who'd chased after him, banging their swords on their helmets, while the acrid smell of gunpowder filled the air. In the distance the bellowing of thunder was deafening. Choco roared his rage, his golden eyes gleaming with hatred of his enemy.

Francisco Villasandro felt a burning pain when the claws ripped through his shoulder, striking deep to the bone. He felt the cat's hot breath against his throat, but his scream of agony was short-lived as the cat's strong jaws closed about his jugular and severed it. Francisco, only son of Don Pedro Enrique Villasandro, knew no more pain.

Lily sat kneeling beside the dead man, staring in disbelief at the blood flowing from his neck and shoulder. She looked up to see a flash of black disappearing into the trees, then there were only shadows.

"¡Madre de Dios!" Diego Calderon muttered in horror when he came hurrying around the fallen tree to find his captain's son lying dead in a pool of blood.

Simon Whitelaw looked down at his arm in surprise, touching the red blood seeping from the wound. Except for the uncomfortable stinging he had only momentarily felt, he would never have known he'd been shot.

He'd felt the tingling sensation shortly after the lookout stationed at the point of the headland had cried out a warning of sighting a strange sail on the horizon. Then they'd heard the distinctive sound of cannon fire, although to the unwary it might have sounded like thunder.

But to Valentine Whitelaw, who'd been watching the last of the treasure being loaded into the boat, it meant the *Madrigal* was being fired upon. He paused, then smiled slightly when he'd heard the *Madrigal*'s response in kind. When hearing that first shot, however, he had glanced around more in dismay than surprise, as if he'd half been expecting such a warning to be sounded.

While several of the *Madrigal*'s crew armed with harquebuses had returned fire against the soldiers appearing over the headland, holding their attackers at bay, Valentine Whitelaw had ordered his men into the boat. Then he'd signaled to the Turk, who had already been running to his captain's side. Looking startled by the order his captain had given, he'd nonetheless accepted the journal and the other leather-bound book that Valentine had handed to him. Tucking the two books inside his caftan, he listened attentively to his captain's quickly spoken words. Once, he shook his turbaned head, and then nodded when Valentine Whitelaw's words sharpened, but there was a look of disapproval on the Turk's harsh countenance as he obeyed his captain and climbed into the boat, taking his seat at the stern.

For the first time, Valentine Whitelaw became aware of his nephew's condition, for Simon Whitelaw had come to stand near him, but he had not complained or even mentioned his injury while Valentine had been giving his orders to the Turk and the rest of his crew.

"Simon!" Valentine now said, staring in disbelief at his nephew's bloodied arm. "Good Lord, lad, you've been hit," he murmured, and before Simon could protest, he'd lifted him clear into the boat, a couple of the mates reaching out to take the lad into their care.

"See he gets proper attention once back aboard, Mustafa! He is in your care. Now row, damn you! Don't let them catch you sitting here on your oars!" he called, pushing with all of his might against the boat to get it well beyond the pull of the tide.

"Lily!" Simon hollered, trying to turn around in his seat. "She's at the pool. I left her there, Valentine! She's all alone! We can't leave her! She will have heard the cannon fire! She will be frightened! She's in danger, Valentine!" he called back, wincing instinctively as another deafening roar filled the air. "We can't leave both of you here! Stop! Don't leave them!" Simon said frantically, and would have jumped into the surf had it not been for the Turk's restraining arms. "He's your captain! You can't sail without him!" Simon said indignantly, not seeing the Turk's grieving face.

"I'll find her, Simon!" Valentine called, already running along the shore, for with his men in the boat there was no longer any return fire to keep the troop of soldiers from descending the headland.

Simon Whitelaw watched helplessly from the boat as it cleared the surf and was rowed with what seemed inhuman strength toward the *Madrigal.*

Valentine Whitelaw had nearly reached the headland separating the cove and bay, passing by the tall pine where Lily had kicked off her slippers and thrown her stockings and garters to the winds, when he spied a small party of Spaniards descending from the slope. And walking amongst them was a girl in no more than her petticoat and chemise; it was Lily Christian.

Despite the sword pressed against his spine, Valentine Whitelaw helped Lily climb into the boat that had been rowed ashore from the *Estrella D'Alba.* He knew it was the *Estrella D'Alba;* he had recognized its castellated towers and the streaming banners and pennants, as well as her coat of arms displayed so proudly for her enemies to gaze upon before being sunk by her overpowering cannon fire. The other ships which had accompanied her had gone in pursuit of the *Madrigal*.

"Valentine?" Lily murmured softly.

Valentine Whitelaw glanced down at her sitting so quietly next to him on the seat. Valentine took her cold hand in his, for the Spaniards had left them unbound, knowing that their captives had nowhere to run.

"My Lily Francisca, I would not have had it end this way," he said, unaware that he repeated another lover's regrets, tearfully spoken over ten years earlier when Geoffrey Christian had sent his wife and daughter ashore on this very same isle.

"They will kill you, Valentine," she spoke huskily.

"I know," he said. Even though he could not understand their Spanish words, he knew, for they had called him *El Tigre*. It would be an honor for any captain, especially Don Pedro Villasandro, to hang Valentine Whitelaw. "Of course, they have to get me back to Spain first," he added, a slight smile curving his lips, which had one of his captors crossing himself worriedly, for the Englishman was supposed to have magical powers—how else could he have wreaked such destruction along the Main?

"They have been talking of your death, Valentine," Lily said, barely able to pronounce the damning words. "You and I will find no mercy from them, or their captain, Valentine," she told him, and glancing at the body that had been wrapped in a length of sail cloth and placed on the bottom of the boat, she continued. "That is their captain's son, Valentine. They blame me and you for his death. So will this captain of theirs."

At that, Valentine Whitelaw did look concerned. Don Pedro's son? He glanced at Lily and realized that she did not know that the man was her cousin. How he had come to die, and why she should be blamed, he had yet to learn, but pay for the lad's death, yes, by God, he knew they would if they ever did reach Spain—but then, perhaps they never would reach their destination, he thought, glancing at Don Pedro's galleon. He did not fear his own death, for he had expected it during every battle he'd fought, but Lily . . . no, not Lily. And he feared Don Pedro would have good reason for seeing Lily Christian dead. It would settle a very old score—an eye for an eye.

The boat had cleared the whitewater of the surf and was

being rowed ever closer toward the entrance to the cove, and to the *Estrella D'Alba*, anchored just beyond the reefs.

"Why did the *Madrigal* leave us?" Lily asked, her angrily raised voice drawing the attention of one of the sailors, whose eyes lingered overly long on Lily's fiery red hair and soft breasts revealed all too immodestly in her thin chemise.

Valentine Whitelaw wanted to drive his sword through the Spaniard for the way he was looking at Lily, as if she were a whore; indeed, had Valentine understood the Spaniards as Lily had, he would have been angrier to have heard Lily referred to as *El Tigre*'s redheaded whore. There had even been some speculation as to what her fate would be before she ever reached Spain and surely met her death there as a witch.

"The *Madrigal* was outgunned, Lily. She would have been sunk had she not fled. Those were my orders," Valentine told her, damning himself now for not having been more vigilant, more suspecting of treachery, but although he had expected that word would have leaked out about the *Madrigal*'s journey, he'd had no idea of the true traitor's identity or that every move he'd made had been anticipated and reported by that unknown enemy.

Lily Christian stared at Valentine Whitelaw's face. She loved him. If he were to die, and in the manner in which these Spaniards were discussing, she would never rest in peace. She could not bear to see him harmed. As Lily sat in the boat, still shaken by the death of the young man who'd given his life for hers and knowing that she and Valentine would soon follow by just as violent a death, she stared at the deep turquoise waters of the cove splashing against the sides of the small boat.

Her gaze shifted toward the headland, where only that morning they'd climbed the stony path to the cave. Then her gaze moved to the great galleon that rode at anchor just beyond the reefs, and where she and Valentine would be taken aboard as prisoners.

Once in Spain, Valentine Whitelaw would be tried and found guilty of being a heretic by his Inquisition judges. Upon sentence, he would be burned at the stake in a public square. Lily closed her eyes, shivering in terror at such a thought. As for her own fate . . . she would gladly welcome death, no matter how painful, if Valentine died.

Lily opened her eyes to see a porpoise frolicking in the blue-green waters. She watched unthinkingly for a few minutes while the porpoise jumped and dived through the purple and orange reefs, disappearing for a minute, then suddenly surfacing with a splash of water and a funny-sounding cry. As she continued to gaze into the clear waters, she saw a large turtle paddling by, intent upon some business of his own, oblivious of the world above his underwater realm.

As Lily watched him drifting into the safety of the deep water below, she suddenly remembered. Her heart started pounding so loudly with the idea that she thought their guards must surely hear and suspect something amiss.

"Valentine?"

Valentine Whitelaw grapsed her hand tighter, thinking she was growing frightened as they neared the tall sterncastle of the galleon.

"Do you trust me?"

"*¡Silencio!*" one of the guards said, raising his halberd threateningly.

Lily lowered her head submissively, her fingers tightening around Valentine's hand warning him not to speak, for she felt the anger surging through him. But he mustn't be hurt or wounded, not now.

"Do you trust me?"

"Yes, of course," he said wonderingly.

"Then jump over the side of the boat when I do. You must follow me, Valentine. I led you to the cave didn't I? I will do so again," Lily promised. "Trust me, please, Valentine," she begged him. "I told you something else about that cave. Remember?"

Valentine stared down at her bowed head. To drown would at least be preferable to burning, he thought. And at least they would be together. "Yes, I trust you, Lily Francisca," he said, but even as he spoke, he found himself remembering her last words about the cave and suddenly he laughed softly, which caused his captor who'd already been disturbed by *El Tigre's* smile of moments ago, to glance in concern at Diego Calderon, leaving his captives unguarded for just an instant.

Lily kept her head down, but she was watching the headland through the corner of her eyes. "Take a deep breath. Now!" she cried, and standing up in the small boat, she jumped into the sea.

Valentine Whitelaw had stood up with her, but had somehow managed to rock the easily overbalanced boat before he followed Lily into the watery depths.

Gunfire sounded after their descent into the aquamarine depths, but the bullets and spears that followed floated harmlessly down into the deep.

The startled guards in the boat continued to gaze frantically into the sea, waiting to see the two surface, some trying to position their harquebuses in the rocking boat while others took aim with their pikes, ready to spear the two heretics like gasping fish when they came up for air.

But the two never surfaced. For almost half an hour, the boat remained in the same position, the crew searching the water, but no sign was ever seen of the two prisoners. The oarsmen even rowed back to shore, searching the beach and the surrounding areas of both headlands, but no sign could be found of either one.

None of them wished to report to their captain, Don Pedro Villasandro, that the two prisoners, one of them the infamous *El Tigre*, had drowned while trying to escape. And that would have been the easy part, for the rest of their task would be harder when they had to inform Don Pedro that his son was dead.

Valentine Whitelaw followed Lily as she swam deeper into the sea, and he suddenly had the fanciful thought that she was indeed the mermaid he'd thought her to be, leading him to his death in a watery grave. He felt as if his lungs were going to burst, but still she swam ahead of him as if born to the sea. Never had he seen anyone move with such ease and grace through the water. Her long hair floated out around her like the seaweed drifting through the water. He kicked off his shoes, paddling all the harder to keep up with her, but she always remained just ahead of him, her pale legs beckoning him to keep following her deeper and deeper into the turquoise depths that stretched into indigo beneath him, and where only fish and turtles and strange undersea creatures—and Lily Christian—dared to roam.

He felt a roar growing louder in his ears and a painful burning in his chest, and it was with a sense of disbelief that he saw her disappear into a coral reef and he found himself wondering if she had gills.

Once inside, however, she was suddenly there beside him, her hand grasping his. Thinking he was about to black out from lack of oxygen, although the sea surrounding him suddenly seemed far lighter in color, he held on to her hand all the tighter, not daring to let loose even if she did head toward the dark corridor he saw in the distance. But Lily started kicking her feet and rising to the surface, pulling him along with her.

Suddenly glorious air filled his lungs and above him he could actually see blue sky and tufts of salmon pink clouds, burnished around the edges from the sunset, drifting by. He breathed deeply again, the air heavy with salt spray and the sound of the sea.

Her pale green eyes met his for a triumphant second before she was diving back down again, her hand grasping hold of his again to lead him into the dark, narrow-walled corridor that wended through the coral reef, and hopefully not out to sea.

He had about despaired of ever reaching land again when his feet struck sand and he surfaced just behind Lily into a cavern formed of rock, and the very same cave he'd been in earlier in the day.

Slipping more than once, he staggered out of the water, his arm flung over Lily's slender shoulder. He was unaware that he was leaning so heavily on her until she stumbled under his weight and they both fell to the sandy floor of the cave, but high enough on the sloping floor not to worry about the rising tide.

Their breath came raggedly as they lay there.

Then Valentine Whitelaw's laughter filled the cave, startling Lily from her fatigue. His laughter was jubilant, deep and rich with triumph.

Suddenly he rolled over and captured her mouth with his, kissing her deeply and stealing from her the breath she'd just caught. "Thank you for my life, my dearest love," he murmured against her lips, then lifting his mouth from hers, he got to his feet and walked quickly to the mouth of the cave.

Lily struggled onto her stomach, staring at the cave entrance where he'd disappeared. Trying to calm her racing pulse, she found herself smiling slightly—they were alive, and he'd called her his dearest love.

As she lay there, dripping wet from the sea, she suddenly began to shiver. She was so cold. She was suffering more from the effect of the traumatic experiences of the day than the coolness of the cave, and with teeth chattering, Lily sat up and wrapped her arms around her shaking chest.

"They are searching the cove for us. The *Estrella D'Alba* is still anchored beyond the reefs. We will be safe here at least," Valentine said as he reentered the cave, forgetting that she might recognize the name of Don Pedro's ship. "Lily?" he said worriedly, seeing her huddled so forlornly against the floor of the cave. "Why, you're shaking."

He knelt down beside her, taking her into his arms and lifting her off the floor. Walking to where a pale shaft of sunlight filtered into the cave, he sat down against the curving wall of the cavern and held Lily in his arms.

His hands moved over her arms and legs, not passionately, but merely to restore the circulation to her cold limbs. The shaft of light held some warmth, and gradually Lily's shaking lessened, but when Valentine caught sight of her face, he saw that it was tearstained.

"Ah, my love," he breathed, placing a soft kiss against each eye.

Lily felt shamed and tried to hide her face from his gaze, but he turned it up to his and stared down into the tormented green eyes.

"What happened on the island, Lily? Those soldiers didn't touch you, did they?" he suddenly demanded, a horrible thought entering his mind when he remembered Lily's dishabille when she'd been led captive onto the beach by the soldiers.

"That young man, Valentine. The Spaniard who died," she said, her voice husky with tears. "He saved my life," she told him, stunning Valentine with the confession.

"He did?"

"He needn't have died, Valentine. I might be the one lying dead right now if he hadn't pushed me away and stepped in front of me. It was Choco."

"Choco?" Valentine asked, not remembering the black jaguar.

Lily nodded. "He was at the pool. I had wanted to find him. I wanted to know if he still lived. I was swimming in the pool when I heard the thunder. I was wading out when I saw him lying in wait in the tall grass. But, Valentine, he didn't attack me. He could have, but he remembered me, I know he did," Lily said, her hands gripping Valentine's arms.

"The jaguar you left behind. Choco," he said, understanding now. But the thunder she claimed she'd heard had been cannon fire.

"I truly think he might have left me alone," Lily said, not seeing the expression on Valentine's face when he thought how close she'd been to death facing that jaguar, for he did not believe that the big jungle cat would have left her alive and his arms tightened around her body, holding her closer to him.

"Those soldiers came into the clearing by the pool. I didn't see them at first, but they saw me in the pool and were coming to take me prisoner so I would not warn you when Choco leaped out of the grass. I don't know who was more frightened. He isn't used to strangers and felt they were threatening him. When they ran, I escaped, only that young Spaniard caught me. We were standing there, just beyond the hut, when Choco came flying over the fallen tree. That was when that man pushed me aside. It was awful," Lily said, beginning to cry in earnest now, her muffled sobbing racking her body.

Valentine's hands were gentle as they caressed her. "He screamed so horribly and there was so much blood. The poor man. I didn't know him, Valentine, and yet he gave his life for me. He was my enemy. Why would he sacrifice himself for me?" she asked, burying her face against Valentine.

Valentine continued to hold her until she had fallen into a restless sleep. He stared at the shaft of light, watching it fade as the sun sank lower, until finally the cave was thrown into complete darkness.

Lightly resting his chin on top of her head, his arms holding her close against his heart, he stared into the darkness. Strange, he thought, that Don Pedro Villasandro, a man who had betrayed so many others, including his wife's sister, should now have to pay so great a price for his sins. Retribution had been ten years in coming, but when it had, it had struck swiftly and cruelly, taking from Don Pedro his only son, and on the very same isle where he'd left Basil and Magdalena and an innocent child to die. It would be a bitter irony to Don Pedro that his son should

e saving the life of the girl that he, years earlier, had passed a
ath sentence on.

"Lily." He said her name softly, caressingly, and settling
mself more comfortably against the damp wall of the cave, he
)sed his eyes for a few minutes of rest. "Lily, you're mine
w," he murmured before he fell asleep.

Lily awoke, startled, her heart pounding. The sound of the
a lapping gently against the floor of the cave reminded her all
) quickly of where she was and what had happened.

She shivered, then hearing the steady breathing of the man
ng next to her, she felt herself relaxing. The heat of his body
d warmed hers while they'd been curled up asleep on the
or of the cave. His arm was heavy across her waist, while his
, was slightly bent and resting between hers, giving her a
ange feeling of shared intimacy with him.

She eased herself onto her elbow and stared into his face, cu-
us to look at him more closely now that he was asleep and she
l not have to face his quizzical gaze.

"I love you, Valentine," she whispered, her breath soft
ainst his face. "I always have loved you and I always shall. I
)uld have died if anything had happened to you. Valentine,"
² said the name again.

He was beautiful, she decided, noting the finely chiseled
)uth and the straight bridge of his nose. His cheekbones were
;h, the flesh taut across his lean, bronzed face. His eyebrows
re not too thick, one even arched slightly higher than the
ner, she thought with a smile. She knew a sudden urge to
ch out and touch his beard, to feel its roughness beneath her
m. A black curl had fallen across his wide brow, and Lily
ew the curling strand would be soft beneath her touch. Her
ze drifted down his body, lingering on his chest and hips and
² found herself wondering unmaidenly thoughts. She
wned slightly, then gazed lower before returning her stare to
face.

Belatedly, she realized that it was dawn, and that she'd been
:ing at him through the silvery light spreading through the
ugh-hewn window high on the cave wall.

She continued to lie in his arms, staring at him, until finally she could no longer resist and she reached out and ligh touched his beard with her fingertip.

She was taken aback to have her finger bitten, then find turquoise eyes staring deeply into hers with a boldness s didn't understand until he rolled over and pinned her benea him. Her eyes widened in surprise as she felt a probing hardne pressing against her.

"And I love you," he said, smiling when he saw her look surprise. "When we share a bed you will learn soon enough th I am a very light sleeper. I've been enjoying your caress for t last half an hour, although I've had a hard time containing n self knowing those beautiful green eyes have been wanderi over me."

Lily was speechless with embarrassment. He was going t fast, presuming too much, she told herself in growing confusi as she met his ardent gaze. He loved her?

"Kiss me, Lily," he said softly, his lips just a breath aw from hers. "Kiss me like you did at the fair. . . . No?" he m mured, his tongue lightly touching her lips when she remair unresponsive.

Lily felt a dryness in her throat and parted her lips, prepa to speak, but his tongue touched hers, and her mouth oper wider under the pressure of his. She remembered the pleas able touching of their mouths once before and found herself sponding to the pressure, her tongue licking against his now the kiss deepened in intensity.

His hands moved along her back, sending a tingling sen tion along her spine. Then they moved around to touch breasts, gently and slowly until they swelled in his hands, nipples rising taut beneath the thin linen of her chemise.

Her lips were still caught by his, his tongue moving agai hers, savoring the warm softness of the entwining. His ha moved lower to encompass her small waist, then slide over curve of her hips and the firm roundness of her buttocks. hand moved down to her thighs, caressing their slender leng then surprising her when one of them lifted up her petticoat slid between her thighs to move along the soft inner flesh where she had begun to feel a slow quivering deep inside. sucked in her breath when she felt his finger touching her so i mately, causing her breath to quicken.

Sensing her confusion at his boldness, and the sensations she'd never experienced before, he stopped, his hand moving away and leaving her feeling oddly empty and longing for those tingling sensations again.

He had never stopped kissing her, and when he finally lifted his mouth from hers, her lips felt numb. "Lily?" he questioned. "You and I belong together. You belong to me now, Lily. I did not realize it at the time, but you have been mine since I first saw you here on this isle. And when I saw you riding along the riverbank, you belonged to me then. Only then I didn't realize the truth. And, Lily, I belong to you. You are my love, my only love. I intend that you shall be mine completely, Lily Francisca. I will not lose you again, not now that I have found you. It only seems right that we should come to know one another as lovers here on this isle. We are already friends, aren't we, my dear? Now I wish to become your lover," he said, his voice low and husky and very seductive.

He was bending over her, his thumb moving along the delicate line of her jaw, his mouth so close to taking hers again. The turquoise eyes were bright beneath the heavy lids that half-masked their expression.

Valentine Whitelaw stared down into her pale face, her lips reddened from his kisses, her breath shallow and coming quickly, her pale green eyes glowing mysteriously as she met his gaze openly. He could see the love in them and he thrilled to that knowledge.

Lily stretched her arms up to entwine them around his neck and pull his head down to hers, their lips meeting in a long kiss that sealed the promise of their newfound love. "The isle has not lost its enchantment," she murmured, losing herself in Valentine Whitelaw's embrace, melding herself to him, drawing from his warmth and strength. And something told her that her mother and father and Basil would have been pleased by the choice she had made this day.

Valentine's hands moved quickly, surprising her by his deftness as he removed her petticoat and chemise, leaving her body bared to his gaze. He stared down at her ivory-tinted flesh, at the soft womanly curves that beckoned for a man's touch. Her breasts were high and firm, the pink nipples hardening under his gaze, but she continued to lie there, not trying to cover herself when his eyes wandered lower to where she had yet to know the full passion of his lovemaking and truly become a woman. His hand reached out to caress her, sliding over her smooth belly to feel the softness nestled between her thighs and letting her experience the growing pleasure his touch would bring her.

He removed his shirt and breeches, his hose pulled off with little care to turning them rightside out. He felt her eyes upon him and allowed her to gaze at him. He stood tall before her, his chest broad and covered with fine black hairs. Lean-waisted, with narrow hips and long muscular thighs, he now gave her the pleasure she had afforded him moments before by letting him gaze so boldly upon her. Smiling, he took her hand and guided it to him, startling her by the vibrancy of him.

He spread out the discarded petticoat, then lifted her up and placed her on it; then he was beside her, pulling her into his arms, his hands sliding over her, caressing her flesh, learning about her body with an intimacy that even she'd been ignorant of.

His mouth was against her breasts, his tongue moving around the pink crest and taut nipple while his hands fondled her. His mouth moved over her body, leaving no part of her free of his touch. When she felt his hands spread her thighs, holding them wide for his entry, her nails were digging into his back, her hips already beginning to move sensuously against him. Her lips clung to his as he kissed her deeply, then she felt his hardness entering her, moving slowly inside of her, until she gasped with the sharp pain of his intrusion against the tender softness, untouched until now.

He paused, allowing her to learn the feel of him, of the throbbing that would soon turn to delight when he moved against her with increasing passion.

He felt her hands spreading against his back, moving lower to hold him closer against her as she began to feel the passion of his embrace increasing, and when she began to move her hips against him, he responded, carrying her with him as he felt her tightness holding him to her, caressing him in a way that left him unable to stop until he'd felt the climax of their lovemaking. He felt her thighs wrapped around him, then heard her moan of pleasure as her hips moved with his, and never before had a

woman seemed so perfect for him, for his desires. They came together at the same time, her eyes so green with surprised pleasure that he felt the full measure of love by having pleased her as
well as having received the ultimate gift from her body.

Their passion spent, Valentine continued to hold Lily close in
his arms, his hands fondling her gently while they lay there, unwilling to break the contact between them. Lily drew a deep
breath, her breasts pressing against his chest. She moved closer,
molding her body to his trustingly, and with her head against his
shoulder and the sound of the sea surrounding them, they
drifted into sleep knowing a shared contentment that came of
their love.

Lily awoke to find the cave empty. She sat up, glancing
around nervously. She felt the coolness of the air against her
bare skin and realized that she had been there lying naked. The
shirt Valentine had placed over her had fallen off. Shivering,
Lily struggled into her chemise and petticoat. Her breasts were
sore from Valentine's caress, and she felt a tenderness between
her thighs. But as she thought of the love they had found, she
welcomed the pain of that first coupling.

Hurrying to the cave entrance, she carefully left the concealing darkness, blinking when the brightness of the sun struck
her eyes. She stood on the path staring out to sea.

The Spanish galleon had gone. Her gaze searched the gentle
curve of beach. Suddenly she saw his tall, lean figure walking
along the sands, pausing now and again as he stared out to sea.

She stood for a moment watching him, remembering, and
she felt her heart miss a beat as she stared down at him, knowing
he was her lover.

"Lily!"

Lily waved back, hurrying down the path to the beach below.
She followed the wandering trail of his footsteps across the
sands, stopping once to pick a couple of fragrant, lush blossoms
from the forest.

By the time she returned to the beach, he had come most of
the distance and was standing watching her. Her arms were
raised above her head, drawing her chemise tight across the
firm, rounded breasts he'd suckled the night before. The breeze
molded her petticoat to her hips and thighs, leaving little to the
imagination, which he no longer needed, for he had tasted of her

body, become a part of her, and, perhaps, he had even planted his seed deep inside that nurturing place.

"The galleon, it is gone, Valentine!"

"I know. I thought she would be. There was no reason for them to stay any longer, thinking we'd drowned in the cove."

"If . . . we ever return to England—" Lily began, twirling around and around as she flirted with the waves, suddenly feeling shy with him as she caught that ardent glint in his eye.

"*When* we return to England," Valentine corrected her, his arms pulling her into his embrace. Her hair was fragrant with the exotic, deep red blossoms she'd woven into the long strands, and her skin smelled of the sea; he kissed her shoulder and wasn't surprised that it tasted of salt. "There is a cove, very sheltered, beneath the cliffs at Ravindzara. There is a sandy beach and the waters are as clear and warm as these. The winds are gentle, blowing in from the sea. You and I will go there often, Lily Francisca. And at sunset, when the sky is aflame, we will lie on a silken rug and make love throughout the night. No one will disturb us, for they will know that the master of Ravindzara and his beautiful bride, who may indeed be from the sea, are wrapped in each other's arms, lost to the world and—"

"Valentine, please, you must listen," Lily protested.

"I do not want to listen," he said, his mouth finding hers and silencing her protest, and despite her intentions she found herself responding wildly to his caresses.

He knelt in the sand, pulling her down on top of him, his mouth never leaving hers while he kissed her, his hands moving over her rounded hips, holding her to him until she became aware of his intentions through the thin petticoat.

"Valentine, not here."

"Yes, here. There is no one to see, and I want you, my love," he warned.

"I have to speak with you. We shouldn't be doing this. What happened last night . . ." she began uncomfortably. "You don't have to feel you must marry me. I would understand. I'm not the kind of woman a man would wish for his wife. You should marry someone like—like Honoria. She would make a far better wife than I ever could. She has all of the graces. I am not a proper person, Valentine. My life had been very unusual. I do not always act in a civilized manner, despite what Basil tried to teach me.''

"I would be bored with anyone else, my love, my only love,'' Valentine murmured against her lips, laughing softly. "Always thinking of others rather than yourself. But I am astounded that you would sacrifice me for what you mistakenly think is right and proper. You will become my wife, Lily. Accept that fact, my dear. Indeed, you are already my lover and, to my mind, my wife. When you allowed me to become your lover, 'twas no dalliance between us. You and I will be lovers forever. Never doubt that. But to make certain you never leave me, we will say our vows for the world to hear. And the church bells shall ring in celebration of our marriage vows. No one will ever take you from me. I hold what is mine, Lily Francisca Christian. Love me now, Lily,'' he said, his lips devouring hers until she had no breath left in a body that was no longer hers, for he had claimed it as his prize.

"You seem so very certain that we will return to England,'' she managed to say faintly when his lips parted from hers for an instant so she could draw breath. "I wish I had your faith, Valentine. The *Madrigal* is gone. She—she may have been . . .'' Lily paused, unwilling even to think such a thought, especially since Simon was aboard Valentine's ship.

"Faith? Yes, I have faith, faith in my men,'' he said with a smile, his narrowed gaze searching the horizon almost impatiently until he felt Lily's hands caressing him boldly and realized that he would have her to himself in this paradise for a little while longer.

It wasn't until early the following day that his faith seemed justified and his search proved worthwhile, for just beyond the reefs, flying the red cross of St. George, was the *Madrigal*, her cannon firing a salute to her captain on shore.

He was a gentleman on whom I built
An absolute trust.

SHAKESPEARE

Chapter Twenty-Six

THE *Madrigal's* sails had seemed to sing, catching the wind and billowing with a thundering song. The curving sheets of canvas had been burnished by the sun from dawn till dusk, while shimmering sea had stretched as far as the eye could see.

Under press of canvas, all her sails set and drawing well, the *Madrigal* had held steady to her course with the westerlies keeping her sails rapping full. Leaving the warm waters of the Gulf Stream that had carried her north, she turned toward home with the wind off her quarter, the gilded figurehead of the sea maid riding the waves as the trim ship gave easily to the motion of sea and wind.

In the *Madrigal's* wake, each trying for the weather gage, were several of her sister ships, their captains crowding on in a friendly but competitive race. But the *Madrigal* remained apart, forging ahead, her captain setting every stitch of canvas as he raced with the wind, scattering the white horses cresting in foaming waves before her bow.

More than the others, he had reason to reach the shores of England.

The *Madrigal* made the crossing in less than a month, almost beating the twenty-three days it had taken Drake ten years earlier to cross the Atlantic after his successful raid on Nombre de Dios.

She was anchored now just below Greenwich, where her

captain had gone ashore for a private audience with Elizabeth. Lord Burghley had received the news of her docking immediately upon the *Madrigal*'s arrival and, on the strength of his own suspicions, had already alerted a troop of guardsmen to stand ready.

Valentine Whitelaw had been escorted into the palace through a back entrance, along a darkened corridor empty of courtiers or servants, with only the yeomen of the guard in full livery to guide him along its narrow length.

The captain of the guard allowed him entrance into the privy chamber. Elizabeth, as was often her custom, had dined alone. The wide assortment of dishes that had been offered for her selection had been tested for poisoning by her yeomen before being served to her. It was a ceremony Valentine had witnessed once before, when a lady-in-waiting had given a spoonful of the dish each yeoman had carried to that man to taste, lest he have been tempted to poison it along its route from the royal kitchens. The gilt plate was now being removed while stacks of correspondence and treatises which needed Elizabeth's perusal and response were being placed across the table in order of importance.

"Your Majesty." Valentine Whitelaw knelt on one knee before her, his head downbent.

"Rise, my captain."

Valentine Whitelaw rose before his queen. Elizabeth stood before her throne in royal splendor; her satin gown was of a brilliant shade of marigold and embroidered with brightly colored silks and encrusted with sparkling jewels; her red-gold curls were crowned by what appeared to be a sunburst of gold tipped with rubies and pearls; a high-standing ruff of the finest lace framed her head and shoulders, while the delicate layers of a lace collarette were starched to unfold like the petals of the flowers she loved to surround herself with. A fragrant rose was pinned to her breast and the scent of lavender floated from the silken folds of her gown when she gracefully took her seat, but she sat rigidly, despite the tall-backed support of her throne, and she ignored the sable rug that might have warmed her knees.

"Away! Leave us!" she said, gesturing impatiently for her maids of honor, ladies-in-waiting, and various officials flocking around to leave.

Valentine Whitelaw continued to stand alone before Elizabeth, oblivious of the rustling of silken skirts and petticoats and the curious glances being sent his way by those insulted officials not important enough to remain during his audience with Elizabeth. He felt her dark eyes on him and finally met her speculative gaze.

"You need say nothing. I can see from the graveness of your expression, Master Mariner, that your voyage has been successful," she spoke harshly, her long, slender fingers straying to the heavy ropes of pearls that dangled from her neck. Her ringed fingers moved nervously along the gleaming coils and were the only indication of her growing unease.

"Indeed, ma'am, although there is much sadness and little victory in finding that we have been betrayed by those we have placed an absolute trust in," Valentine spoke softly, his turquoise eyes shadowed by that betrayal.

The door to the chamber opened to allow Lord Burghley's dark-clad figure to enter, then it closed behind him, shutting off the sounds of laughter and music drifting from the great hall.

Valentine Whitelaw reached inside his doublet, where the leather-bound journal had been safely hidden from all eyes, and withdrew the book. He stepped forward and held it out to Elizabeth.

"My brother's journal."

By her wish, Lord Burghley carefully took the book, half expecting it to crumble to dust in his hand. "You have read it? It proves our suspicions?"

Valentine Whitelaw nodded. "Basil did a fine job. He left detailed descriptions of everything he saw and heard. Names, dates, places, his impressions of the people he met, the gossip he was privy to. It was while at the home of Don Rodrigo, Magdalena Christian's father, that Basil saw two Englishmen he knew well. They were traveling in the company of a priest and Don Pedro Villasandro, captain of the *Estrella D'Alba*. They had just arrived from Spain aboard his ship.

"He was, of course, suspicious of their presence in Santo Domingo. By bribing a fisherman, Basil managed to get aboard the *Estrella D'Alba*. From his vantage point on the balcony outside the captain's cabin, he overheard Sir Raymond Valchamps plotting an assassination—his queen's."

"And the other gentleman?" Elizabeth asked.

Lord Burghley had been quickly thumbing through the book, noting with some surprise the information revealed in Basil Whitelaw's neat hand. Now he held the journal open for his queen to read the name printed therein.

"I will have the warrants for their arrest drawn up immediately. As of the last report I received, Sir Raymond Valchamps had not yet left his townhouse. We may be able to apprehend him before he leaves the city and learns of Captain Whitelaw's return. Even should he try to flee to the coast, we have him in our grasp now," Lord Burghley stated. "We have said nothing of our suspicions of him. Of course, he knew you would have spoken to us concerning his attempted murder of Mistress Christian, but he would have known we had little proof; no more than her word against his. He has behaved as he always has—as if innocent of any wrongdoing. Indeed, I would have been surprised had he tried to flee the country. He would have wished to protect his good name had you not returned. And fleeing to France would have made him look very guilty indeed. However, I had thought him uncommonly calm considering the predicament he finds himself in. I realize now that he had every reason to believe that you would never return to England. He and his friends have been a step ahead of you since the beginning. You have my admiration, Captain, for having managed to escape the trap they surely set for you," Lord Burghley complimented him, a curious expression in his eye.

"With the cooperation of a few good friends, I set a trap of my own, my lord," Valentine Whitelaw responded, then glanced to where Elizabeth sat, lost in thought.

"With Your Majesty's permission, I would ask leave to accompany your guard when arresting this other . . . traitor."

Elizabeth nodded, rising to walk over to the window to stare out on the green banks sloping down to the river.

"I have resisted, until now, believing those allegations you brought to Lord Burghley. I could not believe such treachery could exist so close at hand, but time and time again it has been proven so," she said, remembering others she had trusted through the years who had betrayed her and tried to seize her crown.

Turning from the window, she was momentarily silhouetted

against the light and Valentine Whitelaw realized how very frail Elizabeth suddenly seemed. So accustomed had he become through the years of her reign to seeing her raise a bold face to the world, to hear her damning oaths or rich laughter fill a room that he had forgotten that she was an aging woman. The thick white powder she covered her face with could not hide the lines spreading out from her eyes nor conceal the finely wrinkled and sagging skin of her neck, and the rouge painted unsparingly on her sunken cheeks could not replace the natural color of a young girl's blush. This was a woman who was growing tired of subterfuge, fearful of assassination plots, and of losing friends and companions to death. At this moment, with her usual bravado gone, her queenly duties weighing heavy on her thin shoulders, she looked no more than a weary woman faced with her own mortality.

"I believe Sir Raymond has been making preparations to attend a masque at Riverhurst this eve and since both of our traitors are certain to be in attendance, we could, if we miss Sir Raymond here, apprehend Valchamps and—"

"Never again mention either name while in my presence!" Elizabeth interrupted, her voice shaking now with her rage. "God's death, but I will hear nothing further concerning this matter until both traitors are lodged in the Tower!" she swore, and with her dark eyes burning with rekindled fire and her head of red-gold curls raised proudly, she left the chamber, her maids of honor, ladies-in-waiting, and flustered officials hurrying after her, each praying he or she would not draw her notice and anger Her Majesty further, for her voice was raised shrilly in oath after bloodcurdling oath.

Lord Burghley waited a few minutes longer, until the corridor beyond was almost empty. "Come, I will get you a horse. A moment, please, and I will see to the warrants," he said, guiding Valentine along the corridor.

"I will need three horses, my lord. Mustafa, my manservant and self-appointed bodyguard, will not allow me to leave without him. He would run behind my mount rather than be left behind. And my nephew, Simon Whitelaw, will of course wish to see his family at Riverhurst."

Lord Burghley nodded his agreement. "Of course. And Mistress Christian? She is well and in London?'' he inquired politely.

''No,'' Valentine Whitelaw replied almost regretfully, his finger straying to touch the smoothness of the pearl he wore in his ear. ''She is at Ravindzara.''

''Your home in Cornwall? Ah, that is wise. Now, tell me how it is you escaped the trap I am certain was set for you. I have information that Don Pedro Villasandro sailed from Madrid within a few days of the *Madrigal*'s sailing. There was a rumor, merely hearsay, of course, that he was going to rid the world of a bold Englishman called *El Tigre*. Anyone I know?'' Lord Burghley asked softly, his curiosity as yet unsatisfied concerning that point as they walked along the corridor until their two figures disappeared from view.

Lily Christian stood looking out the windows of the great chamber. She could see the sea in the distance and she longed to spy the *Madrigal*'s sails against the horizon and know that her captain had returned to Ravindzara.

How many days had it been now, she wondered, since the *Madrigal*'s lookout had first sighted the shores of England? With every league that had passed while the *Madrigal* had closed the land, Lily had sensed Valentine's growing impatience. Lying along the land, the *Madrigal* had anchored and a boat had been sent ashore. Valentine had brought the *Madrigal* in close, to hug the shore, so the boat would not have to be rowed a great distance. It took a good crew to make it ashore through the rough seas and dangerous currents that flowed through the rocky mouth of the small cove, but Valentine had not had the time to dock in Falmouth and travel by land to Ravindzara. But fortune had been smiling and the boat had been safely beached in the cove below the cliffs near Ravindzara. Valentine and Lily, the Turk and Simon, and several of the crew had climbed the narrow path to the cliffs above. They'd hurried across the wide stretch of lawns, traveling the short distance through the parkland to where the brick paths meandered through the terraced grounds surrounding Ravindzara.

It had been late afternoon, and through the coolness of the shadows deepening along the walled gardens they had reached the great hall of Ravindzara. This time, upon entering, Lily felt a

welcoming warmth engulfing her, which contrasted sharply
with the cold emptiness she'd felt when seeing Honoria Penmorley standing in the hall to greet them the last time she entered Valentine's home.

The hall was filled with voices raised in merriment. A cheerful fire was burning in the great hearth, where a large mastiff
was stretched out before it warming himself against the afternoon chill. Mouthwatering aromas of a meal in full preparation
drifted through the hall and the great table was being set with
silver plate that gleamed invitingly in the firelight.

A trio of jesting footmen were lowering one of the circular
chandeliers from the beamed ceiling, their at times ribald comments spoken loud enough to cause a blush to color a comely
maid's cheek and draw a disapproving glance from Quinta
Whitelaw, who was arranging an elaborate centerpiece of a ship
of sugar paste, with marchpane figures of animals, candied
fruits, and confections surrounding it, in the center of the trestle
table.

Two children and a curious monkey sat in a row on the long
bench, watching her every move as she arranged the intricate
display.

"Now, Tristram, you may place the flags atop the *Madrigal*'s
masts," Quinta said, holding out three little white flags stained
with berry juice to resemble the red cross of St. George. "Be
careful, dear, for they are very fragile. If you break one, well, I
suppose you will have to eat it, but 'twould be nicer to do so *after*
your dinner."

"I'll be careful, Aunt Quinta," Tristram said, leaning forward to place the flags in proper position.

"When do I get to put something on?" Dulcie asked, her
dark eyes wide with concern as she watched Tristram nearly
knock off the *Madrigal*'s bowsprit, which had been fashioned
from a cinnamon stick. "What happened to those raisins that
were here a minute ago? And the dates are gone too! Did you eat
them, Tristram?"

"Me?" Tristram asked indignantly.

"Cappie!" she said, pointing an accusing finger at the monkey disappearing beneath the table.

"Wonderful, Tristram," Quinta complimented the beaming
boy. "Now, my little one, you have the honor of putting the fig-

urehead into position," Quinta told Dulcie, who squealed with pleasure before staring in openmouthed wonder at the beautiful marchpane sea maid, the tiny body sprinkled with cinnamon sugar and nutmeg.

Raphael had opened a curious eye and raised an offended ear at the high-pitched sound, but when he spied the people standing near the door, he stood up, barking loudly until he recognized them as friends.

"Lily!"

"Valentine!"

"Simon!"

The three voices chorused, causing Raphael to begin barking with renewed vigor, his tail, wagging so enthusiastically, nearly sending one of the marchpane figures to the floor, where it would have quickly disappeared.

Valentine Whitelaw caught Dulcie's flying red velvet-clad figure and swung her high into the air before hugging her tight while she placed a kiss against his bearded face. Tristram's greeting began a bit more sedately, but soon he'd given in to his emotions and returned Lily's embrace with a bone-crunching hug of youthful exuberance.

"I swear you've grown a foot taller since I've been away," Lily said, eyeing her brother up and down as if she'd never seen him before.

"I'm glad you're back, Lily," he confided. "I've missed you. Will you tell me all about the island? What it looks like now?"

Quinta had remained slightly back, watching the scene with satisfaction, but upon encountering Valentine's gaze, her expression had altered subtly.

"Welcome, my dears! Come in! You must be fatigued," Quinta said, sending a couple of maids and one of the footmen to the kitchens for refreshment. "You have ridden all the way from Falmouth?" she inquired, kissing Lily's cool cheek, then Simon's, much to his surprised dismay until she touched her lips to Valentine's, cheeks too, and he hadn't seemed to mind.

"No, we came by boat," Simon responded, not realizing how impudent that sounded until he saw Quinta's surprised expression. "The *Madrigal* lies just off shore, Aunt Quinta," Simon explained, eyeing the empty door to the kitchen impatiently. "We *are* on a mission of some importance."

"How is Artemis?" Valentine asked, calling one of the footmen over to have a word with him before he moved closer to the hearth.

Quinta smiled. "I fear we worry too much. She is far stronger than any of us allow her to be. Until the latest storm brought in such cool weather, she was taking a stroll every day. Difficult though 'twas—her time is very close now—she would not be denied her breath of fresh air as she calls it," Quinta said with a shake of her dark head. " 'Tis Sir Rodger I am most concerned about. I've never seen a more nervous gentleman. Of course, 'tis his firstborn, and if a son, then heir to the Hall and the great Penmorley name. What a responsibility," Quinta remarked, and whether she intended it as a sarcastic rejoinder or not, one could not be certain.

"Ah, here we are. You must be famished. Supper will not be ready for a while yet, but we've some freshly baked bread from this morning, and some meat and cheese from yesterday. 'Twill hold you till supper."

"I'm sorry, but I haven't the time, Quinta," Valentine said abruptly as the platters were placed on the table, and when Quinta looked questioningly at him, he drew her aside and they stood in quiet conversation for some time.

Lily could remember her start of surprise to learn that they would be leaving Ravindzara so quickly. She had thought they would stay overnight, or at least for a couple of hours. She did not like to admit that she was tired, but she found herself huddling close to the fire, trying to soak up some of its warmth.

When Quinta had suggested she might wish to freshen up before eating, thinking they had very little time, she had quickly followed Quinta upstairs to the chamber she'd slept in before, where her trunk had been stored. She had planned to wash, then change her clothes, before returning to the hall for a light repast. They would soon be reboarding the *Madrigal* for the rest of the journey to London. She had been somewhat dismayed, therefore, upon taking her place at the table to find that Valentine had left for Penmorley Hall.

But she'd had little opportunity to think further upon it, for Tristram and Dulcie had been full of questions about the voyage and the island. She'd had no difficulty in recounting the first part of their voyage or when they'd stepped ashore on the island after a three-year absence. Her vivid memories of it had filled the room with the feel of the warm, turquoise waters of the cove and the white sands of the beach, the seductive sounds of the palms whispering in the trades above tall green grasses bringing an aching sigh from one of the footmen who'd often thought of trying to join the crew of the *Madrigal*.

Soon, there had been a stillness in the hall, for all of the servants had gathered close to hear the tale. Slowly, as if difficult still for her to relive, Lily had told them of the young, unknown Spaniard who'd died saving her life when the jaguar had attacked them. Dulcie's squeal when Choco's name had been mentioned had caused more than one of the servants to jump nervously and had sent Cappie scurrying back under the table. Then, hurriedly, Lily had recounted when she and Valentine had escaped their captors and dove into the water to find the passage to the cave. She couldn't hide, however, her blushing cheeks when she'd ended her tale rather too quickly with the sighting of the *Madrigal*'s sails.

Luckily, Tristram was more than willing to answer the countless questions about the underwater passage through the coral and the cave where the treasure had been hidden for so many years. Once, Lily had glanced up to find Quinta's speculative gaze on her, but then Quinta had smiled and turned her eyes away when Simon had taken over the tale, for this was when the real adventure had begun, he'd said, delighting his listeners with his highly personalized account of the sea battle he'd been engaged in while aboard the *Madrigal*. He had the scar to prove the danger of the situation, for he'd been shot; a comment which had had Quinta hovering over him embarrassingly, especially when he'd rubbed his arm for effect.

But he had soon calmed her worst fears and resumed the tale where Lily had left off.

"After I was wounded, I had to leave the isle, for I could no longer be of any use to the captain, but I did so under protest, for Lily was still missing. Had I known the danger she'd been in I would never have gotten into that boat," he stated firmly. "We had almost reached the ship when we saw the captain taken prisoner by the Spanish. They already had Lily. I thought the Turk was going to jump overboard, but he'd been given his orders by the captain and he could do nothing but stand on the deck and stare toward shore," Simon told them, and, glancing around just to make certain that the Turk had gone with the captain to Penmorley Hall, he added, "and I've never seen such a mean look in anyone's eye.

"Well, the first mate had his orders too, and it surprised me to see the *Madrigal* cut her anchor and run. I couldn't believe that we were leaving the captain and Lily at the mercy of the Spanish," Simon said, still disturbed by the thought. "But there were three galleons giving chase and if we hadn't sailed we would have been blown from the water. We sailed away from the island, then entered this narrow channel leading toward another island to windward, but the galleons seemed to be closing the distance and their cannon fire was falling awfully close. Thought they were going to overtake us. Didn't seem to me we had enough sail," Simon said, his voice breaking with excitement as he remembered his own fears at the time, standing on deck and watching the Spanish sails closing on his ship.

"Then, rounding this headland, we sailed right into the ranks of three English ships lying there in wait. I've never been so happy to see the red cross of St. George in my life! The sailors on board cheered when we reached them and sailed right past to leave the Spaniards to fall foul of them. We were almost close enough to see the Spaniards' surprised expressions too when they realized that they'd been tricked. The *Madrigal* hadn't been running scared, she'd been leading them into a trap. She'd wanted them to follow," Simon said with a chuckle of remembered glee.

"Well, fancy that, them English ships bein' there," one of the footmen said, shaking his head in disbelief.

"Well, of course they weren't *just* there," said another, slightly older man. "The captain knew all along there was goin' to be trouble."

"He did, Zeke?" another footman asked.

"Well, of course he did, he's the master, ain't he?"

"Reckon so."

" 'Tis true, Tom. He's the smart one, he is. Always rememberin' our names," Willie agreed with a knowing look in his eye.

Simon Whitelaw stared in amazement at the three before continuing. "Then the English ships opened fire on the galleons. We've got long-range cannon, and you should have seen the masts splintered on board those galleons. They couldn't even get off a raking broadside, but we fired and fired, and the smoke filled the air. By the time we finished blowing away half of their decks there wasn't much fight in them, especially their commander aboard the *Estrella D'Alba,* and they turned tail and ran. We had the best position. Had the weather gage and we, and the other three ships, went in pursuit. What a fight!'' Simon crowed, his dark eyes glowing with happiness, for it somehow made him feel better to think that this time it had been the Spanish who'd been beaten, instead of a lone English ship like the *Arion* ten years earlier, especially since one of those galleons had been captained by the man who'd helped sink the *Arion*—Don Pedro Villasandro.

Lily smiled, remembering how excited she'd been to see the *Madrigal's* sails just beyond the cove. She could also remember seeing Simon waving wildly to them from the boat being rowed ashore, forgetting in his excitement his injured arm and to keep his seat. If it hadn't been for the Turk's restraining hand, Simon would have nearly fallen overboard again.

She could remember turning to Valentine, who'd been smiling and hadn't seemed surprised to see his ship's return. But then, he'd known all along what had been planned. When Simon had raced ashore with his news and the revelation that one of the ships had been the *Estrella D'Alba,* captained by Don Pedro Villasandro, she had been startled, for it had seemed as if history was repeating itself—only this time they had won the battle, not Don Pedro Villasandro.

Lily frowned slightly, remembering a strange look that had entered Valentine's eye when Simon had spoken of the *Estrella D'Alba's* retreat, as if her captain had suddenly turned coward. The *Madrigal's* first mate had been stunned by the *Estrella D'Alba's* sheering off, because she'd left the other galleons fighting alone. Simon had shaken his head, saying that the Spaniard only liked a fight when the odds were in his favor, and this time he'd gotten more than he'd bargained for. But Lily could have sworn she'd almost seen an expression of pity enter Valentine's eyes when he'd said that a man could lose something far more precious to him than a battle or his pride. Sometimes, when the losses were too high, the fight went out of a man.

Lily had questioned Valentine further, wanting to know how he suspected Don Pedro would be lying in wait for them at the island. Valentine had said that he'd been warned that Don Pedro had been watching his movements for some time, and he'd suspected that this voyage would be reported to him. His worst fears, however, had been that their destination would have leaked out, and then, as indeed happened, Don Pedro had already arrived on the island by the time the *Madrigal* anchored beyond the reefs. He had been expecting trouble, but not quite so soon. And he had not been surprised to discover the *Estrella D'Alba* in command, for Don Pedro was the only one who knew the location of the island. He would also have been eager to even the score between them, and knowing something of Don Pedro, he had known the Spaniard would not have sailed alone.

Before setting sail from England, he had spoken with several of his captain friends. Under the pretext of sailing to Alexandria, they'd set sail within hours of the *Madrigal*'s sailing. They'd been given the location of the island, and when the *Madrigal* had made port in Falmouth, they'd sailed on and had arrived in the Indies just a day or so ahead of the *Madrigal*. Staying out of sight, they had waited.

Simon had still been answering questions an hour later when Valentine had returned from Penmorley Hall. It was then that Lily had learned to her indignation that Valentine was not going to take her with him to London. She was to remain at Ravindzara. She had tried to convince him to change his mind, but now that the journal was in his possession she had lost her bargaining power.

Hiding her deep disappointment and her growing fears, she had gone with Tristram and Dulcie to the garden's edge to watch as Valentine had walked away. Simon was returning to Whiteswood, after stopping off at Riverhurst to reassure Lady Elspeth and Sir William that he had returned home safely. He and the Turk would be accompanying Valentine and his crew when the *Madrigal* sailed. Just before entering the parkland, Valentine had paused for a moment, turning to see the three of them standing there watching him. Then he'd waved to them before disappearing beneath the trees.

Lily had stood there, her arm raised in farewell, the remembrance of his kiss warming her lips. When walking through the gardens, he had sent the others ahead, and leading her into one of the shadowy rose arbors he had pulled her into his arms, his mouth seeking hers hungrily. It had been too long since they'd touched, since they'd known the warmth of each other's bodies, for they'd not been lovers since the island.

Once aboard the *Madrigal*, Valentine Whitelaw had kept his distance from her, treating her as he had before their brief, passionate interlude on the island. Lily could still remember the wry smile that had crossed his face when she'd asked him in an uncertain voice if he had grown tired of her. She had even gone so far as to tell him that she would not make any demands upon him, that what had happened while on the island could all be forgotten once they returned to England. They had been alone in his cabin at the time. He'd been sitting at the small table making entries into the *Madrigal*'s log book. He'd seemed stunned, then angered by her remark, and before she'd realized his intent, he'd drawn her down onto his lap, his arms holding her against his chest while his lips had left a trail of fire across her face before finding her mouth. His searing kiss and the caress of his hands against her breasts and hips had left her in no doubt of his ardor, and when she'd felt the hardness of him against her thigh where she sat across him, she had known he still desired her. Holding her face captive in his hands, he had spoken bluntly.

While he was captain of this ship he owed his men the same respect he expected from them, and he would not insult them by having a woman in his bed while they returned to their cold berths each night. Nor would he have any of his men, or others once they returned to England, calling her his whore. She was to be his wife and he would have her treated with the respect she deserved, no matter how he ached to have her lie with him during the voyage.

It had been a long journey to that embrace in the gardens of Ravindzara, when he had whispered words of love against her lips. For an instant he had held her so tightly against him that she couldn't breathe, then he'd released her, staring down into her face as if memorizing every feature.

"Will you trust me, Lily?" he had asked. "As long as I know you await me here at Ravindzara, I will always return here."

Lily sat down on the tapestried cushions of the window seat, curling her silk-stockinged legs beneath her as she continued to gaze upon the wild heath to the west, where it stretched toward the sea. She reached up to touch the ring of Spanish gold she now wore in one ear. Valentine had taken it from his own, and, removing the delicate pearl she'd been wearing he had placed it in his ear instead and stated with a grin, "Now I have something else of yours to bring me good luck."

Lily frowned, wondering what else he possessed of hers? She glanced down at the leather-bound book she held on her lap, her hand caressing the grainy cover lovingly.

It was the log book of the *Arion*, and across its yellowed pages was her father's impatient scrawl, for he'd never been one to sit still for long. But a conscientious captain he had been, and daily observations and occurrences had been recorded in detail. The *Arion*'s position each day had been duly logged and the leagues journeyed from noon to noon, as well as allowances for leeway and the heave of the sea. The distance high land could be seen from seaward had been noted, along with finely sketched drawings of the islands and lands the *Arion* had sighted. There were also beautifully drawn ships, of all types and flying the flags of many countries. Fish, birds, plants, and all manner of exotic creatures and places had been painstakingly reproduced in the ruled spaces beneath the columns where he'd made his notations on each page.

Lily shook her head in amazement. She'd never seen this side of her father. He had always been so boisterous and forceful, full of a daring that had made him a dangerous enemy. Oaths had scorched the air when he'd been angry or defiant, but his laughter had always come quickly. The man who had drawn these beautiful sketches had a sensitive, quiet side to his nature, and only a man of great patience could have captured with pen and brush the images that had filled his mind.

Lily still found it hard to believe that these drawings had been penned by her father's bold hand. But when she saw her own eyes staring up at her from a little girl's face, with a delicate lily and a loving inscription beside it, she knew that these sketches had been the work of her father. She'd found several more portraits that she would always cherish. One had been of her mother, and Lily's breath still caught in her throat when she saw the warmth and beauty of the face that had become a memory. Two other portraits had fascinated her, for they'd been of her Spanish grandmother and grandfather. The one of Basil, wading out of the surf without his clothes, a fish held protectively before him had startled her, but then there'd been another one of Basil, the profile of a thoughtful man, and that had held Simon's attention the longest when she'd showed it to him.

But it had been one very special entry that had left her laughing with joy. Valentine had lifted her clear of the deck, swinging her around when she'd hurried into his arms, his laughter mingling with hers. He'd already read the passage and had placed a red flower from the island between the pages for her to find.

She opened the log to the page, staring down now at the last part of the entry for the day the *Arion* had set sail from Santo Domingo never to return to England:

. . . . Wonderful news. Magdalena is with child. She told me upon my arrival from a bit of raiding along the Main (quite successful—wait 'til I tell Drake what he's now referred being kin to in Rio de la Hacha). My happiness knows no bounds, although I did tell the dear woman that my Lily Francisca was handful enough for Maire Lester; however, she would think to please me more by giving me another child—a son this time. Already she tires me out with ponderings of a proper name. She would call him Francisco, after her father, but I have told her it might not be seemly for an English lad, especially if he inherits my fairness, to answer to a Spanish name. We have decided on the name of Tristram, which does my English soul good, for 'tis a proud name of a noble knight of King Arthur. However, if a girl . . .

Tristram Francisco Christian was rightful master of Highcross and no one, especially Hartwell Barclay, could deny him his place as Geoffrey Christian's son. Over ten years later, her father had claimed for his own a son he'd never even seen and given that lad his name and inheritance, banishing any doubts others would harbor that this boy was not his son and rightful heir to Highcross.

Lily could still remember Tristram's face after she'd showed him the log when they'd arrived at Ravindzara. He'd stood so proud knowing that his father had known of his coming and had selected the name he bore.

The only thing that still puzzled her was the page that preceded that entry; it was missing. It had been ripped from the log. When she'd asked Valentine about it, he had looked away, unwilling to deny or confirm her suspicions that he might have torn the page from the book.

Lily sighed, wondering if Valentine had confronted Sir Raymond Valchamps and the other man. Lily glanced back out the window, her eyes gazing at the sea. It looked molten now, with the sun sinking lower on the horizon. Soon the first star of evening would appear.

Lily smiled, touching her lips with her fingertips. The last night on the island, they had slept beneath the stars. She had gathered up the driftwood and started the fire, much to his surprise, she remembered, until she'd reminded him that she'd lived such an existence for many years on this same isle. He had smiled, taking himself off to hunt for their dinner, but by the time he'd returned, empty-handed, she'd already cooked the sweet meat from a conch and the stone crabs she'd caught, the aromatic blend of herbs she'd collected from the forest adding to the flavor. She'd found fruit to add to their feast, as well as cool water from a small, bubbling spring nearby, leaving Valentine to feel rather helpless for the first time in his life, especially when he saw the bower of sweet-smelling grasses and fragrant flowers she'd made high on the sands.

Lily shivered delicately, her pulse quickening when she remembered that night of love with the stars shining so brightly above, while the sea lapped gently against the sands. Lying naked in each other's arms, their desires reaching a feverish peak and threatening to consume them both, they had formed a bond of such intimacy, of such sharing, that Lily would always feel a part of Valentine Whitelaw.

That evening they'd watched the sun set in a glorious blaze of burning copper, the clouds floating above the waves gilded against a deepening purple sky. The following morning, their bodies bathed in a golden light, they'd watched the sun rising from the sea, the sky aflame with the scarlet of flamingos taking wing.

"Someday, I would like to return," Lily said aloud.

"Buss us a nice one, sweeting! Lift a leg! *Prraaack!*" Cisco said from his perch in the corner of the room, ruffling his feathers to draw Lily's attention from the window. "I'll truss him up prettier than m'lady's hat! *Prraack!*"

"Prraaack, yourself, silly Cisco," Lily said with a laugh, and digging into the pocket of her skirt, she withdrew an almond for Cisco's delectation. He caught it easily in his beak when she tossed it over to him, flapping his wings with pleasure as he giggled.

"Oh, there you are, my dear," Quinta said from the doorway. "I thought I heard someone in here laughing."

Lily's smile tightened imperceptibly when she saw the graceful figure entering the room behind Quinta's tall form.

"Honoria very kindly made a special trip to let me know how Artemis is faring. She also brought over some smoked sausages from the Hall's smokehouse. Quite famous throughout the county, and which we will find most enjoyable, I am sure," Quinta said, gesturing for Honoria to take the comfortable chair nearest the hearth while she perched on the hard settle against the wall.

"And gooseberry tarts—I do confess to making a rather fine one," Honoria reminded her hostess with a complacent look around, her chin lifting haughtily when she saw Lily sitting curled up in the window seat.

"Yes, of course, however could I have forgotten, your goose—" Quinta apologized when interrupted by a rude noise.

Honoria drew in her breath indignantly and turned a suspicious eye on Quinta Whitelaw, as if she were guilty of some indiscretion.

"Lift a leg there, my fine one. Ooooooh, naughty, naughty girl," Cisco crowed, eyeing the outraged woman's flushed face with an unrepentant yellow eye.

"Well, really! What a horrible creature," Honoria Penmorley said, returning the parrot's gaze with one of dislike.

"Goose us one, then! My, aren't we the pretty one. *Prrraaack!* Ease it over here, sweeting! Let's have a look."

Honoria Penmorley's mouth dropped open most unbecomingly as she stared at the parrot in horror. "Can it fly?" she asked weakly, thinking the creature might fly to land on her shoulder.

"Most definitely," Lily said, uncurling her legs from beneath her and smoothing down the green velvet of her skirt before she walked across the room to give Cisco several more almonds to keep him quiet while Honoria Penmorley was here.

"A pity," she murmured, taking her seat again before the window.

" 'Tis a lovely day, not too cold yet. I found the ride over from Penmorley quite enjoyable. We really must do something about the lane, however, since we do visit so often now and perhaps will even more in the future," Honoria rushed into speech as she took her seat, glancing down at her folded hands, and leaving both Quinta and Lily to wonder what she had intended by her casual remark.

"When is Sir Rodger to return to the Hall?" Quinta asked, wasting no time on the pleasantries.

"Any day now, I should imagine," Honoria replied. "I had thought he might return with Valentine aboard his ship. I am certain he will wish to return as soon as possible."

"I did not know Sir Rodger was away," Lily commented politely, feeling she should contribute something to the conversation.

"Yes, he traveled to London to fetch the doctor. The closest doctor is in Truro, and I must say I have not been overly impressed by his skills. Rodger expects the best possible care for his firstborn. A London-trained doctor will, of course, be quite suitable. We cannot have anything happen to the heir," she said.

"No, we certainly wouldn't wish any harm to come to either mother or child," Quinta responded. "Would you care for refreshment, Honoria? We've some fine claret wine, perhaps with a roast apple in it to add a bit of tartness?"

"How kind, but I really would enjoy a posset to take away the chill," she replied. "But please, do not trouble yourself."

"No trouble at all, Honoria. Lily?"

"No, thank you, Quinta."

"Some hot spiced wine, although you've color enough in your cheeks already. Sweet thoughts of someone dear, hmm?" she added, her comment causing Lily's cheeks to brighten even more. "Like a wild rose," Quinta said, smiling thoughtfully as she noted Honoria's tight mouth and the narrowed gaze fixed on Lily's beautiful face.

"That would be lovely," Lily replied, wondering what Quinta was up to.

"Oh, it has just about slipped my mind. We've received word from this Maire Lester. She wrote to me, not knowing where to contact you. She says she is now free to leave her sister's farm, since the woman has returned with her daughter and son-in-law and apparently the whole family, and a rather large one from the sound of it. I gather she's been asked to leave. She says, if it is still our wish, that she will be happy to travel to Cornwall and take over whatever chores we might find for her if we already have a nursemaid. Sounds a reasonable enough request. From what Tristram and Dulcie have said of her, I think I might find this Maire Lester quite an interesting woman. I never spoke with her much when we visited Highcross."

"The children will not be staying here permanently, will they?" Honoria asked, her nostrils looking pinched.

Quinta Whitelaw raised an imperious eyebrow. "I really cannot say, that will be something for Valentine to decide. 'Tis a family matter. If you will excuse me, now," she said, "I'll prepare that posset for you. Young Millie never beats the eggs enough. Always comes out too thin."

Honoria Penmorley glanced toward the fire, allowing Lily a wonderful view of her classical profile. The firelight glinted over her, softening her features in its golden light.

"Artemis and I were just discussing last eve the importance of being a proper wife, and mistress of one's husband's home. A woman must be well accomplished in all of the skills and graces of being a lady and a gentleman's wife. One must be an asset to one's husband, not . . . a hindrance. Naturally, for instance, the wife of a man of Valentine Whitelaw's wealth and influence would have to be a gentlewoman of exceptional qualities, for I am certain Valentine Whitelaw will one day become a knight of the realm.

"A certain standard of respectability would be expected of his wife. Her reputation must be beyond question, her deportment never faulted. She would, of course, be an accomplished needlewoman, well versed in the art of lace-making, silk-spinning, and fine embroidery. For entertaining, she would indeed have to be a competent singer and musician, well skilled with lute and virginal. But, most important, she should have a working knowledge of the household, for she would be required to handle the affairs of the family and staff at all times. It would be of special importance for the wife of Valentine Whitelaw, since he would often be away on a voyage of some duration.

"Yes, 'tis quite a serious matter, matrimony. One must think of one's suitability before accepting a proposal. A mésalliance is so unfortunate for all parties concerned," she said with a sigh. "You must agree with me, being a young woman who has, I am certain, been taught not to aspire to a position she does not belong in. Naturally, my dear, considering your circumstances, especially now that the boy will inherit Highcross, you might think to better yourself. You must guard yourself against such ambitions. I would think it most tragic, for both of you, if you mistook Valentine Whitelaw's intentions as being more than a sense of responsibility toward you. But I am assured that you would never take advantage of his kindness. Well, enough of that, for I am sure we understand one another.

"I am interested, Mistress Christian, in hearing of your *latest* exploits. You do seem inclined for misadventure. What an exceptional life you have led; not quite . . . well . . . what shall we say? ah . . . *respectable*, although I do not mean any offense by the word," she commented with an understanding, pitying glance at the younger woman.

"Here we are," Quinta said, entering the chamber, a maid carrying a tray with several goblets and dishes crowded across it. "I trust I haven't been too long?" she said glancing between the two women curiously, for Honoria, still seated primly in the chair before the fire, was staring at Lily Christian with a satisfied smile curving her lips, while Lily Christian was staring out the window, a faraway look in her eye.

"No, not at all. It gave Mistress Christian and me a chance to become better acquainted. We have discovered that we think much alike concerning many subjects," Honoria Penmorley said, her smile widening as she accepted her steaming posset.

"Indeed, Mistress Penmorley has very kindly helped me to make up my mind about many things which have of late been troubling me, but now I feel my conscience is clear," Lily Christian said, a glint in her pale green eyes as she stared at the other woman, her fingers fondling the ring of Spanish gold in her ear.

* * *

Sir Raymond Valchamps gazed at his reflection in the looking glass, a look of admiration in his eye. Dressed in a black velvet doublet with gold jeweled embroidery, his silken hose of the finest quality, his shoes of the best cordovan leather, the toes fashionably slashed and edged with gold, he looked the princely figure he felt. The ruff about his throat was stiffly starched and framed his face to perfection.

"You fool!" he said, hitting his manservant across the face, when the man held out his cloak. "I told you I wanted the black one lined with sable. This is lined with silk. Would you have me freeze to death on the river?"

"No, sir," the man mumbled, wishing he should be so lucky. " 'Tis below, sir. I was having one of the maids darn a small tear in the hem."

"Through your mishandling I'm certain. Well?"

"I'll get it immediately, sir," the servant said hurriedly, wiping his hand across his bloodied lip as he left the room.

With a slight smile, Sir Raymond set his black silk hat on his head of pale curls, adjusting the high, soft crown to just the right angle, so the narrow brim slanted across his brow. With a silent chuckle he gazed at the dazzling brooch pinned to it, the sapphires, rubies, emeralds, and pearls winking wickedly at him.

He tapped his fingers impatiently against the gold pomander that hung from his neck, wondering where Cordelia was; he could hardly wait for her reaction.

He glanced around his bedchamber, delighting in the great canopied bed supported by gilded posts, its high headboard carved with his initials and armorial bearings, and surrounded by bas-relief figures from mythical scenes. A scarlet coverlet, the silk embroidered with golden threads entwined in convoluted designs, covered the feather mattress and plump pillows.

Above his head was a magnificent mural painted on the plaster ceiling and portraying saints and demons locked in eternal combat. Chairs upholstered in red velvet were placed in front of the hearth with its molded mantelpiece fashioned in the classical style. But his joy was the small stained-glass window depicting the Last Judgment; the bright reds and blues, so savage in intensity, filled him with a sense of his own purpose.

Sir Raymond sauntered across the room to a door set discreetly in the paneled wall. He opened it and glanced into the darkness of what once had been a servant's room and now served as a jakes. With a smile, he felt along the wall, touching the molding. Beneath the curving edge, he found the latch that released the spring holding the secret panel tightly shut.

Few people would have searched here for a secret passage leading down to another passage in the house next door. Hearing footsteps on the stairs, Sir Raymond quickly backed out of the small closet and closed the door.

Swinging his pomander lazily, he waited. He was not worried. He felt certain Don Pedro Villasandro would succeed in his mission, but if the Spaniard failed, and he had to flee England, then he would easily outsmart Lord Burghley's spies. He knew they were watching his house, his every movement. But they were not watching the house next door, and right under their noses he would slip out of England. But so far, he'd had no word from the Spanish ambassador concerning Don Pedro's voyage, nor had he heard from his own spies watching the Pool of London, where the *Madrigal* would dock, if she ever returned to England. He would have time to flee, once he had received word, and his manservant was under orders not to open the door to anyone unless an invited guest.

"Damn you!" Cordelia Howard stood in the doorway staring at him.

"I knew it!" she spat. "My brooch! I had it yesterday, and you were the only one in my bedchamber. I remember now you going through my jewels. Damn you, Raymond. Give it back! 'Tis my most expensive piece!"

"Is it really?" he inquired with malicious pleasure. "I thought the necklace I gave you was your most prized possession. 'Twould seem to me you attach a great deal of sentiment to this insignificant trinket; indeed, m'dear, I fear 'tis a trifle gaudy," Sir Raymond declared, eyeing its brilliancy in the mirror. "Does look rather nice, though, 'pon my hat."

"Give it back, Raymond," Cordelia warned through tight lips, her black eyes narrowing into slits.

"Could it be you desire it because that bold sea captain, Valentine Whitelaw, gave it to you for being so obliging whenever he came into port?"

"You swine," Cordelia said, her hands clenched until her long nails bit deep into the soft flesh of her palms. She moved closer, her silken petticoats beneath her gown of black velvet rustling softly.

"My dear, you really must control that temper of yours. You do realize that when we marry, all of your possessions become mine, and I may do with them as I please. I rather like the jewels in this brooch, m'dear, so I shall have it reset into several pieces," he said, watching her carefully as he toyed with her.

Unable to contain herself, she stormed across the room, but Sir Raymond was expecting her attack and caught her arm, twisting it painfully behind her back.

"Let go, Raymond! You're hurting me. Do you want to break my arm?" she cried.

"Never raise your voice in anger at me again, Cordelia. I do as I please and I answer to no one," he warned, releasing her abruptly.

Cordelia swung around, but before her hand could come in contact with his face, he had caught it, and the back of his hand had slapped her hard across the cheek and mouth, his ring leaving a vivid scratch.

Sir Raymond released Cordelia from his punishing hold and she hurried to the mirror to see the damage to her flawless features. Her dark eyes welled with tears when she saw the cruel scratch.

"Now look what you made me do," Sir Raymond said in growing irritation as he noticed the drop of blood staining the ruffle of fine lace edging his sleeve. "If this doesn't come out, I shall have to change. Damn, we are going to be even later now."

Cordelia Howard stared at her fiancé's image reflected in the mirror, and she despised him. How could she ever have been fascinated by Raymond Valchamps, or even remotely entertained the thought of marrying him? His true character had emerged after she'd accepted his proposal. She had begun to see a fanaticism and cruelty in the man that she'd never suspected. She had always known he had a cruel streak in him, but she'd had no idea how deep it had gone until she'd started spending more time with him.

Before, when she'd spent a few hours or a night with him, he had seemed wildly exciting, and he had been gracious and generous and determined to please her, but once he'd won his prize, he'd changed and she'd found herself engaged to a vicious-tongued, parsimonious man who seemed to delight in tormenting others.

He treated her little better than a servant or a whore, taking what he wanted by demand or force. Cordelia Howard eyed him nervously, for she knew a fear of him that she'd never experienced before, and it came not only of today's incident. She bore the bruises of his previous beatings when something had displeased him and he'd taken his anger out on her.

"Where are you going?" he demanded as she edged toward the door.

Cordelia stopped, and turning around, she pointed to her face. "I need to wash this blood away. I need some water."

"There's some here," he said, indicating the stained water where he'd rinsed his ruffle.

"If you don't mind, I'll get some fresh water in the kitchens," she told him, moving closer to the door.

"Very well. I didn't get all of this out. Better have my man bring up some fresh water when he comes. And where is he, anyway? Sent him down to get my cloak. Simple enough task."

"I'll tell him," Cordelia said, leaving the room.

Once outside, she stood for a moment taking a deep breath to quell her shaking and swore she'd find a way to break her engagement to Raymond Valchamps, even though she knew she would fear for her life if she tried to leave him.

Hurrying down the stairs, she grabbed her cloak and ran to the door, swinging it wide. She nearly cried out when she saw a troop of the queen's guard standing just beyond, their captain climbing the steps to the house.

"This is the residence of Sir Raymond Valchamps?" he inquired.

"Yes. What is this about?" she asked, eyeing the troop more closely.

"And you are?" he continued, watching her suspiciously, she thought, a sudden fear snaking through her.

"His fi—an acquaintance," she suddenly corrected herself. "I was just about to leave."

"You've had an accident?"

"Yes," Cordelia Howard laughed harshly, touching her finger to where the blood had congealed against the corner of her mouth. "I am returning home to see to it. I tripped and fell."

"Then Sir Raymond Valchamps is still within?" he asked with a casualness that did not fool Cordelia.

Cordelia Howard had an instinct for survival and sensed a change in the wind, which could prove fortuitous for her if she acted quickly now. With a smile curving her stiffening lip, she gestured within, where Sir Raymond's manservant had just come to stand by the door, as if prepared to slam it shut.

"Yes, Sir Raymond is still inside. Upstairs, in his bedchamber. 'Tis the first door on the left at the head of the stairs. Is that not correct, Matson?" she asked the stunned manservant.

Matson continued to stand by the staircase, watching the well-armed guard entering the hall.

"Oh, aye, that it is," Matson answered, quick as Cordelia to sense a change in his fortunes, especially as he watched the well-armed guard entering Sir Raymond Valchamps's home. "In fact, ye should be careful, for there's a board on that top step that squeaks like the devil if ye steps on it. Master always complains that he hears it at night, wakes him up, ye know. Aye, he be expectin' me with his cloak here," he said, rubbing his hand over the soft sable. "Reckon he might not be needin' it now," he guessed, glancing over at the captain of the guard.

"Oh, he will still be going out, but perhaps not to the party he had originally planned to attend. I will remember your assistance," the captain said as he began to climb the staircase.

Matson smiled, wincing slightly when his split lip cracked open again. He glanced over at the door where a couple of the guard stood at attention, looking for the lady, but Cordelia Howard had disappeared.

Despite the pain, he grinned wider as he walked back toward the kitchens, thinking Sir Raymond Valchamps would have to make do with the silk-lined cloak after all.

Sir Raymond Valchamps was adjusting the lace ruffle, eyeing critically when he heard a footstep at the door and without glancing up, he said, "Well, 'tis about time you got here. What the devil's been keeping you?"

"We had to get the warrant for your arrest, Sir Raymond," the captain of the guard said from the doorway, his men stepping into the room and grabbing Sir Raymond before he could even get halfway across the room to the door to the jakes.

* * *

Valentine Whitelaw, the Turk a step behind, stood in the
great arched doorway to the banqueting hall at Riverhurst. The
room was ablaze with light from chandeliers swinging from
the high plasterwork ceiling. Colorful murals and richly
embroidered tapestries graced the walls and glowed softly in the
firelight spreading from the great hearth. A long table against
another wall held the sumptuous feast laid out for the assembled
guests, who were watching a masque performed by a company
of players made up of family and friends. A stage had been set
up at the far end of the hall, where George Hargraves, repre-
senting Orpheus, patron of song and dance, strummed a lyre
while the nine muses garbed in exotic clothing circled him. A
painted backdrop of trees and temples, the sea shimmering in
the distance while clouds seemed to move back and forth above
the stage almost magically, created a stunning illusion of a mythical scene as several small children costumed as sprites and
fairies raced across the stage.

The spectators clapped enthusiastically as the final act ended.
In a quiet corner, away from the stage where a small orchestra
was setting up, several groups of gentlemen were gathering to
play cards and backgammon, while the musicians began to play
a slow tune for the guests who were now beginning to dance a
graceful measure, some still clad in their unusual costumes from
the performance.

"I don't see my mother anywhere. She's probably behind
the stage. I thought I recognized a couple of those sprites. She's
most likely seeing that Besty and Wilfred are gotten into bed
without any further delay," Simon said, coming to stand beside
Valentine. "I told the steward to find Sir William. A troop of
guard standing in the hall is liable to cause some comment, Valentine," he advised, for people were already beginning to
glance their way. "I think I'll go upstairs and see if I can find
them," he said.

"I'd rather you said nothing to anyone until I've had a
chance to speak with Sir William and Elspeth, and handle this
matter, Simon," Valentine told him.

"Of course, I understand. You *can* trust me, Valentine. Isn't
that Sir Rodger? I didn't know he was in London. I thought he'd
be with Artemis," Simon exclaimed, watching a tall man disappearing into the crowd of dancers.

"Where?" Valentine asked, his gaze searching the crowd.

"He's gone now. Good Lord, look at George Hargraves," Simon said with a loud guffaw as a short man dressed in a toga and wearing an ivy-leaf crown danced past with a tall goddess in his arms, but so busy was he trying to keep his crown from slipping that he didn't see either man staring at him from the doorway.

Valentine Whitelaw's gaze narrowed. Thomas Sandrick stood against the wall, sipping from a goblet of wine, his head inclined slightly as he listened attentively to what his wife, Eliza, was saying; then Valentine lost sight of him when a crowd of people surged around them, laughter drifting over the strains of music.

"Good Lord! Valentine Whitelaw, you've returned from yet another voyage!" a loud-voiced woman spoke directly beside them. "And your mother will be thankful you've returned in one piece, I might add," she said, turning her critical eye on the younger Whitelaw. "Couldn't believe it when she'd said you'd left to sail with your uncle, after what happened to your father. I can tell you, Master Whitelaw, I wouldn't allow such a thing. You mark my wo—"

"Lady Denning," Simon spoke coolly, sounding quite a bit like his father in that instant.

"Sir Charles escorted you this eve, Lady Denning?" Valentine inquired with seeming little interest.

"Nearly didn't, said he'd something important to handle. But he's glad he did now, for he would have missed seeing George Hargraves dressed up as Orpheus. Not that 'twas supposed to be George, too short for the Muses," she said with a hearty laugh. " 'Twas supposed to have been Sir Raymond Valchamps, but he never showed up. Damned impertinence. And would you believe it? That she-wolf he's goin' to marry comes sweeping in here on the arm of that young buck Raleigh. Never heard of such an improper thing."

"Where is Sir Charles?"

"Over there, playing dice most likely," Lady Denning said, but when she glanced to where she'd seen him sitting just moments before, she frowned. "Well, he was there. Wonder where he has wandered off to now? If I catch him with one of those serving wenches, I'll—" she said through clenched teeth, the light of battle in her eye. "What the devil is a troop of the queen's guard doing skulking back here in the hall?" she demanded, her voice carrying across the room and drawing the curious attention of several people nearby.

"Captain," the Turk murmured, his nod drawing Valentine's gaze across the room.

"There! There he is!" Simon cried.

"Who? Charles?" Lady Denning roared, squinting as she tried to follow where young Simon Whitelaw was pointing.

Sir Charles Denning, who'd been standing just out of Lady Denning's line of sight, gulped, seeing his wife standing with a troop of guard at her back while Simon Whitelaw pointed him out to them, his intentions of following that fair-haired wench into the kitchens vanishing from his thoughts.

"Sir William! Here!" Simon called to his stepfather, waving to catch his attention from across the crowded room.

Sir William Davies glanced up to see Simon standing in the doorway waving to him. Beside him stood Valentine Whitelaw, and behind him, a troop of the royal guard.

Valentine Whitelaw stared at Sir William, their eyes meeting across the great banqueting hall. Words were not necessary, for they both now knew the truth.

Sir William Davies had been the other man Basil Whitelaw had recognized in Santo Domingo ten years ago.

"What's wrong?" Simon demanded, for his stepfather suddenly looked ill. In fact, for a moment, he'd looked like he was staring death in the face. "Where's he going? He saw me waving to him. Is he sick? What's wrong?" Simon repeated again, but his uncle had already disappeared into the crowd, and the Turk's turban was bobbing up and down as he followed in his captain's wake, but Simon had little time to wonder, for several of the soldiers hurried after them, causing a panic amongst the dancing guests as the guard, swords drawn, shoved their way through the finely dressed gentlemen and their ladies, who'd thought for no more excitement this evening than an amusing masque.

Simon Whitelaw stood where he was, staring across the hall to where his stepfather had so suddenly disappeared after seeing Valentine Whitelaw standing in the doorway.

Simon Whitelaw knew the truth. And he felt the same sense

of horror that his father had when discovering Sir William aboard the *Estrella D'Alba* that night so long ago. They had both been betrayed. Simon's jaw clenched as he tried to keep his lips from trembling when he thought of this man, this traitor, who had been his father's friend. This friend had known of his father's death, had done nothing to stop it. Then he had come home to England and married his betrayed friend's widow. This man had married his mother, Simon thought, his dead father's wife, and come to live in his father's house.

Sir William Davies had betrayed his father, then taken for his own everything that his father had loved: his wife, his home, and even his son. While his father had been abandoned on a desolate island, left to die without ever seeing his beloved family again, this man had slept in his bed and taken his wife as his own. All of these years he had shamed them, Simon Whitelaw thought, feeling a deep, burning rage whipping through him.

Now he knew why Valentine had not told him the truth. Why Valentine had been so brooding and quiet since discovering the journal. He had known what his reaction would be as Basil's son, and as Basil's brother he had felt the same rage inside of him.

Simon Whitelaw turned away, drawing his sword as he made his way from the hall and the people standing around, talking in whispers, for the music had stopped with the unexpected entrance of the guard, when the guests had realized something was wrong and had stopped their dancing.

With a certainty he didn't quite understand, he knew where Sir William would be headed. Simon remembered Sir William's great joy and pride when the chapel had been built at Riverhurst. He had spent many an hour praying within the cool, dark walls, where the light filtering through the stained-glass window, painted with a figure of Edward the Confessor, had seemed heaven sent, the rich colors an inspiration to aspire to a higher order of existence.

Simon Whitelaw hurried along the corridor leading toward the chapel, vengeance the only thought in his mind. As he neared the arched portal that led to the chapel, he came to an abrupt halt.

The Turk stood barring his passage.

"He is inside, isn't he?" Simon demanded.

The Turk just stared at him, his dark eyes strangely opaque.

"Let me pass, Mustafa. It is my right to avenge my family's name."

"You do not pass by me, young Master Whitelaw."

"I will pass."

"No."

Simon's hand tightened around his sword hilt. "I don't want to fight you, Mustafa. But I will enter."

The Turk continued to stand before the door, arms crossed before him.

Simon moved closer to the doors.

"Simon! Stop!" Valentine called out to him as he and the guards approached along the corridor.

Reaching Simon, he grabbed his sword arm and held it between them, staring down into Simon's hardened face.

"Mustafa?"

"Sir William inside. When I come down this corridor after you go in opposite way to search, I see him enter. I know," he said. "I know. So I wait," he said with a patient look of understanding on his face. "It is Allah's way, Captain," he explained with a glance at the religious carving cut into the stone above his turbaned head.

"Let me go, Valentine. 'Tis my right."

"No, I feel the same hatred, Simon. We've the same blood in our veins, the same blood Basil had, but that does not give us the right to take Sir William's life. He will face death soon enough, Simon."

"We have a warrant for his arrest. We are here with the queen's authority. It is our duty to arrest him for treason," the senior officer of the guard spoke, but, so far, had been unwilling to enter the chapel where the Turk stood guard.

Valentine Whitelaw stared down into Simon's thin face, and he knew the deep anguish the young man was feeling as he felt the betrayal of one he had come to trust.

"Simon, listen to me. You must remain strong. You must become the man of this family now. Your mother will need you, Simon. Do you know what this will do to her? She has been betrayed far more cruelly than you have. She will know a deepness of despair that you and I will never experience. She loved Basil with all of her heart. She grieved as only a wife and lover could when Basil died. But she started again, with a man she trusted and loved, a man who gave her another life, and two children she could be proud of. She has known happiness with Sir William. This will destroy her, to know of Sir William's treachery. She will believe that he has made a mockery of their love these many years.

"Simon, you will be her salvation. You must be her strength, her will to continue. And what of young Betsy and Wilfred? Are they to be damned for their father's sins? Oh, Simon, listen to me."

Simon stared up into Valentine's face, tears filling his eyes, and he dropped his sword, turning away to bury his face against the wall.

Valentine reached out, his hand heavy on Simon's shoulder for a moment. Then he turned to the Turk. "Let me enter, Mustafa."

The Turk stepped aside, opening the doors.

Valentine Whitelaw would always remember the dark coolness of the chapel when he entered. The chapel was illuminated only by the jewellike tones radiating through the stained glass.

He glanced around, feeling the peace Sir William must have sought within its walls. It would have been a place where he could have come to confess his sins and try to make peace with his own conscience.

It was the place in which Sir William Davies had chosen to die. He had taken his own life.

Quietly, the guards stepped into the shadowy chapel and lowered Sir William's body from where it hung from one of the supporting beams of the high arches.

Valentine Whitelaw turned away. It was over. He left the chapel, glancing curiously at Mustafa, who still stood just outside, never having entered. "You knew."

Mustafa nodded. "It was written in his face. When he saw you, he knew. Then, when I see him enter this place of worship, I knew he will end his life here, not to be dishonored further, or bring more dishonor on his family. It was the only way for a man to end his life."

Valentine walked over to where Simon stared dazedly at his feet. "Come, Simon," he said, placing his arm over Simon's shoulders. "We will face this together."

Simon nodded, looking up gratefully. "I will have to tell Mother, Valentine."

"I know, but we will get through this. At least we have the truth now, Simon. We will start anew and we will become stronger because of that. Basil, Magdalena, Geoffrey Christian, and the others who died because of what happened so many years ago, they will live on through us, Simon. We will never forget them, nor will they have died for nothing."

Lily Christian raced along the cliffs precariously close to the edge as she sent Merry galloping faster than the winds. Her hair was wild, floating out behind her and glinting with a dark, hidden fire. Her cheeks were flushed like the wild rose, while her pale green eyes glowed with a fiery warmth that was kindled from deep within the heart.

Crossing the wild heath, Lily pulled Merry up. Staring out to sea, she felt her heart miss a beat, for silhouetted against the horizon were the sails of a ship: the *Madrigal*.

Valentine Whitelaw had returned to Ravindzara.

"Come on, Merry," Lily whispered in his ear, patting his sleek neck as she nudged him with her satin-slippered heels, "let's go home."

The big white horse galloped faster than before, his long tail and mane flying, his hooves digging deep into the earth. Quickly they passed along the stately lane leading to Ravindzara. When reaching the stables, Lily rubbed Merry's soft nose and treated him to a handful of oats sweetened with honey from the pocket of her green velvet gown.

Hurrying into the house through a side entrance, Lily avoided passing through the great hall, for she intended to look respectable when greeting Valentine after his absence of nearly a month.

Reaching her room, Lily quickly disrobed and sponged herself off with a cloth soaked in rose oil and lavender. A heady blend of jasmine and hyacinth she touched to her throat and breast, and behind her ears and against the throbbing softness of her wrist, the warmth of her body heightening the scent by the time she'd dressed in her gown and arranged her hair to satisfaction.

She was staring at her reflection in the looking glass, when there was a knock on the door, and Quinta stuck her head inside. "I thought this was where you would be. Valentine is back!" she said excitedly. "He is wondering where you are. I'm afraid you gave him quite a scare, racing along the cliffs on Merry. He is a bit angry, my dear," Quinta advised, coming into the room when Lily held out her hand.

"He saw me, then?"

"He stood before the window, never moving, while you and that horse of yours raced along the shore," Quinta said, eyeing Lily curiously. "Good Lord, child, whatever have you done to yourself?"

"Don't you approve?" Lily asked worriedly, smoothing down her skirt with a nervous gesture. She had so hoped to please Valentine with her appearance.

"Well, ah, yes, there is nothing wrong at all. You look, ah, quite respectable, my dear," Quinta told her.

"Good, that is what I hoped," Lily confided.

"You are so in love with him aren't you, my dearest child?" Quinta said, her expression softened. "I believe you always have been, haven't you?"

Lily bit her lip, watching Quinta uncertainly, but Quinta reached out and pressed a kiss against her rosy cheek.

"You do not mind?"

"Mind? I could not be happier. I cannot think of anything that would give me greater pleasure than to welcome you into this family, not that you are not already a part of it, but this way we will never lose you to another. You will become a Whitelaw, and we hold what is ours," Quinta said, echoing Valentine's words spoken so lovingly once before.

Lily stared down at her hands, unconsciously twisting them as she anticipated her meeting with him after so long an absence and after so much had happened. They had received a letter from him, telling them all that had occurred at Riverhurst. How could she seek happiness now, knowing the sadness that Simon and Lady Elspeth were sharing?

"Don't, my child," Quinta advised, taking Lily's sad face in her hand as she looked into her shadowed eyes. "We all must live our own lives. One day, Simon and Elspeth will come to terms with what has happened. Their wounds will heal. I understand from Valentine that Sir William left several letters. One for

Elspeth, and one for his children, and one for Simon. I do not know if Sir William's words will be able to explain what happened. Perhaps one day they will understand him better. He was a very tormented man, Lily. As a young man he believed very deeply in the cause of his Church, and he remained, until the end, a very religious man, but he became involved in something that he had no control over, that drew him deeper into a web that he could not escape from until it was far too late.

"He could do nothing, Lily. If he tried to follow his conscience, he would have betrayed his Church, and his beliefs, and the others involved. And yet, because he chose not to, he betrayed those he loved the most, and in the end he lost everything. He is a man to be pitied. I do not excuse him, Lily," Quinta said, her eyes glinting with the anger she'd felt when hearing of his treachery, "but I cannot hate the man."

Lily touched Quinta's hand understandingly, then said softly, "And Sir Raymond Valchamps?"

Quinta's mouth tightened. "That is one man I feel nothing for. He will go on trial this month. It will not go well for him, my dear. He will meet the fate of a traitor, and it will not be a peaceful death," Quinta told her, then drew a deep breath. "Now, enough of this. You had better go to the great chamber immediately. I do not wish Valentine to come and break this door down trying to find you. He is angry enough, my dear," she warned.

"You think he would, then?"

"Without a doubt. He has been away from you for far too long, and I am not too old yet to understand young lovers."

At Lily's start of surprise, Quinta laughed. "Oh, my child, don't ever doubt that he loves you. I have never seen such a determined glint in a man's eye, unless 'twas when my brother courted his mother. The man was crazed from first laying eyes on her. She was quite a beauty, and a bit wild. Like you, my dear. Besides, you wear Valentine's ring of Spanish gold," she commented when Lily reached up to touch the rough band of gold. "I had wondered that he wears a pearl now. You wear its mate in your other ear. 'Twas not only his most prized possession, but 'twas his good luck charm. I think you must be that now."

"Thank you, Quinta. I do love you," Lily said, hugging her.

Quinta smiled, touched, for she had always liked the child. "Now go to him. You have kept him waiting long enough."

Lily wasted no more time and hurried from the room, flying down the corridor toward the great chamber where Quinta had said he waited for her.

She paused just outside the door, forcing herself to breathe more slowly, then she opened the door and entered the room.

Valentine Whitelaw stood staring out the windows where she had stood for so many long hours watching the horizon for the *Madrigal*'s sails. He seemed more handsome than she remembered. He was dressed as she first saw him, in leather jerkin and breeches, his white shirt so startling against his sun-bronzed skin. The pearl he wore in his ear glinted softly beneath the blackness of his hair, while his neatly trimmed beard made her want to touch the strong line of his jaw.

Suddenly Lily found herself staring into his eyes, and she felt the same sense of breathlessness she'd felt the first time when she'd opened her eyes to find his turquoise eyes watching her so intently, like her *tigre*'s when he was hunting.

"Valentine!" Lily said, holding out her hands to him.

"I beg your pardon?" he said, staring at her as if at a stranger.

Lily frowned. "Valentine?"

"God's Light!" Valentine Whitelaw expostulated, his eyes narrowing in disbelief as he stared at her.

Suddenly his deep, rich laughter filled the room.

"What have you done to yourself?" he demanded, and in a stride he had come to stand before her.

Lily's cheeks paled. "I thought you would be pleased."

"Pleased? I come home to Ravindzara to find the most beautiful woman I have ever known racing along the cliffs, every step of that damned horse carrying my only love closer to the rocks below, then find that my flaming-haired darling has become a Puritan! Pleased? I have seldom known such despair," Valentine said, his lips twitching slightly as he stared at her crestfallen expression. "Would you mind explaining this—this attire?" he asked softly as he walked around her.

Dressed in a plain gray gown of a fine quality of silk, but with no trimmings except for the simple linen collar and cuffs, Lily Christian looked quite somber. But in Valentine Whitelaw's eyes, the worst crime she'd perpetrated had been in confining the glorious thickness of her dark red hair in a tight braid which she'd tucked beneath a prim-looking headdress without benefit of even the merest wisp of lace.

"I can see I have been away far too long," Valentine murmured thoughtfully.

Lily licked her dry lips. "I only wished to appear proper, Valentine. I thought I might be an embarrassment to you if I did not try to act more genteelly. I did it for you," she added faintly, for he had disappeared behind her back.

"Valentine!" she gasped, for he'd pulled her back against his chest and his hands were busy at her waist and bodice undoing the fastenings. "What are you doing?"

"I am going to free you of this shroud," he said against her ear, his breath warm, then she felt his tongue against the ring of Spanish gold, before his teeth bit her lobe gently.

She felt a rush of air against her bare shoulders when he took the bodice from her, then her skirt had fallen into a wrinkled heap at her feet, leaving her standing in the middle of the great chamber in her petticoat and smock.

But before she could reach down and retrieve her clothes, his hands had moved to the offending attifet, and pulling it loose from atop her head, his hands slid into the thickness of her coiled hair and loosened the dark red strands until they fell across her shoulders like a heavy silken veil.

Turning her around to face him, he stared at her for a long moment. "There is one thing missing," he murmured, his eyes half-closed as he gazed into her face, particularly at her lips.

"*Prraaack!* Buss us a nice one, sweeting!"

Valentine glanced over at the parrot who'd just awakened from a nap and who was now strutting on his perch.

"Thank you, Cisco, that is just what I had in mind," Valentine said with a laugh. Then his mouth had covered Lily's, his lips teasing hers for a long moment, touching them softly, then with more pressure until they parted and his kiss became more intimate under the gentle, persuasive probing of his tongue against hers.

His hands held her close in his embrace, until his warmth spread to her, burning her where he touched her.

Lifting his mouth from hers, he said against the reddened

softness of her lips, "Now you look like a woman who has just been kissed by her lover. That was what was missing," he said with a smile.

Lily's arms had moved behind his neck during the embrace, and now her fingers caressed his nape, playing with the black hair that curled there.

"I've missed you so," she said, placing a soft kiss against the corner of his mouth.

"Not as much as I have missed you," he said, breathing deeply of her fragrance. "You smell too delicious to be forgotten easily, and the mere thought of your sweet-scented flesh causes a man a great deal of discomfort," he said, his mouth finding hers for a long kiss before moving lower to caress the softness of her breasts.

"At least I did have this to remind me of you, and what I was missing by being away from you," he said, lifting his mouth from hers and smiling with pleasure as he reached beneath his leather jerkin, holding up a lacey, beribboned garter.

Lily stared in amazement at the garter. "That is mine!"

"I know," he said, keeping his prize out of her reach.

"Where did you find it?"

"On the island. I was walking along the sands and spied this priceless treasure. 'Tis as sweetly scented as its mistress," he said, breathing the delicate lavender scent that clung to the lace. "I have kept it against my heart," he told her, his turquoise eyes bright with love as Lily caressed his cheek, her fingers trailing along the roughness of his beard.

Lily jumped nervously when she heard footsteps beyond the door, her face flushed with embarrassment when she realized she stood in his arms in nothing more than her petticoat and smock, which left her little modesty under his roving hands as she felt his caress along her hip.

With a smile, he released her from his embrace and walked over to where his cloak lay across the window seat. He held it out and wrapped her within its concealing folds.

"We have much to discuss, Lily Francisca, and we have a lot of lost hours to make up for. Come," he said, holding out his hand to her, " 'tis a fairly warm day for winter, and I have yet to show you that cove just below the cliffs. We will be undisturbed there," Valentine Whitelaw said, his fingers closing around hers when she placed her hand in his.

"You are certain we will not be disturbed?" she asked, wrapping the great folds of his cloak around her.

"If no one knows where we are, how can we be disturbed? It will be our secret," he said with a devilish glint in his eye as he pulled her after him out the door.

"*Prraaack!* Buss us a nice one! Lift a leg, mate! Ooooh, where are we off to, my pretty one? *Prraaack!* The cove. No one knows! A secret! *Prraaack!*" Cisco chirped, his giggling laughter filling the room.

This royal throne of kings, this scepter'd isle,
This earth of majesty, this seat of Mars,
This other Eden, demi-paradise
This fortress built by Nature for herself . . .
This precious stone set in the silver sea . . .
This blessed plot, this earth, this realm, this England.

SHAKESPEARE

Epilogue

"GOD bless Queen Elizabeth!"
Dressed in a gown of cloth of gold, with a crimson cloak trimmed in ermine and a golden crown set regally on her red-gold curls, Elizabeth Regina rode in a chariot of gold through the streets of London. Elizabeth, who had been christened in a mantle of purple velvet and anointed with the holy oil entitled for royalty at Grey Friars Church on September 10, 1533, was now celebrating her fiftieth year of birth and the twenty-fifth year of her reign. The only child of King Henry VIII and his ill-fated queen, Anne Boleyn, Elizabeth had been destined to rule the island kingdom and bring about a golden age that would give birth to an empire.

"God save Your Grace!"

Banners of silk, emblazoned with the royal arms, fluttered while trumpets and drums sounded. The Master of the Horse rode behind his queen, leading her white horse draped in gold. The captain of the guard and the royal horsemen came next, riding in close formation. Ladies-in-waiting and courtiers followed, their horses' bridles gleaming with jewels, while the Lord Mayor, churchmen, aldermen, dignitaries, and court officials completed the royal procession.

The narrow, cobbled streets of the city were crowded with the usual congestion of traffic and inhabitants, as well as the country folk who'd swarmed through the city gates from village and town to celebrate their queen's fiftieth anniversary. Footmen dressed in velvet liveries ran before the coaches of nobles to clear safe passage through the rabble, while plainly garbed drivers, with damning oaths and loudly cracking whips, sent their carts and drays into the narrowest of lanes with little regard for anyone's safety. From three-storied gabled houses, oak-framed with lath and plaster walls, bay-windowed shops with creaking signs swinging over the doorways, inns with taprooms and courtyards packed with drunken revelers and weary travelers, and the stately homes of the wealthy the people cheered Elizabeth Tudor's cavalcade as it wound through the streets of London. Nosegays of delicate lavender and rosemary, marigolds, and red and white Tudor roses fluttered down from above to carpet her path.

"God bless you all, my good people!" Elizabeth called to her loyal subjects.

Sir Valentine Whitelaw, newly knighted by his queen, stood on a garland-draped balcony overlooking the street below. His lady stood beside him in a rich cloak of green velvet embroidered with gold and pearls, her dark red hair glinting like fire in the sunlight.

Lady Lily Francisca Whitelaw felt the warmth of her husband's hand caressing her waist. She glanced up, her eyes meeting his for a long moment before he lowered his lips to touch hers in a tender kiss that bound them together. He whispered something in her ear, his lips and words causing her to blush delicately, her pale green eyes glowing with love for him. Beneath her cloak she felt his hand move to rest protectively against her rounding stomach, where the child conceived of that love now moved with life. Lily glanced up in surprise. Meeting the startled look in his turquoise eyes, she knew he had felt the vigorous movement of his child within her. He smiled with delight, and with a sigh of contentment, Lily leaned back against Valentine's chest, feeling his gentle strength encompassing her while his arms held her close against his heart. Soon they would be returning to Ravindzara. The *Madrigal* was riding at anchor in the Thames, her crew ready to board once they'd received their captain's orders to sail.

Tristram Christian stood proudly beside his sister and her husband, dressed in his finest doublet and hose. He was Geoffrey Christian's son, and the world knew it, and he was the rightful master of the ancestral home—although, until of age, he would continue to live with Lily and Valentine at Ravindzara. Every so often, the young master of Highcross, unable to contain himself, would lean precariously close to the railing of the balcony, nearly tumbling over as he sought a better view of the procession passing beneath. His grinning face was beaming with mischief when he glanced back at his friends standing just behind him. The two men, one short and dark, the other tall and fair, each of whom was holding a bawling baby in their arms, shrugged helplessly in response, while Tillie Odell, the triplets' mother, stood between them, her only daughter sound asleep in her arms. She smiled complacently, knowing the Odell brothers would in future have little time or energy for mischievous pranks.

Dulcie Whitelaw stood between her brother and sister, her dark brown eyes glowing with excitement while she watched the celebration, her dainty feet, clad in brand-new silk slippers, never stilled as she stood on tiptoe to toss roses into the crowded street. Her laughter and squeals of delight brought amused grins from those around her, especially from Simon Whitelaw, who kept a firm grasp on his sister's slender shoulders to keep her from flying over the rail.

A look of sadness briefly shadowed his expression when he thought of his mother, and young Wilfred and Betsy, still in seclusion at Riverhurst. Soon, he vowed, he would escort them all to court, where they would walk proudly beside him. They did not bear the guilt or shame of Sir William's betrayal. They had been the innocent victims. Simon smiled. Elizabeth had personally extended to him her wish that his mother would return to court, where she would gladly receive her. He could hardly wait to tell his mother that when he visited Riverhurst.

The rest of the family and close friends stood surrounding them. Quinta Whitelaw, Sir Rodger, Artemis, and their daughter, Elizabeth Mary Rose, held between them, would be returning to Cornwall aboard the *Madrigal*. George Hargraves, overshadowed by the tall woman beside him, was grinning widely at some remark she'd just made. Standing to the right of Valentine Whitelaw, his hand resting lightly on the hilt of his scimitar, the Turk watched the proceedings, a ghost of a smile softening his harsh countenance when his gaze shifted to his captain and his lady.

Soon, he thought, they would be sailing along the rocky coast of this island that had been shrouded in mists the first time he had gazed upon it. A strange, cold land it had seemed then. But now . . . Soon, the Turk thought with longing, he and his captain and family, would return home to Ravindzara, where the sea winds blew warmly against the shore.

Rich pageantry met the eye on every street corner while the roar of cannon fire, commemorating the great occasion, sounded in the distance. But the merrymaking would not soon end, for with nightfall, the skies over London would be ablaze with a brilliant display of fireworks, of shooting rockets and showers of brightly colored stars. Bonfires would be lit in honor of the jubilee, while the revels continued throughout the night.

The bells of the city continued to peal. From every church steeple they rang out in joyous celebration of Elizabeth.